The critics on Anita Burgh

'A blockbuster . . . an excellent reading experience'
Literary Review

'The mix of suspense, romance, humour and good old heart-tugging pathos is irresistible' Elizabeth Buchan, *Mail on Sunday*

'A blockbusting story of romance and intrigue'
Family Circle

'The perfect beach book' *Marie Claire*

'Its crafted writing keeps you hanging in there until the last page' *City Limits*

'Sharp . . . wickedly funny' *Mail on Sunday*

'Ambition, greed and manipulation add up to a great blockbuster' *New Woman*

'You won't be able to put it down' *Good Housekeeping*

'A well-written contemporary story that has all the necessary ingredients to make a great read – and it is!' *Oracle*

'Anita has the storyteller's gift' *Daily Express*

'Sinister and avaricious forces are at work behind the pious smiles . . . Gripping!' *Daily Telegraph*

'A sure-fire bestseller' *Prima*

By the same author

Distinctions of Class
Love the Bright Foreigner
The Azure Bowl
The Golden Butterfly
The Stone Mistress
Advances
Overtures
Avarice
Lottery
Breeders
The Cult
On Call

Tales from Sarson Magna: Molly's Flashings
Tales from Sarson Magna: Hector's Hobbies

Anita Burgh was born in Gillingham, Kent, but spent her early years at Lanhydrock House in Cornwall. Returning to the Medway Towns, she attended Chatham Grammar School, and became a student nurse at UCH in London. She gave up nursing upon marrying into the aristocracy. Subsequently divorced, she pursued various careers – secretarial work, a laboratory technician in cancer research, and an hotelier. She has a flat in Cambridge and a house in France, where she shares her life with her partner, Billy, a bulldog, a Cairn terrier, three mixed-breed dogs and three cats. The visits of a constantly changing mix of her four children, two step-children, six grandchildren, four step-grandchildren and her noble ex-husband keep her busy, entertained and poor! Anita Burgh is the author of many bestsellers, including *Distinctions of Class*, which was shortlisted for the RNA Romantic Novel of the Year Award.

THE FAMILY

Anita Burgh

ORION

An Orion Paperback
First published in Great Britain by
Orion in 1999
This paperback edition published in 2000 by
Orion Books Ltd,
Orion House, 5 Upper St Martin's Lane,
London WC2H 9EA

Second impression 2000

A CIP catalogue record for this book
is available from the British Library.

Typeset by Deltatype Ltd, Birkenhead, Merseyside
Printed and bound in Great Britain by
Clays Ltd, St Ives plc

This novel is about a family and is dedicated to:

Alex (Greg), Ben, Billy, Cath, Emma, Hannah, Holly, Ian, James, Jane E., Jane J., Jane L., Jonathan, Julie, Kate E., Kate J., Lara, Mike, Milly, Nadja, Nancy, Niall, Patrick B., Patrick L., Peter, Poppy, Rebecca, Ricky, Sarah, Savannah and Wilma.

In other words, for better or worse, my family.

Far from being the basis of the good society, the family, with its narrow privacy and tawdry secrets, is the source of all our discontents.

Sir Edmund Leach, BBC Reith Lectures, 1967.

Chapter One

1

Summer 1966

Young as she was, there were times when Jillian feared that her happiness could not continue, that something had to go wrong. What had she done to deserve such bliss?

The top of the car was down, the wind was in her hair, the sun beating down, the Beach Boys on the car radio and Jack was beside her, yet she shivered with a sense of foreboding.

More to distract herself than from genuine interest she pointed towards a lush, flat meadow. 'Jack, just look at that house. Isn't it lovely?'

He pulled up. In the meadow, on the far side of a narrow band of river, nestling among a group of mature trees, was a manor house so perfect in style and setting that it looked like a doll's house placed there by an absent-minded child. Its red brick had mellowed to a warm, dark pink as if in its many summers it had absorbed the heat of the sun. The steep roof was tiled, more blue than grey, and set in it were four dormer windows, like heavily lidded eyes. Beneath it, six long, small-paned sash windows marched in perfect symmetry. Below them were four more and in the middle a white-painted door with a fan-shaped light above, its very width made for welcome.

'It's perfect!' Jillian exclaimed.

'Very English. You really like it?'

'Love it.'

'Then I'll buy it for you one day.' He restarted the engine.

'Can I have that in writing?'

'I never break a promise – and certainly not to you.'

At his words dark fears rushed in. She was sure that the vengeful gods, having overlooked her, would remember, spot her in this little car, and return to punish her and take it all away. She pulled her cardigan tight around her and hunkered further down in the seat of the racing-green Triumph.

'Cold?' Jack glanced across at her.

'No. Just thinking.'

'And that makes you shiver?'

She could see he was smiling. He changed gear smoothly as they approached a steep bend.

'Not the thinking, silly. The thought.' She turned in her seat, the better to see him. 'Are you happy?'

'You know I am, thanks to you.' His gloved hand patted her thigh. She loved it when he did that, as if he were reassuring himself she was real.

'Aren't you sometimes afraid it'll all disappear in a puff of smoke?'

'No.'

'I am.'

'Why should it?'

They were travelling fast now, along a straight stretch of road beside a dyke towards Norfolk. She would like to tell him his speed worried her, but there was no point. If she complained he'd only take it as a challenge to go faster – he was like that. She took off her glasses: if they crashed she wouldn't get glass splinters in her eyes. It was this silly feeling of apprehension that made her do so.

The thought of crashing was a logical worry, given their speed, but her fear for her happiness was more complex. The idea that good luck had to be paid for in some way never quite left her.

'It's probably the fault of your ancestors.'

'Sorry? I don't understand.' She looked at him.

'This idea you've got that it's all got to be paid for.'

'I didn't say that.'

'No, but it's what you meant. I reckon the apprehensions of an ancestor are lurking in your genes so that you think the illogical is perfectly logical.'

She smiled tentatively, unsure if he was teasing her, but he looked serious enough.

'We accept inherited hair colour, talents, so why can't we inherit ideas and fears?' He changed gear and as he explained his theory to her, she realised, to her relief, that he'd slowed down. 'I've been driving too fast, which frightened you, so your mind was receptive to fears and superstitions from long dead great-great-, and a hundred times great-grandparents. Could be a Catholic, Puritan or even pagan granddad slipping in, couldn't it?'

'I suppose so, I never thought.'

'Mind you, maybe my driving was so bad it made you call on our own God – you know, that poor fellow we only talk to in emergencies!' He laughed. 'I'm sorry. I'll drive more carefully.'

Far more likely to be her father's fierce, unforgiving God bothering her, she decided.

Charlie lived in a world of fear, where sex fiends and mayhem lurked, waiting to lure his daughters from him. He rarely saw any good in others but was quick to note the sin. She did not mention this to Jack – she rarely told anyone about it. She found her father's religious intensity embarrassing, not quite nice, something to be hidden. And this obsession with sin had made her a sinner. She'd had to lie and say she was going to Brancaster with girlfriends this weekend. If he had had any inkling of what she planned to do, he'd want to kill her or Jack, or both of them.

She had known Jack for almost three months. Soon after they'd met he'd gone home for the long vacation. She hadn't expected to see him again until the autumn. Instead he'd come back within a week, declaring he couldn't exist without her. All summer he'd divided his time between his parents' home and the flat of a young married couple he knew in Cambridge – where, she knew, he had to sleep on the sofa. Every spare moment she had she spent with him, and it had been time enough to know him, fall in love, and learn to trust him.

She had finally decided that this weekend they would *do it*. Until now they had kissed and fondled each other, inching agonisingly towards making love only to stop before it was too late. It wasn't fair on him, it was wearing her down. In any case, she wanted to go to bed with him – hell, she was the only virgin she knew!

3

'Light me a ciggie, will you?' His voice stopped her analysing, anticipating. They were approaching a bridge, which would take them across the dyke. Despite her short-sightedness, she could see the narrow, steel-grey band of water that crossed the land in a straight, shimmering line almost as far as the eye could see. She handed him the cigarette. The very act of lighting it for him showed how she felt about him. She'd never smoked, never wanted to, not after a life of hearing her father clear his lungs every morning. If anyone else had asked her to light a cigarette for them she'd have told them to do it themselves. But when Jack asked she happily complied, finding it an intensely intimate action and making her feel like Bette Davis . . . or was it Joan Fontaine?

'I love you,' he said suddenly.

'Ditto,' she replied.

'Why can't you ever say it?'

'I do.'

'Rarely. "I ditto you" hasn't got the same ring to it, has it?'

'I'm sorry. I suppose I'm not used to it – being in love, saying it.'

'Good. I'd loathe to be the last in a long line.'

The flat countryside sped by, the sky dominating wherever she looked. Jillian sat hugging the word *last* to her. Did that mean what she hoped it did? That he wanted to be her last boyfriend, that he wanted to spend the rest of his life with her? She must try to say she loved him more often. It was silly to have such a hang-up. He might think she didn't.

'I think it's because I can't ever remember my parents saying it – you know, I love you.' There, it wasn't so difficult to say. 'Not to each other or to me.'

'That's no excuse. My lot never do either – hate, now, they're very good at that. But love? That's deemed sloppy, ugh, beyond the pale. Even my mother, who adores me, never says it. So, madam, it's no excuse, and it hasn't stopped me telling you a thousand times.'

'Who hates who?'

'My mother hates my father and he hates me. He's made a career of it for the past twenty years. Bless his cotton socks!'

4

He chortled loudly, but Jillian noticed that his knuckles had whitened as he clenched the steering-wheel.

'Then I'll make it up to you. I love you, love you, love you, Jack, darling!'

'That's more like it.' His hands relaxed. She sank back into the seat, allowing herself to dream all manner of dreams, a soft, contented smile on her face as they roared across the vast, flat fenlands.

'Smell it?'

She wound down the window and sniffed deeply. 'Ah, yes!' she lied. All she could smell was petrol, but she didn't like to say so. She sat forward, waiting eagerly for that first glimpse of the sea, which still excited her as it had when she was a child.

'Imagine, when we were kids we must have played on the same beach, may even have smiled or kicked sand at each other.'

'More likely the latter. I hated girls.'

'I'd not much time for boys either.'

'Just as well we didn't meet then. We might have loathed each other irrevocably.'

'Oh, my darling, don't even say it.' The love she found so difficult to tell him in words was etched on to her face.

'Don't ever look at me any other way, will you?' He placed his hand on her thigh, and again she felt that jolt of pleasure.

'Here we are.' He turned the car between two gateposts, on which there hung no gate, and up an overgrown drive. Ahead was a solid Edwardian building, fussy with unnecessary embellishments, even a small turret. 'I thought it . . .' Her voice trailed off. He'd invited her to his family seaside house and, she'd expected it to be a chalet, at most a bungalow, not a substantial house like this. Sand, she saw now, was everywhere, in the drive, in the flower-beds, as if the beach had decided to encroach further inland, reclaiming its own. They climbed out of the car. 'Listen,' he ordered.

They stood for a second and she heard the sibilant hiss of the sea. 'Hope it doesn't come as far as this, like the sand.'

'No. Don't worry. There are sandbanks between us and it.

Oh, sod, no!' He frowned as a bright red Aston Martin turned into the gate and accelerated too fast up the drive. A second sports car followed.

Jillian was confused. If they were not to be alone, as they'd planned, maybe this was a sign that she'd made the wrong decision, that she shouldn't sleep with him. Then fear hit her: she had to meet new people and she hated that. All she wanted was to be alone with him, no matter how dangerous that might be.

A young woman emerged from one car in a fluid, elegant movement. Her long legs were deeply bronzed with a tan Jillian doubted had been acquired in Norfolk. Her jet-black hair was cut in a short, angular style, almost brutal in its severity, but she had the face to carry it and large, intelligent brown eyes, made larger by the black line painted around them, which made them seem slanted in a cat-like way. The long false eyelashes fascinated Jillian: she would have liked to try them but never had – she'd only worry about how secure they were. On her full lips was a pink lipstick so pale it was almost white and broad slashes of colour beneath her sharp cheekbones made them look even sharper. Her dress – primary colours fit for any exotic bird – was the shortest Jillian had ever seen. Her toenails were painted gold to match the straps of her flimsy sandals. Jillian stared, fascinated, at them. She felt like a dowdy wren beside this brightly coloured, beautiful, confident, fashionable woman.

'What are you doing here?' Jack asked belligerently.

'Dear Jack. What a sweet welcome.' She leaned forward and kissed his cheek, her height almost matching his six feet. Jillian felt an unpleasant twinge of jealousy.

'I told you to stay away.'

'I was curious. Introductions, Jack. Manners.' She tapped his shoulder bossily.

'Jillian, this is Esmeralda Illingworth,' he said ungraciously.

'Hello, Jillian! But call me Esmée! Esmeralda's such a mouthful and such a horrible name.'

'How do you do?' Jillian shook the manicured hand, aware of her own short nails and that her dress was home-made, in patterned polyester, while Esmée's was pure silk. 'Actually I think it's a lovely name. Exotic, like you.' And she felt herself colour at how gushing she must sound.

'Oh, I like you. What a sweet thing to say. I'm Jack's older sister! He's a brat – don't waste your time with him!' Esmée laughed a glorious, husky laugh which Jillian was certain was due to her obvious relief at learning Esmée's relationship to Jack. 'God, my manners get worse. This is . . .' She paused, almost imperceptibly, as if she was striving to remember his name. '. . . Fabrice. He's French, can't speak a word of English, which is just as well since he'd bore you with what an important little count he is.' She bent slightly and kissed the unsuspecting man. 'And this is Sally Brentwood and Troy something or other.' A sulky-looking, short young woman held out her hand as if it was almost too much effort to do so, while Troy, unshaven, long-haired, sat in the Aston gazing vaguely into space. 'He's a pop star, isn't he, Sally?'

'So he says.' Sally yawned. 'Christ, I'm tired. Is there a bed handy?' She spoke in a small voice with a slight lisp, like a child.

'I phoned Mrs Turner to ask her to make up beds for us. Don't think *you* can have them,' Jack said, a shade sulkily.

Jillian noted the plural and wasn't sure if she was relieved or disappointed.

'So did I,' Esmée said. 'I'm in Mustard and you'll be in the Turnip room, Sally darling. Remember it? Top of the stairs, turn right, third door along. Better toddle off before you fall over, sweetness.' Wearily Sally made her way to the front door, followed by Troy, who had finally decided to heave himself out of the car.

'Poor darlings, they're stoned out of their minds. I'm amazed they got here in one piece. They haven't slept for days. You'll see to the luggage, Jack darling, won't you?' Then Esmée grabbed hold of Jillian's arm. 'You come with me and tell me all about yourself.'

They sat in the kitchen, Esmée with a bottle of champagne in front of her, Jillian with a cup of tea. Fabrice was slumped at the table, his head on his arms, apparently asleep. His long dark hair flopped on to the table and Jillian found herself thinking how unhygienic that was. Why she should worry about it mystified her since she had more important concerns. A surly Jack had gone for a walk after a stand-up row with his sister.

'I should have gone with him,' Jillian fretted.

'Why? He was intolerably rude to poor Fabrice,' Esmée said. 'Still, it shows his French has improved. Honestly, he carries on as if he owns this place and it belongs to us all. I've as much right to be here as he has.'

'Yes.' Jillian was not sure what to say or do. She hadn't actually been given the option of going with Jack, he'd simply stormed out.

'Are you sure you don't want a drink?'

'No, thanks. This tea is fine.'

'Bizarre.' Esmée stretched luxuriously. 'A joint?'

'No thanks.'

'No point in offering you some acid, then?'

'No.' Jillian felt uncomfortable. It was said, these days, that every other person dabbled in drugs. Until now she'd never met anyone who did.

'What do you do? I presume you work?'

'Of course. Doesn't everyone?' Jillian bridled at the sneer she was sure she hadn't imagined.

'I don't,' Esmée answered, and Jillian was aware she had fallen into a trap. 'How did you and Jack meet?'

'At a May Ball.'

'How predictable.' Esmée looked as bored as she sounded.

'No, not really. I was working – I work for a theatrical agency, and we handled some of the acts booked for the balls. I was checking everything was okay.'

'How fascinating. Maybe you can help Troy's group.' The change in Esmée was dramatic: she leaned forward, her face alight with interest. Most people sat up when Jillian told them what she did but she rarely went into detail because, no matter how she liked to pretend that her job was more exciting than most, it was still fairly routine. Her tasks were primarily secretarial in the small, dingy office of a one-man agency that handled third-rate comedians, jugglers, magicians, exotic dancers. Hardly the Beatles or the Rolling Stones. It was only because Pete, her boss, had taken a fancy to her that she'd been at the ball in the first place. Not that she'd encouraged him, since he was old and married, but she knew from his flower-patterned shirts and his long hair that he saw himself as still young. But she'd met Jack, and Pete was a history that had never happened.

'So you know masses of famous people?'

'Not really. We don't handle any of the big groups, just the fill-in acts.' Then she wished she hadn't explained.

'Oh, I see.' Esmée looked bored again. 'You should call yourself Jill not Jillian, then you'd be Jack and Jill. What a hoot!'

'I prefer Jillian for that reason.'

'But I shall call you Jill.'

'I'd best go and look for Jack.'

'Oh, let him stew. He always wants his own way.'

'No, I'll go. I don't want him to sulk, do I?' Jillian laughed uncertainly.

There were no holidaymakers on Brancaster's long beach. The day had turned dull, overcast; a sad apology for early August. A chill wind from the grey North Sea beat at the long grass on the sandbanks, and Jillian pulled the Arran-knit cardigan her mother had made closely around her as she stumbled on soft sand. She stopped and called Jack's name, but the breeze caught the sound and whisked it away. No point in yelling, he'd never hear. She trudged along, closer to the water's edge where the sand was damp and firm. She put on her glasses and looked up into the dunes for him. Maybe he wasn't here. Maybe he'd gone and left her. Come to think of it, she hadn't seen his car but, then, she hadn't been looking for it. She felt panic build, as it did whenever she was alone in a strange place with strange people. She was trying to teach herself to despise this lack of confidence. She'd read an article in *She* magazine about being self-assured, which had made it sound easy, and yet ... Esmée and her friends needed no such advice. Everything about them was different, their skirts far shorter than she'd dare wear, bright colours in contrast to her pastels, thick makeup when she wore the merest flick of mascara. Then there were the drugs ... She shivered at the thought. How could they dare? Where did they find the courage when she didn't even want to drink? She didn't like the taste, except Bristol Milk and Drambuie at Christmas. And, of course, they were rich and she wasn't, and they were confident or at least they appeared so. Oh, hell! Why did she let people frighten her?

Once again she looked back towards the sandbanks, searching for him, just in case. Birds wheeled noisily over her head, squawking and fighting, soaring and dipping. Seagulls were easy to identify, but was that a kestrel? Maybe Jack would know. With relief she saw him standing in the fold of one of the dunes, semaphoring to her. She ran up the beach, waving back. 'I thought you'd gone.' She fell into his arms.

'Why would I do that? God, you look so pretty. The wind has given you such a colour. Come here.' Taking her hand he led her behind the bank and into a small valley between three large dunes. They sank on to the ground. There was no wind here, it wasn't even cold.

'Twenty feet away it's freezing.'

'Marvellous, aren't they, the dunes? No one will find us. I used to hide from my nanny here and I'd watch her going pink, red, puce then purple with rage as she searched for me – puffing about out there.'

'Monster!' She pushed him playfully.

He pulled her to him and kissed her. It was a gentle kiss, a friendly kiss. Jack had a whole repertoire of kisses, from the merest whisper of an eyelash on her cheek to others of such intensity, such longing and passion, that they almost made up for not having made love with him – almost, not quite.

'You know, you're the only bloke I know who kisses in a hundred different ways.'

10

'How do the others kiss, then?'

'Oh, you know. All crushing lips and tongues half down your throat when you've only just been introduced.'

'Yucksville.'

'Exactly.' She lay back in the sand, his arm protectively around her, and snuggled close to him.

'What were you talking to Esmée about?'

'Not a lot. She asked me if I could help her long-haired beatnik-looking friend get work. She lost interest when I told her what it was I did.'

'Sounds like Esmée.' He snorted. 'She's snooping on us, you know.'

'Is she?'

'My whole family snoops all the time. They're incapable of keeping their noses out of my life.'

'Perhaps they worry about you.'

'Not them. She's probably been sent by Dad to find out who I've got with me and what they're like and are they suitable.'

'Heavens! What if she doesn't like me?' She sat up and patted her hair instinctively, checking that her chignon was still neat. He pulled her towards him and one by one began to remove the Kirbigrips that kept it in place. 'Jack, you'll make me look a mess.'

'You should wear it down. You've got lovely blonde hair. Long, soft, silky.' It had tumbled halfway down her back and he stroked it. Gently he removed her spectacles.

'It's as straight as a die, I can't do a thing with it. I *hate* my hair.' She blinked, focusing her short-sighted eyes.

'Well, I don't.' He nuzzled it, breathing deeply. 'Smells wonderful.' He sighed. 'God, I love you,' he whispered softly. Slowly he unbuttoned her cardigan, then her dress. He kissed her, gently at first, but then with mounting passion as his tongue explored her mouth, sending shockwaves down her body. He unclipped her bra, his hands found her breasts and he teased her nipples, which she knew were hardening. She wanted him to suck at her breasts, willed him to do so. As if he read her thoughts, he stopped kissing her and instead nibbled her ear, then short kisses marched down the column

11

of her neck, across her chest and she could feel his breath on her breasts as she writhed with her longing for him to touch them. But he paused, the waiting sweet torture before she felt his warm lips on one breast, sucking gently, softly, as his hands moved lower, searching, fondling. The movement of his mouth strengthened and he was pulling at her nipple, then releasing it, then searching for it. Her body arched with pleasure and she knew that what she wanted, what she feared, what she desired, what she dreaded was about to happen. It was inevitable and there was nothing she could do to stop it.

'Oh, yes, my darling. Yes!' she heard herself say.

He peeled her dress, now bunched at her waist, away from her as he lowered his head, licking, kissing the slight swell of her stomach. She felt his breath, his lips, his tongue on that part of her she had for so long kept sacred. She opened her legs, at first embarrassed that anyone should do this to her before she wriggled from the exquisite wonder of it, half sat and held his head firmly to her as waves of pleasure flooded into her belly. Next, when he kissed her, she could smell herself on him, which only excited her more. When he entered her, his largeness filled her and she rocked with him, riding the surf of joy as he thrust into her, slowly and carefully at first then with mounting confidence as her cries showed that another orgasm was overwhelming her.

3

'Where have you two been?' Esmée, curled up on the sofa, looked up from the book she was reading.

'Out and about.' Jack's arm was around Jillian's waist.

'Well, you both look as if you found a bucket of cream.'

'We went for a walk.'

'And the rest!' Esmée uncurled her long legs and, with one fluid movement, was standing in front of them. 'I can always smell sex.' She laughed and Jillian felt herself redden. 'Hope the sand didn't get in your bum! Who's cooking supper?'

'Not us. We're going out.'

'Where?'

'I thought I'd take Jillian to the Jolly Tar for lobster.'

'Yummy – book us in too.'

'No, Esmée. We want to be alone.'

'How quaint. How dull!' She picked up her book. As she passed Jillian she said, 'You know, you look heaps more attractive with your hair down. I've friends who'd die for straight hair like that.'

'Thanks.' Jillian smiled at the compliment.

'But you know what? You really ought to get fitted with contact lenses – those glasses spoil it all. See yer . . .'

Jillian pushed instinctively at the offending spectacles, which, as usual, had slipped halfway down her nose.

'Esmée's right. You should get lenses.'

She twirled her hair, fumbling in the pocket of her cardigan for a hair pin, all happiness seeping away.

'My darling. Sorry. Sorry. Sorry.' He put his hands together in supplication. 'It's just that you have the most beautiful grey eyes and I want to see them. I want the whole world to see the great beauty you are.'

'Jack, you are sweet.' But she didn't believe him.

'It's the truth.' And he removed the offending spectacles, kissed her eyelids, and that kiss led to another, then another. Within a minute he'd grabbed her hand and they were racing up the stairs into the large room at the front of the house where they collapsed on to the bed, tearing at each other's clothes, wanting each other again, all thought of lobsters forgotten.

They stayed in their room, an oasis of their own, eating picnics gathered from the kitchen when they were hungry, drinking water or beer when they were thirsty. No routine marred their pleasure as they explored each other, body and mind.

'I'd begun to think you'd died, but every so often I was reassured by sounds of unmitigated passion!' Esmée said, as she and Fabrice entered the large, comfortably furnished sitting room, where for the past hour Jillian and Jack had

13

been sitting. She was reading, he mending a model boat he'd found in a cupboard upstairs, which, he told her, he'd built as a child, helped by his older brother, Mungo. It was little details like that that she loved to know. She filed them away in the increasing pile of information she was learning about him. 'Got any cigs, Jack? We're completely out.'

'No, I haven't. I suggest you go to the village and buy some.'

'You're always so crabby with me, Jack. Why?'

'Because you're supercilious and interfering, that's why. And stop trying to embarrass Jillian. I don't like it.'

'Was I embarrassing you, Jill? I'm so sorry. I didn't mean . . . Please, please forgive. Anyone fancy champagne?' She pointed to a side table where Fabrice had placed a tray with the bottle and some glasses, rather like a waiter, Jillian thought.

'She doesn't like being called Jill.'

'Really, Esmée, I'm fine. You're not upsetting me,' Jillian said hurriedly.

'I wish we hadn't come now.'

'I wish you hadn't too, Esmée.'

'I thought we could make it like it used to be – spillikins, charades and mussels for tea.' She pouted childishly.

'Grow up, Esmée. If you wanted a weekend like that, why bring a dope-head like Sally and that oik Troy? I won't even go into what I think of Fabrice, and I'm a Francophile.'

Jillian glanced nervously across the room at the Frenchman, who was leaning languidly against the wall gazing out of the window. He was very beautiful, she thought, with his fine features, pale skin and long, shiny dark hair. But the few times she'd seen him she couldn't help thinking he was posing all the time; he made a point of always sitting or standing in the best possible light.

'Actually, when my divorce is through I'm thinking of marrying him.'

'You're mad! You hardly speak a word of French and he's got no English.'

'Sounds perfect to me – we'd never argue, would we?' Esmée poured the champagne and carried a glass across the

14

room to Fabrice. 'Here you are, *chéri*.' She stroked his face and was rewarded with a lovely smile.

'Has Dad met him?' Jack asked from the table, where he was working on his galleon.

'Yes. Thought he was a poppet. Fabrice agreed with everything he said and left the stage clear for Daddy. Big improvement, he thought, on Toby.'

'Toby was, is, Esmée's husband, Jillian. Nice chap, but looks a bit like a toad.'

'Don't be horrible about toads, I adore them – and I can't say that about Toby. Never marry the first man who asks you, Jill. It's fatal! How was I to know he'd have such nasty habits? But, then, you won't make that mistake, will you, Jill? You're sensible. You're testing the water. So intelligent of you.' Jillian's face grew hot. 'You're quite beautiful when you blush.'

Her colour deepened. Why was Esmée like this with her? Unless . . . No, she told herself, that was crazy. Why should Esmée be jealous of her?

'Anyone fancy some breakfast?' she asked brightly. 'I don't mind cooking it.'

'What a treasure you've found, Jack, to be sure. Don't let her slip through your fingers like the others. Bliss, Jill. Two eggs for me and Fabrice loves black pudding.'

'What about Sally and Troy?'

'I shouldn't worry about them, they've probably OD'd. Don't look so appalled, Jill darling. They're having a long snooze.'

The roomy kitchen was furnished to function as a sitting room too. She'd love her mother to see it, a total contrast to their cramped kitchen. She searched for the equipment and food she would need, getting on all fours to look in the many cupboards.

'I don't often have company in here, that's for sure.'

A pair of very flat feet in battered Hush Puppies were planted beside her, and she looked up to find a plump, pleasant-faced, middle-aged woman looking down at her. 'I thought I'd cook everyone breakfast,' Jillian said.

'That must be a first. Need a hand? I'm Mrs Turner-what-

15

does. This kitchen only gets used when Mrs Stirling's here. A lovely lady. Why she puts up with her family I'll never know.' As Mrs Turner talked she bustled about dusting and rearranging. 'The big frying pan's here. I've said to Esmée, I don't know how many times, she'll miss her mother when she's dead. You never know, do you? Eggs are in the pantry.' She pointed towards a door in the corner of the room.

Jillian reappeared, carrying them in a wire basket, wondering what she meant.

'There, dear, I've put the bacon on for you. You from Cambridge or London?'

'Cambridge.'

'Then you're one of Jack's friends. A right monkey he is. I doubt he'll ever settle. I said to his father, "he'll never settle, your son, you mark my words." He said I'd never spoken a truer word. Mind you, I find I get on better with his friends. Mungo's are always killing things and Esmée's friends are strange, they look ill. Sometimes I quite expect to come to work and find one of them dead. Not healthy, not healthy at all.' She banged down the frying pan, chopped mushrooms, buttered bread in a flurry of movement.

'Why won't he settle down?' Jillian ventured to ask, having put down the eggs on the kitchen table.

'Jack? Spoiled for choice, that's his trouble. Like a bee what can't make his mind up which flower to have, I always say. The girls he's brought here – a battalion of them. Knives and forks are in that drawer there . . .'

But Jillian, not wishing to hear more, had fled.

4

Jack parked his car outside the bay window of Jillian's home off Cherry Hinton Road. 'There's a whole chunk of Cambridge you never see as a student,' he said, and he turned off the ignition. Then he looked up at the neatly curtained house.

She felt angry at his words. This house was her parents'

16

pride and joy, for which they'd worked hard. It was a far cry from the bathroomless terraced house of her early childhood. 'The rest of the world has to live,' she said. 'Not everyone can afford Edwardian piles!'

'What is it, Jillian? You've hardly said a word all the way back. What's wrong? Have I upset you?'

'Nothing's wrong.'

'Come on, it's me you're talking to. Who offended you? Did anyone get at you?'

'Why are you always so paranoid, Jack? Nobody got at me. And, in any case, why should anyone?' She ventured to look at him; his expression was perplexed.

'Are you going to invite me in?'

'No.'

'Oh, I see.' He looked down at his hands in the soft leather motoring gloves she'd given him for his birthday in June. They'd been too expensive by far for her pocket.

'*What* do you see?'

'I thought I asked you to keep your hair down.' He ignored her question. 'I like it better than this bun.' He stroked the large doughnut shape at the back of her head. She bridled at his touch. 'Sorry,' he said, removing his hand.

She picked up her handbag from the floor and buttoned her jacket. She wanted to get out, but she wanted to stay. She longed to cry, but forced herself to smile. 'That was a lovely weekend, Jack. We must do it again some time.' She congratulated herself at how nonchalant she sounded.

'Jillian.' His hand was at her chin and he forced her to turn her head. 'Look straight at me and tell me that again.' As she stared into his face, the face she loved and only last night had studied intently as he lay sleeping beside her, his image shimmered mistily through rapidly forming tears. 'Oh, my darling, what is it?'

She tried to repeat, 'Nothing,' but the word would not form. Instead she gulped air deeply in an attempt to control the sob, which escaped. Then she began to cry in earnest. He held her tight, stroking her hair, whispering softly to her, telling her many times he loved her and wanted her. The

17

sobbing slowly subsided. 'Please explain, Jillian. You owe me that. I love you so.'

'Don't say that if you don't mean it.'

'But I do mean it, that's the whole point. I've never said it to anyone ever before for the simple reason that I've never felt like this before. Believe me.'

'What about the others?'

'What others?'

'The other women.'

'What women?'

'You know, the others. How you won't settle. And . . .' She told him of her chat with Mrs Turner.

'Jillian, listen to me. Mrs Turner is a gossiping old fool who likes to think she knows us better than we know ourselves. Of course I've had other girlfriends – no doubt you've had other boyfriends. And maybe Mrs Turner's right and there have been too many, but it was only because none of them was right. Not like you.'

'I want to believe you.'

'I can only say how it is. I want to be with you every moment. I hate bringing you back here. I hate your job. I hate everything that takes you away from me. I mean, thank God it's the long vac – I'd have got no work done if I'd met you earlier. Please, darling.'

She smiled, tentatively at first, then a wider, deeper smile.

'Thank God! She's listening to me!' And he hugged her tight, as if he'd never let her go.

'He seems a nice young man, Jilly.' Her mother was slicing the remains of the Sunday joint which, with jacket potatoes, was their habitual Sunday-evening meal. 'I wish he'd stayed for supper.'

'He had to get home. Anything I can do?'

'Well, the table's set, but you could just fetch the Branston . . .'

In the dining room she checked the table. Her father would make a fuss if anything was forgotten, which would annoy her mother and make Jillian and her sister tense.

She hung her jacket on the combined hat and umbrella

18

stand in the hall. She checked herself in its small oval mirror and remembered how, for so long, her ambition had been to see herself in it and the sense of pride when she was finally tall enough to do so. She wondered if her face showed that her virginity had been claimed, if she looked like a woman now. But it looked disappointingly the same. She took off her spectacles and had to peer at the blur her face became. *Was* she beautiful, or had he just been saying that? But Esmée had said it too – but was she just being nice? She smiled at this. No, niceness wasn't in Esmée's nature. Certainly no one else had ever said it to her. She knew she wasn't *bad*-looking, but there was a great difference between that and *beauty*. The problem with being so short-sighted was that she only ever saw herself clearly with her specs on. She'd find out tomorrow how much contact lenses cost – she'd use her savings to get some. The money had been meant for a holiday in Spain, not that anything was planned, it was just a dream she had that one day she'd have the courage to tell her father that she wasn't going on holiday with them to the usual caravan site in Devon. She could shelve Spain and –

'Aren't you ever coming up? I'm fed up waiting for you!' Her sister Patsy, younger by three years, was hanging over the banister.

'Coming!' Jillian ran lightly up the stairs, which were covered with the new Axminster runner of which her mother was so proud. 'You can come in,' she said pointedly to her sister. Patsy was never allowed into her room unless Jillian was there, but Jillian knew she often snooped. She'd caught her out several times, laying traps of strategically placed hairs or measuring with a ruler where she'd put something so she'd know if it had been moved. Of course, Patsy always denied it. Jillian wanted a lock on the door, but her father had vetoed that in case there was ever a fire. 'So? What do you want?'

'Tell me everything!' Patsy plopped her plump self down on the bed.

'Why should I tell you, of all people, anything?' Jillian sat down at the dressing-table and unpinned her bun then brushed out her hair, experimenting to see if it looked better falling back or forward.

'Because you're bursting to talk to someone about it – and I'm the only one you can. So, how was it?'

'Very nice. It was a lovely house, you could hear the sea from every room. The weather wasn't very good.'

'I don't want a bloody weather forecast. I want to know if you *did* it?'

'For heaven's sake, Patsy, what a question!'

'You did, didn't you?'

'No, I didn't,' she lied. She didn't trust Patsy. If she told her what had happened, in the next argument they had her sister was likely to blurt it out in front of their parents.

'I don't believe you, so there!'

'Then don't. See if I care.'

'He's dishy. I peeked out of the window at him. I like tall lean blonds myself. Any hope of you shacking up with him?'

'Don't be ridiculous! We only met a couple of months back. So you can quit planning to have this room.' Patsy was always devising schemes for Jillian to leave home so that she could have the larger bedroom.

'Are you on the pill?'

'I told you I didn't do it so I wouldn't need to be, would I?'

She concentrated on twirling her hair in different styles. Talk of the pill had brought her up short. She should have gone to the family-planning clinic, but somehow that had seemed rather calculating, as if she had planned to sleep with him. And what would he have thought of her if she'd said, 'It's all right, I'm on the pill'? Not much, undoubtedly. And it wasn't that easy. Was the clinic sympathetic to unmarried women? She wasn't sure. She'd heard tales of unmarried girls being turned away with a lecture, that the pill was only given to women who already had children. The only other alternative had been their family doctor, and she was unsure if she could rely on him not to tell her mother. So she'd done nothing. They'd been careful, though, after that first time on the beach. Jack had come prepared, she was grateful for that – strange how it was all right for the man to be and not the woman.

'Anyone else there?'

'His sister brought some friends with her. They were on drugs.'

As soon as she'd imparted this information she regretted it for Patsy sat bolt upright with excited interest. 'Drugs! Really? What drugs?'

'They were smoking pot – it's got the funniest smell, I'll never forget it. And I think there was some LSD around.'

'LSD. Wowee! Did you?'

'Don't be daft. I'd be too scared to. In any case, I couldn't see the pleasure in it. They were either comatose or else they were all daffy and giggly. Very anti-social, it struck me, and rather rude.'

'What if the police had raided? You'd have been in the soup then.'

'Well, they didn't. It's unlikely they would because they're a very respectable family.'

'Sounds it with dope-heads all over the place!' Patsy laughed. 'I envy you. I can't wait to try drugs. Live a little – or, rather, live a lot!'

'Patsy, don't you dare!'

Patsy was a constant worry. She'd talked and walked early and, it seemed, had been in a hurry ever since. At sixteen it was as if she were merely biding her time before bursting free of whatever constraints annoyed her. She might have questioned Jillian about sex and drugs but it wouldn't surprise her in the least to find out that Patsy had already experienced both. Where fear corralled Jillian, Patsy had been born without any. Life was for the taking and Patsy could hardly wait to grab it.

'When are you seeing him again?'

'Not for over a month. He's going to Greece with his family, but he said he'd write.'

They both looked up as they heard the front door slam.

'Happiness is home,' Patsy said irreverently. She swung her legs over the side of the bed and stood up.

Their mother called up the stairs, 'Girls. Your father's home. Supper!'

Jillian could remember a time when her father, although not

the happiest of men, had enjoyed a pint at the pub, watching television and the occasional trip to the cinema. He'd relished his food and had had quite a paunch to show for it. Not any more.

Several years back, a colleague at the garage where he worked, who belonged to a small breakaway church calling themselves Friends of Jehovah, had invited Charlie to make up the numbers in the coach they'd hired to go to Wembley to listen to Billy Graham.

Charlie had gone to scoff and came home saved.

All his pleasures were cancelled overnight. Only cigarettes remained. He'd failed to give them up, and although he had cut down dramatically, he still smoked, still coughed.

Mary, his wife, had balked at the banishment of her television to the loft, and had made such a scene that Charlie had been forced to put it back. To Jillian the return of the television was symbolic of the separation that took place within their family. In the evening she would watch it with her mother and Patsy in the sitting room, while Charlie sat in saintly isolation on a hard chair in the dining room.

As religion had taken hold of him it was almost as if he'd contracted a disease. He lost weight, became lean and grey. His face, reasonably handsome when full, became narrow, his eyes sunken so that he had a mean expression, as if he had too much acid in his gut, which he didn't.

'If anyone ever asked me what made my marriage finally go wrong I'd have to say God!' Mary said one day to her sister, Flo. Jillian, overhearing, did not laugh as her mother and aunt did. But resentment towards her father began to grow. She blamed him for changing everything.

As children they'd gone to the local C of E Sunday school, but after his conversion church attendance had become a constant battle. For the sake of peace Jillian occasionally attended his meetings, where the others banged tambourines and sometimes spoke in tongues while she watched but never took part. Patsy refused staunchly to go.

Then one day last year he'd told Jillian he'd put her name forward as a Sunday-school teacher. 'I'm sorry, Dad, but you should have asked me first,' she'd replied, with a courage that took them both by surprise. 'I'm eighteen. I don't have to do this.'

He'd lectured her then. Standing on the hearth-rug, rocking slightly on the balls of his feet, picking up the Bible as if for strength – that Bible never left his side, these days. As he droned on she had found herself acknowledging what must have been lurking in her mind for some time: she didn't like him. And, worse, although she wanted to love him she feared she might not be able to.

In defiance she'd found her job at the theatrical agency, a place he would be certain was brimming with sin. Not that he knew, of course: he thought she worked for a building society. She enjoyed deceiving him: it made her feel she had a little power in her life. Now she schemed and planned to move out and find a place of her own.

Jillian and Patsy took their places at the table and bowed their heads as their father said grace. Both kept their eyes open and both, as Patsy put it, entertained lewd thoughts on principle.

'Did you have a nice weekend, Jillian?'

'Yes, thank you, Dad.'

'We missed you at lunch. I hope these new friends of yours won't mean you'll neglect your family.' Charlie Foster looked sternly at her while helping himself to a jacket potato. 'You've other obligations, you know, than these friends.'

'Yes, Dad.'

'You can't be too careful these days.'

'No, Dad,' she answered automatically, not really listening, but sending a swift glare at Patsy who was smirking.

'Perfect potatoes, Mary. No one does a jacket potato like you. Crispy –'

'– on the outside, fluffy on the inside.' Patsy finished the sentence for him and giggled as he looked across the table at her. 'You always say that, Dad.'

'Because it's always true. So you needn't be all smart with me.' He smiled benignly, almost proudly, at her.

Jillian looked down at her plate. He wouldn't have been so pleasant with her if she'd said that. But Patsy had always been his favourite. Not that it mattered now that she had Jack, she thought. As she watched her parents eat silently she found it difficult to imagine them ever having felt like she and Jack did. Come to think of it, when did they even talk to each other now? But they must have once. If she married Jack she'd want to stay as happy as they were now for ever. *Married Jack*. Well, there, she thought, what a thing to think! And a small, private smile played around her mouth.

'Fancy sharing the joke?'

'Sorry, Dad. Are you talking to me?'

'Well, no one else is sitting at this table with a silly grin on their face, not that I can see.' He looked pleased, as if he'd made a good joke.

'She's grinning 'cause she's smitten,' Patsy said. 'Oh-oh. See that? If looks could kill!'

'I thought this trip to the seaside was with some girlfriends you'd met through your work?' Her father laid his knife and fork carefully on his plate and stared at her.

'It was.' She crossed her fingers beneath the table against the lie.

'She met someone there, didn't you?' her mother intervened. 'He drove her home – ever such a nice young man, Charlie. A student, at Magdalene no less.'

'I've told you I don't know how many times to keep away from those undergrads – they've only one thing on their minds.'

'Haven't we all!' Patsy whispered.

'What was that, Patsy?'

'I just agreed with you, Dad.'

'Right. Well, I'm warning you, young miss, any hanky-panky and you're out. Straight out that front door. Is that understood, Jillian?'

'Perfectly.'

'You didn't . . . you know . . .?'

'No, Dad. Of course not.' She hoped she sounded affronted.

'Right!' he said, as if unsure how to proceed with the conversation.

It never failed to amaze her how lies, which she'd been warned against all her life, tripped off the tongue so easily. The problem was that one lie always led to another.

'Are you awake?' Patsy was at her door.

'I want a word with you,' Jillian said. 'Do you have to be such a creep? Why drop me in it like that? You know what he's like about boys.'

'He's got to know, especially if this one's serious – which he is. I was doing you a favour. And don't give me any crap about not sleeping with him because you did – you look different. All sort of smug and secretive.'

Involuntarily Jillian touched her face. 'Do I?'

'Ha! There! You've admitted it! Brilliant! Has he got a big dick?'

'For heaven's sake keep your voice down! They'll hear. I'm not telling you things like that. I don't want talk like that about something so wonderful. So shut up!'

'Sorree! It was just a joke. But now you've done it, can you imagine *them* doing it – the parents? That is an indisputably grotesque concept.'

'I'm sure we must have been virgin births.' Jillian grinned. It was something she'd never been able to imagine either – and even more impossible now she knew what it was like.

'Tell you what,' Patsy giggled, 'can you imagine Dad with a Bible in one hand and a hard-on in the other?'

At this Jillian collapsed in noisy laughter on the bed and the two sisters rolled about, unable to control themselves.

They were stopped by a sharp rap on the door, which was opened by their father. 'Girls! Girls! Consider other people and how they feel,' he admonished, and was deeply puzzled by the further gales of laughter his comment unleashed.

5

Work proved difficult since the office was the last place she wanted to be. She made stupid mistakes, filing two acts under the wrong letter of the alphabet and jamming the antiquated copying machine. When she was sent to buy her boss a jam doughnut she had to come back to ask him what it was he'd sent her for.

'Am I going to have to cancel my holiday, Jillian?' Pete de Silva asked exasperatedly. 'If you can't remember a flaming doughnut, how can I rely on you to run the agency while I'm away?'

'Honestly I'll be fine. You go. You said yourself it's a quiet time. If anything happens I've got your number. Heavens, Pete, Weston-super-Mare's hardly on the moon, is it?' She laughed, and he did too. 'Now, one doughnut or two?'

'Make it two. Let the holiday begin now.'

She walked quickly along King's Parade to Fitzbillie's cake shop, where she joined the usual teatime queue. As it shuffled along she thought of Jack. Her main worry was that they might have met too soon: they were both so young. Yet she was happy to settle down. All she could ever remember wanting was to marry and have children – in that she was no different from most of her friends. But boys were different, she knew that, they always joked about escaping marriage, calling it a trap. Silly, really, when that's how they all ended up.

Armed with her doughnuts, and a chocolate sponge she bought as a surprise for her mother, Jillian walked back to the cramped office in St Edward's Passage. She was just passing the Copper Kettle when, on the other side of the road, sitting on the wall of King's College, she saw Patsy and a boy, with long, matted hair wearing dirty, torn jeans, carrying a guitar case. She raised her arm to wave, but stopped as Patsy pointedly turned sideways. How odd, she thought, as she continued on her way. And what a dirty, dishevelled character she was with. She'd have a word with her sister about him, she decided, as she turned into the doorway that led to her office up the steep, uncarpeted stairs.

'Who was he?' Jillian demanded, later that evening. Supper over, she had hauled a reluctant Patsy into her room.

'I don't know what or who you're talking about.'

'Yes, you do. You saw me this afternoon outside King's.'

'I never did.'

'Oh, Patsy, don't lie to me. I saw you and I know you saw me. Who is he?'

'A friend.'

'Not one I know.'

'You don't know all my friends.'

'Evidently. Where did you meet him?'

'Not that it's any of your business, but in the market square. He was busking.'

'Is that legal?'

'Oh, come on, everyone's doing it. He plays because he loves to play. He's got a group called Strawberry Jam – isn't that fun?'

'No. Silly.'

'Christ, you're getting so *old*, Jillian!'

'I didn't like the look of him. He was dirty. Mum would have a fit.'

'Mum's not to know! She'd have kittens. Cracker's living in a drum off Mill Road with a crowd of beatniks. She'd never understand him or his friends in a million years – not that they'd ever meet. I wouldn't allow it and Cracker wouldn't want to know. He's ditched all this crap.' She waved her arm vaguely to encompass the room. 'He's free, a free spirit. It's what I want to be.'

'Patsy, be careful. I mean –'

'What? What do you mean? Drugs? So? Your friends take drugs so you can't lecture me there, can you?'

'No, I can't. But don't dabble in anything yourself, will you? Promise?'

'Don't be such a mother hen!' Suddenly Patsy hugged her. 'I love you, Jillian. I know you're only fretting because you love me.'

Later, when she lay in bed, Jillian realised that Patsy had not promised anything.

Being alone in the office was boring, she decided, four days into Pete's holiday. He'd been right, business was dead – the summer bookings were out on the road, the winter parties and concerts had still to come in. She had reorganised her filing system, cleaned the office from top to bottom, and now sat watching the tourists dawdling through the narrow passage beneath her office window. She stepped back smartly as she saw Patsy with Cracker edging their way through the crowd.

There was a clatter of footsteps on the stairs and a knock on her door. She opened it to find Patsy, shiny-eyed and excited. 'Jillian, will you see my friend Cracker? He wants to talk to you.'

She stepped back to allow them to pass. The waft of body odour from Cracker made her move even further away. She went across the office and sat down, glad that her desk was between them.

'I told Cracker you knew all about booking groups and getting people started.'

'Well, hardly.' Jillian smiled apologetically.

'It's not very plush here, is it?' Finally Cracker spoke.

'Pete de Silva only handles a few clients so he can concentrate on them. And he says they're more interested in what he can do for them than what his office looks like.'

'Who's kidding who? And de Silva! What sort of a name is that?'

'On a par with Cracker, I'd say.'

'Oh, *touché*!'

'Cracker's got a demo-tape, haven't you, Cracks? I said you'd help him.'

'Maybe. If we gel.' Cracker stared at Jillian. She found his gaze so unsettling that she had to look away.

'Let's hear the tape,' she said.

Cracker set it up and a loud, crude sound poured into the room. He sat, legs sprawled in front of him, a tantalizing bulge in his jeans, with his head flung back and his eyes closed.

The tape stopped abruptly and the silence was almost a shock.

'Well?' Cracker sat up.

'It's got something.'

'Of course it's fucking well got something. That's why I'm here.'

'The thing is, I don't think Pete de Silva is the right person to handle you. He's tried the odd group, but they nearly all break their contracts and go to London. Here.' She riffled through the large address book on her desk, found a number, scribbled it down and handed the paper to Cracker. 'I'd talk to them, if I were you. It's the agency most of the groups who've ditched Pete go to.'

'Cool.' She presumed that was his way of saying thanks.

'What on earth have you got *on*, Patsy?' Patsy's jeans were covered in bright patches and she wore a patchwork waistcoat too.

'Like it?' She stood up and twirled around.

'Well, it's different.'

'A friend of Cracker's has got a stall on the market. I'm going to make them and sell them; aren't I, Cracker?'

'Sure thing.' Cracker was in the process of rolling a cigarette. He balanced Rizla papers, a pouch of tobacco and a small brown knob of something that looked like an Oxo cube on his knee. He grated this into the tobacco with a small knife he took from his pocket. As he wet the cigarette paper with the tip of his tongue he looked straight at Jillian, his look almost challenging. He lit the thin, badly made cigarette, there was a flare of flame and he inhaled deeply, holding the smoke in his lungs as he handed the cigarette to Patsy.

'No, Patsy!' Jillian was on her feet. But Patsy was sucking at the cigarette.

'I thought you said this was your sister, not your fucking maiden aunt,' Cracker said, through the smoke that escaped his mouth like ectoplasm. Jillian looked at him with loathing as Patsy giggled. 'Don't come on so dreary, Jilly love. Relax . . .' And Cracker laughed too.

'You tell on me. I'll tell on you, it's as simple as that.' Patsy strode along the street towards their house. They'd met on the bus from town.

'I've not taken any drugs,' Jillian protested.

'No, but you let Jack Stirling screw you witless, didn't you? What do you think Dad'll say to that?'

'You're a bitch, Patsy.'

'And what are you? Threatening to tell the aged ones about a harmless smoke.'

'It's not harmless. God knows what it'll do to you.'

29

'Everyone's doing it.'

'They're not. I'm not.'

'Cracker supplies some of the dons, so there! And a few years back one of the fellows advertised in *Varsity* for people to experiment with hallucinogens, so *there*!'

'You're a fool, Patsy.'

'You drink occasionally. I like dope.'

'My friends wash.'

'I knew it would come down to that. If he drove a Jag and wore a suit I suppose that would be all right.'

'It's not just that. He looks so unattractive, dressed like that. And he stinks.'

'I like the smell of him.'

'You're nuts.'

'And you're antediluvian!'

They'd reached the gate. Both stopped.

'Agreed we keep each other's secrets?' Patsy asked, her hand on the latch of the gate.

'Agreed,' Jillian said, with misgivings.

'You're fired!' Pete de Silva, back from his holiday, was towering over her, shaking with anger.

'What have I done?'

'You've been disloyal, that's what. A group called Strawberry Jam – ever heard of them?'

'Why, yes. My sister –'

'Demo-tape. You heard that, I gather. And you heard something in it that you liked so you sodding well sent them packing to Steve Ramshaw at Metropolis. Where's the fucking loyalty in that?'

Jillian sat down again. 'I didn't think you'd be interested.'

'Permit me to be the judge of that.'

'You said yourself, only last month, that groups were more trouble than they were worth,' she said, her voice raised too.

'What if this Strawberry lot are second to the Beatles or the Rolling Stones?'

'I doubt it.'

'Well, I hope you're right, little lady. You need to learn a bit of humility, you do. Acting as if you know best.'

'How do you know?'

'Because Steve phoned me to thank me for sending him such a promising fucking *sound*, that's how!' He punched his fist on Jillian's desk.

'I'm sorry. I did it for the best.'

'Yeah, but whose best? And what's more, *this* . . .' he lifted his leatherbound address book from beside her and waved it threateningly at her '. . . *this* is the result of years of work, of bloody graft, of making contacts, of establishing myself. My business, my livelihood, is contained inside these covers. And what do you do? Hand out the numbers like fucking confetti. You heard, you're fired!' Pete banged out of her office and she heard him pound up the stairs to his own office above where he slammed that door too.

Jillian began to pack the contents of her desk into a box. She'd liked working here, but he had had reason to sack her, she admitted to herself, which didn't make her feel any better.

Chapter Two

1

Jillian was sitting on her bed, reading the three letters she'd received from Jack, which were already in a sorry state from constant handling. Of course, he hadn't written every day as he'd promised, but she hadn't really expected him to, not with all the swimming, sightseeing and holiday things he had to do. She wished he'd written that he loved her, soppy things, real love letters. Instead he'd told her what it was like in Greece, how he only liked some of the food, that retsina was great but gave him a hangover, and that if he saw another statue he'd smash it. That the country was full of German tourists but very few English – he didn't say if he thought this was a plus or not. Jillian was glad though: she knew he spoke no German so he was less likely to go off with a *fräulein*, or did all Germans speak good English? She frowned at such thoughts and returned to rereading her letters. In each he said he wished she was there, which, she supposed, was something. Unsatisfactory as they were, the letters were contact with him, and she kissed the pages, knowing he had touched them, then smelt them, longing to find his scent on them.

She had taken out a book on Greece from the library. She'd never met anyone who'd been there, it was so far away, so foreign-looking. What an unusual family they must be to choose such a place. One day, maybe, she'd go there too. She added Greece to her dream of Spain.

'Jillian! You've a visitor,' her mother called up the stairs.

'For me?' She was surprised: everyone she knew was at work. She checked her hair – she was wearing it loose with just an Alice band to hold it back – and blinked rapidly to stop the soreness in her eyes: the optician had told her to do that when her new contact lenses hurt. She was wearing them for six hours a day now, putting them in for longer than the optician had recommended since she was determined to be wearing them all day by the time Jack was back from his holiday.

One last check and she was on the landing, coming down the stairs. 'Jack!' she cried, and stumbled down the remaining steps straight into his arms.

He held her close and kissed her rapidly. 'Oh, I've missed you. I love you!' he said, even though her mother was standing in the sitting-room doorway.

'But you're not due back until next week.'

'Athens was too hot. My father said it was killing him and we were to move on. So here I am.'

'You're so brown. And even blonder.' She would like to have said, 'And even more handsome,' but she couldn't bring herself to do so, not with her mother there.

'Would you like a cup of tea, Jack?' her mother asked. 'Or lemonade?'

'If it's no trouble, Mrs Foster, lemonade would be wonderful.' He smiled at her, his teeth gleaming an improbable white in his deeply tanned face.

Mary Foster giggled and seemed all girlish suddenly. 'You two go into the garden. I'll bring it out.'

It was gloriously hot still for early September. Initially they sat on the deck-chairs beneath the one tree in the small, neat garden, and the sounds of neighbours either side carried through the wooden fence Charlie had put up for privacy. Soon they sat on the grass so that they could be closer together.

'It was hell without you. I kept remembering those nights we had in Norfolk, the feel of you, the smell of you. I had a permanent hard-on. I kept having to sit down.' He chuckled. After her initial confusion at his bluntness she laughed too.

'What's the joke?' Mary Foster had emerged with a tray of glasses and the jug of home-made lemonade.

'Nothing in particular, Mrs Foster. Just overjoyed to be

together again,' he answered smoothly, while Jillian looked away, knowing she was blushing.

'That's nice.' Mary smiled down at them.

'Your boss is a pain, Jillian. I presumed you'd be at work and he was very short with me. You're not ill, are you?'

'No. I got the sack.'

'The sack? Why, that's brilliant!'

'Not really. I need the money.'

'You haven't got another job, then?'

'No.'

'Fantastic! That's why I'm here – just on the off-chance. I wanted to know if you could spend a few days at my parents' house? Say yes! Please!' He was on his knees, his hands together, pleading in a funny, jokey way.

'Jack, I'd love to but I can't.' She glanced across at her mother. 'We're all going on holiday on Saturday – to Dawlish.'

'Oh, no.' He slumped back on his heels and Jillian bit her lip. She could have cried. This offer, and instead she'd be in a caravan with her family for two whole endless boring weeks.

'You'd much rather go with Jack, wouldn't you?' said her mother unexpectedly. 'If his parents have kindly invited you, then go.'

'Mum!' Jillian could barely believe what she was hearing. 'But what will Dad say?'

'You leave your father to me.'

Jillian scrambled to her feet. 'I'll be quick,' she said to Jack, as she ran across the pocket-handkerchief lawn, intent on packing before her mother changed her mind.

As Jack was loading her bag into the boot, Mary tugged at Jillian's sleeve. 'You will be careful, won't you?'

'Jack's a good driver, Mum. Don't worry.'

'I didn't mean that. I meant – you know.' Her mother couldn't look her in the eye. 'Just play safe, Jillian. Don't get in the family way, will you?'

Jillian could hardly believe that they were having this conversation, it must have cost her mother dear to mention such a thing. 'As if I would!' She leaned towards Mary to kiss

34

her but, as usual, her mother shied away. She did not set much store in kissing, she was fond of saying.

Jillian had no preconceived idea of the Stirling family home, Mede House, but she had certainly not expected anything as lovely and grand as this house, which stood surrounded by sweeping lawns and topiary. A creeper covered much of the front so that the red brickwork appeared to be wearing a green veil. Long, latticed windows with stone mullions stood to attention like soldiers along its length. At the angle formed by two wings was a tall three-sided, oriel window with fine lacy stone tracery on it. One wing was squatter, older, more solid than the other, and at its centre, hidden in a heavily decorated stone porch, was a studded oak front door.

'You *are* lucky to live in a house like this.' She almost sighed as she spoke for, sensational as this house was, it worried her. Here, standing four-square, was the symbol of how far apart her family and Jack's were.

'I don't think about it much, it's just home to me.' He shrugged his shoulders as if not caring, but she sensed he was pleased at her reaction. 'Come in, and welcome to my humble abode,' he clowned, bowing and scraping, making her laugh, easing her concerns.

Inside it was cool. The sun shone through the oriel window, picking up the colours from the stained-glass panels that were set in it but arranged in no particular order. These colours patterned the simple flagstone floor as if shimmering, jewel-coloured rings had been thrown on it.

They had entered a large hall, as high as the solid, darkened beams in the roof. Halfway along one heavily panelled wall was a stone fireplace in which stood a huge copper pot with a complicated flower arrangement. She crossed the room and bent to smell them, only to discover they were artificial, made of silk.

'Oh!' she said, surprised and disappointed.

'Mother won't have real flowers in the house. She says it's cruel, she can't bear to see them dying in their vases.'

'How soft-hearted.'

35

'She should be a Buddhist. She prefers to stay indoors rather than squash an ant.'

'Must make life difficult.' She wasn't sure if he was serious or not.

'Come and see the sitting room. It's my favourite.'

She could see why. The ceiling was heavily plastered like an ornate cake. Huge comfortable sofas were scattered about the room, a mixture of paintings hung on the walls – mainly modern, of animals. The long windows, which covered one wall, looked out on a garden that swept down to a river, and from here she could see that parts of the back of the house were timbered.

'I like this room. It's old, yet homely. Know what I mean?'

'It's lovely,' she replied, noticing another complicated arrangement of artificial flowers. If this were her house, and if she were as rich as these people, she would have fresh, sweet-smelling flowers everywhere. 'How long have your family lived here?'

'About ten years. Fancy a glass of champagne?' He was already uncorking a bottle, which had been standing in a bucket. 'I put it on ice before I left – in the hope you'd come back with me. If you hadn't, I would've drunk it all myself, drowning my sorrows.'

'Wouldn't it be simpler to have kept it waiting in the fridge?'

'Yes, but not as romantic.' She accepted the glass he handed her, beautifully engraved, she saw. She coveted everything she had seen in this house so far, apart from the flowers.

'Ten years, you say. So it's not an –' She stopped short: if she said what she was thinking it might appear rude.

'Not an ancestral home – is that what you were going to say?' He smiled at her: he was amused, not cross. 'No, nothing like that. We're not a grand family – only trying to seem so.' He made a little snorting sound.

'What does your father do?'

'He's a glorified rag-and-bone man.'

'A what?' She gulped at her wine, laughed then choked. Jack slapped her on the back. 'Sorry! That sounded so funny.'

'It's true. When he came out of the army all he had was my mother, two toddlers – Mungo and Esmée – and a baby, me, squeezed into a small flat in Balham, and the gratuity the Government paid to all ex-servicemen. They'd met during the war and eloped against her family's wishes. They thought my father a vulgarian who would ruin their daughter's life. And they were right. They were also concerned about his lack of money, so he set out to prove them wrong.

'He's smart, I'll give him that. He spent a month thinking, then spent what he had on buying up unwanted army saucepans and he was away. He'd buy anything if he thought he could sell it, but army surplus was the making of him. Then he started a factory to produce new-fangled plastic toys.'

'You're joking!'

'No. He spots trends then goes for them. He has a finger in so many pies now. He believes in diversification – "Don't matter if the bottom falls out of one thing, mate. You've always got the other buggers to fall back on –"' he said, in a gruff voice, with a marked cockney accent. 'Everything you see he'd sell if someone offered enough. It's a miracle the house hasn't gone by now. I think the old bastard must be genuinely fond of it.'

'Jack, that's your father you're talking about!' But secretly she admired him for having the courage to be honest. She knew she never would.

'Yes, and he *is* an old bastard. I hate him. I wish he was dead. And don't worry, my sweet, the feeling's mutual.'

Talking about his father had spoilt the mood. Jillian crossed to him, put her arms about him and kissed his cheek. He turned to her, pulled her close and kissed her full on the mouth.

'Someone might come in, Jack,' she said, breathless with her own excitement.

'There's no one here.'

They raced up the staircase, flew along the landing, then another corridor. Her earlier interest in architecture had evaporated; she looked neither to right nor left as he led her to his room, his bed.

37

When they touched each other, even lightly as she just had, their longing for each other ignited and became a clothes-tearing, ripping, desperate need. As she felt his hands exploring her body, his mouth closing over hers, his tongue searching, probing, the excitement mounted. At the touch of their naked bodies she felt the warmth, the velvety softness of him and gloried in her own. Quickly he was straddling her. She writhed in pleasure as he thrust into her. Their bodies entwined in the centre of his wide bed.

Exhausted they lay in each other's arms, satiated – for the time being.

'We never have time for much foreplay, do we?' She sat up in the bed and looked down at him.

'Complaining?'

'No. Nothing like. It's like a craziness comes over me. All I want is you in me. That wonderful hardness filling me.'

'Talk like that and we'll be off again. Let's finish the champagne. I'll go and get it.' And he padded, stark naked, out of the room.

'Should you walk around like that?' she asked, when he returned.

'Why not? I told you, there's no one here.'

'But what if your parents walk in?'

'They won't. They're in Crete.'

'But you said – my mother –'

'I didn't lie. I said Athens was too hot for my father and he decided we should move on. I used work as an excuse to come home and they went to Crete. He'd been there in the war. The last thing I needed was a sentimental journey round old battle haunts.' He grinned mischievously at her. 'I can't help it if your mother jumped to the wrong conclusion.'

'How long before they get back?'

'Two weeks.'

'No! How wonderful. Just us?'

'Absolutely. We can make love morning, noon and night and howl our joy to the heavens. Shall we practise?' And he lunged across the bed for her.

They enjoyed long, lazy days together. They ate when

hungry, slept when tired, made love endlessly. They were not restricted by time so night became day and vice versa.

'Esmée told my mother about you.'

'Why did she do that?'

'Because she's a spuddling cow.'

'What did your mother say?'

'Gave me a lecture on contraception!'

'You can talk to your mother about that? Sounds great. Does your dad know about us?'

'No, but he wouldn't care what I did so long as it didn't cost him.'

'I think my dad would kill me.'

'I thought you said he was a Bible-thumping churchman.'

'He is. He's not so Christian that he wouldn't bump me off, though.'

'Then I'd kill *him*.'

'But if you don't want to be a lawyer then don't do it. Read history if that's what you'd prefer.'

'I'd be cut off without a penny.'

'Surely not.'

'Oh, yes, no doubt about it. My dad wants me to be a lawyer so that I can work for him – a tame lawyer in the family, he reckons, will save him a fortune.'

'Then why you? Why can't Mungo do it?'

'I'm afraid Mungo's too thick. He's a nice fellow but with a few neurones missing, unfortunately for me.'

'What about Esmée, then?'

'She's bright – brighter than me, probably – but unfortunately Dad thinks a woman's place is in the home, that higher education is wasted on the female of the species. I think she got married because she was bored and wanted to get away from here. I like her husband, Toby, but he couldn't control her – no one can – so she did a bunk.'

'Does she work now?'

'No. Dad gives her an allowance.'

'My dad's a bit like that – he thinks the only career for a woman is marriage.'

'What do you think?'

'Me?' Suddenly she was flustered. 'Oh, I don't want to get hitched for years,' she lied.

'And your sister? Does he want the same for her?

'I'm not sure. She's the favourite. And she's clever. She's got more courage than me. If she wants to do something with her life she'll do it and my dad can take a hike – only he doesn't know it yet. I'll probably settle for being exactly what my father wants for me, a wife and a mother.'

'Is that a proposal?' He smiled at her.

'Good God! No!' She covered her face. What must he think of her?

'Just teasing.' He took away her hands and kissed her gently. 'Do you mind Patsy being the favourite?'

'No, not really. It's always been like that. Perhaps if I liked him more I'd mind.' There, she'd actually put into words the thought that had been rattling around in her mind for ages; it didn't seem to be such a big deal either, now she'd said it.

'Perhaps you don't care because you don't love him either.'

She looked up sharply. 'I'd never think like that.' How could he know that that was exactly what she *was* beginning to feel?

'Only because you're conditioned not to. The day I acknowledged to myself that I didn't like or love my father was, I can assure you, a day of blessed relief.'

She frowned, not liking what he said, not approving of it, fearing it – but why should she? She shook her head, shaking the idea away. 'We were meant to meet, you and me. We're soul-mates. Unloved by our daddies. Boo-hoo.' She laughed at him and, as if the laughter was an invitation, his mouth was quickly upon hers and within minutes they were back in bed.

Jillian had had boyfriends before, had been in love before, but never like this. They *were* soul-mates. There was so much they had in common – history, and Henry VIII in particular, was one thing. Neither liked the Beatles, but had hardly dared confess it to anyone else since each had, until now, felt they were the only person on the planet who didn't. They preferred Buddy Holly and the Beach Boys. 'True rockers, that's us,' Jack said. They both wanted to go to America, but that didn't stop them hankering to visit Tibet – one day, when it was possible.

In these days at Mede House, Jack began to educate her on food, the one thing they didn't have in common. Jillian's mother cooked good, plain food. She would not have recognised garlic if she saw it and herbs meant mint for sauce and sage for stuffing. Until now, Jillian had eaten because it was necessary and had little interest in food. She had tried the Italian restaurant in the market square and had quite liked it, and she'd had moussaka at the Varsity, the Greek restaurant in St Andrew's Street. But on the rare occasions they went out to celebrate as a family it was invariably for steak at the Berni Inn that had opened in Trinity Street. Jack was appalled. 'I shall teach you as my mother taught me. I think food, next to you-know-what and wine, is the best reason for being alive.'

She enjoyed sitting at the table in the large, vaulted kitchen watching him cook – peeling, chopping, beating, frying, tasting – like an expert. They had Italian, French, Chinese, Indian dishes, each night something different, each night a delicious meal. She quickly became his avid pupil.

They dissented on religion. Jillian believed in God, though not the fearsome one her father worshipped. Hers was more of a wise grandfatherly type.

'On a cloud with a flowing beard?' Jack asked.

'No, silly, in the wind, the sun, nature.'

'You're a pagan!'

'I never am!'

Jack believed in nothing, which worried her – she couldn't help it.

'When you're dead that's it. Eyes closed, big nothing,' he declared.

'Jack, don't even say it.' She looked nervous, as if afraid her father's God might hurl a thunderbolt at him.

'I think it sounds rather nice. Just like sleeping. I like sleep.'

'I haven't noticed!' she replied gaily, and the sombre moment was gone.

After almost a week of their own particular solitude, they went to London for the day. They shopped in a way new to Jillian. If Jack liked a shirt he bought three or four. One pair of shoes became two. He suggested she should have both when she'd fallen for a short shift and matching palazzo pants, brightly patterned like the Pucci clothes she'd seen in a magazine. 'You'll regret it if you don't buy them.'

'That's ridiculous. Anyway, I can't afford them.'

'I'll buy them for you.'

'You jolly well won't!' She compromised by buying the two outfits but in different colours. She would have had to lie to her mother if he'd bought them for her: the one piece of sexual advice Mary Foster had given her daughters was, 'Never let a man buy you clothes. He'll think it his right to take them off you.'

They went to La Vendôme for a lobster lunch – the first time she'd ever tasted it – and a lifelong love affair was born. She drank half a bottle of Chablis where once a glass had been enough. They went to Cork Street and toured the galleries; she'd never have dared to go in by herself, but Jack was a well-known customer, and fêted, so Jillian relaxed.

The small back seat and the boot of Jack's car were filled with packages and carrier bags. They had thought of going to the theatre, but decided they wanted to go home instead, that they'd already been too long away from their bed.

She had nodded off on the journey – the effect of so much wine, she supposed.

'Oh, sod! No!'

His voice woke her with a start. 'What? What's happened?'

'They're back.'

'Who?'

'My parents.'

'Oh, no! Are you sure?'

'That's Dad's car!' He pointed to a silver Rolls-Royce standing in front of the house.

'I didn't do the washing-up!'

'Doesn't matter.'

'Of course it does. What on earth will your mother think of me?'

'She won't mind. She's not like that.'

Jillian felt apprehensive as they collected their purchases and entered the house. Flitting about in her mind was a silly plan to race upstairs, pack and leave before she met anyone. But all such ideas collapsed as a large man moved towards them, drink in hand.

'Dad! This is a surprise.'

'Evidently,' his father answered, in a deep, rich voice tinged with amusement.

'I wasn't expecting you home for another week.'

'So I see.' Ralph Stirling stared straight at Jillian, who found herself mesmerised by the startling blue of his deep-set eyes. No wonder Jack had such lovely eyes. 'Caught you out, haven't I?' He laughed. The sound began deep within him, rumbled to the surface, exploded joyously and echoed in the large room. At this point Jack dropped two of the carrier bags on the floor and the makeup and perfume Jillian had rashly bought tumbled out and rolled about the stone floor. She swooped on them in confusion, fearing her perfume might have broken. Jack returned a pot of cream to her and she saw that his hand was shaking.

'When you've finished grovelling around down there, maybe you'll introduce me,' Ralph said, amusement still bubbling in his voice.

'This is my friend Jillian Foster.'

'Esmée didn't do you justice, Jillian,' he said, taking her hand in his large one. His smile deepened the lines on his tanned face dramatically so that he looked, momentarily, as if he were wearing a rubber mask. He was casually dressed in slacks and sweater and on his little finger shone a large diamond ring. At his wrist was a chunky gold watch, and round his neck was a heavy gold chain with a large medallion – a St Christopher, Jillian thought. She was fascinated: she'd never seen a man wear jewellery before. He was taller than his son by a good four inches, broader too. His hair, given his age, was too black to be natural but she decided that such a show of vanity was rather appealing. He was a handsome giant of a man – a genial giant, she felt, not an ogre. 'I hope you've been comfortable here, my dear.' Nor was his voice as accented as Jack had made out.

'Thank you, yes. It's a lovely house,' she said, unsure how to proceed.

'It does us,' he said genially.

'So why are you back so soon, Dad?'

'Your mother got sick. She made such a fuss I thought it best to come home. She's in the kitchen, getting dinner. Mungo and Liz are on their way over.'

'I'll go and see her.' Jack moved towards the door that led to the back of the house. Jillian, wondering if she should stay or go with him, decided on hot pursuit. She excused herself to his father and ran after him.

Jack stood at the kitchen sink, his arm around his mother. Though she had her back to the room, her stance was of total weariness. 'Ma, you look done in. Come and sit down. Let me do that.' He led her to a chair at the long, scrubbed table on which, to Jillian's shame, their breakfast dishes sat. 'You should have phoned, Ma, told me you were coming. I could have had a meal ready for you.'

'Communications made it difficult. The telephone system was a scandal.' Her voice was melodious, soft, very feminine. 'And you know what your father's like. My dear!' She began to stand up. 'I'm so sorry. I didn't see you there.'

'Ma, sit. Relax. This is Jillian, the girl I told you about.'

'So, you're my son's little friend. How lovely to meet you. You're making Jack very happy, that's all that matters. Everything else is unimportant, my dear.' Jillian found herself on the receiving end of a wonderful smile, to which the only response was another. She felt, quite illogically, she realised, that she was the one person in the world Theresa Stirling wanted to see.

Theresa had an elegance that did not pander to the extreme fashion of the time, yet incorporated parts of it in her own style. The effect was to make her look younger than her age, which Jillian knew to be fifty since Jack had told her. She had the lovely face of one blessed with fine bones, a beauty that

44

age would improve rather than lessen. Her eyes were a luminous grey. Her fine blonde hair was lightened by a sprinkling of silver which, since it was not camouflaged, presumably she did not mind.

'I'm so sorry about the mess, Mrs Stirling.' Jillian waved at the dishes that littered the kitchen. 'We've been lazy.'

'Far more important things to do than housework, I'm sure.' She laughed and looked at her son indulgently. 'Such a pretty dress you have on. Nylon is so practical, isn't it?'

'Thank you.' Jillian smoothed its skirt – it was her least favourite dress. She assumed that Theresa was making her feel comfortable.

'I'll just get these dishes out of the way. It'll only take a second.' Theresa got up.

'Oh, no, you don't, Ma.' Jack pushed her back into the chair.

'I'll do it.' Immediately Jillian began to collect them. Seeing potatoes in the sink, half peeled, she stacked the plates on the draining-board. 'How many potatoes shall I do?'

'How very kind of you. Are you sure you don't mind? We shall be, let me see ... Are you staying to supper, Jack?'

'No, Ma. Jillian has to get back.'

'Ah, what a shame. Back where?'

'Cambridge. Her mum will put me up for a few days.'

'Such kindness. I love Cambridge. Is your father an academic, Jillian? Where was I ...?' she continued, without waiting for an answer.

'Counting numbers, Ma,' Jack said, with amused tolerance. Jillian was glad she was occupied with the potatoes and turned away from them so that his mother couldn't see the surprise on her face. She felt disappointed that they were leaving; now that she had met Jack's parents and discovered how nice they were she would have liked to stay.

'So it's your father and me, Mungo and Liz and ... You should have come to Crete, it was fascinating. Knossos was unbelievable too, and –'

'Dad says you were ill.'

'Gracious, he does exaggerate. I had a slight chill, that was all. Your father found the antiquities boring and wanted to come home so he used me as an excuse. I was sad. I was enjoying myself . . .' Her voice trailed off with regret, but then, as if catching herself, she sat up. 'But tell me, what exciting things have you been doing?'

'Not a lot.' Jack talked about London, and Jillian could see that he was trying to make what they had done and seen today sound as if it had filled a week.

'Excuse me, should I boil these?' Jillian interrupted.

'Just par-boil. The meat's in. I stopped and bought a rib – your father was literally pining for English food. Such a shame you're not staying.'

'I'll just knock up the Yorkshires for you', Jack put in. 'Then we must be away, otherwise Mrs Foster will be wondering where we are. Liz will give you a hand when she gets here.'

'Do you really think so?' She smiled wearily. 'I want to know all about Jillian.'

'Time enough, Ma.'

'Will you come and stay again, Jillian?'

'I should love to,' she replied, then wondered if she'd said the wrong thing since Jack was shaking his head at her from behind his mother's chair.

'We could go back to my place. My parents aren't due back for another week,' Jillian said, as they drove through the twilight at a fierce pace.

'Not on your nelly! What if they turned up early too?'

'They won't, though. If my dad's paid for two weeks' holiday nothing will stop him getting his full pennyworth. They could have a hurricane hit the caravan site and I bet you he'd be clinging on.'

'We'll be more comfortable in a hotel.'

'But what if they ask if we're married?'

'Then I'll say we are!'

'We look too young.'

'I'll say we're on our honeymoon – a shotgun wedding!' He liked this and laughed, and the tension she'd seen in his house lessened with each passing mile. 'You worry too much, Jillian. Heavens, this is the sixties. We're liberated now.'

'Are we?' She was uncertain. 'I wish we could have stayed.'

'I'm not having you in the same house as my father.'

'What about the weekend your mother invited me to?'

'You can come for lunch.'

'Why?'

'I have my reasons.'

'I think your father's lovely, and your mother's adorable – so charming.'

'She is but, for Christ's sake, Jill, don't let my father con you for one minute.'

He seemed so agitated that she didn't bother to remind him that she didn't like to be called Jill.

3

They found a pub with rooms near Newmarket. She was sure the owners had known she and Jack were not married, but they were comparatively young so nothing was said and they had been at pains to make her feel at home.

'Gracious, I'll get fat at this rate,' she said over breakfast one morning, as she cut into her second sausage.

'Don't you dare!' he said, popping a slice of his third into his mouth.

Jillian had worried about the cost they must be racking up, especially when Jack ordered champagne, for the third time.

'Jack! At pub prices! You shouldn't!'

'Why not? Don't worry, darling, I've got the money. Dad may not like me but he's very generous.'

'I think all that business of him not liking you is all in your mind. He seemed genuinely pleased to see you.'

'You know nothing about it so I suggest you stop giving your opinion,' he said coldly. Jillian looked at him, horrified: it was the closest they had been to an argument in the three and a half months she'd known him.

These days together, though pleasant, were not as idyllic as the week they had spent at his home. She sensed a distance forming between them, as yet a mere shade of difference, which she noticed only because of their extreme closeness before. It was as if, for a week, they had been one person; now, imperceptibly, they were returning to being two. Since they were still happy, still making love, still enjoying being together, she decided it was because they were no longer alone for twenty-four hours a day that the world was intruding on them.

He was right, she told herself. His relationship with his father was none of her business. But, then, since she and Jack were involved, it could equally be said that it *was* her concern. Maybe she shouldn't jump to conclusions too fast. After all, who really knew what went on in a family unless they were part of it? When she apologised to Jack for pressing too much and told him of the conclusions she had reached, she was rewarded with the return of their previous intimacy.

They were both reluctant to leave.

'Just one day more,' he begged, on the Thursday night.

'No, my love. Please don't tempt me. I must be back early tomorrow, get everything straight and the shopping in for my family's return on Saturday.'

When they pulled up in front of the Foster house at lunchtime on Friday it was to see the windows open and the front door ajar.

'Crikey. You don't think we've been burgled, do you?' She looked anxiously at Jack.

'I'll go first. You wait here,' he ordered. But she followed him up the short garden path and was right behind him when, gingerly, he pushed open the front door. 'Anyone at home?' he shouted.

The sitting-room door swung open.

'Where the hell have you been?' Her father stood in the doorway, his face suffused with anger.

'At Jack's, as arranged. Didn't Mum tell you?'

'Don't you lie to me!' He stepped forward so quickly that she hadn't time to avoid his sharp slap across her face.

'Here! I say! Don't you hit her like that!'

'I'll hit her any way I want, young man. I suggest you get out now before I hit you.'

'Oh, yes. You think so?' And the two men squared up to

48

each other just as an agitated-looking Mary rushed in from the garden. She stepped between them and, at the same time, took Jillian's hand and squeezed it as Jillian controlled tears that were not far away.

'Calm down, Charlie, do. Let's have a nice cup of tea and talk about this!'

'Just listen to you, Mary, wittering on about nice cups of tea when your daughter's disappeared and the Lord above knows where she is and in what peril.'

'Mum? Patsy? Disappeared?'

'Don't play this charade with me! No doubt you know all about it, you lying little bitch!' He looked as if he was about to lunge at her again, but Jack stepped forward menacingly.

'I don't believe this is happening!' Jillian said, perplexed.

'You might sneer at my suggestion of tea, but we can't stand here just howling abuse at each other, and hitting people, now can we? Sitting room,' Mary ordered.

They all settled in chairs, except Jillian's father, who paced the semi-circular hearth-rug – worked by Mary.

'When did she go? Where?'

'We had a bit of a row, truth be told,' Mary began.

'Your fault.' Charlie pointed an accusing finger at Jillian.

'I wasn't even here so how can it be my fault?'

'Once she learned you'd decided not to grace us with your presence on our holiday she announced she was doing the same,' Charlie said.

'I told her she was only sixteen and you were older so you had more right to do what you wanted,' Mary explained.

'Rights!' Charlie exploded, as if the word were an expletive.

'I told her your father was already deeply hurt that you weren't coming and that it would be unkind of her not to come too,' Mary ploughed on, ignoring her blustering husband. 'We went to bed, our cases packed. She was sweet, I thought she'd reconsidered. In the morning she and her cases were gone. She left a note. All it said was "Sorry. I'll be in touch." And she hasn't. I'm so frightened.' Mary began to cry softly, as if many tears had been shed more noisily before.

Jillian put her arm around her mother's shoulders and was

49

shocked at how thin she had become in such a short time. 'Mum, you've lost so much weight!'

'She doesn't feel much like eating at a time like this,' Charlie snapped.

'Excuse me, Mr Foster, but have you called the police?' Jack asked politely.

'Of course we've called them. Fat lot of good they are! Said she'd turn up, no doubt, when it suited her. That she was sixteen, that she'd packed her bag so she was unlikely to have been abducted. The fact that this is a good home and she had no need to leave meant nothing to them.'

'Good home! You call this a good home? You sodding hypocrite, Charlie!' Mary's voice was shrill and Jillian was unsure what shocked her most, the shrillness or the bad language. She'd never heard her mother swear before. Charlie stepped back as if she were about to attack him and bumped against the fender, looking alarmed. 'If you hadn't spent your time ramming that sodding Bible down their throats, spending more time on your bloody knees than with your family, this would never have happened.' Mary was shaking now. Jillian tried to calm her, but it was as if her mother had held back so much that now the dam had burst she couldn't stop it from flowing free. 'That bloody church and those mewing, two-faced toads you like to call friends – we'll see if they regard you as a friend now, won't we? Oh, yes, we'll see what your fine friends think of you now!' And Mary sobbed, noisily this time, as if her tear glands had been given another lease of life.

'I don't think accusing each other will help,' Jillian said quietly.

'Help, you say! You're a fine one to talk. What help have you been? Of course, you didn't have the courtesy to leave a phone number where we could contact you, did you?' Her father grabbed at her interruption as if diverting his wife from attacking him.

'There seemed little point since *we* don't have a phone.'

'There are call boxes, aren't there? Took us days to find you! Of course, your mother here, couldn't remember your so-called friend's name. Typical!' He glanced with disdain at his weeping wife. 'And when we do find out the number and ring, what do we find? That you're not even there. And, what's more, his father thinks he's here. So there's a mite of explaining to do, wouldn't you say? I presume you were out whoring.'

'Mr Foster, I must object.' Jack was on his feet. 'How dare you speak to Jillian in this way?'

'So you weren't rutting – fornicating with my daughter, then?' He spat out the words, his face distorted with disgust.

'No, sir, we weren't,' Jack said stalwartly.

'You expect me to believe you?'

'We weren't doing any of those things, sir,' he said, with an almost imperceptible pause before the 'sir'. 'If you must know, we were making love, but obviously from your attitude that is a subject you understand little about.' He put out his hand to Jillian. 'Come, Jillian, I think we should leave.'

'But, my mother . . .' She glanced anxiously at Mary, wanting to go but loath to leave her.

'You go, Jillian. I'm all right.'

'I think I know where she might be, Mum.'

'See?' Charlie said triumphantly. 'I just knew she'd be at the bottom of this. Where?'

'I'm not telling you, Dad. It's up to Patsy if she wants you to know where she is. I can't decide for her.'

'Is she all right, Jillian? Where she is, I mean?'

'She'll be fine,' Jillian said, and forced as much confidence into her voice as she could muster. She stood to leave.

'If either of you were going to do this, why couldn't it have been you? I could live without you!' Her father stared coldly at her. She felt her skin tauten and she tried to smile, to show she did not care, but the result was a rictus of pain. She turned and ran from the room ignoring her mother's 'Wait!'

'Phew, families!' Jack half laughed as they clambered into his car, aware that Charlie, still seething with rage, was scowling at them from the front-room window. 'I thought I was the only one who lived in a madhouse.'

'God, that was awful! Mortifying.' She put her hands over her face as if she could shut out the memory.

51

'Did he hurt you?'

'Feelings more than flesh.' She felt too ashamed to want to make too much of it.

'That was a dreadful thing he said. Probably from the stress. He didn't mean it.'

'He did,' she said bleakly. 'But so what?' She sat up straighter. 'He only said what I knew he was thinking. What's new?'

Jack patted her hand. She wanted to pull it away, for she didn't want sympathy, not now. Sympathy would ensure that she lost control: then her father would have won whatever battle it was he had with her.

'Right. Let's get going.' Jack put the car into gear. 'Do you really know where your sister is?'

'She might have gone off with a bloke called Cracker. He lived in a house off Mill Road. I don't know if he's still there.'

'Let's go and see.'

'I don't know the address. We'll have to ask.'

The first person they asked evidently knew who they were talking about but pretended he didn't. And when Jillian mentioned that it was her sister she was trying to find, the man backed off sharply.

'I don't think he's too keen on family, do you?' Jack grinned at her. 'I'll have a go next time.'

Jillian didn't know whether to be shocked or impressed as she listened to Jack talking to the long-haired beatnik type, obliquely referring to 'stash', 'pot' and 'weed'.

'You're not the pigs?'

'Do I look as if I am? I'm a student. Magdalene.'

'Really! Babbage your tutor? He was mine too.' They shook hands, the unkempt non-conformist and the smartly dressed Jack, but college loyalty transcended all other considerations.

'Don't tell Cracker I told you. He has a mean side.'

'Sure thing. Why have you –'

'Dropped out? I listened to Leary, man. And it all made sense. Peace!' He drifted away.

Cracker wasn't at the address they'd been given and the young woman who answered the door had no intention of helping. 'They've probably gone to London. I gave them the address of an agent,' Jillian said.

'Right. London it is, then,' Jack said. 'I've never been to this area before – only had the odd drink in the Locomotive – but these houses could be pretty done up – lick of paint. Bet you could make a bomb here.'

'*These?* You've got to be joking! They're awful.' And she looked dismissively at the rows of neat Victorian terraces – two windows up, one and a door below.

The agent, Steve Ramshaw, couldn't help.

'Sorry, Jillian. Cracker's got potential, no doubt about it. And egos I can understand when they've made it, but an ego the size of his on the first rung of the ladder – no way. I couldn't deal with him – Knew it all, rejected all advice. As to your sister, never met her. Fancy a job? You have a nice telephone voice, and you're a looker too.'

Outside the agency they stood on the pavement, unsure what to do next.

'I don't think I'd want to work for him.'

'I'm glad to hear it.' Jack put a proprietorial arm around her shoulder. 'He'd be trying to get into your knickers before you knew where you were.'

'Jack! What a thing to say!'

'You know, I can't really see the point of looking for Patsy. If she wants to do a bunk, why shouldn't she? I often wish I could.'

'But – she's so young.'

'And you're Methuselah? Having met your father I'm not surprised she's done a runner.'

'Dad means well, I suppose. He's so scared for us, I think, that he wants to circle us with religion to keep us out of harm's way.'

'Hasn't he heard of vicars' daughters? Wow, they're the worst! A reaction sets in, apparently, and they kick up their heels – and how!'

They were weaving their way along the crowded Soho pavements, but despite all the people he never lost hold of her – that was nice, she thought, and made her feel cosy and safe.

'She'll be in touch, I'm sure. Meanwhile, what about us? Let's go to Esmée's. She'll put us up.'

'Are you sure? She scares me.'

'Esmée! Don't be silly, Jillian. She's all front.'

4

Jillian couldn't fault Esmée's welcome as she ushered them in. 'Of course I've got room for you both. What a lovely surprise. I'll just have to boot a couple of stray dogs out if the squash gets too much.' They followed her along the narrow corridor that bisected the large mansion-block flat. 'You couldn't have come at a better time, Jack. Tedious Toby's here, creating problems. I'll get us something to drink.' She turned into what must have been the kitchen.

Jack pushed open a door on the other side of the corridor. 'Hi, Toby, how's tricks?' he asked, as he and Jillian entered a sombrely lit room. A tall, blond man sat in a large chair. In his pinstripe suit, he looked out of place against the sequined, heavily beaded, brightly coloured cushions that surrounded him.

'Jack. Great to see you.' And Toby leaped up with an expression of pleasure. He just missed being handsome: his face was a little too fleshy and flushed so that his eyes looked smaller than they probably were, but as far as Jillian could see he bore no resemblance to a toad. If he lost just a little weight, Jillian thought, he could be quite good-looking.

'I didn't expect to see you here,' Jack said, when the introductions had been completed.

'I had some stuff to discuss with Esmée. You're a godsend, Jack. Try and get her to see sense, will you?'

'I'm a genius in many things, Toby – but understanding my sister? What seems to be the problem?'

Jillian's eyes had adjusted to the gloom and she looked around her. The room was dark because the windows were covered in black paint on which were stuck gold and silver stars – like the ones her primary-school teachers had given for good work. The walls were painted a deep maroon, and the paintings on them were large and sombre too. One wall was swathed in heavy dark red brocade. The only lighting was from lamps standing on the floor, each shade draped with chiffon. The only true colours were those of the cushions and Esmée's clothes. When she returned with the champagne and moved about the room, the shine of the silk, the sheen of the satin, the glint of the sequins she wore seemed to attract what little light there was and absorb it. Everywhere else was left darker with her passing. She looked like a colourful butterfly caught out in the night.

'Don't listen to a word Toby's saying to you, Jack,' Esmée said. 'As usual he's being an out-and-out bastard.'

'See, Toby? Nothing changes,' Jack said, laughing.

'Don't worry, old chap. If Esmée were nice to me I'd probably die of shock. I'd like your opinion, though. Please, Esmée, just let me put my side to Jack, then you can have your turn. It's about the house . . .'

Toby began to speak urgently and quietly to Jack, who leaned forward as if conspiring, so Jillian, not wishing to intrude, continued to look about her. There was a musty smell in the airless room, which, no doubt, came from the preponderance of rugs and hangings, Jillian wondered if they were Moroccan – she thought Esmée had said she'd been there recently. She could detect stale cannabis too. What would her father think of this? A small smile played around her mouth.

'I think Toby's right, Esmée,' Jack said eventually, sitting back on the ottoman where he'd perched.

'You bloody creep! Take anyone's side but your sister's.'

'It's not a question of taking sides. Toby's put his case and I think he's right. He needs to sell the house, and it's silly to stay married when it's over. Give the poor chap his freedom. He's offered to allow you to sue him. What more do you want?'

'But I won't. I hate to think of anyone in my house.'

'It's not your house, it's Toby's, and if he's to give you any money he needs to sell it.'

'Then why has it got my name on the deeds?'

'Because Toby's a nice guy, if a sucker. If I'd married you I wouldn't have done what he did.'

'But, then, even if you weren't my brother I'd never marry a prig like you. In any case, I don't want his money.'

'The house has got to go and I need your signature, Esmée, please.'

'I might sign,' she said infuriatingly. 'I might even agree to a divorce but, then, on the other hand I might not.'

'If I were Toby I'd divorce you, citing that creep Fabrice.'

'Well, Toby won't. He's a gentleman and you're not.'

'Quite honestly, Esmée, I'm amazed no one's murdered you yet. You deserve it. Now, sign that bloody paper or I'll never speak to you again.'

Jillian felt increasingly uncomfortable as brother and sister shouted at each other. Poor Toby looked close to tears. Esmée had reached the point of telling both men she hated them, when Toby sagged from weariness. Jillian thought he'd given in, but he hadn't.

'You leave me no choice, Esmée. I'll have to divorce you naming Fabrice, Richard, Peter . . .' As he spoke, he was ticking off the names on his fingers. Jillian was amazed that anyone so young could have had so many lovers. 'And I'll find out the names of those three who were tripping in one room in one bed with you.'

'The darlings were happy – but you don't understand about happiness, do you, Toby? Just money.' Esmée was on her feet, bending down to snatch up the paper. 'I'll sign the flaming thing, then. For peace.'

'Oh, yes. So Dad won't find out how you live your life, more like.' Jack was grinning. 'Aren't you ever worried he might just decide to visit you one day, Esmée?'

'No. He's too predictable for that. He'd make an appointment first. You know he would.'

'What about Mum?'

'She's already been here. She thinks the flat and my friends are perfectly sweet. So there, Jack, my *dear* lad.' Esmée tossed the now signed paper back on to the table. 'Right.' She sounded quite normal, not how Jillian had imagined a woman who had been through such a scene might sound. 'You and Jillian can sleep in the end room. It's empty but it might be in a bit of a pickle.'

'Oh, that doesn't matter, Esmée. I can sleep anywhere.' Jillian scrambled to her feet.

'And, undoubtedly, you have,' Esmée said serenely, as she wafted from the room.

'Take no notice,' Jack said, but Jillian's embarrassment had, as always, turned into a traitorous blush.

'Would you be so kind as to witness Esmée's signature?' Toby asked. 'I'd be incredibly grateful.'

Jillian looked worried.

'You're only witnessing her signature, Jillian, not anything that she's actually put it to,' Jack explained.

'Oh, fine.' Jillian accepted Toby's pen.

'If she changes her mind again, will you divorce her, Toby? It could be messy – all over the papers, what with the drugs and Dad's brand of fame.'

'I don't know. All the time she's married to me it stops her taking the plunge with someone totally unsuitable. I mean, have you met the latest – Fabrice? If he's a count, I'm an all-in wrestler. Thanks, Jillian.' He folded the document and stowed it away in his briefcase.

'But what about you? What if you meet someone else?'

'I think marriage to your sister has cured me of wanting membership of that institution for some time.' Toby laughed, good-naturedly enough, but as they stood to say their goodbyes Jillian saw again the sadness in his eyes.

'Toby's nice,' Jillian said, as they changed the somewhat dubious-looking linen on the bed in the end room.

'He is. One of my favourite people. He's straight as a die, kind, loyal, generous. The perfect man for any woman, I'd have thought.'

'So what went wrong?'

'Maybe he's too steady. Maybe Esmée wanted someone a bit more unreliable. I don't know. I've often wondered if, in fact, she's more struck on him than she'll admit, but he's so wrapped up in his work that she's gone wild to attract his attention and even make him jealous. But Toby being Toby rationalises how she is and thinks he should be fair and try to understand her when, the truth is, there's nothing *to* understand. Esmée's a show-off shell of a person.'

'That's a bit harsh, isn't it?'

'I don't think so. You asked.' He looked at her with a puzzled expression.

Patsy might annoy her at times, Jillian thought, but she wouldn't ever speak about her like that to anyone – not even to the man she loved.

'I don't say things I wouldn't say to her face,' Jack added, 'if that's what you're thinking.'

'Your sister's really rather sad, isn't she? Though she pretends otherwise. It would explain the drugs. They're an escape. When she's on them she can forget about Toby and what she's lost.'

'Could be. Mind you, Esmée's always been one for enthusiasms. She never does anything by halves. She's the type of person who never eats one chocolate, she'll pig the whole box. If she likes a piece of music she'll play it *ad nauseam* until you want to eliminate it from the face of the earth. And she's like that with people – she gets a craze for someone, lives in their pocket and then, *zap*,' he clicked his fingers, 'they've gone. And you can say to her, "Where's old so-and-so?" And she'll look at you all blank and say, "Who?" It can get quite creepy.'

'These drugs she uses – pot and LSD – are they addictive?'

'They say not, but I guess the feeling they give you could become so.'

'Have you tried them?' She looked at him curiously.

'Only pot a couple of times. I'd rather have a beer myself.'

'Don't you worry about her?'

'Not particularly. It's her life and she can do what she wants with it.' He seemed detached, almost uninterested, in Esmée's fate, which Jillian found chilling. As if her body sensed this, she shuddered. 'Cold? Come here.' He leaned across the bed and pulled her towards him.

*

They had arrived at Esmée's at a quiet time. After their love-making they had fallen asleep and when they emerged from the end room it was to find many more people in the flat.

'I'm hungry. Let's have a fry-up.'

The gloom of the rest of the flat had not pervaded the kitchen, but looking about at the chaos, the dirty plates, the half-empty tins, Jillian wished it had. The refrigerator contained two bottles of champagne, a tin of cat food – though neither she nor Jack had seen a cat – half a bottle of milk soured solid, one blackened avocado and a clutter of cough medicines, pills and a small case of ampoules. It smelt. Opening the chill drawer at the bottom they discovered why: a chicken, long forgotten, was decomposing.

'Phew! How can she live like this?' Jack stepped back in disgust.

Jillian looked under the kitchen sink and found some rubber gloves and a stack of carrier bags. She selected a Harrods one. 'Best to give the poor thing a decent burial,' she said, as she decanted the chicken into it.

'Give it to me. I'll find a dustbin for it and I'll get some grub *en route*. You stay here – I'll only be ten minutes, there's a shop round the corner that stays open late.'

'I'll clean up.' She looked at the chaos with a sinking feeling. But once she'd started, she found the task wasn't so bad and, in a strange, masochistic way, she quite enjoyed herself. Never before having had to tackle such filth, she discovered that there was a surprising degree of satisfaction to be gained in doing so.

'What a sweetness you are,' Esmée said, pausing in the doorway, looking at her unrecognisable kitchen and down at Jillian who was just finishing the floor. 'How noble. I couldn't face it and the char refused point-blank. It was all becoming a fearful problem.'

'Yes, I can imagine.'

'I've been shopping, though.' Esmée placed two bags on the washed kitchen table. She had spoken with an air of triumph, as if she were looking to be congratulated for doing anything at all.

'Splendid. Jack's gone to the shops too – though I can't imagine where he's got to. He said ten minutes, and that was an hour ago.'

'Unreliable creature. Has no one offered to help – none of those parasites out there?' Esmée waved in the general direction of the rest of her flat.

'I didn't ask.'

'You shouldn't be so amenable, you know, Jill. You'll get put upon. Hell, these shoes hurt.' She sat down and eased her toes out of a pair of scarlet and gold brocade slippers.

'They're lovely. Where did you buy them?'

'What size are you?'

'Six.'

'Have them.'

'I couldn't possibly.'

'Why not? I don't want them. They pinch. I've been trying to kid myself I'm a six but I'm more like a seven. Huge plates. Just look at them.' She lifted her legs and waggled two elegant, slim feet in the air. 'There's a party tonight at Tristram Oliver's. Do you know him? No, you wouldn't, why should you? He's terribly talented – everyone says he's a genius. You'll come?'

'Well, I don't know, Jack –'

'Jack won't want to come, but you don't have to do *everything* he wants to do, or do you?'

'No, of course not. I'd just prefer not to go if he's not going,' she said defensively.

'Sweet. Maybe you wouldn't enjoy it. Tristram's like them all – hates women.'

'Like them? Who?'

'Men, of course, darling. Didn't you know? All men hate all women.'

'That's a lie. I don't. I love women, and especially this one.' Jack had returned and the minute he'd placed his shopping beside Esmée's he'd lifted Jillian in the air, twirled her around, hugged her, kissed her full on the mouth and deposited her back on her feet before she had time to realise what he was doing.

'I must admit I've never seen you so happy before, Jack.'

'Of course you haven't, I haven't felt like this before.'

'I hope it lasts is all I can say.' Esmée took a cigarette languidly from a packet and lit it.

'Esmée, don't say you're finally concerned for my well-being?' He grinned.

'No. Jillian's, actually. Look what the dear girl has done. You could take tonsils out in this kitchen. I think Cinderella should go to the ball tonight, Jack. Party at Tristram's. Coming?' She stood up.

Jack looked at Jillian and must have seen the look of excitement on her face. 'Why not? But only if she'll cook me bacon and eggs.'

'I've nothing to wear.'

'Feed the pig, then come and I'll find you something – at least you've got the shoes,' Esmée said, over her shoulder, as she left the kitchen.

5

Jack had told her that Tristram Oliver lived in decaying splendour on a diminishing trust fund in a large, crumbling house in Chelsea. He let them in with gracious condescension.

'I've never read any of his poems,' Jillian whispered to Jack, as Tristram welcomed the rest of their large party. 'I hope he doesn't ask if I have.'

'You couldn't have read them. He's never allowed anyone to see them.'

'But how come Esmée said he was a genius?'

'That's because he tells everyone he is. And, of course, it implies that she's read the poems so is on the inside track with him.'

'You're a cynic, Jack.'

'No, I'm not. I'm a realist.'

They stood watching the passing parade in the large hall

which, with its sweeping marble staircase, seemed to be the main party room. Certainly the stairs made a wonderful central point and Jillian was amused to notice several people sashay up them, pause at the top then sashay down again, checking they were being watched, rather like mannequins at a fashion show, she imagined.

'My dear Jack. Such sartorial elegance.' Tristram, dressed in a powder blue soft velvet suit with gold epaulettes and a jabot of tumbling antique lace, fussed over towards them.

'You know me, Tristram.' Jack looked down at his neatly pressed grey slacks, his chequerboard jumper in grey and maroon and his blazer; he straightened his tie. 'I always like to stand out in a crowd.' In the midst of this colourful parade, Jack was a focus of difference.

'But, my dear Jack, if people stare at you it's a sure sign you're badly dressed.'

'When Beau Brummell originally said that he was wrong too,' Jack said smoothly. It was at this point that Jillian noticed that whenever Tristram spoke a young woman behind him scribbled in a notebook. Apparently she was not recording what anyone else said. Tristram did not reply but, with a sardonic smile, moved away.

'Got him! He didn't know how to answer – stupid pseud. It's rumoured he's writing a novel,' Jack whispered in Jillian's ear. 'That woman takes down everything he says. What I want to know is whether she follows him into the bog! He did write a lyric once for Bash – you know, the rock group who never quite made it. "Ersatz Lover" it was called.'

'Oh, yes. I remember. It was banned by the BBC, wasn't it?'

'They say *prick*. Shock horror!' Jack laughed.

It was interesting to watch the party, but there was no way she could circulate here. She'd no idea what she could possibly say to anyone. She had a moment of panic when Jack left her to go to the loo, so she stood against a wall and watched.

Despite Esmée's efforts to find her something to wear, she had been unsuccessful. Everything had been too small. She had had one fleeting thought that Esmée had offered her clothes on purpose to show how slim she was beside the bigger-busted Jillian, but she had rejected the idea as uncharitable. She had suggested that perhaps she could borrow one of Esmée's collection of long, flowing dresses – kaftans, Esmée had called them – but Esmée had vetoed the idea saying she'd look out of place if she wore one of those. Now, standing here and watching the umpteenth woman flow past in loose-fitting silk, she found herself resurrecting her first theory.

She stood in her pale-grey Susan Small tailored shift dress, with its Peter Pan collar, wishing she hadn't taken Esmée's advice and worn the brocade shoes, which did not really go with it.

Never one for much makeup, she now felt almost obscenely nude as women with pale painted faces, fluttering arachnoid-looking false eyelashes and liner thick and black enough to remind her of pandas, ambled by.

The eyes bothered her, for people passed her as if they did not see her – or, worse, as if she did not exist. They were devoid of expression, blank, dead, as if they were truly unseeing and she'd wandered into a room full of the blind.

She heard odd snippets of conversation. One young man, dressed like an admiral with long, flowing hair that gave him a Byronic look, was busily chatting up a young girl. 'I'll write a song, bird, just for you.'

'Oh, yeah! And I'm to believe you?' The girl moved away with a haughty toss of her long mane.

Five minutes later he was back with another woman. Jillian felt as if she was listening to a tape-recording as he repeated everything, word for word, but this time with greater success as the girl giggled and simpered with joy.

'Enjoying yourself?' Esmée was dressed in a deep claret-coloured velvet dress with a long chiffon scarf in scarlet and orange floating around her neck. It should have clashed; instead the combination was perfect.

'Lovely.'

'You needn't fib to me, darling. It's not my party. Personally I think they're all pretentious and grim.'

'Then why bother with them?'

'Who else is there? What else to do? Everything is so predictable and boring.' Just for a second Esmée looked sad and Jillian instinctively put out her hand and touched the soft velvet on her arm. Esmée smiled at her as if acknowledging the friendly gesture and, for once, there seemed no front to her, as if she were allowing Jillian to glimpse her real self. 'Don't listen to me! It's the gin, it makes me so doleful. I shouldn't touch it, but I generally succumb.' She laughed, the moment gone. 'I'm so glad you didn't borrow one of my kaftans – look at them, they look like shapeless blobs. But, then, I think people wear them to cover up their fat bits, something you need never do, not with your glorious figure.' Esmée beamed at her, and Jillian felt ashamed of her previous uncharitable thoughts. 'Hell! There's Shirl Founder – old boiler she's turning into. Must go and say hi to the old mainliner for all that.' And Esmée sallied into the crowd, sharp and brittle as before.

The conversation washed back and forth around her. No one invited her to join them and she was far too shy to butt in. In any case, she could have added nothing to the talk for it was all of mysticism, tarot and magical things. And why should they bother to include her? She did not look like them, could barely understand the words they spoke.

In the background there was a constantly playing tape of drums beating and other musical instruments she could not recognise. It was a hypnotic noise, not music as she recognised it but rather like an electronic heartbeat resounding through the large house.

She looked about for Jack, willing him to return. The noise and smell were getting to her. She was beginning to feel she really didn't exist, as if she wasn't here.

'Sorry. I met an old chum.'

'I don't like it here, Jack. It's as if they're all waiting for something to happen and I don't think I'd like it when it did.'

'You are fanciful! They're just a load of exhibitionists who think they're the new order. Imagine what the Martians would think if they landed here!'

'They all look so sad and lost.'

'Stoned, more like. Odd, isn't it? They look at us and think that we're the sad non-understanding ones.'

'Jack! Hi!' Sally Brentwood, with lank, dirty hair and a dark blue velvet trouser suit of miraculous cut, put her hand possessively on Jack's arm. 'Long time no see.' She spoke in a quiet voice, almost a whisper.

'Been too busy, Sal. How's tricks?'

Sal stood on tiptoe and whispered in his ear. From the way her body leaned against his, from the hand still touching him, Jillian knew they'd been lovers, and wished he'd told her. She shuddered.

'Do I know you?' Sally peered myopically at her.

'No,' Jillian said, so as not to embarrass her.

'That's so strange – I feel I know you. Maybe we met in another life . . .' And Sally drifted away even as Jillian bent forward to say she hadn't quite caught what she'd said.

'Why does she talk so quietly?'

'It's the only way she can get people's attention.'

'How do you mean?'

'She's got nothing to say. She's vapid, stupid. But when people can't hear they listen to her intently as if she were saying something worthwhile.'

'You are silly!' She laughed at him. 'Were you lovers?' she asked.

'What a question! Fancy a curry?'

'After those bacon and eggs? You're insatiable.'

'That's why I'm hungry – because I *am* insatiable where you're concerned.' And he looked so hard at her that she felt a rush of excitement.

'I'll get my coat.'

She made her way through the crowd to the room set aside for coats. It was a large well-furnished drawing room. She found a group of women there, kneeling on the floor at a glass-topped table on which were arranged lines of white powder. One woman's head was lowered as she sniffed the powder up noisily through a rolled dollar bill.

'Patsy!' Jillian exclaimed.

'Oh, shit!'

For three days Jillian waited for Patsy to call round at Esmée's as promised.

'If you ask me, she isn't coming. I can't say I blame her. Lecture from older sister? No, thank you!' Jack said as Jillian returned from answering the front door, disappointed yet again.

'It was Whispering Sally. She looks dreadful. She's covered in spots.'

'That's the heroin. It does that.' He poured himself another glass of wine from the bottle in front of him. 'These addictions are bad for one.' He chuckled as he raised his glass to her in a toast.

'If Patsy doesn't come this evening then that's it. I'll have to go back to Cambridge. I've got to get a job.'

'Moving back home?'

'No. I rang my cousin, Michelle, this morning. She says I can bunk down with her until I find a room of my own.'

'That shouldn't be difficult. After all, bedsits are ten-a-penny, aren't they?'

'Yes.' And expensive too, she thought, but she didn't say this since she didn't want to go on about her money problems. He might think she was asking for help.

An hour later Patsy finally arrived.

'We'll talk in the end room, it's quieter.' Jillian ushered her along the corridor, aware of Patsy's excited curiosity as she glanced into the various rooms which, as always, had people lounging in them.

'What a fab gaff! Whose is it?'

'Jack's sister's.'

'Do you think I could doss here?'

'No,' Jillian said, pushing her into the room. But now she had her here she was unsure how and where to begin. Patsy prowled around the room inspecting paintings and ornaments like an expert.

'A friend's got a stall at Portobello market,' she explained. 'He's taught me a lot.'

'You should write to Mum.'

'Have done.' Patsy flopped down on the bed. She no longer looked like a schoolgirl. She wore an odd collection of clothes, primarily black, layered one on top of the other, so that beneath her long skirt were trousers, under her shirt was a jumper and over it a brightly embroidered waistcoat. Around her neck hung at least a dozen ropes of beads, and drop earrings, made from matching beads, dangled from her ears. From a drawstring velvet bag she took a smaller bag and began, deftly, to roll a cigarette.

'That hasn't taken you long to learn.'

'Jillian, before you start let's get one thing straight. I'm not prepared to have you lecture me, I'm here to reassure you I'm fine – OK? That's all.' She flicked a Zippo lighter and inhaled deeply, holding the smoke down in her lungs then exhaling slowly. 'Ah, that's better. No point . . . I suppose . . .' She offered the ill-formed cigarette to Jillian with a sly smile.

'I'm fully aware you're trying to goad me. The effort's wasted. I suppose there's no point in telling you that what you're doing is illegal – you could go to prison?'

Patsy laughed. 'Jillian, you can be such an old maid at times. If I go to prison half of the kids in London would have to come with me.' She inhaled again.

'But why, Patsy? Break away – I can see that. But these people, Cracker –'

'Cracker, phew! He's history.'

'Are you alone, then?'

'No. I live with friends, we look after each other. I eat at least once a day – just like a Labrador. It's dry, clean. And I'm happy. Released.'

'How can you be released if you depend on junk like that and the stuff you were shoving up your nose the other night?'

'What? The coke? Oh, that was a treat. I can't afford that normally. And you miss the point, Jillian. It's this that releases me.' She waved the joint in the air. 'Releases me from all the horror and shit out there.'

'You? What's happened to you that's so awful? Come on.'

'A lot. There's stacks you don't know about and I'm not

telling you,' Patsy replied enigmatically. 'But I'm happy now. Fulfilled. I make clothes for a friend to sell on her stall. A bloke called Troy has asked me to make stage costumes for him and his mates. He's writing a song just for me – imagine! It's all beginning to happen for me.'

'I know Troy. He's a no-hoper to start with. And that must be the commonest chat-up line for innocents like you. And you won't get rich doing that.'

'But, Jillian, I don't want to be rich. See how little you know me? I need enough to buy my food and my stash, then I just enjoy not doing, just being in nature and floating. I've a friend, she taught me to see, taught me to feel, to comprehend the aura of other days hanging there in the cosmos. The being. The loosening of the bonds.'

'You're talking gibberish.'

'You won't understand, Jillian. You don't stand a hope in hell, not till you've learned. Not till you've hugged a rock.' Patsy smiled inanely at her.

'We're getting a takeaway. Do you want some?'

'Always so practical, Jillian. You're Mother Earth, the White Goddess and you're not even aware. That's beautiful, you know, beautiful. Have a chocolate.' She delved, clumsy now, into her velvet bag and produced two chocolates wrapped in tissue. 'See the pretty sugared violet – pretty. You have that one. And stop worrying, stop thinking. Go with the flow.'

Jillian popped the chocolate into her mouth.

The conversation, or argument, did not, nor could it, flow back and forth. There was little point, Patsy seemed to be getting sillier and sillier. Whatever Jillian said made her giggle. To test her she'd said 'seven times seven' and Patsy fell on the floor finding it so funny. As the time ticked by Jillian began to feel . . . she didn't know how to describe it, strange, odd, things weren't right. Different, she finally decided upon. She felt different. But, then, everything was different. And she knew it was when the front of the building fell away and an elephant lumbered by, which was odd when they were on the fourth floor.

'What about that takeaway?' Jack stood in the doorway. 'Are you ordering or coming?'

'Coming,' Jillian replied . . .

The road stretched ahead. She walked with a light step. Patsy was right, she did worry and think too much. She cluttered her mind with the rubbish of fear . . . The worry and fear were noisome . . . Rid herself of that and the silence would come. So natural to walk in the silence.

The sky still had the after-sunset glow and the light caught the underside of the leaves on the plane tree and they shimmered and glowed and she could see them pulsating, could see the life force sap throbbing and flowing through the capillaries – life flowing, life giving. And all in the silence. The blissful silence. She was an eye. There was nothing else to her. This eye saw all, understood all without the need of commentary, without disappearing down unnecessary corridors of memory and speculation . . .

She knew she was walking down the underside of a staircase without being upside-down . . .

The takeaway was crowded. She, the eye, sat down. She saw the other clients – human-shaped, with two arms, two legs, a body. But the heads! A lion smiled at her, the eye blinked in response. A toad sat dripping, a slime of spittle on his jacket, and he quivered and faded and returned with the antennae of the snail probing, searching, watching her eye. Beside her a unicorn sat waiting patiently. She knew it was Jack, she could tell by the unicorn's smile. There was a girl with no cheeks and her jawbone and tongue rattled away as she chattered to her friend, who had an ant-eater's snout. Behind the counter the proprietor, a monkey, leaped and chattered and laughed as he served.

The eye knew exactly what was happening. Because she was in the silence she was not interfering with their basic being, if she'd been thinking and worrying then she was fully aware that her perception would be different. She liked the silence and hugged it to her, knowing nothing was by chance. The monkey winked at her and she knew he knew too.

The walk home was lit by lights, which glowed and pulsated, and when she looked up into the skies it was as if a roof had been lifted and she saw a brightness and a busyness in the heavens that the silence enjoyed. And everything was so clear, so understandable, simplicity itself.

It was necessary for the eye to skirt a large mound in the gutter.
A twenty-foot-high pile of elephant turds . . . and night closed in as
she tripped along.

'You stupid, evil bitch! You could have killed her!'

'Oh, come on, Jack. It was good stuff, the best. I knew she'd
be all right. Don't exaggerate.'

'I'm not exaggerating. And you know how strongly she
feels about all this crap.'

'You shouldn't have, Patsy.' Esmée was talking seriously.
'We're lucky she hasn't had a bad trip. But she should have
been prepared, she should have been accompanied.'

'I'm sorry. I just wanted her to understand. If she did then
maybe she'd get off my back and leave me alone.'

'Yes, Patsy, but that has to be her decision, not yours.'

'Okay, Esmée. You've had your say. Lecture over?'

'God, you're a cocky bitch. You think you know it all,' Jack
exploded.

'Well, I evidently know more than you do!' Patsy snapped.

'Please. What the hell?' Jillian struggled up in the bed.
'Why are you all arguing? Heavens, the weirdest thing
happened last night. It was odd . . .'

'Did it frighten you?' Esmée sat on the bed and took her
hand.

'It was frightening, but I wasn't frightened. Really strange.'
The images were still clear within her mind. 'I must have
been dreaming,' she said, grasping at this for an explanation
but, odd as it had been, she knew she hadn't dreamed it. Was
she going mad? 'A dream,' she said, in a firmer voice to
reassure herself.

'Your kid sister here slipped you a dose of LSD. You were
tripping. I went with you to the takeaway – you sat staring
into space.'

'The eye . . .' she said vaguely.

'I got you back here as quickly as possible.' Jack was sitting
on the other side of her.

'There was this huge pile of elephant droppings, outside the
house. Is it there now?'

'There was a crash last night. A man was killed,' Esmée explained.

'Just before we got back . . .' Jack added.

'Oh, Patsy. How could you do that to me?' Her sister had the grace to look ashamed. 'I think I want to go home to Cambridge, Jack. Now,' she said, and she began to cry, for in a strange way she felt as if she had found something and lost it, but she couldn't quite remember what it was that had gone.

Chapter Three

1

Winter 1966

After the incident with the drug Jillian felt suspicious of people. She could reason that that was unfair, that not everyone she knew was as irresponsible as Patsy. Still, in her new job in a solicitor's office, she always refused tea or coffee made by the others, never accepted a cake and got out of taking a chocolate by saying it gave her migraine.

For someone who had never lived alone, had been afraid of the very idea and the loneliness it might involve, she found, instead, that she relished it. For now she needed to be alone, needed her own silence to think things through, to try to recapture that one moment of knowledge, serenity and peace, which, even as she searched for it, she knew would never return. The sadness she had felt that evening was often with her now: she seemed unable to shake it off.

One thing had not changed, and that was her love for Jack. They saw less of each other, but when they did they made love with as much joy and enthusiasm, and he was always attentive and considerate. She understood why he came infrequently: term had started and his work with it. She was sure that by being patient and not demanding to see him she was helping him. Several times, after they'd made love, he'd fallen asleep immediately, something he'd never done before. Usually they'd talked and she'd found these times the most precious when she'd learned more about him and he of her. But when he slept, she felt an illogical distance building. How could she follow him into his dreams? It was as if, by sleeping, she was losing him . . .

'Am I boring you, Jack?' she'd asked one day, when he woke up.

'No. What on earth gave you that idea?' He stretched, yawning.

'Well, you go to sleep.'

'Because I'm bloody knackered, that's why. You're a demanding minx.' He grabbed her and hugged her tight. 'You're sure it's not the other way around and you're getting tired of me?'

'Don't be silly. I love seeing you. I spend all day hoping you'll come round.'

He kissed her tenderly. 'You're adorable. How can you bore me if I love you?'

And she nestled into his arms, wondering how she could have thought anything so silly.

'You spend too much time alone, that's your problem. And you think and worry too much for your own good.' He spoke kindly, but she'd flinched at his mirroring of Patsy's words that night.

The bedsitter she'd found in the labyrinth of streets off Mitcham's Corner was small, at the top of a four-storey house, but it was hers and it was cheap. There were two rooms on her floor and three on the landing below; she shared the bathroom, lavatory and kitchen with the other occupants of the house. In the kitchen each had a cupboard, but after a jar of coffee and a tin of sardines were stolen she'd learned to keep her supplies in her room. Apart from meeting people in passing she never saw the other tenants or even knew how many people lived there: the Edwardian family house had been converted into a collection of isolated, lonely cells.

Cooking wasn't allowed in the rooms, but even so she'd bought a kettle and had found a Baby Belling in one of the house-clearance shops on Mill Road. It didn't work yet, but as soon as she could afford to get it mended she would. There was a basin in her room, for which she was grateful. It was sparsely furnished but, given its size, what little there was made it seem cluttered. She tended to sit more often on the bed than on the one chair. The table was not only for eating off, but for ironing, for use as a desk and for her bedside light, too. The wardrobe was a pole, angled across a corner behind a curtain. From the window she saw roofs and chimneys, and she'd been told that if she leaned right out she could glimpse the river but she hadn't tried to yet.

Once her books were in, her print of La Goulue hanging and her collection of china pigs had been lined up, it didn't look too bad, she kept telling herself.

She'd been convinced she'd miss the order of her mother's house, but she found she liked the lack of routine – eating when she wanted to and not having to think of others. It wasn't as if there were no routine, but it was hers, not her mother's. She shopped for her basics on Friday. She did her washing in the launderette at Mitcham's Corner on Saturday. She did her ironing on Sunday. It was the independence she was enjoying, despite the fall in her standard of living.

When she had finished her ironing she would go to visit her cousin, Michelle. Jack always went home for Sunday lunch so she could relax, certain he would not phone or turn up and find her not there.

Before the break-up of Michelle's marriage she had not been close to her cousin: they had met at family events but had never sought each other out. That had changed when Michelle, battered by her husband once too often, had thrown him out, changed the locks and begun divorce proceedings. This had rocked the family since divorce had been previously unknown. Michelle's own mother, Flo, had lectured loudly, as if everything had been her daughter's fault. 'Well, you must have done something to warrant a beating,' she had said. Michelle, toughened by the experience, had shown her mother the door too.

Jillian's parents reacted similarly. Mary sided with her sister and there was much talk of the sanctity of marriage vows which, since Mary had never been attacked by her husband, seemed to Jillian unfair in the extreme. Charlie had said, 'That Michelle's no better than she ought to be,' a statement Jillian never quite understood.

So it had fallen upon the younger generation and Michelle's friends to rally round in support. And Jillian had grown to like her feisty cousin, who, having been duped once by a man, had no intention of letting it happen again; Jillian doubted that any man would dare to swipe her now. She did wonder sometimes if Michelle had not gone too far the other way for she found her dislike of men a bit strident. 'Surely they're not all horrible, violent, unfaithful, not to be trusted?' she'd asked, time and time again. But the answer was always the same. 'You don't know what you're talking about.' Finally Jillian had just let her get on with it, not arguing or disagreeing with her.

Not understanding her cousin did not stop her enjoying being with her. Since Michelle had found freedom from her husband *and* mother her home was always bustling with other young people and Jillian found that the relaxed atmosphere suited her, kept her mind off Jack and her own loneliness.

September and October had not been too bad in her little room in the eaves of the tall house. But November was different. November was cold in that bone-chilling way of Cambridge where the wind seemed to have come straight from Siberia.

'I brought that eiderdown you wanted. I left it with the hall porter, it was too big to lug in here.' Mary Foster looked about the chintz-decorated lounge of the Garden House Hotel. 'Pushing the boat out a bit, aren't we?' she said, once they'd ordered their tea – sandwiches, scones and cake, she'd decided.

'A bit of indulgence now and then never hurt anyone.'

'True. You can always rely on a good tea here, too. Your father brought me here for dinner once. An anniversary. It was lovely – all silver service and chafing dishes. Real luxury.'

'You haven't had much of that, have you, Mum?'

'What would I be doing with luxury? No, I've been fine. I've been lucky. Your father doesn't drink. He doesn't hit me.'

'It always seems so bleak to me, that comment, as if one should be grateful, as if it's unusual.'

'If you know what I know about some marriages,' Mary sipped her tea, 'you'd be shocked.'

'Like Michelle? But I'd never marry anyone who hit me.'

'Neither did she,' Mary said tartly. 'Could I have another of those cucumber sandwiches? I don't approve of Michelle's going on about men and marriage. A girl should be grateful to find a husband. But I wish you'd stayed at hers. I don't like to think of you on your own.'

'I'm enjoying it. It's very noisy at Michelle's with people in and out all the time. I see her most Sundays. More than that and I think she'd get me down, she's so bossy – she thinks she knows it all.'

'Just like her mother. Flo was always a bossy moo when we were young. How's the new job? Oh, like that.' She saw Jillian's expression. 'Not too bad, I hope?'

'No. It's the other women, they're not very friendly. And it's boring – conveyancing mainly. I'm looking around for something else.'

'And how's Jack?'

'He's fine. Busy – it's his last year. But we see each other as often as we can.' Her face shone as she talked of him. 'And Dad?'

Mary made a small mewing shape with her mouth. 'Still in the right. I let him rant on – I don't listen half the time. He still blames you for leading Patsy astray.'

'That's funnier than you know.'

'He just can't see people as they are. He only sees them as he wants them to be. Patsy writes, though, give her her due. And she's doing well with her sewing. But it seems a shame. She's got such a good brain on her. I'd always hoped she'd be a doctor.'

'You never said.'

'I wouldn't. It wouldn't matter what I wanted – I'm only her mother – and I didn't want to influence her in any way. So I've always said, "You must do what you want to do." And Patsy says she is. So that's that.'

'And what did you want for me?'

'To find a good man and be happy.'

Jillian laughed, but not in a bitter way. 'So you didn't think I was up to anything else?'

'Oh, yes.' Mary looked up at her, surprised at the question. 'I think you could have done lots of things if you'd wanted, if

76

your father had coughed up for it. I've just always thought that you'd find your true happiness in marriage and running a home, don't ask me why.'

'I'd give up everything if it was Jack.'

'Such a shame you met him when you're both so young – it hardly ever lasts, does it? Oh, look, I've dropped jam on the tablecloth.' Her mother, fretting at the stain on the white linen, did not see the sadness flit across her daughter's face. When Mary looked up, Jillian saw that flour from her scone had ringed her mouth.

'Jillian? It is Jillian, isn't it? Yes, I thought it was you.'

Jillian looked up to see Theresa Stirling, smartly hatted and gloved, smiling down at her.

'Mrs Stirling, hello. Would you join us? This is my mother . . .' Poor Mum, thought Jillian, she'd be mortified if she knew she looked like a clown.

'Just for a minute. I'm meeting a friend. Why didn't you come to our party last month? I was so hurt when Jack told me you didn't want to.' She smiled sweetly.

'I never said anything like that,' Jillian blustered. 'What did he mean?' She flapped her napkin in agitation. She didn't say she hadn't known she'd been invited to a party.

'Well, then, no harm done. Silly boy. I wonder why he said that? Strange.' She moved her head to one side, which reminded Jillian of a small, alert bird. 'Shall I invite you again?' The smile, this time, was almost coquettish.

'That would be lovely.'

'Right, then. I shall arrange it with my errant son.' She stood up. 'I'm seeing him for dinner. Are you coming?'

'No. No, I've things to do.'

'How sad. Well, I'm so pleased to have met you, Mrs Foster. Excuse me, but I spy my friend. À bientôt, Jillian.' And again Jillian was the recipient of her gentle, sweet smile.

They watched the small, slim figure move quickly through the large lounge.

'She's trouble,' Mary said, picking up her teacup.

'Mrs Stirling? She's lovely. It's Jack's father who's the problem.'

'You reckon, do you? If you'll listen to me, you'll watch

77

your back where that one's concerned. Any more tea in that pot?'

2

'You do know you're becoming depressed, don't you?' Michelle looked sternly at Jillian over the glass of rough plonk she'd brought with her. 'I should never have let you leave my place for this poky hole.' She looked about the tiny room from her position on the one chair. Jillian was sitting on the floor feeding the gas meter with shillings.

'I like it. At least it's mine. And it's getting better – I buy something for it each week. See that cushion? I got that last week, and some lovely curtain material from Thoday's.' Jillian wished she hadn't decided to return Michelle's hospitality and invite her round for a spaghetti supper. She did not like her room criticised so dismissively.

'You didn't answer.'

'And at least there's a telephone here – we never had one at home.' Jillian ignored her remark.

'And how often does *he* ring?' Michelle asked abruptly.

'He's busy. It's his final year – crunch time. And I'm not depressed. I don't know what you're going on about.'

'I think he's distancing himself from you.'

'Well, I don't, and you think wrong. And, in any case, at least I have someone. You don't,' she said, with uncharacteristic sharpness. But she was afraid: she didn't like Michelle saying what she was thinking. 'I shouldn't have said that.' She looked ashamed.

'Doesn't matter.' Michelle shrugged her shoulders. 'It's true. I live in a town with ten men to every girl and I can't get a feller. Does wonders for the ego.' And she tossed her head so that her curls, which she could never quite tame, bounced in the light of the candles Jillian was burning because it made the room look prettier and more mysterious than it was.

Michelle didn't have a boyfriend but it was not because she was unattractive: she was too honest. At a dance at the

Dorothy Jillian had once heard her saying to a young man, who innocently asked her for a date, 'You needn't think that a couple of pints at the Mitre and a curry at the Bengal will entitle you to get into my knickers.'

'I never thought any such thing!'

'Oh, yes, you did. Admit it.' The young man pretended to go to the lavatory at this point and did not return.

Jillian often wondered if the honesty was used as a shield to put men off, that after her disastrous, short-lived marriage she was frightened to commit herself again.

'It's your standards that get in the way.' Jillian turned on the radio and tuned into the new Radio Caroline. 'You're too moral.'

'I just don't understand anyone. Every girl I know now is sleeping with a bloke – it didn't used to be like that. It's like the pill came and we couldn't use pregnancy as an excuse any more, and the blokes just think everyone's fair game. It's just not right.'

'I didn't until I was nineteen and met Jack.'

'But ten years ago – even five, probably – you wouldn't have gone to bed with him. You'd have had some heavy-petting sessions and that would have been that and he wouldn't have thought any the less of you.'

'I don't think Jack's lost his respect for me. This is healthier.'

'Is it?'

'I don't understand you, Michelle. You bang on about life not being fair for women. So why shouldn't we be like the blokes? Isn't it double standards if not? They can sleep around and we can't? I'd have thought you'd have been all for more sexual tolerance.'

'Trouble with sexual tolerance is it leads to another type of intolerance. Now if you don't do it, or you don't think sex is the be-all and end-all of everything, you're left out, you're not *with it*. It's made everything worse, I think.'

'Still, it's fun.'

'*If* it's fun. Or are loads of women pretending it's fun? Are we afraid to look old-fashioned and say it's not? To say, "Hang on, I didn't enjoy that. I found it boring, disgusting, painful" – or whatever. No, suddenly the world's full of people having blissful, perfect how's-your-father and I, for one, don't believe it.'

'You're always so certain about everything, Michelle. Don't you ever think you might be wrong?'

'No.'

Jillian felt uncomfortable. Michelle had a way of saying what others didn't want to hear. 'When I listen to you going on about what you think, I think you should be a politician.'

'Me? Join that load of slime? Not on your nelly. That would be a betrayal . . .'

Why was it that something a friend said could be the key to unlock a chest of worries? She had happily accepted the reasons why she saw less of Jack. They were well into the Michaelmas term and he had a heavy workload, and yet when she was in town Jillian saw hordes of undergraduates spilling out of pubs and cinemas or wandering aimlessly around. Not all were tied to their books. Which led her to wonder if he loved her as much and as passionately as he said he did. Surely if he did he would make time to see her, would not be able to get through a day without being with her. Now, when she counted up, she found that a week had gone by since their last date. 'Date', that was hardly the right word. A date was going out, doing things, being seen together. For them, these days, it was invariably him turning up, without warning, with a bottle of wine. They would hurriedly go to bed, her longing for him undiminished, and he'd be away before midnight and his college curfew.

Why, she thought, as she sat on her bed, trying to read a book and failing, had it taken Michelle's sharp comments to make her face these facts? The obvious answer was that love made fools blind – but, then, she'd never thought of herself as a fool. Far more likely that her mind did not want to know the truth and had decided to bury it, as it had when she was a child and a maths test loomed: forget about it and it would all go away.

Nor could she forget about the party at his house she'd missed.

'You didn't tell me about your mother's invitation,' she said at the first opportunity.

'Didn't I?' He was lying on her bed, intent on the ceiling.

'You know you didn't. Why?'

'You wouldn't have enjoyed it.'

'I might have.'

'You're nagging.'

'I'm not. I'm . . .' She wanted to say 'hurt and disappointed' but she thought better of it and kept quiet instead, which hadn't stopped him leaving a few minutes later. She'd not mentioned it again, even if she wished she could.

And here she was again, another evening alone, yet more waiting, heart leaping at every ring of the pay-phone down in the entrance hall – which she always heard because she propped her door open, just in case.

It wouldn't do, she told herself. She picked up the *Cambridge Evening News* she bought each evening on the way home and flicked through it to see what films were on. She'd take herself to *The Sound of Music* and maybe she'd have a curry on the way home. Why not?

Despite being on her own she enjoyed the film, and the music was still jangling in her head as she walked home through the bitter December cold, her hands deep in her pockets. Yes being alone in the darkened cinema was one thing: she couldn't quite bring herself to eat out alone too. She had a tin of baked beans – that would do.

She turned into her street, digging in her handbag for her key. Slumped in her doorway, fast asleep, was Jack.

'Jack, darling, what on earth . . . ?' She knelt down, pleased to see him, furious she'd gone out. 'You must be frozen.'

'I came to see you. You weren't here.' He rubbed his eyes, but his words were slurred.

'I can't stay in all the time just on the off-chance you'll turn up,' she said, helping him to his feet. He stood, wavering slightly.

'Oh dear, sorry I spoke. Sorry I came.' He tried to bow but stumbled and fell against the front door.

'Shush.' She giggled, as she put her finger to her lips. 'You'll wake everyone up.'

'Wake 'em up. It's only nine, for Chrissake!' he bellowed.

'It isn't. It's gone eleven. Now, be quiet and I'll open the door.'

Getting him up the stairs of the tall Edwardian house was difficult. As they banged and crashed their way up, two doors opened and annoyed tenants peered out. 'Sorry,' she whispered, as they climbed the next flight.

'What's their problem?' Jack said belligerently.

'Nothing. They're tired, that's all.' She was still mouthing 'Sorry' to them as they got to her landing and she pushed the recalcitrant Jack into her room.

He stood in the middle of her tiny bedsit, and she had to manoeuvre round him. He looked bedraggled, and very drunk.

'You've torn your jacket. Did you fall over? Just look at you.'

'Don't nag.'

'I'm not. I'm just saying . . . You'd better lie down.'

'You're nagging.'

'Sweetheart, I'm not. You're tired and you should go to sleep.'

'I'm not drunk.'

'Did I say you were? Come on, let me help you with your shoes.'

'Only if there's one thing that would finally put the mockers on us it's your nagging. I hate it. You do understand?' He peered myopically at her, swaying as if in a breeze, before collapsing on the bed and falling asleep immediately.

She made herself a cup of coffee, sat on the chair and watched him as he slept. 'Finally,' he'd said. 'Finally' could only mean that something had gone before, that there was a whole list of things and his thinking she nagged was the last straw.

As she watched him all the love she felt for him, all the dreams she'd had of him, flooded her. It was ending, and she did not know why or what it was she'd done. She felt a deep sadness seep into her veins.

'Hell's bells. Who hit me on the head?' Jack groaned as he sat up on the bed. He made a chewing motion with his mouth, his tongue exploring it, and he grimaced. 'What the hell did I do that for? Shit!' He held his head in his hands.

'Here. Drink this. And I've an aspirin if you want.' She handed him a glass of orange juice.

'Got any Alka-Seltzer?'

'No, I'm sorry.'

'A home should always have Alka-Seltzer in the medicine chest.' He toasted her with his glass of juice. 'You're my saving angel.' He looked at her more closely. 'Come to think of it, you don't look so hot yourself. Did we get drunk together?'

'No. I just didn't sleep very well. That's a narrow bed,' she said, flustered, knowing that with her red-rimmed eyes she looked dreadful.

'You've been crying.'

'I haven't. I think I might be starting a cold,' she lied. 'I can rustle you up some eggs, but I've no bacon.'

'Yuck. No ta. But I'd like a shower, if that's poss?'

'We've a bath, no shower. You have to feed the meter and if the geyser doesn't ignite straight away then whack it with the toilet brush – that usually works.'

'Well, at least that makes you smile.'

While he bathed she made the bed and tidied her room, which, given its size, took all of a minute. Then she sat on the bed and waited.

During the night, unable to sleep, she'd concocted all manner of fine speeches to make this morning. She'd been so determined to have it out with him. What did he mean by *finally*? And if it didn't mean what she thought, then in future she needed to see more of him; she wanted this relationship to be put on a more secure footing. She would say that she felt he only came round for sex now and she was not going to stand for it. And what had happened? What had she said? A fine, glowing, useless zero. She'd talked about eggs! She would, though, she really would, when he came back from the bathroom. She gathered her dressing-gown closer to her as she sat hunched on the bed, mutely rehearsing her ultimatum.

'You look like a little girl sitting there all bunched up in your candlewick dressing-gown.' He bent down and kissed her, towelling his hair dry as he did so. 'That feels better. But I reckon that geyser's a death trap – I opened the window an inch. Promise you do too, or will? I'm sure you could die of carbon-monoxide poisoning in there, no problem.'

'I always do.'

'What is it? You sound so forlorn. Tell Jack.' He sat beside her, his arm round her shoulders, and pulled her towards him. It was such a comfortable feeling to have him hold her like this: she always fitted so well into the angle of his arm. 'See?' he'd often said. 'God made us to fit like this, a matching pair. Aren't we lucky to have found each other?' She snuggled closer, unaware that she sighed. 'Come on, what's bothering you?'

Her heart pounded, her mouth felt dry. 'Oh, I'm being silly ... It's just ... It's Christmas,' she finished.

'Well, there's a bright conclusion. Yes, I'd say you were right. It has a tendency to pop round every year.' He grinned at her.

'No, I mean, I don't know how I'll cope ... this room ...' She waved her arm ineffectually. 'On my own ... my mother ...' But she got no further for she burst into tears. They were genuine tears for Christmas: in all her worrying about not seeing or hearing from Jack, she'd overlooked where and what she'd be doing. She couldn't go home. Michelle and a group were going to Amsterdam and, though she had been invited to join them, she couldn't afford to go. Her other friends had their own families. She would be alone, totally alone.

'Sweetheart, don't cry.' He wiped away her tears with the edge of his towel. 'That's why I was here. My mother was worried about you and you're invited to come to us.'

'What? For Christmas Day?'

'No, for the whole caboodle, days and days of unmitigated excess.'

'But you said you'd only let me be there for a day. That you loathed –'

'Even I make allowances for Christmas. Bring your best long party frock – Mum likes us to dress up. She makes a fuss.'

'How kind of her. Yes, please, Jack. I'd like that.'

'I thought you would.' His hand was at the back of her neck, stroking her. 'I love that soft hair, there, right at the nape of your neck.' He sat up, lifting her hair and his tongue found the spot. His hands moved within the folds of her dressing-gown and cupped her full breasts. 'You smell of sleep and sex,' he whispered, removing the gown. He laid her back on the bed, unwrapped his towel and knelt over her, naked. Eagerly she put her hands up to hold him, to feel the taut smoothness of him and guided him down towards her.

'What a way to start the day!' she heard him exclaim. She felt she wanted to devour him and have him in her always.

There was so much to do between Jack going down for the Christmas vacation and his returning to collect her. Suddenly she had a whole new family to buy presents for as well as her own. Even though she did not know where Patsy was she still intended to find her a present and put it aside until she saw her again.

The only solution was to make a list, not just of presents but of things she had to do. The first item on the list was to get her hair trimmed: she'd push the boat out and go to the hairdressing department in Joshua Taylor. A well-cut hairstyle would give her confidence. The old candlewick dressing-gown she'd had since she was fourteen wasn't up to standard, nor were her unglamorous pyjamas. New ones were added to the list.

What clothes did she have that were suitable for the country? She had jeans and a pair of wellington boots. Maybe she'd get some leather boots, new trousers and a jumper, and what about some shirts?

Oh dear, this list was getting too long, she thought, sucking the end of her biro. 'New evening dress' was added almost as if she wasn't in control of what she was writing. She'd dare to go to that smart shop, Vogue, in St Andrew's Street with its muted grey paint and tasteful, simple window-dressing.

She couldn't take her ragged old flannel. She'd love a new

makeup case – leather and fitted, she'd seen one the other day . . . No. She scratched that out. Too expensive, she told herself, and substituted a new sponge-bag.

From a drawer she took her savings-account book and checked what was left of her holiday-to-Spain fund. It had been heavily depleted by the countless purchases for the bedsit, but if she were sensible she'd manage. Maybe she'd get Michelle to trim her hair.

3

'The family always tease me that I go overboard at Christmas, but I do love it so.' Theresa Stirling was up a ladder decorating the big hall with garlands of holly and fir.

'It looks wonderful, Mrs Stirling. I think the house is smiling its pleasure at being dressed up.' Jillian, her case at her feet, looked around the splendid room in its Christmas garb.

'My dear, what an extraordinarily nice thing to say.' Theresa paused at the top of the step-ladder, clutching a garland to her.

'Mum, do be careful. We don't want you falling and breaking anything, then everything would be ruined for certain. Let me.' Jack helped her down and took her place.

'Thank goodness Jack's back – I know I'll be helped now. The others are useless. Are you all right, Jillian? You look a little pale.'

'No, I'm fine, Mrs Stirling. A bit tired, that's all.'

'When you've finished that, Jack, there's a fire in the drawing room. Shall we have tea there or in the kitchen?'

'M . . . m . . . m,' Jack mumbled, for he had a row of tacks in his mouth.

'I think he's saying the kitchen is his favourite. We'll meet there. First I'll show you your room, my dear, and you can unpack.'

Jillian put away her clothes in the pretty room at the top of the house with a sloping beam and a tiny casement window that looked out over the garden at the back. What she took to be a cupboard door was the entrance to a bathroom ingeniously built into the eaves of the roof. She needn't have bothered to buy her new blue quilted-satin dressing-gown. She lined up her toiletries and makeup on the glass shelf, her brush and comb like soldiers on the small vanity unit, folded her two new flannels and placed her slippers by the door.

The bed was a single one, and she was one flight above Jack's room. Evidently she was being told that there were strict sleeping arrangements here. The staircase had creaked, she'd registered as they'd climbed it. Ah, well, what else had she expected? Her own mother wouldn't have condoned them sleeping together under her roof. She'd never understand the older generation – they must know that Jack and she slept together so why pretend otherwise? Daft, she thought, as she studied her face in the mirror. Mrs Stirling was right, she was looking tired. She pinched her cheeks, like a Victorian heroine, to put some colour back in them. This last week she'd been worried she might be going down with a bug. She'd felt tired and sick and that would have ruined everything, but today she felt a mite better.

Hair brushed, makeup touched up, she wandered down to the kitchen where Jack and his mother were sitting at the large pine table on which stood cups, a teapot and a large Madeira cake.

'Ah, here she is. We wondered where you'd got to.'

'I'm sorry, I was unpacking.' She wondered why she was apologising.

'I was telling Jack I intend to get to know you properly this holiday. You've never enough time to visit us when I ask you – just like Esmée, rush, rush, rush. You young lead such busy lives.' Once again, Jillian caught that wistful note in Mrs Stirling's voice.

'Is Esmée coming?' She glanced at Jack. *Had* she been invited here? And if so, how often?

'It is alleged, though I never know with my daughter. But her room is ready, her bed aired. She may have a flat in London, but I like to think she still regards here as home. Is that tea the right colour for you?' Theresa looked at her watch. 'Is that the time? I must start dinner.'

'Can I help?'

'Jillian, how sweet of you, but no. You go and amuse yourself – there's a television somewhere. Jack and I will manage, we work well together – the old team, I always say.' Theresa's all-encouraging smile was focused on her and although she would rather have stayed Jillian wandered off and marvelled that a house could be so big that its owner didn't know where the television set was.

'You look lost. Can I help?'

'I'm looking for a television or something to do, Mr Stirling.'

'Along here. It's just the ticket.' Ralph strode quickly through a corridor and she almost had to run to keep up. He opened the door into a cosy room with a fire, a jumble of comfortable armchairs and a fuggy atmosphere. 'There should be something to entertain you here in the goggle-box room. There's mags, books and jigsaws over there. Just make yourself at home.' He smiled so pleasantly that, once again, she was puzzled that Jack loathed him. 'Did you hear a car? That's Esmée, the minx, I'll be bound.' Jillian, unsure if she should follow, decided, since he'd not said so, to stay put, and began to attempt the large, complicated jigsaw on a side table. A few minutes later the door burst open.

'Jill, dear heart! What a relief you're here. I was so afraid it would just be Jack and me and the geriatrics. Bliss. Drink? Gin, whisky, whatever?'

'Is there any Dubonnet? I like that, thanks. But I thought Mungo and his wife were coming?'

'They are, but, sweetness, Mungo and his dear Liz were *born* geriatric – they don't count as youth. Sure you wouldn't like a touch of gin in there, liven it up a bit? I insist.' And before Jillian could make a decision a large measure of gin was added to her glass. One tentative sip told her it was a marked improvement. 'I couldn't believe it when Daddy said you were here. You haven't got engaged and not told Esmée?'

'No.' Jillian giggled. 'Why?'

'Christmas – it's sacrosanct. Family only, well, nearly only – boring as hell. You and Jack must be becoming a very serious twosome. *Do* I hear the faint clang of the church bell?'

If only you knew, thought Jillian, but she smiled happily enough since, no doubt, it was expected of her. 'Tell me, Esmée, have you seen anything of Patsy?' she asked, once they were seated, both cuddled up in cavernous armchairs either side of the fireplace. Normally wary of Esmée, she found, for once, that she felt relaxed with her.

'What a hip babe she is! And so talented. She's going to make a bomb – that is, if she doesn't do something daft and become a dope-head.'

'Oh, no! Is she still living with those friends of hers in Westbourne Grove?'

'I don't think so. I think she's moved to a boat on the Thames at Chelsea – you know, those crazy barges near World's End? Don't look so worried, Jill. The boats are lovely, some are like little palaces.'

'I doubt if the one my sister's on is.'

'Probably not.' Esmée laughed. 'But honestly, Jill, she may be young, but she's bright and very savvy. She won't do anything daft.'

'But you just said, if she became a dope-head . . .'

'That's an occupational risk we all take, isn't it? Well, maybe not you. But, then, you drink, so you could become an alcoholic, couldn't you? It's the same thing.'

'Hardly.'

Esmée looked at her so stonily that Jillian decided there was no point in arguing with her, not that she thought she could – she knew too little about drugs and drink. She found she was on her guard again.

'She's working, then?'

'My dear, didn't you know? She's making the most fantastic clothes – they're snapped up as soon as she finishes them. At this rate, if she doesn't watch it, she'll be a success.'

'She wouldn't try anything really silly like heroin, would she?'

'Who knows?' Esmée shrugged her shoulders. 'I'm not my sister's keeper – to misquote.' But then, seeing how downcast Jillian looked, she put out her hand. 'After the Troy England cock-up, I doubt it.'

'Troy? Your friend who was with Sally at Brancaster?'

'The very same. Zap. Dead. He was mainlining like crazy. Most days he was higher than a giraffe's toupée – honest! Then that night, full of God knows what – bennies, bluies, snow, who knows? – he threw up and choked to death. Disgusting! I wouldn't want to go like that.' She shuddered.

'How awful.'

'Bloody stupid, if you ask me. But Patsy was there – she got out before the police were called, don't flap – and it shook them all up. I shouldn't worry, if I were you.'

Jillian looked at her with disbelief. How on earth was she not to worry? And how could Esmée be so nonchalant about it? Jillian studied her drink as if it could give her some answers.

'Where's Jack?'

'With your mother, cooking dinner.'

'Those two. They're their own friendly society. I suppose I'd better drag myself along and say what ho.'

That evening, as Jillian made her way to her room to change, another guest arrived. So she wasn't to be the only non-family member, she thought. From the landing, she saw a woman appear in a flurry of swirling cape, amid gusts of rain-laden wind and a cluster of exuberant King Charles spaniels. She wondered who she was and thought it odd that no one had told her she was coming. She climbed the last flight of stairs to the room in the eaves.

The tradition in this house was that on Christmas Eve the tree was trimmed before a long, formal dinner. An hour later they met in the hall. Esmée was carrying several large boxes of decorations, Jack the step-ladder, his mother a tray of glasses, Mungo the champagne and his wife, Liz, the canapés. They marched in to the sound of 'Hark the Herald Angels', though Jillian couldn't make out where the hi-fi system was.

Mungo looked so like his father it bordered on amusing, Jillian decided: the same build, wonderful blue eyes, deep, rumbling voice, large, capable hands, yet he appeared to lack his father's enormous confidence. Liz, his wife, was big too. Her hair was permed and set too rigidly for today's fashion, Jillian thought. Although she wore makeup, it had been applied clumsily, as if she were not used to doing it: her eye-shadow was a little too bright and her lipstick was smudged. She kept fiddling with the straps of her blue taffeta dress and the pleating over her breasts as if she wished she weren't in it. Her handshake was bone-crushingly firm. 'Hi, Jillian. Welcome to the team!' she boomed.

Theresa flitted about the artfully lit hall, like an exquisite, delicate moth, dressed in soft grey chiffon. She was checking bowls of nuts and fruit, making certain everyone had a drink, handing round the food, asking if people were comfortable, warm enough – 'For Chrissake, Theresa, do stop fussing. Everyone is perfectly capable of looking after themselves,' Ralph barked, from his position in front of the huge stone fireplace in which an impressive log fire burned.

'Yes, of course,' Theresa said, flustered and apologetic. She took a seat, but immediately stood up again, repositioned a poinsettia then sat down. She looked nervous and tense, just like Jillian's own mother, flapping at the idea that Christmas would be ruined if she didn't get everything right. 'Oh, I've just noticed you, Jillian. How pretty you look. What a nice frock. Is it from one of those catalogues I've read about? Something to do with football pools.' She waved her hand vaguely.

'What are you going on about, Theresa? It obviously isn't.' Ralph frowned at her.

'I bought it in Vogue, that lovely shop.'

'My, and expensive tastes too.' Theresa drummed her fingers on the arm of her chair.

'I was a bit worried about the colour.' Jillian frowned: she sensed Jack's mother was annoyed with her and she didn't understand why. She straightened her skirt, and realised that everyone in the room was staring at her.

'Blondes should always wear red.' Theresa smiled.

'Matches the shoes I gave you.'

'Yes.' And she could have wished Esmée hadn't said that either. She was puzzled as to why she was bothered, but she felt defensive against the tense atmosphere in the room, which was equally puzzling.

The clatter and click of dogs' paws on the oak staircase

diverted the attention from her as an avalanche of white, brown and ruby-coloured fur tumbled into the room and skittered about, sniffing and snuffling, exploring every corner.

'Ah! Here she comes.' Ralph stepped forward. His face, somewhat stern until now, was animated by a broad smile.

Slowly, one hand trailing on the banister, a blonde – but in this case not a natural one – slightly stout, heavily made-up woman descended. Her dress was of the fifties: full-skirted, ankle-length, tightly waisted and beaded. There was a sumptuous amount of flesh on display, not hidden at all by the long, beaded chiffon scarf wound round the shoulders.

'Helen, my dear, we'd all but given you up. Come, come by the fire.' Ralph was ushering her forward, fussing in exactly the same way as his wife had, and for which he'd admonished her.

'He doesn't understand we women, does he, Theresa baby? We have our *toilette* to attend to, Ralphie darling.' She spoke in an attractive husky voice, with a slight German accent. There was something familiar about her that Jillian couldn't place, and she wondered if Mrs Stirling enjoyed being called 'Theresa baby' or her husband being 'darling'. Helen sat in a high-backed wing-chair, arranging her billowing skirts and her feet in their silver, alarmingly high, stiletto-heeled shoes, so that Jillian was aware of her fine ankles. The dogs, their exploration over, returned *en masse* to their mistress and sat on the floor around her, making a pretty picture. 'A stranger, I spy a stranger.' Helen pointed directly at Jillian. 'So you're the girl we've heard so much about. Pretty little thing, aren't you?' Jillian wished the floor would open up and swallow her. 'Is that hair natural?'

'Of course.'

'*Of course* be buggered. Mine isn't!' She laughed, a snuffling noise that exactly echoed her speaking voice and her dogs.

'Jack says you're a secretary? Why?'

'It's all I can do.'

'Rubbish! With your looks you could go on the stage.'

'I can't act.'

'My dear, to my certain knowledge that hasn't stopped a

surprising number of actresses. Sage, stop scratching.' She patted one of the dogs. 'Or a model. How tall are you?'

'Five seven.'

'Stretch to eight and you could. Well done, Jack. I like her. An improvement on the last one, you are, Jillian. She was so stuck up her own arse she couldn't see daylight!' Jillian wanted to laugh, but since only Ralph did she thought better of it. 'You and Jack make a pretty pair – blond and tall, you'll have the most divine children.'

'Helen, you do talk such rubbish. You're embarrassing the girl. Can't you see she's all at sea as it is?' Theresa spoke sharply. Jillian winced inside.

'Am I, my dear? Then forgive a stupid woman's rambling. It's simply that when I see beauty I like to make sure that people know they have it. So often they don't. But I'm mortified if I embarrassed you. The trouble is, I'm over-excited to be here. Can you imagine? Last Christmas I had to go to a dreary hotel, everyone pretending to be having the most wonderful time when, in fact, they were all miserable and pining for family. It was dismal.'

'You don't have family, do you, Helen?' Jillian caught the sharpness in Theresa's voice again, which was at odds with her smile.

'I have all of you, my honorary family.' Helen beamed, apparently unaware of the tension in the room. 'Ah, the tree. Do let me help, please do!' She jumped up like a large child. This woke her dogs, who became hyperactive again.

'If you insist,' Theresa said, with a sigh, and followed her to the tree. She glanced at Jack, but he was looking put out, sulky, and held back. Esmée and the others joined in enthusiastically, not helped by the scurrying dogs.

'Now, let me see. I insist we have no other colour but gold and silver. These gaudy reds and greens are for the little ones, not sophisticates like us.' With a dismissive gesture Helen rejected half of the decorations. 'What do you think?'

'You're the Christmas expert, Helen, you must choose,' Ralph said.

He smiled at Helen so kindly that she put up her hand and stroked his cheek. 'Sweet old friend,' she said. 'You see, in my experience the English don't understand the importance of the Christmas tree. The need for symmetry. Such a responsibility.' She spoke with passion, as if the decorating of the tree was, at that moment, the most important thing to her. As she did so the globes of her breasts, protruding over the tight bodice of her dress, wobbled provocatively. Jillian watched her with fascination. Helen was vulgar but strangely attractive; she was partly repelled by her, yet oddly charmed too. She had never met anyone who had such force of character that she dominated a room. She wondered whether Theresa minded. Neither she nor Jack seemed to like Helen, the others she was not too sure about, but Ralph plainly adored her.

Then Jillian remembered who she was. An actress who had been quite famous way back but who, these days, was more likely to be seen on television on *Twenty Questions*. Helen Carter, of course! Her mother would be so excited she had met her.

'Quick, someone, Basil's got a glass bauble in his mouth.' Everyone set to the task of catching the little dog, who had no notion of obeying commands, or maybe he took after his mistress and did whatever he wanted.

4

Jillian, who drank little, was not prepared for the amount of alcohol that was consumed in the evening. As they went into dinner she felt quite woozy and realised she badly needed food.

The dining-room table was a picture. The place-markers were little silver foxes carrying cards slotted into their backs. At each place-setting the cutlery stretched far from each plate and glasses of varying sizes stood waiting. The centrepiece was a low arrangement of gold- and silver-painted cones and leaves with Christmas roses arranged among them. Thick cream candles shone from a multi-branched candelabrum, their light reflecting back a hundred times from individual salt and pepper pots, cigarette boxes, ashtrays, coasters, all polished to mirror brightness. The room sparkled and the table looked as if it had been covered in silver fairy dust.

'Theresa, what a picture! You are so clever, so artistic.' Helen gushed. Theresa said nothing. Perhaps, Jillian thought, she did not want to hear compliments from this woman. But, if Theresa did not like her, why had she been invited for Christmas?

Everyone took their seats; Jillian was between Liz and Mungo and longed childishly to be beside Jack. But at least she could look at him, sitting opposite her, between Helen and Esmée.

'Esmée, we shall have to find lovers, you and me, we're quite messing up your mother's seating arrangements.'

'It doesn't matter when it's just family,' Theresa replied, and Jillian felt a glow of happiness at being included in that description.

'But I know that such things bother you, Theresa. You like everything just so, don't you?'

'I am fully aware that we can't always have what we want, Helen.' There was a distinct edge to Theresa's voice now, which made everyone concentrate on their napkins, then begin speaking at the same time.

They were rescued by the arrival of the first course. A woman wearing a black dress and white apron appeared, bearing a tray of small pastry cups stuffed with velouté of mushroom, as Jillian read on her menu card.

'I thought we should have a Meursault with this.' Ralph began to tell them the year of the wine and where it was grown.

'Here we go . . .' she heard Jack mutter.

'Do you have to, Daddy?'

'Esmée, it's interesting. You know how expert your father is on the subject.' Helen smiled at Ralph, and Jillian could understand how, with some women, age and figure would never matter, they would always remain attractive and sexy.

'Listen or leave, the choice is yours.'

'I'm starving, Daddy, so I'll stay, but *I* don't find it the least bit interesting.'

With the next course of sole with grapes – a new concept

for Jillian, fish and fruit – another white wine was served and another lecture given. Esmée yawned, Jack talked to his mother, but the others listened. Jillian felt uncomfortable. It was hot in the room, but apart from that an alarming atmosphere was building and she did not know what was causing it.

Although the food was wonderful Jillian was horrified when she learned that the venison had been marinating for a week. She resisted sniffing it, which had been her first reaction to the news. She was surprised to find it tasted delicious, tender and aromatic; if she was going to die of food-poisoning at least it would have been worth it.

'If you don't like it, Jillian, I shall not be offended if you don't eat it. I assume you've never tried venison before.' Theresa had noticed her initial reluctance.

'No, but it's lovely, Mrs Stirling.'

'You've never had venison? Good God, where have you been?' exclaimed Mungo, his mouth full.

'Not everyone has had such a privileged upbringing, Mungo. I expect that, coming from her background, there is much that Jillian hasn't experienced. It shall be our pleasure to teach her.' Theresa smiled her magnificent smile at Jillian.

'What, a bit like the poor relation?' Mungo guffawed with such good nature that Jillian could not take offence. Instead she laughed too.

'Exactly.'

'Theresa, watch it,' Ralph rumbled, at his end of the table.

'Watch what, Ralph?'

Yet again, Jillian wished she could disappear, wished they would change the subject.

'Is your work interesting, my dear?' Helen came to her rescue. It was as if there were a competition between her and Theresa as to who had the best smile. Theresa's was the most beautiful, but Helen's the warmest, Jillian found herself thinking. She was kind, this woman, talking to her about her boring job when she couldn't be that interested.

'. . . then pay for it yourself,' Ralph said loudly, and banged his fist on the table so that everything on it rattled and shook.

Everyone looked up to see him glaring angrily at a confused Liz.

'I didn't mean that, Mr Stirling. Honestly. I just thought you'd be interested.'

'Well, I'm not. The nag is useless. It would be kinder to put it out of its misery.'

'Which horse? What's wrong?' Esmée asked.

'Mine, Esmée. Shalimar.' Theresa looked agitated. 'He fell and hurt his back.'

'Liz's mother knows a gypsy who's great at sorting out horses' backs,' Mungo explained.

'A horse chiropractor? Whatever next?' Helen laughed.

'It's not funny, Helen. Mother adores that horse.' Jack had hardly spoken during the meal.

'What's the problem, Dad? If the man can fix the horse then let him.'

'The problem, Esmée, is something you never take into account. It costs. If you start on something like this there's no end to it. The horse is in pain, the vet says there's nothing to be done. I want it shot.'

At this Theresa burst into tears, but quietly, which seemed to Jillian to make it sadder.

'You *must* pay for it, Dad.'

'I *must* nothing, Esmée.'

'I'll pay.'

'Oh, yes? What with? Horses are an expensive hobby, something this family is incapable of understanding.'

'I've offered to sell my brooch.' Theresa sobbed. Despite never having owned a pet, let alone a horse, Jillian felt so sorry for her. If she had the money she'd have given it to her, just to stop her crying.

'Theresa, you claim to love that horse but I've never seen you ride it in the whole time you've had it. The boy exercises it, Liz rides it, you're not even involved with it.'

'That's not true and you know it.'

'It's cruel.'

'No, Dad, it's you who's cruel. Why can't you do it? Why make Mother suffer so?' Jack was on his feet.

'You know even less about horses, Jack, so I'd appreciate it if you would keep your nose out.'

'Well, I won't!'

'Jack, Jack, please. Don't fight, don't ruin yet another Christmas.' His mother tugged at his sleeve, and reluctantly Jack sat down.

'I'll pay for the horse to be treated. How about that? Then you need not argue about it any more.' Helen beamed at them all.

'I can't let you do that, Helen.'

'Ralphie darling, why not? It's my thank-you to Theresa for being so sweet to me.'

'No, I can't allow that. Oh, sod it, I'll pay.' He grinned sheepishly.

'You bastard!' Jack roared, and stood up so fast that his chair crashed to the floor behind him. 'How can you humiliate her so?' He stormed angrily from the room. Esmée went to her still weeping mother to comfort her but looked as if she didn't really want to.

'Oh dear, what *have* I done?' Helen looked anguished.

'It's all my fault,' Liz fretted.

'So I can tell the gypsy to go ahead? Great, Dad.' Mungo seemed impervious to the drama.

'I'm going to my study for a stiff brandy. Anyone who wants can join me there.' Ralph pushed his chair back. As he got to the door he turned. 'You can turn the waterworks off now, Theresa, you've got your own way, as usual.'

Jillian leaned back in the chair in her room and stretched her spine. She was exhausted. What an evening! Theresa had gone to find Jack. Mungo and Liz had sneaked off home. Helen, she presumed, had joined Ralph, and Esmée had decided to return to London, despite having drunk far too much to drive safely. Jillian had tried to stop her.

'You're such a sweet worrier. I'll be fine. I just can't deal with the wrinklies fighting. I hate raw emotion swirling about, don't you?'

Now, washed and in her pyjamas, she sat and waited, hoping Jack would appear. She wanted many things explained to her and she wanted his arms around her. Her body ached with longing for him: it was hard to be in such close proximity and to have to sleep in separate rooms.

She woke at four, stiff and cold, still in the armchair. She climbed into bed and curled up small, shivering, certain she would never be warm again. She tried to quell the hurt that he had not come to her, if only for a chaste goodnight kiss. She told herself his duty was to comfort his mother – why, he might still be doing so. She peered over her eiderdown to see if the light from the landing still shone under her door, but all was dark. Finally, it was her tears, not Jack, that accompanied her to sleep.

5

In the morning Jillian was sick. As she looked at her wan face in the mirror over the basin she vowed she'd never touch week-long-marinated venison again.

A quick bath made her feel better, as did the prospect of new clothes to put on. The dress was deep blue velvet, shorter than she'd ever worn before – nearly four inches above the knee. It was loose-fitting with an optional chain-link belt, which the assistant in the boutique had shown her could be worn as a necklace too, which is what she chose to do with it. She'd bought a pale blue feather boa, which she'd wear later, and her first pair of fine-denier tights, which were German and had cost a fortune. She'd been afraid that her knickers would show when she sat down in such a short skirt. A pair of knee-high boots completed her outfit. With her long blonde hair worn loose, her new panda eyes carefully painted on and wearing the obligatory pale lipstick, she barely recognised herself. But after last night, she needed to feel she looked good.

Two minutes later she felt foolish. Theresa was in a tweed skirt with a pale pink twinset and pearls.

'What on earth have you got tarted up for?' Jack was at the kitchen table, eating toast and marmalade.

'It's Christmas Day. I thought –'

'You look particularly pretty, Jillian. Such a lovely colour and fabric. So loose and comfortable-looking. Why shouldn't she put her glad-rags on, Jack? What a misery you are.' Theresa pushed her son playfully. Jillian smiled her gratitude to her. 'Do you want bacon and eggs?'

'No, thank you.' She felt sick at the mention of food. 'But if there's some tea?' How strange. They were both behaving as if nothing untoward had happened last night.

'Are you all right?' Jack studied her carefully.

'Yes, I'm fine. Just a bit queasy.' Jillian patted her stomach and noticed mother and son glance at each other.

'You won't mind me mentioning it, my dear, but I couldn't help but hear – Well, I thought you were unwell this morning.'

'I was. I'm not used to such rich food.' She said this hurriedly, suddenly aware of the significance of that look. 'Some toast would be lovely,' she added. It was the last thing she wanted, but she knew she must appear to relish it. She sat beside Jack.

When Ralph Stirling entered the kitchen five minutes later, ruddy-cheeked and tweed-suited, he did not beat about the bush. 'My wife tells me she heard you throwing up this morning. Are you pregnant?'

'No, I'm not.' Jillian felt flustered, then sick again. She hadn't given it a thought. Her periods were so irregular – but, now . . .?

'You don't sound too sure.'

'It was the rich food and all that wine. And in any case . . .' Her voice trailed off. She did not know what she had meant to say or even if there was anything to say. She looked at Jack, willing him to speak up, to defend her, but instead he buttered another piece of toast. 'I drank too much,' she added finally, and helped herself to more toast too, as if by munching it she could prove she wasn't pregnant.

'Let's hope so.' Ralph turned his attention to his wife. 'Helen's ready for her breakfast tray, Theresa.'

'How can you? You creep!' Jack's chair screeched on the flagged floor as he got to his feet.

'Watch it.' Ralph pointed an aggressive finger at his son. 'You'll insult me once too often, my lad.'

'Please, it's Christmas, don't start,' Theresa said gently. 'Really, Jack, I don't mind.'

'I hate you. I wish you were dead!' Jack shouted at his father, then stormed from the room. Jillian wondered if she should follow him, but decided he was probably best left alone. From the Aga's warming drawer Theresa took a plate covered with a metal dome and put it on a ready-laid tray.

'Would you like me to take that up for you, Mrs Stirling? If you tell me where to go,' Jillian offered.

'How kind of you. Such kindness.' Theresa cooed which, since it was only a tray, Jillian thought a little exaggerated.

Having negotiated the stairs, her knock on the designated door was welcomed by a chorus of dogs barking and a cheerful-sounding, 'Come in,' followed at her appearance by a boisterous 'Merry Christmas, dear Jillian.'

It was difficult settling Helen with her tray since all the dogs were leaping on the bed in search of titbits and in the general mêlée, slipping and sliding on the satin eiderdown, were falling off and having to climb back on again. Being shouted at made no difference to them. 'I'll just butter them some toast. Could you hang on and take them down with you and pop them out for a pee? You look down in the dumps. You haven't let last night get to you, have you?' Helen looked up from her task. 'You have. Silly girl, stop worrying. This family *thrives*, positively *thrives*, on confrontation. If they didn't have a great big barney at Christmas they'd think they'd failed. Basil, here.' She popped a piece of lavishly buttered toast into one dog's mouth. 'Gentlemen first, with this lot. Like life, really, isn't it? Or haven't you lived long enough to learn that "ladies first" is mere camouflage? The gentlemen only give way on the little things and always end up doing exactly what they want. Rosemary, here, girl.' She patted the bed. 'Come on, give me a little smile.' Jillian obliged. 'That's better. You sit too.' Again she patted the ornate eiderdown, and Jillian sat obediently on the end of the bed.

'Poor Mrs Stirling, though,' she said. 'She'd worked so hard on that food and so much went to waste.'

Helen said nothing, just concentrated on her dogs, but Jillian noticed her purse her lips.

'Ralph tells me they think you might be up the spout. Are you?'

Jillian felt herself blushing furiously. 'No.'

'I hope you're not. All hell would break loose then. Jack really would get it in the neck – both barrels. Do you come to London often? You must look me up, I like visits from the young. I'll give you my card.'

After such a start there was no way that this Christmas could be resurrected for Jillian. She felt embarrassed, insulted and scared in equal measure. She also realised that she was looking into the abyss of her relationship with Jack. Not once had he crept to her room, or kissed her, or told her he loved her or, probably the worst of all, told her that it was agony at night to have her so close and not be with her. She might just as well not be here, she thought, as she idled away an hour alone in the television room and wondered where he was.

'Would you be happier if I left? There'll be trains to Cambridge, I'm sure,' she asked, when eventually he came looking for her. Butterflies of fear scudded around in her stomach.

'I'm sorry. I should never have invited you. It's not fair.'

'I don't mind. It's certainly been different.' She tried to sound amused, spurred on by his apology, which showed that he cared.

'It's no laughing matter. This is my family.'

'I didn't mean it like that.' She grabbed at his hand, but it was pointless; the moment was lost.

On a walk before lunch, when neither had said a word for a good five minutes, she found the courage to ask him if he wanted to end it.

'End what?' He stood, hands in his pockets, hunched against the chill.

'Us.'

'Don't be silly. Of course not. What gave you that idea?'

'We don't seem to be a pair any more.'

'It's difficult here with my family all around.'

'What's left of it.' She regretted the words even as she spoke them, but too late, they were out. He said nothing, just looked at her witheringly and trudged on through the wood, leaving her to find her own way home.

The conclusion she reached was that she'd have been better off in her bedsit than here. She was lonely there, but that loneliness was less painful than how she felt here with the man she loved in the same house, the same room, sitting beside her, yet behaving as if she'd become a stranger to him.

'Are you sulking?' He appeared in the doorway.

'I can't play bridge, you know I can't. I hoped there was something on TV, but there isn't.'

'I'm glad you're not – sulking, I mean. Esmée sulks and I hate it. She phoned, by the way, just to check we hadn't murdered each other. She sends love and says London is safer!'

Jillian didn't dare laugh in case he took that as another carp at his family, but she envied Esmée her safety.

'You know, they're right, you do look peaky. You're not –'

'Pregnant? How the hell do I know? But I wish you'd all stop talking about me as if I was some breeding pig or something.'

'Christ, you're not, are you?'

'I don't think so. But since everyone started on about it I've been thinking. There was that time, last month – you remember? You'd forgotten your French letters.'

'It can't be. I was careful. I'm sure you're not.'

'But what if I were?'

He sat down. 'Need you ask? Oh, come on, Jillian. Don't look all heartbroken. I love you, I'm always telling you so, but that doesn't mean I want to marry you. I'm too young. I've things to do, places to see, adventures to enjoy.'

'And what about me?'

'It's different for girls.'

'Is it?'

'Of course it is.'

'Maybe I don't want to marry you anyway.' It cost her dear to say that, for as she listened to him talk she was sure she heard the death knell of their love affair.

They lurched through the days until it was time for her to leave. Jillian felt a hypocrite as she said her thank-yous. In truth, she was glad to be escaping.

As they motored back to Cambridge his mood lightened. The frown disappeared, he even sang. He put his arm round her as he drove. 'I love you,' he said suddenly. 'Thanks for being such a brick and putting up with me and my foul moods and my crazy family. Bless you for being sane.'

She smiled and hugged herself tight. Maybe it was going to be all right. This had happened before, his family pulling him down, changing him. If she and Jack kept away from them, maybe their love for each other could survive.

In her bedsit they didn't need to speak but fell on the bed tearing at each other's clothes, desperate to get to each other's body, to feel, to touch, to smell, to possess, to be in love.

'Oh, that's wonderful. How I longed for you,' Jack said on a sigh as he entered her, and she could have cried with joy and relief.

Afterwards they lay for a long time in silence, enjoying each other and the moment.

'I kept meaning to ask you, is Helen an old family friend? Only she hardly seemed to talk to your mother.'

'They rarely do. She's Dad's mistress.'

6

Unable to consult her own doctor, Jillian had travelled to London to see one that a friend of a friend of Michelle's had recommended. A doctor who, she had been assured was very obliging, for a sum, where unwanted pregnancies were concerned.

104

Finding the surgery in the warren of streets in Earl's Court was difficult, and she was late. She was let in by a buxom woman with alarming blonde hair piled high on her head like a motorbike helmet. But she was welcoming and friendly and said not to worry about being late and the doctor would be with her in a sec. The waiting room into which she was ushered was evidently his sitting room as well, for she saw the remains of tea on a table and the television was on in the corner. The woman removed the crockery, apologising fulsomely, and Jillian was left alone to wait.

'Presumably it's no surprise ... but I can ... you are pregnant.'

Jillian, sitting on the examination table in the poky surgery in the basement, felt dizzy, sick and terrified.

'I wasn't sure.' Her voice, to her, was a nervous squeak.

'Of course ... you're so vague ... your dates ... I can only assess ... About eight weeks.' He was washing his hands at a small, grimy basin in the corner of the room. The smell of carbolic was heavy in the air. 'Of course ... any decision ... I'm here ... You understand?'

Jillian nodded mutely, but wondered why he only spoke in short bursts, never quite finishing what he had been about to say.

'Cash. No cheques.' He was drying his hands.

'Of course.'

'Good.' He began to take a selection of instruments from a glass chest. Jillian felt the walls press in on her. The pervasive smell of carbolic was overwhelming. With fumbling fingers she started to dress.

'You're leaving?' He sounded surprised.

'I've no cash on me. I'd have to go and get it.'

'Ah, well.' He replaced his cruel-looking surgical implements. 'You'd better ... new date ... not long.'

'No. I mean, yes.' She looked wildly about her, feeling trapped, which was illogical. The doctor was now at his desk, leafing through his diary. 'Friday ... I can fit you in ...' His voice trailed off for she was already running up the stairs to the front door.

*

In the train back to Cambridge Jillian was unaware of her fellow passengers, of the passing miles. She sat with her arms across her stomach, protecting its contents. She'd expected to be muddled, confused, but instead her mind was crystal clear. She wanted the security of her little room. They'd be safe there.

'It was filthy, Michelle. I wouldn't have wanted an animal operated on in there.' She was glad that her cousin had popped in to check how she was. 'He stank too – of booze. Every time he opened his mouth.'

'It was the drink got him struck off.'

'He's struck off?'

'Didn't I say? No, I didn't, did I? I thought you might not feel too confident in him if I did.' Michelle chuckled, but Jillian was in no mood for jokes. 'There's always the gin-and-a-hot-bath treatment,' she said helpfully.

'And have you ever heard that that worked? Never.'

'So, what do you intend to do?'

'Have it.'

'Thank God for that.' Michelle slumped back in her chair.

'But . . . you arranged . . . I mean . . .'

'You thought I approved? Well, in a way I do. I mean, it's your decision, no one else's. You're the one who has to bring it up. Why should others, especially men, say you can't do what you want with your own body? But, on the other hand, I just hate the idea. It seems so wrong and yet, thinking that, I feel I'm betraying you.'

'Poor Michelle, it's all so confusing, isn't it?'

'So you'll get married?'

'I wish I could. But, no, it's not fair on Jack.'

'Fair on Jack? Oh, Jillian, really, you can be so bloody annoying at times. This is hardly a virgin birth. He had his fun, now he pays.'

'What's the point in marrying someone who doesn't want to be married?'

Michelle sat beside her on the bed and put her arm about her. It was too much for Jillian and she felt in her pocket for a handkerchief as she began to cry. Michelle let her, holding her tight, stroking her hair, letting her release her pain and fear. 'This won't help, will it?' Jillian said at last, blowing her nose into the sodden handkerchief. 'No use at all.'

'You're right about shotgun weddings. But have you thought this through? Being an unmarried mum's no fun. What the hell will your father say?'

'I don't care what he says.'

'I suppose you could have it adopted.'

'No!'

'They'll try to persuade you. There are mother-and-baby homes – they'll look after you while you're pregnant and after. But a friend told me they pressurise you into adoption.'

'No, thank you! Can you imagine what they would be like? Like boarding-school or prison or worse. Perhaps I can still work. They'll just put me behind the scenes, clerking or something, so the public don't see me.'

'God, it's still so Victorian, isn't it? Makes me mad. I think we need something stronger. Got anything to drink?'

'There's a little whisky of Jack's.' She moved from the bed.

'I'll do it.' Michelle collected glasses and the bottle. 'Of course, Jack will help out with money – he's got enough of it.'

'No! I don't want him to know. I'm writing to him to tell him it's over and no mention of the baby.'

'Why? Why should he get away scot-free?'

'Because I know him. He'll insist we get married and I don't want that. It never works.'

'I think you're bloody mad.'

'I might be, but it's my right.'

Brave talk with Michelle was one thing. Facing reality alone in her little bedsit was another. There were many hours when the sheer magnitude of what faced her terrified Jillian, so that sleep became impossible and she had to force herself to eat for the baby's sake.

There were good moments, though, for all that. The idea of this little creature growing within her fascinated and amazed her. Already she felt an outpouring of love and a need to protect him – somehow she just knew it would be a boy.

On receipt of her letter Jack had come round.

'Why?' he'd said, standing in her tiny room. 'We get on so well. It was Christmas, wasn't it? Seeing the horror of my family in full flood, that finished you with me, didn't it?'

'No. It wasn't. I felt sorry for them all, especially your poor mother. The humiliation she must have felt at having to entertain your father's mistress.'

'Then what?'

'You said you don't want to settle down, and I understand that. You're too young, I agree. I see that. But I do. I don't want to waste years with you and have you up sticks, one day, and disappear to one of those places you told me you long to see.'

'Waste? You think being with me is a waste of your precious time?'

'I didn't mean it like that.'

'I'm sorry I bothered you. I'm sorry to have been such a bore to you. I'll go.' He stood up.

'Jack, don't. I mean –'

'I understand what you mean. Forget it, Jillian. It was fun, it obviously isn't any more.' He turned, no kiss, no touch, and left.

The loneliness became crushing. Despite not being with him, as the baby grew, her love for Jack grew too. She was consumed with longing for him. Once or twice in her lunch-hour she hid herself by the law-faculty building just on the off-chance that she would see him. Once she did, and it took all her self-control not to race after him and hurl herself into his arms, tell him all and feel safe. God, how she longed to feel safe!

Without Michelle there would have been no one to talk to about this shattering event. She'd no idea where Patsy was, she dared not contact Esmée, and she couldn't face her mother.

The day she told her boss she was pregnant, but that she wanted to stay on, was the worst ever. Not only did she receive a lecture on the sins of sex outside marriage and her irresponsibility at getting pregnant but she was told that he did not want a pregnant woman in his office and given a month's notice. Since, legally, he could have got rid of her after a week he glowed with pride at his own magnanimity.

That night she trudged home, tired and defeated. She had heard stories of a sexual revolution and of women's liberation. That might be so in London, she thought, but not here. Here, she had sinned, she was a fallen woman. Here, pregnancy was still regarded as an embarrassment. Cambridge was two towns: Town and Gown. Gown might be tolerant in its attitude to her and her pregnancy, but Town, which was her domain, was small-minded.

'Jack!' she said, as she turned into the entrance of her building and found him sitting on the steps.

'We've got to talk,' he said seriously.

Her heart was thudding alarmingly as they mounted the stairs. She hoped it wouldn't hurt the baby.

'Why didn't you tell me you were pregnant?' he said, without preamble.

'I didn't want to bother you.'

He laughed a short laugh. 'What an odd way to put it. I've a right to know.'

'I'm sorry.'

'I don't understand. I get a letter, it's all over you say, no explanation. Was this why?' He pointed towards her stomach.

'I didn't want you to feel trapped by it.'

'Why not? You are.'

She did not know how to answer that.

'Do you love me?' She did not reply. He stepped closer and held her face in his hands. 'I asked you, do you love me?' She had turned her head so that he could not see her eyes. 'You do, don't you?'

'I thought towards Christmas that it – we were coming to an end. I just gave us the final chop,' she said, still unable to look at him. He sat down on the bed and pulled her beside him.

'I was in the wrong. It's just –' He sighed. 'I'll be honest with you, I was afraid we were settling into a rut of being together. It was leading to marriage. I wasn't ready for that.'

'I know.'

'But I didn't want to hurt you, of all people.'

'So I didn't tell you about the baby. That's why I wrote. I wanted to protect you from feeling forced into something you didn't want.'

'Christ. You shouldn't have. You shouldn't have had these weeks alone – what it must have been like for you! Michelle told me you'd even seen an abortionist.'

'So it was Michelle. I'd told her I didn't want you to know.' She was angry.

'No, she's a good friend. I'm glad she told me. It's my baby too.' Gently he stroked her stomach. 'Amazing, isn't it? To think "we" are in there.' He looked at her, his eyes full of tears. 'I'm going to be a daddy! Imagine, me!' And he laughed excitedly. 'We're going to get married.'

'No.'

He put up his hand to stop her. 'I want no arguments. This has changed everything, Jillian. You and he need me. There's no question of me feeling I've *got* to, that you're making me. It's my choice – that is, if you'll have me?'

Jillian couldn't answer. Instead she covered her face with her hands and all the loneliness, worry and fear of the past weeks tumbled out, but her tears were of unmitigated joy and relief too.

'Who was it said "All the world loves a lover"?' Jack dropped his bulky duffel bag on to the floor of Jillian's room, placed two carrier bags carefully on the chair and slumped, looking exhausted, on her bed.

'Shakespeare, I expect.' Jillian looked up. She was sitting at the end of the bed, her back against the wall. Her legs, scissored up, supported a notepad on which she had been happily been making a list of all the things a baby needed. But, from Jack's expression, the defeated slope of his shoulders, all contentment was wiped away. 'Oh, Jack, what is it? What's happened?' She pushed herself forward on to her knees.

She'd been about to touch him, but now her hand wavered an inch or two above his shoulder. To her horror, she had seen that he was silently weeping. She sat back on her haunches, unsure how to proceed. She had never seen a man cry before. Would he want to be comforted or left alone? They sat in silence, then Jillian, unable to watch him suffer any longer, shuffled towards him, took hold of him and pulled him towards her, making soothing noises, stroking his hair, rocking him gently, as one day she'd rock their child, she thought. He said nothing for a while, just leaned against her. Then he sat up, took control again.

'The bastard! The fucking bastard! I wish I'd the courage to kill the shit!' At each expletive he banged one balled fist into the palm of the other. Jillian said nothing. 'The bloody bastard's sacked me.' He looked at her, but his anger was such that his eyes were glazed with it and she doubted if he really saw her.

'I don't understand.'

'The full works. I've just been to see my tutor, told him I have to leave college. My sodding father has stopped my allowance, refuses to pay any fees and has disinherited me, cutting me out of his will. He's even taken the car back. I'm amazed he let me walk out with my clothes on my back and my stuff.' He jerked his head towards the carrier bags.

'I'm so sorry,' she said, thinking how inadequate these words were.

'He wants to control me, own me. Well, he fucking well can't.'

'What exactly did he say?'

He picked up her hand and squeezed it. Jillian felt her nerves tingle, afraid that the action meant he was trying to give her strength. He sighed deeply. 'Bottom line is he doesn't want us to get married. It's nothing personal,' he added quickly. 'He told my mother he liked you – for what that's worth. He just doesn't want me marrying someone *he* hasn't chosen for me. Oh, he's been very reasonable, by his lights. Do as I say, you can have everything back – all the toys, all the props he bribes me with. Only to get them back I'm not to marry you. You have a choice – he sent a message. He'll pay for you to have an abortion – no back-street, in an admirable, clean, shiny clinic.'

'No! I can't!' The words shot out and she clamped her hand

over her mouth. She hadn't intended to say anything, not wanting to influence him, never wanting to be accused of playing on his emotions.

'He has an alternative for you – such a generous man, my eye! If you can prove it's my child –'

'He *what*? How dare he?'

'Then he's willing to help support it – note *help*, not fully support – until the child is sixteen, so no university or higher education for this poor scrap. Generous old bastard, isn't he?'

'I wouldn't accept a penny from him. I don't need him. I can support us. I'll manage.' She sat up defiantly as the fine words tumbled out. She had not thought through how. But she realised that she had spoken as if Jack was not included.

'You're not going to have to, my sweet.' He brushed her cheek with a kiss. 'You'll have me to care for you both.'

'But I couldn't let you marry me now. You'd lose your family, your career. I couldn't let that happen. I couldn't live with the guilt. And your father knows that. That's what's so cruel, so manipulative.'

'You see? I warned you but you wouldn't listen, insisted he was a "nice man". Everyone learns about him in the end. But we *are* going to get hitched. What he says doesn't matter. You don't think for one minute I'm going to let *him* control who *I* marry?'

'I want you to marry me for one – no, two reasons only. That you love me and that you want to. Not because I'm pregnant, not to get at your father.'

'Jillian, I didn't mean it like that. Of course I want to.' He leaped from the bed and, in a blink, was kneeling in front of her. 'Darling Jillian, please, please, will you marry me?' His mood had changed completely.

She looked down at him with tenderness, but she was serious too. 'I will, on one condition.'

'Anything.'

'That you never, ever say in any future rows we have that you felt you had to marry me, that you felt forced to.'

'Easy – I promise.'

'I'm serious.'

'So am I. I want to have my own family. I want to look after

112

you for the rest of your life. I want to be a daddy.' From his pocket he took a small jeweller's box and snapped it open. Inside was a beautiful sapphire and diamond ring.

'Oh, Jack, you shouldn't have. The expense!'

'It's second-hand – Victorian. They're cheaper, less purchase tax,' he said ingenuously.

She laughed at his practical explanation amid this most romantic of moments. Then she became serious again. 'Quite honestly, I don't want it. It would be as if he bought it, and I want nothing from your father.' She looked with regret at the pretty ring.

'What do you take me for? A great-aunt died and left me a legacy. I used some of that. I felt exactly the same as you.' He took the ring from the box and slipped it on to her finger.

'It's so beautiful.' She held her hand and moved it so that sparks of iridescent light flew from the ring in all directions.

He was back beside her. His mouth at her neck, his hand searching for her breast, teasing her, awakening her. She turned to him.

'In any case,' he said, much later, as they sat in her narrow bed sipping the celebratory champagne, which had been in one of his carrier bags, 'you worry unnecessarily. Since we'll never row, no one will ever accuse anyone of anything.'

'Never is a very big word,' she said, but she was far too happy to let anything worry her on this night of all nights.

7

Mary Foster was disappointed. 'In this day and age! You're stupid. What my generation would have given to have something like the pill!'

'You didn't need it, not like us. Only in marriage.'

'Didn't we? You'd be surprised, young woman.' Mary looked almost offended.

'Mum, you didn't!'

'Hormones and lust were not discovered by your generation alone, you know. We were just more discreet about it. I don't know why this generation makes such a song and dance. But, of course, young women are expected to sleep with their friends now, whereas we bestowed favours on our young men – and were a lot more selective, I'll have you know.'

'I didn't mean to sleep with Jack. He didn't pressure me. I'd planned to stay . . . you know, for my husband but, well, I couldn't help myself. If you know what I mean?' Amazed to be having this conversation with her mother, she found difficulty in putting into words what she meant.

'I'm glad you did, Jillian. There's nothing worse for a woman than marrying and finding she and her husband are not compatible – that's a torturous prison to be in.' As she spoke she looked deeply sad. 'What I don't understand is why you weren't taking the pill. They tell me it's pink. We always dreamed of a miraculous little *pink* pill!' She smiled.

'I didn't dare. I was afraid Dr Grey would tell you. And you'd lecture me. And we were careful.'

'Not careful enough, though, were you?'

'Oh, Mum, please. It's too late now.'

'It's no way to start a marriage, that's why I'm concerned. He'll never forgive you, ever.'

'It's not like that – he wants to be married.'

'And you believe him? Quitting university, losing his career, his money, estranged from his family – do you really think he'll ever forgive you that?'

'He says so, and I believe him. One day he'll go back to college. When I've had the baby I can work and help him, and he can get a part-time job. He'll be a historian – we've planned it.'

'A historian? I thought he wanted to be a lawyer?'

'That was his father's wish, not his. Now he's free of him he can do what he wants.'

'He'd have been better off as a lawyer. Who's ever heard of a rich historian?'

'Why do you keep going on about money? It isn't everything, you know.'

'Isn't it? You try being happy without it.'

Jillian's meeting with her father was less confrontational. He refused to speak to her but he stared at her with such loathing that she had to turn away, certain that such a look would turn her into a pillar of salt. She packed her remaining possessions and left her childhood home without saying goodbye. She'd thought she'd be hurt and upset but she wasn't. This house and her father were the past; now she had her own future to plan for and look forward to.

'I think you're mad, tying yourself down at your age. And how will you manage?' Informed by Esmée of the news, Pasty had turned up unexpectedly and was helping them move into a small, terraced house off Mill Road that Jack had found for them to rent furnished. It had two bedrooms upstairs, two small rooms and a kitchen downstairs and an even smaller bathroom built on the back. It was good to have a bathroom – most of the houses in that street didn't.

'I can work. Jack's already looking.'

'And his bastard of a father cut him off without a penny? Couldn't the college have helped him out? Don't they have bursaries and things? Couldn't he have got a grant?'

'A grant was out because of his father's income. And any help from the college wasn't enough for me as well.'

'What a freak! I've got a friend who can put a hex on his dad if you like – she's very good. She crashed a car just by thinking about it the other day.'

'Patsy, you don't really believe that stuff, do you?' Jillian was looking at a cushion that had come with the house, she was unsure, given its bedraggled state, if she wanted it here.

'Totally. I've learned more in the past six months than in my whole life. We've been tied down spiritually. Once you free your spirit the whole universe is there, just waiting to be understood.'

'If you're still on acid, you're not learning a thing. It's all illusion. Honestly, Patsy, for someone so clever, you can be a real arse-head at times.'

'Lordy, Lordy, Miss Scarlett, you're learning the lingo!' Patsy laughed. 'This chair stinks.'

'What of?'

'Old people.'

'Every place we saw had the same smell and this was the best one. No one wants to rent to people with a baby on the way. I think it's because the furniture's all second-hand – it probably comes from house sales of old people who've died.'

'Charming! I hope they weren't incontinent on them.'

'Patsy!' Jillian carried into the kitchen the box of china she'd bought over the months and began to unpack it. 'Fancy a cuppa?'

'If I can have a spliff without you nagging me.'

'If you don't say any more about how daft I am – getting preggers, the full catastrophe.'

'Agreed. What's it like having somebody growing inside you?'

'Not much different. I've stopped feeling sick. I'm not pregnant enough for much else, I suppose.'

'Are you emotionally unreasonable?'

'You'd have to ask Jack. I don't think so.' She poured the tea. 'I'm not interfering, but why have you got that daisy painted on your forehead?'

'It's pretty.'

'It looks daft to me.'

'Jillian!'

'Sorry. And you say Dad's giving you money to go to India? Wonders will never cease.'

'Brilliant, isn't it? I've got you to thank for that. Anything you'd have had, I get. So you've done me a favour.'

'But how did you swing it?'

'I said I wanted to go and study other religions at first hand.'

'And he believed you? Well, watch it, won't you?'

'I'll be fine. I'm going with friends.'

'I won't even ask who!'

Esmée arrived with presents for the house – an eiderdown, an electric blanket, a set of saucepans, a crib and a case full of exquisite baby clothes. Jillian accepted everything with gratitude, while concealing her astonishment at the practicality of Esmée's gifts.

'Is this all you can afford, Jack? It's ghastly.' Esmée looked about the room with disdain. Jillian felt quite protective towards it, just as she had for her bedsit. They'd worked hard to make it nice, deciding where to place her few ornaments and books. Jack had built shelves for them from planks resting on bricks. He had his collection of records, several pictures and some wood carvings he'd bought. They'd painted their sitting room deep red so it was womb-like, which had enraged the landlord. Jillian had taken down the polyester curtains and had draped on the rail a brightly coloured red and yellow cotton bedspread she'd picked up in the market.

'We like it. In any case, it's all we can afford. It's only temporary.'

'What are you going to do?' Esmée was rootling in a large bag she had with her and, like a magician, produced a bottle of vodka. 'Always carry iron rations, just in case.'

'What am I going to do?' Jack said. 'Well, Cambridge hasn't that much to offer on the job front, but I've been looking about. These houses go for peanuts. I'm thinking of buying a couple, doing them up, then either selling or letting them. You've no idea the problem we had finding this place. There's a desperate shortage.'

'How will you get the money, Jack?' Jillian wished he'd told her what he was planning first.

'I've a little bit of money left from dear old Aunt Em's legacy. And we'll borrow.'

'Oh dear. Is that wise?'

'Jillian, my love, that's what everyone does. It's what banks are for.'

'But what if it doesn't work out?'

'Then, my love, we lose the lot and have to think what else to do. Any chance of another vodka, Esmée?'

Her February wedding day was bleak. The wind whipped up Castle Hill, turned right spitefully and blasted the steps of the

Shire Hall, a building that looked as if it had been transplanted from an eastern-bloc country and set down on the only hill in the whole town.

'Cheese. And try to stop shivering.' Mary focused her box Brownie.

They all obliged. Then, Esmée's treat, they piled into her car and a taxi and drove to the University Arms Hotel for lunch. Champagne on ice was waiting for them.

'Esmée, this is so kind of you.' Jillian and her sister-in-law were alone in the ladies' cloakroom.

'It's nothing. My parents are being a positive pain in the arse. Somebody had to do something.'

'Jack says it's only your father.'

'Does he, now?'

'Do you know why he's so against me?'

'Is he? He hasn't told me. Perhaps he feels he's losing control. He's like a silly old wounded lion – poor sweetie. I think it must be a male thing.'

'But Jack so hoped your mother would come today. I suppose she didn't dare. Like Mungo and Liz.'

'Got a hairbrush? I seem to have lost mine.'

'My mother wants to help pay for lunch, Esmée.'

'I won't even hear of it. This is my treat.'

'But –'

'No buts, Jill, my poppet. Do you think this green eye-liner suits me or should I go back to black?'

'It's lovely. There's something else, Esmée. I don't know what to do. If I tell you, you won't say anything, will you?'

Esmée paused, eye-liner brush poised in the air, the small palette of colour in the other. 'Lips are sealed. Brownies' honour!'

'I've had a letter – a very sweet one – and a cheque from Helen.'

'So? I'm not surprised. She's a generous old trout.'

'Yes. But what do I do? Jack told me who she is and I don't think he likes her very much. I mean, he'd tear up the cheque, I think.'

'Then don't tell him.'

'But I shouldn't have secrets, should I?'

'How big's the cheque?'

'A thousand pounds.'

'Have a secret.' She turned back to the mirror.

'But what if Jack found out? He'd be furious. I mean, your poor mother –'

Esmée turned back from her reflection. 'Listen, Jill, love. Nothing is ever what it seems – I've learned that. It's dangerous to judge. Helen's a dear woman, as much a victim as anyone. Use the money, enjoy it. If Jack wants to be petty about it, let him.' She scrutinised her face in the mirror. 'There, that's the best I can do – you never know, my Mr Right might be out there waiting for me. Come, Mrs Stirling, luncheon awaits.'

'Yes. Of course. I am, aren't I? Jillian Stirling – sounds good, doesn't it?'

Chapter Four

1

Spring 1972 – Spring 1974

'I thought, after Miles was born, you said you didn't want any more kids?' Michelle, dressed in the baggiest most unbecoming dungarees Jillian had ever seen, her long, curly hair cut brutally short, paused in her task of rolling a cigarette and looked at her sternly, the Rizla paper held motionless to her lips. 'Well, that's what you said.' She licked the paper.

'I don't know why you smoke those disgusting things.' Jillian pulled a face. Already she was regretting telling Michelle she was pregnant again.

'Hang on, there. It's not my fault you're in the club.' She rattled her Zippo lighter, which stank of petrol and even from across the room made Jillian feel queasy. She concentrated on folding the towels ready for ironing, waiting for the wave of nausea to pass.

'Don't tell me you're going to iron those flipping towels?' Michelle's voice brimmed with astonishment.

'It makes them softer.'

'As if you haven't enough to do! You're mad! I never iron anything if I can help it.'

'So I see.'

'Miaow . . .' Michelle said good-naturedly. 'What does Jack say?'

'I haven't told him.'

'Scared to?'

'No. What gives you that idea?' She tested the heat of the iron.

'Because if you weren't you'd have told him first. Not me.'

Jillian started to iron. 'Of course you're right but, then, you always are, aren't you?' She glanced at Michelle to see if she'd reacted to her sharpish tone, but her cousin seemed blissfully unaware of it as she puffed at her cigarette, which looked as if it had gone out.

'So? Why the secrecy?'

'I didn't want to worry him.' She saw that Michelle looked sceptical. 'He's tired and overworked as it is. These house conversions are hard work, especially when he does them virtually single-handed.'

'He's an ideal husband!'

'Don't scoff, Michelle. He works all hours ... It's been hard.' She paused. 'I guess he won't be too pleased. That's why.' She carried on ironing.

'My heart bleeds for him! Honestly, Jillian, just listen to you. He helped you get preggers, or don't you remember? He'll have to lump it. Your Jack pisses me off.' Michelle relit her cigarette.

'I wish you wouldn't say things like that. It makes me feel disloyal just hearing it.'

'Disloyal? You? Him more like.'

'He never is.' Jillian placed the iron carefully on the asbestos pad.

'Oh, no? So what about his parents? Who keeps his life in neat little boxes? Taking Miles to lunch with his grandmother but you're never included in the invitation, are you, as if you're a second-class citizen?'

'It's difficult for him. As it is, they have to meet at his aunt's in Royston.'

'Difficult, my arse. If she doesn't want to see you, he shouldn't go. "Love me, love my bear." That's what he should say to the miserable old cow.'

'It's not Theresa's fault. It's his father who doesn't want her to see me. She doesn't want to lie to him and I don't blame her.'

'The trouble with you, Jillian, is you're always too reasonable for your own good. You'd defend the devil if he popped in for tea. I wish you'd pack in that bloody ironing and come and talk properly.'

'I feel sorry for her. After all, it means she only sees Miles once a month.' She unplugged the iron. 'Fancy a cuppa? Or there's that bottle of wine we opened last night.'

'Need you ask?' Michelle followed her into the kitchen. 'How the hell do you keep everything so tidy? Just look at this place.'

'If I didn't keep it organised it would soon be too chaotic to work in. One day . . .' Jillian said dreamily, as she uncorked the wine.

'Has the old bat seen how you live? This house is too small for the three of you, let alone four.'

'She came once, when we lived in a similar one in Madras Road, when we were first married. I don't think she approved. I loved that house too.'

'She sounds such a snooty bitch.' Michelle moved back into the tiny sitting room, carrying her glass of wine. 'How many moves have you had in the last five years?'

'This'll be the fourth.'

'Christ, you must be so fed up with it.'

'Not really. At least the cupboards never have time to get too untidy. One day I'd like to think we'll be settled, but until then . . .' She sat down. 'You know, we've made money on every house we've converted. It was a brilliant idea of Jack's and he's so good at it.'

'What about you? You help. Don't give him all the credit. You choose the colours, do the painting. Just look at this dark brown, I'd never have thought to use such a bold colour. So when *are* you going to tell Jack about the new baby?'

Jillian pulled a face at the reminder. 'Tonight. I'll feed him first,' she said nervously. 'At least Mum's pleased, but she would be, wouldn't she?'

That evening Jillian made a chicken casserole. She'd have preferred to give her husband steak at such a momentous dinner, but funds would not run to it. Her life was a constant juggling of money.

'Can I stay up till Daddy's home?'

'No, Miles. He'll be late, I expect.'

'Why's he always late? Why does he never read me a story?'

'Because he's always busy. Which one do you want tonight? You choose.'

Miles selected his favourite book, tattered now from its

nightly reading and settled on the sofa to snuggle up beside her. This was one of her favourite moments of the day, Miles fresh from his bath, just the two of them cuddled up together. She began to read the words she knew virtually by heart.

Just the two of them, but only for another six months, she thought later, when Miles was in bed. She dreaded this new baby – not only because of what Jack would think but because she didn't want it. She loved Miles so totally. How could she possibly love another child as much? They had their routine, their involvement with each other and another person might spoil it all.

Life had been hard at times since she and Jack had been married, but they'd weathered it and they were a family, a unit, that she didn't want altered in any way. With Miles starting school next term, she'd planned to go back to work. She'd never given up on her dream of earning enough one day so that Jack could go back to college and get the degree of which he'd been deprived because of her and Miles. Now, because of this new child, how long would that be?

'That smells good.'

'Jack! I didn't hear you. I was daydreaming.' He kissed her cheek as he passed her, making for the downstairs bathroom they'd had built on where the outside lavatory had been, sacrificing half the garden to do so. As usual he'd returned home with his clothes and hair covered in brick dust, his hands calloused from the hard physical work of converting the houses.

'The way you work for us, you deserve a medal.'

'Don't tell a living soul, but I rather enjoy it.'

'Any problems?' she called, as she finished off the meal and he ran his bath.

'We've found some wet rot.'

'Oh, no! How much?' From the cupboard she took the bottle of whisky she'd bought him as a surprise, mixed him a large one with a dash of water and carried it through. Jack was lying back in the bath, his eyes closed. He looked so tired, she thought. The slim man she'd married had been replaced by a far more muscular one – at least the work had done that for him. 'I got you a drink.' She sat on the lavatory lid and handed him his glass. 'Is it going to be expensive to put right?'

'Everything's always bloody expensive.'

'But we had the survey done. Surely . . .'

'I've read the small print. The surveyor is covered whichever way you interpret it.'

'Then what's the point in having it done?'

'The building society insisted, remember?'

'I'm sorry.'

'It's hardly your fault.' He took a sip of the whisky. 'That's good. Pushing the boat out, aren't you?' He smiled across at her. She looked at her hands. Now, with this news, was hardly the best time, but when would be?

'Jack, I've something to tell you.'

'Fire away.' He was soaping himself.

'I'm pregnant.'

Just for a second his face showed the horror he evidently felt, but the next second it was gone, as if she'd imagined it. 'This is turning into some day!' His laugh was false as he rinsed the soap away; so she hadn't imagined the expression, she thought.

'You don't mind?' she asked, as if she didn't know the real answer.

'Not much point is there?' He hauled himself out of the bath and she handed him a towel. 'Did you forget to take your pill?'

'No. That's what I don't understand.'

'You must have.'

'I'll get supper on the table.' This wasn't right, she thought, as she collected the cutlery. This should be good news, happy news. From not wanting the baby she felt suddenly protective towards it. She found herself thinking that it would almost have been preferable if Jack had been angry.

Victoria was born in September. After the trauma of Miles's breech delivery her arrival was far more relaxed. And whereas Miles had given them many a sleepless night, Victoria was a calm, placid child. From within Jillian found for her the reserves of love she'd feared she would not have, and Miles doted on her.

There was yet another move – the fifth. And then another. But this time it was to the house of her dreams. It was Edwardian, detached, three storeys high with large rooms and a big garden. It was close to the station, which Jack, with his eye for property, assured her was an area of the city ripe for improvement.

'I never want to move ever again,' she said excitedly, the day they took possession.

'Then we shan't.' Jack hugged her.

'But can we afford it?'

'I got it for a song. Don't worry. You've earned this. The last few years haven't been easy, have they?'

'No. But they've been fun too. And we've had each other.'

'I think we're going to have to replace these sashes,' he answered.

With so much work to do on the new house, the children and Jack to care for, Jillian shelved once again any idea of going out to work.

'I don't understand you, Jillian. You're bright, you should get a job. Surely you could afford an au pair now.' Michelle was sitting on the stairs watching Jillian strip years of old paint from the banisters.

'Jack says he doesn't want to go back to college, he's happier making money, and things aren't as tight as they were.'

'I didn't mean for his benefit, silly. I meant for you. You're so *domesticated*.'

'You needn't make it sound as if it's a terminal disease!'

'Aren't you bored out of your skull?'

'No, I like what I do. Heavens, it was only a few years ago that this was our ambition, to be wives and mothers.'

'It might have been yours, it was never mine.' Michelle sounded quite put out.

'So? Just because you don't like housework, that doesn't mean I don't. Suddenly it seems that everyone is expected to get a career, any career, and that that, somehow, will make you a better mother.'

'It would make you a more interesting one!'

Later, Jillian mulled over this conversation, as she so often did when Michelle had been sounding off. She hadn't been totally honest with her. She didn't want to admit that there were days when the strait-jacket of her life made her want to scream, when the sheer repetition of her chores made her feel bleak. But she couldn't see any point in confessing this. It was what she did, and no amount of moaning would make it any better. And, in any case, there were other days when the satisfaction of a clean house, the smell of baking in the air, knowing she was good at what she did filled her with contentment and pride.

'Life's confusing!' she said aloud, to her Kenwood mixer, as she switched on the liquidiser and watched the vegetable purée she was making for Victoria churning away.

Was she becoming boring? She tried not to be. She read the papers so she'd know what was going on in the world. She read the book and theatre critics so that she could join in the conversation when they went out occasionally with Jack's old friends from his college days. And, anyway, it was often the other way round: she found them boring with their endless chat about money and who was making how much and who had recently bought what. They had all had such expensive educations to end up talking about nothing – or maybe it was just that she'd never heard them talk about important things. She scooped the purée into a bowl.

And what else was it Michelle had said that had annoyed her? Yes, of course. She'd pointed out that they only ever seemed to meet Jack's old friends, never hers.

'But, Michelle, that's what often happens in marriages. One lot of friends gets dropped.'

'I don't see why. And I see less that they should be your friends rather than Jack's pompous lot.'

'They are a bit, aren't they?' She giggled.

'And the toffee-nosed wives with a bad case of superiorityi-tis.'

'They make me feel inferior without even trying.'

'Don't let them get to you. They're only jealous.'

'Of me? Why? You should see some of their houses, lovely furniture, beautiful clothes.'

'Yes, but they don't look like you, do they? All sleek and fine bones. That short hair is lovely, and Laura Ashley was made for you.'

'I thought you said a female concerned with her appearance was a sexual traitor pandering to the lust of men.'

'Only because I don't look like you!' Michelle hooted. Jillian smiled to herself at the memory. Dear Michelle, she was such a paradox. She began to prepare their supper. She'd bought some scallops and was going to marinate them in vermouth as an experiment.

She was more or less happy, though, and as she pottered about the kitchen she decided Jack was too. After all, they rarely argued, not like some she knew. They'd weathered the lack of money. They had beautiful, healthy children. She was even reconciled with her father, if not his. Mentally she ticked off the list. She should have been deliriously happy, so why wasn't she? Guilt. The word popped out of its own accord. That wretched guilt, which never quite left her. The knowledge that if it wasn't for her he could be like one of his friends, secure, prosperous. It followed her as if she were a witch and it was her familiar.

She laid the scallops in a china dish. Perhaps if she explained to Michelle that it was guilt that made her work so hard in the home to have everything perfect for him? But even as she thought this she knew that admitting it to Michelle would only give her something else to rabbit about.

Still, she paused, remembering.

'I married a paragon. The perfect wife,' Jack was fond of saying. Jillian smiled.

'You're a prat! You're more like his servant than his wife.' She frowned with the memory of Patsy's words from years ago.

'Darling, he doesn't deserve you, you'll make yourself old before your time. Chill out!' Esmée had counselled on a flying visit.

'Well, I don't know. All this talk of female liberation hasn't done much for you, has it? You're worse off than I was. Your father understood a bit of muddle when you were babies. And at least now I've gone back to nursing I've my independence,' her mother had fretted, only last week.

But none of them knew of the guilt she carted about with her, morning, noon and night. She covered the scallops and put them in the fridge to chill.

After weeks of work with the Nitromors the staircase was finished and back to its natural wood.

'You know, Jillian, this pine thing is all the rage. I think we should do stripping professionally. We could put an acid bath in the shed. We –'

'No acid baths,' she said decisively. 'Not with the children around.'

'Well, then, have you ever thought about a shop?'

'Me?'

'Yes, selling pine furniture. Look how everyone raves about the dresser you stripped.'

'Do you think I could?'

'Sure thing. Part-time, of course. We could get an assistant.'

And, with Jack, it was no sooner thought of than done.

Jillian enjoyed working in the shop, meeting people, finding furniture for them if they'd nothing that suited. And, since it was their own business, she could take Victoria with her when she wasn't at the kindergarten.

Insidiously the stock increased. At the auctions she attended to buy furniture for stripping she often bought other things that had taken her eye – a vase, candlesticks, the odd picture. Some she kept, some she sold.

Jack's business was expanding. Soon he needed a warehouse to store the doors, architraves, tiles, pillars, paving stones, the whole contents of a Methodist chapel, pews and all, which he bought. Anything others saw as rubbish Jack saw as architectural heritage and snapped it up, stored it, sold it. Anything that didn't sell he kept. He said its day would come.

'You're more like your father than you think,' she teased him one day. He had returned from an interview at the bank with sufficient backing to tender for the contents of an old Victorian hospital that was being modernised.

'I'm not a bit like him.' He bridled.

'Business acumen, I meant,' she said hurriedly. 'I've been thinking, we're doing so well you shouldn't be working so hard. You haven't been home before nine one night this week.'

'It's necessary. I can't stop yet. I want to be rich – richer than that evil old bastard!'

2

Summer–Autumn 1976

'You look mighty serious.' Jack peered at his wife across the table. Jillian had put Miles and Victoria to bed early, and they were having a candle-lit dinner. It was Jack's birthday, his twenty-ninth, and for once he was home early.

'I realised today that I was growing old.'

'Well, there's a revelation!' He grinned at her.

'Of course, I know each day I'm getting older, but it's not something you think about, is it? I mean, being old is a long way away. Or it was.'

'What brought this on?'

'Dad. I went to see him. He's missing Patsy and even me, I think, not that he'll admit it, but I think he was close to tears. I suddenly saw we were reversing our roles, that he's becoming truly old, that one day, sooner than I thought, he'll become dependent on me. He's changed. He's much mellower.'

'Christ, Jillian, the poor sod's only in his late fifties, isn't he?'

'Yes, but I don't think it's necessarily to do with just his age, that maybe there's a mental ageing too and perhaps they don't run side by side.'

'My dear wife. One, I don't think this is a suitable conversation to be having on my birthday – it gives me the abdabs. Two, I haven't the foggiest idea what you're talking about.'

'Tell you the truth, neither have I!' She laughed. 'He asked me if I knew where Patsy was. I told him India. You'd think she could write and let us know.'

'Esmée says she's coming home at the end of the year.'

'Great! She knows and we don't. When did you see Esmée?'

'I didn't. She phoned. Family business.'

'Oh.' She hated it when he said something like that: it reminded her of how she was not regarded by anyone, it seemed, as part of his family. 'If she phones again, ask her to let me know when Patsy's back. She's got to see Dad.'

'I will, but I doubt if you'll ever change your sister into the dutiful daughter you are. Fancy some more wine? It is my birthday, after all. And there's something I want to discuss.'

'Please don't say it's another move! I like this house.' She smiled warily for she could never quite believe that he wasn't about to sell up again.

'No, not this time. It's something Gary's come up with. I'll just be a mo.'

She listened to him clattering down the cellar steps. Not Gary, she thought. There was something about Gary Frampshore she didn't like but which she couldn't put her finger on. Gary was a friend of a friend they'd met at a party. He was ex-army and had worked in import and export. Now, with money to invest, he wanted to get into property development.

Gary and his clothes were smooth. He was knowledgeable and, Jillian had noticed, could divert a conversation with ease, rather like a rancher sorting cattle at a pass. She often found herself wondering why he didn't want to talk about his parents, his school, his regiment. She could not trust him. Jack thought he was great.

She was also watchful of Cherry, his wife. She was confident and predatory. She'd not made a move on Jack yet, but Jillian felt instinctively that it was only a matter of time before she did. She tried never to leave him alone with Cherry.

Certainly the advent of Gary a year ago had marked a sharp

upturn in their fortunes, she had to admit that. Imperceptibly, at first, things had changed. A new pair of shoes for Miles was no longer the catastrophe it had been. The electricity bill was paid before the final demand. They went out more, had even bought another car, which, now that she had passed her driving test, was hers. Was it Gary who had made these things happen or would they have come about anyway? She liked to think the latter.

'I thought we'd have some champagne.'

'My. What a treat!'

'Justified, I think. Gary wants me to go in with him to convert a block of houses in Hills Road into offices. It's big.'

'How big?'

'Let's just say it'll be the springboard I've been looking for to better things.'

'Like what?'

'Out of Cambridge. Something we can really get our teeth into. London – the City. Office buildings. Warehouse conversions.'

'Warehouses? You're joking?'

'No, I'm not. You could convert some of them into wonderful flats. You'll see.'

'But how?'

'With my good bank record as a builder and Gary's financial expertise we borrow, of course.'

'Oh, Jack, be careful.'

'Silly. Don't worry. It's what everyone does. Never use your own money when you can use other people's.' He was fond of saying that.

Three months later Jillian sat uncomfortably in Esmée's old flat.

'Patsy, can't you come home just for a short visit? You don't even have to stay the night.'

'Great! You want me to flog all the way there and back in a day?'

'It's not the other side of the world. I came today on a cheap day return and I'm hardly worn out! It's less than a couple of hours on the train. Dad misses you.'

'I don't miss him.'

'Marvellous, isn't it? You get all the attention as a child – I'd have given anything for half of what you got – yet you can't be bothered with him now.'

'I don't know why *you* do – not after what he said to you when I scarpered. Mum told me – evil old sod!'

'He *is* our father. He was hurting when he said it.'

'Christ, Jillian.' Patsy rolled her eyes in exasperation. 'Don't you ever get fed up with your placid, accepting-all-the-crap, madonna act? Don't you ever want to break out? Don't you ever want to stop boring the pants off me?'

'Patsy, please. I didn't come here to fight.'

'Don't fucking "Patsy, please" me! Whenever I see you all I get is nag, nag, nag. There's never any "Hi, Patsy, great to see you, how are you doing?" You, Jillian, with your holier-than-thou attitude are a serious pain in the arse.'

'I don't mean to be. I worry.'

'Then don't. I don't want or need your worry. I'm happy as I am. I've my friends, my dope, my space. Do I criticise your lifestyle?'

'There's nothing to criticise.'

'Oh, isn't there? You think not?' Patsy snorted derisively. 'You live with a money-orientated freak, a capitalistic chancer. Grab, grab, grab. Possessions, possessions, possessions – that's all he thinks or cares about. He's no soul, no sensitivity –'

'That's enough!' Jillian jumped to her feet. 'Don't you dare criticise Jack. He works so hard to support parasitic creeps like you. Oh, you can rabbit on about capitalism, exploitation of the workers till the cows come home. But if it wasn't for people like Jack working, paying their taxes, spongers like you and your mates wouldn't have any benefits to cheat on and you'd all starve. Probably a good thing.' She sat down again thinking she'd feel better for speaking her mind, but she didn't.

'At last! You've lost your temper with me. You're showing some spirit. You *do* live! Thank Christ! I was sure you were dead from the neck up.' Patsy was clapping.

Jillian sat stunned, not only by what Patsy had just said but by her own rage. 'I don't understand you, Patsy', she said. 'Just look at this place, look at the mess. Is it any wonder I get upset, that I'm concerned?' She remembered that when Esmée had lived here this room had been dark but pretty; the feel of being in an Arabian tent had been planned and worked out with care. All that had changed. Now graffiti were daubed on the walls, the lovely hangings were tattered and scattered with what looked like cigarette burns. The carpet was filthy and burned too. And over all she could smell the sickening odour of stale takeaway food, cheap joss-sticks, old cigarette smoke and the ever pervasive scent of marijuana.

'I like it as it is, Jillian. Watch it.'

'You just say that. You can't.'

'There you go again. I don't want to clean up, wash up, have it sterile and sparkling. I have other things to do – important things.'

'Like what?' Jillian knew she shouldn't scoff but couldn't help herself.

'So many things that *you* wouldn't understand.'

'Try me.'

'You asked.' Patsy shrugged. 'Okay – here goes. I want to find my inner self. When I reach that point of self-awareness that is inside me, I know it will be wonderful, that I will understand my life and why I'm here. I'll be able to hug a tree and be at one with it, look at the stars and dial into their meaning. Be aware of space and time in the atmosphere.'

'It was a rock you wanted to hug last time.'

'What?' Patsy was puzzled.

'Oh, nothing. And what if you don't like it when you get there?'

'Jillian, you're so prosaic. Your problem is that the way we've been brought up remains an obstacle to you being able to take on new ideas or understand them.'

'I don't see how any of this is an advance or made easier by not doing the washing-up,' she said tartly. 'I'm realising one thing, though. Those drugs you take are making you completely egotistical. All you want to do is talk about yourself.'

'Because talking about me I don't get as bored as if I were talking about *you*.'

'There doesn't seem much point.' She got to her feet.

'No. There isn't.' Patsy stayed seated. 'By the way, I'm moving.'

'Where to?' Jillian was putting her coat back on.

'All of us. To a commune. Remember Sally Brentwood? She's been left this amazing house in the country and she's converting the barns and stable into workshops. I can work there and we all live together, helping each other.'

'And no one does the washing-up. Still, you'll have plenty of trees to hug!'

Why couldn't she and Patsy ever meet without arguing? Were all sisters like them? She looked out of the window of the bus that was taking her to Knightsbridge, at the crowds teeming along the pavements. So Patsy thought her life was boring. She bet most of those people would give anything to have the lifestyle she and Jack were building for themselves.

If anything was boring it was the life Patsy had chosen. As far as Jillian could make out all she and her friends did was plan how to finance and get their drugs, take them, become zombified, and then, when they came down, repeat the process all over again. She wished she'd thought to point that out to her sister.

Patsy still made her clothes to sell but clearly not many of them. It wasn't the business she'd once talked of making. No fear of her settling to a routine, she'd said.

That, in a way, Jillian could understand. Sometimes she'd be standing at her kitchen sink, peeling potatoes, and find herself dreaming of a cruise to the Caribbean, or a visit to Tibet, away from her own routine. But they were silly daydreams. Patsy and Co., though, with their mind-altering drugs, had taken it another step, and for a time, in their minds, could escape. But why? What were they escaping? What was so awful with *real* life that they wanted to run away from it?

Jillian still remembered when Patsy had spiked the chocolate with LSD and, for a short time, she'd understood her. But even then, when she'd experienced that residual sadness, she hadn't wanted to try it again. Why were they so different?

Why, with identical background and upbringing, had they journeyed in opposite directions?

She alighted from the bus, crossed the pavement and went into Harrods. She had an account there now – a surprise birthday present from Jack. Another sign of how well things were going for them. She couldn't imagine what she would buy here: everything looked so expensive. Until now, Marks and Spencer and the odd sortie into John Lewis had been her limit. But Esmée had told her there was a great boutique here, Way In. Maybe she'd find something.

'Jillian, my dear, wait for me.' She turned round to find a pink-faced, puffing Helen Carter waving frantically at her in Separates. 'Oh, my. I thought it was you. I've been yelling fit to bust.' She placed her right hand on her heaving breast.

'I'm so sorry. I was miles away.' Jillian felt mixed feelings at seeing her. In a way she was pleased, she'd liked the woman when she'd met her, though she hadn't seen her since. But this thought made her feel disloyal to Theresa and Jack, who had such definite views about Helen.

'No children?'

'My mother's looking after them. I've got the day off.'

'Thank God for mothers! Have you time for a coffee?'

Jillian glanced at her watch, about to make some excuse. Then, why not? she decided. Did Theresa care about her and her feelings? Did her mother-in-law ever give her a thought?

They made small-talk as they passed through the store to the Dress Circle restaurant, and there was further inconsequential chatter as they waited to be served.

'How old are the little ones now?'

'Miles is nine in August, Victoria four next week.'

'Is it all those years since we last met? Good heavens, if anyone had asked me, I'd have said it couldn't be more than four years since we had that somewhat unusual Christmas at Mede House.' Helen laughed. 'So you've been married how long?'

'Nine years.' Jillian coloured. Telling Helen this, so quickly after Miles's age, reminded her of the circumstances of her marriage, which pained her, even now.

'I wish Esmée was as fortunate as you. You know she's

divorced her French count and married again? Ah, the coffee and cakes. Yum!'

'Yes, an Austrian. She told us when she last came.'

'Have you met him? Dreadfully formal. I can't imagine what she's thinking of. Hans is a disciplinarian, if ever I saw one. But, then, maybe that's what she wants and needs.

'Why did you return the cheque I sent you?' Helen asked bluntly, once the coffee was poured. Jillian flushed again. 'Still blushing, I see. Sweet. It usually goes once people become worldly-wise. But, then, maybe you still haven't.'

'I felt I couldn't accept it – not after what had happened.' She would like to have said 'since you were Jack's father's mistress.'

'Jack made you?'

'Well, yes.'

'You shouldn't have told him.'

'I don't think one should have secrets from one's husband.'

'Of course. Sadly, it's rare for such honesty to last in a marriage. Let's hope it does with you. Gracious, these pastries are wonderful. And I'm supposed to be on a diet! Ah, well, Monday. I'll start on Monday – the cry of all fatties.'

'You're not fat. You're lovely.' Helen was far from fat, just a little plump, which suited her.

'I do worry. If I lose too much I'll age overnight, a thousand wrinkles will appear.' She patted her miraculously smooth, wrinkle-free complexion. 'But back to the cheque.'

'Do we have to?' Jillian had been hoping that the subject had been dropped.

'We do. What reason did he give? I'd like to know.'

'I'd rather not.'

'It was an extraordinarily graceless thing to do in the face of such generosity.'

Jillian, smarting from this rebuke, took a deep breath. 'He said he couldn't accept money from his father's mistress. That he would never forgive the humiliation his mother suffered at being forced to entertain you in her house.'

'Very commendable of him. There's just one problem. I'm not, and never have been, Ralph's mistress. And it was Theresa who invited me.'

Jillian's jaw dropped. 'Oh!'

'It suits a certain person to maintain that fantasy.'

'Who?'

'I'd rather you worked that out for yourself, my dear. I don't think it's nice to malign people, do you? Ralph flirts with me but, then, he flirts with anything in a skirt – he always has. I was engaged to him many years ago, but he married Theresa. End of story.'

'Do you still love him?' Jillian could not imagine what had made her ask such a question.

'Yes, I do. I'm one of those people who fall in love once in their life. I'm lucky that we have maintained our friendship, but I would never have an affair with him and accept his wife's hospitality – that would be such vulgar behaviour, you do see?'

'Well, yes.' She saw, and she didn't see.

'You do know that Ralph was upset that Jack gave up his studies? So foolhardy of him.'

'Then he's an odd way of showing it. It was he who cut him off.'

'Was it now?' Helen's eyebrows arched questioningly.

'Yes. It was malicious of him. We've had a hard time.'

'I'm so sorry. They had a row, I do know that. And Ralph was drunk, of course, when it happened. He'd been to one of those silly masonic meetings. You know, where they roll their trousers up and lie about in coffins – so infantile, but that's men for you. He came back to find a sheepish Jack saying you were pregnant. The stupid man lost his rag. He wrote later and apologised, offered to reinstate Jack's allowance. Now that was a hard thing for him to do.'

'I never saw any letter.'

'How odd. That money you thought came from me, it was from him too. I swore I'd never say but promises can be so inconvenient. He knew Jack would tear it up if it came from him so he got me to send it to you.'

'How silly.'

'My sentiments exactly. I mean, he and Jack have backed themselves into their corners and neither knows how to get out.'

'It doesn't help that he's banned Theresa from meeting me.'

Helen replaced her cup on to its saucer. '*Did* he? That's most interesting.' She picked up her cup again. 'Isn't this coffee excellent? Not the easiest thing to find in dear old England, is it? So, what do we do?'

'About the coffee?'

'About Ralph and Jack making friends.'

'I'm not sure if I want them to. I mean, that Christmas, the business over the horse.'

'Ralph can be a bully, I agree. And why he does it I don't know. But I can assure you it's only ever when he's had too much to drink. He can be like Attila the Hun then – otherwise he's adorable.'

'Bet the poor horse wouldn't have thought that.'

'But no one was listening to him properly that night. He was concerned for the horse's welfare. It was in pain. He didn't want to see it suffer.'

'Then why?'

'I can't explain, my dear. I loathe to gossip. Suffice to say that Ralph and Theresa have problems. The horse was symbolic of that. You know, things are often not as they seem.'

'Strange, Esmée said that too.'

'The girl's no fool.'

'But, then, what's real and what's not? I mean, who do you believe? I don't understand.'

'It took me a long time. And sometimes I look at them all and wonder if they're worth a candle.'

Jillian had much to think about on the journey home. As soon as the train moved out of Liverpool Street station she went over every detail of her conversation with Helen. She debated with herself whether to tell Jack she'd seen her, and ask him about the letter, why he'd not accepted his father's offer. But he would be angry.

There was another factor, the new generation, two young people who had every right to know their grandfather and make up their own minds about him. After her own father's behaviour to her, she would have had every reason to keep them away from him – people who knew what he had done would have understood – but she didn't think she had that right. And when she saw her father doting on her children and the love between them she knew she had been right to forget her pride.

Perhaps she should do something, and do it alone, not tell Jack until she'd done it. He'd be angry, but it might be worth it. There was only one way to find out. She would write to Ralph and ask him if he'd like to meet his grandchildren. Then, alone, she would take them, and then she'd decide what was to be done.

3

'Mum, I'm sorry I'm late.' Jillian looked up at Mary from the floor where she knelt as her excited children hugged and kissed her. 'They were at sixes and sevens at the hairdresser's. Victoria, calm down, do, you'll make yourself sick.' She extricated herself from the scrum, picked out a Hamley's carrier bag and from it took the presents she'd bought them. Victoria grabbed hers and raced to the corner of the kitchen as if protecting her gifts. Miles, always quieter, took his more calmly and sauntered out to open it in private in his room. 'A "Thank you, Mummy" would be nice,' she said, good-humouredly. 'Have they been all right?'

'Good as gold. It's always a joy to look after your tribe.' Mary looked at her granddaughter, her smile brimming with love and benevolence.

'You're about as useless with them as I am, I reckon.'

'It's nice to spoil them, isn't it? Childhood flies by. I mean, it seems like yesterday that you were that age. You look done in. Fancy a cuppa?'

'Lovely.' Jillian slipped off her shoes and wiggled her toes with pleasure. 'I expected to find Jack in charge. He said he'd come home early.'

'He phoned. He got held up, some drama or other. I don't

139

mind. I've nothing to rush home for.' Mary clattered about in the kitchen. 'Promise me something, Jillian. In the two years you've had this house I've managed to learn my way around this kitchen, the only one of yours I've been able to do that. Please don't move.'

'I've no intention of doing so. I'm determined to stay here for ever.'

Mary put the pot and mugs on the table, clearing a space among the paints and Play-Doh. 'Did you see Patsy?'

'I did. She's off to live in a commune.'

'How did she look?'

'Patsy is Patsy – she probably never goes out in the daytime, like a vampire. My, this tastes good.' She didn't tell her mother her concerns for Patsy, not wanting to worry her. 'I met Helen Carter.' She told her mother of their conversation.

'What will you do about Jack's father?'

'I don't know. I thought I might write to Ralph.'

'I'd phone, if I were you, and speak to him. Letters get lost.'

'What do you mean?'

'It's obvious. Since Jack never received his father's letter what's to say his old man will get yours? Someone must have intercepted it.'

'Mum, don't be silly. You've just said they can get lost in the post.'

'And pigs might fly. None of mine ever have – though a few from the bank going AWOL wouldn't have gone amiss. When it does happen it's invariably someone up to no good. No doubt his mother in this case.'

'Oh, Mum! You've always had a thing about Theresa. How many times do I have to say it? She's a sweet woman, dominated by her husband.'

'So when was she last sweet to you?'

'Oh, you know what I mean. If Miles made a mistake and had to get married I'd try not to blame the girl – that's so illogical – but I bet it would be quite difficult.'

'Hm. And I'll bet you something. If your father had been a lord instead of a stores clerk, she wouldn't have minded one bit.'

'I don't think she's that sort of snob, Mum.'

'Trouble with you, Jillian, and it always has been, you only see good in people. Do yourself a favour and see some evil now and then.' She took a sip of her tea. 'Think it through, Jillian. In whose interest would it be to lie about Helen being the old man's mistress? It's unlikely Jack would – he obviously believes it too. No, that Theresa's made it up, for some reason or other. That's why Helen left it to you to work out, except you're too naïve. She wasn't to know that or that you'd need your wise old mum to tell you.'

'I find that impossible to believe about Theresa.'

'Believe it. It'll save you a lot of trouble further down the line. You mull it over, my girl. Right, let's change the subject – that family annoys me. So, is Patsy coming home to see your dad?'

'No. She gave no reason,' Jillian fibbed.

'Your father's hardly the best company in the world, is he? I can see that.'

'What happened between those two, Mum? They were always so close.'

'I don't know, and to tell you the honest truth, Jillian, I don't want to. It's their business if they fall out with each other.'

'What about you? If she doesn't come to see him then she doesn't see you either.'

'I'll go and see her in her commune. From what I read in the papers these communes sound fun – free love an' all. I might even pack my bags and join her!' Mary laughed.

'You don't worry about Patsy, do you?'

'No, I don't. She's got her head screwed on. She's curious, she wants to find things out about people. She might experiment with different lifestyles, but she'll not lose control, not that one.'

'You mean drugs?'

'I do. I think more danger lies in making too much fuss about them. If I thought she was the type who could become addicted, try heroin, rubbish like that, then I'd worry. Alcohol, drugs, it would all be the same.'

'You hardly bump into the types she mixes with in the pub. They pong! When she got back from India I banned that

Afghan sheepskin jacket she's so proud of, it niffed so. And when it got wet in the rain, phew!' Jillian wafted the air.

'You worry too much, Jillian. You can't be responsible for everyone, you know. What if I told you I'd taken drugs in the past?'

'You?

'Benzedrine – don't they call it speed now? It was the only way we could stay awake sometimes. I knew loads of other nurses and auxiliaries like me who took it, and soldiers, people like that. People who had to work long hours and stay awake. Of course, you could buy it at the chemist's, no problem, then. But I don't think it damaged me. And I tried cocaine once, but I thought I might like it too much so I only had it the once. You see?'

'Maybe she'll be sensible like you.' Jillian fiddled with the handle of her mug. 'Gracious, that's a difficult thought to get my head round. You! But, then, you weren't living with the sort she does. They sleep all day, they've no ambition, they sneer at everything, they're anarchists.'

'They're young. In five, six years they'll all be worried about mortgages, insurance, their children's education. Just like the rest of us.'

'Dad wouldn't think like that.'

'Ah, well, no. But, then, he doesn't understand about happiness and pleasure.' While she had been talking about Patsy and her own past, Mary had sounded light-hearted and happy. At the mention of her husband, she seemed immeasurably sad.

'Mum, what is it? What's happened?'

Mary sighed deeply and looked at her worn hands. 'Nothing. Nothing new.'

'Tell me. You're not normally this low.'

'I lied.'

'Sorry?'

'Just then when I said nothing new. There is.' Mary poured herself another mug of tea. Jillian waited patiently while she fussed with the sugar and milk, certain that her mother was prolonging the process, giving herself time to marshal her thoughts.

'Yes?' she said finally, when Mary seemed no closer to telling her.

'This'll come as a bit of a shock, I expect. I'm thinking of leaving your father.'

Jillian's hand shot to her mouth.

'You see. I said it'd be a shock. I'm sorry but, well, there it is. I've made my mind up.'

'Where will you live? How will you manage?'

Mary put out her hand and took Jillian's. 'Bless you for that! No lecture, no "How could you?" No "At your age". I'm fifty. I've got a good ten years' work ahead of me, maybe more. I've been offered a permanent post as an auxiliary – male medical. I've been part-time up until now, as you know. I can live in the hospital until I sort myself out.'

'Is there someone else?'

'There might be. I've no intention of leaving one man to take up with another straight away. It isn't a sudden decision. I'd always planned to go when you and Patsy left home, but Charlie was so cut up – Patsy going, falling out with you – that I hadn't the heart. Maybe I should have. I begin to think he'd be quite relieved to see the back of me.'

'Surely not, Mum. He loves you.'

'No, he doesn't. He hasn't for years. If we hadn't married during the war, we never would have when it finished. It would have been pointless. That bloody war – it changed him. It's hardly surprising, God knows what sights he saw. It altered a lot of men. He came back a depressive, but refused to acknowledge that he was. It was everyone else who was in the wrong. I've often thought that's why he got this religion thing. And it hasn't helped him. He's getting worse, and I've had enough. I might be selfish, but we only have one life.'

'You're not selfish, Mum, not at all. It hasn't been easy for any of us. If I'm honest I'm amazed you've stayed as long as you have. But there must have been good times, you'll have those memories.'

'Just because a memory seems happy to others it doesn't mean it was.' They both sat with the tea cooling in front of them, Jillian unsure what more she could say, Mary looking as if she were miles away. 'You're happy with Jack, aren't you?'

'Yes. Very. I'm lucky.'

'You would tell me if you weren't? You wouldn't be like me, pretending all was well when it wasn't? Wasting time, wasting life.'

'I promise.' She touched wood hurriedly. 'But I'm not planning on anything going wrong. I love Jack and I'll fight tooth and nail to keep things this way.'

'I think I'll touch wood for you too.'

With the children in bed Jillian prepared supper. What, if anything, should she discuss with Jack? Her talk with Helen? Her mother's shattering news? What a day!

'Darling, you're so late.' She stood in the kitchen doorway taking off her apron. 'And you look whacked.'

'I am. I need a drink.' Without pausing to kiss her he made straight for the sitting room and the whisky. Jillian followed with ice in the new bucket she'd recently bought. She found Jack sitting, his head bowed, staring at the new carpet, one hand holding his glass, the other dangling limply between his knees. His whole bearing spoke of exhaustion and, she feared, worse.

'Jack, what's happened?'

At her voice he seemed to shake himself out of wherever he'd been. 'Sorry, love. I've been doing too much – rushing around. How was London?'

'There's something wrong, Jack. Tell me, please.'

'Nothing. Nothing I can't handle. Ice – that was thoughtful of you but, then, you always are. You're always one step ahead of whatever it is I want, aren't you?'

'I try to be.' She looked at him with a puzzled expression. There was a sharpness in his tone that made what he said more a criticism than a compliment. She sat in the chair opposite and waited, not sure if she should speak or whether silence was called for. But the silence became oppressive as Jack's inspection of the carpet continued. 'I've made some chowder, in case you haven't had time to eat,' she ventured.

'Great,' he responded.

'Do you want it on a tray in here or in the kitchen?'

'I'd rather have another drink.'

'Shouldn't you eat first?'

'Don't fuss, Jillian, do me a favour.'

She poured him another drink, though she added more ice than before in an attempt to water it down, and returned to the kitchen. She laid the table, and pinned up Victoria's latest painting on the noticeboard, which had more of her art on it than notices. She mustn't exaggerate, she told herself. After all, he'd said little, it was just – She sighed: she knew him too well. And she was tired too – London always did that to her – and it was making her over-sensitive.

She sliced the bread and put the small flat parcel containing the Liberty silk tie beside his side-plate. She smiled as he entered the kitchen, glass in hand. He crossed the room, put his arm round her and kissed her full on the mouth. Her body responded immediately, as it always did to his touch.

'I'm sorry, I didn't mean to snap at you.' He gazed at her as they broke apart.

'I didn't even notice, honestly. Come, have some soup.' She poured the chowder from the saucepan into the ornate French china tureen they'd bought at the auction last week. 'Doesn't it look lovely in that?' She sprinkled some chopped chives on the top. Then she ladled it into the Victorian soup bowls, part of the dinner service they'd found at the same place last month.

'You love all your bits and bobs, don't you?'

'One of the best things about starting out with nothing is how much everything matters when we've had to wait and plan for it. I feel sorry for rich people. They can't appreciate things half as much as we do.' She looked with satisfaction at the pine dresser, laden with her collection of teapots and china, the old rocking-chair she'd stripped and varnished and for which she'd worked the cushions. She meant it, they were lucky.

'So, how was your day?' He began to eat.

'Extraordinary. You're never going to believe this, but my mother's thinking of leaving my father.'

'Good God!' His spoon clattered on his plate. 'Are you

upset? No, you're not. But then I crash in in a grump and you're dealing with this. Jillian, I'm sorry!'

'Don't be, really. It doesn't seem that big a deal. I suppose I should be shocked and sad – only I'm not. I couldn't live with my father, so why should she? She said she thought Dad would be quite relieved it was over, though how that squares with his church I'm not sure. Still, it's their life.' She ate a little, still unsure what to tell him. But they'd never had secrets, so she wouldn't start now. 'I met Helen in Harrods. We had a coffee.' She saw him stiffen.

'Did you? How is she?'

'Fine. Bubbly, as always.' She paused for a second. 'Your father sent that cheque when we married, not Helen.'

'I thought as much. I didn't say so at the time, but it was another reason not to accept – you know the other.'

Jillian studied her bowl. Was tonight the best time to mention that Helen had denied being Ralph's mistress? Maybe not. And, given his tiredness, it would be unwise to launch the idea of meeting Ralph and letting him see the children.

'You didn't mind me seeing her?'

'Not particularly. Just as long as you don't expect me to.' He pushed away his bowl, the chowder only half eaten.

'You're not hungry?'

'I'll just pour myself some more Scotch. I've earned it.' He went to the sitting room to get it. He rarely drank like this, he could go days without bothering, yet tonight he was about to have a third, it might even be a fourth. Don't mention it, she told herself. If he wants to get drunk, let him.

'I think we should talk,' he said, returning with two glasses. 'It's time,' he added, ominously to her ears.

'What is it? What's up?' Jillian sat tense. Her heart thumped. She felt as if her skin was covered in insects as fine nerve-endings activated, aware of trouble. She was terrified that he was about to say he'd met someone else, that it was over. She had no grounds to believe this, yet from the first day of her marriage she had never allowed herself to believe that it wouldn't end one day. Was this it? She sat, hardly breathing, as he mixed the drinks, swearing at the ice-cube tray. She wanted to scream at him to sit down, to tell her.

Wearily Jack pushed a glass across to her. 'We're in a mess, Jillian, financially.'

She felt her stomach contract with a different fear, but despite the seriousness of what he had said she could not help feeling huge relief. 'But we're doing so well.'

'Were, is better. I've got us in a mess, Jillian. I'm sorry. I've spent the past month floundering about, working all ways to sort it out but I can't. I think we'll go bust.'

'But how?'

'Simple. I moved off my patch. I shouldn't have listened to Gary. He was so desperate to buy that property in London – you remember, the office block? We paid too much. All the time we were dealing in property here we were fine. I know Cambridge, I know the value down to the last penny. I should have stayed here.'

'But can't you sell it? Everything sells eventually. You've always said that when a house was stuck on the market.'

'Not this time. The bottom's fallen out of the market – everything went up too fast. I thought it would go on for ever. We borrowed to buy, the market has collapsed, we can't keep up the interest payments and the bank wants its money back. You can't argue with a bank.'

'Oh, my God. The shop? This house?'

He shrugged listlessly. She wanted desperately to cry but fought back the tears.

'Gary suggested burning the bloody thing down and getting the insurance money.'

'He would. Typical of Gary. You told him where to go?'

'For a minute it was an attractive proposition.'

'Jack. Even for a minute? That would be criminal.'

'It would save our bacon.'

'I'd rather start again, from scratch, than have you go to prison.' She picked up the whisky he'd poured her. She needed this. No wonder he'd rushed for the bottle as soon as he came in. 'This is all Gary's fault, I bet.'

'I went into it with my eyes wide open.'

'You wouldn't have but for him. I never liked him, never trusted him.'

'You never said.'

'Would you have listened? I thought it best not to say.'

Jack banged his glass onto the table. 'Why do you always have to be so bloody submissive? Why can't you tell me what you're sodding well thinking? Why make me out to be an ogre?'

'I'm sorry, I –'

'And stop fucking well saying *sorry!*'

'Yes.' She sat rigid, twisting her glass round and round in her hands. She waited a minute, but he remained silent. She would not let him see how much his words had upset her. It was no time for her to be feeling sorry for herself. 'We should list all our assets and what we owe and –'

'I've done all that.'

'And Gary?'

'Mortgaged up to the hilt.'

'But why does our home have to go?'

'I put it up as part of the collateral. And we still have a shortfall.'

'What about . . .' She paused, as she tried to work out the best way to approach the subject.

'If you're about to say what about approaching my father the answer is an emphatic no. I'd rather rot in hell than go begging to him.'

'No, I wasn't going to suggest him,' she lied to Jack, for the first time in their married life. Inspiration came to her. 'Doesn't your mother have money?'

'No. I couldn't, he'd know.'

'Something'll turn up,' she said reassuringly. 'Come to bed. It'll look less doomy in the morning.'

'Don't be so thick, Jillian!'

Before, when they'd had nothing, there had been only themselves and a baby to worry about. With growing children, the anxiety and fear were multiplied a thousand-fold.

'We can get emergency housing, I'm sure. I've paid enough

148

in bloody taxes.' The next morning, after a restless night, Jack was pacing the kitchen like a caged animal.

'What, and get split up? Me in a B-and-B somewhere awful and you in a doss-house. Never! We have to find a solution. I could work full-time in the shop. I've been neglecting it. I could –'

'It's sold.'

'What?'

'I sold the shop.'

'When?'

'Last week.'

'And you didn't see fit to tell me?'

'I didn't want to upset you. And, what's more, if I hadn't acted then it would have gone to the bank, like this house. There wasn't time for discussion.'

She looked away. Getting angry wasn't going to help. 'Well, there must be something we can do.'

Jack stopped pacing, laid his palms flat on the kitchen table and loomed over her. 'Listen, Jillian, and listen carefully. There is no solution. We're wiped out. Unless a buyer for that building materialises in the next month we are kaput. *Compris*?'

She hated it when he talked to her as if she were an idiot. It was her life too. They were her kids. She picked away at the label on the tomato-ketchup bottle, as if it was an annoying spot. 'I'm not stupid, you know.'

'Then stop acting as if you are, making asinine remarks like that.'

'Our arguing isn't going to solve anything and is even stupider than my remarks!' She was angry with him. The rage had built up during the sleepless night she had suffered. Question piling on to question, worry fuelling fear and turning it into anger. She'd hoped to control it, but he was making it difficult for her. 'What I don't understand is how you could have borrowed so much when, if things went wrong, you must have known it couldn't be paid back,' she ploughed on. She had to have answers: surely he could understand that.

'I didn't expect anything to go wrong, did I?'

149

'But surely you should allow for the unexpected.'

'If I could have foretold this property crash I would have. If you don't take risks you get nowhere in this life.'

'So much? Risk everything?'

'Why don't you shut up about matters you know nothing about?'

'I know how to budget. I know when we can afford things and when we can't. I know how to put aside for a rainy day. I know not to spend a whole week's housekeeping on one item, on something we could do without.'

'How on earth you can sit there and equate my business affairs with your housekeeping budget beats me.'

'I'd have thought the parallel was obvious. I guess you're not as smart as I thought you were!'

'Dear, darling, supportive wife. Thank you for that.' He turned on his heel.

'Where are you going?'

'Out.'

'What will you do?'

'Use my limited intelligence to try to sort this mess out for you and the kids. Happy?'

4

As he opened the door to her Charlie looked suspicious. Since she had known of the impending change in her parents' lives she had thought it more polite to ring the bell. He had the air of a man who expected the heavens to fall in on him at any moment.

'It's only me, Dad!' Jillian managed to sound cheerful, something she hadn't achieved often in the last few days. 'You look as if you're expecting the bailiffs.'

'And what would you know about them?' His smile was somewhat tentative.

'Don't even ask. I might tell you.' She stepped into the familiar hall. Since everything had changed she had, illogically, expected the house to change too, but the hat-stand was there, with fewer coats to be sure, the grandmother clock wheezed asthmatically as it always had, the runner was resplendent on the stairs, still barely worn. In the present upheaval of her life it was a relief to find it so. 'I thought I ought to come.'

'So, your mother's told you?'

'The other night.'

'She didn't hang around, did she?'

'Better to learn from her than gossip.'

'I suppose you're right. I'm out the back,' he said, leading the way through the immaculate kitchen into the laundry room they'd had built on only last year then into the yard, where he was planting bulbs in pots.

'I'm sorry, Dad.'

'Nothing to be sorry about, Jillian. What's done is done.' His fingers were lovingly pressing down the dark loamy compost. 'I expect you'd like a few of these, brighten up the house in winter.'

'Lovely, thanks.' She decided not to say she wasn't sure how long she'd have a home to put them in. 'But you're all right?'

'Never better.' He tapped a flowerpot, ensuring that the soil was evenly distributed.

'I was worried about the church. What they'd say. You know . . .' She felt uncomfortable, wary that he might construe anything she said as criticism of his beloved church.

'These things happen. If they can't accept me as I am, then of course I shall leave. Maybe find somewhere else that understands. Can't be helped.'

'No. Of course not.' She was surprised but, at the same time, relieved he was taking this attitude. He was less likely to be hurt.

'I saw Patsy in London. She sends her love,' she lied. She had decided on the way here that it would be kinder.

'How is she? Eating properly? Looking after herself?'

'You know Patsy.' She hoped he'd interpret this as an affirmation.

'I've not been a fair father to you, have I, Jillian? I'm sorry.'

151

'Don't be silly, Dad. I don't know what you mean.' She felt confused and embarrassed suddenly.

'I don't know why I was as I was. I think I was always afraid you'd do something daft. I was trying to protect you.'

'Me?'

'Ironic, isn't it? You've turned out so solid and reliable, married and with kids, and it's our Patsy who's gone off the rails. You see, you were always the beauty, any fool could see that. And beauty can be a dangerous thing. Little Patsy, compared to you, was always the ugly duckling. I suppose I thought she needed boosting and you taking down a peg or two. I'm sorry.'

'It's all right, Dad. In any case, I've never seen myself as beautiful.' She laughed at the very idea, but felt touched and saddened by his speech, the longest she'd ever heard from him. So much explained and such a simple explanation. She bent forward and kissed his cheek. 'I'm glad you told me.'

'And you don't mind? You know, your mum and me and everything.'

'Dad, all I want is for you both to be happy. It's your life. Will you stay here?'

'I can't see me moving. Mind you, I've some sorting out to do and I might have to sell up. Your mother put as much into this house as I did so it's only fair she has her share.'

'Of course. I hadn't thought.' She'd had a plan this morning for her father to buy their house from Jack, using his savings as a deposit. By doubling up the children in one bedroom and taking a couple of lodgers she had hoped she could pay his mortgage repayments, with interest on top, for the outstanding amount. There was no point now in even broaching the subject.

'Are the kids all right?'

'Fine.'

'You know, Jillian, I'm glad you're not too put out. I couldn't bear not to see the grandchildren.'

'As if I'd ever stop you.'

'Is that a promise?'

'Of course. What a silly worry to have. Still, I must be on my way, things to do, you know.'

'It was nice of you to call.' He brushed the soil off his hands and led the way back to the front door. As they reached it the bell rang. A middle-aged man stood on the doorstep. 'Oh, hello. You've come about the room, I expect?'

'If it's convenient,' the man said, glancing, nervously it seemed to Jillian, in her direction.

'No time like the present, I always say. Well, Jillian, thanks for calling.' He ushered her quickly through the doorway. 'Pop inside, mate. I'll just be a second.' He walked his daughter down the path.

'Are you taking in lodgers?'

'Every little counts,' Charlie said, opening the car door for her.

As she drove away Jillian found herself wondering if her father had always used so many clichés.

After nearly two weeks of mounting tension Jillian decided she must act. She was certain that both she and Jack were at breaking-point. If the amount he was drinking, the rowing, the sulking silences and her yelling, unfairly, at the children were taken into account, she had already waited too long.

In their nine years of marriage she'd lied to Jack once, but now she was embarking on the biggest betrayal of all.

The traffic, since it was a Sunday, was light – she'd chosen the day especially. It was the first Sunday in the month and Jack always took the children to see his mother.

When she'd telephoned Ralph yesterday she was sure he'd sounded pleased to be hearing from her. And when she'd checked that he'd be alone, he'd sounded intrigued.

As she drove along she could hardly believe she was doing this, and once or twice she wished she could turn back. But she knew she couldn't, that for the sake of her family someone had to do something.

In their years together she'd always looked to Jack to deal with the big problems in their lives while she handled the smaller ones – as it should be, she had often told herself. Yet when something as catastrophic as this occurred, it was evident that Jack was not capable of solving it. It had been a difficult idea to adjust to.

How could he have done this to them? She banged the steering-wheel in frustration. To want to be rich so badly that he risked them becoming poor again. It was the thought of the children being deprived that made her anger feel like a lump stuck in her throat. Once again she supposed she'd have to scrimp and save: the local jumble sales would see her searching again through piles of discarded clothes to dress her family. 'Here we go again!' she said, as she drove towards her father-in-law's.

A car inching out of a farm gate caused her to swerve and forced her to calm down. What use would she be to the kids dead? She and Jack should have talked: she'd tried only last night in a last-ditch attempt, but it had ended, as it often did now, in an argument. It was frightening at how rapidly her life was disintegrating around her; it was out of her control. Until she had decided on today's action, she told herself firmly.

If Ralph wouldn't help she did not know what they would do. If she could feel all this anger and resentment, then Jack could too. As she blamed him, did he blame her? The awful truth was that if he hadn't married her because she was pregnant, none of this would have happened; he wouldn't have had to prove himself to his father.

Was the moment she'd always dreaded getting nearer? The day she'd always thought inevitable in the past, that fear that only their new financial stability had helped to fade. 'Financial stability!' she said aloud, on a bitter little laugh. In these past days it was as if she'd been waiting for the words she'd often heard him say in her imagination: *'I never wanted to marry you. I only did it out of duty.'*

Just thinking them made her feel sick, made her guts spasm, made her hands clench the steering-wheel. For how would she live without him? He was her life, she loved him, her anger changed none of that.

As she turned into the driveway of Mede House, Jillian could not remember when she had felt this nauseous with nerves – probably the last time she'd been here, she supposed. She parked the car, checked herself in the rear-view mirror. As

154

she stood in front of the heavy oak door she took a deep breath to steady her nerves, but found it did nothing for her.

'You see, Mr Stirling, I didn't want your wife put in a difficult position – seeing Jack, as she does, she'd be honour-bound to tell him,' she explained, once settled in the drawing room, which hadn't changed one iota since she'd last been here – even, she'd swear, down to the artificial flowers in the vases.

'And you don't think I will? That I've no honour?' He laughed at what he clearly thought a good joke.

'I didn't mean that. Oh dear. I'm getting off on the wrong footing.'

'You are a bit. You see, I didn't know my wife was seeing Jack – she declared she never would if he married you – but, then, I'm not surprised. Silly things are often said in the heat of the moment, aren't they?'

'Well, yes, but I thought . . .' There was no point in digressing and asking what he meant – and hadn't he vowed never to meet her? For a second her conversation with Helen in Harrods replayed in her mind. 'I brought you these. I thought you might . . .' From a briefcase she took an album in which she'd placed the best pictures from the preceding years. 'You can keep that.'

'Thank you, my dear.' He flicked through the pages. 'They're bonny children. A credit to you. I imagine you're glad you didn't get rid of Miles.' His large frame shuddered as he closed the album. 'It would have been wicked, wouldn't it? It's too easy, these days, from what I hear.'

Jillian felt the room reel, uncertain if she'd heard right, if she was daydreaming. Or was he becoming senile? Had he forgotten he'd offered to pay for an abortion? He didn't look any older. A doubt formed. But she'd have to think about that later. Not now! She accepted the glass of champagne Ralph handed her.

'What seems to be the problem?'

'Jack has overstretched himself. He borrowed heavily to buy an office block in London. Our bank is foreclosing and we face losing everything.' Said like that it all seemed so simple, so unimportant, with none of the terror and misery they were suffering in the words. She wondered if, perhaps, it would have been better if she'd been more histrionic about it.

'And you hope I will help you out?'

'Yes,' she said simply.

'And why hasn't Jack come to ask me himself?'

'He knows nothing of my visit. If he did, I don't know what he'd do. He certainly wouldn't ask you himself and if he found out you were offering help he wouldn't accept. I'm asking you, I'm afraid. The children . . .' She waved her hand at the photo album on the table in front of them. 'There is no one else I know to ask.'

'You propose?'

'That you buy it. Anonymously.'

'Just like that?'

'I'm sure this property collapse will pass and then it will be easy to sell. Jack got too ambitious too quickly. We were doing fine all the time he worked in the town he knew.'

'You're angry with him?'

'I'm . . .' She had been about to deny it, but then, 'Yes, I'm very angry. All along I've worried about his borrowings and his overdrafts. It was not the way I was brought up. In my home if we didn't have the money we couldn't have whatever it was we wanted. It was as simple as that.'

'Of course, business isn't that simple – ever.'

'I know. Jack tells me constantly that you have to speculate to accumulate, but surely that doesn't mean risking the very roof over your children's heads.'

'Does he know you're so angry?'

'I think so, but it's difficult to talk about it. We both get so het up.'

'When you came here first, you were such a sweet, trusting soul. What a fool he's been.'

'He meant it for our good,' she said hurriedly, not wanting him to think she'd gone so far as to dislike Jack – it was far more complicated than that.

'You sure it wasn't to get at me? That he wanted to succeed, to be richer than me? I think that's more like it, my dear. Stupid boy. Ah, well! Yes, I'll do it. Give me the details.'

'You will?'

'I'll do it for you and those kids – not for my son. I'll have a company I own purchase it. He knows nothing about it so he won't ever find out I'm behind it. It'll be our little secret.'

At this, and to her utmost surprise, Jillian burst into tears. All the worry of the past few weeks and the relief now that she and Jack could get back to where they used to be rolled themselves up into a cascade of weeping.

'Here, there's no need to carry on like this.' Ralph fussed about her.

'I don't know how to thank you, Mr Stirling.'

'There's no need. And although I never see you, well, why not call me Ralph?'

'Thank you. But I must be able to do something. I know – I could bring the children. Would you like to meet them?'

'That won't be necessary.' Ralph stood up abruptly, a strange expression on his face. She got to her feet, feeling as though she was being dismissed. She would never understand this family, she thought, as she said a flustered goodbye.

A week later, as Jillian was preparing supper, the kitchen door burst open and Jack rushed into the room, waving a bottle of champagne. 'We've got a buyer! Did you hear me? A bloody wonderful buyer!' He did a jig, then pulled her towards him and danced around the kitchen with her, while the children clapped with excitement.

'Are you sure?' she asked, when Jack had quietened down.

'Positive.'

'You always say things can go wrong. Until the money's in the bank you can't be sure.'

'This company wants the block like yesterday. Some American operation, making the most of the collapse. They've put down a deposit. I've no fears. They want a quick completion. Shit, Jillian, that was a close one.'

'Never again.'

'Never. My nerves won't stand it.'

'Nor mine. I was so afraid.'

'Well, it's over – or nearly. No bangers and mash for us tonight. Put all that away. Phone the babysitter. You and I are

157

going out on the town to celebrate our wondrous benefactor. God bless his soul!'

Autumn 1977

'Turning off every bloody light in the house is dangerous, Jillian. Do you have to? I've just tripped over one of Miles's cars.' Jack spoke pleasantly enough, but she caught an underlying edge in his voice. But having been to the brink of financial ruin, Jillian worried constantly that it might happen again. Unless she was vigilant and cut corners, economised and counted the pennies, she feared their home would be put at risk again.

'I'll get lower-wattage bulbs for the hall and staircase then.'

'And be like a French flea-pit hotel! You'll be wanting timer switches next. No, thank you!'

Jillian turned back to the washing-up, thinking, What a good idea!

'What's for supper?'

'Cottage pie.'

'Not mince again! Cows aren't just made of mince, you know, there are such things as steak, rib and topside. Jillian, love, come here, sit down.' He waited for her to dry her hands and settle at the table opposite him. 'Don't you think you're making too much drama of these economies of yours? You'll be buying scratchy bog-paper next.'

'I think we should be careful – just in case, you know.'

'No, I don't know. Last year we had a scare. It won't happen again, I promise. I'm keeping to Cambridge. No more London.'

'I know, but that land out at Fen Ditton was so expensive. And times are still hard, the property market is still dodgy, you said so yourself.'

'Jillian, recessions never last. The good times always return. Those who keep their nerve and use the bad times are the ones who come out smelling of roses. That land was a forced sale, it was relatively cheap. When we've built those houses we'll be as rich as Croesus.'

'But I don't want to be so rich. I was happy as we were. I like this house and the life we lead. What do we need more money for?'

'You know why. I'll never rest until I can look my father in the eye and say, "So, I did it! And here's a cheque for all the money you spent on my education!" I'd enjoy doing that.'

Paying his father back was a new addition to his ambitions, she thought. If he ever found out the truth, he'd work even harder and take greater risks so that he could give Ralph that money as well.

'I'm sorry I'm a worrier. I can't help it. It came when Miles was born. Worrying is obviously part of being a mother – it comes with your milk.' She smiled at him, blanking out the fear she felt whenever she thought of what she'd done.

'Let me do the worrying. That's *my* job. I don't want you bothered with it.' He patted her hand.

How near to collapse he had come, how close to pulling them all down. Already he seemed to have forgotten. She sighed. 'I'll get some steak, then.'

'Brilliant! That's better.'

'How about whitebait for starters?'

'That's more like it. Life is for enjoying, you know.'

It was all right for Jack, she thought, as she shopped at the local supermarket. He didn't do the budgeting. In theory anything left over from the housekeeping was hers to spend as she wanted. She might have done – once. Now, if there was anything over, she salted it away. She put two steaks in her trolley – she'd cook something cheaper for the children.

She remembered a conversation she'd had with Michelle years ago, soon after she'd married. 'You're daft, you know. You should be putting away any money you can. You never know what the future holds,' Michelle had counselled, with her usual cynicism.

'Like what? You're always expecting my marriage to end in disaster. I can't think why.'

'I don't know anyone who's truly happily married. What happens if Jack –' She stopped.

'Runs off with a dizzy blonde years younger than me?'

'Something like that. Or maybe a financial catastrophe of some sort.'

'I hope he won't find another woman. And he's becoming so successful. But if we did split – God forbid – the new divorce laws would look after me.' She was touching wood as she spoke.

Michelle had been so right. She often was. Not that a blonde had hurtled over the horizon, but had Jillian known that the property collapse was coming she'd have saved, just as Michelle had advocated. Now that things were getting better, she was not going to make the same mistake again. Unknown to Jack, she'd opened a building-society account, and once a month she bought a Premium Bond. She'd won twice, a couple of hundred pounds only, but she'd added that to the account.

'Jillian! You look deep in thought.'

'Michelle. Gracious, I was just thinking about you.' Jillian placed the fish in her trolley.

'Not bad things, I hope.'

'Well, sort of, I suppose. Just how you're right so often – it can be annoying.' She was smiling now and Michelle, who had looked concerned, grinned broadly.

'My friends tell me that. You shouldn't be buying that melon, by the way, it's South African.' Michelle pointed at it Jillian's trolley.

'If we don't then surely the workers who grow them will suffer even more,' she said, reasonably.

'It's the principle, that's what counts.'

'They're on special offer, *that's* what counts.' She patted her melon as if it were a baby's head.

'I despair of you, Jillian. Who'd ever think we were cousins?'

Jillian, carefully made-up with her new Mary Quant false eyelashes, dressed in a pale pink mini with her new white leather boots, was in stark contrast to Michelle, in paint-spattered denim dungarees, Dr Scholl sandals, her face devoid of makeup. They both had short hair, but Jillian's was highlighted – the blonde was fading now – and skilfully cut. Michelle's was mousy and looked as if it had been attacked with garden shears.

'Oh, I don't know, my mother says we've both got our Scottish gran's grey eyes. I wish I'd met her, don't you? Have you got time for a coffee? Or is there some campaign you're involved with for the Brazilian coffee-bean workers?' They were walking towards the checkout.

'Your life must be so dull, cousin, only thinking of your little nuclear family when there's so much in the wide world that should be concerning you.'

'I can be concerned about a million things but who's interested in what I think? Or what I do?' She loaded her shopping on to the conveyor-belt, making sure that her melon was far enough away from Michelle's grasp.

'You're antediluvian. The silent majority matters. Don't you understand?'

Jillian slapped down the bag containing her steaks.

'I don't know why you poison yourself with dead flesh –' Michelle began.

'Do me a favour, stop bullying me, please, just for a minute.' Jillian laughed to cover her irritation. As she packed her goods and Michelle was being dealt with by the checkout girl she wondered if her cousin was as opinionated and bossy with everyone or just with her. Was there something about Jillian that made people zone in on her to harangue and lecture? All her life it had been happening – her father, her mother, Patsy, Michelle. She'd read an interesting article the other day in *Cosmopolitan* that said there were people who were victims – not that she'd agreed. But there was definitely something about her that made people think they could say whatever they wanted to her when she'd never dream of doing it to them. For a start it was rude.

'So. What were we talking about?' Michelle asked, when they had emerged from the supermarket.

'You were lecturing me.'

'I never was! Lecturing! What a thing to say!'

Jillian pushed open the door of the coffee bar, which was

161

handily close to the supermarket. They shoved their baskets under the table and ordered coffee and a Danish pastry each. Michelle found her tobacco tin in the pocket across her bosom and began the ritual of rolling herself a cigarette.

'Instead of being so concerned about meat and my health, why don't you start with your own? Give that filthy habit up for a start.'

'Do I sense a slight irritation with me?' Michelle inhaled deeply on her thin, mangled-looking cigarette.

'Not really. I was just wondering why everyone takes it upon themselves to tell me what I should be doing or thinking. Thank you,' she said to the waitress, as she deposited their coffee and cakes.

'Because we love you and don't want you hurt.' Michelle forked a large piece of pastry into her mouth. 'My, these pastries get better and better.'

It wasn't the answer she'd been expecting and she couldn't think of a response.

'How's Jack? Still beavering away amassing a fortune?'

'Hardly. We get by.'

'I saw he'd bought a Jag – gas guzzlers, polluting the environment. What's wrong with a bike?'

'You don't like Jack, do you?' Why had this never occurred to her before, Jillian wondered.

'I dislike what he stands for – the capitalistic pig.'

'Don't be so naïve, Michelle. Your half-baked politics would be funny if they weren't so sad.'

'I think buying up property and harassing the poor tenants to get out so he can make a mighty profit is gross.'

'He doesn't do that. Here in Cambridge? Don't be silly.'

'No, in London.'

'He doesn't work in London.'

'Doesn't he?'

'No.'

'Ah, sorry, then I've got him muddled up with someone else.'

'Yes. You must have.'

'I visited Patsy at her commune the other day. Have you been?'

'No. I haven't been able to find the time.'

'You should. It's an eye-opener. It's paradise.'

'Really?'

'Oh, yes. Everything's shared. No one's stuck doing the lot. They have a rota of work. There's ten of them so it's only every nine weeks that it's Patsy's turn to cook. She could be babysitting or gardening or doing the laundry, instead. It's so liberating.'

'I wouldn't want anyone else looking after my kids.'

'That's because you've been brainwashed into thinking that if you did you'd be a bad mother.'

'I haven't. I enjoy it. I don't understand why everyone harps on so.'

'Because housework and child-rearing are terminally boring pastimes. It's suited men all these years to make us think that it's what we, and we alone, were born to do. I mean . . .'

When Michelle was in full flight like this, Jillian had learned over the years that it was best to let her get on with it. She'd heard it all before. She'd probably finish by accusing Jillian of being stuck in a rut.

'You know your problem, Jillian? You're stuck in a rut and the tragedy is you don't even know it.'

'Oh, yes, I do. But, you see, I like my little rut.' Jillian snorted inwardly at how predictable Michelle was.

'How can you?'

'I haven't been hurt like you. Jack's a good husband. I'm content. I don't have to hate men. I like them. I feel sorry for you, Michelle. It must be difficult carting around so much bitterness.'

'Well!' For once Michelle was speechless. She sat with her cake-laden pastry-fork poised halfway between her plate and her mouth.

'Still, I must be going. My treat.'

'But we've only just got here.'

'I'm in such a rush, Michelle. I've so many wifely duties to attend to.' She made her way to the cash desk, where she turned and waved merrily to her startled cousin.

Michelle's hint that perhaps Jack was involved in London property again rankled with Jillian as she drove home. While she unpacked her shopping she felt the old fear return. If he was lying about his business to her, she'd never forgive him.

Today wasn't the first time Michelle had sown the seed of an idea that would never quite go away, but today she'd surpassed herself. Jillian *was* happy and content. She didn't want a career, never had. She was a wife and mother, two honourable positions any woman should be proud of. And yet, just recently, she'd found herself wondering if Jack really noticed what she did – he complained about light bulbs and mince, but when was the last time he'd complimented her on the smooth running of his home?

'This is stupid,' she said aloud, to the empty kitchen, and put the kettle on. This was her lot, she'd chosen it, she'd wanted it. What was getting into her? 'Stupid woman,' she added, for good measure. She made the tea. 'Pull yourself together,' she told herself, using the words her mother would use.

'Good for you, Jillian. I'd love to have seen Michelle's face. She's a bossy cow.' Jack was spreading out the plans for the new housing estate on the kitchen table to show Jillian. They'd had dinner but he hadn't mentioned the steak.

'I think she means well.'

'Kiss of death that, my mother always says.'

'She's been hurt, that's her trouble. Violent husbands don't just hurt women physically, the pain is mental too.'

'She probably asked for it.' He smoothed out the plans.

'She what?'

'If I'd been married to her I'd have probably whopped her too.'

'Jack!'

'Well, she's an irritating creature. Too opinionated by far for a –' He stopped abruptly.

'Were you going to say "for a woman"? I don't believe I'm hearing this. There's no excuse for hitting anyone.'

'Sorry I spoke.'

'And because she's a woman, can't she have opinions? I have opinions. Shouldn't I have them?'

'You're not so strident with yours.'

'Maybe because mine usually coincide with yours.'

'Probably.'

'What if they didn't?'

'Jillian, what on earth's got into you tonight? You're so edgy. Do you want to look at these plans or not?'

'Of course I do – but you shocked me. I thought I knew you.'

'You do. Now, can we drop it? See? This new architect we've employed has got another two houses in. What do you think?'

'Aren't the gardens on the small side?' Jillian peered at the plan spread before her.

'We're aiming to sell to professional couples, not families. They won't want to be bothered with gardens.'

'How can you be so sure? The first thing most people do when they buy a house is to start on the garden. Otherwise they'd buy a flat. I think you should make them bigger.'

'Sometimes you can be insufferably irritating when you're rabbiting on about things you don't know about.'

'I beg your pardon?' She looked up from the plan.

'Well, you are.' He shuffled his papers and had the grace not to look at her.

'I thought you were asking my opinion.'

'I was.'

'Then why get ratty with me when I give it?'

'I wasn't.'

'You could have fooled me.' She pushed her chair back and stood up. 'You might not be aware of it but sometimes you are *insufferably* pompous – you must take after your father,' she added for good measure.

'Look, Jillian –' he began, but he was interrupted by the ringing of the phone, which he answered. From his tone she knew it was his mother. There was always a softness when he spoke to her. She attacked the grill-pan with a Brillo pad to distract herself. Why was she upset? All these years she'd accepted him seeing his mother without her, she'd understood, it hadn't bothered her. Or had it? Had she been suppressing resentment over the past ten years that needed the almost-row they'd just had to make it race to the surface?

She scrubbed away at the grill-pan, more slowly now. Ever since her visit to Ralph she had kept a lid on the odd things her father-in-law had said about Theresa and seeing her and abortions. She had feared that if she examined these matters too closely she would not like what she found. But, really, she should say something, shouldn't she?

Jack returned from the phone. 'That was Mum.'

'I gathered.'

'She wondered if I could change my visit with the kids this month. She wants to see us on the Saturday. I said yes.'

'Then you'll have to unsay it, won't you?'

'Sorry? Why?'

'Saturday morning Victoria has her dancing-class and Miles has football-coaching.'

'It's hardly the end of the world if they miss one week.'

'I disagree. And, in any case, I've arranged to take them to visit my sister in the afternoon.' She hadn't, and she was appalled at the swiftness of her lie – she who'd vowed never to lie to her husband.

'Your sister is unlikely to be going anywhere. She won't mind. Heavens, when was the last time you saw her?'

'Exactly. It's time I did. I've neglected her.'

'It could be said that she'd neglected you – it's easier for her to get to you than vice versa. Phone her or send a carrier pigeon or smoke signals or whatever is the best way to communicate with her in Tepee-land.'

'No.' She spoke emphatically. 'I'll cancel if I can go with you to see your mother.'

He didn't reply immediately. 'I don't think so,' he said slowly, almost deliberately.

She turned back to the sink. Funny, she thought, how often she worked things out here, how washing-up helped her concentrate. Like now. She must have this out with him. She needed to know and had a right to know. 'She doesn't want to see me. That's it, isn't it? It was never your father, it was your mother all along who rejected me, wasn't it?' She turned to look at him, curious to see how he took this.

'Don't talk so daft.' He appeared calm.

'And it was she who wanted me to have an abortion. You've lied to me all these years. Why?'

'I don't know what you're wittering on about. You know we have to meet this way because of my father.' Now he looked put out, she decided.

'No, Jack. Please don't lie to me any more. I know. Your father didn't even know you were meeting your mother until I told him.' She sat down, feeling strangely at peace when all evening she had felt so jittery.

'You told him? When did you see my father?' She noted the expressions that flitted across his face – surprise, anger, pain. She didn't want to hurt him, but if he wasn't straight with her over this what else was he capable of hiding?

'I wanted to build bridges with your family.'

'You didn't answer me. When?' He was standing now, glaring at her, leaning menacingly over the kitchen table.

'Last month.' Fourth lie, she thought. When would they end? But it was necessary, he must never know that his father had bailed him out.

'Where?'

'I drove over to Mede House.'

'You took the kids?'

'No. Just their photographs. I wanted us all to be friends. I thought this feud was silly.'

'Well, I don't. Don't interfere in matters that don't concern you.'

'But they do! They're my family too. My children's grandparents, for heaven's sake! But I was in for a shock. It transpired that it was your sainted mother who was against me all along. Well, she conned me hook, line and sinker.'

'You don't mean you believed my father? That evil old sod would twist everything to his own ends. My mother would do nothing to hurt us. I can't believe you went there when you knew how I felt about him.' He stood glowering at her, his fists balled as if he was consciously controlling them – from hitting her?

'I thought I had the right.'

'You've many rights, but not that one.'

He turned towards the door.

'Where are you going?'

'Out. I might just hit you if I stay.'

The door slammed.

Jillian sat at the table for some time. He'd behaved as if he knew she was right, that he knew that what she was saying was the truth. These problems were not of her making. She'd been a good wife and mother, and how dare Theresa stand in judgement on her? Only last month Miles had asked why she never went to visit his gran, and she'd lied to him, said she didn't want to go. No doubt he'd asked Jack too, and what lies had *he* told the child?

Lies. Was a totally honest relationship impossible? Suddenly she felt very tired and decided to go upstairs for a nap. An hour later Jack appeared in the doorway. He sat on the edge of the bed. 'Darling, I'm sorry.' He took her hand.

'So am I.'

'Jillian, I don't understand. What's happening to us? Why did we row like that?'

'I don't know.' Jillian slumped back on the pillow. 'That's not true. I do know. Everything's piling up again. All the worry is coming back.'

'What is it, Jillian? Tell me, please.'

'Michelle said you'd bought another property in London, even though you promised me . . . You never tell me what you're doing. I have to find out from my cousin. I've been so worried ever since I got in. Everything is so secretive, and then your mother phones and there's more secrets. It all got to me.'

'Who's talking? Would you have told me you'd seen Dad if this hadn't blown up?'

'Probably.'

'I wonder. Look, Jillian, arguing won't get us anywhere. We've never argued. Why, I watch friends of mine battling in their marriages and I thank God we're never like that. I'm sorry if my dad had a go at you – do you see now why I keep away from him? I'm sorry I snapped at you.'

'I'm sorry too. It's been a bad day one way and another and I think Victoria might be going down with something.

Michelle always rubs me up the wrong way – she's so goddam bossy.' She managed to laugh.

'Phew! Thank goodness that's blown over. Fancy a glass of wine? I bought a case of claret, I'd like to try it out for size.' He was already moving towards the door.

'This London thing. You haven't gone back to speculating there, have you?'

'Michelle talks a load of twaddle. Haven't you grasped that?'

That night Jillian couldn't sleep. They had settled in bed, a mite fuddled from the wine, and made love instantly. Evidently it had worked for Jack, for he had quickly gone to sleep. But Jillian lay in the darkness, staring at nothing, only the occasional flash of headlights playing across the ceiling as a car passed on the street outside.

It was true what he had said. They never rowed. But it was she who tended to back down at the first hint of trouble. How many times had she apologised not because she needed to or had done anything to justify it but, rather, to keep the peace? Her mother had often teased her that she'd rather crawl a hundred miles backwards than have a confrontation. What was changing her?

It had started last year when she'd been so afraid they were to lose everything, when fear for her children's well-being had transcended her guilt and her gratitude that he'd married her.

Gratitude. What a word to choose! What did that say about her? She could just hear Patsy – she'd hit the roof if Jillian ever said that to her; Patsy would think if anyone had to be grateful it must be Jack, that she'd married *him*! She wished she had a scrap of Patsy's confidence. She turned on to her other side. She would take the kids to see Patsy on Saturday, after all – she'd turn the lie into truth.

She wondered if lying was like adultery, easier after the first time. Esmée had told her that. 'Darling, I'd worked myself into such a state about it; the sin of deceiving poor boring old Toby. Would I be marked with stigmata on my face telling all and sundry I'd strayed? When I did do it it was boring. I felt exactly the same, and after that it was easy, too easy,' Esmée had drawled, inhaling deeply on a cigarette, making light of what to Toby must have been a catastrophe. And pretending she didn't care, when Jillian had a sneaking idea that Esmée did.

One thing she was certain of: she'd never be unfaithful to Jack. The idea of another man kissing her, his hands touching her where Jack did, entering her was too disgusting to contemplate.

If Jack died she knew she'd never remarry. But what if she died first? She couldn't imagine him on his own. How would he manage? But, then, even if it was selfish of her, she would hate to think of him with another woman – ever. She was too jealous for that. She'd been lucky to have Jack for he'd never given her any cause to worry where other women were concerned. If someone flirted with him he'd invariably laugh as he told her all about it later. So that jealousy, of which she was not proud, could be sealed away. Her mother had once asked Jillian if she was concerned when Jack was late home or away on business and she had been able truthfully to say that she wasn't, that he wasn't interested in other women.

While her jealousy was controlled he, it seemed, had none. She wished he had a little. Often, when other men flirted with her, she would have liked to see a spark in him. All he did, however, was say that because they fancied her they were only confirming his good taste. It was a compliment but often she thought it somewhat back-handed.

Silly, that was just a small complaint. She was *so* lucky. Why shouldn't she be grateful? It was a good word for the way her life had panned out – even with tonight's little upset.

Jillian puffed up her pillow and turned it on to the cool side. That was better, she thought, as she nestled into it. If Jack had broken his promise and was involved in London properties again, what could she do about it? Not a lot. If she nagged he'd turn on that blank look, as if he'd spring-cleaned his mind. He'd always defend himself by saying that what-ever he did, the hours he worked, it was all for her and the children, even though she knew it was hatred for his father that powered his ambition. One thing she was determined to do, though: she'd been to see his father, so what was to stop her going to see his mother and having it out once and for all with her?

6

It was such a glorious day, but Jack's absence made it imperfect. She almost hadn't come, wanted to cancel at the last minute when, at breakfast, guilt at what she was doing overwhelmed her.

'Mum will be upset I've not brought them with me,' he'd said pointedly. 'She looks forward to it so much.' Jillian said nothing, but concentrated on clearing up Miles's spilled orange juice. Maybe she should relent . . . 'I don't know why you're being so selfish,' he'd added, and that had decided her.

She had only read lurid tales in the press about communes so she wasn't quite sure what to expect, and had been pleasantly surprised by the lovely old house that had been left, fully furnished, by an elderly aunt to Sally Brentwood, who was now living with Crispin. If the group had allowed someone to be its leader, Crispin would have been the natural choice. Older than the others, suave, more confident, she wished he was involved with Patsy rather than Sally. She felt her sister would be safer with him. He didn't look as if he was on drugs as some of the others did – wafting vaguely about with a silly smile, raising a limp hand in greeting to Jillian. 'Man,' they said, as if the drugs had made them all inarticulate.

They were walking in the neatly tended vegetable garden. Patsy was cooking this week and they had strolled out to pick herbs for the vegetarian lasagne she was making. Miles and Victoria were racing ahead happily with the gaggle of children who lived here.

'They all seem very content.' Jillian watched them playing tag between the fruit bushes.

'They are. We all care for them – they have so many people

loving them.' Patsy snipped at a bunch of chives, which she added to the parsley she was already holding.

'But they would have that in a normal family set-up – grandparents, aunts and uncles.'

'Oh, yes? And how many *normal* families do you know? Certainly not ours. And how often do we see any of our relatives?'

'That's true.' Jillian held out the trug and Patsy put in the herbs. 'But Mum might be right. Remember how she always used to say that her family get-togethers were like World War Three?'

'Jack's with his mother, you say? I don't know why you put up with it.'

'It's complicated. Even more so now I'm pretty sure it's she who's avoiding me – though Jack won't have that. He blames everything on his father.'

'Mum's always believed that that woman would be trouble for you, that she was the clinging type who'd resent you in her son's life.'

'But she was always so sweet to me – and kind.'

'Because she's clever. We had a woman here who initially we all adored. She was so amenable and smiling when all the time she was turning one against the other. None of us had been aware it was happening until a couple left all hurt and upset, and rows were erupting and cartels setting up – all down to sweet Lucy, who just sat and smiled through it all as if butter wouldn't melt in her mouth. Ugh! Come the end, I wanted to knife her.'

'Theresa's got a smile like that – you couldn't imagine her having one bad thought. She does sigh a lot, I did register that.'

'Ah, the martyred madonna, a common form of the species. Often they masquerade as earth mothers too. Earth mothers, my arse! They're like Attila behind it, causing bloodshed and mayhem wherever they roam.'

'How do you get rid of someone who causes problems here?'

'We call a meeting – a gathering, we call it – and whoever

172

has a grievance tells it as it is and we debate it and vote on a decision.'

'How grim! Isn't it embarrassing?'

'Can be, but it's better than ill-feeling festering unspoken. I'll just pop over there and get some lettuce.'

How right that was, Jillian thought. What if she and Jack sat down and she told him of her fears and worries, honestly, openly? Even, perhaps, tell him of her guilt about their shotgun marriage. But to be open she'd have to confess about his father and the money, and she could never do that. And Jack, too, would have every right to say what he felt, what he wanted, his own fears, his own regrets, and she knew that she didn't want to hear that.

'Crispin's nice,' Jillian said, as Patsy returned with the lettuce.

'He's all right – a bit of an old woman over the furniture, though, and he gets at the kids too much about it.'

'It doesn't seem to make much difference.' Jillian had winced at the childish daubs on the walls, the battered, ravaged furniture – lovely antiques she'd love to own. She had had to stop herself shouting at an eight-year-old using a chesterfield, covered in what looked like old silk damask, as a trampoline.

'I don't understand his obsession with belongings. They don't matter, people do.'

'But they're such beautiful things – I'd have thought you, of all people, would have seen that. I'd rather hoped you and he . . . you know . . .'

'Crispin and me!' Patsy hooted. 'No way, he's too prissy for me. And those jeans, they're so tight that if he farted he'd blow his boots off.'

Jillian laughed loudly as they made their way back along the path towards the gate in the old red-brick wall. 'Miles, Victoria, this way,' she called. 'Is there anyone special?'

'You must understand, Jillian, we don't work that way here. We don't want to own each other. We all love each other.'

'I see.' Patsy could mean only one thing and the idea of free love shocked Jillian. But she hadn't come here to disagree

173

with her sister. On the drive over she had resolved that whatever she found she'd stay mum.

'You've changed. I expected a screeching avalanche of disapproval.' Patsy pushed open the back door.

'It's your life. You must live it as you want.' Jillian knew she sounded prim, but she couldn't help herself. She followed her sister into the huge kitchen. 'I'd love a kitchen like this.' One whole wall was of cupboards in pine. There was a black-leaded range – unused, she noted – two electric cookers, a vast porcelain sink with a wooden plate-rack, large windows overlooking a cobbled yard littered with tubs of geraniums, a squishy sofa, a table for sewing, another for sitting at, a third for food preparation.

'I'd have thought you'd want a Poggenpohl kitchen – isn't that the one that's all the rage?'

'I've got one. I'd rather have this. It's the space – my kitchen's a quarter the size. Would you like me to peel the potatoes? Are you putting them in the lasagne?'

'No. It's just that the men need stoking up, they work so hard – so we serve tatties and bread with everything. Do you want to taste my bread? It's wonderful, though I say it myself.'

'I'd love some – I'll see to it, and for the kids too, if I may. You're content here, aren't you?' She sliced the rough brown soda bread.

'Very. It suits me. I don't want children, but I have everyone else's to enjoy.'

'I never knew that.'

'I'd always thought I did. Then I watched mothers and I decided not for me. The fear that something might be wrong with them and to love that intensely – I couldn't get my head round it.'

'It's the down-side of the bliss. You can't have one without the other.'

'There's enough down in life without adding to it. But you're not happy. What's up?'

'I am. Whatever made you say that? Everything's fine. We had a bit of a money problem a year ago, but that's over. The kids are well, Jack's Jack and I'm me. We just chug along and I'm fine.'

'I can't understand how that can be when you've subjugated everything about yourself just to care for them. You're a modern slave.'

'I'm no such thing.'

'I bet you even have sex when you don't want it – always the dutiful wife.'

'Look, Patsy, I don't want any arguments.'

'Did we always argue when we were children?'

'You know, I can't remember. Perhaps. But then we tended to have a common enemy to gang up against – Dad. So maybe we didn't.'

'That was a shock, wasn't it?'

'The split? Yes, but if they're happy – that's what counts, isn't it?'

'I didn't expect you to be so understanding.'

'Divorce happens. I've friends who've split up after a couple of years. At least Mum and Dad were together for thirty-five or whatever.'

'I didn't mean that.' Patsy paused in chopping the onion on the board in front of her. 'You don't know, do you?'

'What? What's wrong? Is Dad ill?'

'Look, if they haven't told you it's because they don't want you to know. It's got nothing to do with me.' She returned to her chopping.

'Tell me! What? I've a right to know. If you do I want to too.'

'Don't tell them I told you, then. It's Dad, he's got a lover.'

Jillian sat down with evident relief. 'So? That's great. Mum's got a feller.'

'So has Dad.'

It took a second or two for her to understand the implications of what Patsy said. 'You don't mean . . .? But Dad . . . he was so against sex! Let alone –'

'There you go! I'd say he was obsessed with sex. Now we know why. It's a case of the most repressed being the goer! Actually I'm quite proud of him. At least he's doing his own thing.'

'Oh, my God, how sad.'

'I knew *you* wouldn't approve.'

'No, I mean how sad that they lived all those years together and it was all a lie. How Dad must have suffered, pretending to be something he wasn't. And Mum too. Oh, Patsy, how tragic for them.'

Jillian had always felt that judging someone on first impressions was shallow and unfair. But on meeting her mother's lover, Rob, she had been alarmed to find she didn't like him. He was polite enough, and attentive to her mother, so she wondered why.

They had been invited for tea – as always Mary had made too much, including a trifle especially for the children. The conversation was general and Rob was very open about himself, that he was divorced with two grown-up children and that he worked for a pharmaceutical company.

Watching him talking with her mother and Jack, not saying much herself, she realised, with a shock, that she resented him. He was acting as if he was well settled in her mother's flat and belonged there, and Jillian didn't like it.

Why not? Why shouldn't her mother be with him? She looked happy enough. He was her choice, it was nothing to do with Jillian. And yet . . .

'You're quiet, Jillian. Cat got your tongue?'

'No, Mum. You lot are talking enough without me adding my twopennyworth.' She forced out a laugh. There was something about Rob, something she couldn't quite put her finger on. Perhaps it was because he was being too nice. So? What could be more natural than that he should want them to like him? Yet she felt that they weren't meeting the real Rob.

Victoria was playing with the box of Lego Mary kept here for her. Miles was deep in a comic. Rob offered Jack a whisky. Jillian and Mary were clearing the plates, and she followed her mother into the kitchen.

'Well, what do you think?' Mary, eyes shining with excitement, swung round to face her daughter, shutting the kitchen door for greater privacy.

'He seems very nice. Shall I wash and you dry?' She filled the sink with water and suds.

'Nice! That's a bit limp! He's wonderful – I'll dry, I know where everything goes. He's making me so happy. I feel like a teenager again.'

'I'm glad,' Jillian fibbed.

'I think he's going to ask me to marry him pretty soon.'

'But you're not divorced from Dad yet,' Jillian blurted out.

'Oh, that! But I will be soon.' Mary waved her hand, as if divorce was a minor impediment.

'How long have you known him?'

'A month.'

'Is that long enough to really *know* somebody?'

'I thought you were my daughter, not my mother!' Mary stacked a pile of plates into a kitchen cabinet. 'One day, one week, one month, one year – the length of time is irrelevant, provided you're in love. And I am. For the first time in my life I really know what it feels like to be a woman.'

Jillian busied herself checking each fork as she washed then rinsed it. She did not want to look at her mother. For a month now, ever since Patsy had blurted out about her father, she had been debating with herself what to do. She hadn't told Jack because she feared he would joke about it. Michelle was the obvious one to discuss it with, but she hadn't, for that would have seemed to be a betrayal – Michelle was only her father's niece by marriage, after all. And how could she talk to her mother? How foolish her mother must feel. Since Mary hadn't told her she didn't want her to know, and Jillian decided it was best to go along with that for her mother's sake. She was too embarrassed to discuss it with the one person she should. What could she say to him? 'Dad, I hear you're a homosexual. Don't worry. I understand.' It wasn't that she was censorious, she wasn't. If that was how he was, so be it. But for all that, for all her reasonableness, she wanted him to be 'normal', she wanted him to be her father again, as if in her discovery of his sexual orientation he had ceased to be. They had not had an ideal relationship, but that hadn't stopped her hoping and longing that one day it might be.

'Seen your father recently?' Mary's question made her jump, almost guiltily.

'Yes. About two weeks ago. He seems fine. Content.' She fumbled for words and wondered if her mother was about to broach the subject.

'I'm glad he is. We're both better off. We should never have married in the first place – incompatible, that's what we were. Still, water under the bridge.' Mary neatly folded the tea-towel, scanned her small kitchen. 'Everything looks ship-shape. Come and have a sherry.'

And the moment had passed, it was not to be discussed.

If she'd felt nervous about seeing Ralph she felt doubly so at the prospect of meeting his wife. This time she hadn't telephoned to arrange an appointment; there was no need. She knew that on the first Friday of every month Theresa drove to Cambridge to shop and always took tea at the Garden House Hotel before returning home.

It seemed decades rather than just eleven years since she and her mother had met Theresa here, she thought, as she entered the hotel lounge. That had been the time Mary had warned her that Theresa would be trouble and she hadn't believed her.

Selecting a table that faced the door so that she could see her mother-in-law the minute she entered, Jillian ordered tea and cakes. She wished she could banish this stupid nervous-ness. Why should she feel so scared? She was a grown woman of thirty. A wife and mother. Pull yourself together, she told herself firmly.

'Mrs Stirling!' She half stood as she called out the woman's name. It had been getting on for six years since she'd seen her and she did not appear to have altered at all. Still slim, still immaculate, still fluttering so that the waiters were already descending upon her, eager to attend to her. 'Mrs Stirling,' she called again and waved. Seeing her Theresa looked hesitant, as if she wasn't going to cross the room to her.

'Jillian, what a surprise.' She had recovered her composure swiftly, and this was said with her customary gracious smile.

'I must admit I barely recognised you, with your lovely hair cut so short.'

'It's easier to manage.' Jillian patted her hair self-consciously. 'With the children.'

'Of course. How are the dear children?'

'They're fine, though Victoria has a cold.'

'Give them their Granny Stirling's love, won't you?' She began to turn away.

'Mrs Stirling, I want to talk to you.' She rushed the words out before she lost total confidence.

'Do you? I'm afraid I'm running a little late.' She glanced at her watch.

'I won't delay you long.'

'Very well. I'll be at my usual table in just a minute,' she told the hovering waiter, and gracefully took a seat in an armchair opposite Jillian. 'So?'

'I'm . . . I'm not sure where to begin . . . It's . . .'

Mrs Stirling folded her hands in an exaggerated gesture of patience. 'Most people begin at the beginning.'

'You don't like me, do you?'

'What an extraordinary question, Jillian.'

'Not really. I never see you.'

'But circumstances preclude that. Jack has explained to you the invidious position I'm in. I send you presents on your birthday, at Christmas.'

'You're my mother-in-law. You live thirty miles away from me. Don't you think it's odd that we don't meet?'

'No. My husband doesn't wish us to have contact with you. I'm sorry, but I am of a generation that believes wives should do what their husbands want them to do.' She spoke slowly, as if explaining to a child.

'You need not lie to me.'

'Lie? I beg your pardon!'

'Yes, Mrs Stirling. You *are* lying. Your husband has no objection to me. Nor, I gather, did he want me to get rid of Miles when I was first pregnant. I have a nasty suspicion – no, more than that, a certainty – that *that* message came from you.'

'Are you feeling unwell, my dear? Life is so stressful, is it

179

not?' She talked calmly, sweetly, as if at the sick-bed of a friend.

'You don't seem to be registering. I've seen your husband and I've talked to him.'

Theresa snapped open her Hermès handbag, removed a gold compact and studied herself leisurely in its tiny mirror. It gave Jillian the first glimmer of triumph that she was, after all, discomfited: she was playing for time. Theresa snapped the compact shut and replaced it in the handbag, which she closed decisively.

'Very well, Jillian. I don't dislike you – why should I? There's nothing to dislike about you. You are a cipher, you are what other people make you. So, you are my son's dutiful, caring, efficient, I gather, wife. But you're not the person I think his wife should be. You were so young when you met that I was not concerned, it was only a matter of time and the little affair you were having would end. I was happy for him to sow his wild oats before settling down with someone suitable.' Anyone seeing them together would have presumed from the confidential way she leaned forward and the ever-present smile that here were two women having a friendly conversation. 'But then, of course, you trapped him. And he, gentleman that he is, found it necessary to marry you. And that made me extremely angry with you and unhappy for him.'

'That is grossly unfair. I did not trap your son. My pregnancy was an accident. It takes two, you know.' Jillian felt flushed with anger and appalled at the cool, calculated way Theresa spoke to her.

'You need not raise your voice to me, young woman. You invited this conversation, and you cannot blame me if you don't like my answer to your question.' There was no anger in her voice, just that relentless coolness. 'You are, of course, correct. I did want you to have an abortion. But, of course, I could not say that. In the end, though, it did not matter who said what, did it? Not when you came sobbing from the abortionist's and, kind boy that he is, he preferred to turn his back on his family than upset you. I told him he would rue the day.'

'But why? What have I done? I'm a good wife – you've just said as much. I don't understand.' She was finding it difficult – so many emotions were scudding about inside her – but she had to try, had to put her point across.

'Now there is no problem. Of course not. You live in this city which, let's face it, is a unique place where the oddest people fit in. Who and what you are is insignificant. It's one of the reasons I've never liked Cambridge, it's a shiftless society. But what happens when Jack realises his ambitions and you go to London? There you will move among society, entertaining the best, the most important people. There, Jillian, I fear that you will become a serious liability to my son. Put baldly, you are not good enough and never will be. This is not your fault. It is your background. You were raised in a different, unsuitable environment. Not to beat about the bush, you are working class and so you will remain.'

'And what about your husband? Isn't he working class and proud of it?'

'He's a man, it's different. And he's rich. Much can be forgiven the seriously wealthy.'

'I don't believe what you are saying!'

'Oh, I'm saying it, Jillian, and you would be wise to believe it.' She stood up. 'Jack has made a disastrous marriage, in my opinion, and I, for one, shall be more than content when it's over. Now, was there anything else you wished to discuss?' Unbelievably after such a tirade, Theresa, smiled at Jillian, who sat, white-faced, in front of her. 'Then I must be going.' She collected her bag, smoothed her skirt, to all intents as if she was merely saying goodbye to a friend. 'And, Jillian, you'd be wise to heed my advice not to repeat a word of this meeting to Jack. I shall deny everything and, I can assure you, my son will believe me. Good day.'

Jillian sat rigid in her chair. She felt exhausted, as if she'd been beaten. She watched the small, elegant woman move across the room greeting friends as she went. No one would speak to someone like that – she must have dreamed it. She would wake up, find herself in her own bed: it had been a nightmare.

'Will that be all, madam?' A waiter stood over her.

'Yes. Thank you.' She fumbled for her purse, blinded by tears.

Chapter Five

1

Summer 1978

The confrontation with Theresa Stirling had shaken Jillian to the core. That someone could loathe and despise her so much, to be waiting, with longing, for her marriage to fail, was a terrible shock. She'd presumed that, with time, the painful memory of their confrontation would fade. Yet a year later, while she was going about her daily tasks, Theresa's words would worm their way without warning into her mind. Like now, as she polished the silver. She could see her mother-in-law's beautiful, smiling face as the venomous words spilled from her pretty painted mouth – 'trapped', 'unsuitable', 'working class', 'liability'. She buffed the fork in her hand, as if by rubbing hard the image would go away. It rarely did.

Sometimes at night, when sleep was elusive, that scene would clatter into her mind. There were times when she'd think of all the things she should have said in reply. Smart-arsed, cutting responses, the sort that only occur too late to be of any use.

That woman had made her angrier than she had ever been. She rubbed at her chest as if she had indigestion, but it wasn't, it was this anger swelling like a growth inside her whenever she thought about that day. She resented this ugly lurking fury: she who had never hated anyone now had to face the fact that she was quite capable of this destructive emotion. Often she'd find herself imagining pushing Theresa under a bus, or taking the phone call to say she was terminally ill!

'If only I could talk about it to someone, it wouldn't be so bad,' she told herself. But who? Michelle and Patsy would inevitably trot out their well-worn opinions about her submissive weakness. Her mother was too happy, and she didn't want to spoil that for her. Her father would be offended. How on earth could she tell Esmée how much she hated her mother? And Ralph was married to the woman! She was too afraid to tell Jack in case his mother's parting words that he'd never believe her were the truth. She needed a friend. She had acquaintances but she hadn't any *real* friends, not the sort she could confide in. She'd always thought that she had no need of friends for she had Jack. Now she did, and there was no one. That she was sure was why the anger festered. She stood up to answer the telephone.

'I'm in Cambridge – an interview on the radio. If Jack's not in, might I call round?'

'Helen! I'd love you to.'

'Well, my dear, you've really only yourself to blame,' Helen said, after listening to her report of events as they sat either side of the fire taking tea. 'You've let this go on too long. I mean, after all those years of barely seeing her you might have twigged a little earlier that she wasn't exactly enamoured of you.' Helen's astoundingly green eyes, in her smooth-complexioned face, twinkled kindly.

'I know. I suppose I'm a bit of an ostrich. If I don't say anything or think about it, it won't happen.'

'Commoner than you think, my dear. I've a friend married to a philanderer. He makes no secret of it but, bless her, she thinks if she ignores it it'll all go away. I do it too. I'm told I've got a particularly nasty type of anaemia – there, I said it, horrible word! – but I pretend I haven't, certain it will disappear.'

'Helen, I'm sorry. How awful. Not serious?'

Helen held up her hand. 'I shouldn't have mentioned it, seeing the concern such a little word can bring. I'm fine. Forget I said it. I forbid further discussions. Any more tea in that pot?'

'Helen, do you know why she hates me so? Theresa, I mean. It can't just be because of my background.'

'Why not? She's a dreadful snob. Though with what justification, I don't know. Her great-uncle by marriage was a lord. She didn't tell you? Why, I'm amazed, she normally does *ad nauseam*. Such a tentative link, but she seems to think that it makes her more upper class than she really is. In fact, her father was a dentist. She'd never admit it – not grand enough, you see. Poor soul, to be so deluded. And that, added to her gross possessiveness of her son, well . . .' Helen pursed her red-painted lips in disapproval.

'I love my son to distraction, but I'd want him to be happy. If the right girl comes along I'll be delirious.'

'*If*'s a big word. What if she's awful and he can't see it but you can? And what if she causes him nothing but grief? Say she has an affair with someone and hurts him bitterly, what then?'

'I'd hate her.'

'Exactly.'

'But I haven't had an affair. I've done nothing to hurt Jack.'

'Perhaps, in Theresa's book, you have. Not being good enough for him – as she so charmingly put it.'

'I thought you'd understand.'

'My dear, I'm only playing devil's advocate for you. Don't look so unhappy. She's been abominably rude to you. Unforgivably rude and cruel. I think you should discuss it with Jack and let him know how you feel.'

'Oh! I couldn't do that! She warned me she'd deny everything. What if he didn't believe me, as she said?'

'Then it would show he didn't love you.'

'Then I can't, can I?'

'Isn't it better to know the truth?'

'Not necessarily.'

'You're being an ostrich again. I'm sorry I can't be of more help.' She looked about her at the room. 'You've done this house up so well. You could make a career out of house-designing – it's all the rage in London.'

'I haven't time!'

'Of course, your little shop.'

'We haven't got it any more.' She decided not to explain why.

'How sad. I thought it so wise of you to have something in

store to do for when the children have gone and you're not needed so much – my married friends with children tell me it's essential.'

'Do you regret not having children?'

'I used to. But now, when I look at the world – the promiscuity, the drugs, the violence – I don't think I could deal with all the worry. Life was much simpler when I was young.'

'You're such a lovely person. Why on earth did Ralph marry Theresa and not you?'

'Oh, he had no choice. She vamped him and seduced him and he, silly, weak man, allowed his hormones to triumph over his morality. She was pregnant and the rest is history, as they say.'

'She was *what*? *Pregnant*? She *had* to get married?'

'Dreadful hypocrisy, in the circumstances, isn't it? But that's Theresa.'

'Knowing that doesn't make it better, it makes it worse. Then she really does hate me!'

'Oh dear, I shouldn't have told you. Gossip can be so damaging. If it's any consolation I wouldn't be in the least surprised if Theresa has simply forgotten why Ralph married her – for her own convenience, you understand. But, unfortunately for her, I remember. I've a memory like an elephant's for a thousand things.' Suddenly she looked wistful.

'I shouldn't be asking you such questions and waking up those memories. I'm sorry.'

'No, no, my dear. Don't be. It was a long time ago. It hurt for years but fortunately that sort of pain fades with time. We have our friendship, and I'm grateful for that – but I'll never go there for Christmas again, not after last time. World War Three, wasn't it, dear?' She laughed.

'But why does she allow the children to think you're Ralph's mistress?'

'Oh, only Jack does. It's handy for him, gives him yet another excuse to hate his father. Mungo and Esmée know I'm not.'

'Why do they hate each other so?'

'Ralph hasn't been a kind father to Jack. And Theresa has seen fit to add her bit of poison – you can't blame the boy.'

'But why?'

'Ah, my dear Jillian, I'm happy to talk about me and my indiscretions, but you can't expect me to tell you any more about others. I've done enough damage for one day. You wouldn't by any chance have a teeny-weeny gin about the house? It's past tea-time now.'

It dawned on Jillian that the Theresa incident and her talk with Helen had brought her to a watershed in her life. Until now she'd always thought about herself in relation to others – Jack, her children, her parents. Now she was thinking more about herself and their relationship with her. She decided that for too long she'd worried about her role as a wife and mother, striving always to be perfect, for who could be that? Helen had worried that she shouldn't have told her that Theresa had had to get married too, but it had been a form of liberation for Jillian: it was good to know that it wasn't just her to whom this had happened, and if Theresa felt no guilt, why should Jillian cart it around with her for ever more?

It felt to her as if she were seeing things now as they really were and not as she wanted them to be. Why hadn't she seen before that she and Jack were different with each other? Correction: Jack was different with her. She had not changed how she felt or behaved with him – or, she wondered, had she?

He'd been so irascible with her the other night, and in front of Gary too, just because she'd been a bit slow in understanding something. The awful thing was that she had to acknowledge he often was and that she'd accepted it. Now, though, she had to face the fact that it didn't hurt her feelings as it once would have. This could mean only one thing: that they'd both changed towards each other.

She sat in her kitchen – where else? She smiled to herself as she thought these things and wondered what Jack really thought of her. If someone asked him what she was like, what would his answer be? What did they talk about, the two of them? Their house, their children, money. That, she decided, was about the sum of it. Once they'd talked about so many things, now it was only the mundane. He knew so little about her, what she thought, what she dreamed of, but then, she realised, she was as guilty of that as him. When had they last sat down and talked, *really* talked, like the adults they were, about world problems, politics, religion? If he didn't know her, she didn't know him either and that was a scary thought.

And then she began to wonder about the future and what there would be to talk about when the children had left home and they were alone? 'What shall we have for supper?' Would that be the main talking point? She managed to smile at that. But the problem was that whereas once she'd been content in her role, seeds of discontent were emerging. And she was becoming aware that if she questioned one thing it led to another. She hated to admit it, after all this time, but in some ways Patsy and Michelle were right. She needed to stop just accepting, she must start doing. There was more to being a good wife than a clean cooker and knickers.

'Your father phoned. He's invited me to lunch at the University Arms,' she said one morning, with a pounding heart. 'Do you mind if I go?'

'Why should I? So long as I'm not expected to turn up.' And Jack returned to reading his newspaper.

The guilt at her clandestine meeting was eased, but was replaced with a new fear: he didn't care any longer who she saw. Another change.

2

'I hear you saw Helen last month. I'm sorry about my wife's rudeness to you, Jillian. I'd no idea you'd seen her.'

'Oh, it was ages ago. I'm over it now,' she lied, as she accepted the menu from the hovering waiter in the cavernous dining room of the University Arms Hotel.

'It's not how I think about you – you do realise that?' Ralph Stirling unfolded the napkin across his lap.

'Thank you.'

'In fact, I think the opposite. I think you're too good for Jack.'

'Please.' Her brow knitted.

'I'm sorry. I shouldn't have said that. Does he know you're here?'

'Yes. I told him. I nearly didn't but I don't like secrets. He doesn't mind. Of course, he still doesn't know about your generosity with the money.'

'So many secrets. What a family we are!' He ordered some wine.

'Helen says your wife hates me because she's a snob.'

'She is. But I think it's a bit more complicated than that. She's over-protective of Jack.'

'I've often wondered, and Jack will never explain, why your relationship is so damaged. Will you tell me?'

'No.'

'I'm sorry I asked.' She smiled apologetically.

'Don't be. You've every right to ask. I'd just rather not explain. My old dad used to say, "Never complain, never explain." I've heeded his words.'

'There's something else I'd like to ask.'

'I don't promise to answer.'

Their starter arrived. She waited for the waiters to stop fussing. 'Why do you never want to see my children?' she asked bluntly.

'I don't like children.'

'Not even your own grandchildren?'

'Not particularly. Just because you like children it doesn't mean the rest of the world has to.'

'Is it because they're Jack's children?'

'Possibly.'

'You're a strange man, Ralph.'

'So I've been told. Good claret this, isn't it?' he asked, bolting the door on that particular subject of conversation.

They ate awhile in silence, Jillian wondering if she hadn't gone too far with her questions but, after all, she had to live with the consequences of their feud.

'Esmée gave me my wedding reception in this hotel.'

'She's a generous girl. She told me all about it, you know, and how lovely you looked.'

'Oh.' Jillian looked abashed. 'I wish I saw more of her.'

'So do I. Dear Esmée, she's a constant worry. If only she could be happy. She has the looks, and so much personality, generosity of spirit but . . . she always ends up with no-hopers who give her sadness.'

'She's not . . . ?'

'I'm afraid so. First Toby, a good man, I wish she'd stayed with him. Then there was the dreadful French count, the formal Austrian, now the laid-back Aussie – he's gone the way of the others.'

'I didn't know about the Australian, Jack never said.'

'He probably didn't know. It was all over in a flash. He was a sheep farmer with millions of acres and millions of sheep, but could you honestly imagine Esmée living in the back of beyond, cooking mutton for the shearers?'

'It probably sounded romantic at the time. Where is she now?'

'America, a film producer. She was over this weekend with him. He seems a nice enough fellow, but whether he's strong enough for her . . .' Jillian saw that he was distressed, put out her hand and held his reassuringly. 'I don't know why she's so restless.'

'Because she'll never find someone like you. That's why.'

'I'm sorry? I don't understand.'

'You and she have such a good relationship.'

'We fight.'

'Ah, yes, but never seriously. She loves you and no other man ever comes up to her expectations of what she thinks a man should be like – like you. You're unique, Ralph.'

'If that's so, I'm to blame. Why? Have I loved her too much?'

'No. How could you do that? It's just that if you're lucky to have such a relationship with your father it's going to be hard ever to find it again – there's no matching blueprint.'

'I hadn't thought of it like that. And I suppose it could be the same for men, couldn't it? But that's not so. Jack and

Theresa have a good mother–son relationship but he's got you.'

'Yes,' she said simply, but thought, If only you knew. 'What if she had children?'

'Esmée? No chance of that. There's something wrong with her plumbing.' He waved his hand vaguely.

'I didn't know.'

'Perhaps I shouldn't have said. Poor old Liz keeps trying, but with no luck – odd, when she's got the hips for it. Looks as if I'm to have no grandchildren – from that quarter.'

Jillian looked down at her plate so that he could not see he'd hurt her. He'd added 'from that quarter' a little too quickly. Evidently he had no intention of building a relationship with her children which was what she had continually hoped.

As she always made lists, of shopping, things to do, cupboard contents, she decided now to make a list of her life, the pros and cons, and she ruled a third column for what she should do about them.

PROS	CONS	ACTION
I love Jack.		Tell him every day.
		We must talk more!
The kids.		Another one?
Lovely home.		Keep it!!!
	Not trendy enough.	Try and do better!
	Getting dowdy.	New clothes!!!
	Fear of moving.	Talk to Jack honestly.
	His mother.	Ditto.
Good health.		Exercise more.
	Never any time.	Get up earlier.
	Bothered what people think.	Ignore them (try to)
	Too secretive.	Talk to Jack re Dad.
	Worry too much.	Try meditation.
	Am I boring?	Do a night-school course.

Try to be more independent!!!	A job?
Garden.	Do it!
Mother's relationship	None of my business.
Father's relationship	Ditto.

She counted up her list and finding there were more cons than pros she struck through it with irritation. She was making difficulties for herself. She knew her weaknesses, she didn't have to list them. She also knew her strengths and it was they she must concentrate on. Still, it was interesting.

She pulled the pad with the rejected list towards her. She'd occasionally thought about having another child. Yet there it was in black and white. Why not?

The other idea, that of doing a night-school course, attracted her too. But what? Languages? Maybe she could do art. That might be fun. Or a course in antiques appreciation? Then maybe she could open an antiques shop and work full-time. 'Yes!' she said aloud. She could. She could do so many things if she set her mind to it. What had started as an idle exercise had had a positive effect, after all.

'Jack, what would you say to us having another baby?' She had just brought a whisky and soda to him in his study.

'I'd say no.' He looked up from the papers he'd been working on.

'Oh!' She felt enormously let down so that the little 'oh' that had emerged bore no relation to how she was thinking.

'You did ask. I'm only being honest. You needn't look as if it's the end of the world – you weren't serious, were you? Oh, hell, you were.' He stopped what he was doing and took her hand. 'Darling. Think it through. We've two wonderful kids – that's enough for anyone with the overpopulation there is. Imagine the nappies, the sleepless nights, then tell me that's what you want to go back to.'

'I thought it would be nice. We can afford it.'

'That it would be and having the money are hardly the right reasons to bring another life into the world, are they?'

'I suppose not.' There he was again, speaking to her as if she were a child who had to have things simply explained.

'Haven't you enough to do? If you're feeling unfulfilled then why not look about for a job? Something secretarial – earn some pin money?'

'I am fulfilled. I don't think you'd like it if I got a job. It might affect your comfort.' There was irritation in her voice. Had he always patronised her like this? She shook her head slightly. Maybe she hadn't been totally honest in her list, maybe she should have added to her cons column that Jack, at times, looked down on her too. 'Maybe I'll enrol at night school this September.'

'Now you're talking! What a good idea.' He returned to his papers.

3

Autumn 1978

'He's a creep. I'm glad you agree.' Patsy was looking at Rob.

'I didn't say that.'

'*C'est moi*, Jillian. I know what you're thinking, even when you don't know yourself.' Patsy was resplendent in a kaleidoscopic mix of colours and fabrics, her cheek painted with a large iridescent lightning fork. Her hair, more frizz than curls, hung almost to her waist. Her bare feet were deeply tanned and calloused from rarely wearing shoes. She smiled at everything, not out of courtesy, but as if it was a source of secret amusement to her.

Jillian chose to ignore her sister's claim to telepathy, a new one to add to her insistence that she was psychic, and looked at her mother. 'Still, Mum looks happy.' Mary was talking animatedly across the room to her own sister.

She was dressed in a short-skirted pale pink copy of a Chanel suit. Round her neck hung a collection of chains and pearls, and her hair had been highlighted and recently permed.

'Shouldn't someone point out that that skirt's too short with her varicose veins?' Patsy adjusted the long Paisley shawls she had thrown over her shoulders.

'And spoil her wedding day? No way.'

'She's too old for that hair too.'

'I thought you were into peace and loving everyone?'

'I am.'

'You sound quite bitchy to me.'

'I'm not! It's the truth. She should be told to protect her from herself.'

'Mum looks nice. She's only a little bit too old for it!'

'Jillian, you can't spend your life sitting on the fence, you'll get piles!' And Patsy wafted away in a swirl of chiffon, velvet and satin.

'You look pleased with yourself. What's new?' She'd been joined by Michelle who, making no concessions to her aunt's wedding, was dressed in her customary dungarees.

'I'm surprised you're here, Michelle. I thought you didn't approve of all this tribal malarkey of female subjugation in marriage?'

'You can't expect someone as old as your mother to comply. It's people of our age who shouldn't be in domestic bondage. Speaking of which, where's Jack?'

'He's late but he'll be here.'

'Where is he?'

'Business. You know Jack. Actually, I *am* pleased with myself. I signed a lease on a shop in Trumpington Road this morning.'

'Really? What sort of shop?'

'Nothing you'd approve of, Michelle – antiques, you know, bourgeois trappings.' She sipped at her glass of Asti *spumante* and wished she'd got Jack to supply champagne.

'Jack's idea, I presume.'

'No. You presume wrong. He doesn't know. It's my project. I intend to surprise him.'

'Then I do approve. Independent Jillian. That's good. And, in fact, if you look at antique-dealing it's a form of recycling, isn't it?'

'I love you, Michelle.' Jillian was laughing.

'And I love you too, Jillian. You're shaping up nicely – even if it's taken time.'

The next morning Jillian and her family stood on the pavement in front of the white-painted shop. Victoria, almost unable to contain her excitement, was jumping from one foot to the other.

'So, what's the surprise you promised me?' Jack was puzzled.

'This.' Jillian took a key from her raincoat pocket, unlocked the door and ushered them in. 'Isn't it sweet?'

Victoria, still bouncing, giggled. Miles uninterested, swatted at a cobweb in the window.

'Victoria, for heaven's sake, stand still.' Jack glared at his daughter as he inspected the empty premises which, given their size, took only a minute. 'So?' He emerged from the tiny storeroom at the back. 'What are you telling me? That you want me to get this place for you? If so, what for?'

'No, Jack. I've already got it. I took a lease on it.'

Jack had been checking the meters in a dusty cupboard and cracked his head on door-frame when he turned round quickly. 'You've what? You didn't say.'

'No. I wanted to do it all myself.'

'Isn't that being a bit secretive?'

'I don't think so.' Jillian could feel her excitement seeping away. 'I might not have pulled it off – there was a lot of interest. These properties on the main road, and so close to the Fitzwilliam museum, don't often come up. The museum will be a bonus – extra passing trade.' She knew she was babbling but she so wanted him to be enthusiastic too.

'It's too small for pine furniture.'

'I don't want to sell that. I'm going to have a few small

195

pieces of mahogany – Regency, if I can get it. Side tables, canterburys, nests, that sort of thing. No, I want to concentrate on pretty objects. Pictures, candlesticks, ornaments, snuff-boxes. The things that make a room ...' There, she was prattling again, but she didn't like his frown. Maybe today was not a good day to have brought him to see the shop: he hated his routine of breakfast and the Sunday papers to be interrupted.

'And how is it to be financed?'

'Ah, well. I've saved a little, and I went to see the bank and they were very helpful.'

'Dexter didn't tell me any of this,' he said, referring to their solicitor.

'No, I went to another company. I saw Colin Coleridge, a nice Scotsman. He did all the paperwork for me. He's promised to be one of my first customers. I've talked to a lot of people, they all think it's a good idea. I'm going to call it Objets – French and sophisticated.' She was nervous, unable to control her chatter. She'd expected him to be pleased for her, but although he'd said nothing she knew he wasn't.

'Any more secrets?'

'It wasn't meant to be. I just want to prove to myself that I could do it. Arrange everything. That I could be independent.'

'Is dependency on me so awful, then?'

'No. It's just – Miles, Victoria, why don't you run up the road to that nice café and cake shop and buy us some buns for tea?' She took money from her wallet.

'It's Sunday.' Miles kicked at the skirting-board.

'It's open. It always is. Go on. Daddy and I will follow you.' Reluctantly Miles opened the door.

'Don't you like Mummy's shop?' Victoria piped up. 'I think it's lovely. She's going to sell dolls too and I'm going to help her.'

'It's a lovely shop, Victoria. Now do as Mummy says.' Left alone, Jack reinspected the shop more carefully this time. 'It needs work doing to it.'

'Yes. Painting and shelving. I know. I built that into my figures.' She brightened at his interest.

'How will it pay for itself? It's very small, you won't have much turnover. Not like the pine shop.'

'No, but there's a flat above. It's let at a good rent. That will go towards expenses. And with just myself there'll be no wage bill or insurance to pay. Oh, please say you like it, Jack.'

'I do. It's a good position, and done well it's a good idea. Also, you've an eye for antiques, you've proved that. It's just that ... well, things are good for us. We're doing fine. I don't see the point.'

'The point is I want to do something, not just work at home, and I'd like to prove myself.'

'Who to? You don't need to prove yourself to me.'

'That's nice. Myself, actually.'

'Well, I think you're mad. A shop is a big tie. I'd have thought you'd enough to do. And what about the children?'

'I've thought that through. They're both at school and in the holidays Victoria can come here with me. I can make her a play area in the storeroom or she can go to that holiday club for children that's been set up down near the Round Church.'

'And Miles?'

'Jack, since Miles got his bike I hardly see him, he's out with his friends.'

'A latch-key child.'

'Oh, hardly. Thousands of women work.'

'Yes, but you don't have to.'

'But I want to,' she said, quite firmly. They let themselves out and walked along the road in silence. Of course he was right, she *had* been secretive: she'd been afraid he'd object and say no. But the biggest secret of all wasn't just her need for independence, as she'd claimed. It was bigger than that. Security. Jack had frightened her when bankruptcy loomed, and she never wanted to be put in that position again.

*

Despite its size the shop did well. She'd enjoyed working in the pine shop but she enjoyed this more. She liked nothing better than to scour the auction rooms, bid for stock, be successful and scurry back to her shop to clean and display it, then sell it quickly. She was busier than she'd dared hope, which had one advantage: all thoughts of having a baby were erased from her mind.

'What I like about this shop is that I can always find a present that's spot on.' Colin Coleridge watched as she wrapped the small still-life of a peach and roses.

'It's a lovely painting.'

'It's for my mother's birthday. She loves roses.'

'You know you told me to look out for any silver snuff-boxes for you? Well, it isn't for snuff, it's a pill-box. Early Victorian.' From the drawer of the desk she used as a counter she took out the ornate filigreed box. 'I put it aside for you to see first.'

She watched him as he took it to the window the better to see it. True to his word, Colin had become a regular customer in the few months she'd been open. Upon first meeting him she had presumed he was in his forties – he was greying and he stooped slightly as if already weary. It was a shock when, last week, he'd told her he was only thirty-seven. Something was bothering him, she was certain. There was an air of sadness about him. She would have liked to ask him what the problem was but, of course, she couldn't.

'It's pretty. I'll take it, and any more you can find. You know, Jillian, I like your honesty. A lot of people would have claimed it was Regency and charged accordingly.'

'What would have been the point? You know more about them than I do. I mean, you're such an expert. I should be learning from you.' She laughed, but stopped when she noticed he wasn't even smiling. 'Colin, are you all right? You look – well, so weary. Sit down. Would you like a coffee?'

'It was just . . . the way you said . . . No, I'm being silly.'

'Tell me. What?'

'The way you said I was an expert, as if you meant it.'

'I do. You are.'

'Not everyone would agree with you.' She detected a bitterness in his voice and waited, wondering if he was going to enlighten her or if she should make the coffee – unless that would stop him? She'd make the coffee, she decided, and moved towards the storeroom. 'My wife thinks these are a waste of time and money. That I'm a fool,' he blurted out.

'Well, I don't know her, but she's wrong. These boxes are difficult to get hold of and when I do find them they've gone up in value.'

'They do, don't they?'

'Yes. And, no doubt, it's your money?'

'Exactly. So I can do what I want with it.'

'Yes. Why not?' This time he joined in when she laughed.

'Tell you what,' he said, 'you make the coffee and I'll run up the road and get us some cakes.'

After that he often called in, since his office was just around the corner. Sometimes they indulged in a cake, sometimes just coffee, but always a chat. She liked him, he was amusing, and she loved to hear his stories of his life on a croft in the Highlands. Of the sacrifices he and his family had had to make to see him through law school.

'Don't you miss Scotland?'

'Aye, but Morag's happier here. She likes the shops,' he joked.

The more Jillian heard of his wife, Morag, the less she liked the sound of her. She appeared to be a demanding, discontented woman – not that Colin ever said anything against her: he didn't need to. Just learning of his wife's ambitions and acquisitiveness was enough.

'Who's that? An admirer?' Michelle asked one day, as Colin left when she entered the shop.

'Don't be silly. He's a customer.'

'Um. He looked quite smitten as he said goodbye. Quite touching. Not exactly an oil painting, is he?'

'I think he's got a very pleasant face. I suppose you want coffee?'

'I'll make it. You look whacked.'

'It's been a busy day.'

'You do too much. This shop, the kids, waiting hand and foot on your lord and master.'

'Michelle! I don't. I've a cleaning woman now, and that's made all the difference in the world. I send the sheets to the laundry. I'm almost a woman of leisure!' But she *was* tired and she *was* doing too much, she knew, but she couldn't let up, even with the help she paid for herself. When she'd opened the shop, she had promised Jack it wouldn't affect him. A guarantee that became even more important to keep when he reported, after a visit to his mother, that Theresa was concerned at the effect Jillian's working might have on the children. She had doubled her efforts to make everything run smoothly so that that old bitch had no cause to complain.

'*Leisure.* I'm surprised you even know the word. You're bloody mad. He's using you,' Michelle said, as she returned with the mugs of coffee.

'He's not. How many times do I have to tell you that this shop was my idea? I enjoy it. And, Michelle, stop hating men so.'

'You'll see,' Michelle said ominously.

'I won't. I like men. I like being treated like a lady. I don't mind being referred to as a girl. It's great to be a woman. Lighten up,' Jillian teased, but her cousin didn't respond. She put her arm around Michelle's shoulder. 'I know, you've had a hard life, but it'll get better, I'm sure.' To her consternation Michelle began to cry, quietly at first, trying to talk, then louder until speech was impossible. Jillian waited for the storm to subside, gesticulating apologetically to a customer who, stepping into the shop, looked startled and backed out. 'What is it?' she asked.

'Shane came round last night.' Michelle paused again to sob.

'Your ex? He didn't hurt you?'

'No. He's going to Australia!' she wailed.

'Isn't that good? I thought you hated him.'

'I do.' Michelle cried even louder.

Jillian, who was as confused as Michelle, decided the best action was to make more coffee.

4

People were strange, she thought, as she cycled home. She'd long ago given up using her car to get to work. There was nowhere to park so, like every other inhabitant of the city, she'd bought herself a bicycle with a large basket on the front to put her shopping in. Poor Michelle, all those years of pretending to be tough and hating men when all the time she'd been pining for her husband. Sad. She stopped at the shops on Hills Road to buy their supper. At least with Jack working such long hours she always had plenty of time to cook dinner for them. She'd do chicken breasts in a tarragon sauce. Time was when she'd have been appalled at such extravagance and have bought a whole chicken to do other things with it, but not now. And the children? Spaghetti – they could never get enough of that. She cycled on. She hoped she'd done right in advising Michelle to follow Shane, if that's what she wanted. But she'd miss her and her bossy ways. Still, she thought, as she chained up her bicycle outside the house, when people asked advice, nine times out of ten they only wanted what they'd already decided to be confirmed.

'Jack? Is that you? You're home early.'

'What's this?' he asked, as Jillian entered their bedroom to change out of her working clothes. He waved a sheet of paper at her.

'Oh, that! It's a list I made a few months back. You know me and lists.' She laughed, but felt embarrassed, racking her brains to remember what she'd written on it.

'I see. Are you showering?'

'No, just changing.'

'I'll go and pour us a drink.'

He'd slipped the list into his pocket, she'd noticed. She hoped he didn't want to discuss it. It was meant to be private. But when she entered the kitchen to get their supper the list was on the table beside their drinks.

'I'm doing chicken with tarragon.'

'I'd like to talk about this first.' He tapped the paper.

'Oh, don't bother with that. I was being silly one day and made it.'

'But what's this about my mother?'

'Nothing. Just that I still feel disgruntled about not going with you to see her. That's all. I'll do the spuds.'

'Sit down, Jillian, please. This one here.' He stabbed at the paper. '"Too secretive. Talk to Jack? Dad." Secretive about what? My father? Yours?'

'It's nothing, honestly. I'd rather not discuss it.'

'Well, I'd rather you did. We shouldn't have secrets. Is he ill? Are you worried about him? Tell me.'

'He's not ill.' She sighed and sat down at the table. 'It's difficult to tell you – to tell anyone.'

'Try me.'

'Well ... you know he has a lodger? Well ... he isn't really. He's his partner.'

'Partner? I didn't know your father had set up in business.'

'He hasn't. He's his lover.'

Jack choked on his drink and the gin and tonic spattered his sweater. He jumped up, grabbed a kitchen towel and dabbed at it. 'He's what?'

'Dad's a homosexual, Jack.'

Jack sat down with a bump on the kitchen chair. 'Since when?

'Since he was born, I suppose. I don't think you become one.'

'But you and Patsy ...'

'He tried to pretend he wasn't, or fought it ... or something,' she finished lamely.

'That's disgusting!'

'He can't help it, Jack. He must have been through torment.'

'What has your mother to say?'

'I don't know. I've never discussed it with her, or him.'

'And how do you feel?'

'Sad for him. It must have been dreadful.'

'Well, that's it. Miles doesn't go there again.'

'Jack! Really! He's not a paedophile, for goodness' sake. He loves Miles, he wouldn't hurt him.'

'He's a pervert!'

'You're talking as if you're from another generation! He didn't choose to be – he is. It's as normal to him as your heterosexuality is to you.'

'You said yourself it was sad.'

'I meant because he'd had to live a lie all his life. And think of what that must have done to him and my mother – torn them to pieces.'

'You're wrong. You should be ashamed.'

Jillian jumped to her feet. 'Well, I'm not. He's my father, I love him and I'll stick by him.' As she shouted the words she suddenly realised what she was saying and how clearly she saw her relationship with her father now. How could she have ever thought she didn't love him or that she had lost him just because he was as he was?

'You can do what you like, but don't expect me to and don't take my son there.' Jack, too, was on his feet and heading for the door.

'Where are you going? We've got to talk.'

'Out.'

'Do you know, Jack? Whenever there's a problem that's what you do and say. Scuttle out, run down to the pub. Anything but face reality. But this time don't think you can come back and say sorry.'

'I shan't. I've nothing to be sorry about!' He slammed out of the kitchen and the front door banged with equal ferocity.

That night Jillian slept in the spare bedroom, but she need not have bothered for Jack didn't come back.

*

203

'I'm sorry,' he said, standing in the kitchen doorway the following morning as Jillian cleared the remains of breakfast. She said nothing. 'Did you hear? I shouldn't have let off steam like that.'

'No, you shouldn't have.' She stood, straight-backed, as if by holding herself rigid she could contain the hurt she felt.

'It was the shock.'

'Did you have to stay out all night? I had to lie to the children this morning when you weren't here. Don't ever put me in that position again!'

He stepped into the kitchen. 'You're really angry with me, aren't you? Hell, I've said sorry.'

'Just saying it doesn't make everything automatically right again. What did you expect? He's my father and I love him and no one, not even you, can speak about him like that.'

'You've never been like this with me before.'

'There's never been anything to be so angry about!' She swung round to the sink, turning her back on him. She looked out of the window, but the garden had disappeared in a shimmer of tears she was determined he wouldn't see.

'I'm sorry I spoke the way I did. But I can't help how I feel. My apology makes no difference to that. I still don't want my son under the same roof as him. Is that understood?'

'And who explains to Miles?'

'You do. You're his mother and it's your father.'

'Thanks a bunch.' She did not dare face him: she felt that if she saw him she would want to hit him. She stood, clutching the rim of the sink, until she heard the door close and his footsteps on the steps.

'Dad, there's no point in beating about the bush. I know about you being gay, Dad, and living with Hal. I want you to know that I love you and I respect you.' She waited awkwardly in the small kitchen of her father's house for him to say something. Why was it that so many dramas in her life happened in kitchens?

'That's nice of you to say.' Her father smiled kindly at her. 'You seem upset. What's happened?'

'It's Jack. He doesn't understand. He's banned Miles from coming here. He says you're – perverted.' She had difficulty saying the word to him.

'Ah . . . well . . . I think we'd be better off in the dining room, don't you? More private, like.' He led the way into the familiar, over-furnished room. Strange that now her mother and the offending TV had left he still preferred this uncomfortable room. They settled on the hard chairs. Her father splayed his hands flat on the table and studied them intently before looking up at her. 'I think the problem with this family is that we never really talk. You know, thrash things out – put our cards on the table.' Trust Dad to have a cliché ready even now, she thought. 'So. It's time to put things straight. Tell your tolerant husband from me that I'm not a homosexual, I've never been and never will be.'

'But I was . . .'

He held up his hand to stop her. 'I don't know what it is about the world today, but it seems to me to be obsessed with sex. But not everyone is. I'm not. I never have been. Hal feels like me. We're good together but, listen carefully, we don't share a bed. We are true friends and I love him, certainly, but as my friend.'

'Dad, what can I say? I'm so sorry.'

'It's not your fault, it's mine. I should have discussed it with you all. I did wonder – Patsy. It was Patsy who told you? Your mother and I had had an argument one day. I'm not blaming her. If there's a victim in this sorry tale it's your mum, the way she put up with me and no sex for all those years – and her so attractive and vibrant too. She's a good woman, your mother. But in her anger – well, she shouted at me that I was a poofter but I wouldn't admit it, and she wished to God I would go and get on with it so she could be free.' He put his face in his hands as if to shut out the memory. 'Unfortunately Patsy heard. I didn't know at the time, I found out later. But what your mother said made me stop and think. I'd been so selfish for so long. She should leave me and get on with her life – a normal life. But I love her, Jillian, I always have and I always will.'

'Oh, Dad.' She slid her hand across the table and took his.

'But there you go. We never talked it out and we should have. I knew back in the war when I was with the lads and they couldn't wait to get a bit of how's-your-father, and I had no interest, that something was wrong. But selfishly I hoped if I got married it would get sorted, only it didn't. It was wrong of me to marry her.'

'Dad, are you saying we're adopted?' The thought hit her with the force of a train.

'Lord, no. Don't start worrying about that. No, I can do it, it's just I don't want to, not with women and not with men. The few times ... you know ... with your mum ... We were lucky. I always said you were my little miracles.' He managed a smile, despite his obvious embarrassment at discussing such matters with his daughter.

'But you said yourself that if the brethren at the church didn't like you as you were then they could lump it.'

'I meant divorce, dear. Nothing else. See what a world we live in – even you thought I meant sex! Fancy a cuppa now that's all out of the way?'

'Trouble is, Dad, I couldn't believe Jack last night. What he said, his attitude. I thought I knew him, now I'm not sure.'

'That's life, Jillian. Who ever really knows anyone?'

5

Winter 1979

Their twelfth wedding anniversary was approaching. Jack had said nothing about going out to celebrate – they usually went to the Red Lion at Whittlesford. She wondered if she should book it anyway. She pulled the phone book towards her across the kitchen table. What if he didn't want to go? That misunderstanding over her father should have been like a summer storm, soon over and either forgotten or something to be laughed about. She sighed. It hadn't proved that simple.

True, she had been angry with Jack. Angrier than when they'd faced bankruptcy. That was strange, she thought. But it was as if, like a dam bursting, all her accumulated anger about other things had broken free. They should have talked. How often had she thought that? Why hadn't she done something about it? But then the deluge might have been too much for them to survive. She was angry about so many things – his mother, money, his patronising attitude towards her, his secrecy, his dirty socks on the floor and the way he coughed in the mornings! All the things, big and small, which they should have thrashed out and never had. Now she doubted they ever would.

Still, Jack had been to see her father, even though she knew it was because he distrusted her explanation. Poor Dad, it must have cost him dear to explain his sexuality to his son-in-law. He had done it for love of Miles, she was sure, and at least Miles was allowed to visit his grandfather again.

Had she been so naïve as to hope that everything would settle and they would go on as they had before? How could they? Things had changed, she had changed. That wretched anger had seen to that. She knew she loved Jack, this life, her home. But she had also learned that her longing for security was only a dream that could never be fulfilled. Hell, the very act of living was insecurity itself, she thought, as she looked up the Red Lion's number.

It was bitterly cold on the February morning of their anniversary. Jack, it seemed, had forgotten. He had rushed out, not even stopping for breakfast. She felt foolish now that she'd booked their normal table. She telephoned the restaurant and cancelled it. If he'd forgotten she had no intention of reminding him.

As she sat at her kitchen table she looked about her at the room she'd worked on and decorated. They had done well for themselves in those twelve years, despite their ups and downs.

They had lived in this house for nearly six years, the longest ever. The children were happy in their schools, Victoria at the local primary, Miles now a day-boy at the Leys. She had faith in the local doctors. The shops were handy. And, of course, Jack had been right: they had bought this house when this area was unfashionable and had watched it become desirable as, in their street, house after house had been bought and done up.

Later that morning, in the shop, rearranging a display of Staffordshire pottery, she looked up as the door burst open. An excited Jack rushed in. 'Happy anniversary. Bet you thought I'd forgotten!' He held out an enormous bouquet of red roses.

'They're lovely. So that's why you rushed out so early. Sweet.' She buried her nose in the lovely blooms, but they smelt of nothing.

'That's not all. I've a surprise. I phoned your mother and she's picking the kids up from school. We're going out to lunch.'

'But I'm working in the shop.'

'No, you're not. We'll shut it!'

'But Colin Coleridge is coming in to look at a box I found for him.'

'No, he's not. I've seen him and put him off.'

'When did you see him?'

'I had to pop into his office to sign some papers. I told him then.'

'Well, lovely. Should I dress up?' She smoothed her jeans.

'No. Just as you are will do.'

Parked further along the road was a brand new E-type Jaguar, pillar-box red, the leather smelling new and pungent.

'Jack! It's lovely.' It was, but if it was an anniversary present it was more for Jack than her: cars were of little interest to Jillian.

'Oh, this is a minor surprise, not the main event. Get

in.' He held open the door for her and she slid in. 'Before you say anything, we can afford it.' He put the ignition key in the lock and the powerful car growled into life.

'I wasn't going to.'

'Oh, yes, you were. I know my wife. Look, I didn't tell you before since you're such a worrier, but for the past four years I've been expanding in a serious way, doing a lot of deals, making a lot of money.' The car slid smoothly down the road.

'Why should that worry me?' she asked lightly. 'I can't think of anything nicer.'

'I've been developing property in London. *That* would have worried you.'

'Jack! You promised.' So Michelle had been right all along.

'See? I knew you'd be cross. But there's no need. It's all right, my love. I've not made us bankrupt this time. Instead I've made us a sodding fortune. We'll never have to worry again.' He banged the steering-wheel triumphantly. 'We're rich.'

Jillian's mind was in turmoil. On the one hand, how could she be anything but happy with this news? Happy at his obvious elation and joy. But niggling away was the knowledge that he hadn't told her before, that he'd kept this secret, that he'd been risking everything again. He hadn't the right to do that. It wasn't fair. She had begun to relax, had stopped worrying. Was she going to have to start all over again?

The red car overtook everything on the main road out of town. Jillian felt herself pressed back into the seat as it accelerated. Still he wouldn't tell her where they were going. Looking out at the passing scenery she guessed Norfolk, and wondered why.

They left the main road, purred through the flat country lanes and finally into a gateway and up a rutted drive. He stopped the car in front of a rose red, Queen Anne house, the one like a doll's house she'd always admired.

'There you are.' He waved his hand at it.

'I'm sorry?'

'That's the surprise. It's ours. I bought it for you – as I promised I would that first time you saw it. Happy anniversary, darling.'

'Jack!' was all she could say and she looked at him in astonishment. 'I don't believe it.'

'Are you pleased?'

'It's wonderful.'

'Then come and see.' He opened the car door.

They stood on the gravel forecourt, looking up at the house. It had a beautiful symmetry and the red brick, mellowed by two hundred years of weather, was a soft, kind colour. He pointed out the lead insurance marker on the side of the wall. 'Bet we'd get a pretty penny for that.'

'Don't you even think it. What's it mean?'

'If it caught fire and the firemen came and they weren't paid a retainer by that particular insurance company, they'd piss off again.'

'Charming.'

They walked into the hall through the wide white door. Ahead was a sweeping, intricately carved oak staircase, black with age. The walls were panelled and a large window on the stairs allowed the sun to filter in through the overgrown ivy. They explored the drawing room, the morning room, the dining room, the huge kitchen with pantries, laundry rooms and still more rooms clustered about it. There were four main bedrooms and four above, hidden away beneath the steep, blue-tiled roof.

'Pleased?' he asked, in the half-panelled room he'd decided would be theirs.

'It's amazing. I can't believe it. But there's so much work to be done.'

'And you'll turn it into a gem, I'm sure. You'll have to give up working in the shop. You'll have no time.'

'But I love the shop, meeting people.'

'You'll have people to meet here – lady of the manor, you'll be. I bet you'll have to open things – you'll have to get an opening-fêtes hat for sure. My mum's got a cupboard full of them. You know what really upsets me? That my father won't be visiting to see what I've done. I'd have loved to see his face.'

'And your mother?'

His smile disappeared fleetingly. 'Oh, I'm sure she'll want to nose around. She'll think I'm living as I should be at last – no more grotty city houses! Still, lunch! It's in the car.'

Jillian crossed to the window. Theresa might approve of the house, but it was unlikely she'd ever approve of its mistress. She sighed. Was it an anniversary present or just the triumphant cocking of a snook at his father? She sighed again, more deeply. She gazed out at the garden, the meadow beyond, and glimpsed a river in the distance. The setting was perfect. The children would love this space, the huge bedrooms. The silence . . .

She was elated at his gesture, overwhelmed. Why spoil it by seeing other motives, thinking about his parents? But . . . There was a huge *but* that she could not ignore. She was happy where they were. She had told him so many times that she never wanted to move again – ever. And yet here they were. She'd only ever lived in the city and she'd no idea if she'd like living in the country. She had said she loved this house all those years ago, but only as a passing remark.

And yet? She opened the window wide, listened to that silence, broken only by the songs of birds as yet unknown to her. How on earth could she say to Jack, 'I didn't mean it, I don't want to live here.' She couldn't, that was the bottom line.

'Jillian, you coming?' she heard him call up the stairs.

He'd brought a blanket, which he'd spread on the bare floorboards in the large hall. Beside him was a picnic basket packed with goodies, the champagne already open.

'When we've eaten I'm going to make love to you – just us, in this empty house. Imagine!' He smiled at her. 'Happy?'

'Delirious,' she replied, pushing all doubts into that dark place deep in her mind.

Chapter Six

1

Spring 1980–Summer 1982

From not wanting the upheaval of another move, Jillian astounded herself by how quickly she adjusted to living in the countryside. She had the house to thank for this. She had fallen rapidly in love with it. 'It's as if the house is a person,' she explained to her mother who, now she had a car, often popped in to visit.

'So you're not lonely?' Mary was measuring the hems of the spare-room curtains Jillian was making.

'A bit. Not many come to visit – it's as if we live in Outer Mongolia. Cambridge people are so static.'

'Mind you, you've never had a lot of friends, have you? Very wise. Friends can cause so many problems. You're better off without them, I always think.'

'You are funny. What a daft thing to say.' Jillian looked up from her tacking.

'Not really. There are always undercurrents – jealousy. You know what I mean?'

'No.'

'There's the obvious jealousy of other people's partners ogling yours. Not funny! But there's the other type too, jealousy of possessions, the you've-got-more-than-me syndrome.'

'I don't know anyone like that.'

'Don't you? Why did Michelle go on at you all the time about what you'd got, up in arms when you wrote that you were thinking of having a swimming-pool put in? Jealousy.' Mary wagged a finger to emphasise her point.

'That's Michelle. Actually, you're right in a way, but I'm not sure it's jealousy. I met a woman from Victoria's old school in Cambridge at the PTA. I invited her for dinner and to spend the night – I wanted to be friends with her. Do you know what she said? That it was no use their coming, they could never return the hospitality. It's as if our money is making a barrier.'

'I understand that. Some people don't like being beholden. I'm like it myself.'

'But we don't flash it around. It could still be Spag Bol in the kitchen, if that's what people want. I mean, Jack's made this money but it hasn't altered us, we're still the same.'

'Don't be silly, of course you're not. Money changes people, always does. And there's that Cheryl creature.' Mary added.

'Cherry,' Jillian corrected.

'She fancies your Jack.'

'You've noticed too?'

'See? I'm right. Best do without them.'

'But we don't have many friends. I've never felt the need. And a social life is difficult with the hours Jack works.'

'Where is he this week?'

'Spain. He and Gary are building a golf course.'

'I didn't even know he played golf. Why don't you go with him? Take a break.'

'Too much to do,' she said quickly. She wasn't about to tell her mother that although she'd asked if she could go with him Jack had said no. It had led to an argument. How she longed for those days when there'd never been any! She shuddered at how petulant she must have sounded, complaining that she bet Cherry was going and why couldn't she? Jack had done what he always did when they argued; he'd walked out of the room, which always left her feeling more frustrated and angry. It was all right for him: last week he'd spent three nights in London at a flat he'd bought for overnight stays, and when she'd complained about her lonely evenings, he'd asked her if she'd prefer him to be splattered on the A11, tired out as he'd been.

'Still, you can't complain, can you?'

'What? Oh, no,' she lied.

'Look what you've got from Jack working so hard. I never thought to see one of my daughters living in this style. It's

213

such a beautiful home and you've done it up a treat. And such lovely furniture. You're a lucky girl.'

'I know. It scares me stiff at times, the amount I'm spending. That's why I decided to make these curtains. It makes me feel better to be saving a little. But Jack doesn't mind – he wants it perfect and it seems I've *carte blanche*.'

'Whatever that is when it's at home. I liked that blanket chest in the hall.'

'Irish Chippendale. It's lovely, isn't it? But a house like this, it deserves the best. I don't think the old brigadier who owned it before us decorated an inch of it in the fifty years he lived here.'

They worked on in silence. Jillian was pleased at her mother's praise. Certainly she'd worked hard on the house. She'd spent hours in the library poring over books with illustrations of Queen Anne houses and how they had looked so that the restoration would be correct for its period. She had visited museums for the right colours and fabrics to use, and if she was unable to find the correct paint colour she mixed it herself. She had felt like an alchemist as she added a little of one colour, more of another and a smidgen of something else. She noted down the quantities so that it could be easily reproduced, much to the amusement of the painters and decorators. However, they did not laugh when, once the colour was on the walls and she had decided it was wrong, they had to redo it all.

'I saw Miles. He's settled now. He said he hated being a boarder at first.'

'I didn't want him to be. He could have gone as a day-boy – I'd have driven him in. But Jack insisted. He said it would do him good.'

'Funny lot, some English, aren't they? Shoving the kids off to school like that. I'd have hated not having you and Patsy at home with me. Still, you've got Victoria and she loves the local primary.'

Jillian pulled a face. 'Jack's sent off for prospectuses for her too.'

'Never! She's only eight. What on earth's he about?'

'Not to send her now, when she's ten or eleven.'

'And you don't want her to go? Then put your foot down. Insist she doesn't go. She's your daughter too.'

'Yes,' was all she said. But it wasn't that easy. When he made his mind up about something, Jack was difficult to budge. Sometimes she wondered if the reason she gave in so easily was because she didn't want an argument – her usual excuse to herself. Or was the real reason that, this way, life was easier?

When Theresa had called her a cipher, she hadn't really known what she had meant by it and had had to look the word up in the dictionary. A 'nonentity' she'd read. Is that what she was? Was that how everyone saw her? She threaded her needle. Certainly she had no great political opinions, no great social conscience, apart from thinking that everyone should be happy. She had sold flags once for the RSPCA and had collected clothes for Oxfam, but compared with Michelle and Patsy, who always had causes to fight for, opinions to voice, she did nothing. The trouble with listening to other people, she thought, was that if you didn't watch out it was too easy to believe what they said.

Theresa was wrong. To her immediate family Jillian was sure she was not a nonentity. To them she was important, needed, the person who kept them healthy, who was the cement of the family. That's how she saw herself, but sometimes she wished someone would tell her that that was how they saw her too.

'How's the shop doing?' Mary interrupted this line of thought.

'Fine. I don't get in as much as I'd like. I do Tuesday and Friday afternoons. But Penny, my assistant, is great. I can rely on her.'

'Shame. You enjoyed that little shop.'

'Still, when this house is finished I'll be able to go back to it, *when* being the operative word.'

'Heard from Michelle?'

'I told you, a letter last week moaning about the swimming-pool. I think she's happy.'

'It seems daft to me, going halfway round the world to live with a man who hits you.'

'Maybe he won't any more.'

'You reckon?' Mary snorted her disbelief.

As the house became closer to completion, Jillian became more involved in the village. Within the first year she had joined the WI, not that she would ever tell Michelle! She could just imagine how loudly her cousin would laugh. She went to church because, as her mother wisely pointed out, that would be the best way to get to know the community. She joined the flower-arranging rota, a monthly luncheon club and was soon on the committee set up to save the church steeple.

The following year, when the invitation arrived to open a local fête, she looked at it in horror. 'Me? Open the fête? I couldn't do any such thing.'

Jack laid down his newspaper and looked at her seriously. 'Of course you will, if you're asked. It's your duty.'

'Why?'

'Because we live here, because it's expected of us.'

'Don't be silly. Famous or titled people do that sort of thing. Not ordinary people like us.'

'Speak for yourself. I'm not an ordinary person. My mother does it all the time. She thinks it's a pain but she knows she has to do it.'

'I'm not your mother,' she replied sharply. Any mention of Theresa always put her on edge.

Sitting nervously on the platform in the community hall of the next village, wearing a brand new hat, and waiting to open the sale of work, Jillian was sure she was about to throw up. She had practised her speech, borrowing Jack's tape-recorder, but her voice sounded artificial with a strangled accent, not a bit like her, more like the Queen when she was young, she'd decided. Today her nerves were not eased by Jack sitting in the front row grinning broadly at her through-out her ordeal. Halfway through her little speech, she noticed, to her horror, that he was wearing odd socks, faltered and floundered and, far too quickly, declared everything open.

'That's the last time I do that,' she said, as he drove her home.

'I thought you made a perfectly wonderful Lady Bountiful. And that hat looked great.' He was still grinning broadly.

'You did the socks on purpose, didn't you?'

'I didn't want you to look miserable. But it misfired and you looked as frightened as a rabbit.' He found this funny, but Jillian couldn't see the joke. 'I doubt if anybody else noticed. I expect everyone looks like that when they open things. You were a good girl, I'll say that for you.'

'Oh, thank you, Jack,' she gushed falsely. 'You do realise you're being very patronising?'

'Dearie me, we are in a grump.'

'What do you expect? After all, I'm just an ordinary person, aren't I?'

'As I've said before, speak for yourself, my darling.'

2

Summer 1983

'You've changed, Jill, my love. You used to read *Vogue*, and *Harpers*. Look at this lot – *Homes and Gardens*, *Ideal Home*. What's happened?' Esmée, on one of her surprise flying visits, looked up from the garden lounger and, from her expression, did not think much of Jillian's choice of magazines. 'Are you, perhaps, in danger of becoming a little *hausfrau*?'

'I've always been that, or haven't you noticed?' Jillian placed the tray of wine and glasses on the table.

'But how can you exist without dear *Cosmo* telling you how to keep your man interested?'

'I don't need it to tell me that, I've grown up.'

'I wish I had.' Esmée sighed. 'I mean, three husbands down and God knows how many affairs. I'm just a walking disaster! I've reached the point where I'm having to think it wasn't *all* their fault and maybe I'm to blame.'

'Well, that's a turn-up.' Jillian poured the wine. 'Which nationality next?'

'Oh, don't! I'm such a failure.' She looked as if she were about to cry.

'Esmée, darling, I'm so sorry. That was a crass thing to say. I meant it as a joke and it's not a joking matter, is it? Forgive me?'

'Silly. I don't blame you. Joke away. I *am* a living comedy. I loved Hans and I wanted it to work. But we disappointed each other too much.'

Jillian handed her the wine and settled herself on another lounger. 'Do you want to know what I think? I told your father my theory. You were such a daddy's girl. You'll never find that sort of love again, no matter how hard you search.'

'You think so?' Esmée brightened at this and sat up expectantly.

'I do. My sister was the apple of my father's eye and I've lost count of the number of partners she's had. She just never got round to marrying any of them.'

'And you didn't get on with your dad?'

'You could say that. We've reached an understanding now. But, you see, when I met Jack he was the first man to love me totally. Dad hadn't. So Jack's my template, your father's yours. I think I'm lucky it was that way. I never had an endless search.'

'It can't be that simple, though, can it? I'm afraid I have to take some responsibility. After all, I am selfish, and I'm opinionated, and extravagant. And I do flirt – that upset Hans dreadfully.'

'You'll find someone else, Esmée. Just look at you, you're stunning. You always make me feel like a country cousin.'

'You? Don't be ridiculous! I wish I could wear white as well as you do. It's that hair, of course. Blondes always look marvellous in white. It just drains me. It's almost become a signature for you, hasn't it? I can't remember when I last saw you in colours.'

'It's simpler. My whole wardrobe is beige, grey, white. Everything intermingles and matches – it saves time.'

'But the long skirts and all those petticoats – it's so feminine, so dreamy. I could never get away with it.' Esmée looked at Jillian admiringly. She was in an ankle-length white cotton skirt with a long white cotton shirt tightly circled with an ornate silver belt, and her hair was shoulder length again.

'Jack calls it my upmarket hippie look. It would be a bit out of place in London, I suppose.' She straightened her skirt, pleased by Esmée's compliments, especially since she had always admired Esmée's dress sense. 'But I refused to go into tweeds and twin-sets, it just wasn't me.'

'Ghastly! Don't ever! I've been worried about you ever since Mother said you looked like a ghost.'

'When has she seen me?'

'Oh, around. Snooping, no doubt. She's always snooping.'

'She'll always hate me.'

'You shouldn't have married her precious son.'

'But we could have been friends. She misses out on so much with the children. Now Jack's so busy he doesn't get to see her nearly as often. I'd happily have taken them, but she made it impossible.'

'My mother is incapable of being friends with anyone.'

'Really?' She was so used to hearing Theresa's virtues extolled by Jack that she was surprised to hear her criticised, especially by one of her children.

'Darling, don't look so shocked. My mother's a bitch – it's probably where I get it from. Actually she isn't too well. Didn't Jack tell you?'

'He said she'd got very vague.'

'That's an understatement! Poor old scone forgets everything. It was funny at first, you know, forgetting our names and which day of the week it was. Now it's getting everyone down. Jack especially. He stays away. Creep.'

'What's wrong?'

'Old age, I suppose. I don't think I'll bother with it myself. I'll just pop my clogs before I get there. Now, about my friend. Are you sure you don't mind her coming to stay?'

'Esmée, any friend of yours is a friend of mine.' She trotted out the well-worn cliché.

Caroline Bruce, who preferred to be called Cara, was not an easy person to be friendly with if you were a woman, Jillian decided. She did not even think her particularly attractive, but supposed men would. She was of mid-height and tended to the skinny. Her hair was long and artfully highlighted so that it looked natural, but Jillian knew that the effect was achieved at considerable cost. She played with her hair constantly, stroking it, twirling it, flicking it – often quite violently, so that it swished through the air as if she were making sure people noticed it. While her body was thin, her face was slightly podgy like the as-yet unformed face of a teenager. Her lips weren't full, so she pouted constantly to make them seem so. However, her eyes were large, round and a beautiful blue – and she used them to advantage, often looking wide-eyed with innocent astonishment.

'All she needs is a baby-doll nightie to complete the Lolita look,' Esmée said, puffing angrily on a cigarette as she perched on Jillian's kitchen table where both had retreated to get away from Cara's relentless sweetness.

'I thought you said she was a friend of yours.'

'Hardly. I met her at a party in London. She was so lost and sad I felt sorry for her.'

'You what? And then you invited her here? Oh, Esmée!'

'Yes, but only for the weekend. How was I to know she'd stay on? For a whole boring week. You shouldn't have asked her to.'

'I didn't. Jack did.'

'Men! What suckers they are.' Esmée topped up her glass of wine. 'Where are they now?'

'Jack's teaching her whist.'

'Whist! Everyone can play whist – you learn it at your mother's knee.'

'Not our Cara, apparently. She said bridge was too hard so he's teaching her whist first.'

'Jack loathes bridge.'

'I know. Odd, isn't it?' Jillian laughed. Without doubt Cara was the most ridiculous, false person she had ever met. Why, this morning she'd seen her clasp her hand over her mouth in child-like surprise at seeing a beetle.

'I can't stand that Tinkerbell voice either. I think I'll get her to lose her temper. Then we'll see what happens to it.' They sniggered together, united in their conspiracy.

Finding a subject with which to goad Cara proved difficult. Apart from herself, nothing interested her. Finally Esmée was forced to ask her where she had her hair coloured.

'What on earth do you mean, Esmée?' The pout increased. 'This is my natural colour.'

'Oh, come on, Cara. We're friends here. Whoever did it has done a great job. I just want to know who it is so I can go there too.' She leaned forward, smiling sweetly. 'It must knock years off you.'

Instead of losing her temper, tears welled in Cara's eyes and slid beautifully, like dew on a pink rose petal, down her face.

'Esmée, you bitch, look what you've done! Poor Cara.' Jack leaped up from his chair, searching in his pocket for a handkerchief. 'Here, Cara. Take this.'

'Thank you so much, Jack,' Cara said, in her breathless little voice, making it sound as if Jack had presented her with a costly jewel.

'Oh, really!' Esmée said, in disgust. 'She's putting that on, Jack, can't you see?'

'Esmée!'

'Why are women so horrible to me, Jack?'

'Because they're jealous, Cara.'

'I'm not jealous of *that*!' Esmée exploded.

'You see, Jack.' And some judicious dabbing at tears followed.

'What has got into you, Esmée? Cara's our guest. How can you be so rude to her?'

'Your prick seems to have overruled your head, Jack,' Esmée said.

Jillian looked out of the window and wished this would all end, wished Esmée had never started it.

'Do you have to be so goddam vulgar?'

'And do you have to be so bloody pompous?'

Once started, brother and sister continued to hurl abuse.

'You're such a bitch it's no wonder all your relationships fail! You're inadequate.'

'You call me that? You've never grown up. Without a strong woman, you're a baby in nappies. Without Jillian to hold your hand and sort out your problems, you're a great big sodding nothing!'

'What do you mean? What problems?'

'She's lost her temper. You both have. Now calm down, do. What on earth must Cara think of us?' Jillian smiled tentatively at Cara, not really caring a hoot what she thought. This argument was getting out of hand. Any moment now Esmée would be spilling the beans about her deal with Ralph.

'What problems?'

'Ask Dad about rescue packages,' Esmée shouted.

Floors did move and slap one in the face when one was shocked. It happened to Jillian as she braced herself and pressed herself against the wall.

'What does she mean, Jillian?' Jack turned to face her.

'I haven't the foggiest.' Her voice emerged, high-pitched and thin.

'I want to know.' He loomed over her menacingly. 'Tell me.'

'I said, I've no idea what she's going on about.' She saw his hand lift, watched, fascinated, as it moved swiftly through the air and, oddly, felt nothing as he slapped her across the face.

'Jack! What the hell!' Esmée leaped towards him, pushing him out of the way. Jillian's hand went to where he had hit her more from a reflex action than from pain. She looked at him with horror.

'Please don't fight,' Cara wailed. 'Please. I can't bear it. Jack, don't be violent, please. You remind me of my daddy.' And she began to cry silently, prettily, flapping his snow-white handkerchief helplessly in the air.

Jack glanced from Jillian to Cara, as if uncertain how to proceed, as if shocked to the core by what he had done.

'You bastard!' Esmée spat at him. 'Come on, Jill. Let's put some ice on that face.'

They were in Jillian's bathroom. She peered at herself in the mirror. 'I think it'll be okay.'

'I can't believe he hit you. He hasn't done it before, has he?'

'No. Never. But, Esmée, how could you say that? How

222

could you put me in such a position? Now he knows it was his father who helped him that time. Does your mother know?'

'No, just me. I'm sorry. I lost my temper when I saw him fawning over that silly bitch downstairs. I mean, you're worth dozens of her and he can't see it.'

'Jack and Cara? Oh, Esmée, don't be so silly. I'm not bothered by her.'

'I think you should be.'

'She's too thick for Jack, for starters.'

'She's not thick. Make no mistake.'

Despite her hurt feelings and the shock she was feeling, Jillian giggled at the very idea.

'Well, I warned you. Will you be all right here?'

'Yes, of course. Why? Are you going?' It wasn't 'of course': she dreaded being alone here with Jack, unsure where his anger would take him, what he might say to her. She busied herself applying lotion to her face so that Esmée wouldn't see how upset she really was.

'I don't want to stay here now. Not after that. I hate confrontations.' And Jillian saw that Esmée was shaking. 'Still, I expect he'll apologise.'

Jack did not apologise. Instead, when he came upstairs, he began a relentless interrogation. She insisted that she didn't know what Esmée meant. He followed her downstairs, firing questions at her, anger barely controlled, as they went into the kitchen. He trailed behind her as she went from kitchen to pantry and back again.

'Jack, I want to go to the loo. Surely you won't follow me there.'

She sat in the lavatory and rested her head in her hands. Now what? She'd give in, she knew she would. The evening was young. If he went on like this . . .

'Where are you going, Esmée?'

'Antibes. I'll call.' They kissed.

'Jack, your sister's leaving, won't you say goodbye?'

'Not unless she tells me what she meant.'

223

'Get stuffed!' Esmée called over her shoulder.

Jillian confessed at one o'clock in the morning. Once the words were out, she waited, sitting on her bed in her cotton nightdress, for his reaction. She expected an explosion of anger, feared he might attack her again. Instead, he sat on a stool and took an inordinate time studying his hands.

'I'll never forgive you, Jillian,' he said finally.

'I'm sorry, Jack. But what was I to do? I was desperate.'

'You don't go to my father with a begging-bowl. I have my pride.'

'And I had the children to consider. We were about to lose our home, don't you understand?' Jillian felt her own anger rise.

'Oh, yes, Jillian. I'm fully aware what your priorities are.'

'What does that mean?'

'You know damn well what. My mother said you were devious. How right she was.'

'I am not devious. It wasn't easy to go to your father – I thought he hated me. But I did it for us. And he was happy to help – he wanted to help you.'

'Me? You, more like. I'm surprised he didn't screw you too.'

'Don't be ridiculous!'

'Maybe he did. Maybe when you meet him for your so-called lunches you slip up to one of the hotel bedrooms.'

It was her turn to slap him, and she did, hard.

'Don't you ever accuse me of being unfaithful to you! I never have been and I never will.' She was breathing fast and deeply, anger, hurt tumbling in her mind.

'I wouldn't make promises like that. You might not be able to keep them.' He rubbed his face distractedly. From his pocket he took out a notebook, sat down and calmly began to write down figures. She found this quiet, seething anger more alarming than the shouting and ranting had been.

'What are you doing?' She knew even as she asked.

'Working out how to pay the old bastard back.'

'No doubt you'll be at it half the night. I'll sleep elsewhere.' She collected dressing-gown, pillow, toothbrush, then, with as much dignity as she could muster, she left her room, only to bump into Cara, who smiled at her in an insufferably smug way.

The following morning as Jillian made her way to the kitchen she fancied she was walking through a miasma of hurt feelings and anger, that tendrils of it touched her face, that it was everywhere.

She shook her head as she pushed open the door. She was tired, she had hardly slept, that was why she was being over-imaginative. She hadn't seen Jack yet, and she dreaded seeing him in case his anger was still as strong.

She made her tea and went across to the window, which looked out on her rose garden. Throughout the night she had gone over everything again and again. If she could go back in time, would she have handled everything differently? And, again and again, the answer was no. Jack had been in the wrong then; she believed he was in the wrong now.

The sound of bicycle tyres on the gravel outside reminded her that it was eight thirty and that the cleaning lady had arrived. She wished Gwen had called in sick – the last thing she needed was to talk to anyone. But still, she told herself, life had to go on. It didn't stop just because she and Jack were rowing.

'Morning, Gwen.'

'Morning, Mrs Stirling. Nice day. Your hubby's late getting away, isn't he?'

'We overslept. Dinner was heavy last night.'

'Oh, doesn't do you no good, that, leads to nasty indigestion. Drawing room or dining room?'

'Drawing room, please. Sorry, it's a bit of a muddle.'

Should she cook breakfast, she wondered, as Gwen clattered out with her cleaning paraphernalia. She couldn't face it herself, that was for sure. And what about Cara? At least she'd go now that Esmée had. Who'd want to stay with this atmosphere in the house?

Jillian concentrated on tidying the kitchen: she'd gone to bed and left the dirty dishes. She wondered if Gwen had noticed and, with an untidy drawing room, put two and two together to realise that trouble was brewing.

It was nine when she finished, and there was still no sign of Jack. Perhaps she should take him some tea. He'd be late for his appointments at this rate.

Feeling silly, she knocked on her bedroom door. Somehow, in the circumstances, she didn't feel she could just walk in. She pushed it open, carrying the tray in her other hand.

'I thought I'd better . . .' She found herself talking to an empty room. 'Jack?' She turned round in time to see a fully dressed Jack emerging from a guest bedroom. Cara's room. 'Jack?' She looked at him, clutching the small silver tray as if it were a life-belt. 'Jack?' The blood drained from her face, she felt cold, then violently sick. 'Jack.' It emerged as a near whisper. In turn he looked at her, and she wished he hadn't for his expression was hard and full of loathing. He said nothing but ran swiftly down the stairs. She stood still, certain she could not move, that she would never move again. His study door banged. Then she heard the front door open. Movement returned to her. She dropped the tray – tea splashed the walls, her carpet. She raced down the wide oak staircase, skidded across the hall, opened the wide white door. 'Jack, wait.' And she hurtled out on to the circular drive waving frantically as his car moved down the long drive. She ran after it, futilely calling his name. He accelerated. Her shoulders slumped, she stood dejected, then trudged back to her house. Looking up, she saw a curious Gwen peeping from the drawing-room window. A sudden movement of a curtain in one of the bedrooms made her glance up. Cara!

She pushed open the front door and climbed the staircase. She did not knock and stormed into the room. 'Get out!'

'Jillian. Good morning.' Cara smiled.

'You heard me – I mean it!'

'Gracious, Jillian, you seem to be in a bit of a state. Has something upset you?' she asked, in her little-girl voice.

'You know bloody well it has. I want you out within the hour. You understand?'

'But why? What have I done?'

Jillian felt herself shake with almost uncontrollable rage. 'Don't do the innocent baby-doll act with me. I'm not taken in for one minute. You slept with my husband.'

'I did no such thing. Why should I? Just because you're having a little local difficulty don't blame me.' She swung round on the stool before the dressing-table and studied herself in the mirror, smiling with evident satisfaction at what she saw.

'I repeat, I want you to go.'

Slowly Cara moved round, her dressing-gown swinging open to reveal her naked body.

'No, Jillian. I'm not going anywhere. Why should I? Jack hasn't told me to go and in any case, I like it here, I like your style of living. If you don't like my presence, I suggest *you* go somewhere.' She spoke in a normal voice, with not a hint of the breathless little girl.

'How much do you want?' Jillian's voice had changed too. It was hard, decisive, as she realised just how mercenary Cara was.

'Are you bribing me?'

'Yes. No doubt you have a price to get out of my house and my life.'

'I doubt if you've got enough – after all you're just the little wife around here, aren't you? Little Goody Two Shoes, little *hausfrau* and other stories.' She laughed. 'Five hundred quid,' she added abruptly.

'Two fifty.'

'Three.'

'Done.'

3

Lists! Make a list, her inner voice said. Calm down, she's gone. Forget it. It's nothing. The cuckoo clock she'd bought on a holiday in Switzerland made its grating, grinding noise as the mechanism prepared to hurl the cuckoo out of the little front door. She looked up, waiting for it to appear, as she often did. It had never lost its charm for her. How Jack had teased her for wanting it. 'It's pure kitsch, it's ghastly!' he'd declared, as they'd stood in front of the shop window, an excited Victoria urging her mother on and Miles taking his father's side. 'It's disgusting,' he said, using his then favourite phrase.

'I don't care if it's kitsch, I love them. I've always wanted one. Every year I put it on my Christmas list but I never got one.'

'Then you shall have one, ghastly as it is.'

'Oh, Dad!'

'Ladies should be spoilt, Miles. It's a good thing to remember.'

'Could Mummy have one with an oom-pah-pah band too? Look, one of the big ones.'

'Certainly not, Victoria. One cuckoo's quite enough for any family.'

How long ago was that? Not long, three years, perhaps – they'd been living here. Such happy memories . . .

'I've done upstairs, Mrs Stirling. Changed that Miss Cara's bed. You should have seen her bathroom. What a mess. Don't know where she's coming from, I'm sure.'

'I'm sorry, Gwen. She won't be back.'

'Can't say I'm sorry to hear that. Here, Mrs S, are you all right? You look real peaky.'

'Do I? Oh, it's nothing. I think I might be getting a cold. Where's my purse?' She busied herself getting Gwen's money together, wanting her to go, longing to be alone.

'I've another half-hour to do.'

'Forget it, Gwen. Everything's perfect – as always with you.'

Gwen beamed at the compliment. And after a profusion of 'If you're sure' and 'It don't seem right, leaving early' and countless 'Well, I'll be on my way', she finally left.

Jillian studied her face in the mirror she had hung in the kitchen, to check herself before answering the door. *Did* she look peaky? Was her misery etched on her face? She looked tired, certainly, and had dark circles under her eyes. What now? What to do to stop the fear that was building up inside her? Even her lists weren't helping. She looked down at them on the table, the pages covered with more doodles than lists.

Aimlessly she wandered into the family room, where the television reigned, and switched it on. She rarely watched TV

– there was always so much to do. She'd have a drink. That was something else she never did – drink during the day.

In the kitchen she took a bottle of Chablis from the fridge, washed an apple, cut a slice of Cheddar then carried them back to the TV room. She'd hardly settled when the phone rang. She looked at it with loathing – she wouldn't answer it, she didn't want to speak to a soul.

The television burbled on. She did not watch it but sat hunched, her unhappiness cloaking her. On the coffee table was one of their large photo albums, which she always kept up to date, the pictures neatly pasted in as soon as they came back from the developers, each annotated with place and date – her great-grandchildren would never wonder who was who. She flipped it open. Jack's face smiled up at her – but, then, would those great-grandchildren know who they really had been? What was there in Jack's face to tell them of how hard he worked, of his pride, of his intelligence – of his adultery? She flicked the page quickly, her family, the people she loved, frozen in time. To her great-grandchildren, it would seem they were always laughing and smiling, that they knew only happiness. That they lived in a world where the sun had always shone or the log fire roared beside a perfect Christmas tree, or that they had sat at a beautifully laid table groaning with luxuries. She'd started these books as a record of their lives – but suddenly she knew they weren't. Life wasn't all holidays in the sun and celebratory meals for birthdays and Christmas. The photographs were an artificial representation of it. As was her life, she realised, just like Theresa's fake flowers, which had been symbolic of that family too.

If she forgave him – if – how would their life be, their marriage? At five past nine this morning, her whole world had changed. Could it ever be the same again? Could trust be resurrected? She remembered Esmée saying one day, when Jillian had suggested she try for a reconciliation with one of her lovers, 'There's no point, Jill, darling. A love affair is like a beautiful piece of broken china. Even if it is mended, the cracks remain.'

'Oh, I don't know. That Spode jug of mine, I had an expert restore it. You'd be hard pressed to see the joins.'

'Maybe. But *you* know they're there,' Esmée had replied. So true, so very true. She poured herself some more wine.

One incident, though, she thought, as she sipped her drink. One stupid act of betrayal. Was it enough to destroy sixteen years of marriage? Was Cara, whom they barely knew, important enough to cause its collapse? It seemed inconceivable. It seemed – stupid.

He'd been angry last night. Not just angry but furious with her, enraged with her. Hating her, momentarily. But still, if the roles had been reversed she wouldn't have done this. She would never betray him – ever!

The bottle was nearly empty. 'It's a quarter full,' Esmée, the perpetual optimist, would have said. She wished her sister-in-law were here now – or did she? Did she really want anyone else to know what had happened, to know her shame?

'We're the perfect Stirlings,' she said, raising her glass to the room. 'We'll stay that way.' Why should anyone else know? No one but Gary and Ralph knew they'd looked financial catastrophe in the face. Why should anyone be told of this? She emptied the last of the wine into her glass and downed it in one. She suddenly felt total exhaustion – not tiredness, but the leaden feeling she'd experienced when the children were born, as if her body had not one more ounce of energy left in it. She curled up in the large armchair. 'I love you, Jack,' she told the television, as finally sleep claimed her.

Jack was away for forty-eight hours, a nightmare two days for Jillian, during which there was no scenario she didn't imagine, no fear she didn't know intimately. In that time she did not go to her shop, did not telephone anyone but sat, drinking too much, the answerphone switched on so that calls could be filtered. She would only pick it up when he rang – only he didn't.

Her heart lifted at the sound of his car and she ran to the door, glad that, despite her misery, she'd made herself up and dressed in clean clothes.

'Jack, I've been so worried,' she said, opening the door before he could.

'I'm sorry about that.' He swept past her.

She followed him up the stairs, along the landing and into their room. He marched towards his dressing room. 'Jack, please. Listen to me.' Still following him, she saw with horror that he was pulling out his black leather case. 'I've decided to forget it, Jack. To forgive you,' she said hurriedly. It wasn't what she'd planned, but panic had taken over.

With slow deliberation he placed the pile of shirts he'd picked up on the dressing-table. 'I beg your pardon?'

'I said it's all right. It's over.'

'What's over?'

'You and Cara. What happened between us. I've thought about it. I don't think what you did is sufficient grounds for us to split up.'

'You don't? How nice of you. I don't agree.' His voice and his expression were cold, so withdrawn that it was as if a stranger spoke to her.

'Jack? Please?'

'*You* betrayed *me*.' He stabbed at his chest with his finger. 'And I can never forgive you.'

He might just as well have hit her again for the skin of her face contracted with shock. She leaned on his trouser press for support, convinced that her legs were about to give way as she watched him scoop up the pile of shirts and pack them in the case.

'We've got to talk.'

'What about? You've forgiven me, I haven't forgiven you, that's all there is. Unless you've something else to say. I haven't.'

'I'm sorry, Jack. It was wrong of me. I should never have told your father.' She faltered over the words as she betrayed herself.

'And?'

'I should never have asked him for the money. I deceived you and I apologise.' She felt tears, hot with pain and humiliation, collect in her eyes. She stood tense, watching

231

him closely. She saw him relax, minutely at first, a tiny softening of his shoulder muscles.

'You mean it?'

'Totally.'

'Very well. I'll forgive you this once. But if you ever do anything like that again we're finished. Is that understood?'

4

Summer 1985

'Could you possibly park that thing round the back?' Jillian looked with dismay at Patsy's Dormobile, every inch of which was painted in swirls of primary colours.

'Don't want the posh neighbours to see it?' Patsy grinned at her from the driving seat.

'No, nothing like that. I don't bother with the posh neighbours. I don't want the goldfish frightened,' she lied.

She walked to the rear of the house as Patsy, a very overweight Patsy now, was clambering out of the van in her customary layers of clothes.

'I think I preferred it when it was painted with flowers. That was pretty.'

'Ah! Flower power! And what a con that was. Jillian, this is Ash.'

'How do you do, Ash?' She put out her hand to Patsy's latest hippie lover.

'Right on,' said Ash. As inarticulate as the rest, she thought, as she ushered them in.

'We're off to the rock festival on Midsummer Common and need a bath. We shan't be staying.'

'I hoped you were.' She saw too little of Patsy, these days, for their relationship to be as strained as it once was.

'Oh, come on, Jillian. Jack loathes me being here. Mind you, I don't enjoy it much either, but I like your bathroom.'

'He doesn't loathe you. You amuse him.' She ignored Patsy's last remark.

'Oh, great. "Meet my weirdo sister-in-law. She's always

good for a laugh. Don't listen to anything she has to say – her opinions, what she'd die for – it's all crap."'

'What on earth's the matter with you? You're so grumpy.'

'And I suppose you never are? Perfect wife, perfect mother, perfect sodding everything!'

'Well, since you like my bathroom I presume you'd like a bath?'

'Do you realise you're impossible to goad? It's bloody annoying.' Ash seemed to find Patsy's annoyance highly entertaining.

'I know you too well, Patsy, to let you get at me. Bath?'

'I do. Ash doesn't.'

What's new? Jillian thought, but she didn't say. 'Maybe Ash would like to watch TV or something while you're, upstairs?'

'TV is the opiate of the masses,' Ash intoned.

'Yes, Ash,' she said. She'd heard that one before. 'Well, perhaps you'd like some tea or a book to read?' She doubted if Jack would be too pleased at Ash being in his library, but what else was she to do with him? As far as she could make out he didn't smell.

As she prepared the tea she found herself wishing that Patsy would phone before she turned up. She didn't like to suggest it, though, because she was certain her sister would take umbrage and then she'd never see her. Still, if she carried on being as prickly as she was this afternoon maybe that wouldn't be a great loss. Patsy was thirty-five now, she should be settled, not rattling about the country in that childishly painted van. She took Ash a cup, then went upstairs to her sister. Patsy was out of the bath.

'Why did you quit the commune?' Jillian asked, sitting on her bed, while Patsy, at the mirror, was drying her long, dark hair, wrapped in a white bath-sheet that made her look even fatter.

'Sal – remember Sal Brentwood? I decided she was evil so I split.'

'Sal? Evil? Bit of an exaggeration, isn't it?'

'No. She was like a spider in a web, luring people in with

drugs as treats, freaking them out into zombies, getting bored with them then casting around for some new victim.'

'I'd have thought she'd be a zombie herself by now, the tripping she's done.'

'Doesn't touch her. There are people like that – they take whatever they want and they survive while destroying everyone else around them. It was when I realised she was enjoying it, like some sort of power, that I got out.'

'How odd.'

'Not really. You must know people who can drink everyone else under the table and not slur a word yet they encourage everyone else to get legless. She's like that.'

'How creepy.'

'Evil, like I said. I reckon she's caused at least three deaths. I don't want to be part of it any more.'

'And you?'

'I dabble, but moderation in all things – except grub.' She happily patted her thighs.

'I didn't like to say . . .'

'No, but you were wondering. I decided they were right. Fat is a feminist issue.'

'Oh, Patsy! Not another crusade.'

'Sorry, but you know me, I've got to have a drum to bang otherwise I get bored.'

'What's being thin, then? Not feminist? Where does that leave someone like me who never puts any on?'

'Well, you're a victim, to be sure.' Patsy was checking her pores in the magnifying mirror.

'Me? I don't diet, I've never had to. I'm lucky.'

'And you'll never get fat running this barn of a place and waiting hand and foot on Jack. That's being a victim – a victim to his male chauvinism.'

'Patsy! You still talk a load of rubbish.'

'No, I don't. You look washed out, thin, circles under your eyes and sad. Your eyes are full of misery. What's going on?' She swung round on the stool, her hands on her substantial thighs. 'Tell me.'

'There's nothing to tell.'

'And I'm to believe you? I'm staying here until you tell me.'

'It's all so stupid. Way back, nearly eight years ago, I persuaded his father to help us out of a mess. But I never told Jack. Two years ago he found out.'

'So?'

'You know how he hates his father. He can't forgive me. He can't forget I went behind his back. He . . .' She couldn't stop the tears. Patsy doled out Kleenex and waited patiently for her to continue. 'That's bad enough,' she said, 'but since he discovered, he's been working even harder, he's mortgaged things, he's sold things – stuff he really liked. Shares have gone. I've been so scared we'd lose this house.'

'What a dork! Why did he do that?'

'Pride. He refuses to be beholden to him for one penny. It's okay, though. He's done it, paid his father back, and he's making money again. Sometimes I wish we had nothing, we were happy in those days. Only the other night I talked to him and asked him why, now he's paid his father, he couldn't forgive me. He said it was impossible. He said his anger with me was lodged in his chest like a brick.'

'Then I hope he gets indigestion. The creep!'

'I wish I hadn't told you if you're going to be rude about him.'

'Then I won't – but it's hard!' Patsy grinned. 'Why does he hate his father so?'

'I don't know. I think it's a personality thing.'

'Taken to extreme lengths, isn't it? There has to be a reason. Do you think the old man molested him when he was a kid?'

'Patsy! What a bizarre thing to think. Of course not.'

'How do you know? We feminists hate for a reason.'

'Then what is Ash doing in your life?'

'I've needs, like everyone else.'

At this Jillian laughed. 'Oh, how funny! You sound just like Mum.'

'Great! Thanks a bunch! That's made my day.' She yanked angrily at her hair.

'What's up? I've told you my problems. It's your turn to tell me yours.'

'Nothing's up. I just get pissed off with this family thing, okay? You're always seeing people in other people – actions,

noses, talents. Look at you with Miles. "He's his dad to a T."'
She aped Jillian's voice. 'He isn't. He's himself. His own
eighteen-year-old self. It gets up his nose too. And, in any
case, I think he's much dishier than his dad.'

'Miles told you that? When have you seen him?' It hurt
that Miles had confided in Patsy rather than in her.

'I see him,' she said, in a tone that implied she wasn't about
to explain anything further.

'I'm sorry you feel so grotty, but sniping at me isn't going
to help, is it?'

'Oh, I don't know.' And Patsy grinned at her impishly: the
irritable mood had passed. 'Which reminds me, talking of
Mother, she says you never go round. She always has to come
here.'

'I know. It's Rob. I don't like him. I avoid him.'

'He hit her.'

'No! And she's still with him?' She looked away not
wanting Patsy to guess that Jack had hit her, if only once.

'Pathetic, isn't it? She says she walked into a door! Bah! I've
heard that one before. I told her she was weak and to get the
hell out of there. Does she listen? I think you should go and
see her. Seen Dad?'

'About once a month too. He's fine. I think he's happy.'

'Bully for him,' Patsy said.

'Why do you dislike him so?'

'Must take after your husband,' Patsy replied gleefully.

After a tour of the house to inspect new acquisitions and
give a lecture on being overworked and having the wrong
priorities, Patsy kissed Jillian goodbye. 'Look, here's a number
you can phone if you ever need me. I travel about, but phone
base every so often.'

'Thanks. If I ever have an emergency I'll call,' she said
blithely, in the way of one who thought it unlikely she
would.

'There's something rotten in the state of Denmark. You
might have to,' Patsy said darkly.

'What are you going on about?' Jillian gazed at her sister,
once more back behind the wheel of her Dormobile.

'I can't put my finger on it, Jillian, but there's something rotten in your life, your house. I don't like the vibes one little bit.'

'Right on!' Ash contributed, as the overladen Dormobile lurched off down the drive.

5

A couple of days later Jillian was in her shop. She intended to go to her mother's when she closed for lunch, determined to find out if Patsy's suspicions were true. Her sister's dislike of Rob was enough, Jillian was sure, to exaggerate the situation. Look at the way she'd spoken about Jillian's home and life, quoting Shakespeare, over-dramatising. It was probably nothing, but she'd better check it out and, anyway, she didn't go to see her mother as often as she should.

'Colin! I'm so glad to see you.' She smiled at him as he came through the door. 'How lucky.'

'I checked with Penny which day you'd be here. I hardly see you since you moved. I'd hate to lose touch.' He had called in to pick up an exquisite Regency silver box she'd found, and which she'd asked Penny to keep for him.

'How kind of you to say that.' She felt oddly flustered.

'Well, you know what I like to collect.'

'Of course.' She felt even more foolish at stupidly misunderstanding. 'But Penny knows always to look out for silver boxes for you.'

'She does, but she's not as selective as you are. When you phone and say you've got something for me to see it's never a wasted journey. After six years you know what I like.' He was prowling about the shop. 'Your husband's in partnership with Gary Frampshore, isn't he?'

'Yes. Do you know him?'

'Only through a client.' He was picking up plates and looking at their backs. He didn't seem able to keep still, she thought, as if he were nervous.

'Why do you ask?'

'Oh, nothing, just curious.' Now he picked up a small

237

figurine of a cat. 'I like this. It's my wife's birthday and she collects cats.'

'I could gift-wrap it, if you want.'

He continued to wander about the tiny shop until she said, 'There you are,' and handed him the parcel, decorated with gold and silver ribbons.

'That's a work of art in itself. Thanks. How much do I owe you?'

'A hundred and fifty for the cat and two hundred for the box, please.'

'And the wrapping?'

'Oh, that's free, like in France.'

'That's kind.' Colin paused, staring at her so intently that she wondered if there was a smudge on her face. She put up her hand without thinking. 'I suppose it's a bit of a cheek. And if you say no, I won't mind . . . you know, be offended.' He looked at her quizzically now, as if waiting for an answer.

'I'm not sure what I might be saying no to?'

'Didn't I say? Oh, stupid of me. I wondered if you'd have lunch with me.'

Her first reaction was to say no. Instinctively she felt she shouldn't. It was nothing she could put a finger on, but it was the way he looked at her sometimes that rang warning bells. And, also, she shouldn't because she found she wanted to.

'So, what do you say?'

'Yes. Thanks.'

They walked the short distance to the river. She sat at a table in the pub – all the outside seats had been taken – while he went to order their drinks and sandwiches. He looked much happier, she decided, not as depressed as he had when she first met him. As a result he was a bit better-looking, not that he'd ever be handsome, not like Jack. Or was he just one of those men who improved with age?

'You look deep in thought.' He placed their drinks carefully on the table. 'Can you share them?'

'I was thinking you looked much happier than when I first met you.' She felt as if she had been caught out somehow, and she had in a way, she supposed, comparing him to her husband. Whatever next?

'Do I? That's good news. I decided to take control of my life, it's made me feel better about myself. I'm glad it shows.'

'Was it out of control, then?'

'You might say that! Cheers!'

Her lunch with Colin had been pleasant, a nice break in her routine. It had been a perfectly innocent meal between two friends – yes, she'd decided she could call him a friend now, not just an acquaintance.

He'd talked about Scotland again and how he never wanted to go back. How much he loved Cambridge and the varied social life. She learned he had two children, one just a baby, and surmised that he did not get on with his wife. He was lonely, she decided. But that was all. He hadn't made a pass at her, not even a hint of one.

As she buffed up a silver rose-bowl she found, to her amazement, she was quite disappointed that he hadn't. Although, as yet, it was only a faint glimmer, Jillian knew guilt was building; she was an expert at recognising it. Why should it be there when she'd done nothing wrong? Why shouldn't she flirt with a man a little bit? After what Jack had done with Cara ... She paused in her polishing, not liking this thought. She'd forgiven Jack, but it seemed she'd never forget. Never. No, she'd nothing to bother herself with over Colin, he was just a nice friend. And then, suddenly, she knew where the problem lay. She'd been out to lunch, enjoying herself, instead of going to see her mother as she'd planned. That was it. She felt better for identifying it, but it didn't make it go away. 'Tomorrow,' she announced, buffing the silver harder.

The following day was glorious. She did not always enjoy the drive along the busy main road into Cambridge, but today, with the sun shining, the roof down on the new drophead coupé that Jack had bought her as a surprise present, and with lighter traffic than usual, the journey was a pleasure. First she popped into the auction house to see if there was anything of interest, then she did some shopping, and it was mid-afternoon before she knocked at the door of her mother's flat.

'Where the hell have you been?' was her mother's tear-stained welcome.

'What's up? Why are you crying?'

'I've been calling you all bloody day. Where the hell were you? All you do is shop.' Her mother turned into the small hall of the flat. Nonplussed, Jillian followed her.

'I didn't know you were trying to get hold of me. I'm not a clairvoyant.'

'Congratulations, you got here,' said another voice.

'Patsy! What are you doing here? What's going on?' The atmosphere in the room was tense. Small tendrils of fear stabbed at her heart when she saw that Patsy was crying too. 'What's happened?' But both women were too upset to answer her.

'I think it's best you sit down, Jillian.' Rob, whom she had not noticed before, took her arm and led her to a chair.

'I don't want to sit down!' The fear was very real now. People only told you to sit down when they were afraid that what they were about to say would make you fall down. 'I want to be told what's going on. Has something happened to Jack?'

Patsy snorted derisively. 'Typical!' she said. 'It's as if no one else exists in the whole wide world but him. I feel sorry for your kids, Jillian, I really do. You're obsessed with that bastard!'

Jillian was perplexed: what on earth was Patsy going on about?

'It's your dad, Jillian. There's no easy way . . . I'm afraid, my dear, he's dead.'

Her legs gave way beneath her and Jillian sank down on the chair. 'But he can't be, he hasn't been ill.'

'No, my dear, it was an accident, in his car.'

'When?'

'Early this morning.'

'I called you. We've been phoning all day. Why didn't you answer? We needed you here.' Her mother spoke accusingly.

'I'm sorry, I didn't know. I wish I had.'

'Bet you wish you'd been to see him more often now. I hope you feel guilty.'

'You're a right one to talk, Patsy. When was the last time you saw him? I'm not his only daughter.'

'Girls! Girls! This is no time to argue. Calm down now. I'll make some tea,' Rob fussed.

'Mind your own sodding business!' Patsy snapped.

'Patsy, don't speak to Rob like that.' Their mother was plumping up cushions with agitation.

'He's no right to interfere. Tell him to keep his nose out of things that don't concern him.'

'Don't be silly, Patsy, my dear, what affects your mother affects me.'

'What? Like hitting her when the mood takes you – you evil prick. And while we're about it, don't call me dear. I hate you almost as much as I hated him.'

'I really don't know why you go on like this, Patsy. Charlie was always a good father to you. What *has* got into you?' Mary was wringing her hands.

'Because he abused me.' Patsy's gaze swept from one to the other as if to assess their reaction to the statement.

'I've never heard such rubbish in all my life,' Mary stated. 'You just make remarks like that to draw attention to yourself. What a thing to say!'

'Look at your mother,' said Rob. 'See what you've done, as if she hasn't enough grief. You're nastier than I thought.'

'Rob, please,' said Mary. 'It's the shock. She doesn't know what she's saying.'

'Yes, I bloody well do.'

'You said something about tea. I think that's a very good idea. And I wouldn't mind a nip of whisky to go with it.'

Patsy stood up, as if uncertain whether to go or stay. She looked wary now, frightened. But the crying had ceased.

Jillian felt as if she were observing a play in which she had no part. Since she had no part she had no lines to say. She was not crying, or grieving, she was feeling nothing, just waiting for some tea, but inexplicably she wanted to sleep.

When Jack entered the room she realised she hadn't even heard the doorbell ring.

'Are you all right, darling? I've just heard the news. An articulated lorry on the A11. Christ, what a shock.'

'Who told you? I didn't phone.' Mary looked even more anxious, as if she was alarmed that the news was out.

'It was on the local radio. A friend –'

'On the radio? Well I never. Did they say his name?'

'Yes, Mary. His full name and where he worked. I'm so sorry – and for you too, Patsy.'

'Don't waste your sympathy on me, Jack.'

It was Jack's turn to look confused, which pleased Jillian, as if she were not alone in this bizarre drama.

'Patsy's in a bit of a tizzy, Jack. It's the shock, we think,' said Rob, entering with the tea.

'Ah, I see,' said Jack.

'You might as well be told. Patsy has chosen today to accuse her father of molesting her, Jack.' Mary spoke in a normal conversational tone, which somehow made her words even more shocking.

'How convenient when he isn't here to defend himself,' Jack replied.

'You don't believe me! Any of you! How could you not believe me? Especially you, you're my mother.'

'And today I could wish I wasn't.' Mary's tone was chilling. This made Patsy cry again, longer and louder.

'I don't think you're helping your mother and sister much, Patsy,' Jack said. 'Ah, tea, what a good idea.' He accepted a cup from Rob. Jillian looked at her husband – Jack didn't even like tea. Everything was different today. Why? But then it was as if she stood on a rail-track and an express of black horror bore down upon her. With shattering suddenness she was fully aware of why she was here and why people were crying and she wished she could escape, but there seemed nowhere to go.

'Of course you wouldn't believe me, would you, Jack? Messy business, incest. Almost as bad as Dad being a poofter, or was that worse in your book? Got to keep the precious image going, mustn't let the neighbours know. It's obviously from you Jillian has learned such startling stupidity.'

'And what does that mean?' Jack demanded.

'That everything in the garden at Fen Manor is hunky-dory. Mustn't let the neighbours know you're an out-and-out two-timing bastard. Keep the perfect family image going, all blond and beautiful.'

'You having a bad trip or something, Patsy?'

'Scared I'm going to spill the beans?'

'Jack, what does she mean? Two-timing who?'

'Come on, Jillian, don't say you don't know because I wouldn't believe you. I just feel sorry for anyone involved with your husband. You've spent your life criticising me and my friends and my lifestyle. But I wouldn't swap the honesty of my life with the hypocrisy of yours. Mind you, you're naïve. Look at Dad and how he pulled the wool over your eyes. Do you realise, Jillian, both the men in your life are lying bastards?'

Jillian swung into life. She was on her feet, across the room, had grabbed hold of Patsy's hair and yanked it hard. 'How *dare* you? Don't you ever speak about my husband like that. You're a jealous bitch!' She punched her, Patsy slapped her back. 'Stop saying these evil things about my father.' She pushed so hard that Patsy toppled over. 'You can't have it both ways! You can't accuse him of being homosexual and molesting you, it doesn't make sense,' she yelled.

By nightfall, exhausted but home at last, sitting in her favourite chair, a large whisky in her hand, she began at last to cry. Jack was at her side and held her tight, rocked her gently. Neither of them spoke. There could be no words to comfort her. But the tears she shed were like a balm.

For over an hour she cried, then slowly words returned. And once she started to talk she couldn't stop. She talked about her father, her childhood, of how it had been long ago. She spoke of her pain for him in his confusion; the awful loneliness he must have suffered when all of them were together and he was isolated from them. And the guilt they must all carry and which would never go away. How cruel it was that, as they had been getting to know each other, he had had to die! She blamed herself for she'd had years to cement that relationship and she had visited him only once a month.

He poured her another whisky and coaxed her into eating a sandwich. 'Oh, Jack. What a dreadful day.'

'Not one of our best.' He kissed her forehead. 'Not helped by your nutty sister, that's for sure. I reckon she's tripped to the moon and come back barmy.'

'Such awful things she said.'

'Did you believe her about your father? Why has she never mentioned it before? You don't keep quiet about something like that. And it isn't as if you lived in a mansion – your mother would have known even if you hadn't twigged.'

'I don't understand anything. He loved her, certainly, but only as her father, I'm sure. You don't think . . .' She looked at him, the whole horror returning.

'Not for one minute. The last time I saw Patsy she was rabbiting on about hypnosis and regression, rubbish like that. And she'd had a rebirthing. Maybe that's where she got the idea from, or someone fed her the notion.'

'Do you think so? Oh, I do hope so!' But even if it had happened, Jillian didn't want to know. And so much had been said today. There were still other questions whose answers she feared.

'What did she mean, Jack? Are you having an affair?' she asked, with all the courage she could muster.

'I haven't the foggiest what your sister's motives were. No, I'm not having an affair. Are you?'

'Don't be silly, Jack. I'd never be unfaithful to you – ever. But after . . . But if you were still seeing . . .' She faltered. It was hard for her to say the name. 'You . . . Cara . . . then I'd want to know.'

'Well, I'm not, so there's nothing to know.'

Jack and Rob made all the funeral arrangements, for which Jillian and Mary were grateful. Of Patsy there was no sign. The day of the row Ash had come to pick her up in the Dormobile and no one had heard from her since.

In the time between her father's death and his funeral Jillian went, most days, to be with her mother. In a strange way she looked forward to seeing her. An intimacy between them had emerged. And even if it was only temporary Jillian was determined to enjoy it and remember it.

They talked themselves hoarse as they went over again what Patsy could have meant. Unlike Jillian, Mary had no sense of guilt about Charlie. 'He should have been open with us, not strung me along like he did. And why you should feel any guilt beats me. He was awful to you, so cold always, as though you weren't his. And you were. I was often tempted but I never strayed. You've my word for that.'

'Mum, don't. You don't have to reassure me.'

'As to Patsy, I don't know what wickedness has got into her. Why would your father molest her if he had no interest in sex? Tell me that.'

'Another cuppa?' Jillian suggested, slamming the lid on that particular Pandora's box.

'We'll be pickled in tannin at this rate.' Mary followed her to the kitchen as if she didn't like to be left alone.

'Mum, there's something else Patsy told me. I've got to ask. Has Rob hit you?'

'Oh, really, that girl. She's such a drama queen. I walked into the bedroom door in the night, going for a pee – it happens as you get older. Rob has never laid a hand on me. Oh, I know he's got his faults – he's a know-all, he's always got to top your story with one of his own, and he's a bit pompous. But he's kind, he cares for me, he's there, and we're good in the sack. What more can I ask? And shut your mouth, Jillian, you look gob-smacked.' She pushed her daughter playfully.

Jillian didn't know what to believe, not any more. All her previous assumptions seemed to have shifted.

The funeral was a nightmare. Patsy arrived with Ash five minutes before the cortège left Charlie's house. The fight between the sisters had created an atmosphere that rode with them in the limousine along the Huntingdon Road towards the crematorium. Mary was upset that cars were overtaking them. 'They shouldn't,' she said. 'There's no respect these days.' But such concerns seemed irrelevant to Jillian, who sat beside her mother holding her hand tight.

They were a small group at the service, in the modern, soulless chapel with its canned music, and the vicar, who had not known Charlie but spoke as though he had. Halfway through the service Jillian realised that her father's companion was not there.

'He's in hospital,' Mary explained, when the service was over. 'He was driving. I hope he dies. If he hadn't been speeding . . .'

'Shouldn't we go and see him? They were very fond of each other.'

'Not likely. He can rot in hell as far as I'm concerned.'

'I thought your father belonged to some sect,' Jack said. 'Why didn't they conduct the service?'

'They didn't like his lifestyle either,' Patsy said.

'You'll come back for tea, Jillian?' Mary asked.

'Mum, if you don't mind, I'm whacked.'

'Suit yourself.'

'I feel sorry for Rob,' Jack said, as he drove along the familiar road.

'Why?'

'Your mother was divorced from Charlie, but she's grieving like a widow. It must make him feel a bit insecure. Perhaps your father was the love of her life, after all. Did he have anything to leave?'

'There's the house, and a bit in the bank.'

'I suppose he left it to his friend?'

'No. Didn't I tell you? He left it equally to Patsy and me.'

'Well, that's good news. Those houses go for a pretty penny these days.'

'I expect so. But I gave my share to Patsy.'

The car swerved. 'Are you mad? Why do a stupid thing like that?'

'Patsy has so little, and I have too much. It seemed only fair. There's no point in going on at me. I've already instructed the lawyer.'

'Is that fair on the kids? And what about me? Honestly, Jillian, I think you could have discussed this with me first.'

246

'I'm sorry, Jack. I didn't think you'd mind. Compared with what we have it's so little.'

'Money, my dear wife, is never little.'

Chapter Seven

1

Summer 1986

Jillian noticed that the death of her father had brought her and Jack closer. He had sensed her vulnerability, she decided, and consequently, in the following year, was more attentive than he had been in ages. And he had realised she had suffered a double loss with her father's death and her alienation from her sister.

'Look, Jillian, if Patsy wants to play silly buggers then let her get on with it.'

'But, Mum, I think she's unhappy.'

'If she is I'm not in the least surprised – and who caused it? *She* did.'

Her mother's reaction to her younger daughter's plight shocked Jillian. How could she be so cold, so rational? She was certain she could never be like that with her own children.

'Rubbish! You don't care about me. You prefer Miles to me anyway. And Dad over everyone. It's always been like that.'

Victoria stood in front of her, blonde, beautiful and sulking.

'Victoria, you do exaggerate. Just because I don't think it's a good idea for you to go to Amsterdam with your friends.'

'Their mothers haven't said no.'

'Then they're stupid.'

'And, of course, you're not!'

'In this case, no. I just know more than they do about drugs and the people you're likely to meet there.'

'We're going to the Rijksmuseum, Mother.' Victoria spoke with the barely controlled rage of thwarted youth.

'Correction, my love, you're not going anywhere.'

'I hate you!'

'I expect you do, but you'll get over it.' As Jillian turned back to her ironing she fell forward on to the board as Victoria shoved her violently from behind. 'What on earth!' She recovered her balance. 'Victoria, why did you do that?'

'Because I hate you! I wish you were dead!' She burst into tears and fled from the laundry room, the door crashing behind her. From the noise she made, pounding feet on the stairs and doors slamming, Jillian was able to chart her progress through the house.

'It's the strain of her school work, no doubt – she's not as bright as Miles. Take no notice.' Jack seemed unconcerned by his daughter's outburst.

'But to say that to *me* of all people – I can't get over it.'

'Kids talk to their parents like that.'

'I didn't.'

'Well, you're the exception, then. Could you sign these papers for me? There's a sweetie.'

'What happened to the Ten Commandments? Where? Here?' She pointed with the pen at the papers Jack had pushed in front of her. 'You know, honour your father and your mother.'

'Oh, that crap!' Jack laughed.

'That's not the attitude to take, Jack. I think this is serious.'

'Well, I don't. She deserves a break. Next year when the run-up to GCSEs begins she won't be able to. And this one needs two signatures.' He pushed another form towards her.

'You're not going to let her go when I've said no?' She looked at him aghast.

'Of course not, we'd have to agree.'

'I'm afraid for her.' She bent to sign her name.

'Have you thought you might be overreacting? Just because your sister's a junkie doesn't mean everyone else is. She's probably telling the truth – she probably does want to go to the Rijksmuseum. After all, she is doing history of art. Thanks.' He shuffled the papers into order.

'My sister's a pot-head – there is a difference.'

'If you say so. Can't tell the difference myself.'

'The difference is hard drugs kill and soft ones . . . well . . .'

249

'Fuck up your memory, your relationships . . .'

'Oh, you know what I mean.' She laughed. 'What are they? What have I signed?'

'Just some papers for the lawyer, nothing important. So, what do you think?'

'About Amsterdam? I'm not happy about it.'

'She wouldn't hate you any more,' he wheedled.

'I couldn't believe she said that. And accusing me of loving Miles more – and you.'

'I should bloody well hope you do. I'm your husband. And you probably do love Miles more. You're a woman and mothers favour their sons. Look at me and my mum and dad.'

'I'd rather not.' The very idea that she could be with Miles like Theresa with Jack horrified her. 'No. I love them equally, I really do. It's your family that's odd. And, of course, I love you, but it's a different love from what I feel for them.'

'So she can go?'

'Have you listened to a word I said?' She was teasing.

'Avidly. But . . .?'

'Oh, I suppose so. You're probably right – I'm an old mother hen, I can't help myself.'

In some ways Victoria had a point. She was wrong about the love, but Jillian could see how she might have reached such a conclusion. She spent more time with Miles, more effort trying to understand him; she must watch herself, if Victoria was misinterpreting her actions.

Victoria, although prone to sulking, could at least usually be talked or cajoled out of it. Now, she sensed that Miles was angry about something and he was harder to deal with. 'Are you worried about something, Miles?'

'No. Why? Should I be?'

'I just wondered. I sense that something's bothering you.'

'There isn't.' But his surly expression belied his words.

'If you'd talk to me about it, Miles, maybe we could resolve it.'

'I've no idea what you're talking about, Mother.'

His use of 'Mother' rather than Mum or Ma, was a sure

indication that he was angry with her.

'Do you love me?' she dared to ask.

'Of course. Can I go now?'

She'd watched his face intently at this question, but his expression was bland. He grabbed at his books as if in a rush to escape her and her questioning.

'Honestly, Jillian, for an intelligent woman you can be dumb. Any lad of nearly nineteen when asked a question like that will run for the hills. You're embarrassing him,' Jack said, upon his return from a business trip.

'Has he told you he won't be here this Christmas?'

'I think taking a year off between school and university is a damn good idea. I wish I had. It'll be the making of him.'

'But India?'

'Oh, Jillian. Let them grow up and make their own mistakes.'

'That's not fair, Jack. I do. I don't smother them, I never have. But you read such stories in the newspapers.'

'Then *don't* read them. He's off, it's all arranged, and I'm happy to help the lad. Could you repack my case for me?'

'You're not going again? You've only just got back.'

'Business is business, my love. And stop worrying, do.'

'I hope you'll be back in time for your birthday. I've written to Esmée.'

'How do you know where to contact her?'

'Her bank, of course.'

'You're not going to make a fuss, though, are you? I don't want a cast of thousands telling me I'm forty. I'd rather forget I am.'

'No. Just us,' she lied.

2

'Hasn't anyone ever told you? It's not chic to answer the phone on the first ring.'

'Why ever not?'

'It implies, Jill, that you were waiting for my call, having nothing better to do with your time.'

'But, Esmée, I *was* waiting for your call – nothing else.' Jillian was happy to hear from her sister-in-law.

'How did you know it was me?'

'Come off it, Esmée. Who else has a voice like yours? It's unique.' And it was. Esmée's voice was not only low and husky from too many cigarettes and too much gin, but also held a hint of laughter just below the surface. Her strength was still that she found her life and the people in it inordinately funny.

'It's odd, though. I've been thinking about you a lot recently. Where are you?'

'You always were a bit psychic.'

'I never knew.'

'Oh, yes, you do. You just don't want to admit it. Tell me, are you sitting at your kitchen table making lists? Please tell me you are. It's how I always imagine you.'

'As a matter of fact I am. For the birthday. It's to be a surprise. You're not to say a word. How predictable of me, I suppose.'

'Don't ever alter, will you? Promise me. Stay predictable.'

'Esmée, what's the matter?' She had heard a catch in the familiar voice.

'Can I come to stay? Now?'

'Of course you can.'

Later, the call completed, Jillian stood staring out of the window at the meadow beyond. If Esmée was upset it would be because of some man – it always was. She turned away and went across to the table. There was no doubt, she thought, pulling her list towards her, she was *predictable*. It sounded so boring, but it was the only way she knew how to be and still keep control of everything. Was that all that separated her from a life of chaos like Esmée's – lists?

What other words did people use to describe her? She'd lost count of the times she'd been told how lucky she was. One thing the years had taught her was that luck didn't enter into it. The only lucky factors were accidents of birth that had made her attractive, intelligent and healthy. The rest had been down to hard work, compromise, attention to detail – and lists, which might be an obsession with her, but without them the lifestyle they all took for granted would never run as smoothly.

She got up and went to her small desk, took out her notepads, in which she'd written the menu of every meal she'd served to guests. New people were listed with their hobbies and children's names. That was how perfection was achieved. She flicked through them to check past buffet parties. If nothing could ever be totally perfect she could make it as close as it could be.

She must get on. There was Esmée's room to check. And then it struck her that she wasn't alone in her predictability. Her sister-in-law was guaranteed to lead a rackety life. She was amazing. Despite being well into her forties all the drink, drugs and late nights of her youth had left her physically unscathed. Esmée couldn't have chosen a better time to come: not only would she be company while Jack was away on yet another business trip, but she could talk to her about Victoria. Victoria liked her aunt which, in the girl's present mood, would be a great help. On Saturday, Jack's actual birthday, she would ask Esmée to distract him and take him into town while everything was set up for his surprise party.

Two hours later she heard the crunch of tyres on the gravel of the drive at the back of the house. She ran to the door and held it wide open. 'Esmée!' But she paused in her welcome, for the woman who climbed out of the car looked tired and bedraggled, not at all her usual self. 'Esmée, what's the matter? You look done in.'

'I'm knackered, and so would you be if you'd driven non-stop across Europe then got no sleep last night. So, let's try again, shall we? Hello, Jill, wonderful to see you.'

'I'm sorry, Esmée. You look brilliant. Is that better?'

'There's no need to lie to me. I know I look a wreck, I just don't want others to say it. But, for God's sake, get me a gin, I'm gasping.' She took her bag from the back of the car.

'Just the one? It's not like you to travel light.'

'Yes, it is. It's the new me. It's easier to do a bunk with one bag.' They went along the back hallway towards the kitchen. 'Is the birthday boy here?'

'No, he's in Spain on business. You'll have to make do with me.'

'There you go! What did I say? You never change, still putting yourself down. Will you ever stop doing it? I came to see you, if you must be told. I couldn't care less if I see my brother or not. He's a pain and always has been. In any case, what's he doing in Spain? He hates Spain.'

'Building another golf course, I think.' Jillian was pouring Esmée a large gin and tonic, which Esmée decided was not big enough and, with a grin, signalled to her to add more gin.

'He hates golf too. What's got into him?' She accepted the glass from Jillian and sipped it suspiciously. 'Ah, that's better. Spot on.' Glass in hand, bag in the other, she followed Jillian, who carried a silver tray with ice bucket, gin and tonic. 'You didn't put another glass on. Aren't you joining me?'

'It's a bit early in the day for me.' Jillian pushed open the door to the drawing room.

'You know, you have the most appalling ability to make people feel in the wrong.'

'Sorry. What have I done?'

'"It's too early for me!"' Expertly Esmée mimicked Jillian's voice. 'That immediately labels me a lush.' She pretended to look affronted.

'I'm sorry. I didn't mean to.' Jillian smiled. Once upon a time just a hint that she was upsetting Esmée would have sent her into a tail-spin of anxiety.

'And, for heaven's sake, stop saying sorry! It drives a body mental.' Esmée sank on to the newly covered Knole sofa. 'Nice.' She stroked the soft, powder-blue French velvet upholstery. 'You've got good taste, I must say.' She looked about the elegant room with approval. 'If you don't know what he's doing out there, why not? Doesn't he tell you everything he does?'

'You know Jack.'

'Evidently I don't. And it sounds as if you don't either. I

suppose it all goes back to that schemozzle about you asking Dad to bail him out. Still sulking, that sounds like Jack.'

'Well, yes. I suppose so. He's never fully trusted me since.' Jillian was glad she hadn't told Esmée about Cara. It was something she'd decided was best kept secret. 'But don't let's spoil now by talking about that.' And reminding me of that woman, she thought.

'I've been riddled with guilt over letting the cat out of the bag. Typical of me.'

'You never told anyone else?'

'No one. Dad and I occasionally mention it. He wasn't surprised, you know, when Jack paid him back. He said he'd always reckoned that you'd confess in the end. He likes you enormously, you know. He regrets how infrequently he sees you.'

'That's nice.'

'Don't sound so surprised, everyone adores you.'

'Your mother doesn't. Victoria hates me at the moment. Miles hardly speaks. He's gone to India and I have this sneaking idea it's to get away from me. I still irritate my sister. Oh, yes, I'm flavour of the month with a horde of people.'

'Teenagers aren't supposed to like their parents. Of course Miles hasn't gone because of you, don't be paranoid. He's doing what the young *should* do – finding out what a creaking mess the world is. He'll settle like an angel after that. And there'd be something distinctly wrong with Victoria if she wasn't being a monster. And your sister has been away with the fairies for so long that does her opinion matter or even count?'

'You didn't explain your mother,' Jillian said slyly.

'My mother is a pigheaded woman – you should know that by now. Maybe, now she's in the state she is, she'll see the error of her ways. Though don't hold your breath, will you? Any chance of another?' She waved her empty glass expectantly in the air. Jillian thought she was drinking far too much too quickly but said nothing as she replenished Esmée's glass. 'Thanks. Getting here is like reaching an oasis of calm.' She took a long draught. 'I went to see the wrinklies. Poor Mummy *is* in a bad way.'

'Jack said she was. In fact he rarely goes to see her now, it upsets him so.'

'Typical of Jack. Just when she really needs him he shoves his bum in the air and his head in the sand.'

'It's hard for him.'

'It's hard for us all. She's going gaga in front of our very eyes. It's grim.'

'How's your father managing?'

'In the circumstances, considering she's been such a bitch to him, he's being a positive sweetie. I'd hoped to be here for over a week, until the birthday and maybe give you a hand – not that you'll need one – but I don't think I should. I've got to get back and hold Daddy's paw. Poor darling, he looked lost with no one to hate. And no one's getting any sleep – she's got a bitch of a nurse who won't do nights. The one we had walked out – something Mummy said to her in one of her lucid moments – and it's proving difficult to get a replacement. Mummy will wander – half the time naked. The gardener found her almost on the road the other day. So we're taking it in turns.'

'How awful for you all. Maybe I could get over one night and help out?'

'Why on earth should you? After the way you've been treated? No way. It'll be better next week – Mungo and Liz will be back. They're plodding around Europe buying horses, as if we haven't got enough. Any more mother's ruin?'

Jillian decided to pour herself a drink too, relieved her assistance wouldn't be needed.

'How is Mungo?'

'Dear old Mungo. He's such a lovable character, or should be, but I fear that only Liz truly loves him.'

'I think Mungo would run a mile if he heard you say that. Excuse me.' Jillian stood up and crossed the room to the ringing telephone. 'Jillian Stirling,' she said.

'Is Esmée with you, Jillian dear? But, then, if she is maybe it wouldn't be such a good idea to speak directly to her. Perhaps I should tell you first. What do you think?'

'I'm sorry, I don't know.' She racked her brains, she knew that voice, but for the life of her could not put a name to it.

'Well, neither do I. I did hope you'd know what was best.' This was spoken not as a reprimand but as if the person was genuinely confused.

'Look, I'm terribly sorry, I don't wish to appear rude, but I don't know who you are.' There, she had said it, and if they were offended so be it.

'Why, it's me, Helen Carter. Didn't I say so? How silly of me. I simply hate people who do that, don't you? I'm so sorry, my dear, but I'm in such a state that I don't know whether I'm coming or going.'

'Helen, hello. How lovely to hear from you.' Jillian turned her back on Esmée and the room. She could hear panic in Helen's voice. 'I think you're right. It would be better if you told me.' She cupped the telephone receiver with her hands. 'Is it Theresa?' she whispered.

'Good gracious me, no. It's Ralph. He's collapsed. He phoned me earlier today, and asked me to come. I think he had a premonition. He was alone. I didn't get here quickly enough – I tried but I had meetings I simply had to attend. The doctor was here when I arrived. They say there's no point in even moving him to the hospital. Please, my dear, come quickly. Bring Esmée but don't let her drive, will you?'

As she replaced the telephone Jillian felt stunned. She stood a moment, collecting her thoughts, trying to work out how best to break the news to Esmée.

'Crikey! Who was that? You look as if you've seen a ghost. Forgive the cliché. Come and sit down.' Esmée placed her glass on the table and jumped to her feet.

'Esmée, my love, I think you must sit down. That was Helen. We've got to get to your parents. I'm afraid your father has collapsed.'

'Daddy?' She sat down. 'No, that's not possible.' She stood up again. 'Why he was fine at lunchtime. I said to him should I stay, and he insisted I came to see you. If he'd been ill he wouldn't have let me go, would he?' The words tumbled out, gathering pace as fear took hold.

'I doubt if he knew he was going to be ill. I think we should get going right now.'

The drive was a nightmare: it was late and the headlights, which she had meant to have fixed, were off beam. She could not drive fast, and Esmée's entreaties to her to hurry did not help. Nor did Esmée's interminably going over what could have happened and asking innumerable questions to which Jillian had no answers.

Helen had not exaggerated the seriousness of Ralph's condition: he was in bed, comatose, his breathing laboured and noisy. To see such a large, vital man laid low was sad – like an oak tree felled by lightning, Jillian thought.

'Why won't you take him to hospital?' Esmée asked the harassed-looking doctor. 'He shouldn't be here. We don't have the facilities. He needs a specialist. Who's the best? Get him – now.' She spoke urgently, shaking the doctor's arm as if to make him understand her better.

'Esmée, I fear your father is dying, and I know he would wish to do so here in his own bed.'

'But surely there's something you can do to stop him dying. Give him something – an injection. What is it?' She flicked her fingers with impatience. 'That stuff, you know – adrenaline. That's it!'

'Esmée, I promised Ralph that in a situation as grave as this I would not "strive officiously" to keep him alive.'

'How dare you? Call yourself a bloody doctor? I'll report you! I'll have you struck off! I'll ruin you! That's a promise.' Esmée was shouting in her panic.

'Esmée, my dear, don't. This is what your father wanted.' Helen came forward and put her arms out to her. 'He told me the same thing. And, no doubt, his lawyer too. If you truly love him, you'll let him be at peace now.' As Helen spoke, tears were tumbling down her cheeks, but she did not brush them away. It was as if she was not even aware of them.

'Helen! Oh, Helen.'

And Helen wrapped Esmée in a tight embrace, as if the strength of her hold on her would protect her from the truth.

Esmée calmed. 'Now come with me. Sit with him. Hold his hand. I'm sure he'll know you're here.' Jillian looked at the two women sitting on Ralph's bed, one either side of him each holding a hand, united in their sorrow, and felt she was in the way. Quietly she tiptoed out of the room. She needed to get hold of Jack. She closed the door and walked towards the stairs.

'Hello, how are you, my dear?' Theresa, ghost-like in a long white lace-trimmed nightdress, padded along the corridor towards her. 'Such a lot of noise, what's going on?' She smiled her beautiful, deceptive smile. 'Hello, how are you, my dear? Such a lot of noise. What's going on?'

'Perhaps I should take you back to your room.' Gently Jillian took hold of her mother-in-law's arm.

Before they had reached the door a bad-tempered-looking nurse appeared.

'There you are, Theresa. You mustn't wander off like that. I'd only gone to the loo,' she explained to Jillian. 'When I came back she'd gone.'

'I've told you before, young woman, my name, to you, is Mrs Stirling. Kindly do not forget it.' And she swept in a very dignified manner back into her room.

'She is a trial,' the nurse said. 'One of the old school. Mrs Stirling this and Mrs Stirling that. A right pain!'

'I think it would be better to use her surname – she's of that generation that doesn't like familiarity.'

'And who are you?'

'I'm her daughter-in-law,' Jillian replied, finding it hard to say, since she rarely thought of herself in that way. 'I'll sit with her if you feel you should be with the doctor and Mr Stirling.'

'Not my job. I'm employed to look after Madam, no one else. As it is, I'm doing them a favour staying tonight. I don't do nights.' With this she went into the room and shut the door behind her. Jillian supposed she should feel sorry for Theresa, having such an unpleasant woman to look after her, but then she thought they probably deserved each other.

She went to the kitchen, where there was a telephone. She

could try to contact Jack, for even though he disliked his father he should know that he was ill.

First she tried the hotel in Spain where he normally stayed but was puzzled to be told there was no booking in his name. She left a message on the answer-machine in his flat in London. Maybe she had got it wrong: maybe he was at the complex they were building in Florida. When she telephoned, the manager of the works there could not have been more helpful, but he did not know where Jack was either. She made herself a cup of tea before telephoning the one person who would know where he was, and with whom she loathed to have any contact: his partner, Gary.

'Jillian, I'm sorry, I haven't the faintest idea. Has he done a runner?' She did not bother to answer his crass question, but could easily imagine the glint of his gold tooth as he smiled at his own cleverness. 'But I know he's not in Spain. We're both going over next week. Probably up to no good, if you ask me!' He laughed uproariously.

'If he does contact you, would you please tell him to telephone me at his father's or to come over. It's urgent.'

As the night wore on, Jillian lost count of the number of cups of tea she made, the brandies she poured. And, despite the nurse's efforts, Theresa kept wandering from her room to Ralph's.

'She knows something's up, poor thing.' Helen looked at her with sympathy as the nurse led her away yet again. 'I just hope, for her sake, she isn't aware exactly what.'

Five minutes later she was back again. 'Hello, my dear, and who are you? Such a long time since you were here. Why?'

They would smile and reply inconsequentially.

'Hello, my dear, and who are you? Such a long-time since you were here. Why?' Theresa would repeat these words as if she was at a party or receiving guests. It was maddening, but nobody knew how to stop her. And there was such an innate dignity each time in her greeting that nobody felt they should stop her. Only once, Esmée, asked for the umpteenth time how she was and who she was, broke with the strain. 'I'm your sodding daughter. Shut up, do.'

'Hello, do I know you?' Theresa replied.

Halfway through the night, Jillian heard Jack's car. She ran down to the hall and was opening the door for him before he had time to knock.

'Jack! You got my message. Thank God!'

'Gary told me to come here. Is it my mother?' His face was etched with stress.

'No, it's your father. He's had a stroke.'

'You got me here for him?' He looked at her angrily.

'But the doctor says he's dying.'

'Good.'

'Jack, you don't mean that.'

'I bloody well do.' He moved towards the door as if about to leave.

'Jack, put aside how *you* feel. Your sister and your mother need you.'

'All right. I'll go and see the old bastard, act the dutiful son, but for my mother, no one else. I need a drink first.'

'It's in the kitchen, it seemed the easiest place to set up the drinks. We've certainly hit the brandy,' she chattered, as she led the way. She poured him a large whisky and soda. 'How did Gary know where you were? He told me he'd no idea.'

'Old Gary always knows where to find me. You know that.'

'So why couldn't he have told me?'

'He's allergic to wives asking the whereabouts of their husbands.'

'But you said you were going to Spain.'

'I never did.'

'You did.'

'What is this, a bloody inquisition?'

'Don't be silly, I was curious that's all.'

Jillian dithered about whether to go with him to his father's bedroom and finally opted to accompany him. As they walked into the room Theresa had a moment of lucidity.

'Jack!' she cried, with pleasure at the sight of her son. She leaped from the chair, ran lightly across the room and into his arms. 'How sweet of you to come, my darling. Your father is dying,' she said, with a rising tone to her voice. There was no question that she was delighted.

'I thought you might want me here, to hold your hand, Mum. I haven't come because of him, you do understand?'

'Can't you let this hatred drop, even now?' Esmée asked, anger, fear and grief distorting her face, so that in the half-light she looked much older than her years.

'No, Esmée, some bitterness goes too deep.'

'I don't understand you. He's your father.'

'Oh, no,' Theresa intercepted. 'No, he's not. That's why he hated us.' And Theresa laughed, which, if anything, was even more chilling than her tone earlier.

'Oh, dear God,' Helen said, from the other side of the bed.

'What do you mean?' Jack grabbed at his mother's arm.

'Don't listen, Jack. The poor woman doesn't know what she's saying,' Helen begged.

'I think she does. Mother, say that to me again.'

'Hello, my dear. How are you? It's such a long time since I last saw you. Hello, my dear. How are you?' The moment was lost and Theresa slipped back into confusion.

'I would rather not say. It really is none of my business. Please, Jack, don't you see the impossible position I am in?' Helen twirled the glass in her hand, studying its contents. They were in the kitchen, having been asked by the doctor to leave for a few minutes while he tended his patient.

'Helen, we've known each other a very long time. You have to tell me – I've a right to know.'

'But you never particularly liked me so, quite honestly, I don't see why I should help you now.'

Jillian looked at Helen with astonishment. She was always so kind. Why on earth should she choose now to stand on her dignity? Esmée crossed the room, sat down at Helen's feet and took her hand in hers. 'Helen, I know this is a dreadful time for you too. And this family has never been kind to you. I understand why you wouldn't want to help. I can only beg you to tell all you know. There has been too much bitterness, please don't let it continue.'

Helen began to cry, gently, dabbing at her eyes as if she

didn't want them to see. Esmée patted her hand. Jack looked irritated as he poured himself another large drink. For the first time Jillian noticed that his hands shook.

'It just doesn't seem right, Esmée. It's your parents who should be telling you.'

'How the fuck can they? One's at death's door, and the other might just as well be.' Jack banged his glass on the table.

'I hope for your sake, Jack, that you don't ever become old.' Helen had stopped crying but still looked immeasurably sad.

'Jack, being unpleasant is not going to help! Get a grip.' Esmée looked up at her brother from her position on the floor.

'And what do you know about how I feel?'

'Well, since you hate Daddy so much, you must be very relieved that he isn't your father,' Esmée snapped back.

'Esmée, Jack, don't fight, please. Helen, quite honestly, with Mr and Mrs Stirling unable to, I think you should tell all you know. I mean, neither of them can be hurt now,' Jillian put in.

Helen fussed with her hair. 'I understand what you're saying, Jillian. But, oh dear, this is when I need Ralphie. It still seems wrong . . . a confidence is a confidence . . . but then . . .' She paused for what seemed an interminable time, shook her head, as if to concentrate her thoughts. 'But you're right, Jillian. The voice of reason always. Sweet child. Yes, Jack, I'm afraid it is true. Ralph isn't your father and he knew that he wasn't. Your mother is not one of my favourite people, but to give her her due, she was honest with him. It virtually destroyed their marriage. They never lived as husband and wife after that, as I'm sure you're all aware. It might have been better if they had parted then rather than continued with this charade of a relationship.' Jillian noticed how bitter Helen sounded at that. 'But your father is an honourable man and the other gentleman did not want to know about you, Jack – he literally broke your mother's heart. And, of course, there were Mungo and Esmée to consider. You see, even in those days the mother invariably had custody in a divorce and Ralph could not bear to lose you two. The only way he

263

would have got custody, was to sue your mother for a divorce, citing the other man. But then the whole world would have known of her shame, and that he could not do. So there has been this appalling unhappiness.' Helen rested her head back, massaging the back of her neck. She closed her eyes and sighed. A tear squeezed itself between her eyelids and trickled down her rouged cheek, and Jillian knew that she was weeping for her part in this sorry tale.

'Oh, how dreadfully sad.'

'Yes, Esmée, it was. But with the war on, unfortunately it was a common tale. The husband away . . . and the bombs . . . not knowing if one was going to live or die. It was too easy for some to stray. Your mother had been seeing this man for a year – he'd avoided military service, but I won't go into that.' Her pursed lips marked her disapproval. 'When, eventually, your father returned from the war it was to find your mother pregnant, and, of course, there was no way it could have been his.'

'I suppose you couldn't get abortions in those days?'

'Ah, yes, one could, given the money. Which, of course, Theresa had. She decided not to.'

'Because she wanted Jack so badly?'

'No, because she hoped the other man would stand by her. And he didn't.'

'You're a fine one to moralise, Helen. Was that when you started your affair with my father?' Jack asked sardonically.

'No, Jack. My love affair with your father ended the day he married your mother. When, by the way, she claimed she was pregnant by him. But on the honeymoon she had what she said was a miscarriage. Very convenient! Mungo came much later. It's a trick that's been played often enough, and men continue to fall for it.'

'I don't believe you.'

'Jack, I don't care if you do or you don't. It's immaterial to me what you think.'

At this point there was a tap on the door, and the doctor appeared. There was no need for him to speak. His face said it all.

The drive home through the night was a repeat of a drive Jillian remembered so many years ago. The car was different, they were different, but the situation was the same: with Jack in a temper, they had fled from his father and family. Jack sat clutching the steering-wheel, knuckles white. Jillian hunched low in her seat, unsure of what to say or even think. She felt in shock. Not only was there a death to contend with, but this new-found information to digest and adjust to. Jack would need all her support as he came to terms with this discovery, she was sure.

She felt a deep sense of loss at Ralph's sudden death. Larger than life, he was one of those people who seem indestructible. And now he was gone. She could not claim to have known Ralph well, but, apart from that awful Christmas night when he had been so drunk, he had only ever been kind to her, generous too. And she'd known, even before Esmée had told her, that he liked her. She wished she had known the full story before, for then she and Ralph would have been united against Theresa and so much else would have been clear: her dreadful possessiveness, her lying, her hypocrisy.

The more she thought about what had happened, the more everything made sense. Ralph had not been a monster: rather, he had been an honourable, if misguided, man. He had cared for Jack, educated him, been generous to him, when many a man would have turned his back on somebody else's child. In her anger at Jack's choice of Jillian as his wife, Theresa had, no doubt, demanded that Ralph cease keeping him at Cambridge, believing it would make him return to her. And when Ralph tried to repair the damage she'd destroyed the letter. How cruel Theresa was, and how very wrong about her son and his love for her. In the darkness Jillian allowed herself a small, satisfied smile.

When she had first seen Theresa this evening, so confused and pathetic, she had felt sorry for her, but no more. Theresa's deceit had liberated her from that. She did not hate her, but now she resolved that the best thing for her own equilibrium was to try to persuade herself that the woman did not exist. At such an idea she shivered, shocked at her detachment and coldness; and, like a distant echo from the past of another journey with Jack, she momentarily feared that a wrathful God would come to punish her.

'Are you cold?' Jack glanced across at her.

'No, just thinking.' She paused, wondering if he would remember that other conversation, but of course he didn't, it was silly of her to hope he would – it was women who remembered such details.

'I suppose you want to talk about it all.'

'Not unless you want to.' The resigned irritation in his voice made her shiver again. 'I'm here, if you need to.'

'Well, I don't. I never want to speak about it. You understand?'

'Of course.' She would like to have put out her hand to touch him and reassure him, for that was what she would want in his place. But she didn't. Between them was a huge barrier, almost tangible, in the cramped confines of the car. Why it should be there puzzled her, and frightened her too.

In his anger he was driving too fast, but she hunkered further down in her seat so that she could not see the road and could pretend that they were not travelling at this speed. She closed her eyes.

The scrunch of gravel on their driveway woke her.

'Good gracious, I must have been to sleep.'

'Evidently.' Jack switched off the engine.

'I'm sorry.'

'What are you sorry about?'

'I should have stayed awake for you.'

'Why?'

'In case you wanted to talk, of course. And I never think it fair of the passenger to fall asleep.' She climbed out.

'Did you think I might crash in my grief?' He spoke sharply with brittle amusement in his voice.

'No. But I always like to keep you company on a drive.'

'So I've noticed. But tonight it wasn't necessary. I had much to think about and decide.'

'And what have you decided?' She followed him into the house.

'You'll find out, in good time. I need a drink, do you want one?'

'I'll get the ice.'

When she entered the drawing room, Jack was slumped in his favourite chair, his eyes closed. He looked older. She wanted to kiss him, but something stopped her – that same distance she had felt in the car. Instead she poured their whisky. She looked about her: the room had not changed. It was the same room in the same house but they had returned to it a different couple.

'Here's your drink, my darling,' she said. 'I suggest you have this and then go to bed. It's nearly four and you look done in.'

'Jillian, will you do me a favour? Just this once, stop fussing and leave me alone.' He took the glass.

She felt hurt. She knew it was stupid to feel this way; it was selfish of her. She should be concentrating on his feelings, not hers. 'I'm sorry, Jack. I should have thought, of course you want to be on your own.'

'For Christ's sake, stop being sorry all the time!' Jack shouted, and with one swift movement sat up in the chair, picked up his glass and hurled it at her.

Sleep was out of the question. She tossed and turned to the sound of the dawn chorus. Of course, he hadn't thrown the glass at her, she reasoned; he was just angry and had thrown it at nothing. And his anger wasn't for her – what had she done to deserve it? No, he was just angry with everything.

By seven the bed was too rumpled and uncomfortable. She took a quick shower, dressed in jeans and a T-shirt then went downstairs. She had decided the best thing to do was to carry on as normally as possible. And the most normal thing she could do was to cook them both breakfast.

Before entering the kitchen she peeped into the drawing room and, to her immense relief, saw that he was asleep. At least he had had some rest, there would be so much to do in the next few days, she thought, as she went into her kitchen. She put the coffee percolator on, then began a list. The children would have to be told; but how to get hold of Miles, *en route* to India? They didn't even have a schedule of where he was to be or when. She would phone the Foreign Office – they would know what to do. What about Victoria? She crossed to the noticeboard on which was pinned her daughter's end-of-term examination timetable. She ran a finger down the list – English today. Should she wait until the exams were over before breaking the news? She would telephone the headmistress and act on her advice. Now, where was she? Oh, God, the party. What on earth to do? All those people to put off . . . or maybe, given the circumstances, they could still hold it. *Discuss J.*, she scribbled. It would no longer be a surprise party but that couldn't be helped.

She looked up as Jack entered the room. 'Coffee?'

'Thanks.' He sat at the table.

'Bacon and eggs?'

'I couldn't.'

'You must eat.'

'I don't have to do anything.'

'Of course. I think I might have a boiled egg.'

'Eat what you want.'

As she collected the saucepan and a couple of fresh eggs she realised that the antagonism was still there.

'We need to contact Miles somehow.'

'What? You're thinking of calling him back for the funeral of a man not even related to him? He really will thank you for that.'

'We need to discuss whether they should be told. I mean, where do we begin? How do we explain that . . .?' Her voice trailed off.

'That I'm a bastard? Simple, we just tell them.'

'It's not that easy.'

'Of course it is. You just tell them.' He spooned sugar into his coffee.

'I'd already sugared it,' she said, but he ignored her or,

perhaps, he hadn't heard. 'Maybe it would be better to let them continue to think that Ralph was their grandfather.'

'They didn't even know the man.' Jack enunciated each word deliberately.

'You need not speak to me as if I was a child.'

'Then don't act like one. Stop playing this charade of happy families.'

'Jack, you're upset. I understand.'

'You don't understand anything, you never have.'

Jillian turned towards the saucepan and gently lowered the eggs into it. She watched the churning water. She mustn't react, she must keep calm, he had had a momentous shock. She must be patient with him, she told herself.

'Did you really think I would go to that old bastard's funeral? You live in another world, don't you?'

'We might know the truth, but there's no reason that the rest of the world should. If you don't go, then of course people will gossip.'

'Do you think I really care what people think?'

'Yes. Why else do we live the way we do?'

'Without doubt, Jillian, I think you are the stupidest person I know.'

She sat down sharply, folding her hands on her lap so that he would not see them shaking. She knew that the moment she had always dreaded was about to happen; that everything was about to change. She held her breath as if that would delay him speaking.

'You think I'm angry because he's not my father. You've got it all wrong. I'm relieved that he isn't. Now I know that all the hatred and the anger was not my fault, don't you see? It wasn't me, it wasn't some glaring fault in me.'

Jillian felt dizzy with relief. 'I know you're confused now, Jack, but I think you'll see it differently eventually. I've been thinking about it too. Ralph was honourable to bring you up as he did. I'm sure if you looked at him in that way . . .' She knew she was on dangerous ground, but she felt for his sake she should say what she thought. She must help him see it that way: he'd feel better if he did.

'Crap! What upsets me most is what fun he must have had

with my mother. How cruelly he treated her.' He banged his fist into the palm of the other hand with frustration. 'Oh, shit! All those wasted years! I needn't have grafted in the way I have. I needn't have done so many things I hated doing. I could have done or been anything I wanted instead of having to prove myself to him. Do you realise the whole catastrophe of my life would never have happened? I could have been free. I could have gone where I wanted. Done what I chose. I need not have been lumbered with this hideous domesticity that was forced upon me.' He stabbed his forefinger at her.

'Jack! You don't mean this.' Jillian sat rigid on the hard pine chair.

'Oh, yes, I do. You can't imagine how many times I've dreamed of this moment. Of being honest. Of saying what I think. I never wanted to marry you. I did it to spite him – to prove him wrong, to show him, my father, how a real gentleman should behave. And I needn't have done it! That's why I'm angry with him, with you, with the whole lousy mess.' He stood up abruptly.

Jillian's hands were in the air now, pushing at nothing but trying to push his words away. 'I can't listen to this,' she cried. 'You didn't say it. I didn't hear it.' He looked down at her, and there was such loathing for her in his face, the face she loved, that she had to look away. He said no more but left the room.

Jillian sat motionless for some time. The early-morning June sun poured through the windows, which normally would have given her great pleasure but which today she did not even notice. Although shocked at the scene that had just taken place, she was not surprised. Had she not waited all the years of her marriage for this? There was a strange satisfaction in knowing that, despite all his denials, all his protestations of love, she had been right: he resented her and their union. The guilt that had never left her had, perhaps, been a preparation for this, a way of limiting the shock.

Suddenly she reached out jerkily for the pot of marmalade. She screwed the lid back on. Then she undid it. Like a soldier wounded in war, assessing the damage to his body, she sat quietly and assessed the damage to her soul. Sadness, rejection and the ever-present guilt played follow-my-leader through her mind. And then, with no warning, at first slowly, then gathering momentum a voice deep inside her said, 'Here, hang on a minute! Are you going to let him get away with that?' This voice would not stop, but berated her, encouraged her, goaded her until she leaped to her feet and rushed from the room.

Jack was packing. His large leather hold-all lay open on the bed, surrounded by shirts, ties, underwear and socks. Her new-found anger dissipated rapidly to be replaced by fear.

'What's this?'

'What does it look like?' He was balling his socks the better to pack them.

'I always pack for you. Let me.' She picked up a shirt, preparing to fold it, her movements slow to delay his departure.

'I am perfectly capable of packing my own case. I'd rather do it myself.'

'But you'll make a mess and everything will be creased.'

'For Christ's sake, Jillian, stop fussing. I can't stand it. It drives me bloody mad.'

'I don't know what you mean.' She hugged his shirt to her.

'I mean the way you witter and flap about like an old woman. "Make sure you do this. Have you got enough of that? Is that damp? Don't want you getting a chill! Eat it up, are you ill, are you well? Did your fucking bowels move this morning?" Do you want me to go on? There's plenty more like that. I'm a grown man and you treat me like a fucking child!' He was shouting at her, his face ugly, distorted with his rage.

'I don't speak to you like that.' She was aware that she was shaking and folded her arms so that he could not see. 'I care for you, I always have. It's my job. It's what I'm here for.'

'Ah, I'll admit you've been the perfect housewife, you made sure of that, didn't you? There was no question that anyone could criticise you on that level. But, dear God, did you know how fucking boring you are?'

She stepped back, as if he had physically attacked her. She

cleared her throat. 'I think . . .' she began, unsure how to continue. 'I admit I've worked hard to prove I was good enough for you. So that you could never regret being with me. What was wrong in that?' She took a deep breath, aware her stomach was churning, her nerves jangling. 'But that was only a part of it. I wanted everything perfect because I love you. It was all I had to give you, don't you see?' She could hear the tightness in her voice, caused by the battle she was having not to burst into tears.

'Don't give me the sob-story, please. No one does anything they don't want to do. You enjoy slaving away, always on the go, martyring yourself.'

'I never have. I've never complained to you or anyone.' The sheer effrontery of what he said threatened to take her breath away. 'I see what I do as my role, my part of the bargain.'

'What bargain? I give, you take?'

'You give money, the wherewithal to make our lifestyle possible. I give my time, my love, my efforts. But I'd lie if I said I love every minute of it. I don't. There are days when I wake up and think, Not that same bloody routine again.' He stepped forward as if to say something. 'Let me finish. You're right. I didn't contribute money – but I did a lot else. And if you think back, Jack, I'm for ever thanking you for this life. When was the last time you thanked me for doing anything? And don't you ever consider I might sometimes like to be doing something else? You get away from here regularly, you travel, see the world. Don't you think sometimes I would like to be free too?' She leaned now upon her white and gold dressing-table, half sat on it, unsure if her legs would support her if she stood. Her anger had returned in full.

'Free! Free? You think I'm that? I work my bloody guts out for you.'

'Don't lie to me, Jack.' She was shouting too. 'We both know that everything you did was to spite your old man. There was no other reason. If, as you so politely tell me, you didn't want to marry me, you would hardly have worked your "bloody guts" out for me, now would you? Grow up, Jack. I'm sorry for your pain, for finding out that he was not your father. But don't take your anger and your disappointment out on me. I didn't deserve this.' She pushed herself away from the dressing-table and, her head held high, she stalked from the room. On the landing she leaned against the wall. She felt dizzy, she felt sick, but most of all she felt angry.

'I'm going then,' Jack said, coming into the kitchen, and placing his black leather bag on the floor. 'I'll call this evening, when I get there.'

'Where are you going?'

His tone was normal, the anger had left his face.

'I told you, Spain.'

'I thought that was next week. Do you have to go?'

'Yes.'

'But we need to talk.'

'I have to think. To sort my head out. There's been too much . . .'

'Of course. I . . .' She felt vulnerable now that her anger had drained away at the sight of him. 'What about the funeral?'

'I've already told you, I'm not going to that. You can't expect me to.'

'Then your birthday. You'll be back for that?'

'Yes.' He bent down to pick up his bag. He looked at her, then glanced away guiltily as if, she thought, he were ashamed.

'Jack?'

'Jillian, I shouldn't have spoken to you in the way I did. It was unforgivable of me. You were right, you didn't deserve that.'

Quickly she stood up, crossed to him, her arms held out in front of her. 'I'm sorry too, Jack. I hate to argue with you. I love you.' She sank into his embrace.

'Sorry.' He kissed the top of her head. 'I'll phone.'

At the door he paused and blew her a kiss.

Such sharp mood swings were almost too much to deal with. In the past twelve hours she had gone from grief, shock, despair, to anger, reconciliation and almost normality. Of course, it was that word 'almost' that bothered her. She would have liked to pretend that those cruel scenes had not taken place; that it had been a bizarre nightmare. Only she couldn't. The memory of his anger and bitterness would remain with her always. He had said he was sorry, but she knew that nothing could ever be the same again.

So what was she to do? What did she want? She wondered why she even bothered to ask herself these questions. Somehow she would have to create the illusion that everything was all right, that he loved her and regretted nothing. And this awful sadness that weighed heavy inside her must be kept secret from the world.

5

Ralph's funeral was impressive. Jillian was glad that she had telephoned Helen Carter and suggested they go together, for Helen was in no state to go on her own. The woman who had always been so vital and full of life seemed in this past week to have shrunk and her spirit was sadly diminished.

'I don't know how I shall go on, knowing he's no longer here. You see, Jillian, I could always telephone him if I had any problems, and he would always solve them for me. Now, without him, I'm afraid of life, of everything.'

'It's hard, I'm sure. I can only imagine what you're going through. But I just know you'll cope, you're that sort of person. And Ralph would want you no other way.' Even as she spoke, she felt that her words were woefully inadequate.

'But he was the love of my life. And without that love what is the point?'

Jillian linked her arm in Helen's and shuddered at the bleakness of her words. Jack was not dead, but she understood exactly what Helen meant.

Despite her grief, Esmée was managing admirably. It was she who had made the meticulous plans for the service, the interment and now for the wake back at the house, in which Ralph's personality still seemed present.

'It could be a new career for me, don't you think? Funerals

arranged, distance no object.' She laughed but she sounded more like someone trying desperately not to cry, Jillian thought. No doubt with all the arrangements to be made she had been kept busy. She would probably need a lot of support in the weeks ahead. 'I presume Jack's birthday party is still on this Saturday?' she asked. 'I mean, I don't want to miss it.'

'I wasn't sure what to do, but I haven't cancelled anything.'

'Then don't. A good thrash is what we'll need, when this is over. I'm disappointed Jack didn't come. Daddy supported him for all those years and it seems a bit petty-minded not to come to lay him to rest.'

'It's difficult for you, Esmée, but it's nigh on impossible for Jack. He's devastated. And he had to go to Spain, on business.'

'Oh, sure, we mustn't let death get in the way of greed, must we?' And Esmée laughed again, a hollow laugh tinged with hysteria.

It was a mistake, Jillian felt, that Theresa was there, for she had no idea what was going on. She wandered around making polite conversation, smiling constantly, the gracious hostess she had always been. Since Ralph had not wanted people to know she was ill, she was looked at askance by many, and her progress was followed by shocked comment.

'She insisted on coming. Short of locking her in her room there was nothing we could do,' Liz explained to Jillian. 'Everyone thinks it's an awful tragedy she's like this, but I'm not so sure. Just look at her! She's having a lovely time, she hasn't a clue that old Ralph's gone. She's spared the tears and recriminations. And, to be quite honest, she's much nicer now she's batty. At least the smile these days is genuine.'

'I didn't know you didn't like her, Liz?'

'Hated her, Jillian. She loved nothing better than to put me down, just because I'm a bit on the large size, and I've never been one for feminine wiles. Of course, she couldn't do that with you. She wouldn't have got away with it because you're too lovely.'

'I wish I'd known. I could have done with an ally.'

'One thing I learned early on with this family was to keep my own counsel. Nothing personal, you understand? But there was enough friction already without adding to it. And it would have played right into Theresa's hands – if she got an inkling that we were becoming pals she'd have moved in to separate us, just like she tried to do with you and Jack. Just like she tried with me and Mungo, only dear old Mungo's too sweet and too canny. Without doubt, though, Theresa is the ma-in-law from hell!'

Jillian, like everyone else, had regarded Liz and Mungo as nice but dim, and had rapidly to reconsider this. 'But why? You're a good wife to Mungo, and I try my best with Jack. You'd think she'd be pleased for them, wouldn't you?'

'My mother says it's quite common with mothers of sons. They can't deal with another woman being fussed over in the family when, until we moseyed along, they'd been the queen bee. Pathetic, isn't it?'

'I hope I'm not like that with my son. Mind you, I don't think he thinks I'm the queen bee.'

'Where are your children? I was looking forward to meeting them.'

'Jack didn't want them to come. In the circumstances,' she said obliquely, unsure if Liz knew about Jack's parentage.

'What a shock that was! If Mungo's been left the bulk of Ralph's fortune, he says he wants to work out some way of sharing it with Jack.'

'What a wonderful person you married.'

'I think so.' Liz beamed.

Ralph's will was not that simple. After the friends had left, only the family and Helen remained for its reading. Jillian, not regarding herself as a true member of the family, was leaving when Esmée stopped her. 'I think you should stay.'

'He won't have left anything to Jack.'

'No, but he might have left something to you.'

Just as everyone was sitting in the drawing room for the will to be read, Theresa had a lucid moment.

'What's that woman doing here?' She pointed menacingly at Jillian.

'I asked her to stay, Mother.'

'This is my house, Esmée. I shall say who is to be invited and who is not.'

'It doesn't matter, Esmée, I'll go.' Jillian searched around on the floor at her feet for her handbag.

Liz leaned over the back of the sofa. 'Don't rush off, she'll be doo-lally again in a minute.'

She was right for, within a minute, Theresa's mind was wandering again and she had to be led away by her nurse – a new one, with a pleasant face, Jillian noticed.

Mungo's plan to share with his brother was not to be. Most of Ralph's vast fortune was to be put into a trust. His wife, Esmée, and Mungo were the beneficiaries. In dry legal words, Ralph explained his actions: he had felt that neither Mungo nor Esmée had the necessary expertise to manage the fortune he had amassed and that the trustees he had appointed would be far more competent.

'Fair enough,' Mungo said good-humouredly.

'I'd have lost it all in divorce settlements!' Esmée smiled.

Of Jack there was no mention.

There were legacies for servants, for faithful employees. The Lord Whisky Sanctuary Fund was mentioned, as was a home for aged horses. There was a large bequest in trust for Helen, the income from which would protect her for the rest of her life. The capital would revert to the family trust upon her death.

And then, just as everyone thought that the lawyer had finished, he read out a recently added codicil. Ralph had set aside a sum of money for Jillian Stirling to claim in the event of Jack Stirling deserting her.

As promised, Jack had telephoned when he arrived in Spain. Jillian did not hear from him again but, then, she hadn't expected to. He was never very good at keeping in touch. Nor did she phone him. When he was on a business trip she did not like to disturb him unless it was important. But after she returned from the funeral on Wednesday, still saddened and alone in the house, she needed to speak to him, to be reassured that he loved her, no matter what he'd said in pain and anger.

'Mr Stirling is no longer staying with us,' the heavily accented voice of a receptionist told her.

'Is he flying home?' She was pleased at the prospect.

'I really could not say, madam. Mr Stirling left no instructions.'

The call was disconnected. What could be better than that Jack should return a couple of days early for his party?

Immediately she telephoned his flat in London – she always thought of it as his flat, not theirs. She wanted to leave a simple message of welcome on the answer-machine: she liked to do that when he was returning from a journey. But he had forgotten to switch it on, and she listened to the ringing tone, imagining it echoing through the empty rooms. She went to bed in a much happier frame of mind, certain she would see him in the morning.

Organised as she was, there was still much to do and Thursday flew by in a welter of preparations. She was puzzled that he had not arrived. On Friday she had to drive to Victoria's school, having arranged for her to take the weekend off. She was stabbed with guilt as she remembered the lie she had told the headmistress, saying an elderly relative was visiting, but she did not think the school would regard a father's birthday party as reason enough for two and half days away.

Jillian waited, hiding her impatience, as her daughter insisted on saying a lengthy goodbye to her best friend.

'You'd think you were saying goodbye to Emma for ever, instead of a weekend.'

'I wish she could have come.' Victoria said, twisting round to wave a last goodbye. 'I suppose everyone will be geriatric.'

'My darling, your father's only forty. That's hardly one foot in the grave.'

'Sounds old to me. I'm sure I'll be bored witless.'

'I bore myself. Or didn't you know?' Jillian smiled at her daughter.

'What does that mean?'

'Think about it.'

'I can't be bothered. I want to stop in Cambridge. I've got to get something to wear.'

'Victoria, that can't be necessary. You've got a cupboard full of clothes. Wear the blue Laura Ashley.'

'Laura Ashley – you have to be joking! I'm never wearing that again.'

'In any case, I haven't got time. The house is upside-down, there's so much to do.'

'I knew you'd say that. I could have put money on it. You're so predictable, Mum. And I don't know why you're flapping – everything will be all right, it always is.'

'Thank you for your faith in me, but the answer is still no.'

'Dad said I could have a new dress.'

'When?'

'When he came to see me last week.'

'He didn't tell me. Did he say why?' Jillian asked, making her voice sound as if it was an idle query. Victoria had a secretive streak and never liked being probed – a bit like her father. He must have had second thoughts about telling her that her grandfather was dead, she decided.

'He said he was off to Spain and he felt like a hug.'

'How strange.'

'Not really, I'm immensely huggable. Mind you, I did wonder if he'd come to talk to me about his father dying, but he didn't.'

'How do know about that?'

'Mum, the school buys newspapers, you know. And we are allowed to read them. Not everybody treats us as kiddiwinks.' Without looking at her Jillian knew her daughter would be rolling her eyes with exasperation at the stupidity of adults.

'I didn't think.'

'Obviously not.' Victoria paused, but Jillian sensed she hadn't finished. 'As it is, I'm fairly hacked off. I would like to have been told – by either of you.' She hadn't finished. 'It looked distinctly odd my not knowing the old codger was dead, of having to read about it in a newspaper when somebody pointed it out to me. And I had to pretend I knew. That wasn't fair, Mum. After all, I had a right to know – he was my flesh and blood. In a normal family I'd have met him, wouldn't I?'

'Yes. But then I'm never sure what a normal family should be like.'

'Granny Stirling, before she went gaga, said it's your fault we never met him. That he never forgave Daddy for marrying you when you weren't suitable. And, what's more, she said you're jealous of her because Daddy loves her so. If that's so then you're responsible for us being cut off from half our family, and I don't think that's fair either.' Victoria spoke quickly, urgently, as if she'd been mulling this over, practising it even.

Jillian had to hold the steering-wheel tight. Now was the moment when she should tell her daughter the truth about Theresa, that she was an evil old snob who lied. She took a deep breath to dampen the spurt of anger she felt, controlling herself. 'It's not a subject I wish to discuss. I'm sorry we embarrassed you over your grandfather's death but your father and I thought it was for the best.'

'Nothing aggravates me more than to hear adults say that – it's a total cop-out. Now, can we go shopping in Cambridge?'

'I suppose so, if you're very quick.'

Of course Victoria was not quick. She dithered between two outfits, which to Jillian looked identical. And it was only when Jillian spoke sharply to her, taking her by surprise, that she made up her mind. She sulked mightily when Jillian refused point-blank to shop for shoes, so the drive back to Fen Manor passed mainly in silence. She did not want to spoil Jack's birthday, she would wait until it was over, but he was going to have to talk to Victoria about her attitude. There was no point in Jillian doing it, for she knew her daughter would not listen to her. She never did. And was it such a surprise, when Theresa had made sure so assiduously that they had scant respect for her?

Jack was still not back, but she had plenty to do. First, though, she checked the messages on her answer-machine. To her joy the first was from Miles, to say he would be arriving at Heathrow and if no one was there to meet him he would hire a car. Three were from Esmée, each giving a different arrival time. The caterers and the bank had called. The rest were from Gary, Jack's partner, in ascending order of irritation, demanding that she telephone him the moment she returned. Her initial reaction was to ignore him, but then she dialled the number. As she waited for the connection she looked at herself in the mirror which hung above the desk and wondered if she would have time tomorrow for a shampoo and blow dry.

'Gary? It's Jillian obeying your orders to call.' She couldn't resist saying that.

'Where the hell have you been? I've been calling for hours.'

'I had to go and collect Victoria from school for the party. You're both still coming, I hope?' She hoped nothing of the sort, but she did not wish the man ill so a mild stomach upset that would prevent him attending would suit her very well.

'Has Jack been in touch?'

'Not since last Saturday.'

'Do you know where he is? If so, I've a right to know.'

She did not like his belligerent tone, nor did she like the wisp of fear that flitted through her mind. Still, she had no intention of letting him know that she had no idea where Jack was. 'He'll be back some time today. It's his birthday tomorrow, don't forget. He wouldn't miss that.'

'I hope for your sake you're right.'

'What does that mean?' There it was again, a clenching deep in her gut, a certainty that all was not well. She brushed the idea away. 'You're so enigmatic.'

'I'm driving over.' And the line went dead. Again Jillian looked at her reflection. What an unpleasant man he was. And, no, she would not have time to go to the hairdresser's. And, no, she was not going to let him wind her up. Of course Jack would be here – any minute now. Back in her kitchen she prepared a light supper, just a quiche and some salad she'd decided – keep busy, don't think.

'Anyone home?'

'Esmée! I didn't hear you. I'm so glad you came early. Victoria's already here. Miles phoned. He's back from India. I don't suppose you've heard from Jack by any chance?'

'He's cutting it a bit fine, isn't he? Or haven't you told him about the party?'

'No. I thought about it but he said he'd be back for his birthday so I didn't bother. Now I'm concerned that he's got tied up somewhere but isn't worried because he thinks it's just him.'

'He's an inconsiderate sod, not phoning. Darling, you look worried. Don't. I reckon he's got an allergy to the flaming instrument. He's always been the same. I live on the phone and he wouldn't touch it. Still, I'd better go and see my adorable niece. Don't bother – you're busy – I can look after myself. Am I in the usual room?'

As Jillian continued with the supper she felt glad for Victoria that she got on so well with Esmée, that she had someone older to talk to. If she couldn't have a close relationship with her daughter she would prefer Esmée to fill the role more than anyone else she knew. How strange it was, the way life and relationships turned out; once she'd been so afraid of Esmée, now she regarded her as her best friend.

The rickety noise of a clapped-out engine made her look up hopefully. She had invited Patsy to the party. She missed her and regretted their falling out. She would like to be friends again. Patsy had not replied to the invitation but, then, she wouldn't have expected her to – such social niceties were not for her. She went to the back door but it was the jobbing gardener come to do a last cut of the grass. She liked the sound of the mower, the smell of the new-cut grass – sounds and smells of an English summer. Then the telephone rang again, interrupting her simple enjoyment. At this rate she'd have to take the thing off the hook.

'Well, of course I met the Rolling Stones. I knew everybody. The sixties were very busy. Weren't they, Jillian?'

'Sorry, what did you say?' Jillian looked up as Esmée and Victoria, arm in arm, entered the kitchen.

'Your daughter doesn't believe that we were part of Swinging London. I think the poor cretin thinks we were born this age!' Esmée laughed as she sat down at the table. 'The young are so distrusting, I mean ... Heavens, Jillian, what on earth's the matter? Love, what's happened?'

'It's nothing.'

'Don't be bloody daft. You don't look as if it's nothing.

Victoria, be a little angel, and piss off for five minutes, will you?'

'Why?'

'Because I say so. Because I wish to speak to your mother in private. And I don't want you sulking and skulking. Is that understood?'

'I don't sulk.'

'Yes, you do. It's the prerogative of the very young, so make the most of it. You won't get away with it later. Now, scoot.' Esmée waited for Victoria to go, which she did with bad grace. 'This looks like a double-gin situation.' Esmée crossed the kitchen to the fridge and collected the bottles of gin and tonic. 'Is it Jack? Have you heard from him? Is he not coming? Is that why you look so down in the dumps?'

'No. Something else.' Her voice was weak, as if the effort of speaking was almost too much. 'It was the bank manager – he's an old friend. He was asking for Jack. He wondered if I knew where he was. And if I knew why he had cleared all the money from our account.'

6

The bank manager was not the only person querying Jack's movement of funds. Jillian and Esmée had no time to discuss the bank's call before Gary and Cherry arrived in a squeal of brakes and scattered gravel.

'So, where is he?' Gary asked, not bothering with a preliminary greeting.

'Good afternoon, Gary,' Jillian said pointedly.

'This is no time for sarcasm, Jillian. Are you going to tell me where the shit's scuttled off to?'

'Do you have to be so rude? Still, yes, I suppose you do, you don't know any better, do you, poor soul?' Esmée leaned languidly against the cooker. 'Anyone for a drink?'

'Esmée, sorry, do help yourself.' Jillian turned to Gary. 'I told you on the telephone, he'll be back for his party. You'd have seen him tomorrow in any case.'

283

'You seem very laid-back about all this. I wish I shared your confidence.'

'Anyone hungry?' she asked, hoping they were, so that she would have something to do. Since the call from the bank she had been left with a strong sense of foreboding.

'I thought the countryside was supposed to be quiet. It's like Piccadilly Circus out there.' Esmée peered out of the window. 'It looks as if your prodigal sister has turned up, unless, that is, you have many friends who drive about in psychedelic vans.'

'Patsy!' Forgetting food, forgetting guests, Jillian rushed out to the backyard. Until now she had been able to control herself, but at the sight of Patsy, larger than ever, even more oddly dressed, clambering backwards out of her van, she burst into tears.

'What's this? Come on, it hasn't been that long.' Patsy grinned at her. 'Well, this is a damp welcome.' Her smile faded. 'Love, what is it?'

'I'm sorry . . . Seeing you . . . I just lost it . . .' Jillian flapped her hand impotently, unable to continue.

'Esmée, what's going on?' The group from the kitchen was now standing on the steps.

'You might well ask, Patsy.'

'Who are you?' Gary asked bluntly.

'I could ask the same of you. Majored in charm, did you?'

'There's no need to take that tone with my husband.' Cherry flicked her mane of bright-yellow hair defiantly.

'I'm Jack's partner, if it's any business of yours.'

'So you're the creep.'

'Patsy, please, don't. You'll only make matters worse.'

'Then somebody tell me what's happened.'

'I don't think we should be discussing matters with people who aren't involved with Jack.'

'She's my sister, Gary.'

'So you're the druggie.' At this Patsy gave Gary a withering look. 'It would seem your brother-in-law has done a bunk.'

'You're going to look mighty silly when he turns up tomorrow. Not only that but I'd be fully prepared to say you've slandered my brother. Shall we sue? What a jolly jape!'

'You think you scare me, Esmée?'

'If Gary's right, bickering among ourselves isn't going to help. If Gary's wrong, then behaviour like this could make for bad blood between us all,' said Patsy.

'Mum!' They looked up at the window from which Victoria was leaning. 'Telephone,' she yelled. The rush to return to the house was like a stampede. They all piled into the kitchen.

With pounding heart, Jillian grabbed the receiver off the wall. 'Yes,' she said breathlessly praying that it would be Jack.

'Jane of Jolly Jeeves here, Mrs Stirling. We were wondering if we could bring some of the food over tonight. It'll make things easier in the morning.'

'I'm sorry, Jane, that won't be possible.' With no explanation she hung up. 'It was the caterers,' she said.

'I think your sister's right. We mustn't fall out. And poor Jillian looks done in. I think we have to sit down and pool what we know about Jack and his movements. Then, perhaps, we'll reach a conclusion. What do you say?' Cherry said, with quiet reason.

'Do you think we'd be more comfortable in the drawing room?'

'I don't think this is a social event, Jillian,' Esmée remonstrated. 'It doesn't really matter where we discuss this. I've always loved your kitchen. Let's stay here. In any case, it's nearer the ice for the gin.'

'Well, if you don't mind . . .' Jillian looked up. 'Now, who could that be? Jack?'

'I'll go and see.' Gary was halfway out of the kitchen already. The others waited but no one spoke. Victoria ambled in, looked about her, said, 'Hi,' but, when no one responded, wandered out again.

When the door opened Miles entered. 'Thank God you're all right, Mum. I thought something must have happened to you. I mean, Dad's message was so cryptic.'

'You've heard from your father?' Gary jumped in.

'The British consul got hold of me. Though how the hell he knew where to find me is a bit of a mystery. Makes you think, doesn't it? Do they spy on us?'

'What did he say, Miles?'

'I didn't meet him. There was just a message that I was to return home as quickly as possible. I thought the consul wouldn't go to all the trouble of finding where I was unless it was an emergency. So I came.' He dropped the large haversack he was holding on to the floor. 'If there's a drink or any grub going, I'd love some.'

'I'll make some sandwiches.'

'You sit down, Jillian. You've got things to discuss, I'll do the food,' Cherry insisted.

'I'm sorry to say this, everyone,' Gary said heavily, 'but it sounds to me as if Jack arranged for Miles to be sent for so that Jillian had some support. You see, Miles, your father and I were due a large sum of money this week, a bridging loan for the purchase of a building, due today. The vendor has included some severe penalty clauses if we fail to come up with the dosh. The loan was paid to us, but unfortunately it didn't go into the company account – for a very good reason. All cheques written on this account require both our signatures. I haven't got to the bottom of it yet, but it would seem that some prat at the bank, presumably instructed by Jack, paid the money to another bank. Of course, they said they could not give me any information, but after a little judicious bribery I discovered it's no longer there. The only conclusion is that Jack has taken it. Now we have to find out where.'

'I can't believe that! Not Dad!'

'One of the sad facts of life, Miles, is that every embezzler or crook is somebody's son, husband or father.'

'I'm sure there's an explanation, Gary. An error. A misunderstanding. There *has* to be. I mean, Jack's got expensive tastes, these days. He would need an enormous amount of money to keep up his current standard of living.' Esmée wasn't smiling now.

'He has. This loan was for three million. I haven't had time to check if other accounts we have are in order.'

Jillian felt as if the walls of the room were closing in on her. If all this was true, then was it possible he had engineered those dreadful scenes with her? Had he done it so that she would hate him and not mind him going? Had this always been his plan? Had he waited until his father died – he would not have wanted Ralph to know he was a criminal. She shuddered at that word and pulled her cardigan closely to her, as if being warmer would make this nightmare go away. Or had Ralph's dying simply happened at an opportune time, and he had grabbed it, knowing full well that because of the shock he had received, she would make excuses for him, understand his wanting to get away, and thus gave himself precious time. So many theories clattered about in her mind that she thought her head would burst.

'It sounds to me as if my brother was planning this. He isn't the sort of person who would act on the spur of the moment. To get away with this, something of such magnitude, he had to have bank accounts arranged and a bolt-hole. I thought it was odd the other day, Jillian, when you said you had no idea where he was. You always used to know. If you didn't, he has been planning this for some time, with or without an accomplice,' Esmée said.

'He has an accomplice all right. I loathe her. Why men are so stupid as to fall for the little girly-voiced helpless baby-doll act beats me every time. But that's men for you, isn't it?' Cherry waved the bread-knife at them to emphasise her point.

'Shut up, Cherry,' Gary snapped.

'Do you have to add to her worry?' Patsy asked angrily.

'Cara!' Jillian and Esmée said, in astonished unison.

How nice it would be, thought Jillian, if she could faint, and wake up to find it was all a nightmare. Instead, she knew that she must get everything into a rational order, to prove not only to herself but to them that this was all a dreadful mistake. But she feared that it would be hard to persuade herself he hadn't gone.

'Miles, I think we should go and check your father's desk. No, Gary, I want to do this with my son, thank you,' she said, sufficiently firmly for Gary to sit down again. 'Thank you, Cherry, you're being such a help.' She smiled at her, realising that Cherry had been just that.

In Jack's study she found what she dreaded: his desk was empty. Jillian didn't feel surprised: it was as she expected.

'When could he have done this? And why?'

'I don't know, Miles. But there's something else you should know. I'm afraid your grandfather is dead.'

'I know – it was even in the Indian papers. Seems everyone knew Grandad.'

'When we got back the night he died, your father and I had a row. I went to bed and left him down here. I presumed he'd slept in the chair, but perhaps he was clearing his desk then.'

'What was the row about?'

'I'd rather not say, Miles. It's something I'd rather forget.' She looked away from him, not wanting him to see her eyes, certain that the pain was still there. 'He was upset, he'd had some very bad news, and I think it was that that made him do this.'

'Mum, this is very serious. If Gary's right he's looking at prison. And, if Cherry's right, he deserves it.'

An hour later they were still in the kitchen. Jillian's mother and Rob had arrived, summoned, to Jillian's annoyance, by Patsy.

A ring at the doorbell made them all start. For a precious second Jillian hoped it was Jack, before sense reminded her that he had a key and, in any case, never used the front door.

'I'll go.' Miles returned a few moments later with Ed Kingsman, the bank manager.

'Gracious, Ed. What are you doing here? The party isn't until tomorrow.' Jillian realised how rude she sounded and added quickly, 'This is a lovely surprise.'

'Miles telephoned me at home and suggested it might be good idea if I came. Thank you, Miles, a whisky and soda would be fine, but you'd better make it a small one.' He placed his briefcase on the floor, but as he nodded at the group, Jillian noticed he frowned as if not pleased to see them.

'Perhaps you can shed some light on what Jack is about.' Gary plonked himself on the chair nearest Ed.

'You're Jack's partner, aren't you? I'm afraid there's nothing I can tell you. I'm Jack's personal banker, as you know. We've nothing to do with his business interests.'

288

'Ah, come on, don't give me that. How much has he got in his accounts with you?' Gary persisted.

'I'm sure you're aware I cannot discuss a client's business.' Ed Kingsman sipped his drink appreciatively.

'I have not mentioned our telephone conversation to anyone, Ed, but I think his partner has a right to know, and everyone else here is family.' Jillian leaned across the table towards Gary. 'Jack's cleaned our account out.'

'Oh, dear God, no!' Mary exclaimed, adding to the shocked gasps, trying to grab her daughter's hand to comfort her.

'Please, Mum, don't. And, Ed, I think you should know that Jack has a mistress. Gary has phoned her, but her flatmate told him that she has gone, she thinks, to South America on holiday.' Jillian spoke calmly, as if of everyday matters.

'You didn't say, Jillian, about another woman. I thought it was just the money.' Mary looked shocked.

'Just the money!' Gary exploded. 'It's my life we're talking about here.'

'And sorry I am for you, Gary, but my daughter's world is shattering about her.'

'Christ, someone give me a gin,' Esmée said.

'And what about the party? Has anyone thought about that? I mean, you don't want to be bothering about that, do you, Jillian? I think it should be cancelled.'

'It's too late, Mum. The caterers have cooked all that food. I can't let them down.'

'The point is, Jillian, do you really want to face all those people tomorrow, who by then may have heard what's happened? All gossiping as you pass by,' Esmée asked.

'No. It's the last thing I want.'

'Then cancel.'

'But how? I don't want the party, but I don't know if I could face putting everyone off either.'

'Jillian, undoubtedly you have lists and more lists of names and telephone numbers. You don't have to do it, the rest of us will. I suggest we just say that something has turned up and the party has been put off. Patsy and I can do it between us.'

'If you think so. I'll sort out my master list.'

'See? what did I say? This woman has a list for everything.' Esmée smiled at her.

Jillian was aware as she searched for it that the others were talking about her, for their voices were suddenly lowered.

'Here we are.' She returned to them with a notepad. 'Why has everyone stopped talking? What were you saying?'

'Just general chit-chat about what my brother is.'

'I was saying, it could be worse, at least you've got this house.' Her mother smiled encouragingly at her.

Jillian wished they would all stop smiling at her like that; it was similar to the smile you gave someone who has just announced she is terminally ill.

'I'm afraid, it's not that simple,' said Ed. 'He remortgaged the house a few weeks back.'

'But it's Jillian's house. I well remember when they bought it she told me, "Mum, don't worry." That Jack had put it in her name so that if anything bad ever happened creditors wouldn't be able to take it away from her. That's right, isn't it, Jillian?'

'That's what he said.' Though Jillian knew he'd put the house in her name for two reasons: certainly, the first was that something could be salvaged from any catastrophe. The second was to prevent her running to his father again for help.

'Then there's no problem. Sell it, buy something smaller, and invest the rest,' Patsy said practically.

'Except it isn't Jillian's to sell. She signed the papers, which transferred ownership to her husband. Then he took out the mortgage.' Ed looked gloomier by the minute.

'What the hell did you do that for?'

'Because I didn't know.' Jillian remembered now the stack of papers Jack had given her to sign. 'I didn't think to ask what I was signing.'

'You prat. You deserve to lose it.'

'Patsy!'

'She'll be all right. You know me, Mum, I never did set much store by money and my sister's lifestyle. Now, she'll be able to find herself.'

'You always did talk a load of crap, Patsy. But your timing tonight takes the biscuit.' Esmée glared at her.

'Hang on a minute. It won't be binding. To do something like that a woman has to have independent legal advice, otherwise it's not legal,' Cherry, who until now had said little, added brightly.

'I know what Ed is about to say. I signed something saying I had been advised by my lawyers and that I understood the implications of signing. Isn't that so?' Ed did not answer, merely bowed his head. 'I know it sounds stupid to you, Patsy, but I trusted Jack. I had no reason not to.'

'Still, you've got that nice car.' Mary beamed.

'We lease all of them,' Gary said.

'And my car, Gary? The one Dad gave me for my birthday?'

'Sorry, Miles.' Gary shrugged his shoulders.

'They don't have to know at school, do they? I couldn't bear the shame.' This was Victoria, who had sat silent so far.

'I doubt, at this rate, that that will be a problem. Your mother won't be able to afford the fees.' There was a look of satisfaction on Patsy's face as she said this.

'You should have stopped him, Mum. How could you let this happen to me?' Victoria sobbed. 'I hate you. No wonder Daddy left you!' She stood up, pushing herself away from the table. 'It's all your fault! Gran said he should never have married you.' And with that, Victoria flounced from the room. They heard her run up the stairs crying hysterically.

'That one needs a good clip round the ear, if you ask me.'

'Well, no one *is* asking you, Mum.' Jillian, white-faced, rounded on her mother. Rob quickly poured her a drink.

'Then Oxford's out for me too,' Miles said, the truth slowly dawning. 'Oh, fucking great!' He kicked at the door of a kitchen cabinet. 'You must have known, Mum. You must have had some inkling. Or are you too thick for that?'

The silence that ensued was heavy with embarrassment, and everyone found something on which to concentrate rather than Jillian and her son.

'Yes, I must be – I'd no idea. Your father didn't confide in me,' she said, with quiet dignity.

'You can help, Patsy. Jillian gave you her share of your father's house. You'll have to give it back,' Mary said.

'I'll do no such thing!'

The row that ensued swirled about Jillian as she sat transfixed at the table. Everyone had an opinion. Everyone knew better than she what she was to do. Everyone, it seemed, was far wiser than she. Everyone had seen this coming. No one had a good word for Jack.

'Shut up! Shut up, all of you!' Jillian sprang to her feet. 'I want you all to go, now. I've had it up to here! I can't take any more. Do you understand?'

'We're only trying to help, Jillian.'

'Being wise after the event and slandering my husband isn't helping. For Christ's sake, go!' As she marched from the room everyone stood slack-mouthed with astonishment. No one had ever heard Jillian lose her temper before.

Chapter Eight

1

Although Jillian hadn't expected to sleep, she did, deeply, for the whole night. When she first awoke she felt rested, well and happy. Then, like an avalanche, everything flooded back. She lay for a while in the large bed she had shared for so long with Jack, and part of her still refused to accept what everyone said had happened. But another, larger part of her knew that it had.

Looking at the ceiling above her, she remembered that only last week she had discussed with Jack the possibility of having it painted to look like a summer sky. He had laughed at her and said how naff it sounded, but if it was what she wanted she must go ahead and do it. Even as he had spoken, he had known that the house was no longer hers, that it would be sold. She had lost her husband, her marriage and her home. But like so many people, faced suddenly with bereavement, she could not cry.

Vaguely she could hear someone moving about. At eight it was far too early for either of her children to be up. Did that mean someone else had stayed last night? She hoped it wasn't her mother: she didn't think she could face her concerned agitation this morning. If Gary was still here she would go out, she decided. She felt sorry for him too. At least at thirty nine, even if the prospect was daunting, she was still young enough to think of starting again – but how old was Gary? In his mid-fifties she was sure, and to face bankruptcy at that age would not be fun. Perhaps he was afraid, too, that his young wife would leave him now the money had gone. Odd that her mind flitted about, even now.

Or was it? Last night it had been so easy to think only of herself, and the effect Jack's actions would have on her, but it wasn't that simple. She might be at the epicentre, but the shockwaves would radiate out, affecting untold numbers of people: friends, colleagues, shopkeepers, builders. 'How could he?' she whispered, to the empty room.

But her immediate worry was for her own family. What effect would all this have on them? She'd been shown a glimmer last night. How would her children be with her this morning? She did not look forward to seeing them: the memory of their bitterness and anger was still too sharp. Last night she'd tried to comfort Victoria, but her door was locked and she had ignored Jillian calling her. Miles, she was sure, had got drunk – she'd heard someone falling up the stairs in the early hours. Would they still be furious, blaming her? Or were they dreading facing her too?

What a mess it all was! But lying here would solve nothing, she told herself. Where had she read that one of the first signs of depression was an inability to get out of bed? She decided to take a long bath, which should make her feel half human again before going to meet whoever it was clattering about downstairs.

'Esmée,' she said, as she walked into the kitchen, 'I'm sorry about last night. I was abominably rude.'

'Don't be silly. It's us who should be apologising to you. Everyone got over-excited, and probably a bit pissed, and said things they shouldn't.'

'Who else is here?'

'Just me. I'd like to have scarpered with the rest, but I was a smidgen over the top and the thought of being breathalysed – too boring, sweets. So I took the risk of your ire having dissipated by morning, went to bed and crept down early, hoping to make amends by fixing you some breakfast.'

'I didn't mean *you* to go, just the rest. Where are they?'

'Patsy went off with your mother. That poor little bank manager scuttled off to his cocoa soon after you sailed out. I think he was a bit out of his depth, don't you? Gary and the relentlessly groomed Cherry stayed a bit longer – he was questioning me mainly. I do believe he thinks I know where Jack is, and I'm holding out on him because of family loyalty

– if only he knew! But I must say, I thought him much nicer than I expected and, much to my surprise, I thought Cherry was an absolute poppet.'

'I'd always presumed she didn't know how to boil a kettle, but she came up trumps last night. But I've disliked Gary for so long it would take me a long time to change my mind about them. Don't forget it was his expansion plans that got us into trouble last time.' She accepted the cup of tea Esmée had made for her, though it looked dubiously weak. 'What did you think about Patsy's reaction to Mother's suggestion that she give me that money back?'

'Not in the least surprised, were you?'

'It was a lot to ask, but I'd like to think that if the circumstances were reversed I'd give it to her.'

'But there, my love, is where you differ from your sister. You're a caring individual and she's an egotist – a lot of the druggies I've met are. I suppose you can't blame the poor dears, it's from all those years of contemplating their own navels so assiduously and scrabbling and scratching about to get the wherewithal to buy their stash. It becomes a habit not to share, I suppose.'

'All the same . . .' Jillian's voice trailed away to nothing.

Esmée sat down beside her and took her hand. 'Dearest, listen to Auntie Esmée. You're going to have to grow a tough skin. No doubt Patsy will be the first of many to let you down. If you believe everyone will, then the ones who don't will be a bonus. It's going to get tough.'

'I realise that.' Her voice was sharp and she pulled away her hand. She hoped Esmée would not continue to lecture her.

'You look deep in thought. Penny for them.'

She began to say, 'nothing', then changed her mind. 'I hope everyone doesn't start handing out advice to me. The first thing I've got to learn is to manage on my own, and to make my own decisions – whether they're the right ones or not.'

'Glory be, Jillian's being assertive. You must forgive we busybodies, but you've always been so placid and acquiescent that bullies like me just swoop on you with joy – a victim to

lecture!' Esmée grinned at her. 'Message received and understood. There's just one thing before you go all independent
on us. The kids. I want to take over the expenses of their
education.'

'Esmée, I couldn't possibly let you. It's a small fortune. I
could never repay you.'

'To begin with, I don't want to be repaid. I have the small
fortune and it'll be a change to spend it on something
worthwhile rather than the latest fellow. And if you won't let
me you're being selfish. You shouldn't let your pride deprive
your children of something they want and need. What's
more, and most important, you would deny me the pleasure
of doing it.'

'Put like that . . .'

'There's no other way. So you'll let me? Good. There's just
one thing. I shan't do this if they don't apologise to you for
last night's little scene.'

'But if this is on offer, of course they're going to apologise,
aren't they? Some apology that will be.'

'Not if they don't know what I plan until after they have.'

'I understand why they behaved as they did. It upset me,
but they were shocked too, they saw their futures crumbling
before their eyes. Their father has left them.'

'Jillian! Jillian! When will you stop? They were disgusting.
You're facing a much greater catastrophe. You're older, for
starters. Did you blame anyone? I bet you won't even blame
Jack eventually – you'll come up with some half-baked reason
for why he's such a shit. No, don't make excuses for them,
they've got to learn, and fast, that they have to think of
others.'

Jillian burst out laughing, Esmée looked at her in surprise.
'What did I say? What's funny?'

'You. Imagine you talking like this! Why, when we first met
you didn't give a fig about anyone. Did you?'

'No, for far too long I thought the world existed just for me.
Unselfish types like you have it easy. It's been a hard lesson to
learn – with a lot of heartache and pain along the way. And
the mess my life is in shows I'm still learning. Altogether

more reason, then, to make sure Miles and Victoria don't make the cock-up I have.'

'Dear friend. You're not a fraction of the monster you think you are.'

'Bah! Then you think I'm a bit of one. Cheeky!'

As if on cue, Miles, looking fragile, stumbled into the kitchen. 'Why didn't somebody stop me? Never again! I'm going on the wagon for life.'

'Have some tea.' Esmée picked up the teapot.

Miles sat down at the table. He looked everywhere except at Jillian. 'I was dreading coming down, Mum. My behaviour last night was unforgivable. As if you don't have enough to cope with, I make matters worse by blathering away. I shouldn't have reacted as I did, especially in front of everyone. All I can say is I'm sorry.'

'Miles, I do understand. There's nothing to forgive.'

'Great,' said Esmée, opening the fridge door. 'One down, one to go. Now, Miles, I've never done this before, but I'm willing to have a bash, if you're willing to try it. Bacon and eggs?'

The weekend of Jack's disappearance everything was as usual. Jillian stuck to her normal routine of getting food ready, making beds, tidying the house. Miles had gone to see his best friend to plan their evening out, which was what he always did when at home. The only difference had been that he had asked if she had minded him going. Victoria was in a sulk, but since she so often was there was nothing untoward in that either. Jillian had been quite relieved when she had announced she was catching the bus into town. She had said it in a confrontational way and looked almost disappointed when Jillian had agreed and had asked her if she had enough spending money.

As the day wore on, the sun shining, Radio Four burbling in the background, Jillian began to think, in a strange, detached way, that there must be a simple explanation for everything. That everyone, including herself, was overreacting and that Jack would appear at any moment. Then she would feel ice cold with fear that he had gone for good.

'If he doesn't come back today do you think I should call the police?' Jillian asked Esmée, as they sat at the kitchen table drinking yet more coffee.

'In the circumstances, do you think that's wise? After all, you don't want to be the one responsible for having him arrested, do you?'

'But have you thought, Esmée, we only have Gary's word that he's gone off with the money? What if Gary has stolen the money and is putting up a smokescreen?'

'It's a possibility, I suppose. But he seemed convinced and he *had* spoken to the bank.'

'But had he? Or did he just say that?'

'What I can't get over is this business about Cara! Well, I ask you, if he was going to take a mistress can you really see him choosing her, of all women? And we only have Gary's word that he has.'

'Yes,' Jillian said, too mortified to let Esmée know how true that probably was.

'On the other hand . . .' Before Esmée had time to finish the telephone rang.

Jillian leaped up to take the call. 'Yes, Mum, I'm fine, really . . . I slept like a log . . . No, Mum, it's very kind of you . . . Esmée's here, I'm not alone.' She rolled her eyes in resignation at her friend. 'Thanks for calling, Mum,' she said decisively and replaced the receiver. 'She's the last person I want to see at the moment.'

'Totally understandable. They always think they know best, don't they? And I mean, the world has changed so dramatically since our mothers were young – how can they possibly understand the problems that we have?'

'Exactly,' Jillian replied, but not without a flash of discomfort at the memory of Victoria telling her she was too old to understand how she thought.

'Dearest heart, your optimism is commendable and I hope you're right. But there's a teensy-weensy thing you've forgotten. Your bank and the manager's concerns? I just mention it *en passant*.'

'What was to stop Jack moving our accounts to another bank? And before you say it, just because I didn't know

298

means nothing. He may have had a disagreement with the manager. But is Ed going to admit that he offended one of their most important clients? Of course not, he'd be busy covering his tracks, fast. And I know what you're going to say next, this house, and why did he do that? Simple. He might have needed some money in a hurry, maybe a property he had to make a quick decision on. His life was full of deals like that. Jack never bothered me with the details of the business. Once it annoyed me, but it was his way. He protected me. He didn't want me to worry. And I respected that. So there's nothing sinister or stupid about me signing papers when I didn't know what they contained. I frequently signed things. We are a married couple. It would never have crossed my mind to ask him what they were.'

'You should know best. I hope ... I don't want to be a doom merchant ... I just think it's a good idea ... if you consider the alternative ... That's all.' Esmée spoke in short bursts, as if she was finding it difficult to say. She went on, 'If you're sure you're all right, I think I'd better get home. I called the nurse this morning before you came down and mother is being impossible. Poor Liz is at her wit's end.'

'I'm fine.' In a way Jillian was relieved. She wanted to be on her own: she had marshalled her thoughts so that now she was certain she was right, and the last thing she needed was others' negativity.

'Let me know when that little creep has apologised to you, and then I'll talk to her. I've already asked Miles to pop over when he can.'

'It's very sweet of you, though I don't think it's going to be necessary,' Jillian said stubbornly.

'At least we'll be prepared.'

By early Saturday evening Jillian was drunk. Miles and Victoria were highly amused when they returned home to find her fuddled, muddled and giggly. She swore them to secrecy. 'This is our little con-sp-tera ...' She took a deep breath and tried again. 'Conspiracy!' she shouted triumphantly. 'You see, if you take a run at a word like that, you can do it, if you take it unawares.'

'I think you should get tiddly more often, Mum.' Victoria giggled with her.

'I don't think we should go out to this party, Victoria, do you?'

'Don't be silly. You go. I'm very happy here.' And Jillian was.

2

It was a mystery why people drank too much regularly, she concluded the next morning, when the thought of food made her nauseous. She decided to clean the laundry room. She told herself it was overdue and that she had been planning to do it for ages. She should talk to Victoria and tried to plan what to say, but couldn't think of anything that would be remotely helpful. She was also afraid of Victoria's raw emotions, that by being exposed to them she would lose control. She tugged at the washing-machine to clean behind it.

'Daddy's missing, my life is in ruins, and you choose to sort out the laundry room. I just don't understand you.' Victoria stood in the doorway looking down at her.

'It's my way of coping.'

'Have you seen my blue blouse in there? You know, the one I lost.'

'No, but I haven't been looking.' At least, she thought, Victoria was consistent. She doubted if her daughter would ever stop putting herself first, no matter what the circumstances. Such an idea pulled her up short; she knew Victoria had faults but normally she made excuses for her. 'Do you want any breakfast?' she asked, to make amends.

'I've had some chocolate. You were very drunk last night. I don't know what Daddy will say.'

'Since it was because of him I don't think there's much he can say,' she replied sharply. 'I'll make some coffee.'

Miles was already in the kitchen. 'I thought you'd be

groaning and moaning in your bed.' He grinned at her. 'I'm getting breakfast. Don't faint.'

'How very kind.' The kitchen already looked chaotic but she said nothing. 'Was it a nice party?'

'Not really. I couldn't stop worrying about Dad. I don't believe all that crap Gary was spouting the other night. He's always been jealous of him and he's ridden on his coat-tails long enough.' Miles waved a fish slice to emphasise his point. 'I'm worried something's happened to him, that he's had an accident, lost his memory or something. Dad isn't a crook, I know that,' he added staunchly.

'I'm so glad you think like that. I've been wondering all morning if we should call the police.'

'I have. The local plod is on his way over.'

Constable Bowman was a very serious-minded young policeman. Jillian knew him for he had lived in the village for almost two years.

'What seems to be the problem, Mrs Stirling?' he asked, setting down his notepad on the table.

'I'm sure I'm panicking about nothing but my husband did not come home when I expected him to. I thought he would be back from a business trip to Spain last Wednesday. It was his birthday yesterday and we were to have a party, but he didn't come home.'

'Is this usual?'

'He's not very good at keeping in touch. You know how it is, he's always too busy to be phoning home. But he's quite a baby where his birthday is concerned and he wouldn't have missed that for the world.'

'You didn't worry before today?'

'No, I just assumed he'd turn up. I've telephoned the local hospitals, and the ones close to Heathrow. But they had no one fitting his description.'

'I shouldn't worry about that, Mrs Stirling. If he'd had an accident then you would have known very quickly. A businessman like him would have a lot of identification on him, wouldn't he? He's not been worried about anything?'

301

'No. Nothing.' She watched the young man making his notes neatly and carefully. 'Not that I'm aware of,' she added.

'So there could be something?' He looked up expectantly.

'Well, yes, I suppose so. I mean, there could be something I don't know about is what I mean.'

'No problems . . . you know . . .' He glanced at Miles and Victoria, who were listening intently. And he twisted his ring as if to emphasise it was marriage he was talking about.

'Nothing. We are very happy. Very.'

He took down a few more details as to where Jack had been, the name of the hotel, his address in London and telephone numbers where he might be contacted. His portable radio, strapped to his tunic, crackled into life. He bent his head to speak into it. 'I'll make a report of this, but don't worry. Mr Stirling doesn't strike me as the type to lose his memory.'

'Is there a type?' asked Miles.

'I must be getting along.' He ignored the question. At the door he turned. 'The best bit of advice I can give you is to pray for rain.'

'I'm sorry?'

'People that go missing, you'd be amazed how many come back when the weather changes.' He laughed as if it was a huge joke.

'I'm sorry, Constable, but I don't find my husband not returning home the least bit funny. I think you know the way, perhaps you'd like to see yourself out.'

'What a prat!'

'What a defective!'

'He probably meant well.' She wished now she hadn't been quite so sharp with him.

Her belief that Jack would return diminished hour by hour. She blamed herself: that if they had not involved the police she would not be feeling like this. By talking to Constable Bowman they had in some way made it real. She knew that a report was now at the police station. He was filed under Missing – it was official. On Monday morning she felt low and was glad that the children, as normal, were still asleep. She did not want them to see her like this. She had completely forgotten that Victoria should be back at school, and so phoned the headmistress and lied, saying she was unwell.

She drove into Cambridge to keep an appointment with the bank manager, and another with Dexter Reeve, their solicitor.

As if to reiterate what he had said when she had seen him, Ed Kingsman had produced all the papers relating to the transfer of the house, the remortgaging, and the statements of their empty accounts. One by one she looked at the documents, which confirmed her dire position.

'Then I have no money. What do I do?'

'Have you nothing of your own?'

'Nothing.' She had decided it was better not to mention her legacy from Ralph for fear it might be taken away from her. She would worry about that later.

'I always believed Jack made you an allowance.'

'He did. But since we moved to Fen Manor there was rarely anything over to salt away. It's an expensive house to maintain.'

'What about the antique shop?'

'I make enough to cover the costs – it would never support us. If you remember, I borrowed from you to set it up. I think it will have to go.'

'Regrettable.' Ed looked pained. 'Perhaps you could live in the flat?'

'The tenants have a two-year lease.'

'What are your immediate needs?'

'I made this list as you suggested.' She handed over the sheet of paper she had worked on last night. 'I expect I've forgotten some things – I did it in rather a hurry. As far as I can make out these are my outstanding bills.'

Ed studied her accounts; she waited anxiously.

'This is rather a large amount, Jillian. I hadn't expected it to be quite so much.' He rearranged his spectacles and looked down again.

'The party expenses have pushed it up. And May's bills are just coming in. And there was my present to Jack.' Gold cufflinks, solid, heavy, and far too expensive. 'At least I'll be able to sell that.' She managed a wan smile and Ed, unsure if that was what it was, smiled back faintly.

'For such a sum I shall have to consult with my area directors. An overdraft of this size is outside my discretion.'

'Then there's a chance of the bank helping me?'

'I can't promise. But I'll do my best.'

From his tone and the way he avoided looking her in the eye she knew he was just being polite and that he held out little hope. He probably didn't have the stomach to tell her to her face and, no doubt, in the next few days, she would receive a letter from him to that effect.

'Once I've sorted out the shop I shall get a job,' she said, as if it was a matter of course. She wondered if it would be so easy: she had long forgotten her secretarial skills. What were left was her knowledge of antiques and the ability to run a home.

Sitting in the small waiting room in the solicitor's office where once she had worked and had been unhappy, she realised how tired and demoralised she was. Perhaps it had been unwise to have the two meetings on the same day. But she had worked on the principle that it was best to get them both over and done with. So little had changed in this room since she had been employed here: the same prints on the wall, the same dreary curtains, out-of-date magazines and, she was sure, the same Swiss cheese plant in the corner.

Dexter Reeve was working on some papers when she entered his office. He looked up, smiled pleasantly enough, said he'd only keep her a minute and to take a seat. She watched him – a grey-suited, plain-featured, short, rather plump young man, whose somewhat exotic name did not really suit him: a Dexter should be handsome and tall. Her Jack was both and yet he had the plain name.

She had never really liked Dexter, but was not sure if her attitude was unfairly coloured by the fact that his father had sacked her when she had confessed she was pregnant and unmarried. Watching Dexter now, importantly signing some papers, she wondered if he knew that about her. She would rather have used another firm of solicitors but Jack had decided on this one and she had not protested. Now, when she thought about it, it struck her as insensitive of him. It was strange that she hadn't thought that before . . .

'So, Jillian, you're looking very pretty today.' Dexter rubbed his somewhat podgy hands and looked at his pink, shiny nails as if pleased with them. No, she thought, it wasn't just because of his father that she didn't like him: he had a self-satisfied air that set her teeth on edge. 'What can we do for you?'

'I assume you've heard the news?' He spread the sausage-fingered hands palm upwards and gave a minimal shrug. 'Then I would have thought it was self-evident. I need some help and advice. I have just been to the bank and the situation is grim. Jack has left me with nothing. I was wondering if you knew where he was, and if you know of any funds that I could call upon?'

'I'm in a very difficult position here, Jillian. I know I have acted for you both in the purchase of various houses, but primarily I regard myself as Jack's solicitor. I think perhaps it would be better if you found yourself another legal adviser.'

'I don't understand, what circumstances?'

'Why, any divorce, of course.'

'But I don't want to divorce Jack.'

'You don't?' Dexter looked surprised and somewhat put out. 'I was led to believe you would.'

'Jack told you this? What else did he tell you? How much *do* you know about all this? You have to tell me, you do see that?'

'I'm afraid I don't. You are forcing me into a conflict of client interest here.'

'He spoke to you, didn't he? You knew what he was planning. You know where he is.'

'I know nothing, Jillian.' Like the bank manager, he could not look at her. But Ed had avoided eye-contact from embarrassment. Dexter was doing so out of guilt, she was sure. Once again his hands came in for close scrutiny. 'I could recommend another firm to you. Kenner and Tate, perhaps.'

'I don't believe this. You do understand he has taken money that isn't his?'

'That's a very serious accusation, my dear.' She looked at him and felt an overwhelming rush of anger and dislike. She stood up abruptly.

'I have a friend I can consult. Colin Coleridge.'

'Coleridge? I'm afraid you're seriously out of date, my dear. He left town some time ago. Gone back to Scotland, I heard.'

'Dexter would you stop calling me your dear. I find it rather offensive.' She stood and said this with as much dignity as she could muster, and also to cover her disappointment that Colin no longer lived and worked here.

As she drove home Jillian felt sick. Last week she had had everything a woman could want materially.

Materially. Now that was a strange word for her to choose. Not that it wasn't true, it was just that last week she would have said she was happy and loved and thus she had everything a woman of her age could desire. The difference was that today she knew that the love she had cherished and nurtured so carefully had existed only in her imagination. The life she thought she had did not exist. The beautiful, contented family, admired by everyone they knew, was a charade. As she faced the truth that for so long she had shut away, the road dissolved into a watery mirage. She had enough wit to pull into the side of the road where she stopped the car.

There, alone, cars flashing past, she did not so much cry as howl her frustration, anger, loneliness and fear. She beat a tattoo on the steering-wheel with her hands. She threw back her head against the seat and screamed until she could scream no more.

3

That evening Esmée, her mother, Gary, the bank manager, everyone she knew, it seemed, telephoned.

One by one they asked the same question. 'Are you all right? You sound strange.'

'I think I'm getting a cold.' She explained the huskiness of her voice. She reassured them that she was fine, she was busy, she would do nothing silly. Finally she took the telephone off the hook, not wanting sympathy, kindness, pity; just peace and time to come to terms with her new situation.

She left a note for the children and went to bed. With her she carried a tray and a bottle of whisky. She got ready for bed, removing her makeup with her usual care. She poured a large drink, and sat for some time looking at it. 'No, that's not the way,' she said aloud, picked up the glass, carried it to the bathroom and poured the whisky into the basin.

The next morning Jillian was up at six. It really was strange, she thought, as she made herself an early-morning cup of tea, that despite how she felt, she was sleeping deeply in a way she had not for years – dreamless, childlike sleep. She looked out of her kitchen window at the dew that still decorated the plants. It was going to be a glorious day. The garden on which she had worked so hard looked heartbreakingly beautiful in the early-summer sun. Was it only last week that she had said to Jack that she thought this year was going to be the best for the roses they had planted? Now this garden she loved would belong to someone else. She would not be here when the house went on the market, she decided. She would just move out and someone else could sell it. Without the furniture, it would not attract the best price, but that wasn't her problem – not any more. This thought cheered her a fraction as she collected cleaning materials.

'What on earth are you doing, Mum?' It was three hours later and Miles stood in the doorway of the drawing room, a can of Coke in his hands and an indulgent smile on his face.

'I'm getting some of this ready to sell.'

'Poor Mum. Is it ours to sell?'

'I'm only polishing the pieces that are mine – presents from your father and things I bought myself. I'm in a rush since I've no proof that they're mine – I've no receipts. Had I known what was going to happen . . .' She smiled a bit bleakly. 'I'm telephoning a dealer I know today to get him over here quickly.'

'Good for you. I promise you, though, that one day I'll buy all this back for you.'

She could have cried at the emotions in her young son's face – despair and frustration that there was nothing he could do. It was not fair that he had to deal with all this just as his own adult life was beginning. 'I shall look forward to that. Thanks.'

'Have you got a minute to talk? Only I've made some decisions.'

Jillian stopped polishing and sat down, patting the chair beside her. 'I'm all ears.'

'I went to see Aunt Esmée yesterday. Had she told you she was prepared to pay for me to go to Oxford? It's kind of her. Only I don't want to take her up on the offer.'

'Did she tell you something about your father?' She needed to find out how he had reached this decision. But, just as important, she did not want to burden him further with the tale of his father's illegitimacy.

'Only what she thought of him, which isn't much. I was in total agreement with her. You see, Mum, I never really wanted to go to Oxford. It was just that Dad was so keen that I should. I suppose I didn't want to let him down. Only it's he who's done the letting down, so I think I'm free now to do what I want to do.'

'Which is?'

'I want to work in the hotel trade. I went to see the manager at the Garden House and he gave me a lot of good advice. He's got no vacancies there but he's given me the names of some friends of his. And I bought a copy of *Hotel and Caterer* – it's a trade magazine. See?'

'You're not doing this out of some misplaced pride, are you?' She looked up from the glossy magazine he'd handed her.

'No. I never told you that this is what I wanted to do. I suppose I thought you wouldn't approve. Dad had such grandiose plans for me.'

'Probably because he was never able to realise his own. But the hotel trade? I should think it could be fascinating – if you got into the right place, of course.'

308

'I'm not suddenly deciding this, Mum. Honest.'

'You must do whatever you want, Miles.' But she was still concerned that he'd turned Esmée down out of loyalty to herself. 'Still, I've got some news for you. Your grandfather left me some money, should I ever be desperate.' She chose her words carefully, then realised she was doing so to protect Jack – why should she bother? 'Actually, he left it to me in case Jack ever left me. He was far more perceptive than I.' She laughed bitterly. 'I haven't mentioned it before for fear that your father's creditors might be able claim it against his debts. We could use that money to send you to Oxford if you don't want to use Esmée's.'

'Mum, honestly, it's what I want. You use the money. Is there enough for you to buy a house or flat for yourself? Because that's what I think you should do. I shall be living in, so you would only need something big enough for you and Victoria. Aunt Esmée told me she's waiting for her to apologise then she'll pay her school fees. I reckon hell will freeze over first. You know what she's like.'

'I think Esmée's being a little hard on her. Poor Victoria, she's only fourteen – too young to deal with all this. We've all had one hell of a shock. We're all suffering.'

'Have you any idea why he's done this? Cherry said he was having a male menopause and he'd be back. But, to be honest, Mum, if he came home I don't think I'd ever want to speak to him again.'

'Don't say things you may regret. Not now. It's a dangerous time for us all. I find myself changing how I feel all the time. One minute I'm so angry with him, so bitter, and then I understand what has happened and perhaps why.'

'What?'

'I realise now ... Well, that's not strictly true. I think I always knew that one day this would happen. You see, the lie was committed before you were born. He told me he wanted to marry me because of you but he didn't. He only did it because he thought it was his duty. And he's an honourable man. All those years must have been dreadful for him.'

'Mum, that's a load of crap. Honourable is the last word I'd use. Is it your fault, then, that he embezzled all that money?

Did not wanting to be married and a father make him a criminal? Come off it! He could have left you a hundred times in the last nineteen years. He wasn't that unhappy or he'd have pissed off long ago. So stop blaming yourself. He's a selfish bastard, Mum. He met this bit of crumpet and he lost his senses. The opportunity arose for some easy money, he took it and to hell with the rest of us.'

Several days later, after hours of battling with figures that would not add up as she wanted them to, Jillian decided to do some gardening. It had always been a good standby in the past when she needed to think. As she was tugging at a particularly recalcitrant weed, she heard a car racing up the drive. Not visitors, please, she prayed. But it was the postman and she relaxed. If she weren't about he would leave the mail inside the back door as usual. This morning, however, he appeared around the side of the house.

'Saw you from the drive, Mrs Stirling. That's the ticket! Don't let the weeds take over – fancy doing mine when you've finished?' He grinned as he held out a letter from the top of the pile. 'Recorded delivery, if you wouldn't mind signing.'

She got to her feet, her heart sinking. Such a short time ago, the post had been something to look forward to. Now it was something to dread. A recorded letter could only mean bad news. She opened it with shaking hands.

The letter was from Gary's solicitor. It said he was holding her responsible for the money Jack had stolen, informing her that a garnishee order had been placed on her bank accounts. She began to laugh. The absurdity of the situation was almost too much. 'What accounts? The madness!' she said aloud. She offered a silent prayer of thanks that she had had the foresight not to apply for her legacy from Ralph. She would bide her time, maybe buy a flat but put it in the children's names so it could not be touched.

As she entered the kitchen the telephone shrilled. She placed the rest of the mail on the table and answered it. 'Did you get a recorded-delivery letter?' Gary asked, without announcing himself.

'I did. And I had a good laugh.'

'It's only a formality.'

'But you know I've got nothing. I mean, this letter is absurd.'

'There'll be a queue of creditors, no doubt. I wanted to register my claim and be first in line. I hoped to get hold of you before it arrived but ... You all right, Jillian? Only if there's anything that Cherry and I can do, you've only to ask.'

'Thanks, Gary. How about paying my bills, finding me a home and supporting me for the rest of my life?'

'Yes, well ...'

'Joke, Gary, joke.'

Once the conversation was over she read the letter again and reached the unpleasant conclusion that the letter had been sent because they had a sneaky idea that she was involved in some way, that she too was embezzling money. Great, she thought. One thing was certain; she would be wise to get her possessions out quickly before Gary started to claim them as Jack's.

An hour later her gardening was interrupted again as another van pulled up outside. It was her old friend Windy, come to see her furniture. Why he was called Windy no one knew.

It took less than half an hour to view, discuss and agree a price.

'I'm sorry about all this, Jillian. What a bastard for you,' Windy said, as he peeled off notes from a huge wodge he carried in his back pocket. 'No doubt the last thing you want is a cheque.'

'You know, then?'

'It's all over Cambridge.'

'These are my things, Windy. I haven't sold you anything that was Jack's,' she said anxiously.

'It wouldn't have bothered me if you had. Good luck to you, I say. Do you want me to look at anything else?'

'I'll think about it,' she answered quickly, for the temptation to raise more money that way was almost irresistible.

'Well, don't think for long – restraining orders can appear from nowhere like a tornado. Now, you're happy with that?'

'You've been very generous, Windy. I appreciate it.'

'As far as I'm concerned you're still trade to me, and we have to stick together now, don't we?'

'If you hear of any jobs going – shop assistant, polishing, restoring – give me a ring, will you?'

'Will do.'

Windy, huge and with the strength of two, loaded her furniture into the back of his van. Her possessions, her precious things – gone! She turned back into the house. It had saddened her to part with them, but not as much as she'd expected. A week ago she'd have said the loss would break her heart; today she counted the banknotes before stuffing the money in an old tea caddy. Her priorities were changing.

If Gary could write that letter making a claim, did that mean the money Ralph had left her was at risk too? She needed a solicitor, and quick, but if she found one she liked and trusted, how the hell was she supposed to pay him?

She picked up the rest of the mail and glanced through it. There were too many buff envelopes for comfort, several circulars, which she immediately threw away. There was one letter, hand-addressed in writing she did not recognise, posted in Cambridge. She ripped it open, unfolded the sheet of writing-paper, and had to sit down quickly, for the handwriting was Jack's.

My darling Jillian,

Saying sorry is, I know, useless. I have, no doubt, hurt you irremediably. I wish there could have been some other way, but there wasn't. I knew that if I confided in you, I would never have had the courage to leave.

I wanted you to know that it is nothing you have done. You were a good wife to me. It was the circumstances of our life together which ate away at me until I felt domesticity was stifling me. You often spoke of your feelings of guilt, well, you've no need of them now, I've taken all that guilt to myself.

I can't really explain why I'm doing what I have. It's like a compulsion, I know that if I don't go now I never will. Ralph dying made me think. I'm getting older, the approach of my fortieth birthday made me stop and wonder what I had done with my life and where had all the dreams gone? I wanted to taste life again – to live.

I have no guilt over the money I took – Gary has ripped me off enough times. And if he could have set it up and stolen it himself I have no doubt he would have done so.

I'm sorry about the house. I know how much you love it. But there was no other way. The deal was going bad on us, I knew. We were facing losing everything and I couldn't do that to you again. I'll be honest and tell you I had it planned for some time.

The past few days must have been agony for you and I'm sorry for that too. I have opened you an account in a Swiss bank – the number is on the enclosed paper; memorise it then throw it away. Please tell no one about this – not even the kids.

I do love you, Jillian, in my way. I'm sorry it's not your way.

By the time she reached the end of the letter she could barely see the print. But these tears were tears of rage. How could she ever have imagined that she knew him? How could anybody be so selfish? He was a selfish, inconsiderate child! And the letter was nothing but a muddle. He was lying even now: on the one hand, he'd planned it, on the other, he was protecting her from losing everything – and yet that was precisely what had happened. 'Oh, come off it, Jack. Who are you kidding?' She spoke aloud. She sat down. 'To live again . . .' Did he not realise the sheer brutal cruelty of that statement? She pulled the envelope towards her. Inside was another piece of paper. On it was the account number of the bank in Zurich: five hundred thousand pounds had been deposited in it. She stared at it in disbelief.

Miles entered the kitchen, his face still puffed with sleep. 'What's the time?'

'Eleven.'

'You look shattered, Mum.'

She said nothing but pushed the letter across to him, which he read as she put the kettle on. Victoria ambled in, looking even sleepier than her brother. 'Any breakfast?'

'I'm busy, Victoria. Can't you get some for yourself?' She

really must insist she go back to school, but at the moment she did not have the energy to face the inevitable row.

'You're making tea for him. Why can't you do it for me?'

'Tea isn't cooking breakfast. Please, Victoria, not now. No dramas. I've had enough.'

'Crikey.' Miles put the letter down. 'That's a lot of money, Mum.' Miles leaned back in the chair. 'At least it will make things easier.'

'What will make things easier?' Victoria grabbed at the letter.

'Let go of it.' Miles pulled it back.

'If you can see it, why can't I? See? It's always the same, you let him do whatever he wants.'

'Let her read it, Miles. He's her father too.'

While she made the tea Jillian's mind was in turmoil.

'Brilliant! Can I have those new shoes now?' Victoria looked at her, all hint of sulking wiped away by a broad smile.

Jillian took the letter and placed it safely in her desk. 'I was gardening. I think I'll go and finish that bed.'

Why was it, she wondered, that glorious weather made the situation worse? As if the glory of the day underlined a wonderful world she couldn't really appreciate. No doubt she would feel much better if it was raining. Of all the mood swings she'd had recently she decided that anger was the most productive. Odd for someone who had spent their life controlling it. But, she realised that when she was aroused, as she had been by that letter, she felt more positive, more in control. In fact, that letter had made her feel much better.

She looked up from her weeding as yet another vehicle drove up. It was becoming a very busy day, she thought, as she went to see who it was.

Constable Bowman stood by the door.

'Any news, Constable?'

'Sorry, Mrs Stirling, nothing. But this is Inspector Heath.'

'How do you do?'

'Mrs Stirling, I have to tell you I'm from the Fraud Squad. Certain information has been given us pertaining to your husband. It would help us if I could ask you some questions.'

'Of course, do you mind the kitchen? We seem to live there, these days.' She led the way. She could not help but smile at the guilty expressions on her children's faces as she entered with the uniformed constable. 'Sit, do.' She crossed the room, opened her desk and removed Jack's letter. 'This might be of some use to you.' She held it out to the inspector.

'No! You can't do that! It's not fair.' Victoria rushed across the room and dived to snatch the envelope from her mother's hand.

'I refuse to become a criminal too, Victoria. I'm sorry.'

'I hate you. You're a smug bitch.'

'Then I'm sorry for that too,' Jillian replied calmly.

4

Spring 1988

'What a blast! This is just like the little house you and Jack started out in. Sweet.' Esmée looked about her at the small sitting room of the terraced house Jillian had bought two years ago with Ralph's money. 'You're such a genius, you could make a rabbit hutch cosy, couldn't she, Helen?'

'I always said that was where her talents lay. Dearie me! If you don't mind, I've simply got to sit down.' Helen, flushed and fanning herself with a newspaper, flopped into the wing-chair.

'Can I get you some water?' Jillian was concerned: she didn't look well.

'I might be an old trout, my dear Jillian, but I feel I could do with something stronger.'

'Look, we brought supplies.' From a copious shoulder-bag Esmée produced a bottle of gin, another of champagne and a large one of tonic. 'Helen's been to see a blood man here at Addenbrookes Hospital. The vampire, we call him. He's got fangs. We waited hours, didn't we, Helen?'

'Don't listen to her, Jillian. He's a dear man and well thought-of.'

'And he said?'

'Oh, I'll be seeing all of you out,' Helen said dismissively.

Jillian felt sure she'd had bad news, but if she didn't want to talk about it, she wouldn't make her. 'You must have strained your shoulder carrying that lot.' She collected glasses from the Regency corner cabinet.

'I see you managed to salvage some of your lovely furniture. I'm so pleased for you.'

'No. Esmée –'

'Jillian, shut up!'

'No, I won't, Esmée. Why, you're embarrassed by your good deeds! Unbeknown to me, Helen, she went to the auction at Fen Manor, bought all this,' she encompassed the room with a wave of her hand, 'and gave it to me.'

'Dear Esmée.' Helen took her hand and squeezed it. 'Her father's daughter.'

'Well, I couldn't stand it. All those grim people salivating over Jill's bits and bobs. I had to rescue some. Where's the horrible teen daughter? At school?'

'Just. If the phone rings my heart sinks. It's invariably the headmistress with another complaint. She's *wayward*, they say.'

'Pain in the arse, more like. Poor kid. Missing the creep, I suppose. Won't let you say a word against Jack, that sort of thing?'

'Exactly.'

'Well, at least she saw the error of her ways and apologised to you – or she wouldn't be there at all.'

'Yes. I'll get some nibbles.' Jillian left the room, not wanting Esmée to guess from her expression that she'd lied to her. Victoria had never apologised: if anything, she was worse. She blamed Jillian endlessly for her father having absconded. Jillian had been patient with her, understanding her pain, but finally her patience had run out. One day she'd tried to point out that she had had nothing to do with Jack turning into a thief, which had made Victoria hysterical. She'd screamed abuse at her, far worse than she had before. It was after that scene that Jillian had decided that they would both be better off if Victoria was away at school for a large chunk of the year, and that was when she'd allowed Esmée to believe the apology had been made.

'Here we are. I've some olives. Not much, I'm afraid.'

'Perfect.' Helen beamed. 'I was in Claridge's the other day for tea and met your charming son. He recognised me, wasn't that dear of him?'

'Was he in his breeches and gold braid? He says he feels a prat dressed up in that footman's garb.'

'My dear, he looked adorable. And he's so good at his job.'

'He loves it. But he's ambitious. He says he wants a string of hotels one day.'

'Shadows of his father – hope not!' Esmée snorted.

'Esmée says you've two jobs? I do hope you're not doing too much.'

'No. I'm fine. I work in John Lewis, in the china department. I like it. I've always enjoyed selling, and china in particular. And three evenings a week I work in the Pickerel. It's a pub opposite Jack's old college – I enjoy the company.'

'So you're not lonely?'

'Gracious, no. The shop has the most fantastic social life, if you want to be part of it. They've loads of societies. I'm thinking of joining the drama one. The other women have been very sweet to me. Occasionally I'll see someone I knew from before – from my previous life, I call it.' She giggled. 'They look a bit askance at me working in a shop, but that's their problem, not mine. No. I'm far more content than I ever dared hope I'd be.'

'You've inner resources, that's why. Esmée, my dear, are you ever going to pour that gin?'

'I'll do it.' Jillian jumped up.

'And your mother and sister?'

'Mum's fine. I'm so busy I don't see her as often as I should.' Which was only a half-truth. Her mother wasn't all right. She was becoming depressed. Jillian had tried to find out what was wrong, but Mary would simply put on a buttoned-up look that brooked no further discussion. But it was true, she had little time to spare. 'And Patsy's a traveller now. She has a gypsy caravan, one of those lovely painted ones, and a piebald horse, and they plod around the West Country. I quite envy her sometimes, she's so free.'

'Are we ever really free? I don't think so. We're always marked by other's actions, often more so than our own, don't you think? Ah, bliss. Thank you.' Helen sipped her drink. 'Might I just ask – perhaps a little more gin would make this perfect?'

'How's your love life?' asked Esmée, lighting a cigarette.

'Non-existent.'

'Ditto. It might be looking up, though. I met this lovely American. He's a plastic surgeon – I thought he might come in handy one day.'

'But you tried America – the film producer.'

'Don't talk about him. All that sniffing and snorting cocaine up noses quite puts one off! No, this one's sweet, and I thought I'd give him a fling. I'm just going to settle Mummy in a home and then I'm off. Poor Liz can't cope any longer. I told her she mustn't so we're stashing the old biddy away.'

'Best thing for everyone,' Helen said matter-of-factly. Jillian admired Esmée for having the courage to do the one thing that shocked everyone else rigid and leave her sick mother.

'Well, I'm amazed you're not inundated with men,' Helen said.

'Cambridge is full of them, Helen, but they're all so young! They don't see women of forty-one.' Jillian laughed. 'I did have one little drama. Gary came round soon after the kerfuffle and tried it on.'

'Not *the* Gary – all tinted hair and gold medallions?' Esmée asked.

'The same. It was odd. I don't think he *really* wanted to seduce me, just that he thought he ought to try. Almost as if it wouldn't be polite if he didn't. Anyhow, he looked quite relieved when I slapped him down.'

'Sad.'

'It is in a way, isn't it? Sort of fighting age, got to keep pulling the birds, kid everyone he's younger than he is. And I'd grown to quite like him. You know, he'd other reasons to be angry. Jack had been stealing from the business on a regular basis. Not enormous sums that would show up too

318

quickly but added together . . .' She frowned. 'I feel so guilty that we were living partly on stolen money.'

'Don't be so wet, Jill. It wasn't you stealing.'

'You know what I mean.'

'No, I don't. And you must stop thinking that way. It was Jack. Everything's Jack's fault.'

'Esmée! People do things for a reason. I think he always knew Ralph wasn't his father and it affected him deep down inside and made him a crook.'

'Or it could be hereditary,' Helen interrupted. 'You see, his father was a crook. Not as spectacular as his son, more a petty thief, I think it's fair to say,' Helen continued. 'He was what we used to call a spiv, a wide-boy. During the war, which of course he didn't fight in – something to do with his feet if I remember correctly – he was always a reliable source for anything on the black-market, such as stockings, coffee, cigarettes, whisky, those little luxuries that make life so much pleasanter. Benjie could always find them for you. That's how Theresa met him. She wanted some cigarettes but, of course, he gave her a lot more! He was devastatingly handsome, blond, blue-eyed, just like Jack. She was potty about him and, of course, quite lost her senses. Everyone warned her that he was no good, but would she listen? Of course, everyone was appalled at her choice, but I never understood quite why they were. She'd already shocked her snobbish family by choosing Ralph as a husband. She liked a bit of rough.'

'And this Benjie, where is he?' Jillian wanted to know.

'Gracious, my dear, he went to the thieves' kitchen in the sky – or perhaps it's down below – a long time ago. When Theresa became pregnant, the war conveniently ended and dear Benjie ran away to America. I hear he was shot in some gang battle.'

'Goodness. How could she have been so disapproving of me?'

'She's a silly woman. As hard as I try to feel pity for her now that she's in such a muddled state and so pathetic, I find it very difficult. The past will keep popping into my mind. It's dreadfully unChristian of me but I keep finding myself thinking that it serves her bloody well right.'

319

'I keep finding things out. Life with Jack was like a huge jigsaw puzzle with bits missing and I keep finding them. That story of Benjie is another piece to fit. And I had a letter from a woman who'd had an affair with Jack soon after Miles was born. She wrote to tell me I was well shot of him. All those years ago and I never twigged. It makes me feel such a fool.'

'Dear Jillian. Don't. The wife really *is* the last to know. And if you're honourable, of course you presume everyone else is.'

'There must have been others and so Cara wasn't an aberration, she was inevitable.'

'If it's any consolation, Jill, I've found out that Europe is littered with Cara's cast-offs,' Esmée said. 'Jack is safe all the time he has money, but if he loses it, our little bird will fly away fast to the next richly appointed nest. She's a whore, though no doubt she'd sue me if she heard me say so. That's what she is, though. She does it for money. The only difference between her and a prostitute is that the prostitute is honest.'

'But why?'

'Jill sweets, better not to ask, especially where men are concerned.'

'No doubt they'd say the same of us.' Helen laughed. 'Do you still miss him, Jillian?'

'Yes, I do.' She looked away, not wanting Helen to see how much. At the start of this period of her life she had longed for him with a physical ache that at times had been unbearable. But as the weeks became months she still missed him but not as painfully, or as frequently. However, she was glad that she was always so tired at night when the longing was worst.

'I still love him, you see.' He had been the first and only one for her. She could disapprove of him, she could be angry with him, even bitter – but she could not get rid of the love.

'Don't lecture me,' were Victoria's first words as she hauled her trunk to the car, expelled, as Jillian had feared, for smoking cannabis.

'I wasn't intending to. If you want to ruin your life, get on with it,' she said, already feeling her good intentions disappearing, replaced by mounting annoyance. There were times in her life when she wished she smoked and this was one of them, she thought, as she tapped the steering-wheel, still smarting from the headmistress's coolness.

'See? I knew you wouldn't be able to resist it.' Victoria climbed into the seat beside her, waving goodbye to her assembled friends, clenching her fist in a salute of triumph at which the others cheered and giggled.

'Proud of yourself, I see.'

'They're my friends and I'll say goodbye to them any way I want.'

'Some friends! I note that none of them has been as stupid as you.' They were at the bottom of the school drive waiting to turn into the road.

'You don't know anything about it. Everyone smokes dope these days – we're a different generation.' Still stationary, Jillian turned in her seat to look at her daughter, whose eyes flashed with not quite enough belligerence to mask the tears. At the sight of them she decided not to say anything. 'You might have put yourself out and turned up smart instead of in jeans. Honestly!'

They were unfortunate words for Jillian's momentary sympathy dissipated rapidly. 'Look, Victoria, you've been a fool. Don't try the smart-arsed approach with me.' She swung the car into the road.

'Tut-tut, Mumsie. Such language. What will the neighbours say?'

'I don't give a damn what anyone says – not any more. I just wish you'd stop and see that the one person you've damaged with these actions is yourself. But you're too dumb to realise it, aren't you?' She knew she was driving too fast, but it was as if her anger was drawn into the foot on the accelerator. She forced herself to slow down.

'I don't know what all the fuss is about. You'd think I was mainlining the way the droopy-drawers head went on at me. Why sack me? Everyone else gets away with it.' The sullenness was back in her voice. 'I might just as well have done heroin.'

'Not everyone does heroin, for a start. And don't think I don't know what I'm talking about because I do. And I can assure you of one thing, Victoria, if you want to go down that particular road then you travel on your own. I will have nothing to do with you and I will not help you.'

'Call yourself a mother?' Victoria sneered.

'And while we're sorting out a few home truths you'll have to get a job. I can't afford to support you.'

'You can use the money Aunt Esmée gives you for my education.'

'That is to educate you, not to support you in idleness.'

'What job can I do? I'm not trained in anything. Miserable sods! Eight weeks to my GCSEs – they could have waited.'

'That school has been patience personified towards you. They made every allowance they could because of the upset over your father. You brought this upon yourself.' She slowed down again at traffic lights as they approached Bishops Stortford. She had been here often with Jack – so long ago. She shut her eyes tight to blank out that line of thought.

'Exactly. They should have made double the excuses for me and the trauma I've suffered – thanks to you.'

'Thousands of kids' dads leave home and they don't all rush to smoke pot.'

'You bet? So, what great career have you lined up for me?'

'There are plenty of waitressing jobs around. I suggest you apply for one of those.'

'Me? No way.'

'I'm not too proud to work in a bar.'

'You needn't boast about it. I was mortified you'd stooped so low. I never told any of my friends.'

'It feeds and clothes you – or it did until now.'

The atmosphere in the small car was heavy with animosity. But Jillian was determined that this time she would be firm with Victoria. The girl's attitude was making it a lot easier for her to do so. She found, to her amazement, that she disliked her daughter for all the trouble she was creating – she'd never expected to think like that.

'I think I'll split and go to London.' Finally Victoria spoke.

'Yes, you do that,' Jillian replied, to her daughter's astonishment. The surprise silenced Victoria for the rest of the whole journey home.

322

Chapter Nine

1

Summer 1990

'I don't understand you, Jillian. You're letting Victoria run wild. She was telling me that most nights she stays out and you don't care what time she comes home. That can't be right.'

'Of course I care. But, Mother, she's eighteen. I have no legal right to stop her doing whatever she wants. What's your suggestion? That I throw her out on to the street? A lot of good that would do.' Jillian tested the potatoes she was cooking for the supper she had prepared for the two of them. Recently she had made a concerted effort to see her mother since Mary's depression was, if anything, worse. Once a week she invited her round on her own. She was always hopeful that Mary would eventually confide in her. Jillian was sure it had something to do with Rob, but she was also aware that her mother was of a generation to whom discussing problems was anathema.

'I think you should talk to her. Jillian, you didn't buy steak, did you? It's far too expensive.' Mary's conversation, as always, flitted from one topic to the next.

'When do you and I go out? Rarely. So I thought it was about time we had a treat. I've got strawberries too, I'm warning you.' She turned back to the cooker. Then she realised that, for the first time, she had forgotten that today was the fourth anniversary of Jack's disappearance. Did that mean she was getting over him?

'By the way, I had a letter from Michelle.' Jillian broke the silence. 'She's good at keeping in touch.' She stirred the Roquefort sauce she was making. 'Her business is going well.'

'I never understood her following that Shane to Australia

when he beat her up so bad. Still, there's no accounting for taste, is there?'

'She's not with him any more. In fact, reading between the lines, I think our Michelle is in love.'

'With a man or a woman?'

'Mum, you –' She nearly said 'sound like Jack' but stopped herself in time. 'It's the idea of Michelle selling skin-care products I can't get my head round.'

'She's an attractive woman.'

'I didn't mean that. It's just that she was always against makeup and stuff.'

'I've always admired Michelle. She wouldn't have put up with half the rubbish you had from Jack.'

She was about to begin. 'Right, it's ready, put this dish on the table for me, Mum.' Jillian said to forestall her.

When they were settled, the wine poured, Mary started again. 'The one thing I will say about us is that we always talked things through.'

'Mum, that's not true, we never did. I don't once remember us sitting round the table as a family and discussing problems.'

'But we never had problems like you go in for.' Mary neatly cut the fat from her steak. 'The price of meat nowadays, they should trim the fat off – I think,' Mary prattled on, unaware of the frown on Jillian's face.

'You make it sound as if I engineer them. You don't think I enjoy Victoria's behaviour, do you? Sometimes, Mum . . .' She trailed off.

'Then talk to her. She's lost.'

'It isn't that simple. From past experience I know she's not going to listen to me. She's goading me into a confrontation. She wants us to have a great big barney and I don't intend to give her the satisfaction.'

'But you can't go on like this. You look dreadful and she looks worse.'

'Thanks a bunch. When did you see her?'

'She pops round.' Mary did not look at her.

'Are you giving her money?' Mary did not answer. 'If you

are, stop it. She needs to get a job and if you do that she never will.'

'She's got to have something.'

'Why? I feed and clothe her. I refuse point-blank to give her money to spend on drugs.'

'Oh, she never does!' Mary dropped her knife and fork with a clatter. 'Not Victoria, she's far too sensible. In any case I asked her about that fuss when she was given the boot and she says she was set up at the school, that she thought it was an ordinary cigarette. It happens, you know.'

'Yes, but it wouldn't happen to Victoria. She's far more likely to be the one doing the setting up.'

'What a way to talk about your own daughter.'

'She lied to you, Mum, I can promise you that.'

'She doesn't lie. Really, Jillian, what's got into you?'

'But it's the truth, Mum. Just because she's my daughter there's no reason why I shouldn't acknowledge what she's like. Please listen to me. I'm not sure if what I'm doing is the right thing, but I know you're not.'

'If you say so.' Mary sounded far from sure. 'But I can't help feeling sorry for the girl. After all, she idolised her dad. That's what's caused all this, hasn't it?'

'I don't know, Mum. She was an angelic little girl. A friend at work told me that if you have a good toddler she'd guarantee a disruptive teenager and vice versa. She was a bit iffy before . . . but she's got worse.' Oops, she thought, she'd stopped herself just in time from mentioning Jack. 'I suppose it could also be argued that it's genetic. Look at Patsy. Maybe she'll end up like her.'

'I know you've never approved of your sister's lifestyle but I can't see the harm in it. She lives her life as she wants. She doesn't give a monkey's about anyone and I admire that. And it isn't as if she's a junkie, now is it?'

'I sometimes think how wonderful it would be to be that selfish and free! But that doesn't alter the fact that I think Patsy is an extremely dangerous woman – just like her friend Sally Brentwood before her. Young kids see that, despite all the drugs, they manage their lives and they think they can do the same. But maybe they're not the same. Maybe they're addictive types and don't know it. The Patsys of this world lure them into a web of drugs and addiction.'

'You do exaggerate. Our Patsy would never hurt anyone. She's not like that.'

'Not intentionally, but she's too selfish to change her lifestyle if someone like Victoria, easily influenced, happens along.'

'You've always been too hard on Patsy. She hasn't had an easy life like you.'

'Easy! You think mine's been easy? You think I didn't work hard to maintain our lifestyle, that everything just happened by itself? That I didn't work all the hours God gave to keep all the balls in the air? I thought you of all people would understand.'

'You needn't get huffy with me if the truth doesn't suit.'

'Then don't say something like that. Patsy can never do any wrong in your eyes, can she? I live a conventional life, I've done everything people expected of me. Sometimes I think I put my life on hold for everybody else. Patsy is self-obsessed, always does what she wants, with no regard for anybody else, and *she*'s never criticised. It's not fair.'

'Really, Jillian, pull yourself together. You sound like a child. You were always jealous of her. That steak was very nice, dear.' Mary laid her knife and fork on the plate. 'In any case, I've always found that people only do what they want to do, so if you wanted to martyr yourself, doing housework, that was your choice.'

Jillian collected the dirty dishes and, smouldering with anger at her mother's words, went to the kitchen to collect the strawberries. Almost defiantly she opened the second bottle of wine.

'What about this business of Dad molesting her as a child?' she said, upon returning. She had vowed never to open the subject again but she wanted to hurt her mother as she had just been hurt.

'I don't believe it. It was a horrible thing to say. But I said at the time she was attention-seeking.'

'There you go! But Patsy said it, didn't she? She isn't all perfect, is she? She has faults and so has Victoria.'

Mary was upset. 'Your father doted on her, as you well know.'

'That's what she said, though.'

'It's no good blaming someone else for your problems.'

'I'm not.'

'Sounds as if you are to me.' Mary fiddled with her napkin. 'But then, today of all days, I suppose it's understandable, isn't it?'

'More wine?' Jillian topped up their glasses, ignoring the question.

'Pushing the boat out a bit, aren't you?'

'I feel like a drink.'

'Any news of Jack?'

'None whatsoever. The police tell me that they had a report he was in Bournemouth but it was a false lead.'

'I can't see our Jack in Bournemouth.'

'He's not our Jack any more,' Jillian said tartly.

'Well, I'm glad to hear you say that. You can't moon about him for ever. You should be out and about trying to find a new husband.'

'What? And end up terminally miserable like you?' The question was out before she could stop it. To cover her confusion she poured more wine into her glass, slopping half of it on the tablecloth. Quickly she was on her feet and in the kitchen, ostensibly to get a cloth. She returned to find her mother staring blankly into space while tears rolled down her cheeks.

'Oh, Mum, I'm so sorry, I should never have said that. Please forgive me.' She was beside her mother, intending to comfort her.

Mary brushed her hand away. 'Just look at me, silly old bag! This won't pay the rent!' She stood up abruptly, swayed and sat down again.

'Mum?'

Mary looked up at her. She started to speak, stopped, clutched at her throat and was racked by a sob. 'I can't go on!' she said. She cried now, a great gulping noise, as she fought for breath between sobs. Jillian, who could not remember having seen her mother cry before, stood transfixed and horrified. Gingerly she patted her mother's shoulder. Her touch seemed to galvanise Mary into a greater paroxysm of weeping. At the sight of this misery, Jillian's legs gave way too and she sat down. She gulped her wine desperately.

'I'm sorry.' Mary looked at her with a tear-stained face. 'I shouldn't have . . . It was . . . I've been bottling things up. You shook me . . . caught me unawares.' She dabbed at her eyes somewhat ineffectually with her hankie. 'Must have been the drink – you know me, never touch it. Just as well.' She laughed a very shaky laugh.

'I think you should tell me, Mum.' Gently Jillian took her mother's hand.

'There's nothing much to tell. Rob's a bully and a bastard, and I should never have left your father for him. That's all. And now that I'm over sixty it all seems much worse and I don't know what to do.' She looked as if she was about to cry again, so Jillian squeezed her hand encouragingly.

'Does he hit you? Patsy said . . .'

'What an idea! Silly Patsy. What made her say that? No, nothing like that. I wouldn't have stood for that. No, he gets at me in other ways. Whatever I do, it's never right, his ex-wife did it better. I'm ugly. I'm fat. I'm clumsy. I'm stupid. Who else would ever want me? I'm old.' And the tears welled again.

'He sounds insecure. Isn't that what some people do, make you feel inadequate because they're afraid of losing you?'

'But it's getting worse and it's true. I *could* cope years ago, when I was younger. But now I'm over sixty everything's changed.'

'What's being sixty got to do with it? You don't look your age – you're a good-looking woman. I hope I look half as good when I'm your age.'

'It's awful – I can't explain. All the years, they've just slipped by so fast. Where have they gone? What have I done with them? What am I doing with my life? When you're young you think you'll live for ever and then you get to this age and you start working it out. How much longer have I got? Will I see my grandchildren married and settled? I don't

328

want to die.' She began to wail again. Jillian waited patiently for this bout of crying to subside.

'Mum, don't you think you're like this because you're so unhappy with Rob? He demoralises you – is it any wonder that you feel so depressed? Goodness, you've got years yet. Please, don't talk in this way.'

'Maybe you're right. I don't know any more. I'm just permanently sad.'

'Do you think you should see the doctor?'

'What good would that do? No, I've got to sort this out myself.'

'Should I talk to Rob?'

'No, no. That would make matters worse.'

'You know what you should do? Leave him.'

'And live by myself? I couldn't Jillian, I'd be too scared.'

2

Spring–Summer 1992

As the years slipped by with no news of Jack, Jillian wished sometimes that she knew where and how he was. Some nights his presence seemed so strong that she felt he was there in the room with her and missed him painfully. At other times she felt nothing but contempt for him. Then she thought of him as dead and out of her life for ever – since he might just as well be. Often it was as if her previous life had been a dream and had nothing to do with this Jillian.

'Mum, can I come for a few days?'

'Miles, need you ask?' Her voice brimmed with pleasure at the thought of seeing him after so long – over a year, she'd worked out.

'Mum, I've something to tell you. Something nice.'

'You're getting married?'

'You're a witch.'

'How lovely.'

'And I thought I'd bring her to meet you . . .'

As soon as she replaced the receiver Jillian flew into a panic over bed space – two bedrooms! Maybe Victoria wouldn't mind sleeping downstairs. Or could she run to buying the sofa-bed she'd been thinking about. Gracious, what excitement!

'This is Maxine Weaver, Mum.'

'I'm so pleased to meet you.' She took the young woman's hands in both of hers in a genuine warm welcome.

'How do you do, Mrs Stirling?' Maxine smiled, but with a start Jillian saw that it was with her mouth only. The smile did not go as far as her eyes.

'Well, yes, come in, do.' Suddenly Jillian felt stupid, as if she'd been gushing when she knew she hadn't. 'I'm afraid it's very small.' She wondered why she had said that.

'You should have seen our last house. Mum made it beautiful, didn't you, Mum?'

'I tried.'

'You told me.'

For an awful moment Jillian wondered if Maxine was stifling a yawn. 'Tea? Or a drink?' she asked, suppressing such an idea.

'Drink for me.'

'Tea, please, Mrs Stirling.'

'Do call me Jillian.'

'If you wish.'

There it was again. A voice of barely concealed boredom. Was she here on sufferance? She had so often imagined this moment and what it would be like. She'd been certain she'd adore whomever Miles chose, and secretly hoped he'd fulfil the biggest compliment a son could pay a mother and choose someone who looked like her. Daft of her.

Maxine was tiny, barely five foot, Jillian guessed. While she herself was blonde – if a bit faded, these days – Maxine was dark with large, brown eyes. Jillian was slim, and Maxine had a voluptuous figure. Jillian smiled frequently, and Maxine smiled hardly at all.

'So congratulations, Miles. When's the wedding to be?' She forced happy expectation into her voice.

'Mum, you've got to stop him. He can't marry her, she's awful!'

'She's probably shy of us. It's never easy meeting your boyfriend's family.'

'There you go again, being reasonable. Why can't you be honest for once and say you hate her?'

'Because I don't, silly, so how could I?' Jillian smiled at Victoria's exuberant dislike: it could so easily swing the other way and Maxine become her best friend.

'But you don't like her?'

Jillian concentrated on the washing-up so as not to have to answer.

'I'm glad they went to a hotel. I didn't want to give up my bed for her.'

'It's made it easier.' Though, in fact, Jillian had felt disappointed they had gone. She'd decided they could have her room and had even made up the bed. Miles had wavered, but Maxine had been adamant. 'We don't want to put you to any trouble, Mrs Stirling,' she'd said, with that smile that wasn't a smile.

'She's got to be mustard in bed, that's all I can think. Why else would he be with her?'

'Victoria, you're winding yourself up.'

'With reason. She's so superior she's looking down her nose at us all the time.'

'I expect she was a bit surprised by this house.'

'So? We've got nice things. If she's sneering at how we live then she's sneering at you, and I won't have it!'

'Victoria, that's so sweet of you.' Jillian was touched by her daughter's staunch defence, especially when she thought they had drifted too far apart ever to be this close again. Yes, that was it, tonight they *were* close and united.

'She knows about Dad. She made a snide remark. I don't know how I stopped myself from swiping her.'

'What?'

'I can't remember. But it was snide . . .'

'Victoria, if you can't remember it can't have been that bad.'

331

'She's loathsome.'

'Darling, you think no one would be good enough for your brother. That's what all this means. She's not right in your eyes.' Or mine, she thought, as she gave Victoria a big hug to try to blot out her own concerns.

Boyd and Vanessa Weaver ran a country-house hotel in Berkshire. Miles had taken a job there as an under-manager and had fallen in love with the boss's daughter. It was a lovely hotel, beautifully furnished, full of flowers, pot-pourri and whispering guests. It should have been perfect, but it wasn't. There was a rigid formality to it that made the occupants look uneasy.

'Why's everyone whispering?' Victoria asked, doing the same.

'I don't know. Maybe they're overawed by the house.' Jillian managed to speak normally.

The large ornate arrangement in the hall was made of artificial flowers. They reminded Jillian of her mother-in-law and she shuddered. She hoped they were not an omen, for those flowers of Theresa's, so out of place in that lovely house, had become symbolic of everything else that had been false there.

Their room had everything they could possibly need, from headache pills to a miniature decanter of sherry. Victoria was happy in the bathroom, sniffing the various bath products. Jillian looked at the carefully selected books.

'It's just like being in someone's house. It's so well thought-out.' Except for the flowers, Jillian thought, as Miles appeared at the door of their room.

'Everything all right?'

'This room's got everything.'

'The Weavers know what they're about. A sachet or two of Crabtree and Evelyn, tissues in lace-trimmed boxes, a thimbleful of sherry and you can charge – how you can charge! All those odds and sods and you can add a good fifteen to twenty quid on the bill. It's cost you a pound and the punters think they're getting it all for free. Can't be bad, can it?' Miles grinned proudly.

'You wretch. You're spoiling it. You sound so . . . commercial.' And like your father, she thought, but she didn't add that. 'Do you get on with Maxine's family?'

'Dad more than Mum. I work more with him. She's a bit of a fusspot. We just say, "Yes, Mrs W," and then do it how we think. But it's no problem, we shan't be staying here.'

'Oh, I presumed you'd continue working with them.'

'No, I want more than this. I want a big hotel to run. I'm thinking of Paris for a couple of years, or maybe Zurich – pack in the experience.'

'You really like this work?'

'I love it! It's different every day. And there's so much to learn. Right, are you ready? Then we'll go and meet my future in-laws. And, Victoria, don't sulk. This is a big day for me and I don't want you messing it up.'

'Honestly, Miles, you speak to me as if I'm nine instead of nineteen.'

'Your body might be, but your mind's stuck at nine!'

The best way to describe Vanessa Weaver, Jillian decided, was professionally gracious. The house was gracious, as was the food, the ambience, the curtains and the conversation. But she felt that it was all a charade. That this was Vanessa being the perfect hostess to them, not their friend. Nothing was said, no rude or dubious remarks were made, but Jillian could not get rid of the idea that Miles and his family were a great disappointment to the Weavers.

Jillian had always dreamed that one day, when Victoria married, she would invite her fiancé's mother to discuss every aspect of the wedding. She would welcome this woman so that in no way would she feel excluded from the excitement of the planning. Part of the dream was that when Miles married, hopefully, his future mother-in-law would include her. As with so many daydreams this was not to be.

As the wedding day approached, Jillian heard nothing from Vanessa so she telephoned to ask if there was anything she could do to help. Vanessa was curt. There was nothing for Jillian to 'bother herself with.' 'I've got everything under control,' she said, with a heavy emphasis on the I.

Miles's family was booked into the local village inn for the weekend of the great day.

'Give her a bell. Say you want to help with the flowers.'

'I don't like to, Mum. If she wanted us to help she would have asked.'

'You're too soft, Jillian. I'm going up to the church to see what's what.'

'I wish you wouldn't, Mum.' But Mary would not listen and sallied forth to do battle, only to return a quarter of an hour later ruffled and put out.

'Well! She's got a bad case of the Lady Bountifuls, hasn't she?' Mary flounced into the bar. 'She was all smarmy smiles and how kind of you, but the bottom line was that she wanted the flowers done her way. I couldn't possibly have the breeding to know what was the right or the wrong way. Blow her! And then, when I asked if we might see the wedding presents, I was told it was not convenient and that we'd have to wait until tomorrow like everybody else. But we're not just anybody, are we? We're Miles's family.'

Mary was hurt. Jillian was not surprised. Her own feelings weren't damaged, but she was concerned for the future. She had hoped to be gaining a daughter, but she was seriously worried that not only was that not so but that she had definitely lost her son.

'So, how was America?' Jillian asked, as she ushered Esmée – who as usual had just turned up with no warning – into her little house.

'Large.' Esmée slipped off her jacket, kicked off her shoes and, in her normal elegantly effortless way, seemed to float into the armchair.

'And the plastic surgeon?'

'Still slicing people up, no doubt. But not me. All he wanted to talk about were other women's boobs – I ask you!'

'Would you like some tea? I've only got cooking sherry. If I'd known . . .'

'Darling, don't fret. As you know Auntie Esmée never travels unprepared!' And, laughing, she produced a bottle of vodka from her usual voluminous handbag. 'Simpler than gin, I don't need the tonic.' She waved it in the air. 'I suppose you've no ice.'

'I might have.' Jillian collected glasses and ice from the small kitchen.

Esmée poured the drinks. 'So, my little nephew's married. How was it?'

'It was a lovely wedding . . .' Jillian began. 'Oh, what the hell! It was awful. I felt in the way, as if *his* guests were only tolerated. It wasn't how I'd imagined it would be, more fool me.'

'And the blushing bride?'

'She doesn't blush for a start. She's never been anything but polite to me, but I don't think she likes me or anyone to do with Miles.'

'The jealous, possessive type?'

'No, I don't think so. More the cold, emotionally frozen sort. There's just no warmth there and it's so worrying.'

'And Miles?'

'He's besotted with her. I don't think he sees any fault in her. Which, of course, is as it should be,' she added hurriedly, knowing that even with Esmée she should not be so disloyal.

'Probably good in the sack.'

'That's what Victoria says.'

'Of course it won't last. Poor Miles.'

'It's done now.' She sat up in her chair. 'How were the adventures?'

'Numerous.' Esmée stretched. 'But nothing worth hanging on to.'

'I quite expected you to stay there.'

'Me? No. I love America – so busy and vibrant – but I'm a staid old European at heart.'

'Staid is hardly the word that springs to mind. Thanks.' She accepted her own glass.

'I saw Jack.'

Jillian's glass paused in its path to her mouth. 'Did you?' she said carefully.

'Yes. Sends his love, though I pointed out that I doubted it would be appreciated.'

'Is he all right?'

'He's fine. Jillian, you're such a sweetie. I'd have bet anything that's what you'd ask.'

'Where?'

'South America. He's got a flat overlooking the sea. He's working, importing stuff, I gather. He said he was dreadfully ashamed at what he did. Says he doesn't know what got into him. I pointed out that it was me he was talking to, no need to lie. That he was just a crook at heart. Do you know what he said? "Like my father."'

'He knew all along?'

'Yes. You were right. Our mother told him years ago and he never let on. I'd have blabbed it to everyone, wouldn't you? Well, probably you wouldn't. No, all that angst about his daddy not liking him, all put on. How did you guess?'

'After Theresa blurted it all out he was never curious about who his real father was. But I wasn't sure. I could have been way off beam because the hardest part has been the realisation that I thought I knew him and I didn't.'

'Who ever really knows anyone?' Esmée looked up. 'I've a letter for you and a message.' From the same capacious handbag she extracted an envelope. Jillian put it on the small table beside her. Esmée watched her intently. 'He wants to know if you'll join him?'

'No,' Jillian said simply, and discovered she was not surprised at the question or her answer. 'He must be between women for him even to ask.'

'Are you going to read your letter?'

'Later will do.'

'Excellent!' Esmée poured more vodka. 'I was so afraid you'd be over the moon with bliss. He never deserved you. Helen told me she thought you were sad and still pining for him so I was almost afraid to deliver his note and his request.'

'I'm sad because I've had to learn there are no for-evers. And I pine for what I thought I had – somewhat pointless since evidently it was all in my imagination. And how could I ever trust him again? Then there's poor Victoria. She's still a handful. Honestly, Esmée, she might be twenty but with her moods it's like living with a teenager. It's as if she's frozen at the age she was when he left.'

'Like she doesn't want to grow up and take on responsibilities?'

'Exactly.'

'I know how she feels. Poor Victoria. Well, we shall just have to love her even more, shan't we? Good old TLC.'

'And that's harder to do than you think.'

'You do realise I can't give you Jack's address if you're not going to join him?'

'Afraid I'd shop him?'

'Well, you are fearfully moral, aren't you?'

'I wouldn't, but I'd rather not know where he is. Then I don't have to lie to the police – they keep in touch, you know.' She drained her glass, declined more. 'Have you eaten?'

'No, but I'm taking you out. And don't flap, I've booked myself into the Garden House.'

As she prepared to go out Jillian studied her face in the mirror. Had she changed? Were the past six years marked on her face? She didn't think she looked too bad. She wondered what Jack would think. She smiled at her reflection. How strange life was. All those years of longing for him and dreaming of being with him, and then when the opportunity came she could turn it down without a second's thought.

This day, she saw, was another watershed in her life. She had been through a trial and had emerged the other side. There was a future, after all.

'I've a proposition, Jillian. You don't have to decide in a rush – take your time.' They were at the pudding stage of their meal at Panos's restaurant, fussed over and made to feel important as always by the proprietor, Genevieve. 'I'm looking for a partner.'

'And?'

'I want you to help me run a hotel.'

'A hotel? You? Where?'

'Scotland. My great-aunt Fiona has turned up her little toes and she's left me her mansion, lock, stock and barrel. I want to convert it into an upmarket pad. It eats money – like feeding a dinosaur Maltesers.'

'Why not sell it?'

'I'd prefer not to. Dear Aunt Fiona lived for that house – she adored it. She left it to me because she knew I loved it too. Only, even with my money, it needs to wash its face.'

'But I don't know anything about running a hotel. You need a professional.'

'That's exactly what I don't want. This hotel will be like a home from home – and who ran her huge house like clockwork? You. You'd be perfect.'

'But I've got no money to put in.'

'I don't want any money. I want you.'

'It's a very attractive idea, but . . .' She looked down to hide her disappointment. 'I . . . I can't leave Cambridge.'

'Why not? Victoria? She's old enough to paddle her own canoe.'

'No. It's my mother. She's very unhappy and depressed. I can't leave her.'

'Then bring her with you. There are plenty of cottages and she can live in one of them.'

'You mean it?'

'Of course. And the dreaded Victoria can work as the kitchenmaid!'

'You reckon?'

'Look, I've been very professional and I've done loads of figures and business projections. The bank manager almost fell off his chair with shock.' Esmée cleared a space on the pink linen tablecloth and laid out charts and lists. She settled down to explain them to Jillian.

'Can I think about this?' Jillian asked, an hour later, as the taxi drew up outside her house.

'Darling, take all the time you want,' Esmée said, and was driven off to her hotel.

For days Jillian wondered what to do. As always she made her endless lists of pros and cons, but even though the pro list was the longest, she delayed making a decision. She broached the subject with her mother, who at first said she 'couldn't possibly', but then, 'On the other hand' and 'It would be selfish', and then, 'Why not?'

'You know, my mother was Scottish and I was born there, but I can only just remember it before we left for England. I'd like to see it before I die. What about Rob?'

'Mum, only you can make that decision. After all, only you know how unhappy you are. And stop going on about when you die!'

'What if it doesn't work out? What if the business fails? Then where would I go, and how would I manage?'

'I'm keeping this house. Esmée says she wants no money from me so I'm going to let it. If the worst comes to the worst, we've got this to fall back on.'

A week later Mary had made up her mind and so, consequently, had Jillian.

'I saw Patsy, and she said I should go for it. After all, what have I got to lose?'

'That's great,' said Jillian, covering her irritation at learning that because Patsy had agreed it was all all right. None of her own arguments had meant a thing to Mary.

'How can you even consider it? I'm not going to go and live in the back of beyond. I'd die of boredom.'

'Victoria, why don't you just come and see it? You might change your mind.'

'No way. I don't want to live with a load of haggis-eaters in skirts!'

'I'm going.'

'I know your last concern is for me.'

'I haven't made my mind up definitely. I want to see the house for myself too, but I promised Esmée that once I have I'll decide one way or the other. I'd be happier if you were there with me.'

'No, you wouldn't. You don't give a toss about me.'

'That's not true, and you know it. But while you're hurling insults around, perhaps you should think this out. You're an adult now. You can't rely on me to be around all the time. And you'll be off soon, married or shacked up with someone,

339

no doubt. And where does that leave me? Just think a minute, will you? This is a wonderful opportunity for me. It will be hard work but it will give me a measure of security that I don't have at the moment. Don't you see that?'

Victoria had the grace to look guilty. 'Is Gran going to see the house?'

'No, she said she would rely on my judgement.'

'I'll come, but I won't like it. I might go to London.'

'We're agreed, then. If you don't like it, I'll help you get settled there. But give Scotland a chance.'

3

Autumn 1992

As if Scotland knew it was on trial it could not have looked more beautiful and more seductive. Esmée had met Jillian and Victoria at Inverness station off the sleeper from London, which had been an adventure in itself. Given the hour, Jillian was surprised that her sister-in-law was even awake. She was even more surprised to see how alert and fit she looked.

They stopped at a viewing-point on Struie Hill, and clambered out of the car. Below them, stretching as far as the eye could see, was the Dornoch Firth in all its beauty in the early-autumn sun. Far to the west Jillian could see the mauve and purple smudge of distant mountains. It was as if they stood on top of the world and that they were the only people in it. She took a deep breath of air, so clean, so clear it was like inhaling pure oxygen. All her senses were at work and acute, and she was aware of them in a way she had not been for a very long time. The awesomeness of the view had silenced them all, including Victoria.

'I'm sorry this is such a mess,' Esmée apologised as, a little later, they bounced along a rutted driveway. Rhododendron bushes, evidently untamed for years, brushed against the side of the car as if clamouring to welcome them. 'Right, we're nearly there. Close your eyes, I want to surprise you,' she said, after five minutes more of the rattling drive. Jillian did as she asked, but Victoria peeped through her fingers. She heard her daughter gasp. 'Victoria, you wretch. Keep your eyes closed! Keep them closed, Jillian,' Esmée shouted. 'You can look now. Welcome to Altnahany.'

Ahead, with rough grass growing right to its edge as if it was resting on a bright green cloth, stood a large house, which, despite its size, had a lightness to it. At either end were round towers with pepper-pot roofs. It was harled in pink, and the steep mansard roof was tiled in a bluish grey slate that seemed to have been chosen to tone with the hills towering behind it. Long casement windows glinted in the sunshine. The massive oak doorway stood welcomingly open.

'Esmée, I'd no idea it would be as beautiful as this.'

'She's something else, isn't she? I think of her as a woman. She's lovely and graceful. What do you think, Victoria?'

'It's lovely. Is there a town near by?' Victoria asked, in a reasonable tone.

'About five miles away, along the glen. It's not exactly a jumping joint. There are a couple of bars, several shops and they do have the odd ceilidh.'

'What's that?' Victoria asked.

'It's a general singsong, and people recite poems and play the bagpipes and there's dancing. Actually, they're rather jolly. Though I doubt if it would be of interest to you, Victoria.'

'Oh, I don't know,' she replied, to Jillian's astonishment.

'Of course, if you came we'd have to get you a car and you'd have to have driving lessons. Wouldn't you?'

'I suppose I would.' Victoria failed to keep the excitement out of her voice.

'What do you think?' Esmée asked, as they sat in the plush, somewhat over-furnished, drawing room, their tour of the house complete.

'It's fantastic! Can I have a room in one of the towers?' Victoria's face was animated. Jillian could not remember when she had last seen her daughter look so eager and happy.

'Of course, Victoria, sweetheart. You must have whichever room you want. But it will have to be the topmost, because of

341

the fire regulations. The guests must be protected but we can burn to a crisp and no one will mind. And you, Jillian? Do you think it's a goer?'

'It's a beautiful house. Such lovely furniture and things in it. But it's going to need an enormous amount of work.'

'Mum, don't say you've got doubts. I'll help. I can paint. I'll do the washing-up – anything. I've only just got here and I adore it. It's like I've always known this place. Please don't be a spoilsport, please say yes, Mum!'

'Actually, Victoria, it was the expense for Esmée that was worrying me. Guests in hotels, these days, demand so much. People want *en suite* bathrooms – I counted at least eighteen bedrooms but only two bathrooms.'

'The bathrooms are a bit antiquated. Mind you, I think we should keep the old baths and loos – they're bliss and would cost an arm and a leg in London. There's a third bathroom in the staff quarters – that's even grottier. I don't think Aunt Fiona's generation cared much for washing, do you?' Esmée laughed.

'Not if it gets too cold here in winter. My mother was born in Aberdeenshire and she says she can remember the cold and how they had to break the ice on the water in the morning. Her mother had a constant battle keeping her children clean.'

'Mum, really, that's because Gran's mother only had peat fires. Gran said they smelt wonderful. Can we have peat fires, Aunt Esmée? You're just putting up difficulties, Mum.'

'I'm not. But I'd be doing Esmée no favours if I don't point out any drawbacks I see.'

'Make a list, Jillian. You know your system – write down the advantages and disadvantages. Let's do that.' Esmée handed her a notebook and pen. 'See, I got this ready for you. I know how your mind works.'

'I can tell you already, Esmée, that I would love to help you make this into a hotel.'

'Yes!' Victoria punched the air.

'The position is perfect. That view of the loch with the mountain behind is breathtaking. It's not on the main road and everything tells me it should be, but perhaps we could get permission to put up a sign pointing people towards the glen road. Then its isolation might become an advantage. You say you have some salmon fishing and a small amount of hill for stalking. I think that would be necessary, here. But . . .'

'Oh, no, there always has to be a but with you, Mum, doesn't there?'

'Victoria, leave your mother alone. I want to hear what she has to say. So be an angel and shut your cake-hole for a mo.'

As usual Victoria did as Esmée asked, and Jillian wondered, not for the first time, how she dealt so easily with her.

'The but refers to expense. You want an upmarket hotel, Esmée, but this furniture is worn and threadbare, I saw holes in the curtains and paint chipped off the radiators. People like your aunt don't mind what others think of them, but the sort of people who'll come here to stay will expect everything to be tarted up a bit.'

'I accept some changes will be necessary but not too much. Part of the charm of this house is its dilapidated look. A friend of mine has totally ruined their lodge – ghastly naff tartan carpets, frilly curtains looking like tart's knickers, everything decorated within an inch of its life, totally out of keeping with a hunting lodge. All it lacks is the Gideon Bible. I couldn't do that to this place.'

'I agree. But I think there's still a lot that we'd have to change – those curtains for a start. They must be a hundred years old.'

'I like them,' Victoria said defensively, jumping to her feet. She crossed the room and shook the drapes. A cloud of choking dust billowed out.

'To add bathrooms, you're going to have to alter the proportions of some of those lovely rooms. Will you get permission to do so? It must be listed, surely?'

'Yes, it is, and I've already thought about them. I'd hate to carve out little boxes to put the bathrooms in. But I've solved it – like this.' She pulled a sheet of paper out of a folder, on which she had done some sketches of the first floor – cleverly turning some rooms into two bathrooms and giving each remaining bedroom its own.

'That's neat. But that way you lose bedrooms, and surely

we need at least a dozen people to stay to make the whole operation viable. And what about the fire regulations?'

'Mu-um . . .' Victoria whined. With one look Esmée silenced her.

'At the moment we can only take six because there's no fire escape. But I've made inquiries and a man is coming to see me about installing one. Once that's in we can use the upper floor. Then, if we exclude Victoria's room in the tower, we should be able to sleep a good eighteen – if not twenty. And we shall be rolling in lovely loot. Don't look so worried, Jillian. I've got the money to do this and to do it properly. I might know nothing about running hotels but I know one hell of a lot about staying in them. I intend to make this hotel the most sought-after in Scotland. And, even if you're still wavering, I think we should have some champagne to launch this whole project.'

'I'd agree with that.'

'Does that mean you're saying yes, Mum?'

'There's still a lot to discuss. But let's say I'm three-quarters of the way there.'

Victoria rewarded her mother with a passionate hug and a kiss – just as she once had, but so long ago.

Jillian couldn't sleep but for once it was not through worrying. It was obvious, even to her untrained eye, that this house had enormous potential. She felt she had been right to play the devil's advocate and put up all the possible problems they could meet. It would have been too easy just to agree – after all, Esmée would look after her if it succeeded or failed, she was sure of that. But she felt that she would be cheating if she didn't tell Esmée everything she thought.

The kitchen, spacious and with generous windows, was wonderful for a family. There was an enormous pine dresser along one wall on which was arranged china, its glaze cracked with age. The large, uneven table was bleached nearly white from interminable scrubbing. The double ceramic sinks were deep, with overhead wooden plate-racks, and the Aga, which looked as though it must have been one of the first ever manufactured, was caked with black burned-on grease. Nothing would pass the stiff health regulations that must be in force, she thought, and yet it was a kitchen that some would spend a small fortune trying to recreate elsewhere.

In the middle of the night she got up and took out a book she had borrowed from Cambridge Library, a manual of hotel management. It listed rules and regulations by the page. As she read, there was no doubt in her mind that the kitchen would have to be gutted, that the beautiful black Caithness stone flooring would have to be changed, or at least covered, to satisfy the authorities.

They would have to get estimates on the work to be carried out – she began to scribble, making lists under Kitchen and further lists under Bathrooms. And neither of them, she remembered, had gone to see or discussed the condition of the boiler. Even if it worked, it must be for solid fuel and would have to be converted to oil. If not, they would need a man to shovel coal into it full-time.

As dawn approached Jillian looked out of the window to see the moorland opposite tinged the most extraordinary golden pink as the day crept up the glen. She opened the window, took a deep breath of the gin clear air, and the cobwebs she had felt from too much champagne last night disappeared. She listened. Last night she had thought there was a profound silence here. Now she understood how wrong she had been. A breeze was rustling the leaves of the enormous beech tree that stood beside the house, as if protecting it from stronger winds, and in the distance she could hear the busy rushing of the river, and imagined the salmon forging their way to the spawning-grounds – survival of the species.

She wanted so much to stay here. In a strange way, although she had never been here in her life, she felt she had come home.

Esmée reassured Jillian that she had done her sums and was fully aware of just how much she was going to have to spend.

'I've rattled around for too long. I want to settle here. I want no more husbands, maybe the occasional lover – I mean, have you seen the bottoms of some of the young foresters hereabouts? They're the answer to a maiden's prayer.'

'Some maiden!' Jillian teased.

'Men aside, I'm going to do this anyway, Jillian, if you join me or not. But I'd rather you did.'

It was the cottage Esmée had suggested for Jillian's mother that finally settled everything one hundred per cent. It was perfect.

'It's a quarter of a mile from the main house, Mum, so you're close but we won't get on each other's nerves,' she reported happily over the telephone. 'According to Esmée, it was the head gardener's in the days when her aunt had an army of them. It's in the old walled vegetable garden. There are fruit trees and you'll have such fun restoring it.'

'It's not too big?'

'No, two bedrooms, the sitting room, a tiny dining room, kitchen and bathroom. You'll be so snug.'

'It'll be like coming home.' Mary's voice cracked.

'That's how I feel! Odd, isn't it? Must be those Scottish genes you gave me.'

There was a sob at the other end of the phone and Jillian realised her mother was crying. At that, any lingering doubts were doused.

Victoria decided to stay in Scotland with Esmée while Jillian returned to Cambridge to hand in her notice and arrange a tenancy for her house. Her packing was minimal: as the house was to be let furnished she had only her most prized possessions to worry about. It looked as if the removal van was still necessary, however, as Mary, unable to decide what to take and what to leave, opted to take everything.

Jillian was sad to say goodbye to the friends she had made since Jack's disappearance but was touched by the small gifts they showered on her, and the promises they made to save like squirrels until they had enough money to come and stay with her in her new venture. In turn she promised them all a healthy discount.

346

Saddest of all was saying goodbye to Helen Carter. She was now well into her seventies and, although she played it down, the anaemia was catching up with her. 'At least I've got my marbles, not like poor Theresa. I gather she's driving the staff in the home mad. Poor Liz is terrified she'll get thrown out and they'll have to have her back. Mungo is riddled with guilt as it is – and I can't imagine why since she wasn't a kind mother to him. No doubt he inherited his character from Ralph,' Helen said, with a marked degree of satisfaction. 'At least Esmée saw through her.'

'She never says anything bad about her mother.'

'She wouldn't. She has that stubborn loyalty too. I've never understood it myself. My mother was a cow and I was quite happy to tell her so. I popped her into a home as fast as I could, no guilt, nothing. I've always thought you get the old age you've earned in life. Loyalty's fine, provided it's not blind, so I do hope you're not being stupidly loyal to that fiend Jack.'

'I had a letter from him asking me to join him.' Jillian pulled a face.

'The conceit of the man, after what he did! I suppose he believes he's the love of your life and you'll never find another! Bah! He isn't, is he?'

'Heavens, no, I'm over him,' Jillian said, lying through her teeth.

'I'm so glad you're starting this business with Esmée. For one thing, you'll probably meet a delicious Scotsman in his kilt. But Esmée needs to settle too. She's had such a sad life – she's always attracted to flashy egotists, more in love with themselves than they can ever be with her. No doubt she thinks each time he's something different, unaware of this weakness in her. She should have stuck with dear Toby. You'll be a steadying influence on her.'

'Good gracious! How dull that makes me sound.'

'Not at all. We all need rock-like people in our lives, the type that doesn't go to pieces at the drop of a hat.'

'You didn't see me when Jack left!' She could laugh now at the state she'd been in.

'Yes, but you went to pieces in private, and that shows your strength. There's too much public angst for my taste, these days. Misery and grief should be too personal for others to see,' Helen stated emphatically.

Although Helen promised to book into the new hotel as soon as it opened, they both knew, even as she said so, that it was unlikely she would.

It was inevitable that there should be a confrontation with Rob.

'Who the hell do you think you are, interfering in my life?' he said, the minute he entered her house.

'I'm not.'

'Persuading your mother to leave me and run away to the Highlands. That's not interfering?'

'It's her decision. She wants to come.'

'She says you said you wouldn't go without her. If so, don't you think that's coercion?'

'That's right, I wouldn't have gone. And I'm happy she wants to come too. I didn't make her decide one way or the other.'

'Can't cope on your own, is that it? You like to give the impression that you're so cool and organised and clever but you still need your mum. You're pathetic!'

'No, that's not the reason. I wouldn't have left her here with you when you make her so unhappy. That's the truth. I'm sorry to be so blunt but you made me.'

'Why, you arrogant bitch! Your mother and I would have been happy if it hadn't been for you. She deserves some happiness after that pathetic poofter she was married to, and you intend to spoil it for her.'

'I think you should leave, Rob. I don't wish to hear you speak of my father in those terms. He was a good, honest man. Yes, he made her unhappy too, but the difference is that he got no pleasure from it, unlike a sadist like you. So go, before I really lose my temper.'

'You, lose your rag? I doubt it.' He snorted with contempt. 'You have to have feelings to do that, and you're sadly lacking in that department. It's no wonder your husband scarpered, poor sod, living with a frigid cow like you.'

She threw a vase at him and enjoyed seeing it glance off his forehead. 'Fuck off!' she screamed, and she was not sure if it was the vase or her language that made him scuttle out like a frightened rabbit.

It had taken her four weeks to arrange her return to Scotland. She and Mary were to meet on Cambridge station. Jillian waited on the platform, looking anxiously at her watch, wondering where her mother was and if she had changed her mind. The express for Liverpool Street thundered into the station. There was no sign of Mary. Jillian sighed with exasperation. She was not prepared to wait any longer and clambered on to the train. She settled in her seat and opened a magazine.

'Going without me? That wasn't very nice.' Mary had appeared.

'I've no home left, Mother, the lodgers are already in. I had no choice.' She moved over to make room for her.

'No, I'll sit opposite. I prefer to sit with my back to the engine. So does Rob.' She shuffled along the seat.

'What? Rob's coming?' Jillian looked wildly about her.

'That got you, didn't it? Just joking!'

4

'I'm sorry about my mother's constant moaning,' said Jillian, much later, as the two friends were sitting over a last whisky. Mary, exhausted by the journey, had long been in bed. 'Her furniture should arrive tomorrow and then she'll move into the cottage. Isn't it strange how one lives all one's young life with one's parents, just accepting them as they are? But then there's a change, and now I spend one day with her and want to scream!'

'It's the nature of things, I suppose. And it isn't just we who change. They do too. They get set in their funny ways and they slow down.'

'So much so you want to shove them! At least, I do, and

then comes the guilt!' Jillian grinned sheepishly. 'I don't understand her, she told me she was so miserable with Rob. She complained he belittled her and made her look foolish in front of their friends. Yet on the way up all she did was witter on about whether she'd live to regret leaving him!'

'Some people are happy being miserable. Perhaps your mother's one of them.' Esmée looked at her watch for the umpteenth time. 'I wish Victoria would come back. She is inconsiderate,' she said.

'You sound like a mother.'

'God forbid. I told her which train you were on.'

'I don't mind, if she's making friends. That would be wonderful for her. Do you know the people she's met?'

'The parents, not the offspring. They have a lodge thirty-odd miles from here – nice people. No doubt they've been up for the grouse. I expect they'll be going back south soon. She'll probably be bored out of her skull by then.'

'Esmée, don't frighten me. A bored Victoria is hell on earth to live with.' She declined more whisky. 'I just hope she hasn't been giving them her opinions on animal rights. She can get quite carried away with that one.'

'And quite right at her age,' Esmée said staunchly. 'I was saving every four-legged creature on the planet between the ages of ten and twenty. I was very ardent. I wouldn't even speak to people if they ate meat.'

'What happened? You devoured your steak tonight with enthusiasm.'

'One problem was I never met a male veggie. Then it became such a hassle I gave it up. In fact, I lied a lot of the time and was a secret meat-eater anyway. All the lying necessary to hide my dreadful secret began to get me down. Aha,' she held her head on one side to listen, 'I hear a car.'

Five minutes later, a radiant-looking Victoria bounced into the room. She's stunning, Jillian thought. She had never seen her daughter look quite so beautiful.

'A successful evening, I gather?' Esmée looked up at her niece, who enthusiastically planted a kiss on her cheek.

'I think I'm in love.'

350

'In my experience there's not much thinking to be done. Either you're in love or you're not.' Esmée smiled tolerantly at her.

'I feel all quivery inside. I can't wait till tomorrow. I die a thousand deaths every time we say goodnight.'

'That sounds like love to me, doesn't it you, Jillian?'

'Hi, Mum.' Finally Victoria kissed her too and Jillian felt a small frisson of jealousy that it was Esmée she was confiding in and not her.

The excitement of the work, the plans to make and the dreams to confess to each other made the next few days fly by. Now that Jillian's bits and pieces had arrived, her first priority – at Esmée's insistence – was to arrange the small apartment at the back of the house, which was to be hers. She had a bedroom and sitting room far larger than most people enjoyed, and the bathroom, a relic of an earlier age, was to be updated. She had set to painting the walls – pale yellow, she'd decided, with white gloss on the wood.

'I didn't know you liked yellow.' Her mother appeared in the doorway. 'I rang and rang but nobody came.'

'We've got to fix the bell – it's a pulley system and it's broken. And, yes, I've always loved yellow. I thought it would be a good colour to have in winter when it gets cold. How are you settling?'

'The rooms are on the small side.'

Carefully Jillian painted around the window-frame. 'I've got some old curtains I can redo to fit these windows – you remember, the ones I had with poppies?' She had decided on a new tack of ignoring her mother when she moaned.

'I never liked them much – I like plain things myself.'

'I thought . . .' She was going to remind Mary of the plans to decorate the cottage with Laura Ashley, but decided against it. 'Settling in?' she repeated.

'I'm worried about my carpet.'

'What about it?' Biting her lip in concentration Jillian finished the last sweep of paint and stood back to admire her handiwork.

'I wanted to re-lay it – with a bit of cutting and patching it'll fit. But if I do that it'll become fixtures and fittings, won't it? If I move I don't want any trouble about the cost of it, do I?'

Jillian forced herself to lay the paintbrush carefully on top of the tin. She wiped her fingers. 'Are you planning on moving already?' she asked, with studied calm.

'No. It's just that I think it advisable that we set out what's what right at the beginning.'

'Yes, Mum. I see that. But a square of carpet – well, honestly!'

'I worked hard to buy that carpet. Axminster, it is. And I –'

'Mum. If you move, I will personally replace your carpet with Axminster or Wilton. Take your pick. Does that settle it?' Was her mother always so ungrateful? Esmée had had the chimneys swept and a new porch built on the cottage – all of which Mary knew – but she hadn't heard her say thank you for anything.

'Not much of a view, have you? Not like mine. All you can see is trees.'

'I like trees.'

'Bit odd, isn't it, poking you away in the back here, in the old servants' quarters, I'll be bound.'

'Yes, they are. And, no, I don't think it's odd. We'll need all the space in the front for guests.'

'Esmée's room's in the front with a view. So's Victoria's – she showed me.'

'Temporarily. Once the fire regulations are sorted they'll move too.'

'You reckon?' Mary snorted, in disbelief.

'Yes, I do. In any case, this makes sense. I'm the one who'll be here all year round. The main part of the house will be shut up – we don't expect guests in the depths of winter. I think over the kitchen will be the best possible billet with the heat from the Aga rising up. Shall we have some tea? I could do with a break.'

'I don't see why you're doing your own painting and decorating.'

'I like doing it – and every penny saved . . .'

'Well, take my advice and watch it. Before you know where you are you'll be treated like an old family retainer on a pittance.'

'Yes, Mother.' Jillian ground her teeth.

Driving into Inverness on her own came as something of a relief. They had been at Altnahany for two weeks now, two exhausting but fulfilling and exciting weeks – but for Mary.

If asked, she'd have described her mother as optimistic, contained, but positive in her attitudes. Not any more. Had Rob changed her so much or had Jillian always had a wrong image of her? It was interesting, she thought, that since Jack had gone she'd seen so many people differently. She was far more aware of Victoria's failings. She'd changed her mind about Gary, and Cherry had turned into a star. The only conclusion to reach, since she had also imagined her marriage to be perfect, was that her conclusions about virtually everything had been invariably wrong and had to be re-examined.

She looked about her with pleasure. The leaves were changing colour and the rowans especially promised to be a blaze of colour shortly. The air was a tonic she still revelled in, each morning treating her lungs to huge gasps of it. The river ran alongside the single-track road, which followed its path through the narrow glen. The water was dark brown and its speed made it froth as it flashed by.

Having negotiated her way through the unfamiliar streets of Inverness and parked, she located the solicitor's office in a dour, dark building.

In the waiting room, she leafed through an out-of-date magazine. After all the dramas over Jack when, for a time, she had seemed to live at her lawyer's, she had vowed never to see one again. Esmée however had insisted on this meeting.

'We must have everything tied up legally between us.'

'Quite honestly, Esmée, I can't afford lawyers.'

'I'll pay.'

'But you pay for virtually everything as it is.'

'It'll be classed as setting-up finances and it'll go against our taxes.'

'I just don't think it's necessary. I trust you.'

'After what my brother's done to you? You're bonkers!'

'You're not your brother. I hate lawyers. I think I've acquired an allergy to them.'

'But this one's a perfect poppet. You'll adore him.' And brushing aside all her objections, Esmée had set up this meeting. She had probably been right.

'Mrs Stirling?'

Jillian looked up at her name.

'When I saw the name, I hoped it was you. I told myself it probably wasn't. It's a common enough name in these parts.' Colin Coleridge held open the door to his office. 'What on earth are you doing up here?'

'I could ask the same of you,' she said as she settled in the comfortable leather chair opposite him. 'This is a nice surprise.' And they grinned idiotically at each other. 'Didn't Esmée explain?'

'I don't know. My partner was dealing with this business partnership you're setting up, but he's gone down with flu. I gather your sister-in-law has asked us to answer any queries you might have.'

'But you're an English lawyer – isn't Scottish law different?'

'I read Scottish and English law. We're a rare breed, those qualified in both. It's come in handy more times than I can remember.' He shook his head as if in disbelief. 'Jillian Stirling, here. I can't get over it. You do know it gets incredibly cold in winter? Or will you only be here from the spring to the autumn?'

'I intend to spend all year here. Esmée won't – she'll probably winter abroad – but I don't mind the cold. It's such an exciting venture. I'm looking forward to it. It'll keep me out of trouble!' She was giggling nervously.

'Speaking of which, I heard about your husband. I'm sorry it happened – and to you of all people.'

'I think everyone in Cambridge heard the gossip.' She was aware that she had spoken tartly. She'd felt so pleased to see him, happy with her new start in life, but even here Jack's name came up.

'That was clumsy of me. I'm sorry. I'm afraid I was involved – through one of my clients. I don't listen to gossip.' He looked straight at her as he spoke.

'I'm sorry. I was being bristly. But you do get defensive, you know.'

'I can imagine. Still, we're here to discuss your future.'

'I hope it's a shade better than my recent past.' She laughed, which lightened the atmosphere in the room considerably.

'Surely it will be. You're in Scotland now.'

'But you said you knew because of a client? I was told you'd left Cambridge years ago.'

'Jack's affairs, and those involved with him, were numerous. In fact, now she's dead there's no harm. It was old Aunt Fiona who told me. She invested in him.'

'Oh, no!' Her hand shot to her mouth.

'Still, water under the bridge.' He pulled a folder towards him. 'Your sister-in-law has set up a company of which you are co-directors.'

'Really? She never said.'

'You're called, let me see, Rowan Hotels Ltd.'

'How nice. I was admiring the trees on my way here.'

'The situation is as normal for a company. You both have to give six months' notice of resignation, profits to be shared equally on top of your salary. But here is where things differ. Should you become bankrupt she releases you of any debts.'

'I couldn't possibly allow that.'

'My colleague assures me she is insistent on this – otherwise there's no business. She'll sell up and return to England. I gather this is her way of making amends for her brother's actions.'

'She's done so much already. She put my daughter through school, not that she was in the least bit appreciative. And she offered to support my son through university, but he declined. He's working in the hotel trade too.'

'Will he join you?'

'I shouldn't think so. He's very ambitious. He won't rest

until he's manager of the Ritz or something equally grand. We'd be too small for him.'

'I thought your interest was antiques – especially silver boxes.' He nodded towards a glass-fronted cabinet.

'How lovely. You still have them all.' Jillian got up and crossed the room. 'I particularly liked that Georgian snuff-box. Oh, look, there's that pretty Victorian card case with the thistle. I was so excited when I found that one.'

'They don't look right in my digs and, since I spend most of my day here, I thought I'd have them where I can see them.'

'They must be worth a pretty penny now. You invested wisely.'

'Mainly thanks to you.'

'I did nothing. I just phoned you if anything of interest turned up. You decided to buy them.'

'But you never once wasted my time.'

'You were easy to please.'

They smiled at each other as if neither was sure how to proceed.

'I was –' they said in unison and laughed, then said, 'After you,' and laughed again.

'I was just wondering, why hotels?'

'It was Esmée's idea. She says the world is divided into those who are guests and those who entertain them, and I'm in the second category, that I've been running an unofficial hotel for years, so why not do it and get paid for it? And in a way she was right. I do love organising and I've missed that in the past few years.'

'As soon as you open I'll book in for a weekend.'

'We'll give you a special rate.'

'Never! I wouldn't accept. You must start as you mean to go on – discounts for no one, especially family and friends. They won't appreciate it and will think you're mad to do so.'

'Very well, then. I'll charge you double!'

'I wish I hadn't spoken – and me a Scot!'

They went through the papers. Any points she didn't understand he explained to her. She was reluctant to sign, and worried that she should talk to Esmée first but, as Colin pointed out, if she didn't she'd moved for nothing. Friendly blackmail, he called it. She signed.

Their business finished, Colin invited her to lunch and she accepted. He took her to a small French restaurant, Girvin's, where, he assured her, the food was excellent. In truth she didn't mind what the food was like. It was an age since she had been taken out by a man and it was rather nice to contemplate being the centre of his attention. 'Excuse me,' he said suddenly, 'I've just got to have a wee word with a friend.' He went to another table.

While she pretended to be studying the menu, she was actually studying him. He had changed from when she had known him as a customer in her shop in Cambridge. Then she had thought him ten years older than he was, now he looked ten years younger. She remembered him as stooped, with the manner of a man who had been badly treated by life. Today there was no sign of a stoop and, as he joked with his friend, he looked far from miserable. His hair, which she remembered as prematurely greying, was now white, and he was far from handsome, but nothing could alter that, she thought. He had a high, domed head, small eyes, too slight a nose to suit a man's features, but it was the face of a highly intelligent man – which, if she was honest, was all it had going for it. But, then, Jack had been the most handsome man she'd ever known and where had that got her? But Colin Coleridge had a nice body, now that he wasn't all hunched up, and a neat behind and, she was sure, muscular thighs. She moved in her seat as if she was uncomfortable, but she wasn't. It was her thoughts that were troubling her: he was her solicitor, for goodness' sake, and she was eyeing him as if she were a teenager. Quite ridiculous, she told herself firmly.

'Sorry about that. Business. Decided yet?' he asked, on returning to their table.

'It all looks delicious. I think I'd like the salmon. After all, now I'm here I should eat the local produce.'

'There's an abundance here. Fish. Venison. You must stock the cheese made by the Stones, a family who live in Tain, they make the best Caboc and Crowdie.' It was not a

357

scintillating conversation, but she found herself hanging on his every word. They talked of many things: about Scotland, England, politics in general. Neither spoke about themselves. For Jillian it was a relief that he did not question her about Jack and her marriage – but she longed for him to tell her about his.

'Would you like more wine?'

'Heavens, no! Not if I'm driving. One glass is quite enough.'

'If you don't mind, I think I will.'

'Please, don't let me stop you. Perrier will do me fine.'

He beckoned to the wine waiter 'You're in Scotland now. You'd best get used to the local sparkling water – Caithness or Highland Spring. It won't do to be stocking the foreign competition.' He was smiling: it was no reproof but it was something she should remember.

'Drinking at midday doesn't stop you working?' She regretted the words as soon as she had spoken them, for a wary expression came over his face. She was flustered, unsure what to say next. 'I always go to sleep – I mean if I drink at lunchtime.' He didn't reply and she looked at her hands. 'I didn't intend to sound critical.'

'It's not you. It's me. You see, just for a second, well, you sounded like my wife!' He grinned. 'She was always nagging me. Never stopped.'

If she had been Esmée, this was the point at which she would have said something smart, but Jillian didn't, of course. She had registered that he spoke about his wife in the past tense. What did that mean?

'She was probably right. I did drink too much.'

'Some people do when they're unhappy.'

'I don't now. This is an exception. I've taken the afternoon off, so work is no problem.'

'Honestly, Colin, you don't have to excuse yourself to me. You do what you want when you want.'

'I'd like it clear . . .' He paused and took a deep breath before continuing. 'I'd like to see you again – that is, if you want to and if you're free.'

'I'd like that very much.' She smiled as her heart beat at an unseemly rate.

'Mum's got a feller! Ha! Would you believe?' Victoria was jumping up and down as if she were two rather than twenty.

'Don't be so silly. He's an old friend from Cambridge, that's all.'

'Oh, yeah? So why are you slapping on the war-paint?'

'I'm not. As you get older you need a little more help from Estée and Coco. You'll learn.' Jillian peered at herself in the mirror and wondered if Victoria was right and she had overdone her eye-shadow. But no, she decided, she hadn't, and the colour – a soft grey – could hardly be deemed garish.

'You shouldn't wear blue eye-shadow, it's the pits.'

'It's grey.'

'You could have fooled me.'

Jillian laid down her mascara on the dressing-table and swung round on the stool. 'Victoria, if all you can do is criticise I wish you'd go, it's annoying.' It was making her edgy. She was nervous enough without her daughter adding her pennyworth. Silly, really, she thought, as she returned to her mirror and continued to apply her mascara.

'Are we to meet him, then?'

'Yes. He's collecting me at seven. I'm not like you. I'm open about things.'

'What does that mean?'

'How long have you been seeing Rory? And have we been properly introduced?'

'You've met him.'

'I don't call a "good evening" through a car-window meeting someone. Not someone as important as he evidently is to you.'

Victoria rummaged around in the old box, which had been Jillian's grandmother's, in which she kept her costume jewellery.

'Is it?'

'I'm not sure what you mean. But just because a bloke's dating me doesn't mean he has to go through the tedious drag of meeting my family.'

'Why not? Are we so gruesome?'

'It's just heavy, that's all. Tea and cucumber sandwiches. He'll think he's being set up for matrimony or something.'

'That's silly. I'd hate you even to be thinking of matrimony at your age. You're too young.'

'Age didn't stop you.'

'No. Times were different.'

'And, of course, you were pregnant, weren't you?'

'Yes, as a matter of fact I was. But we'd have married anyway.'

'Really?'

Jillian swung round, but not quickly enough to see her daughter's expression.

'Looking back I *was* too young,' she said hurriedly, feeling such a confusion of emotions – anger, surprise, annoyance, embarrassment. 'So, are we to meet Rory?'

'I don't know. Maybe.' Victoria stood up. 'Right, I'm off. Have a nice time.'

'When will you be back?'

'I don't know.'

'Where are you going?'

'London.'

'Isn't this a bit sudden?'

'No.'

'Who with?'

'Rory, of course!' And she slammed the door behind her.

'Why's she so secretive with me?' Jillian was in the drawing room, nervously sipping mineral water – Scottish, not French.

'Weren't we all?' Esmée was mixing herself a large gin and tonic.

'I can't remember. I don't think I was.'

'Oh, come on, I bet you didn't tell your mother you'd slept with Jack.'

'Of course not – but I didn't hide him away. I wanted them to meet him – well, perhaps not my dad but my mum certainly.' She sipped at the water.

'She's off to London.'

'I know.'

'There, you see? I've only just heard but she tells you, not me.'

'Maybe she thought you'd try to stop her.'

'Stop Victoria? I might just as well try to stop a tank. Where's she staying?'

'Rory has a flat with a group of others. It's best, Jill darling. She'd only moan non-stop and drip buckets of tears over the carpet. Let her go.'

'I'm not trying to keep her,' Jillian answered sharply. Why was concern always interpreted as hanging on? 'I just like to be told her plans. Is that so unreasonable?'

'No, of course not.'

'And why won't she let me meet him? Is there something about him that she knows I won't like?'

'What? That he's wall-eyed?'

'Don't be daft. No, if he's into drugs or he's a criminal.'

'All the criminals I know are amazingly respectable in appearance. Look at Jack.'

'That's true. Drugs, then.'

'He looked all right to me.'

Jillian's head jerked up. 'You've met him?'

'Yes. Didn't I say? We had lunch together the other day. He's a bit beefy for me. You know me, I like them lean and hungry. He's an actor – or, rather, he wants to be. Victoria says he does a "Death where is thy sting" to die for.' Esmée laughed, but Jillian didn't. She held this information to her as if to ward off the jealousy that arose too frequently these days, knowing that Victoria was far more at ease with Esmée than with her.

'Lordy, Lordy, Miss Jilly, I haven't upset you, have I?' Esmée rolled her eyes clownishly.

'No, of course not. I'm sorry. I'm not quite here – it's nerves, like a first date, ridiculous.'

'Not at all. You cling to it. I remember such joy and anticipation of the night ahead – quite delicious.'

'Correction – the evening ahead.'

'Go for it, babe. You never know, stuck up here in the wilds, when the next opportunity might present himself. By the way, did I tell you? I've bought a mixed case of Moniack wines. I thought we should try them and, if we like them, stock them.'

'Colin mentioned this spring water too.' She lifted her glass.

'Is his name really Colin? Such a shame. It doesn't exactly set the blood on fire, does it?'

Jillian thought Colin a rather nice name. They were travelling down the glen road and she wished he wasn't driving quite so fast. She was rapidly learning the dangers of these single-track roads and the exuberant young Highlanders' driving style.

'You're quiet,' he said suddenly. His voice made her jump.

'I was just thinking what a nice safe name you had.'

'Boring, you mean.'

'No. It's an honest name.'

'I hate it. I prefer Col, but my son's called that, so I'm stuck with Colin. I think you'll like Hamish and Fenny. We rely on friends for entertainment – the place isn't littered with restaurants like down south.'

'What do they do?'

'Ah!' He laughed loudly. 'How English to ask.'

'Is it?'

'Yes. They're people, nice people, that's all that matters.'

'I was just asking so that I'd know what to talk to them about.'

'Are you sure you were? Sure you weren't trying to place them socially?'

'No, I'm not like that.' She felt a bit offended, as if he were reprimanding her.

'I'm glad to hear it, you wouldn't last long here if you were.' He laughed again. She wasn't sure if she liked his laugh as much.

'I think it's rather patronising to refer to them just as nice people. They must have something that defines them as individuals.'

'Psst . . .' Colin sucked in his lips. 'A bit tart, aren't you?'

'Yes, I am. And justifiably. I really don't want an evening of being told how I should or should not be. What water to drink or not drink. What food. I am who I am, Colin, take me or leave me. Simple.'

Colin pulled the car into one of the passing places to allow passage to another vehicle coming in the opposite direction. Windows were wound down, greetings exchanged, introductions, or sort of, were made. 'That's Charlie MacNeil, the forest ranger. Great guy, you'll enjoy great crack with him.'

'Really?' She knew her voice sounded uninterested, which she wasn't, but the evening was already such a let-down. Perhaps she'd allowed herself to set too much store by it.

Colin didn't immediately put the car into gear. 'Look, Jillian, I'm sorry. I'm behaving like an oaf, I know I am. But – this'll sound daft and you'll be running for the hills – I've so looked forward to tonight. I wanted it to be a success. And now I'm making a balls-up of it.'

Involuntarily she put out her hand and covered his as it rested on the gear-stick. 'I was being too prickly. If you want the truth I feel exactly the same.' She smiled shyly at him.

'I won't pontificate again, I promise. It's just . . . this will sound even dafter to you, but I really want you to like it here.'

'If it's all right with you, I really would like to know what Hamish does.'

'Hamish is an artist, though he calls himself a painter. He does watercolours to sell to the tourists, but they're not what he enjoys most – if you're lucky he'll show you. It's virtually impossible for him to make a living doing that alone so he does a bit of ghillying and planting for the forestry. He drove the school car for a bit. And Fenny's the health visitor. Enough?' He grinned sheepishly at her.

'Enough.' She grinned back.

Jillian liked Fenny immediately. She was small and dark-haired, with a clear complexion, her skin so pale it was almost white; her eyes were large, luminous and grey. She was beautiful. Jillian supposed that some people would have found her a little too abrupt, but she saw this as down-to-earth. Fenny was a woman who said what she thought, a trait that, as a prevaricator, she admired in others. She could imagine that she would be a good nurse, devoted to those who really needed her but giving short shrift to malingerers.

She was not so sure about Hamish. The only artists she had met were rather thin and wan-looking from, she'd always presumed, years of scratching a living and not being understood. Hamish, however, was a giant of a man, not only in height but in breadth also. Everything about him was large, his head – especially his nose – his feet, hands, which looked more like those of a labourer than an artist, his voice, which boomed, and even at the first meeting, his character too. With his long straggly red hair and equally red bushy beard, he was like a caricature of a Highlander from a Hollywood film, except that in place of a kilt he wore heavy, hairy tweed knickerbockers.

Hamish did not like the English, and made no bones about it, neither did he excuse nor explain himself to her. It was as if she had been personally responsible for the Highland clearances, of which she knew nothing but resolved to learn as much as she could. He had firm ideas about who should have the privilege of living in his country – 'white settlers' he called them. His attitude towards Jillian eased slightly upon hearing that her grandmother had been Scottish, even if from Aberdeenshire, which to Hamish came a poor second best to his beloved Highlands.

'Take no notice of him, Jillian. He's away with the fairies half the time, and the other half the malt's usually got him,' Fenny reassured her, in her beautiful soft accent of the Isles.

The food was delicious: lightly poached salmon with leeks. When Jillian asked from which river it had been caught, the other three were highly amused.

'Best never to ask, Jillian. What you don't know you can't tell.' Hamish roared with laughter.

They had drunk a lot of wine and Colin had consumed quite a few nips of the Famous Grouse also. He had had far too much to drive, but Jillian sat in the car, hands folded neatly on her lap, and tried to convey a calm she was far from feeling. After his reaction to her remarks about drinking at lunchtime, she did not dare point out that perhaps it would be better if she drove.

'Hamish liked you – that's quite rare, you know.'

'You could have fooled me.'

'He doesn't show his paintings to everyone.'

'They were good. I meant it when I said I'd love to buy one when I could afford to. But he's a bit OTT about being Scottish, isn't he?'

'He means it.'

'I hope there aren't too many like him. It might make life a bit difficult.'

'I shouldn't worry. It's the people who don't live here all the time he's against. The ones who come for the shooting and fishing who aren't part of the community. You'll be here all winter and you'll be employing people and spending money.'

'Still, the others who just come for the sport bring in a lot of money too.'

'Logic isn't Hamish's strongest point.'

When they arrived at Altnahany Colin accepted her offer of coffee with an alacrity that, while flattering, was also alarming: she did not want to rush anything. She'd admitted to herself, if not to Esmée and Victoria, that she would like a relationship with him – but not too quickly. She needed time to get used to the idea. Time to adjust to the concept of being in another man's arms when only Jack's had held her.

'I'm afraid we're a bit like a builder's yard,' she apologised, as she opened the front door and they stepped into the half-painted hall.

'That's an unusual colour.' He looked at the cherry-red walls.

'Esmée says we need a warm colour to kid ourselves in winter that we're not freezing half to death. It's looking good, isn't it? I'm home,' she called. Half of her hoped that Esmée was still out, the other half that she was back – just in case. She shivered at what 'just in case' might mean. 'This way.' She led him to the long, elegant drawing room. 'This is our oasis of civilisation.'

'It's a glorious room. You could spend a week just looking at everything.'

'Aunt Fiona was quite a collector, as you can see. Now we

have to decide what to keep in here and what to store. At the moment you'd never squeeze enough guests in between the whatnots and the what-have-yous.' She looked around with pride, almost as if she owned the room and its contents. 'I'll go and make the coffee. If you're cold switch that fire on.'

They sat either side of the electric fire which, with winter drawing in, was barely enough.

'No Esmée?'

'Not yet. She's out to dinner.'

'And your daughter?'

'She's gone to England. She's in love – and feared fading away without her loved one.' She laughed, which neatly covered up how little she knew of Victoria's friends. 'I'm hoping my son will be coming for a few days soon. I'd like to pick his brains.'

'Handy.'

A silence descended, and Jillian tried hard to think of something to say, but her mind stayed stubbornly blank.

'Jillian.' Something in his voice made her look up. 'There's . . .'

'Yes?' She was not sure if she liked his tone, as if he was preparing himself to tell her something he knew she wouldn't like.

'I think I should be straight with you.'

'It's considered advisable.' She tried to smile, but from the rigid feel of her mouth she needed no mirror to tell her she'd failed.

'You know I'm married?'

'Well, yes, sort of. Like me. I've never got around to a divorce. It's on my list of things to do.' She attempted a none-too-successful laugh.

'I don't live with my wife. However, I'm here because of her. She wanted to move back to Scotland and if I was to see my children I had to come too.'

'I understand that. Your children should come first.'

'The thing is. I doubt if I'll get a divorce.'

'Ah, I see.' She trotted out the words even though she didn't.

'Morag is Catholic.'

'So?'

'She doesn't want us to divorce.'

'In this day and age?'

'I know, I know. But there it is. She wants to stay married.' He shrugged his shoulders as if that were an end to it.

'But you could divorce her without her consent surely?'

'I could, but imagine the upset. I fear she'd use the children and stop me seeing them.'

'She doesn't sound very nice.'

'She's very principled.'

'Odd principles.'

He bent forward and took her hand in his. 'I knew you'd find it difficult to understand. I don't blame you. I just hoped.' He smiled diffidently. 'I wanted you to know. I didn't want you to feel deceived.'

'I appreciate that.'

'You do? And you're not going to throw me out?'

'It's not your fault. I feel sorry for you. I . . .'

But she did not finish the sentence for Colin had left his chair and was kneeling on the floor in front of her. 'Jillian, that makes me so happy to hear. I don't want to scare you off by rushing things, but I'm going to all the same.' He laughed nervously, as did she at the sight of him on the drawing-room carpet. 'All those years in Cambridge, well, I never said anything. What was the point, with Jack Stirling in the picture? But the thing is, I still feel the same . . . believe me . . . don't laugh . . . but I'm sure I love you.' He put up his arms and took hold of her clumsily. At first she resisted but then, aware of the pleasant, comforting feel of a man's body so close to hers, she relaxed. 'Oh, Jillian . . .' He sighed.

'Anyone home?' They heard Esmée call from the hall and, like guilty teenagers, jumped back from each other. By the time Esmée entered the room they were sitting primly opposite each other, the electric fire between them an inanimate chaperone.

'In a pig's ear.' Esmée snorted disdainfully.

'I've never known what that meant.' Jillian slid the large, heavy kettle on to the hotplate knowing full well what it meant, and also fully aware of what Esmée was about to say since she had already thought it herself.

'Put simply, darling, he's lying his little cotton socks off. Whoever thought to hear such claptrap ever again. This is the nineteen nineties, for goodness' sake. In our parents' generation maybe a wife could hang on to a husband who wanted to do a runner, making everybody's life hell, in the process. But not any more. He's telling you that because he doesn't want a serious involvement with you.'

'Why do you always have to be so cynical? Even today there are people with serious religious principles. Just because you haven't got any, doesn't mean they don't exist. Heavens, he could be fed up that I'm still married.'

'It's hardly the same, is it? I mean, you will eventually be free. It doesn't sound as if he intends to be.'

'He didn't say that!' Jillian said sharply.

'There's no point in taking your disappointment in him out on me. You told me what he said. I didn't ask you to tell me anything. I'm giving you my opinion – if you didn't want to hear it you shouldn't have told me in the first place. He's having you on and I'd ditch him if I were you.'

'Well, you're not me, and I don't intend to. Heavens above, you talk as though I want to marry him. And you talk about generations moving on. I just want to have some fun, for a change. I'm not hearing wedding bells, I'd just like to have a lover. Is there anything wrong in that?'

'Yes. It's wrong for *you*.'

'Look at all the affairs you've had.'

'Exactly. Which is why I know what I'm talking about, why I don't want you doing the same because you will get seriously hurt. You might think all you want is a fling but you're not the sort, Jill. You'll get deeply involved, whatever you're telling yourself now.'

'I won't. Your brother hurt me so badly that no one can ever hurt me that much again.' She poured the boiling water on the tea leaves. 'And, what's more, what is it about me that all my life people have seen fit to tell me what I should be doing all the bloody time, as if I've no sense, as if I knew nothing? I'm fed up with it.'

'Only because we love you and want to protect you.'

'I love you, but I don't presume to tell you what you should be doing.'

'That's because you're not an interfering cow like me. And you've got better manners.'

'I can't even be cross with you, can I? There are times I wish I could.'

'Don't even think it, sweetness. The rest of the world is always getting at me. You stay as you are. But I promise you one thing. I've had my say and I'll never say it again, and if catastrophe comes along, I swear I won't say "I told you so!" '

'Tea?'

'You are funny. We talk about you and the dangers of this relationship, serious heavy-duty stuff, and you offer me tea. So sweet. No, not for me, I think I'll have a brandy.' Esmée went to collect the bottle and returned to the kitchen. 'By the way, I'm going south for a few weeks. You'll be all right here, won't you?'

'Of course. Anywhere nice?' Jillian made her response sound upbeat. In reality she was far from happy at the prospect of being left alone in this isolated house with so much work to be done. She didn't feel she was in any position to say anything, though.

'No, not particularly. I've just had enough of the Highlands for a while. I'm getting restless.'

There was something in her voice, nothing Jillian could put her finger on . . . it was just that she sounded different. 'Are you all right, Esmée?'

'Fine. What a funny question.'

'Your voice sounded odd.'

'I'm tired, that's all. You must begin to worry about yourself, and stop worrying so much about others.' Esmée smiled fondly at her.

Winter 1992

The worst part about being left alone in the large house was the night-time noises of such an old building. Jillian would lie in bed, unable to sleep, and fantasise about them, imagining the house as a creaking geriatric hauling itself in and out of bed. Or, when the wind blew loudly through the trees, she would feel as though she was on a great sailing ship plunging through the waves. Those were the good nights. On others she would imagine a whole gang of burglars and murderers creeping about downstairs. And after one particularly violent storm in which the wind had howled about the house and shaken it to its foundations, she quite expected to find that one of the turrets had been ripped off and shot into the heavens like a rocket. Every morning she told herself what a stupid, imaginative fool she was but, for the first time in her life, she acquired a dog.

The obsession of dog-owners for their pets had always mystified her, yet within days of the arrival of her cross-breed Alsatian her view changed. She hadn't realised the comforting companionship that a dog could give, the sense of security. Now she could sleep all night, with Prince curled up on the floor beside her bed. He followed her wherever she went. When she was alone in the evening she talked to him about her day, the problems that had occurred, the decisions she had had to make. He would sit listening to her, head cocked, ears alert, tongue hanging out, and she was convinced, though she never said so to anyone, that he understood everything she said.

The near argument she had had with Esmée about Colin need never have taken place since she had not heard from him again. Why he did not call, when he had said he would, puzzled her. She could not remember anything about that evening to which he could have taken offence. Because of what he'd said she knew she had not imagined his interest in her. She had written to Fenny to thank her for the meal and only hoped that Colin's change of heart would not prevent her seeing her again. When Victoria, giggling unmercifully, had asked her on the phone how it was going with Colin, she had confessed that she thought she'd been dumped but added that she couldn't care less. There must have been something in the way she said it, though, for evidently Victoria did not believe her, since in the next sentence she was advising her to telephone his office and ask to speak to him. But Jillian could not have done that: it would have been too forward.

Fortunately, the builders had now started work in earnest, and her days were full, seeing to them, dealing with the architect, sorting out the paperwork necessary for the various planning applications. And she was busy doing what she enjoyed most: going through the house from the cellars to the attics, emptying cupboards, and making an inventory of everything she found. Since she had no idea where in the world Esmée had gone to relieve her boredom, she had to wait for her to call so that she could tell her of the wonderful find she had made in an outhouse: a complete dinner service for fifty people, which meant there was no need to buy new china. Also she had found boxes and boxes of cutlery and a tea chest full of copper pans. The linen cupboard had proved sheer bliss: she found stacks of pure white linen sheets, lace-bordered pillowcases, soft blankets and fat silk eiderdowns by the score. They had decided that the bedding would be of the best quality in their hotel; there was not to be a duvet in sight. The savings pleased her enormously for she was always conscious of how much this venture was costing Esmée and in this area the bills would be cut dramatically. They had already had a commercial washing machine installed and in that she carefully washed all the linen. Unfortunately, she soon discovered, ironing it was a nightmare.

'The problem is, Esmée, that these sheets were last used when your aunt had an army of servants to do them for her,' she explained when Esmée finally telephoned.

'Could we not get a woman in just to do the ironing?'

'I was hoping to keep the wage bill down to a minimum.'

'You do what you think is best. But I never intended that

you should spend your life ironing. If you don't want to get someone in, and those arrangements I leave entirely to you, then we will have to buy new bed-linen that's easier to look after.'

'I've wondered about getting a commercial iron, you know, one of those flat bed ones,' Jillian said, somewhat diffidently.

'Why didn't you?'

'They're very expensive. I didn't like to.'

'Jill, sweetheart, I left you with money in the bank for things like this. If you need one buy one. Any news of Colin?'

'No. But I've reached a decision. I'm never going to argue with you about men ever again. We could have fallen out over him.'

'Me fall out with you over a man? You have to be joking.'

Over a month had gone by without Esmée. The winter was taking hold with a vengeance, and Jillian was learning that life in the Highlands was one long battle to keep the cold at bay. Although she saw her mother during the day they tended to hole up in their respective homes in the evenings. Jillian was glad: her mother's choice of television wasn't hers, and Mary's constant quibbling could quickly pull her down. Jillian was beginning to think her mother regretted the move and was building up a store of complaints, enough to give her an excuse to leave. She knew she should talk to her and find out what the problem was, but she kept putting it off. So much was exciting and new, and she didn't want her mother to spoil it. She was also finding out that, now she had Prince, she liked being alone. After all, she had only herself to consider. She ate when she was hungry, she watched whatever she wanted on television, she could go to bed when she wanted. She could be totally selfish; it was a new experience for her.

'Jillian, it's Colin.'

Despite having practised various cutting remarks, her heart leaped at the sound of his voice with its pleasant brogue, and she said, 'Hello, how are you?' Worse, she accepted his invitation to dinner.

All the way to Inverness she told herself how foolish this

was, but it didn't make her turn the car to go home and stand him up. That inner voice argued with her, telling her it was about time she enjoyed herself, that since he'd behaved so atrociously there was nothing wrong in her using him then ditching him when she felt like it.

'I expect you wondered where the hell I've been,' he said, the minute she appeared.

'No,' she lied, but decided she had not sounded convincing. 'I've been so busy, such masses to do,' she added.

'I've been ill.'

'I'm so sorry. Nothing serious, I hope?'

'Appendicitis.'

'When?'

'The day after I saw you. I had to fly down to London on business and was struck down at a friend's house and rushed into hospital. I was very lucky. It was about to burst and that can mean curtains, they said. I'd had a gyppy tum for a bit but put it down to indigestion – referred pain, the docs called it.'

'I'm so sorry.' She controlled a smile, for he sounded like a boy telling her excitedly of his adventures. 'But you're better now?'

'Right as rain.'

'Did they not have a telephone in this hospital?' she asked, with deceptive sweetness, quite pleased with herself.

'I was only in for a day and a bit. They discharged me just as I was getting round to calling you. At first my friends took me in. I wanted to call you but I couldn't face them taking the you-know-what, which they would have. I should have written but I loathe letter-writing – it always comes out sounding like a legal document and heavens knows what you would have made of it. And then my wife came to collect me and drove me to her place. I couldn't telephone from there.'

'Why not? I thought you were separated. Do her religious principles go so far that she expects you to live like a monk?' She was sharp, but it was better to know everything now and get it over with. She wished she hadn't felt so happy to see him, and how, in some strange way, she found him attractive – still.

'Oops, you're angry. I don't blame you. It sounds odd. It wouldn't if you knew Morag. She's got a temper on her the like of which I'd hate to see on anyone else. I can't face it – not after all the years I put up with it. I admit, where she's concerned, I'm a total coward. Anything for the sake of peace. She's jealous, you see. She doesn't want me but she doesn't want anyone else to have me either. Not that anyone in their right senses would.'

'Why don't you move somewhere else and then she wouldn't know, would she? You could have a dozen women in tow.'

'An unlikely idea, looking as I do. Why, I'm amazed you don't mind being seen with me, someone as beautiful as you.' He looked at her with admiration and pride. 'And too late now. I'm well established here professionally. It would be financial suicide to start again at my age. And then there are the kids. I have to see them – if I don't then I feel only half alive.'

'Then we shall have to be discreet,' she said quietly, suddenly aware that she was going to have an affair with this man, that she wanted to. She had been alone for too long.

He followed her home. It was exciting to be driving along and to see his headlights reflected in her rear-view mirror; exciting because they both knew where this invitation for a coffee and a drink would lead. As she drove she thought of the night ahead. It made her drive faster. She wanted to be at home, in bed, making love to this man . . .

'Shameless hussy!' she said aloud, and hooted with laughter as she used one of her mother's favourite expressions. 'I am!' she cried. But still . . .

She slowed at a roundabout. What if they didn't gel? What if they were no good together? She didn't love him, she fancied him, and between the two was a mountainous difference. She couldn't believe she was doing this. Faithful-to-one-man-Jillian was driving through the night to a bed of lust! One-man woman! She pushed that thought away abruptly. Jack was the last person to be thinking of tonight.

On Struie Hill she slowed down: she'd lost sight of his

headlights. She stopped and looked anxiously behind her. Then she saw a shaft of light in the blackness of the moorland.

'Hell! You drive like the clappers.'

'Do I?' She smiled. If only he knew how staid her driving normally was. She produced the enormous key that opened the front door. 'It's still cluttered with builders' junk. Watch where you step, we might break our necks. Prince!' She hugged the dog, who bounded towards her.

'You didn't have him before.'

'No, I was lonely. He's good company. We'll be better off in the kitchen – at least it's warm in there.'

'God, this is a great barn of a place. It must cost an arm and a leg to heat.'

She told him about the new boilers. How odd, she thought, to speak of such prosaic things at a time like this. 'And, of course, we've got the Aga. That's what keeps the kitchen warm. Brandy?' She picked up the bottle from the table where she had placed it before leaving – as if she knew this would happen, as if she had planned it.

Jillian lay in the dark. Beside her, Colin's breathing was deep and regular. It sounded content, of one who slept soundly. But she could not sleep, and lay thinking, wondering and investigating how she felt. Colin had made love well, one moment gentle and considerate, the next forceful and passionate. She found it exciting, a new experience. Even though she had only one man with whom to compare him, she realised that he was an experienced lover. She was lucky and yet . . . The sad truth was that she had felt nothing, and she should have and she did not understand why she hadn't. She had been surprised at how easily with a look, the slightest touch, he could arouse her and make her think of physical feelings she had shelved for over six years. And it wasn't as if he had taken her by force: she had wanted him to make love to her.

As quietly as possible she got up and wrapped herself in her new wool dressing-gown. She crept downstairs and into the kitchen to put the kettle on. All her adult life, the kitchen had been her place of refuge, where she went when she wanted to think. She pulled a chair towards the Aga, and sat hunched, hugging the rail for warmth.

Had she not enjoyed it because she felt guilty? That because Jack was alive she still regarded herself as married to him? Maybe she was more like Morag than she cared to admit. It was ridiculous! No doubt by now Jack would have had an army of other women and never suffered even the slightest scrap of guilt about her. If she was right then perhaps it meant that she could never be free of him. Steam emerged from the spout of the kettle. She stood up and made the tea.

Had she expected too much? Was it possible for sex to be good the first time or did it take years of being together to make it really work? No – her memory took her back to a beach in Norfolk where, when she had given Jack her virginity, it had been perfect. Or had it? How would she have known? She had had nothing with which to compare it. Had it always been the earth-shattering experience she remembered with Jack? Or had she, in her misery and frustration after he left, pined for a perfection that had never been?

She resumed her seat and sat sipping her tea, staring into space. When she and Jack had been together, she felt sure that they had never had any problems in that area of their marriage, that Jack had been content with their sex life, and yet . . . was that why he had had the affairs?

'There you are – this place is so big I feel I've been on a route march to find you.'

'I couldn't sleep. Tea?'

'Lovely. What time is it?'

'Five.'

'Christ!' He rubbed his eyes with the back of his hand – again she was reminded of a young boy. 'I didn't make you happy, did I?'

'Don't be silly, of course you did.' She busied herself fetching cup and saucer.

'Jillian, my love, I know when it's being faked. All the sighing and groaning in the world doesn't fool me. I'm sorry.'

376

He took the tea from her and pulled another chair up close to the Aga.

She looked at him, huddled in a blanket gazing at her with genuine concern. What was the point in pretending? 'It wasn't your fault, it was me. You were wonderful.' She could say that in all honesty. 'I wanted you to make love to me, longed for it. I like you enormously . . . but when it came to it . . .'

'Perhaps you need to love me. Some people are like that – well, if I'm honest, some women are.' He grinned almost apologetically as if for the whole male sex.

'Esmée says she loves one-night stands.'

'Does she? Or is she just saying it? But, in any case, you're not Esmée. Has there been anyone else? I mean, since your husband left.'

'No, you're the first. Not because of me not wanting to. I did. I just never met anyone I wanted to sleep with.'

'Then I'm honoured.' He made a little half-bow, which as he was swathed in his pink blanket, was not quite as dignified as he had no doubt intended.

'Perhaps I'm rusty.' She smiled.

'Unlikely. It's like riding a bicycle – once done never forgotten. Much more likely that, deep inside, you are riddled with nasty interfering little tendrils of guilt. I shall make it my life's work to get rid of them. You have been warned.'

She laughed. She liked this man. Esmée could warn her all she wanted but she felt safe with him, for he was honest and she did not feel he was playing games with her.

He stayed the whole weekend, and Jillian waited in some trepidation for her mother to appear. Not once did he pressure her into going to bed with him – and her respect for him grew. At night they slept curled up together, and when she woke to find him there, warm, safe, comforting, she began to wonder if, after all, this wasn't the best part of sleeping with a man.

He offered to help her with any legal work – 'For free,' he added. 'I bet you never expected a day would dawn when you'd hear such an offer from a lawyer!' She accepted – it would be her way of helping Esmée out a bit.

'Don't let Esmée put on you,' he had counselled over dinner on the Saturday.

'It's more likely to be me doing that – I've no money to contribute.'

'If she's getting you on the cheap then you are.'

'I don't think she is, though. I have a roof over my head, and my mother is housed. I have my keep. I think I'm paid adequately.' It was the only other blot on the whole weekend. She hadn't wanted him to be like everybody else and lecture her. 'Would you mind if we changed the subject?'

'None of my business?'

'Something like. More potatoes?' she asked firmly.

As Jillian feared, Colin's car, parked at the front, had been noticed.

'Do you think it's right and proper, entertaining here when you're alone?' Her mother had bustled in with an apple tart she had made – an excuse, Jillian decided, since she had never done so before.

'Probably not.'

'People will talk.'

'They undoubtedly have already.'

'You don't care, do you?'

'Not particularly.'

'You would have once – you've changed.'

'I needed to. But it's very kind of you to bring the tart over. We shall enjoy that with our dinner.'

'He's staying another night?'

'Probably.'

'Well, I never thought . . .'

'Neither did I. Mum.' She smiled, such a contented smile that it enraged Mary, who insisted on giving her yet more of her mind. If only she knew, Jillian found herself thinking. One guilty night and only innocence after.

Even from her limited knowledge of men, Colin's behaviour was unique. Over the next few weeks he did not force himself on her, but waited patiently for her to change her mind about him, to resolve the confusion she felt. For nothing had changed: she still wanted him as a lover. The problem occurred as they made love: mentally she would draw back. She tried to hide from him how she felt but he always knew, and would kiss her gently, whisper, 'Another time,' and hold her tight. This always made her feel safe and secure at the time, but in the light of day she knew they could not go on like this. She could not expect his patience to last for ever. She knew he was convinced that she still pined for Jack – and what man would play second fiddle indefinitely?

In every other respect she was an ideal lover for him, she fussed over him, making him feel the most important man in the world. She cooked for him, ironed his shirts, sewed on buttons, did all those little things a woman of her generation chose to do for the man she loved – except that one thing.

She might have started this relationship with ideas that she would use him, make him into a convenience for her, but she had realised that she wasn't that sort of woman. As the weeks passed she began to appreciate him, and grew fond of him. Eventually that fondness had become love – for a very dear friend.

They saw each other once in the week, when she would drive to Inverness, and every other weekend, when he wasn't with his children, he came to stay with her. What would happen when Esmée and Victoria returned she did not know, and chose not to think about it for the time being. She had settled into a pleasant routine.

7

Colin introduced her to his friends, who were writers, painters and musicians rather than the solicitors and accountants she had expected. None were particularly successful but all somehow scraped a living on the fringes of their chosen professions. Once she'd asked him if he chose them because he envied them and would have liked to do something free and artistic.

'Me? I can't paint for toffee. I can write you a fine will, but never a novel.' She didn't entirely believe him. 'And I've obligations,' he added. 'Or does that make me sound dull?'

'I admire a man who is aware of his responsibilities.'

Not like Jack, she thought inevitably. She wished a day would dawn when ideas, words, smells, noises would not remind her of him. Sometimes she saw herself as a widow who, though getting on with her life, still kept alive the memory of her long-dead husband. But a widow need not feel guilty about remembering, it was what was expected. She had buried no one, but still could not rid herself of him. It was not fair on Colin, or herself.

Apart from seeing Colin's friends she was also asked out alone. She discovered that more people lived permanently in the Highlands than she had realised. She was usually invited to lunch: a two-hour drive to a host was quite common, and nobody fancied a long drive home at night when the weather could turn vicious within minutes. Some of the houses she visited were enormous, and she shuddered at the cost of heating them. She learned quickly that clothes had to be thick and warm wherever she went.

In the country in England she'd found it difficult to meet people, but here it was the opposite. The news that Esmée's sister-in-law was at Altnahany had caused quite a stir.

It was explained to her that due to the lack of organised entertainment, people relied on each other for company. She was rapidly 'taken up'.

They were old-established families, some rich in money, possessions and history. Others were rich in background but lived a Spartan life since 'the lodge' took every penny they had. As far as she could make out, none of these people had jobs as such, but creaked along with shrinking dividends, the odd paying-guest for the shooting or the fishing, and the occasional money-making scheme – from mushroom-growing to selling honey or raising llamas – which, she gathered, invariably failed.

In the short time she'd been here she'd been to more lunch parties than she'd ever been invited to while she was at Fen

Manor. And she'd worried about being lonely! The women were charming, full of advice and tolerant of their husbands. Some of the men drank and one, whose collar was somewhat frayed, had a booming voice as if by shouting he could disguise from the world the precariousness of his finances. It seemed to her that they spoke mainly of the killing they had done or the killing they intended.

Initially she had thought that these new acquaintances were no different from their English cousins, except they were fitter, hardier and drank more. She was wrong. They appeared the same, but they were different. She noticed that there was a mutual respect between the landowners and the crofters, ghillies, the people who worked for them. This was something she'd never witnessed among the same class in England with its Them and Us social divide.

'We depend on each other, Jillian,' one hostess explained, when Jillian remarked on it. 'We live here in isolated areas and need each other. This is no place for airs and graces. Who'd come to help you if your house was burning down if that was so?'

When she reported this conversation to Hamish he spluttered angrily. 'Cock and bull, all of it! I'll give you, they're one step up on the English and the Arabs who settle here. But not much. I'm disappointed in you, Jillian, going over to the other side.'

'You make it sound as if I was dying.'

'You might just as well if you're going to hang around with that lot. You do realise it's only because of the big house, Altnahany, that you've been invited? If they knew your full history they never would.'

'From that am I to assume that you do know, Hamish?' She was teasing: she knew Colin had told them about her and Jack. They had asked, had been his simple explanation. It was strange that she did not mind them knowing but would hate other people to find out.

'I do that.'

'Everything?' she asked, in mock horror.

'I never told them everything. I need to keep some things

to myself.' Colin smiled the secret smile that lovers give each other across a room. It always made her sad when he did.

'I'm disappointed. I thought you'd have more taste than to socialise with a load of parasites. They parade themselves as Scots, farting about in their kilts, and all of them were born in London.'

'Hamish, you make politics out of everything. Do stop, for heaven's sake – he'll be going on about the North Sea oil next, if we don't watch out. It's boring,' Fenny admonished him. 'Have you heard from Esmée? Is she well?'

'Not a word since a phone call last month. But that's Esmée for you.'

'And you've no idea where she is?'

'Hopefully not getting married again. But, no.'

'If she calls, give her my regards, tell her I'm thinking of her.'

'I didn't know you knew Esmée.'

'Not well. But we have met . . .'

Without doubt, though, of the people she had met it was Hamish, despite his dogmatism, and Fenny for her sense that she admired most. She was always sorry, as now, when the evening ended.

As they turned into the driveway of Altnahany, it never ceased to amaze her how beautiful the house was, especially in the moonlight. It rose from its grass base a glowing, mystical-looking place. Each time she saw it like this she would think how lucky she was. She wished it was hers.

'Hamish doesn't mean everything he says, does he?'

'About the English? Too right. Culloden was yesterday to him.'

'Some of the things he says have come as a shock. I hope it's not going to be a problem. I'd no idea the extent of the bitterness against the English here. I've got some books on order from the travelling library so I can learn more of Scottish history.'

'Hamish will be pleased.'

'You don't feel like him?'

'No. But I understand him. What the English don't understand about the Hamishes of this world is the fierce pride of the Highlander. Until they do, there'll always be trouble.'

'Well, I think it's all silly. We're all British, all one nation.'

'I shouldn't say that too often if I were you.'

In December Victoria returned home. Jillian had assumed she had come early for Christmas. She hadn't. When she met her daughter at the station and saw the bedraggled figure dragging her case along the platform, obviously all was not well. She had planned that they would have breakfast, do some shopping and meet Colin for lunch. She cancelled everything and they drove straight home. On the way back, Jillian tried to find out what was the matter, but Victoria sat mute and miserable. It was not until they were safely in the kitchen that she gave way, and burst into tears, flinging herself in Jillian's arms.

'I found Rory in bed with my best friend,' she sobbed out. 'And they were my sheets. I bought them!'

'My darling, I'm so sorry.'

'I didn't know what to do.'

'Of course you didn't. Best you came home.' Jillian patted her daughter's shoulder. She was aghast at the misery and pain in Victoria's voice and felt worse than useless in the face of her torment.

'I never want to leave here ever again. I could never face them.' She blew noisily into her handkerchief and took a long sip of the brandy that Jillian had poured her. Jillian braced herself, sensing there was more to come and Victoria was building up enough Dutch courage to tell her. 'But, Mum, there's more. I think you should sit down.'

Jillian felt the familiar lurch of her heart at such ominous words, but did as she was told.

'I had an abortion!' The words hung in the air between them.

'Oh, no!' Jillian exclaimed, before she could stop herself, her voice tight with pain. 'I mean, are you all right?'

'You didn't mean that at all. Your voice was full of disapproval. I knew it would be. I knew you'd take that attitude.'

'I'm not taking any attitude, I'm saddened, that's all. Sad for you and sad for the baby.'

'It wasn't a baby – it was a thing, cells, only cells,' Victoria shouted, then began to sob again. Jillian did not believe that this was at all how she felt, and the loud heartrending sobs seemed to confirm it. Jillian wanted to cry too.

'Victoria, I *am* sorry. It can't have been an easy decision for you to make.' She tried to sound calm and reasonable when she felt such anger inside her – at the man.

'You're a right one to talk! I know about you.' Victoria's face, ugly from crying, peered at her from behind folds of Kleenex.

'I don't know what you mean.'

'Yes, you do, you wanted to do the same. It was only Granny Stirling interfering that stopped you, otherwise Miles wouldn't be here now. So don't give me any sob-sister crap.'

'Your grandmother is an evil, lying old cow. She wanted me to do it and I refused! How often do I have to say it?' Jillian's voice rose.

'You needn't shout at me.'

'I'm not shouting! I'm angry – with her, at the world, at everything!'

'It wasn't you who had to go through with it.'

'I know. And I sympathise with you for that, but please don't ask me to approve, because I can't.'

'Christ, Mum! How can you say that to me? You mean, if you'd known you'd have tried to stop me?'

'No. It's your life, your body. I don't have the right to impose my views on you.'

'So what are you doing?' Victoria shrieked.

'I can't lie to you.'

'So you'd rather I was a single mum?'

'I'd rather it had never happened.'

'Well, it did. So grow up. Do!' And Victoria stamped from the room.

Somehow they got through the day. Victoria shifted from wanting affection and reassurance to being angry with Jillian as if she had contrived her misfortune. Several times Jillian

384

was convinced her daughter was searching for some excuse to lay the blame at her door. Well, not this time, sister, she thought.

Fortunately it was a weekday so she did not have the complication of Colin being there; she'd not told Victoria he often slept here. But as she lay in bed she wondered if Victoria was sobbing the night away. She could not sleep and instead stared into the darkness, worried, fretted and grieved for the child who would never be. Sometimes she'd wondered how she'd react if Victoria ever came to her with news like this. She had presumed she'd be understanding and sympathetic. She'd known exactly where she would stand. Only she hadn't. Not when it was real, not when it was her grandchild.

'Any hope of someone coming to meet me at the airport?' The call from Esmée came as a complete surprise.

Jillian was relieved to get away from the house and the oppressive atmosphere.

'Esmée, you've lost weight!'

'Brilliant, isn't it?'

'But you weren't fat before. It's not as if you'd much to lose.'

'I love you, Jill, I've no need for a mother with you around!' Esmée kissed her swiftly.

'How is your mother?' she asked, out of politeness and also because she had a morbid curiosity about the woman.

'Mungo's still riddled with guilt – I tell him I'm not so why should he be? The home she's in is adorable – all chintz and dear old ladies slurping their tea and not a neurone working between them all. Gracious, it's good to be back. Just smell that air.' Esmée stood beside the car breathing deeply. She coughed. 'A mistake, methinks. Why am I such a romantic? The air stinks of aviation fuel! I'll wait for the Struie.' She got into the car quickly. 'Who's coming for Christmas?'

'It's just us and my mother, if you can put up with her.'

'Why shouldn't I? I think your mother's an absolute poppet.'

'That's because she's not your mother.'

'She's still moaning?'

'Nothing specific. Just that everything is vaguely wrong for her, if you know what I mean. And ... if it's all right with you, I wondered if I could invite Colin.'

'Of course, my darling, we need someone to bait.'

'You wouldn't?' Jillian turned in the driver's seat, worried.

'Don't be silly. I shall be a perfect angel to him. Has he moved in yet?'

'Hardly. It's not my place to invite him.'

'Jill, dear heart, there are times when you sound so quaintly prim. I adore it when you do. I'm hardly at Altnahany and he'd be company for you. If you want to shack up with him, go ahead. You won't hear a peep out of me.'

'I doubt that his wife would approve of that.'

'He's not still playing you both along?'

'Remember, Esmée, we promised not to discuss this subject. It's closed,' Jillian said firmly, as they left the main road and began the ascent over the Struie.

'Apart from the grim wife, I assume all is going well. Are you in love?'

'I'm very fond of him.' She had no intention of trying to explain to Esmée how confused she was.

'Those are the dreariest words in the English language after "Time, gentlemen, please". Or, what about, "Don't you think you've had enough?"' Esmée laughed.

'What about "Of course we can still be friends,"' Jillian added.

'How about "Come to supper, it's only pot luck!"'

They played the game as they drove along, making each other laugh. Jillian realised how much she had missed her friend. 'I've a myriad things to tell you.'

'If it's business, leave it until we're home and I've bathed and got a drink in my hand. Do pull over. This is my favourite place in the world.'

Jillian swung the car into the viewing-point lay-by and turned off the engine. A faint drizzle was falling so they stayed in the car. 'What a shame, you can't see far.'

'Whatever the weather, there's always a magic to this view.'

Esmée stretched contentedly. 'I'm sorry about Victoria. Messy business.'

'She told you she and Rory had split up?'

'Just as well. He was a self-satisfied little creep. Thought he was God's gift in his tight jeans – you know, the sort of man who thinks he's the only one with a dick and that he's better at it than anyone else in the world. They strut around, and they're invariably useless in the sack. No, not him, I meant the termination.'

'You knew?'

'Darling, I arranged it. She phoned me yesterday and said she'd confessed all. Poor little bitch, it can't have been easy.'

Jillian turned slowly in her seat. 'And you didn't think to call me and ask me what I thought?'

'No, I didn't. Victoria asked me not to but, in any case, I guessed you'd be all sentimental and insist she have it and you'd bring it up or something crass like that.'

'I think "crass" is a rather unfortunate choice of word. But yes, that's what I would have advised her to do. And what would have been wrong with that?'

'It wouldn't have been her decision. Heavens, Jill, it's her body. She must do with it as she sees fit.'

'I'm not going to get into an argument with you over this – we'd never agree. That apart, once she'd decided I'd like to have been there for my daughter, as I am now to see her through this difficult time.'

'I don't see any need for any fuss. Everyone has terminations, these days.'

'Everyone doesn't. Honestly, Esmée, you do make such sweeping statements and always presume everyone thinks like you.'

'Oh dear, I think we have a teensy-weensy bit cross Jillian here.'

'I'm more than cross. I don't think you had the right not to tell me what was happening. I think, sometimes, you take too much upon yourself. I think it's easy to trot out your glib excuses but then you wouldn't really understand, would you? You've never been a mother.'

'Ouch!' said Esmée, as Jillian put the car angrily into gear.

8

Winter 1992–3

For Jillian, as a child, Christmas had always been a let-down. Later, she saw that her anticipation had been so great that disappointment was inevitable. But all her adult life she had endeavoured to erase the memory of those childhood Christmases, of which her father had never approved and at which her mother had always worked too hard, and the tension she had often felt.

In the last few years, lack of money and space in their tiny house had prevented her making any great fuss. This year, though, they had a big house which, with its lovely large rooms, said to her that it had waited a long time for the fun to begin. The only disappointment was that, because of his work, Miles would not be joining them.

'You do know that, apart from the dog, we shall be women only – a veritable coven!' Jillian pointed out.

'And what's happened to your surly little Scottish advocate?'

'He can't come, he's spending Christmas with his children. And before you say anything, Esmée, I totally agree that he should.'

'*Moi*? Say an infinitesimal word? Really, Jill, what do you take me for?' She returned to her book. 'Just one thing,' she said, five minutes later. 'Have you met these kids yet? Just asking!'

'No.'

'Why not?'

'The time hasn't been right,' Jillian said, and her look ensured that Esmée said no more. The truth was that she'd suggested several times that she should meet Col and Sammy, but Colin never thought it was a good idea and now she wondered if it ever would be. 'I was relying on you to bring a man back with you from your travels, Esmée.' Jillian had forgiven, if not forgotten, her spat with Esmée. They'd drawn up a pact never to discuss it again.

'We should have a party.'

'Oh, no, not a party!' Victoria slumped back in her chair.

'Victoria, my dear child, I do wish you'd snap out of it – just looking at you fills me with gloom to the bottom of my soul.'

Standing behind Victoria, Jillian shook her head warningly at Esmée. Not surprisingly, her daughter was depressed and getting worse with every passing day. Jillian had tried to talk to her but Victoria had made it plain that she did not wish to discuss anything with anyone. But Jillian knew it was more that she did not want to talk out her problems with her mother, for she often heard her in Esmée's room talking nineteen to the dozen. Of course, there were matters she would not want to discuss with her, she had never wanted to confide in her own mother. But, as much as she loved Esmée, she worried that she was not the best influence on Victoria.

'Of course a party. I think we should invite absolutely everyone we know, not just the nobs but all the people working on the house. It'll be such fun.'

'Haven't we left it a bit late?'

'You're always so negative, Jill. Of course we haven't.'

'I shan't come,' said Victoria, sounding like Eeyore.

'Good. Most considerate of you, in this present mood. Come on, Jill, it's time you made one of your famous lists. Now . . .'

Victoria, after inspecting the fridge and finding nothing to her liking, hugged the dog noisily. She riffled through a magazine and Jillian was amazed at how much noise that made too. She tuned in to Radio One, sighed exaggeratedly and left the kitchen, slamming the door violently behind her.

'Noisy little bitch,' Esmée complained.

'I don't think that's the best way to deal with her, Esmée. You'll make her depression worse.'

'She's not depressed. She's bored.'

'Really, Esmée, what a thing to say!'

'It's the truth. She's bored out of her tiny little skull. It's not surprising, is it? She's stuck here with us old bags and she needs a fellow.'

'I'd have thought, in the circumstances, that that was the last thing she needed.'

'Jill, my dear one, I hate to have to say this to you but, quite

389

honestly, you don't understand her. She's not feeling the guilt that undoubtedly you would have felt. She might be a scrap concerned that she isn't, if you get my drift, but she's got herself stuck here, making all those dramatic statements that she's never leaving. Now she doesn't know how to extricate herself. She'll come to the party, you mark my words. Lists – come on, woman, there's no time to lose.'

Mary was not sure about the party. 'It'll mean a lot of extra work for you,' she announced.

'I like the idea. In any case, Esmée's got in a firm of party planners and they're doing everything. All I have to do is make sure we know who's coming and who isn't.'

'Mixing the types like that, it won't work.'

'Of course it will.'

'The upper classes will be insulted and the lower will think they're being patronised.'

'Mum, if all you're going to do is find fault, could you possibly go and do it somewhere else?'

For one awful moment it looked as if Colin would not be able to come. He had arranged to babysit for his wife while she went out to a family dinner. There was no point in asking her to make other arrangements, he explained, she would be too cross. Jillian longed to tell him he was being a wimp, but found herself wondering if she wasn't wasting her time with him, that perhaps Esmée had been right all along. It was as well she had said nothing, though, for two days before the party Colin's wife's dinner was cancelled so he could come.

Esmée's party was an enormous success. From her visits when her aunt was alive she knew so many people. The huge dining room had been filled with ten small tables, each seating six. There was only candlelight so everyone looked prettier and younger. Esmée's seating plan meant that they were all mixed up, no wife sat with her husband, no sister with a brother. There was no table for the young, which Victoria had said would be a huge mistake – what self-respecting young person would wish to sit with wrinklies?

Hamish had declined their invitation, but he'd done it in verse, which made them laugh.

> If I sit with a toff
> I'll only scoff
> And be rude and unreasonable
> And drunk
> And unseasonable
> Safer by far I'll sit wi' a dram
> And scheme and dream
> Of Devolution, Our own Revolution.

As the party progressed and everyone relaxed, Jillian was aware that she watched Colin constantly. She'd occasionally felt jealous of the hold his wife had over him, but she'd never concerned herself about other women until now. And there were some attractive ones here tonight, she noticed. She spent the evening in an agony of suspense – wanting him.

Esmée had been right. Victoria, saying she was only going to put in a short appearance for politeness' sake, came to the party. Dressed in a dramatic velvet dress, low-cut and expensive-looking, that Esmée had bought her, she looked beautiful. The 'just showing her face' turned into a place being set for her. And although she didn't say so, she was evidently having a great time.

Mary, her hair rigidly set and smartly dressed in a black skirt and white blouse, with a stole of Forbes tartan – which, she was at pains to explain to everyone, she was entitled to wear – was enjoying herself. Her colour was suspiciously high, but so what, thought Jillian, seeing her mother truly laughing for the first time in an age.

The station-master's wife was sick and, as Jillian led her from the dining room, she reassured her it must be the rich food. But she'd noted that there were far more empties on this particular table than any of the others. A local shop-keeper had to be carried off to bed in the middle of dinner when he'd simply toppled over into his plate.

'Is he ill?' Jillian fretted, thinking he'd had a stroke.

'No, drunk. He's famous for it,' his large, organising wife reassured her, as she led the way upstairs to a guest bedroom.

Fenny said, 'He'll be as right as rain in the morning, you'll see. Don't worry, Jillian. You've seen nothing yet.'

There was an air of anticipation, which doubled when the reels began. Tables were packed away, chairs rearranged around the edge of the room. A piper appeared, though Jillian had not thought to arrange one – Gregor, it seemed, never travelled without his pipes. And then the wildness began as the dancers twirled, hurled and roared their excitement to the world. Jillian found herself caught up in it and danced as she'd never danced before, picking up the movements as she went along.

She could not remember when she'd last been so happy, just allowing herself to be swept along with everyone else's joy.

'Having a good time?' Colin grabbed her round the waist. 'You Scots certainly know how to enjoy yourselves.'

'But of course. Mind you, we don't go mad at Christmas. You just wait for the New Year, then we really let ourselves go.' He swung her round, caught her, kissed her and she knew, for sure, that tonight was going to be all right – at last.

'Seen your daughter?' He nodded across the room to where Victoria was gazing with admiration into the face of a young man. 'She looks besotted.'

'Doesn't she?' Jillian said, hoping that this time her daughter was on the pill.

The New Year passed without Jillian joining in the celebrations. Everyone had tried to persuade her differently, telling her what fun it was, a spectacle she should not miss, how deeply she would offend people if she did not take part. She had heard of the momentous drinking binge that Hogmanay invariably became, but it wasn't that which stopped her: it was simply that she had never enjoyed seeing the old year pass.

'If it's been a good year, I'm sad to see it go. If it's been an awful one, I'm scared of what more the New Year might bring me. I've never been able to see it as a time of celebration.'

From the expression on Colin's face, she was not explaining very well.

'But, don't you see, that's exactly why you should celebrate. In a crowd you won't be so sad or scared.'

'Look, you do whatever you want, but please leave me out of it.'

'I will.' He stood up to go. 'Much as I love you, I couldn't not see the New Year in. It wouldn't feel right.'

Victoria was at a party at her new boyfriend's house. While relieved to see her daughter happy, Jillian could not help fearing that it was all too fast too soon. She was certain that Victoria was filling the void left by Rory and her lost child by hurling herself into this new relationship and love with almost hysterical commitment. 'She'll learn,' Esmée had counselled, before going south once more.

The following morning she found Colin asleep in his car on the forecourt, the engine running and him with a monumental hangover.

'I had to come and see you. I missed you,' he mumbled.

'That's sweet of you.' She smiled while worrying about the state he must have been in to look like this. Certainly he should never have been driving.

'I kept phoning you, but it was always engaged.'

'I took the phone off the hook.'

'My, but you're an odd woman, Jillian! You've got to let up, you know, and learn to enjoy yourself. You can't go on like this.'

'Oh, yes, I can if it means not looking like you do.' She laughed at his bleary-eyed expression as he leaned on the car, still uncertain if he could stand up when he let go.

'The English are a weird lot.'

'Not nearly as weird as you Scots! Coffee for you and bed, I think, don't you?' she said briskly, but smiling indulgently at him.

The work on the house continued apace after New Year. Every day brought its excitements. A bedroom might be finished, new treasure was found frequently, for she was still sorting through Aunt Fiona's accumulated possessions. There was the exploratory discussion with the Scottish Tourist Board who, having viewed what she had done so far, declared that undoubtedly she would get the highest rating.

'I'm Ewan Milner. I run the Clansman, the big mausoleum by the loch. I thought I'd stop by and see if you needed any help.'

'How very kind of you. Come in.' Jillian ushered the man into the hall. He was of middle years, pleasant-faced with the complexion of someone who spent much time outdoors. His Barbour was old, the wax cracked. He wore faded tweed plus-fours and thick hairy socks above well-worn brogues.

'My, but you've made a difference here.' He looked around the newly decorated hall. 'And you've restored the Caithness flagstones – magic.'

'You knew Aunt Fiona?'

'She graciously invited me for the odd dram.'

Jillian turned quickly. His voice had sounded pleasant enough, yet she wondered if he was being sarcastic. But he was smiling, his grey eyes disappearing into the breadth of his smile. 'I never met her, unfortunately.'

'She's a great loss. Are you sure you wouldn't prefer me to remove my shoes?'

'Good heavens, no. There's mess enough with the builders. I begin to think they'll still be here when the first guests arrive.'

'How are bookings?'

'None yet.'

'They'll come. I'll send any overflow to you. We're not as busy as in the old days but sometimes we're full.'

She offered him a drink. She'd presumed that the Clans-man's manager would be a rival, not offering help.

'I saw your licensing application was granted.'

'I was terrified it wouldn't be, me being a woman.'

'Maybe once, but even the Highlands move with the times. Want some advice?'

'Naturally.'

'Don't leave all these knick-knacks around, they'll get lifted. Only heavy ornaments. Locked cabinets for the rest.'

He indicated the pretty porcelain and silver bric-à-brac in the drawing room.

'Even here?'

'Especially here.' He laughed. 'The great British public thinks you won't notice or, since they're paying, that they've a right to it.'

'You don't sound as if you've much time for tourists.'

'They're a living.'

'Oh dear, such cynicism.'

'It comes with the trade.'

An hour later, as she let him out, she thanked him fulsomely. He couldn't have been more helpful or generous. He'd even invited her to pop over one evening for dinner, if she wanted. She'd accepted with pleasure.

The decisions on what sort of food they should serve had still to be finalised. On the phone from New York, Esmée was airily vague. 'Make it whatever you want, dear heart. You're doing the cooking. You choose.' Jillian dug out her old cookbooks and scoured them for suitable recipes. She resolved to serve only Scottish and English food – no quasi-French dishes here – and she intended to have a set menu so that everything was fresh.

Not having cooked much game or fresh salmon before, she searched Inverness for more cook books. The more she read about Scottish food, the more interested she became in it. Even if she'd no intention of serving French food, she couldn't ignore the influence of that country on Scotland, because of the Auld Alliance, Colin had explained.

'Did you know that haggis comes from the French *hachis* meaning meat minced, cut up small?' she asked Colin on whom, at the weekends, she practised her new dishes.

'No, I didn't, and I wouldn't tell too many people either. They, like me, wouldn't want to think that the haggis was anything else but Scots!'

The more she delved the more fascinated she became, and she realised that here was a cuisine in its own right which had nothing to do with English food and that out there on the moors, in the forests and rivers, was the most abundant larder in the world. She made notes and collected information, with a notion at the back of her mind that one day she might be able to do something with it all.

Once more she stood waiting at Inverness airport for the flight from London. Miles had called to say that, having worked Christmas and the New Year, he had a week off. She wasn't disappointed when he said Maxine couldn't come.

At the sight of her, Miles rushed across the arrivals hall and swept her off her feet in a huge bear hug. 'I've missed you so much, Mum. Why on earth did you have to come and live this far away?'

'Fate!' She returned the hug. It was then that she saw Maxine approaching. As usual she was smiling the smile that wasn't. 'Ah, Maxine.' Jillian injected pleasure and surprise into her voice, but feared it didn't sound convincing.

'I changed my mind. I hope you don't mind.'

'Why, of course not. You're a lovely surprise.' What a hypocrite I am, she thought. She had been quick to criticise Maxine's false smile, yet what was she now doing?

'I said we should call. My mother hates guests being sprung on her.'

'Maxine, you're hardly a guest, you're part of my family.' Or should be, she thought, as she linked her arm with Maxine's and they walked towards the door. She couldn't be sure but she thought Maxine tensed slightly, as if she did not want such contact. Jillian disentangled herself, pretending to search for her car keys, which she knew were in her pocket.

'I'd hoped we'd have snow,' Miles said excitedly, kicking at the newly fallen flakes.

'I was worried about getting here because of it. I can't take you my favourite way, it's closed – blocked on the summit – but the main road's fine. Things don't stop in Scotland for snow, not like in England. They're impressively organised in the Highlands.'

'I expected Victoria to be here,' Miles said, as he loaded their bags in the boot.

'Your sister is an occasional visitor at Altnahany. She's in love.'

'Again?'

'Again.'

Miles sat beside her on the drive back. She could see Maxine in the rear-view mirror sitting quietly, smiling occasionally as Miles talked non-stop about her and their new flat, their plans and finally how happy he was, how happy she made him.

'Miles, you'll bore your mother rigid. Talk about something else!' She laughed softly, but looked pleased.

'Don't stop him, Maxine. I like to hear all this. It's music to my ears!'

'How's Gran?'

'Finding little joy in the world. I think she'll be disappointed if this hotel venture is a success. She moans about it non-stop.'

'At least you haven't got Rob.'

'No, that's a blessing. He'd interfere, I'm sure. She rarely mentions him so I can only presume she's not missing him.'

'And Victoria's feller?'

'He's very nice. Gregor Macpherson. His family live on the west coast – they've got a fish farm. I think he'll take it over when his father retires.'

'Victoria, the wife of a fish farmer out in the wilds? I don't see it myself.'

'It's early days yet. They've only just met.'

They stopped in Tain to shop. 'I want to serve only local produce. And the cheese I just bought is made here in Tain. I'd like you to try it,' she explained, once they were on their way again.

'It seems a dreary place,' Maxine said, from the back of the car.

'Tain? I think it's a dear little town. You can get whatever you want there. And the people are welcoming and even forgive me my Englishness.' She laughed to cover the

397

annoyance she felt at Maxine's dismissal of the little town. She was surprised at how fond she had become of it.

'You should have the name of the hotel painted on the panels of this car. Better still, get a monospace, for carting guests from the airport.'

'You think so?'

'I know so.'

'I want to pick your brains.'

'Well, I'm the expert,' he said, with mock conceit. Jillian caught what sounded suspiciously like a snort coming from the back seat.

Fortunately she had put Miles in the biggest and best bedroom. She showed them their room then raced downstairs to make the tea. Of course, she thought, thinking how fortunate it was that she'd chosen that room, it said a lot about her relationship with her daughter-in-law. Why should the fact that it was the best room matter? It should be irrelevant which room she'd chosen. But the truth was that the woman made her feel edgy, as if – as Victoria had said on first meeting her – she was sneering at them, that she didn't fully approve of her. How arrogant! Just like her mother, Vanessa.

On the drive she hadn't liked to hear that Miles had shelved his plans to go to Paris to learn more about the trade. He'd announced they were staying at the hotel in Berkshire, and Maxine's father was not retiring. So where would that leave Miles? There were moments on the trip back when she thought his exuberance was more for effect than real.

How ironic life could be. She'd have given anything to have her own mother-in-law like and accept her; now here she was thinking the same about her daughter-in-law. All she wanted was to get on with Maxine and do away with these barriers.

What could she have done to merit this coolness? Surely Maxine wasn't jealous of her? No! She dragged the kettle across the Aga. Mothers were jealous of daughters-in-law, not the other way round. Oh, well . . . 'Let them get on with it!'

'On with what?'

She jumped. 'Miles! Was I talking aloud?'

'You were! Going bonkers here on your own.'

'Probably.'

'Nice dog. What's he called?'

'Prince.'

'What earth-shattering originality!' Miles laughed. 'Maxine says you don't like her. That's not so, is it?'

'What nonsense. Of course I like her if you love her. But I don't really know her,' she replied warily.

'She's mega-beautiful, isn't she?'

'She's lovely,' she said guardedly, not seeing her in quite the same light. 'Look, I've made tea and scones for us. We'll have it in the drawing room. I've lit a fire.' She led the way, Prince padding in front. Upon entering the room they found Maxine idly leafing through a magazine. 'I'm sorry about the choice of magazines, Maxine. Once I only took *Harpers* and things like that. Now it's all *Ideal Home* and practicalities.'

'I don't normally bother with either.'

'Well, we've plenty of books.'

'I don't read much.'

'Really? I couldn't exist without my books. Still, there's masses to do, even in this weather. Television, I've bought loads of videos. There's a giant jigsaw. The forest is lovely for walks – Prince would like that.'

'I'm not too keen on dogs.'

Then what the hell does interest you? she longed to ask. She poured the tea and wondered how Miles, with his intelligence, could possibly live with someone so devoid of interest in anything.

'This is a great place, Mum. Handled right, it's got huge potential.' Miles took the cup she handed him to Maxine and fussed about her as if she were an invalid. 'Of course, you're going to have to get a board put up on the main road. How else will the punters know you're here?'

'I had thought about having one but is it necessary? I'd hoped to rely on bookings.'

'Never knock passing trade. You'll have fallow times when the odd skull passing by will be manna from heaven.'

'Skull?'

'Punters – skulls in beds. Getting them there, that's the

name of the game. And then keeping them, or at least getting them to return.'

'Gracious. You sound like a friend of mine. Do you help your parents in their hotel, Maxine?'

'Not if I can help it.'

'Ah . . .' Jillian passed the scones. If Maxine didn't like the business Miles was in, how long could this relationship last?

'You don't seem to have many rooms.'

'Potentially we've got eighteen. But we're only using six to begin with. We'll see how it goes.'

'You won't make a fortune on that number.'

'We're not looking for a fortune, Maxine. We just want the house maintained and a lifestyle out of it.'

'Place this size, Mum, you'll be pushing your luck. Can't be done.'

'There seems no point in all the expense of complying with the fire regulations if no one comes.'

'What are you charging?'

'That was one of the things I wanted to discuss with you. I don't know.'

'Price is critical. Too much and they won't cough up. Too little and they're suspicious they won't get good service. Is there a local hotel?'

'Yes, a big one. The Clansman. Quite famous too.'

'Then top them by a fiver, perhaps even a tenner. After all, this borders on a stately home.'

'Yes, but I'm an amateur. Ewan, the manager there, is a professional, like you.' She couldn't stop a note of pride creeping into her voice.

'Use the house-party crap. "Welcome to my home, sample the delights of a bygone age." That way, if things go wrong, which they will, you'll have intimidated them into pretending they really are house guests.'

'Really you're a grandiose B-and-B, aren't you? Not a hotel,' Maxine added.

'Yes, I suppose so. Except I'll be cooking dinner, not just breakfast.'

'No chef?' Maxine looked appalled.

'Not yet. When we get on our feet.'

400

'At this size it's just as well too. Get a woman to help with the food prep and washing-up. Chefs can be an expensive pain – they're all ego.'

'I'd also hoped you'd help me with the brochures. I've got the photograph proofs to choose from. And I –'

'You haven't got your brochures out? Mum, it's February! They should have been ready by the beginning of January. People plan their holidays straight after Christmas.'

'I never have. January? You're joking!'

'I'm not. Masses book then. You leave it too late and you've empty beds. Then you're vulnerable to having to do deals. The punters know you're desperate and they'll screw you into the ground on price.'

'I never have. What, negotiate the price?'

'Too right they do. Mum, you've got a lot of learning to do –'

At about nine o'clock Victoria bounded into the dining room where they'd just finished eating. She never slunk into the house now, but moved with an exuberance that mirrored her happiness.

'Miles! Fab! Love you!' Victoria hurled herself at her brother. 'I came back especially for you. Aren't I sweet?'

'Adorable. Bet you smell of fish.' He sniffed exaggeratedly. 'You shouldn't be out alone at this time of night.'

'Don't be ridiculous. This is Scotland. I'm as safe as houses. Oh, hello, Maxine. I didn't notice you,' Victoria said, with a smile so that Jillian was fairly sure she wasn't being rude. Maxine's expression made it clear that she thought she was.

'Mum, are you awake?' Victoria pushed open Jillian's bedroom door and peered in.

'Are you ill?' Jillian sat up in bed. She peered at her alarm clock. 'Victoria, it's only seven!'

'I couldn't sleep. Mum, what's he doing with that woman? She's ludicrous. All she thinks about is how she looks and what colour nail varnish she's wearing. He must be bored witless.'

'Evidently he isn't.'

'Can't you do something?'

'What? Trip her up on the stairs? Don't be silly. They're married and that's that.'

'It's as if you don't care.'

'I care. It's just none of our business, that's the bottom line.'

'Do you think she wants children?'

'I assume so. I haven't asked.'

'I don't think she does. She wouldn't want to ruin her figure for one thing. And if she did poor Miles would have to become a new man overnight. God, Mum, it's a disaster!'

Jillian had been concerned at what Miles would think of Colin and his role in her life. She need not have worried unduly.

'Mum, we're going.' Miles stood in the kitchen, looking sheepish.

'Where?' Jillian asked, even though she knew the answer.

'Back south.'

'But you've only been here two days.'

'I know. I'm sorry. But . . .' He turned to go.

'But what, Miles? Why? I'd so looked forward to your visit. You've only seen your grandmother once and she's excited about coming over for dinner tonight. And I so wanted you to meet Colin. I don't understand.'

'I'll apologise all the way to Inverness. I'm sorry, but we're going and there it is,' he said, with an exaggerated finality, as if hiding behind it, afraid that he might lose any argument she made.

'Has Victoria been rude to Maxine?'

'No. Why should she be?'

'You don't like it here? Or is it Maxine who doesn't like it here?'

'Mum!' He looked so pained and could not look her in the eye. It told her everything she needed to know.

'Very well. As you wish. There's a train in an hour.'

'Won't you drive us in?'

'I'm afraid I can't. I've an appointment with the health inspector in an hour.'

'Victoria?'

'She isn't here. I'll have to call you a taxi.' She spoke briskly to hide the mammoth wave of hurt. Telling herself not to overreact was not working.

'This is a bit off, Mum.'

'You better than most, Miles, should know the importance of the health inspector. If your wife is so rude that she wishes to terminate your visit there is little I can do about it.'

'This isn't like you, Mum.'

'Yes, it is. Before you go, Miles, one word of advice. If you can't control her now you never will.'

'For Christ's sake, Mum. It's not a question of *control*. This is the nineties, I don't *control* the woman in my life.'

'Then why is she allowed to control you?'

Fortunately for Jillian the health inspector's visit distracted her. There was only one problem: the worktop of the magnificent dresser that covered one wall of her kitchen was going to have to be covered in plastic as were all the shelves. Wood was a dreaded enemy in the hygiene battle the man explained to her. Otherwise the new flooring over the Caithness stone in the kitchen, the new sinks for vegetable preparation, as opposed to washing-up, the huge island work-station, the storage facilities, the dustbin placement, all passed muster.

To distract her even further the printer came for the final decisions on the brochure and the tariff leaflet.

That done, only then did she face the bleakness of the idea that her son was involved with a woman who did not like her, did not want to be involved with her and, worse, had no intention of ever being so.

'I like Maxine,' said Mary, over the soup, which they were eating in the kitchen. Since it was just the two of them now, there was no point in opening the dining room. 'I can't say the same of her mother, but she'll do. Pretty little thing. I can see why Miles married her. Of course, you know your trouble?'

'No, Mum, but, no doubt, you're going to tell me.'

'You're possessive.'

'I'm not.'

'You always have been. I've always thought that's what drove Jack away.'

'Mum, you're on dangerous ground here. That was not a fair thing to say. I don't wish to discuss Jack with you, okay?'

'Suit yourself. But boys don't like being possessed.'

'Loving my son is not possessing him. I've always looked forward to meeting his girlfriends.'

'He's happy with Maxine.'

'He doesn't seem so to me. He's too intent on telling us how happy he is. Why?'

'To shut you up, I expect. You always worry too much about other people and not about yourself. You're quick to find fault in others, but never yourself.'

'Mum!'

'You can "Mum" me all you want, but who else is going to tell you?'

'I worry because I love him. I want everything perfect for him.'

'Exactly. Proves my point. *Possessiveness*.' Mary waved her soup spoon belligerently.

Chapter Ten

1

Spring 1993

Suddenly and dramatically Victoria dropped Gregor. From being the most wonderful creature on earth he became a demon, unkind, inconsiderate and lousy in bed. But at least she was not pining and being dramatic at the end of this affair. Jillian suspected there was someone else.

The change in Victoria was for the good: she was unusually helpful; she asked if Jillian would give her a list of things to do, so that she would know what was expected of her and could plan her free time around it.

'Sounds like you're turning into a list-maker just like me,' Jillian teased.

'It's done you well, hasn't it? No harm in copying.' And Victoria produced a notebook.

'If you're going to help on a permanent basis then we should put you on a formal footing. Receptionist, office manager, something like that.' Jillian was pleased at the way things were going.

'Hell, no! I don't want to do this for ever. But I suppose I must think about doing something, though . . . not waitressing!' She grinned broadly.

'What do you want to do?'

'I thought about modelling, but I'm too old.'

'Is twenty-one too old?'

'Aeons too old.'

'Heavens above! How dire!'

'I don't really want to mess up the summer – the lodges will be opening soon, with Easter coming. Heaven knows where that might lead. But come the autumn . . . well, I've been a layabout long enough. Don't laugh, but I think I'd like to go to college and do my GCSEs and my A levels.'

'I'm not laughing, I think it's a splendid idea. You're an intelligent young woman. If you put your mind to it you could do anything.'

'That's what Esmée says.'

'Oh, you told her?'

'I didn't think you'd mind. You see, I need money and Esmée's offered to support me. I couldn't ask you, you've so little, and I didn't want to say until I knew how she felt.'

'It's kind of her, but I can't see how we can possibly accept. She does so much for us already.'

'Oh, she doesn't mind. She says it gives her a buzz to see people enjoying her money while she's in the land of the living.'

'Dear Esmée . . .'

Mary had had a nasty bout of flu and Jillian wrapped her up warm, bundled her into the car and brought her to the big house so that she could look after her better. She was not the easiest of patients, being capricious and petulant. If Jillian made her tea, she wanted coffee; chicken soup and she fancied tomato; give her extra pillows, she wanted them taken out; open her window as requested, she wanted it shut. Jillian was not worried about her: the doctor had assured her that she'd be fine, just needed careful nursing, but how she longed for that improvement to come and her mother to be safely back in her own cottage.

During this time she interviewed and arranged her staff – a grand word to use for the two women she finally employed. She could not believe her luck at finding Margaret, middle-aged, happy, kind and keen, with the loveliest of smiles, who took a great pride in her appearance. She had worked here many years ago as a housemaid for Aunt Fiona and loved the house, almost, Jillian decided, as much as she did. And it was Margaret who introduced her daughter-in-law, Gretchen, who would help when they were very busy. Jillian watched the easy friendliness and obvious affection between the two women and envied Margaret.

She could have done without a call from Esmée to say she wouldn't be there for the opening. They had argued. Esmée tried to bluff her way out of it, but Jillian was angry.

'Honestly, Esmée, I've done everything – I didn't mind, I've enjoyed it. But I did expect you to be here to give me moral support.'

'Sorry. No can do!'

'I just don't believe that anything else could be so important.'

'Well, it is.'

'Has anyone ever told you you're selfish?'

'And has anyone ever told you you're getting like your moaning Minnie mother?'

Two phones were slammed down simultaneously. When the phone rang a minute later Jillian snatched it up knowing it was Esmée.

'Darling, I'm a selfish creep. I'm so sorry. I'd be with you if I could – honest.'

'And I do go on. I'm sure you have your reasons.'

But worse than Esmée not coming was when the hotel sign she'd placed at the end of the glen road was defaced: 'Wite Setler, Pis Off' was crudely scrawled in red paint. Margaret had seen it on her way to work. 'Load of stupidity. Dinnae take nae notice of them!'

'But who'd do a thing like that?' She felt sick.

'There's always the odd hothead in any village. Why, they cannae even spell! Now you forget about it.'

'Margaret, try and find out what the gossip is, will you? Who did it?'

'Maybe it's best not to know.'

But Jillian insisted. It was such a small community she needed to know.

'I tried to warn you. The English aren't liked hereabouts.' Hamish accepted the dram she offered him.

'It's so ridiculous. Esmée and I are trying to create a business and give work to people. Then this.'

'They were probably drunk,' Fenny suggested.

'It doesn't make it any better, though, does it? Drunk or sober, they hate me.'

'You should tell everyone about your mother.'

'She might have been born in Aberdeenshire but I know she doesn't regard herself as Scots. She was only four when they left, for goodness' sake.'

'Once a Scot always a Scot.' Hamish helped himself to more whisky.

'But I'm not. I'm English and I'm proud of it, and why should I pretend otherwise? I'm not responsible for North Sea oil!'

'Don't mention that!' Fenny said in mock-horror and laughed. When Hamish joined in so did Jillian. 'Try not to worry, Jillian. You're well liked here. I hear only good things about you. And I reckon Margaret would die for you.'

'So. How about the painting? Where from? I suggest under the beech tree.'

The three trooped from the house to inspect where best to paint the picture she intended as a present for Esmée.

One of the best *good* things that happened was the arrival of the brochures, which Jillian thought looked wonderful. Certainly, if she had been looking for a place to spend her holiday she would have been seduced by the looks of Altnahany. With trepidation she placed advertisements in the *Sunday Times* and *The Lady* and could not believe it when the phone rang with several inquiries. It looked as if they would really be in business. Each brochure she sent out was accompanied by a hand-written letter from her. She had taken Miles's advice and was promoting the house-party angle.

A week later, when she received the deposit on her first booking she felt elated and nervous at the same time. Maybe it was going to work after all.

Just before Easter the final reservation came: they were to be a full house of six, all of whom had booked for bed, breakfast and dinner. And then Colin's landlady died, from cirrhosis of the liver.

'And there was I, so frightened of the old trout I was smuggling my Scotch into the house.'

'Maybe she was so strict about booze to camouflage her own liking for it. What will you do now?'

'I was hoping you might ask me to move in with you.' He spread his hands in a gesture of quizzical pleading.

'You'd like to?' She could not keep the surprise from her voice. 'What about your wife?'

'I've talked it over with her. She says she doesn't mind. I think she's met someone, so I suppose it quite suits her.'

Jillian felt a shiver of annoyance that he had seen fit to discuss her future with this woman whom she had never met. She stood silent, weighing up whether to say something, phrasing it in her head, but decided it sounded so petty.

'So? Been struck dumb?' He kissed her cheek.

'Sorry, I was just thinking it over.'

'Is there anything to think about? I thought you'd be pleased.' He grinned apologetically.

'I am in a way. Of course I am. And the children?'

'That's what I mean about her having someone. She seems to think it would be a good idea if they came for the odd weekend.'

'So that she can get some quiet nooky, I presume.' The spiteful remark was out before she could stop it.

'I didn't think you'd mind.'

'It might not be so easy when the hotel opens. I mean, how do I look after your kids and work as well? The winter's fine but the summer?'

'I'll help you, I promise. Jillian, don't spoil it, this is what I've been dreaming of happening. I love you, I really do.' He put his hand out to her, gently touched her cheek and smiled diffidently. As always, when he looked at her appealingly, she relented. And, as usually happened on such occasions, if Victoria was away, they fell into bed. All their problems in that quarter had been happily resolved.

Although she had agreed to his moving in with her, she'd told him she would have to discuss it with Victoria first. 'She's not your keeper,' he'd said, disappointed at this delay.

'It's her home too,' she'd replied, and Colin, seeing her stubborn expression, did not persist.

Jillian practised all manner of ways to tell her daughter that her lover was moving in with them but when it came to it all the subtle approaches came to naught. 'Colin wants to move in with me,' she blurted out, as they stood leaning against the Aga watching the rain fall in torrents.

'Permanently?'

'Yes.'

'Like marriage?'

'We haven't discussed that. In any case, I'm still married to your father.'

'But you needn't be – you've been apart for lots more than five years.'

'That's true. I just . . . well . . . no. I don't think I'd ever want to be married again.'

'That's fine.'

'You don't mind?'

'I think I'd have minded if you were going to get hitched. As it is, if you want to live with a dork – well, it's your life, isn't it?'

'What's a dork?'

'Colin is.'

'That's hardly an explanation, is it?'

'A wet, drippy fool best describes him.'

'Victoria! What a thing to say.'

'You asked, Mum!' Victoria grinned mischievously. 'Look, you do whatever you want. If he makes you happy then go for it. All I want is for you to be happy. I'll be away soon. Miles has his own life. It's time you had yours.'

'Thanks. You make it much easier. We get on so much better these days, don't we?'

'Yes. I don't resent you any more. I guess I've grown up a bit.'

'Did you resent me before?'

'Yes. I've thought about it a lot. I can't say I was overjoyed with the conclusions I reached either. When Daddy was with us I was jealous of you, he loved you so.'

'Did he? I don't think he did. Why else would he have dumped me?'

'Oh, Mum, I don't think he meant to. It was a mid-life crisis.'

'Yes, you could call it that! Problem was, he made his crisis mine and I could have done without that.' She laughed. That's better, she thought. She could laugh about it now. There had been a time when she felt the tragedy had marred her for life and that she'd never be happy again. And she was, sort of. 'And after? Why did you resent me then?'

'Oh, easy. I blamed you for him going. Gross of me, but there you are. I was just a thoughtless, stupid child. I can see it all now. I ought to say sorry for having been such an unmitigated cow to you.'

'Bless you.' Jillian put her arm around Victoria's shoulders and squeezed her, willing the wave of affection she was feeling to transfer to her daughter.

'Any info on the sign vandals?'

'I think Margaret knows but she's not telling.'

'Evil bastards. People!'

'You can say that again.'

'How's the old advocate?'

'Moving in.'

'Good God, his wife gave permission?'

'E-s-m-é-e,' she warned.

'Well, if it makes you happy.' Esmée's voice, shadowed by a slight echo, bounced off a satellite.

'It does. He makes me laugh. I think I'm one of those women who's best living with a man.'

'Bizarre. Living with them, I mean. I got over that syndrome years ago. Nowadays the minute they want to move their trouser press in I hear alarm bells. "Bye-bye, lover," I say, as fast as I can, and move on to the next.' Jillian wondered if she really thought this way or was just making a joke of her loneliness. 'How are the bookings?'

'Easter's full. Can you believe it? I'm really excited and looking forward to it . . .' She talked for a while of the business and future plans. Perhaps, feeling about Colin as she did, it was better Esmée wasn't there. But what would happen between them when she did come? Why was life so complicated always? Correction, she thought, it wasn't life, it was the people in it.

'If you ask me it's all wrong.' Her mother, who was batch-baking some cakes for her new freezer looked up with a hot, flustered face as she deftly moved them on to a rack with a spatula.

'Mum, I asked you out of courtesy, since you live here. Colin's moving in, whatever you think.'

'Doesn't seem much point in asking me my opinion then, does there?' With a clatter Mary threw the baking-sheet into the sink. 'And when's this momentous event taking place?'

'Easter.'

'You're a fool. You've all those guests and then he's taking up residence too. He's using you.'

'He's not. His mother could say the same of me. It's to our mutual benefit.'

'Then watch the petty cash.'

'What does that mean?'

'What it says.' And, infuriatingly, Mary began to do the washing up.

'Mum, could you leave that a minute and explain that last remark?'

'Very well.' Slowly and deliberately Mary dried her hands. 'You needn't look so shocked, it's happened to you once. That Jack running off with the proceeds. It could happen again.'

'He's a respected solicitor. He'd lose everything if he took a penny from anybody.'

'You think? Some of the worst people on this planet are in the most respected occupations – you've only got to read the *News of the World* to see that!'

'Well, I'm not worried.'

'Then I think you should be. He's a country lawyer – hardly in the league of a London man coining money like it's going out of fashion. He's got a wife and kids to support, all of which takes a lot of readies.' Mary neatly folded the tea-towel, placed it on the table and stroked it. 'And, of course, he's got his little problem,' she added, and nodded.

'What little problem?'

'He drinks.'

'All men drink.'

'No, they don't, not like him.'

'Oh, Mum.'

'You mark my words. And another thing –' The tea-towel was unfolded and the refolding process began again. 'While we're about it, what's the point of living in sin with one man when you're still in love with another?'

'You mean Jack? No, I'm not. I've thought about it a lot. I love the Jack I knew and our past, but I can't love the man he has become. You needn't worry on that score.'

'Then divorce him.'

'Why bother?'

'You're hiding behind him. If you're married to him you can't marry Colin. That, to me, speaks of a woman who'd rather not be alone, not a true commitment. I can tell you from my own experience it's better to be alone.' At which the tea-towel was picked up and hung over the rail.

The weekend before Easter Colin moved in. Jillian made time to cook a special celebration dinner of welcome. They sat contentedly, enjoying the last of the wine at the end of the meal. It was pleasant to know that there was to be no more packing of bags, that he was here permanently.

'Where shall we sleep Sammy and Col? In this barn of a place I'd like them to be quite close to me. I don't want them wandering around in the night getting lost and frightened.'

'I planned to put them at the back of the house with us. Not only will they be near but it's warmer in winter. They can have a room each and I think we should take them to Inverness and let them choose the colours and wallpaper. Perhaps we could get some posters of pop-stars and foot-ballers, or whatever they want.'

'That would be great. That's very thoughtful of you, Jillian. I can't tell you how grateful that makes me. There's just one problem. Where do I sleep?'

'With me! Where we've just put all your things, where we always sleep when you come here.' She felt uncomfortable. She knew what he was going to say next. She sat upright as if she could ward off his next sentence.

'I can't sleep there when they're here. It wouldn't be right. I promised Morag they wouldn't be exposed to any of that.'

'Any of what?' she asked, in a controlled voice.

'I don't want them confused.'

'Aren't they confused already?'

'I'm sorry, Jillian, but on this I agree with my wife.'

'And what if we get married? Are we still to have separate bedrooms?'

'We can cross that bridge if and when we come to it.'

'I see.' She felt hurt by his answer, which was illogical and unfair of her when she didn't wish to marry him. 'But shouldn't they know that their parents have separated and that you've found somebody else to love and live with? They'll find out sooner or later.'

'Morag and I have discussed this at length and this is the conclusion we have reached. I'm sorry.'

'And what about Morag and her man? Will they be having separate beds?'

'We don't know there is someone. I haven't asked her.'

'Why not?'

'I don't think it's any of my business.'

'But how we live our lives is hers?'

'I knew you were going to be difficult about this. Morag said you would be.'

Agitated at the way the conversation was going, he picked up the bottle of wine and, seeing it was empty, opened a second. While he did this Jillian tried to ignore his last remark. 'I'm not being anything of the sort. I understand how you feel and, if that's what you want, then I'll make up another room for you. But it will have to be on the top floor.'

'I was rather hoping I could use your room and you move out just for when they're here.'

Jillian had heard people talk of a red mist of fury that overcame all control; violence was a natural consequence.

Until now she had not known how literally they had meant it. She had to grip the side of her chair tightly to prevent herself hurling something at him. 'I don't think that's a good idea, Colin.' She was amazed at how calm she sounded. 'No, you'll have to move. If not, it's obvious to me that this is not going to work.'

'Fair enough.' He shrugged, as if it was of no importance to him. 'Still, we've plenty of time to work that out. They won't be here for four days.'

'Four days? They can't come here in four days' time! Our first guests arrive in four days' time.' She knew she was repeating herself, but could not believe what she was hearing.

'It's the Easter holidays. I've got them. I assumed you knew.'

'Well, I didn't. It just isn't possible, Colin.'

'You needn't do anything for them, I'll look after them.'

'I'll have no time for them and that'd be guaranteed to make them feel unwanted.'

'They won't mind.'

'But I will.' Her voice was shrill. 'After Easter will be best. It will give us time to get to know each other. Not this weekend.'

'I think you're being unreasonable, Jillian.'

'Look, Colin, don't push your luck.'

'Then what shall I do with them?'

'What you would normally do, of course.' She failed to keep the irritation out of her voice at the sound of a whine in his.

'Usually I take them to my mother's, or on a trip.'

'Then I suggest that's what you do.' She stood up and began to collect the dishes. She must keep busy. She must keep the red mist at bay.

They had not done anything so silly as not to speak to each other after their disagreement, but there was a change in atmosphere, a slight distancing between them and, on Jillian's part, a marked wariness. When alone she worried that perhaps she had made a mistake in agreeing that they live together, that it was all too soon. She should have taken more time to weigh up the pros and cons, which she'd have done automatically in the past. She had asked Victoria and her mother's opinion on whether Colin should move in or not, but had she asked herself? And, in truth, with the hotel opening she had far too much on her plate already without Colin's children. At forty-six, how was she going to find the patience to deal with a pair aged ten and fourteen? She understood Colin wanting only the best for his children but did he not owe her some loyalty too? How long was she to be kept as a dark secret? Surely, if he really loved her, as he said, he would want the world to know and that would include his children.

Fortunately she had to concentrate on the opening of the hotel and was forced to put such concerns to the back of her mind.

With only six people due – the most they could entertain without fire doors and a fire escape – she supposed that Maxine was right and it was more of a guest-house than an hotel. But she still used the word, not just because it was on the now restored board at the beginning of the glen and the new one at the bottom of the drive, but because it had a nice ring to it.

It was with distinct trepidation that she waited for the first arrivals. She had checked their bedrooms so many times that her calves ached from running up and down the stairs. She had made enough puddings to feed an army. She had polished the silver twice and buffed the glasses until her arm ached.

The flowers in the hall, sent by Esmée to wish her luck on her opening night, were straightened and fussed over for the umpteenth time. How she wished her friend was here. She shifted two lilies and decided they looked better that way. Two seconds later she'd put them back to their original position.

The sound of wheels on the gravel drive made her check herself in the hall mirror. Her stomach churning with a plague of butterflies, she threw open the front door, and stood smiling a welcome.

The guests were a bank manager and a teacher from Dorset, a pilot from Neasden, with a very pretty woman, and a miserable-looking Edinburgh doctor with a spiteful-looking wife. These last two turned out to be the life and soul of the party; so much for first impressions, Jillian told herself. They loved the rooms and thanked her for the little extras she had put in them: fresh flowers, small decanters of sherry and whisky, a tin of homemade shortbread, sparkling water, ice in Thermos buckets, Kleenex, shampoo and proper bars of soap. What was nice was that they bothered to tell her how pleased they were with everything, especially the enormous bath sheets. Everyone commented on them. 'If there's anything I've forgotten please let me know, this is all new to me,' she said ingenuously.

'Below stairs', as Victoria referred to it, was all a-buzz with excitement. Jillian found Margaret repolishing all the silver and glasses, with such enthusiasm that she did not have the heart to say she'd done it all twice before. Her heart sank when her mother appeared: the last thing she needed tonight was the voice of doom in the background, but Mary was excited too.

'I didn't want to miss the fun. What can I do? I don't want to get in the way.' So Jillian set her to fold the napkins, catch up on the ironing and arranged for her and Margaret to turn down the beds when the guests were at dinner. 'I think this is going to be one of the best things you've ever done, Jillian.'

'Thanks, Mum, that's just the sort of thing I need to hear.'

Victoria looked stunning, in a long, straight dress of green crêpe chiffon which, with her blonde hair, made her look like a mermaid. She was to do the front of house. She would see to drinks, discuss the menu, and generally fuss over the guests.

'Did they mind it being a set menu?' Mary asked, watching her daughter put the finishing touches to the meal.

'I was so nervous telling them, but the doctor said he couldn't think of anything nicer than just being told what he should eat. The pilot's wife said that if the menu had been long she would have been deeply suspicious of how much was from the freezer. I can't wait to see Ewan and tell him.'

'Who's Ewan?'

'Haven't you met him, Mum? He's the manager of the big hotel called the Clansman – you know, in the next glen, the one by the loch. He said we'd never get away with it. He said people would expect at least four choices at the price we're charging.'

'I must say I'm surprised.'

'I've got back-up for everything, in case people don't like a dish or they're on diets or vegetarian.'

'You've done enough puddings here for your dining room and the one at the Clansman too!' Margaret looked up from her polishing.

'Put that down to nerves. I shan't do it again.'

Victoria was a whirlwind of movement, racing in to replenish the ice, panicking over how to make a dry martini. 'This is exhausting, I shan't do it every day, Mum, it'll make me an old woman at this rate.'

'I'm going to put honesty books in the drawing room so that when you're not around they can pour their own.'

'I bet you'll lose a lot of money with people stealing the booze.'

'Mum, I could have guaranteed you'd say that.' Jillian laughed.

Everything was going smoothly, too smoothly, she feared.

'Ma, what shall I do? Some people have just turned up.'

'We can't take more than six, I explained to you.'

'No, they say they're local, they want dinner.'

'I hoped that would happen, but not quite so quickly. How many are there?'

'Just two. Either they're mother and son or he's a gigolo.'

'Tell them fine. I'll just do this meat and then I'll be out. Don't forget the wine list.'

'Do you have enough food?'

'Yes, I cooked for us too, so we'll have to make do with a snack. Now, who can that be?' She wiped her hands before picking up the telephone. She expected Colin.

'Hi! It's Ewan. I thought I'd just ring to wish you good luck.'

'How thoughtful of you.'

'I was thinking, if you finish early enough why don't you and Colin pop along for a nightcap?'

'Colin's away. I'd love to, but I doubt if it'll be possible.'

'Well, try. We've quite a party going here.'

Confident that everything in the kitchen was under control she put on some makeup, brushed her hair, removed her large cook's apron, took a deep breath to steady her nerves and sallied forth. Even then she had to pause at the mahogany door that led into the drawing room. She felt so nervous and knew how an actress must feel on a first night, waiting for the curtain to rise.

The room, with the eight people in it, Victoria making nine, looked just as she had imagined it might when she had been alone here and the room seemed so vast that every sound echoed. This evening, with the curtains pulled against the cold night, for spring was late arriving in these parts, the lamps lit, a fire burning, it seemed to have taken on a new life. The noise of people talking and laughing, the clink of ice in the glasses, classical music on the stereo made for a good, friendly atmosphere as if a party was about to begin – just as she and Esmée had planned.

'Ah, here she is.' A large, imposing woman, with a tightly permed hairstyle sat on the sofa. So large was she that the doctor, who had appeared of normal size upon his arrival, seemed to have shrunk in stature. Her face had a high colour – caused by the weather or whisky, Jillian wondered. She wore a taffeta tartan skirt that did little to minimise her bulk, and her silk blouse, with its fussy lace jabot was tight across an upholstered bust. 'I'm Dotty Pearlman. Dotty in name only, I hasten to add.' She laughed loudly at her obviously often repeated joke and everyone joined in. 'I was an old friend of dear Fiona's. I simply had to come and have a snoop and see what you had done to the dear place.' Dotty did not so much speak as proclaim.

'You're most welcome.'

'We were overjoyed when we heard on the grapevine that you were here. The house has seen such happy times that it will be nice to know it's to see them again. Such courage you have. A hotel! I wouldn't know where to begin.'

'So far it's been fun. I'll let you know in six months whether it still is.'

'Have you many bookings?'

'Quite a few in the summer.'

'I suppose it's a very short season here,' Justin Black, the Dorset bank manager, chimed in.

'Easter to October, really, or so I'm told.'

'Then if you have no guests you must come to dinner at my lodge. We're only a couple of miles up the glen. I should regard it as an honour to entertain members of dear Fiona's family.'

'But . . .'

'I'll have no buts. Let's say next week, shall we? I'll give you a call.'

'That's very kind of you but I don't think I should.'

'Nonsense, of course you can. Now where is my son. Lachlan? Typical! He's chatting to your pretty daughter, Mrs Stirling. What a lovely creature she is. Lachlan, manners!' she barked. A tall, muscular, dark-haired young man excused himself from Victoria, with a resigned expression, at his mother's bidding.

'The house looks wonderful, Mrs Stirling. You must have been so busy. It always smelt so fusty in the old days.' He smiled, which made him even better-looking. Jillian was certain that if he came for dinner again she would have no problem in getting Victoria to help.

'What a thing to say, Lachlan. Of course it didn't smell. I do apologise, Mrs Stirling, but you know the young.'

'But he's right, Mrs Pearlman, it was very musty. I'm glad we got rid of it.'

'It must be expensive to maintain,' Justin commented.

'If this venture doesn't work, I'm afraid it will have to go. It has to be able to pay for itself. The owner doesn't want to live here all the year and it would be too expensive to keep just as a holiday home.'

'The owner? Aren't you the owner?'

'Gracious, no, I wish I was. It belongs to Esmée Stirling, my partner. She's in America at the moment.'

'So you're not Esmée? I was led to believe ...' Jillian wondered if it was her imagination or if there was a subtle change in her voice, a faint note of affront, as if in some way she had been cheated.

'No, I'm Jillian Stirling.'

'So you are a Stirling?'

She had not imagined it, for now the voice had changed again and was warm and friendly.

'Yes, Esmée's my sister-in-law.'

Mrs Pearlman sank back on the cushions as if everything was all right again.

'Mum, did you ever meet anyone as gorgeous? Mum, I think I'm in love.'

'Again?'

'You always say that. You're so mean!' But Victoria was laughing.

'He's certainly a good-looking young man. And nice with it.'

'What a useless word to describe him. I think he looks like Byron.'

'I only hope he's got better morals, especially if he's got a sister.' Mary laughed from the sink where she and Gretchen were doing the last of the washing-up.

'What's Gran mean, Mum?'

'It's a joke, dear. Byron fancied his sister. Honestly, I sometimes wonder what was the point of your father and your aunt spending all that money on your education. Have you finished, Margaret? I think we should toast Altnahany, don't you?' From the fridge she took the bottle of champagne she had chilled in the hope that the evening would be a success. She had not dared think it would be this good. All that was missing were Esmée and Colin, who should have been here to share it with them.

They sat around the pine table sipping champagne, congratulating each other on how well it had gone.

'Do you know the Pearlmans, Margaret?' Victoria asked,

unable to stay too long off the subject of her latest infatuation.

'Everyone knows Dotty Pearlman. She's on the council and if there's a committee she sits on it. Aye, she's a very powerful lady hereabouts. She's many enemies and isn't one to get on the wrong side of, if you'll forgive me for saying.'

'She's a bit scary,' Victoria confessed.

'She certainly helped this evening go with a swing.'

'Aye, she can do that all right.' Despite Victoria's pleas, Margaret refused to be drawn further but put on her coat. 'Ready, Gretchen?' Soon they heard the banging and belching of Margaret's battered old car, a noise that Jillian supposed would soon be familiar.

'She didn't like her.'

'Victoria, you don't know that. She just said she was powerful, and she would be.' She stood up from the table to answer the telephone.

'Jillian, I've been a pig,' Colin said, without preamble.

'I'm so pleased you phoned.'

'You mean that? I shouldn't have presumed so much.'

'I overreacted too. I just needed a bit more warning, that was all.'

'Just because they're my kids I can't expect you to put yourself out for them.'

'It was just this weekend. I suppose I panicked.'

'We'll never argue about them again – ever.'

'Agreed.'

'How did it go?'

Excitedly she told him of the evening. 'And we had some locals who dined. A Mrs Pearlman and her son.'

'That old bitch!'

'I gather you don't like her?'

'Few do. She's trouble. The less you see of her the better. She's caused problems for loads of people I know.'

'She seemed nice enough.'

'Well, she isn't. And if Lachlan shows any interest in Victoria lock her up. The old trout's been casting about for a rich bride for him for ages.'

'Then she wouldn't get much luck with us.'

'You must be tired out.'

She hadn't given it a thought until Colin said this, she had been so hyped up with excitement, but now she realised she was exhausted and her feet ached. When she got off the telephone it was to find a note from Victoria and Mary saying, 'Well done, goodnight.' She thought of Ewan, but it was too late to go, and without Colin it wouldn't be much fun.

Jillian was fully aware that one successful evening did not mean she could relax. The result was that she did not stop from morning until she collapsed into bed at night. To her surprise she was soon to learn that the worst meal to prepare was breakfast. In her family it had always been such a simple meal, but served professionally it wasn't. They wanted juice, or porridge or cereal. Eggs had to be cooked in different ways and, since this was Scotland, some wanted kippers. Marmalade was not enough, and there were requests for jam and honey. Brown toast for some, white for the rest. And, of course, oat cakes. She had expected coffee and tea, but was thrown when asked for chocolate and Bovril. When it came to clearing the table, she was amazed at just how much crockery and cutlery had been used. While she could cook dinner for twenty and not bat an eyelid, breakfast was going to be a different matter. The day had barely begun and she was tired out. She was going to have to organise herself better in the morning, that was for sure.

'If you want I can come in and do them for you. Why, when I worked at the Clansman I might do sixty breakfasts when they were full.' Jillian had confided the panic she had been in when Margaret arrived for work.

'It's so silly of me to get into such a fuss. It's kind of you to offer, but I must learn how to manage better than this.' As she spoke Jillian was preparing picnic baskets for those who had ordered them last night. And, determined that they would not have just boring sandwiches, she had got up at six to make quiches and scones.

'You could get those at the cash-and-carry,' Margaret volunteered.

'Probably, but I'm happier making fresh for them.'

'At this rate you'll have to charge them double. They wouldn't get this at the Clansman!' Margaret spoke from a position of years in the catering trade.

'Well, we'll see, but with only six I think I should at least try.'

Once the guests had been sent off for the day, Jillian went to check how Margaret and Gretchen were doing cleaning the bedrooms. Here was another shock: although two rooms were neat and tidy, the third was in chaos, towels on the floor, water everywhere and nothing put away.

'Do you think the bank manager lives like this at home?' Jillian was collecting pieces of paper scattered all over the floor and stacking them in a pile on the desk.

'Probably not. I think people make messes like this because they're paying and someone else will clean it up. Getting their money's worth.'

'How strange. I never have. If anything I'm tidier in a hotel, aren't you?'

'I've never stayed in one, so I wouldn't know. But this isn't bad. You should see some of the things I've had to do. Not pulling the lavatory chain is a favourite. And you know, Mrs Stirling, I've been meaning to say, I think you'll regret supplying that expensive soap and all the bits and bobs. They'll nick the lot.'

'Surely not.'

'Surely yes. Not everyone, of course, but by the end of the season you'll be amazed at what's been lifted.'

While Margaret attended to the drawing room and the dining room Jillian started preparing the evening meal. She had hoped to do some paperwork, but this was not to be. Some people turned up looking for lunch and she had to drop everything to attend to them.

'Where's Victoria? Why can't she help you?' her mother, who had popped in, asked.

'She's gone to Inverness with friends.'

'She should be helping you.'

'I don't want her to feel she has to. In any case, that wasn't part of our bargain. I want her to stay here because she wants to.'

'You always were too soft on your children. And these casual people, you should have said you didn't do lunches.'

'It's all turnover, Mum. At this stage I daren't turn anyone away.'

'It will be no use if you make yourself ill.'

'But I won't, will I, Mother?'

'No need to be shirty with me. I only came to offer help.'

'That's kind of you, Mum.'

'But I don't think I will now.' Mary turned on her heel and stalked out.

Once the casuals had been served, Jillian went to her office and on the computer, which Victoria had taught her to use, she began a guest file. As she had once kept a file on food and wine she'd served her guests in her home, she had decided to do the same here but expanded. Not only would she list the food served but their likes and dislikes, the names of their children and pets, in other words any information she could ascertain about them: It would be invaluable when people returned for visits as she hoped they would: they would feel remembered and cosseted.

She interrupted her task to serve the pudding, then returned to her computer. Ten minutes later, having worked out what she could charge them, she returned to the dining room and found it empty. Their car had gone from the forecourt. Quickly and fearfully she checked to see if anything had been stolen. This time she was lucky. She decided to put the incident down to experience and, in future, to take the car numbers of guests, especially casual ones.

When Ewan appeared on a friendly visit to see how her first day had gone she told him what had happened. 'Were they going north?'

'They said so.'

'Then you should phone ahead to a couple of hotels and warn them. Give a description of them and their car. In turn they'll warn others. They won't do it again – it's our own security network.'

'Does this happen often?'

'Too often. I tell you, the great British public is constantly on the make.'

'Ewan, you're so cynical.'

'No I'm not, I'm a realist. Here, are you all right? You look funny.'

'I'm fine.' His words reminded her of Jack and had made her feel quite strange.

Four days later, when she stood on the front step and waved off her first guests, she could genuinely say she was sad to see them go, even the untidy, inconsiderate bank manager. In her own bank later that day, when she made her first deposit, she wasn't sad but elated.

3

Summer 1993

Everyone in the household was relieved when Lachlan Pearlman telephoned to speak to Victoria. To say the girl had been restless was an understatement: she had paced the house like a caged tiger.

Victoria returned from her first date with him glowing with happiness and declarations of love. Jillian thought that Victoria was too like Esmée for comfort. Esmée fell in love easily, was like a woman possessed at the beginning, then tired of her new love when the initial excitement faded and was away looking for another.

In the face of her daughter's happiness, however, Jillian dismissed her anxiety and was happy for her, laughed with her and looked forward to her confidences.

Colin returned home from his week away with the children. He wanted to apologise again and go over the old ground, but Jillian stopped him. 'Colin, let's forget it and get on with our lives.'

She particularly liked this in Colin, that he was able to say he was sorry, even that he had been in the wrong. Of course, Jack had too, but there was a difference: with her husband she had never been sure if he meant it or was just going through the motions.

Although Victoria and Lachlan were seeing each other regularly now, the promised invitation to dinner from his mother never materialised. 'Just as well, she's an unpleasant old besom. She's a finger in every pie. Interferes with everything and everyone. Her poor sod of a husband topped himself. We all thought it was because he couldn't live with her.'

'Lachlan seems nice enough.'

'I warned you about him, didn't I?'

There was nothing Jillian could do. Victoria was a woman now and must take her own chances in life. She could not protect her all the time. This thought stopped all others in their tracks: 'Good heavens,' she said to herself, 'I must really be changing!'

The first weekend that Colin's children were with her went far better than Jillian had hoped. There were no bookings so she could concentrate on them. She made hamburgers and trifle, and they hired a couple of videos. Understandably, Sammy and Col were wary of her to begin with; they were quiet children and said little. She did not rush things, spoke to them as if they were young adults rather than children and made sure that she did not monopolise their father.

Neither she nor Colin had discussed the sleeping arrangements again. Without saying anything, Jillian, had made up a bed for him on the top floor of the house. But when night came it was to her room he came. She snuggled up close. 'Colin, I'm so pleased –'

She got no further, he placed a finger over her lips. 'Shush, it never happened,' he whispered.

The next day was fun. They went to Inverness to choose the wallpaper and paints for their rooms. The children seemed amazed when she told them they could have any colour scheme they wanted. 'Black, if you like.' She laughed at their surprise. Sammy chose purple paint and wanted gold and silver stars scattered over it. Col went for orange and green. Even if she shuddered at their choice Jillian gamely wrote out the cheque.

But allowing the children to decorate for themselves was a mistake: more paint seemed to be on them and the floor than on the walls. When she was not cross but, instead, held her sides laughing, the surprised expression appeared again on their faces. 'Morag would have had a fit,' Colin explained later.

It had been fun having them and, despite her busy schedule, she was sorry when they left. 'Still,' she hugged Sammy, 'it won't be long and you'll be back here.' She and Victoria saw them off.

'Poor little scraps. They don't seem to have much fun,' Victoria remarked.

'What makes you say that?'

'Didn't you notice? They seemed scared half the time, as if at any moment they were going to be in trouble.'

'Not really. Only over the paint, but Colin explained that Morag doesn't like mess.'

'And the rest. They take life too seriously for kids,' Victoria said, for all the world as if she were an old woman.

Neither Jillian nor Colin was prepared for the angry telephone call later that evening. Colin said little, not that he didn't try but because he couldn't get a word in.

'What on earth was that about?'

'Morag is furious I slept with you.'

'She quizzed the children?'

'Evidently.'

'That's awful.'

'That's Morag. She's angry about the paint too.'

'But there was nothing on them. I checked all their clothing before they went back.'

'No, she thinks it was over-indulgent of us and she doesn't like it.'

'Then she'll have to lump it. This is Esmée's house, not hers, and Esmée would love their attempts at interior decorating.'

'I think we're going to have trouble,' Colin said mournfully.

'Only if you allow it,' Jillian answered decisively.

Business, although not good, was not too bad. Jillian often popped into the Clansman to see what their figures were like.

'Ten skulls I had last night. Hardly worth opening,' Ewan complained.

'I had no one.'

'You haven't got our overheads.'

'True. Still, it's early days. Maybe the tourists will come with the swallows.'

'And maybe they won't.' Ewan's pessimistic expression made her laugh. She was glad they got on and that, although in competition, she never felt it. In fact, Ewan could not have been kinder, sending guests when he was full, offering her advice, letting her have provisions or drink if she ran out of anything. 'We hoteliers', he was fond of saying, including her, and it made her feel proud when he did. She was really doing something: she was turning into a professional.

With the approach of June she inevitably thought more about Jack: it was his birthday month and it was the month he had chosen to desert her. June would never be the same again.

With the advent of Colin she hoped that the memory of Jack was fading, that she'd let go of the past and was grabbing at her future.

'What are you going to do about Jack?'

Her mother was guaranteed to destroy this new equilibrium, Jillian thought, as they sat in her kitchen where she was, as so often now, leafing through her cookery books looking for new ideas. 'Like what?' she asked.

'Like getting a divorce. Isn't it seven years this month since he did a runner? You could divorce him for irretrievable breakdown, couldn't you?'

'What would be the point?'

'It would regularise everything for a start. You could remarry.'

'I don't want to remarry.'

429

'What about Colin? It's not good for him, a professional man, to be living in sin like this.'

'I don't think it bothers him. In any case, we don't want to marry. We're happy as we are. And, for goodness sake, no one uses *that* expression these days!'

'I do. So, hiding behind Jack, are you?' Mary said, with a knowing sniff.

'No, I am not.'

'Nothing more convenient, is there? "Of course I'd love to marry you, Colin, but unfortunately I'm still married to Jack." Oh, yes, very handy.'

'Mum, you can talk such a load of cobblers at times. It's not like that at all.'

'You're not hoping he'll materialise some day and want you back again?'

'Mum!'

'All right, then, he might be rich again, you don't know. You could get some money from him.'

'I don't want any.'

'Don't talk so daft, of course you do. Everyone needs money.'

'I'm content here. Esmée pays me well.'

'And what if something happened to Esmée?'

'You always see the black side. What can possibly happen to her?' She laughed.

'She could die.'

'We could all do that. Mum, don't be such a doom merchant. I was having a lovely day.'

The trouble with talking to her mother was that, so often, she would say something that either made Jillian stop and think long and hard, or that Jillian was thinking but would rather not put into words. She had been fully aware for a couple of years that although free to divorce, she knew she didn't want to. She did not know why. She would not take him back, she was certain of that, which left her with the second of Mary's theories, and she had a nasty idea that that was the truth. She did not want to marry Colin and, if she didn't want to, the inevitable question loomed: why not?

Her life settled into a busy pattern. It seemed with this business that she was either full and turning people away, or with no guests whatsoever. She was either exhausted from too much running about or tired out of boredom.

'Esmée, we've got to make a decision.' Jillian spoke firmly to her sister-in-law on a late-night call from America. 'Do we continue or not next year? If we continue, then we have to sort out the fire regulations. Six guests are not nearly enough. I talked to the local hotelier and he says we should be looking at fifteen minimum, and he knows what he's talking about.'

'It's entirely up to you, Jill. You're the one doing all the work. If you want more guests, then we go for the fire regs. Victoria tells me you're working yourself silly, and I don't want you making yourself ill with overwork. Could you manage with more rooms?'

'I'd need more help but, yes, I think I could. I love the work and the challenge and, quite honestly, Esmée, I'm happier when we're full and I'm rushed off my feet.'

'I leave it with you, sweetness. You do whatever you want. By the way, I met Jack. He sends his love. He's looking awfully well and he's doing splendidly.'

'How nice.' No matter how hard she tried she could never keep the bitterness out of her voice. 'Esmée, when are you coming home? We were supposed to be doing this venture together.' She knew why she asked. Esmée had riled her in talking about Jack. She didn't want to know anything about him.

'Aren't I the proverbial delinquent? I will come soon, I promise faithfully.'

'But if you could at least give me a telephone number to call.'

'Impossible, darling, I never know where I am or when. Don't fuss, you're managing wonderfully without me!'

She was, but she felt let down by Esmée, and wished she was here. There were times when she thought that Esmée was avoiding her, and avoiding coming home, but that was such a silly idea.

Seven years of living alone was a long time. She had become

accustomed to being a single woman and she found there was much to adjust to now she was sharing her life. They were watching television. Or, rather, Jillian was half watching it. The programme about a desert was not particularly interesting and halfway through she picked up the remote control and switched channels.

'Here! I was enjoying that.' Colin leaned forward in his chair, bristling with indignation.

'I didn't think.' She laughed to cover her embarrassment and clicked the television back to BBC 2.

How thoughtless of me, she thought. What's got into me? But then, for all those years, she'd had only herself to consider when choosing what to view – Victoria rarely sat still long enough to watch anything.

There were other things, too. She had got into the habit of eating her supper at around six thirty. It meant the pots and dishes were cleared away in good time, leaving the evening free to do as she wanted.

'I hate eating early,' Colin had answered, when she broached the subject to him. 'I like to unwind after a day's work, take a bath, have a drink.'

'Of course. We'll eat at eight, then,' she'd replied, and felt a little sad at the loss of this little freedom. Jack had been the same. Strange that when she had poured his drink and taken it to him while he unwound in the bath she had never thought it would be nice to have time to relax after work. But with Colin she thought it, even if she refrained from saying so.

More of a problem was their sleeping together. She hadn't minded when he came for the weekend, probably because she knew he was only there for two nights. Now she found she resented this other body beside her seven nights a week. She'd liked the vastness of the bed all to herself. She'd also grown to like the bedroom being her private space, somewhere she could retreat to. Now it was shared, his possessions scattered about and his things in her bathroom too.

Prince had been banned. She'd felt guilty as she'd explained to the dog that he must sleep downstairs. He'd looked at her with his patient, adoring brown eyes and she'd

432

had to look away. Really, she lectured herself, you need professional help for mooning over a dog, preferring his company to Colin's!

Colin was untidy too. He seemed not to have any idea what a coat-hanger was for, that toothpaste tubes had lids, that shaving foam was easily wiped off the side of the basin, that body hair could be rinsed out of the bath.

'That's the laundry basket.' She pointed to the Ali Baba basket in the corner of the bathroom.

'So?' He looked at her quizzically.

'So, socks and underpants just love being put in one!'

'Do I detect a slight frisson of irritation? A hint of controlled anger masked by a lovely smile?' He grinned, razor poised.

'You could say that, yes.'

He bent and picked up a pair of boxer shorts which, with elaborate ceremony, he deposited in the basket. 'Better?'

The next day he'd forgotten and she was back to picking up for him, just like she had for Jack. Odd that with him she'd never minded, but had regarded it as part of her wifely duties. Now it annoyed her. So did that mean she'd never feel for Colin anything like what she had for Jack? More likely it was because she had changed, she told herself. She was a person in her own right, she'd lived too long as someone else's adjunct.

As Colin watched his programme on deserts, Jillian sat deep in thought. How was she to achieve the balancing act of being a different woman in the old setting? She did not want to lose the person she had become. On the other hand, she didn't want to be constantly complaining that he didn't do his share. In other words, she supposed, she was thinking she didn't want to become her mother. God forbid!

'Fancy a cuppa?'

'No, but I'd love another whisky.' He didn't even look up.

The season progressed and with it her expertise. She did not flap nearly as much; instead, she often congratulated herself at how calm and collected she was becoming. Her reputation for cooking grew and often the dining room was packed with

433

locals as well as house guests. And the high spot of the summer was when she catered for a wedding reception. Even the weather obliged as the bride, preceded by a piper, walked up the drive to the skirl of the pipes to make a memorable entrance. The house glowed on this occasion, and she was certain it was not her imagination.

Her life, though happier, was not devoid of problems. Miles always phoned each week to chat, but recently he had not seemed himself. He sounded depressed and monosyllabic.

'He's unhappy. It's Maxine I'm sure.'

'Honestly, Mum, just because you didn't like her it doesn't mean he doesn't.'

'You weren't too keen on her either, if I remember.'

'She's too superior for comfort. But I think they get on all right. No doubt Maxine's trained him,' she added gleefully.

'Victoria, don't say things like that!'

'It's probably because he's got a new job. He did right to move away from his grim ma-in-law. Stop fussing, Mum.'

Mary's advice hardly helped. 'He's an adult and now he's got to make his own mistakes. He's got to be allowed to get on with his own life, Jillian. Your job's over.'

If only she could call Maxine's mother and ask if she knew of any problems. But it was out of the question. A card at Christmas was their only contact. Jillian had hoped at the start that Maxine and Miles's marriage would bring the two families together as friends. She knew now that this had been a naïve idea. She, of all people, should know that happy families only existed as a card game.

Yet because her children were grown she wondered why she was expected to cease to worry or want to help them; that doing so was intrusive of her. The loving hadn't lessened with each birthday that passed. In fact, it seemed to her that the worry and fear for them increased in ratio to their age.

Days could pass by without her thinking of Jack. And then she'd hear a snatch of tune on the radio and thoughts of him would scud into her mind: she would remember another time, another place, another Jillian. Sometimes she felt sorry for that Jillian, her fears and her guilt, but at others times she would be irritated at how she'd allowed herself to be. There were times when the memory was happy and so strong that she would long for the past, for she had found that the happiest memories were the hardest ones to bury. When that happened she busied herself doubly so as to slam the door shut on thoughts that would get her nowhere. Far better to spend her time worrying about her children, her friends, her business – and, she would add hurriedly, Colin.

Esmée called rarely these days. She had told Jillian airily to do whatever she wanted but once the architect had drawn up the plans for the fire escape the bill was horrendous. From her own rudimentary accounting she knew they were a long way from making any profit yet. If only Esmée were there to take some of the responsibility.

And Morag was a problem. Whenever the children had been to stay at Altnahany a row would follow. There was always something that they had done or said that annoyed her and resulted in a screaming match on the telephone to Colin.

'We're having a new bathroom fitted. It's pink with gold taps,' Sammy had told Jillian proudly.

'How lovely,' she said. 'I wish I could have a new bathroom too.'

With Morag in the equation, there was no such thing as an innocent remark. To her the remark meant that Jillian was criticising her for having a new bathroom, that Jillian was interfering in Morag's financial affairs, and that she was making the children take sides. That unless Jillian refrained from criticising her she would have to reconsider Colin's access to them.

'She means it.'

'Oh, for goodness sake, Colin, you're a lawyer and you, of all people, should know your rights. You're letting the woman run circles around you.' Jillian didn't even bother to hide her exasperation.

'You don't know her.'

'No, and I hope I never do!'

The worst part of all this upset was that every time there was a scene Colin would get depressed and his drinking, enthusiastic at the best of times, increased alarmingly. A

435

couple of times she had had to apologise to guests when he'd nodded off in the drawing room. That he was tired from overwork was the excuse she used. But the idea took shape that Colin might, as her mother had warned, have a drink problem.

It was interfering with their lives. It annoyed Jillian that he was so uncontrolled, it annoyed her even more that he would take a bottle of whisky from her hotel store and half the time not pay her for it. Yet she was scrupulous about paying for anything she used. And it was upsetting to her that, these days, they rarely made love. He was either asleep when she went to bed, or several times when he had tried he had been unable to perform. She had told him, in the time-honoured way of women, that it didn't matter when, of course, it did. She was not being perverse: from not wanting him to make love to her she had learned to enjoy their sex life. She had, if she was honest, become used to it again and to be deprived was hard.

Victoria's relationship with Lachlan went from strength to strength. Finally the invitation came to dine with Dotty Pearlman. Victoria was beside herself with excitement. 'I think he's going to propose, Mum. That's why you've been invited.'

'How wonderful,' she replied, though she felt her daughter was far too young at twenty-one to be contemplating marriage – but, then, who was she to say that, when she herself had been even younger when she had married Jack? 'Why does my going to dinner make you think he's going to propose?'

'His mother will want to discuss everything with you, I expect.'

'How strange, when I'm not marrying him.' She grinned.

'It's not having a father. I mean, normally his father would talk to my father but his is dead and mine's pissed off. There's just one thing, Mum. I don't want Colin to go.'

'Why ever not?'

'Because he'll get drunk and embarrass me.'

She could not argue with her daughter's comment but was in a quandary. 'I don't want to hurt his feelings.'

'If he wasn't such a piss-head you wouldn't have to, would you?'

Fortunately the situation did not arise since Colin refused point-blank to go to the Pearlmans. 'I might be many things, but not a hypocrite. I wouldn't accept her hospitality if she were the last person on the planet!'

It was her mother with whom Jillian discussed her concerns about Victoria.

'You can hardly compare it with your circumstances. You were pregnant, she's not. She's choosing to marry, you had to.'

'Thanks, Mum, for those few kind words!'

The Pearlmans' house was a good hour's drive away, which was nothing in these parts, but hardly 'a couple of miles up the glen'. The gates of the house were in need of paint, and the drive in need of resurfacing, some weed-killer and a good gardener. Rhododendron plants, grown wild, lashed at the car as they drove along.

'Creepy Hollow.' Jillian pulled an exaggerated spooky face.

'It's lovely when you get there. It needs work doing on it, but quite honestly it would knock spots off Altnahany.' Victoria spoke defensively.

They drew to a halt in front of a large, imposing house that had certainly seen better days. Stonework was crumbling, a section of pediment lay in a forsaken flower-bed, the dolphin on a decorative fountain gasped as if in its death throes since no water gushed from its mouth and the basin was green and slimy with only rainwater trapped in it. The front door bore evidence of a hundred dogs' impatience to gain entry.

'It surely needs work,' Jillian said, as she climbed out of the car. But Victoria had not stayed to listen: she was already racing up the moss-encrusted stone steps calling Lachlan's name, pushing open the door, disappearing inside.

If anything, the exterior of the house was in better condition than the interior. Marks on the wall showed where paintings had once hung. There were some nice pieces of furniture but they were all sadly neglected and in sore need of a good polish.

'See what I mean.' Victoria twirled around in the front hall. Jillian was spared having to comment as Lachlan and his mother entered.

Drinks were served in a room that had once been beautiful but, given the neglect that seemed to pervade the whole house, appeared to have given up. The first sip of her drink took her breath away with the strength of the gin and the lack of tonic. She had learned in the time she had lived here to sip slowly for such depth charges were commonly served.

'Mrs Stirling and I need to talk. Or may I call you Jillian since I would be more than pleased if you called me Dotty? Now run along, children, and do whatever it is young people like you do.' Given these words it was not surprising that Victoria was giggling fit to bust by the time she left the room. 'Such a happy daughter you have, Jillian, always laughing.'

'Thank you, yes, she's fairly sunny.' She should have added 'these days' but didn't.

'I'm glad that Colin Coleridge decided not to come. I don't like him, there's no point in beating about the bush.'

'Fine,' she said, and wished she'd the guts to tell her that he did not go much on her either.

'He drinks too much.'

'Don't we all?' Jillian said, as icily as she could, looking pointedly at Dotty's glass.

'The little ones seem set on getting married.'

'Do they?' She wondered how long Victoria would tolerate being referred to like that.

'Oh, yes. I said to Lachlan it would be better if we mothers had a little chinwag first and sorted everything before any formal announcements were made. Don't you think?' Dotty leaned forward, her chins and breasts in constant movement, reminding Jillian of a fruit jelly she had made last week for Colin's children.

'I'm not sure what it is you need to have sorted out.'

'I thought it would be right and proper if you gave me some indication of the size of the settlement you intend for Victoria. Such a sweet girl.'

'I'm sorry, but I'm not sure what it is you have in mind.'
Jillian felt as if she had strayed into a Jane Austen novel.

'Well, it is customary in my circle for the father of the bride
to make her an allowance.'

'Really?' Jillian said, as noncommittally as she could, while
thinking that this must be news to most brides' fathers. 'I
wasn't going to settle anything. You see –'

'I'll be straight with you, Jillian. Since my poor dear
husband passed on, times have been hard for us. As you see,
this house is crumbling about our ears. But on his deathbed I
swore to him that whatever I did I would ensure that the
house would be cared for, for our son to inherit.'

'Ah, I see.'

'So, as much as dear Lachlan would adore to support dear
Victoria to the standard . . .' At this she waved her hand
vaguely in the air. 'It will not be possible.'

'In other words, Lachlan needs to marry a young woman
with good prospects.'

'Exactly, Jillian. I knew the moment I set eyes on you that
here was a sophisticated woman of the world who would
understand such niceties.' She settled back with a deep sigh of
satisfaction and her moving flesh subsided from its previous
agitation.

'Oh, I understand, Dotty. The only problem is that I have
no money to settle on Victoria.'

'Then her father?' She leaned forward, her flesh on the
move again.

'We have had no contact with him for years. And if he were
here, I wonder if he would approve of such arrangements in
this day and age.' Jillian congratulated herself at the calm way
in which she was handling this.

'But her grandfather? I have heard . . .' Again she waved her
hand vaguely as if too sensitive to admit that she knew, no
doubt to the last farthing, what Ralph had been worth.

'He was a very wealthy man, certainly. But he left her
nothing. I am employed by Esmée Stirling to run the hotel for
her. I have nothing of my own. I hate to disappoint you,
Dotty.'

It seemed as if a valve hidden somewhere in the folds of

Dotty's skin had been opened to release air, for she looked suddenly smaller and certainly paler. 'I have been misled.'

'I don't think so. I've never made a secret of the set-up at Altnahany.'

'When I had dinner there you implied –'

'I implied nothing. I corrected you when you thought I owned it.'

'You said you were a Stirling. Why, your brother-in-law, Mungo, was in the *Sunday Times* on the hundred richest people list.'

'I'm a Stirling by marriage but that doesn't mean . . . Oh, Dotty, I am sorry to disappoint you.' Suddenly she felt sorry for the woman, who looked close to tears.

'Then there can't be any marriage.'

'Isn't that up to Victoria and Lachlan to decide?' Jillian spoke quietly, her sympathy rapidly changing to anger.

The dinner that followed was cool, not just the atmosphere but the food also, which was tepid and tough. It was, they learned, a ragoût, though of what Jillian did not like to ask. Given the social chill, they left early. Lachlan and Victoria, unaware of the talk between the mothers, clung sweetly to each other.

'That meal looked like sick,' Victoria announced, with a shudder, on the drive home. 'And that wine, ugh, it was disgusting! Bet we have fat heads in the morning. Mrs Pearlman's very grand but I don't think the poor dear has much money, do you?'

'It would appear not.' Jillian had decided it was best not to tell her daughter of anything that had transpired.

'The house is falling about their ears. Lachlan says he wishes it would fall down and then he could do what he really wants instead of looking after the land for his mother. Do you think she's always been fat?'

'What does he want to do?'

'Run a club.'

'What? A nightclub?'

'Don't be silly, Mum, they went out with the ark. No, for clubbing. Like the Ministry of Sound place in London. Only here.'

440

'I see,' Jillian said, while her mind screeched, *'Drugs! Ecstasy!'*

'Lachlan said his mother was going to ask you for money tonight for me. Like a dowry. What a gas! As if I was Elizabeth Barrett or someone. I fell about laughing – I mean, it's so antiquated. I told him there was no danger of that since you haven't got a bean. He was mighty pleased, I can tell you.'

'His mother wasn't.' Since Victoria knew so much there was no point in secrecy any more. 'She says there can be no marriage.'

'She what?' Victoria swung round in the car seat. 'She can't say that. If we want to get married we will.'

'What if she tries to stop it?'

'She won't. Lachlan loves me. He won't let anyone come between us.'

Jillian sent up a silent, fervent prayer that her daughter was right.

4

Autumn–Winter 1993

The season ended and, while having made no profit, the loss was far less than Jillian had feared and the accountants were optimistic that in the following year – with better advertising and word of mouth – business would improve.

Jillian could look back on these months with a marked degree of satisfaction. She could not say that she had liked it all but she had liked most of it. She had enjoyed the work, the cooking, meeting new people. The downside was the regulations, which seemed to multiply by themselves. Without Ewan to help her she would have been sorely pushed to understand some of them. But he was always at the end of the phone, calming her down, telling her how to navigate through the local authority rules.

The majority of the guests had been appreciative. There had been some, though, whom she hoped never to meet again. One woman accused her of having mice and would not believe the man from Rentokil who identified the droppings as bats' – a protected species – so there was nothing she could do.

Then Prince, attacked by a guest's dog, bit back, and the commotion made by the owners was greater than the initial fight had been. It had cost Jillian dear in vet's fees.

There was the fat man who broke the bed and the honeymoon couple who did likewise. And the woman who removed all the soap every day, just as Margaret had predicted, not only in her bathroom but in the public lavatories too. Since she and her husband were guests for two weeks their suitcase, when they left, was considerably heavier.

One man was a no-show, that creature who enrages hotel and restaurant owners more than anything. 'Bill him, you've got his credit-card number,' Ewan advised. She only had that since Ewan had told her always to take it when accepting bookings.

'How can I?'

'No problem. Just bill him for everything but food and drink. It's within your legal rights.'.

This no-show was the first of a spate of cancellations, as if he had inflicted a virus on them. Each one used the same excuse: their grandmother had died. She and Ewan laughed. But she still didn't use the credit-card numbers. How could she? They might have been telling the truth.

All these people, though, were soon forgotten in the deluge of praise and thanks of others. She received flowers, chocolates and invitations to come and stay. With some of them, when it came time to give them the bill she hated to do so since it was like giving one to very dear old friends.

Colin's children came less frequently than she had hoped they would. Morag said they were afraid of the house and that it was haunted. Since they'd never said anything, her first inclination was to ask them outright if this was so, but Colin thought that any questioning would imply he was criticising their mother. Far more likely, she thought, that they didn't want to come because of Morag's interrogations

442

and sniping when they returned home. But she bit her tongue and said nothing since, she argued with herself, they were his children and she must not interfere.

Colin's drinking continued. He'd been fun when they'd first met but now he was invariably depressed or asleep.

'She won't rest until she gets him back,' Hamish advised her. He was still working on the oil painting of Altnahany for Esmée's present, when she came back – *if* she came back.

'But I thought it was Morag who kicked him out. That it was she who suggested he move in with me.'

'Is that what the wee man told you? Well, then, if he did it must be so.' Even though she plied him with her oldest malt whisky he would not say any more.

Inevitably she had quizzed Colin. They rowed, he shouted at her to stop interfering, asked if she was calling him a liar, and slept on the top floor. She needed to know and felt she had a right to know. Her sense of insecurity increased when he announced that he would be spending Christmas with his *family*, as if she were not his family now.

Miles, who had visited for a long weekend in the autumn when trade was slack, was happier. Jillian felt relieved.

'You've got the look of a settled man.' She looked at him affectionately.

'It's the new job. I like it and Maxine likes it too. There's more for her to do, what with the health hydro. And we've a disco and a conference centre.'

'It sounds huge.'

'It is, over two hundred beds.'

'But I thought you were happy working at her father's?'

'I changed my mind. It's nicer for Maxine. That's what matters, after all.'

'What did her father say to you leaving them?'

'He wasn't pleased, but Maxine needs people, lots of people. He saw that she'd been getting depressed at their place.'

'I wish she had come, I hardly know her.'

'She would have only she's too busy,' Miles answered, a mite too quickly, she thought.

'As long as you're happy.'

'Oh, I am Mum, I am.' So why didn't she believe him?

About Victoria she had no such fears. Lachlan had refused to stop seeing her. As far as she could gather, not wishing to pry and have Mary accuse her of interfering, there had been an almighty row and Lachlan had left home. Victoria had asked if he could stay with them.

'Victoria, I don't think that's such a good idea.'

'You don't like him. You don't want us to get married.'

'I think he's a fabulous man, and I admire him for standing up for you. But don't you see? If he comes here you'll give Dotty more to moan about. You'll become doubly the enemy.'

Victoria agreed mournfully with her logic. Lachlan found a bedsit in Inverness and worked at Marks and Spencer. Jillian was told that his mother was not only furious but mortified also. That her son should become a shop assistant, she was heard to exclaim often, and what would her dear departed have had to say about that? The general consensus was that he would have been as proud as punch of his son.

When Victoria asked her if she minded them going to London for Christmas to stay with Lachlan's uncle, Jillian hid her disappointment well and began to plan a celebration around herself and her mother. From Esmée there was not a peep. But that plan was thwarted when Mary announced she was off to England to spend Christmas with Patsy.

'You'll get nut cutlets or worse for Christmas Day.'

'At least I won't put on weight like most years.'

So Christmas loomed, a day to be dreaded, which had never happened in her whole life. She wondered what she would do. Not cook, that was for certain. Maybe she would get an oven-ready meal from Marks. She'd watch television and read; she'd never done that before. Making these plans made her think of another Christmas when she had expected to be alone, but that time Jack had come and rescued her. She felt ridiculously low at the prospect and had to chivvy herself out of it. It was just another day, that was the best way to think of it, forget all significance, and forget all those Christmases of years past.

'Why not spend it with me?' Ewan asked, upon hearing of her plight.

'I couldn't possibly.'

'Why not? Oh, you English are so formal. Would I have invited you if I didn't mean it?'

'Probably not.'

'So, there you go. You're spending it with me. I shall be opening the bar in the morning but that's all.'

'No guests.'

'I had the odd inquiry but not enough. What with having to pay staff double time for working over the holiday, it would have meant trading at a loss.'

'I did think about doing it, but Esmée and I always promised ourselves that we would keep Christmas and New Year free.'

'And where is the famous elusive Esmée?'

'Still in America, as far as I know.'

'Not much of a partner, is she?'

'I couldn't say that. She's been incredibly generous to me,' she said defensively.

'You want to watch that, it's too easy to feel such gratitude that you then get put upon.'

'You sound just like my mother. But, no, not Esmée, she's not like that. When I was setting up I got a bit warped having to make most of the decisions myself. But the worst is over now. It's more that I miss her, and I would like her to be part of the fun.'

'You call this business fun? I can't wait to retire and fish all day, every day and the punters can go and get stuffed.'

'Why do it if you hate it?'

'Because I live in the real world where work is usually something you loathe but it has to be done to keep body and soul together.'

'I work.'

'My dear Jillian, with six guests you're merely playing at it. Still, next year will be harder when you've your planning regs through. How's that going?'

445

'Fine, the last thing I heard. And I've got the estimates in. They're likely to break the bank.'

'Fire regulations never come cheap, but it'll work out cheaper than being burned to the ground and sued by the corpses' families.'

'We're insured.'

'Not if you break the law you're not.'

Jillian had not known that and sighed inwardly with relief that she hadn't given in to the temptation of putting in extra guests when they had been full and she had had to turn casuals away. But, next year, everything would be different. Next year they would be more like a real hotel and would have room for eighteen.

Jillian enjoyed her Christmas with Ewan, who hadn't minded her bringing Prince: he curled up contentedly with Ewan's black Labrador, Bessie. He had a flat on the top floor of the large, sporting hotel. It was an eerie sensation walking through the dust-sheet-covered, deserted rooms which, come the spring, would be full of fishermen and holidaymakers – she was learning that there was a distinct difference between the two and that they rarely mixed in the bar at the end of the day.

Ewan was amusing company and a brilliant cook. 'You have to be, in this racket. Most chefs are either drunkards or mad and often both. I realised early on I had to be able to step into the breach if necessary.'

His cynicism about his chosen profession made her laugh. He did not take it seriously, trusted no one – especially his guests – and had a healthy disrespect for most of them. 'It's something about hotels that brings out the worst in people, as if they've got to show off, and become demanding and irascible. I always go self-catering myself. I don't want to lumber some other poor sod with my foibles.'

He drank with relish but, she was happy to see, not to get drunk. He told her he was a widower, his first wife having died ten years before.

'And you haven't wanted to remarry?'

'Haven't met the right person. Lena and I got on well as a

team. We met working in a hotel in Manchester. She knew the business and this is not the easiest life for a marriage to work in, as I'm sure you're aware. For a long time I missed her too much. Still, I'm over that now.'

She would like to have asked how she died, and wondered from his expression if he really was 'over' it, as he claimed.

'And you?'

Jillian never liked talking about Jack. But Ewan was different, she told him much more about Jack and her feelings than she had ever told anyone else. It was probably because she knew he understood about loss. There was another reason, though: she knew she could trust him. He might go on about the guests in his hotel but she'd never heard him say anything bad about anyone else – gossip was not in his nature.

During the evening when a storm blew up, the wind rushing wildly across the loch, the trees bending to the ground in the path of its wrath like rows of curtsying women, she gladly accepted his offer to stay. It was too bad a night to risk the glen road, which was heavily forested.

Back home the answer-machine held messages from Miles, Victoria and her mother, and one from Patsy saying it was time they saw each other again. That, she thought, was probably the best present of all. The fifth message was an even bigger surprise: Michelle had called from Sydney to say she was returning to England the following year and could she visit? Could she! Jillian hugged herself with pleasure at the prospect of seeing her again. Esmée had called, as she had hoped she might, but as usual had left no number to ring back – really, she was odd the way she kept her whereabouts so secret, and it was silly too. From Colin there were six calls of ever greater incoherence as the drink took hold and his anger at her absence increased. There was nothing she could do but wait for him to ring again. Not only would it be difficult to phone him in case his wife answered, she found she did not want to. Instead she began the preparations for supper, having invited Ewan, as a thank-you, back to Altnahany for Boxing Day.

447

'You had no right not to be here. What do you mean you spent the night at the Clansman? It's closed.' Colin, back from his family Christmas, had stormed into the house and not even bothered to take his coat off before coming to find her in the linen room.

'And hello to you too.' Jillian continued calmly to fold the sheet she had been ironing.

'Why didn't you come home? I was phoning all night and at my wits' end.'

'So why didn't you call the Clansman? You knew I was spending Christmas there. I couldn't ring you, now, could I?'

'There was no reply.' He looked surly.

'I don't believe that. We were there all the time and the telephone rang several times so it was working. But why are you so angry with me? You're shouting at me as if I had done something wrong. There was a dreadful storm and Ewan and I thought it safer if he put me up, that's all.'

'Oh, I'm sure he did.' He snorted.

'And what does that mean?'

'I wasn't born yesterday.'

'Are you implying that I slept with him? How dare you even think it?'

'That's what the whole village will be saying, you can bet on that.'

'I'm not in the least bit interested in what people say. If they want to think that, let them. I don't care.'

'Then you should.'

'What concerns me is what you think. What did you want? That a falling tree killed me? Or perhaps that I had spent a miserable Christmas alone here.'

'It might have been more tactful, yes.'

With great deliberation she placed the linen on the table. 'I see. You can spend Christmas shacked up in the same house as Morag and I don't have to mind.'

'She *is* my wife.'

'And that's not cause for me to be concerned? Grow up, Colin. Now, if you've finished your little rant, I've work to do.' She turned her back dismissively. He lunged across the room, grabbed hold of her shoulder and swung her round to

448

face him. She looked at his face, distorted by anger. 'Don't even think it, Colin,' she said coldly.

In the next few days the atmosphere between them was chill. Both thought they were in the right, both refused to compromise and neither was prepared to say sorry. This surprised Jillian who, in the past, had often apologised for something she had not done for the sake of peace. This time she was as intransigent as others had been in the past.

It was Colin who cracked, returning home with a bouquet of flowers for her, a bottle of champagne and regrets. 'I was jealous. And I was being a fool.'

Esmée, Patsy and Michelle, she knew, would all have felt a sense of triumph and accepted his apologies with a degree of hauteur. 'I was being silly too. I'm sorry, I should have thought of your feelings.' She kissed him full on the mouth.

5

Winter–Spring 1994

Jillian could laugh now at the goose she had once been, who thought when everything was going well that something was about to go wrong. Her new good fortune was based on her hard work. There were no vengeful gods to punish her, to vent their spleen on her. I make my own luck, she was fond of reminding herself these days. And, despite the ever-present worries that were part and parcel of being a member of a family as well as running a hotel, she was more content than she could remember having been for a long time.

'Jillian, I'm afraid I've some bad news.' Colin was calling her from the office. 'Your planning application for the fire escape has been turned down.'

'Why? We were assured that everything was fine.'

'There's been an objection.'

'Who? The National Trust for Scotland said it was okay, the

fire people, the tourist board. So, come on, who?' She was beginning to relax, it must be a joke – a not very funny one.

'Ever heard of POSH? Preserve Our Scottish Houses? No, neither had I. It seems it was set up yonks ago and had become virtually defunct but now it's been reactivated – it would seem for your benefit.'

'Why me?'

'Ah, well, that's what I'm in the process of finding out. They suggest that rather than the standard steel fire escape you have chosen it should be encased in a purpose-built tower to match the existing ones.'

'Another turret? You're joking! It would make the house look like Disneyworld. And, for heaven's sake, how much would that cost? Thousands.'

'Exactly. It looks like someone doesn't want you to succeed, if you ask me. And who, I've been asking myself, have you crossed? Supposing I said the initials D.P.? I'll know for sure tonight.'

After Colin had hung up, she went over and over in her mind who could be behind this. Colin couldn't be right. Why should Dotty do this to her? Their children were living together, she wouldn't want them harmed, as Victoria would be if she went out of business. Of course, there was the uncomfortable thought that she had an anonymous enemy, the one who had defaced her sign, and she was still no nearer to finding out who that was. Or it could be someone from her past, or even Jack's past, who did not want her to be a success. Or perhaps there was someone who loathed Esmée, or even her late aunt, about whom she knew nothing.

'I was right. Dear Dotty Pearlman has put the mockers on it for you. Not that you're supposed to know. No doubt you'll get a commiserating telephone call from her any day now.'

'So how is she involved?'

'She isn't, directly, but cronies of hers are. I expect she's got someone on one of the POSH committees, or all of them perhaps. I wouldn't put it past her.'

'How do you know?'

'Someone who hates her as much as I do told me.'

'But why?'

'She needs her son back to marry an heiress and save that creaking house of hers with which she's so obsessed.'

'I can understand that, especially a house that has been in the family for generations.'

'But it hasn't. Her father was a crofter and her father-in-law was a tinker. Lots of Pearlmans are. Once they were that literally, panning for freshwater pearls, and made a good living. Her father-in-law sadly took to the bottle and amounted to little – in fact, he was found dead in a ditch one day. Her husband was something else. Clever and astute, he played the markets and from nothing made a considerable amount of money. If Dotty hadn't wanted to be the grand lady she'd be all right, but she wanted to cock a snook at the locals who, she felt, had slighted her. And dear old Lachlan senior hated her so much he left everything to charity, except for a small trust for his son. It's all they've got.'

'How sad.'

'Jillian, there are times I'd like to throttle you. This old cow is trying to ruin you and you feel sorry for her!'

'But I don't understand why. And Lachlan loves Victoria, I'm sure of that.'

'I hope you're right. But pause a mo. What if he isn't that in love with her? You help her, don't you?'

'With her rent, yes, while she's studying. I buy food, help out where I can, and Esmée helps out with the costs.'

'So, you go bust, no rent. Then what does he do? You do know he's not working?'

'No, I didn't. Victoria didn't say.'

'She probably doesn't want you to know but he was sacked for stealing. If he has no job, no money, the girlfriend can't help, where will he go? Back to Mummy. That's what she's banking on. He's her son, so who's going to know him best?'

Poor Victoria, was Jillian's first thought, to find out that first her father and now her boyfriend was a thief. But why had she said nothing about it? Too ashamed, she supposed. But, then, what was there she could have said to her daughter? Hadn't she been down that road herself? If Jack

451

had told her what he was doing, had not deserted her, might she not have stayed with him, protected him?

'You should thank your lucky stars you'd got your drinks licence organised. One of the committee asked me if it was true that you were involved in an embezzlement case down south – and guess who'd pointed him in that direction?'

'The bitch!'

'That's better, my love. A bit of temper in the circumstances won't hurt you.'

'So what do I do?'

'You've got good allies. The tourist board, for starters, who like what you're doing. I've had a word with a couple of highly placed old coves who don't like her much either. We'll make this a hiccup. But it will have put you back a year, that's for sure. You know bureaucracy – everything takes time and then some more.'

Fortunately for Jillian it was winter and she had time to decide what to do. Her fear was that, by trading a further year with insufficient income to cover the costs, her losses would multiply. In the way of any debt, it would take far longer to recover from than it had taken to accrue in the first place.

Ewan's advice was blunt. 'On these numbers you'll go bust. If it were me I'd shut up shop until I'd sorted this problem. Open in a year.'

'But the staff?'

'You'll have to let them go.'

'I can't. There's so little work here for them.'

'Then you'll be a philanthropic bankrupt.'

'You make it sound so easy but it isn't. I've grown to like them.'

'I'm being practical. How about letting one of them go and then doing bed and breakfast only, no dinners? Even then, with a barn of a place like this, you're pushing your luck.'

Jillian spent the evening doing sums and reached the unpleasant conclusion that Ewan was right. Telling Gretchen, but especially Margaret, that she was going to have to close was one of the hardest things she'd ever had to do. 'There,

Jillian, don't you fash yourself. We're used to it up here. Jobs come and go, but I'll be back as soon as you need me,' Margaret reassured her, which only made her feel worse.

As was normal in her life, she decided that when catastrophe struck, it divided, like an amoeba, and reproduced more.

It was spring, she was busy in her kitchen preparing dinner and Michelle was due to arrive. She looked up at the sound of a car parking at the back of the house. Surely that could not be her? Across the back courtyard where this year, with time to spare, Jillian was attempting to make a garden, Victoria appeared. There was something in the way she was walking that brought Jillian's hand to her throat.

'Victoria darling, what is it? What's happened?' She had opened the back door.

'Mum, Lachlan's left me.' Victoria managed, before she burst into tears.

'Come in, it's cold . . . I'll make us some tea . . . Here, sit by the Aga . . . Oh, darling, don't cry, please . . . Be brave.'

'But I love him so!'

There was nothing she could do but put her arms around her daughter. She held a grown woman but she rocked her and comforted her with soft words just as if she was still her little child. If only there was something she could do, if only she could kiss away this pain as she had kissed away so many others in the past.

'Tell me everything,' she said finally, when the weeping had subsided and they sat either side of the warm Aga, each holding the rail and a mug of tea as they had so often in the past.

'It's been hard. You see, Lachlan lost his job.'

'I know.'

'How did you know?'

'Someone told me.'

'You didn't say.'

'I thought you'd tell me when you wanted to.'

'He didn't steal, that's all lies. He was set up. You do realise.'
In her agitation she looked close to crying again.

453

'If you say so.' Now was not the time to argue with her. 'Have you had a row?'

'You could say that. We'd so little money, you see. He kept on at me to ask you for more. He'd get angry when I refused. He said you were rich. I told him you weren't but he said you were lying, that everyone knew you were, that you'd been involved with Dad and must have a fortune salted away. He kept on and on at me.' She bowed her head. 'I didn't tell you, but I've been working in the evenings, in a bar. I didn't mind, honestly, but with my studying it was hard. I think he should have tried to get a job too. But he wouldn't. He just lay around all day smoking dope and watching the television. If I said anything he said I was nagging and I sounded like his mother. He said if I really loved him I wouldn't mind. But I did love him. God, how I did.' This last sentence was too much for her and at the memory of that love she feared she'd lost she wailed again. Jillian sat patiently, waiting for this new storm to pass. 'And then . . . I'm frightened you'll be cross. I'm afraid to tell you.'

Jillian tried to smile reassuringly but fear gripped her heart. 'Try me,' she said, with forced bonhomie.

'I'm pregnant.' The word tumbled out, sounding like a lament.

'Darling, that's wonderful!' She was not sure if it was or it wasn't but she could not think of anything else to say that might help or guide, not in these first moments of knowing.

'I can't get rid of it. Not again.'

'Of course you can't.' She knew her voice was full of the relief she was feeling. 'Who would expect you to?'

'Lachlan and his mother.'

'Ah, I see. Is this why you rowed? Is this why he's left you?'

'When I told him first he wasn't best pleased. But I thought he'd come round to the idea. I'd told him about . . . the other, you know . . .' Unable to talk of that other time she looked at the sodden handkerchief in her hands and twisted it all ways. 'I said we didn't have to get married, that I didn't want him to think he had to. But that I wanted to keep it. And he agreed. Then his mother appeared and she called me such awful names and she insisted that I get rid of it, and we had this row

454

and the neighbours came to see if I was all right. Oh, Mum, it was dreadful.' And she covered her face with her hands as if to blot out the image. 'Then she went and we calmed down and he even said sorry and we had a laugh about his mum and what a battleaxe she is. But when I got up in the morning he was packing. He said he didn't want the child, he didn't want me. That it was my responsibility and he was going.'

'My poor darling.'

'But it was the way he was, Mum. He wasn't shouting, he wasn't cross, he was just cold and unfeeling, and it was as if all those months together meant nothing, that *I* meant nothing to him, and he went. And I sat and I cried and I couldn't stop, I thought I'd never stop . . .' And as if to prove the point the tears tumbled again.

Jillian would have walked past the woman who got out of the car for she bore no relation to the Michelle she had known and had last seen twelve years ago. It was not just that Michelle had aged, as no doubt she had too. No, this woman was different. Her hair, cut fashionably short, was streaked blonde but not by the sun. She was slim and dressed in a smart, short-skirted pink suit that reminded Jillian of candy-floss. Her face was skilfully made up and the inevitable wrinkles carefully disguised.

'Michelle, you look wonderful.'

'Different? I take everyone by surprise.' Michelle laughed with delight at the expression on Jillian's face.

'Yes, well, come in. I've made you a cake.'

'I'd hoped you had. I remember your cakes.'

Jillian led the way.

'My, this is grand. It's Esmée's, you say? Lucky bitch, she's had such an easy life.'

'I wouldn't say that.' Jillian pushed open the drawing-room door where the fire was lit and the tea-table laid. Once her cousin was seated she poured the tea. 'So, what happened to the dungarees? I'll be honest, I think I like you better like this.'

'I burned them – remember it was once bras we burned?

Well, I did, not you. I had a bit of a hard time in Cambridge last week. Some of my old mates looked at me a bit askance – they thought I'd deserted them.'

'Can you blame them? What happened?'

'What always happens when a woman changes her style out of all recognition? A man, of course.' Michelle grinned broadly. 'I fell in love. And I suppose you want to know all about him. He's called Matt. He's got his own video business and is doing really well. And he's twelve years younger than me.' She said this with a challenging look, as if she was used to people not quite approving.

'Good for you. He's obviously doing wonders for you.' Jillian smiled.

'I didn't think you'd approve. You were always so proper.'

'Oh, God, doesn't that sound awful! I suppose I was. However, that Jillian doesn't exist any more. And I think in any case she was a bit of an act. If I stayed on the straight and narrow it was because I hadn't the guts to stray, like you and Patsy.'

'How is Patsy?'

'I had a phone call at Christmas but we hardly ever see each other. We had a bit of a falling out, and it isn't totally resolved but I hope it will be.'

'Families! Don't tell me. My mum's having hysterics about Matt. I just block my ears. I mean, when do these mothers stop? I'm forty-eight and she's *still* telling me what I should and shouldn't do.'

'It's hard to stop mothering. I try to close my eyes and let them make their own mistakes.'

'Your kids make mistakes? I don't believe it! You were the perfect family and they the perfect children as I remember. I envied you so much, especially your total love and commitment to Jack. You never needed or wanted anything or anyone else, did you?'

'I thought you despised me.'

'No, I worried about you and what would happen if anything went wrong. I was jealous, more like. I was horrified to hear what happened with Jack. If I could have afforded it

I'd have flown home to be with you. You must have been devastated.'

'It was hard, but I got over it. Now I can look at it and see that benefits came out of it. I changed, and I had to change. It's wrong to live your life sublimating who you are for fear of losing someone. It makes everything a charade. It's not fair on either yourself or the other person to be so dependent and so unreal, is it?'

'Like me with Shane. Whatever induced me to follow him to Australia I'll never know. And for ages I blamed myself for what happened out there. I knew what he was like so when he hit me again I felt it was my fault for being there. That's a bit muddled, but do you get my drift?'

'What happened, then?'

'Three months' bliss and then he whopped me again. I was in hospital for a week. He came with flowers and apologies. But I was lucky, not like some poor bitches I know who are either trapped financially or believe their man when he says he won't do it again. I didn't go back to him and I got divorced. A man like that never changes. They're weak, actually, and that's how they'll remain. I got a job and made a new life. I love Australia and I'm going to stay there. This is just a holiday. I even see Shane occasionally and I guess I've forgiven him. Have you been able to forgive Jack?'

'I could never forgive his behaviour to his children. They don't hear from him.'

'He always was a cold bastard.'

'But I never saw it, not until the end. That's what's so strange. And now poor Victoria has met another . . .' And she told Michelle of what had transpired today.

Outwardly Michelle might have changed, but inwardly her anger for her cousin's child was as forceful as it had once been for Jillian.

'Will you go and see him? Have it out?'

'No. Victoria doesn't want me to and I have to respect her wishes.'

Michelle's arrival could not have come at a better time for Victoria. Not only did she distract her but she also had a mass of practical advice to give her, her rights as a single mother, what forms to ask for, the agencies to contact. 'Comes from my days of working with women's groups. It pisses me off, this happening to you. Just as I start to think that maybe I was too hard on men in general, another creep crawls out of the woodwork. Irresponsible pricks on legs. It makes me weep.'

Such words did not make Michelle weep but they did Victoria: she was not ready to hear her Lachlan called such things, and Jillian feared that if he lifted his little finger she would race back to his side. And she was afraid for Victoria and her vulnerability, puzzled why women, and she included herself in this, were prepared to put up with so much simply because they were in love, or thought they were.

'I'm sorry. I should have kept my big mouth shut. See? I haven't changed totally,' Michelle apologised, as Victoria ran from the room and crashed into a concerned Colin.

Despite the dramas of the day, the evening was pleasant, the meal delicious and Colin did not go to sleep but seemed interested in everything Michelle had to say. He was concerned for Victoria's plight, and practical with his advice, but he was equally concerned at the effect it might have on Jillian.

'She can't stay here,' he announced, when Michelle had gone to bed and they were sitting over a final nightcap.

'Why not? Of course she can. Where else can she go?'

'Jillian, be practical. You're not working now but when the baby's here you'll have a hotel to run. You can't do it all.'

'I won't be doing it all. The child is Victoria's, and she'll be looking after it. Heavens, the house is large enough. The guests need not even hear a squeak out of it.'

'That's not what I meant. Do you really reckon Victoria will take full responsibility for her child? If you think that, then you're a bigger fool than I took you for.'

'I beg your pardon? What does that mean?' Jillian was affronted.

'If you let Victoria walk all over you and, no doubt, scarper and leave you holding the baby, then you're a fool. That's what I mean. For Christ's sake, Jillian, your fifties are just over the horizon. It's time to loosen up, do what you want, not lumber yourself with another child.'

'I don't see it as being lumbered. But even if I did, and I was nearly seventy, I would do the same thing. My daughter needs me and so will her baby. I don't regard it as a sacrifice but as a privilege. And if that's going to be your attitude you either change or I'm afraid we're finished.'

'Come on, be reasonable. I don't want to end my days babysitting someone else's brat. I was married to a pumpkin-eater, always nagging for another child, feeling only alive when carting a newborn baby about. I'm not going down that road again.'

'This conversation is ludicrous. She's my daughter, for heaven's sake. Her life is in a mess, and you want me to throw her out? I can't believe we're having this conversation. That you could think like this even for a minute –'

'Well, I do. And while we're having a little heart-to-heart I don't go much on your friend either.'

'What friend? Michelle? She's my cousin. What's wrong with her?'

'She's too opinionated by far. You sure she's not a dyke?' The ugly word hung between them.

'Michelle is a strong woman and a good woman. Why is it that when inadequate men meet women like that they always accuse them of being lesbians? You sound just like Jack and look at what an inadequate he was.'

Colin leaped to his feet and his hand slammed down hard on the table so that everything on it shook. 'Don't you dare compare me to that defective! He's a sodding crook. He deserted you, left you penniless. I care for you, I look after you.'

'Do you? Oh, really? Well, that's news to me. When you're not drunk you're slinking off to your wife. I might have been left penniless but at least I pay my way now, not like you.'

'Meaning?'

'When did you last buy me a present? When did you last pay for a bottle out of the cellar? When did you ever give me any money for your keep?' She was standing now, and this time she banged the table.

'So this is what we've come to? Arguing over a few pennies.'

'It's not a few, it's pounds and pounds going down your gullet and I can't afford it, not any more.'

'Right. You don't have to. I'm sorry to have been such an inconvenience to you.' Colin stalked from the room.

Jillian's anger supported her as she cleared the table and loaded the dishwasher – even as she made herself a last cup of tea. But then there was a change. Fear began to take hold: the fear of being alone again.

In the morning when Jillian walked into the kitchen, it was to find Michelle and Victoria already up, the former making tea and toast.

'Poor kid's been sick.'

'You all right now?'

'How long does one throw up for?' asked a wan-looking Victoria.

'Not long.'

'Your mother was one of those annoying women who never had morning sickness and sailed through her pregnancies, looking even more beautiful.'

'Mum would.'

'I had my moments.'

'What's it like, Mum? Is it as bad as they say?'

'I told her she needs a water-birth and to drink raspberry-leaf tea. She doesn't need doctors and hospitals and all that high-tech crap ruining a beautiful moment.'

'And I thought you'd changed, Michelle! You could have fooled me.' Jillian didn't laugh. 'What you don't need, Victoria, is other women telling you what you should and should not be doing. You have this baby how you want it. And don't listen to other people! The way some women go on, you'd think there'd never been a normal birth in the history of mankind.' She patted her daughter's hand.

'You didn't say what it was like.'

'It hurts. It hurts like hell, actually, whatever you take, whatever you do.'

'Now who's scaring her?' Michelle leaned forward, her old aggression back.

'I'm not. I'm telling her the truth. I was told that if I did this, that and the other, it would be painless and perfect and it wasn't, and I'd have much rather known the truth than be told a pack of lies and suffer the shock I did – and, might I add, a huge sense of failure that it wasn't as I'd been told, so therefore it had to be my fault.'

'Thanks, Mum. I knew you wouldn't lie to me. You know, Michelle, you're right, this toast is making me feel better.' She helped herself to another slice. 'What's up with Colin? He looked like thunder when he left for work. He could hardly be civil, could he, Michelle?'

'We had a bit of a barney. We both said things we shouldn't have.'

'Good. Has he left?'

'From that, Victoria, is one to gather you don't go much on your mother's choice of a lover?'

'He's a piss-head, I don't trust him, and I think she could do better.'

'Remind me never to ask you for a reference.' Michelle laughed.

'He's using Mum and she can't see it. She puts up with him because I think –' She stopped.

'So, Victoria, what is it? Give us the benefit of your opinion,' Jillian said, but even as she did she wondered why she had: the last thing she wanted to know was what her daughter thought.

'I think he's here because she's afraid of being alone. There, I've said it. And Gran thinks the same.'

'Well, there's a comfort,' Jillian said, with heavy irony, as she pulled the kettle on to the hotplate. Why she was shocked she had no idea. After all, her daughter was only putting into words what she knew deep down was the truth.

'Did you like him, Michelle?' Victoria asked.

'I can't say I was madly impressed, but I didn't think Jillian would appreciate my opinion. I used to annoy her like mad when we were young, putting my oar in when it wasn't

461

wanted, always telling her where she was going wrong. Bloody cheek, when you think what a mess my own life was in.'

'Colin didn't go much on you either.' Jillian couldn't stop herself: she felt so annoyed, so irritated, she wanted to lash out at someone; she wanted someone else to be hurt.

'I gathered that. It doesn't bother me one way or the other.'

'He hasn't gone, has he, Mum? You're going to have him back, aren't you?'

Jillian didn't answer but spooned the tea into the pot.

'Mum?'

During the morning Colin had phoned to apologise. It seemed churlish not to accept. And when he returned that evening it was with a giant teddy-bear for a baby who was little bigger than a tadpole.

Four days into her stay Michelle suggested to Victoria and her Aunt Mary that they go on a trip to the Summer Isles. Jillian knew why they were going: Victoria was still seething with anger at her for patching up her argument with Colin and Michelle felt in the way. But she couldn't live her life for her daughter, she told herself.

The few days alone with Colin came as a relief, helped by him not drinking all the time. When Victoria and the others returned Jillian had a job. 'Ewan's asked me to help out at the Clansman for a few weeks. It will be invaluable experience for me.'

'I think Ewan fancies you,' Victoria teased.

'Honestly, you do talk rubbish. He's a good friend and a colleague.'

'When do you start, what do you do, and what is he paying you?' asked Mary, with her usual practicality.

'The Monday after Michelle has left for Australia. I'm working in the office, reception, the bar, wherever I'm needed. And he's paying me the going rate.' Like a little girl, Jillian poked the tip of her tongue out at her mother.

'I was only concerned.'

'Mum, don't fib. You were being nosy.'

Working at the big hotel was different from running her own small enterprise. Apart from the residents' lounge there was a public bar too. It was noisy, busy, and sometimes, when the drinking got out of hand, it could be frightening. But Ewan was always patrolling when she was on duty there, on the barman's night off, keeping an eye on things, keeping the exuberance controlled.

Jillian liked the reception work best. It was years since she had done any serious secretarial work and it was amazing how quickly her skills returned, even though their computer was much more powerful and complicated than hers. She learned where wastage was most common, where pilfering was easiest and how to juggle bed occupancy. She loved the bustle of the big hotel, where there was always someone to talk to, something needing attention.

'Tell you what, forget the Altnahany project and come to work for me permanently. You're good.' Ewan grinned at her over his mug of coffee. They were in his office, taking a well-earned break.

'Much as I'd love to, Ewan, I can't give up on Altnahany. For one thing I love the house too much and, second, I've got to show that Pearlman woman I can do it, just to annoy her.'

At first when she had worked in the public bar she had been treated with caution and some suspicion. But as the weeks wore on the locals relaxed, became more friendly and, she felt, had begun to trust her as they became used to her.

She was bending over a table, wiping the surface, when a man she did not know pinched her bottom. 'How much do you charge?' He grinned, revealing blackened teeth and breath foetid with whisky. 'Less than your daughter, I reckon, since you're older.'

Her skin crawled with invisible creatures as the meaning of his words sank in. She stood frozen with shock, but one of the regulars, an enormous forestry worker, lunged forward and grabbed the man by his shirt collar.

'Apologise to the lady,' he demanded.

'What lady?' the man asked, unwisely.

The fight that ensued was short. The stranger and his companions were soon overpowered by Jillian's customers, summarily beaten and unceremoniously hurled out of the door. She stood transfixed while all this was happening, unable to speak or move. She felt as if she had strayed into a Wild West film. Her protectors returned, wiping their hands, smiling triumphantly. By now Ewan had been summoned and was offering whiskies on the house.

'Who were those men?' she asked.

'They've been working on the Pearlman land,' Jock, a ghillie, informed her.

'And did they say anything about my daughter to you?'

There was a great shuffling of boots and a steady studying of the mud on them.

'I would like to know.'

'I'd rather not be saying.'

'Jock?'

'Best leave it, Jillian.'

'No, I can't, Ewan. If somebody has been spreading rumours about my daughter I have to know who. You must see that.'

'Tell her, Jock, you'd better.'

'He said he was told she was on the game.' She was sure the huge, bluff man blushed as he spoke.

'Who told him?'

'Lachlan Pearlman.'

'Jillian, wait!' Ewan called after her, but she took no notice for she had not even heard him. She ran out of the bar door across the car park, the wind from the loch tearing at her skirt. She felt sick and her hands shook as she opened the car. She fumbled for the ignition, and started the engine. The small car kangarooed down the slope and on to the road. Ahead was a lorry. She swung the vehicle out sharply from behind it and had to swerve violently to avoid an oncoming car. The near collision made her take stock, calm down a little, but it did nothing to decrease her speed.

The large bell-pull came away in her hand. She pounded on

the heavy door, but no one came. She pushed it open and stalked into the hall, where she paused as if wondering what she was doing there. Then, from the back of the house, she heard the noise of a radio and someone laughed. The sound galvanised her and she ran down the dark, musty corridor towards it.

'How dare you, you lying bastard?' she shouted, as she entered the kitchen. Lachlan looked up from the table and the local paper, which was spread out in front of him. His mother turned from the sink and a man she did not know stood up politely. Jillian knew she must look like a wild creature, for her emotions had taken total control of her. Even if she had wanted to stop she could not for she had allowed the red mist full rein.

'Jillian, what has happened? Calm down. What a to-do!' Dotty moved towards her, wiping her hands on a tea-towel, smiling welcomingly.

'Don't smile at me like that, you hypocritical bitch. I'm warning you, Lachlan, if I hear one more slanderous word from you about my daughter I shall sue you through every court in this land. And that goes for you too.' She swung round to face Dotty.

'We don't know what on earth you're talking about, Jillian. For goodness' sake, sit and take a deep breath. A whisky, perhaps?'

'Your son has been implying that my daughter is a prostitute. I want him to stop.'

'Perhaps I should introduce you to my cousin Fergus, who is, I should point out, our solicitor.' Dotty spoke with a light tone, but there was a menace in it for all that.

'Good. Then he can advise you that what Lachlan is about is dangerous in the extreme.'

'Now, you listen to me.' Dotty pointed her finger threateningly at her. 'There's nothing my son has said that isn't the truth. She might not have accepted money but your daughter, according to my son, is a nymphomaniac who has slept with virtually every friend he has!'

'Dotty!' Fergus interrupted, frowning.

'How could you say these things, Lachlan? I just don't

465

understand you. You make her pregnant and desert her, and then go round saying these intolerable things.'

'If it's his.'

'Dotty, have you not heard of DNA? If he's disputing that he's the father, I shall insist on tests. You can't get away with that one in this day and age. And I shall make certain now that Victoria goes to the Child Support Agency and you will cough up for the rest of its childhood.'

'Of course, Fergus, what you must realise is that we can't blame the girl. She comes from a criminal family, you see. So what can one expect?'

Jillian was halfway across the space that divided them wanting to hit her, wanting to scratch her, to pull her hair, anything to release the boiling anger inside her. But in the split second it took, sense took over. Of course, Dotty wanted her to attack her, wanted her to damage her. Then who would be suing whom?

'Without doubt, I think you are the *most* despicable woman and you, Lachlan, are a poor apology for a man.' She turned on her heel. 'By the way, the fire escape. I heard this morning, my plans have been accepted. You failed with that one, Dotty. I advise you not to try any more nasty tricks.'

She walked from the kitchen then sped to the hall intent on getting away from this house and these people as quickly as possible.

On the driveway, beside her car, stood Ewan. At the sight of him all courage failed her and she stumbled towards him and fell into his arms. 'Why?' was all she could to say.

'Come on, Jillian. Let's get out of here.' He led her to his car.

'But mine?' she said, between sobs.

'I brought old Freddie, the potman, with me. He's driving it back. You see, we hoteliers think of everything.'

A few miles further along the road he pulled into a lay-by. Below them was a wooded valley, a river gushing through it, its peaty water frothing brown. The sun was shining, the curlews were wheeling, it was a beautiful view and a perfect day, and she could see none of it. He sat quietly as she told him what she had been told and what she had said. 'Jillian, my darling, you should not be bothering yourself with trash like them,' he said quietly, and she did not even register that he had used the endearment.

7

Autumn 1994

'What did I tell you? Don't get embroiled with that Pearlman woman!' Colin, just back from work, waved the bottle at her questioningly. She declined a drink: in her present hyped-up mood alcohol was the last thing she needed.

'I am embroiled, as you put it, already. We will be sharing a grandchild in three months' time, or have you forgotten?' She was sharp with him, she knew, but she had expected sympathy not criticism.

'Then you shouldn't have rowed with her.'

'Oh, no? So what do you suggest I do? Allow them to slander my daughter and get away with it?'

'People take whatever that old cow says with a pinch of salt.'

'You could have fooled me. Has anyone told the men in the bar she and her son talk rubbish? Evidently they thought they were on to a good thing.'

'You've only yourself to blame. If you didn't work in the Clansman you wouldn't hear the gossip.'

'And that would make it better? Not hearing it would make it all go away? Oh, come on, Colin. Talk sense.'

'I am. It's you who are letting emotions get in the way. Now, from what you say, you've really put the cat among the pigeons. She'll go for you in a big way.'

'Still, I've got you to care for me,' she said, with heavy sarcasm, which he chose to ignore.

'What's for supper?' he asked.

'Nothing. I haven't had time to make anything. Ewan suggested we all went to the hotel and had dinner with him.'

'He would. Dear old Ewan, the white knight to the rescue.'

'He was very kind. He needn't have come rushing after me. I was in no fit state to drive back.'

'Never misses an opportunity does he, creeping Ewan? Never trust a man who wears suede shoes, that's what my old mum used to say.'

'I reckon your old mum is about as stupid as you are.' She picked up her coat. 'I'm going so you must please yourself. Victoria, are you ready?' she called out as she went into the hall.

Victoria lumbered down the stairs. Poor girl, Jillian thought. As if being on her own wasn't bad enough she was one of those women whom pregnancy did not suit. She had put on far too much weight, her hair was lank and straggly, she had spots and her feet had swollen so much she could only wear her sneakers. 'You sure you want to come? I can bring you something back, if you like.'

'No. I need to get out. If I skulk, Lachlan will think I'm ashamed and hiding from the gossips, and I've nothing to be ashamed of.'

'That's my girl.' She put her arm around her daughter as Colin, looking sheepish, appeared in the hall too.

The Clansman was busy. There was a late surge of holiday-makers who had come to enjoy the autumn colours, and the brilliant weather that the Highlands often enjoyed late in the year, while England was damp and fog-bound. As well as the guests there was a meeting of the local Rotary club. They had a drink in the bar but there was no sign of Ewan.

'Some host,' said Colin.

'He must be held up. I'll go and see if there's a problem.'

'Yes, you do that.'

'Oh, Colin, don't be so pathetic.'

Jillian found Ewan in the kitchen, hot and harassed.

'Bloody chef threw a wobbly! And we've seventy for dinner, our max. Bastard.'

'Has he gone for good?'

'Too bloody right. They only try that on once with me. What's worse is that my back-up's away at her cousin's wedding in Ullapool. Excuse me.' Adroitly he heaved one of the large meat dishes out of the huge commercial range and began to baste it.

'Can I help?'

'I couldn't let you. It's your evening off – and after today! No way.'

'I'd be pleased to.' Already she was taking off her silk jacket and covering her dress with a chef's overall. 'Stella,' she called, to a waitress who was flying by, 'could you let Colin and Victoria know I'm helping out and tell them to go in to dinner without me. Now, Ewan, where, what?'

'You could be doing the starters, I've half done them. We'll need more smoked salmon from the chill room and salad and . . .'

For two hours they worked flat out with no time to talk and no time to sit.

'Jillian, you were a star, I could never have done it without you. Hungry? Fancy a steak?'

'Perfect. Can we join the others?'

'Natch.'

In the dining room, now almost deserted, she found a sleeping Colin, a space cleared in front of him, his head resting on his arms.

Victoria was stoically eating the last of her pudding, which she did not look as if she was enjoying. 'Mum, how can he be so humiliating? He went off before the pudding, even. It's so embarrassing. Everyone was staring. Why does he do it?'

'I tell you what, I don't think I could work every day in the kitchens here, it was hard work.'

'You've got to talk about it and about him, Mum. You've got to stop making excuses for him, and stop changing the subject.'

'I don't have to talk or do anything.' She looked at her daughter with a cool, level expression. Of course Victoria was right, it was just . . . not now, not yet. 'Here comes my food.' She smiled at Ewan, who was crossing the room with a tray.

'Ah, Sleeping Beauty, I see.' Carefully Ewan placed the heavy tray on the table. 'Never mind. We won't have to share this particularly nice bottle of Châteauneuf with him. Want a glass, Victoria?'

'I'm not allowed to drink. I'm pregnant, or haven't you noticed? Mum, I want to go. Why are all the men involved with my mother so thick?' She stood up, abruptly and clumsily.

'Victoria! How dare you speak to Ewan like that? No, we're not going. Sit down and wait until I've finished eating.'

Ewan was on his feet. 'It doesn't matter, Jillian. If she wants to go . . . Freddie can take you home, Victoria, it's on his way.'

Victoria attempted to flounce from the room but, given her size, she looked ungainly instead. At the door she faltered and came back to the table. 'I'm sorry, Mum.'

'And so you should be.' She wasn't ready to forgive her yet.

Jillian waited for Ewan to return from seeing Victoria to the car. 'Ewan . . .'

'Jillian, she's tired and overwrought. Forget it. Our steaks are getting cold.'

They began to eat, the slumbering Colin opposite them.

'Am I involved in your life?' Ewan asked suddenly. 'Only . . . well, you know, if ever . . . I think what I'm trying to say is that if ever you want me to be, I'm here. Involved, I mean.' He looked bashful.

'Ewan, how sweet. Thank you. You're a good friend.'

The next morning, as Jillian was cooking their breakfast, a contrite Colin entered the kitchen and shuddered at the sight and smell of bacon cooking. 'Jillian, I'm sorry. I let you down, embarrassed you. I was so bloody tired.'

She continued to cook. She heard him cross the kitchen and sensed him standing behind her. 'Aren't you speaking to me?'

'We can't go on like this, Colin. I've had enough.' Still she concentrated on the frying pan.

'I only got drunk because of you.'

'So I'm to blame? And how do you make that out?' She laid down the fish-slice and turned to face him.

'I was jealous. I didn't like you working matily away with Ewan. And look at how calm and collected you are, as if what I do doesn't matter to you any more.'

'If I didn't care you wouldn't still be here, Colin. You're a

470

fool to get drunk in public – you'll be losing clients soon. But it's your life and you must do with it as you wish.' She turned back to the frying pan.

'See! What did I say? You don't give a fig for me! You can't even be angry with me.'

'Oh, I'm angry, Colin. Very angry. But what's the point in shrieking and shouting? You'll do what you want, you always do.' She broke an egg into the pan. The door slammed as he stormed out.

Understanding of her predicament came from an unlikely source. 'It's put you in a bit of a spot, hasn't it, this drinking business?' Mary began.

'So you heard?'

'News travels in these parts.'

'What do you mean, a bit of a spot?'

'Well, I presume, even for you, he's gone too far this time. That at last you're beginning to think that life on your own might be better, even if you *are* scared of it.' Mary did not pause in chopping the fruit for the Christmas puddings, although Jillian had stopped weighing the ingredients. 'But you're lumbered with this feeling of responsibility to him. If you did throw him out, what then? He might drink more and fall under a bus and where would that put you? Riddled with guilt, if I know you.'

'Exactly.' Jillian sat down at the table.

'You needn't look so surprised.'

'It's just . . . you've never made any secret of what you think of him.'

'That hasn't changed. It's you I'm concerned about. You need a holiday, if you ask me. Get right away from this place and him.'

'I can't afford one.'

'Then ask his nibs. He gets enough from you.'

'He couldn't help. His wife has asked him to pay for her new conservatory.'

'She what?' Mary looked disapproving. Jillian continued weighing the ingredients. 'But he doesn't live there.'

'No, but Morag always gets what she wants.'

Mary pushed the dish of chopped fruit towards Jillian. 'He's planning to go back to her.'

'What makes you say that?'

'Conservatories, that's what.'

'Sorry?'

'Whoever heard of a man spending that sort of money on a house he had no intention of living in?'

The talk with her mother clarified things for Jillian. She'd meant it when she said she'd had enough. Colin had to go. But it was he who made her change her mind and give him one last chance.

The incident at the Clansman had had more effect on him than all her reasoned talk or any amount of nagging. He was genuinely ashamed at having fallen asleep in such a public place. From that night he took control of his drinking.

He had a small whisky upon returning home from work, and instead of wine was drinking non-alcoholic beer with his dinner. He was more alert, more fun again, he took an interest in what she did, and the regular deep depressions, without alcohol to feed them, deserted him. Even Victoria acknowledged what a nice man he could be if he wanted. Mary counselled caution.

Although they were no longer open because of the fire regulations, if occasional guests appeared Jillian took them in. But they were so few and far between that she was wondering if it was worth it.

'No point,' Ewan advised. 'Sit down and work it out. Extra heating, electricity. You can't cover it with the occasional casual. If the Clansman can't, you certainly can't.'

'But my overheads are far less.'

'It's all relative, though, isn't it? We take in more. Fancy a snack? I was just about to have a sandwich and a glass of wine. Join me?'

Once they were settled in Ewan's small office, he said, 'I was sorry to hear about your sign being vandalised again.'

'It's so annoying, it's such a lovely sign. I called the police this time, but they said there was nothing they could do, they haven't the man-power to keep a watch on us. But haven't you heard the latest? Weed-killer on the drive. Some of the rhododendrons won't be around next year. And a letter suggesting that, for the sake of my health, I should leave Altnahany. I think Dotty's behind it.'

'Or hotheads.'

'But I've made no enemies – not that I know of.'

'Ah, there you have it. You wouldn't necessarily know, would you? There are some odd sods about and this place has its share of them. They're envious.'

'But, apart from the Pearlmans, I've met only lovely people. I've made more friends here in two years than I did in a lifetime in England.'

'But there are always bad apples. Don't you think Dotty's got too much to lose to take up crime?'

'I thought it was her because the spelling in the letter was atrocious. I think it's the same person who did the sign. But it's someone pretending they're not educated. Most of the words beginning with P are spelt with a B. No one spells that badly.'

'Hamish does. He's dyslexic.'

'You're not accusing *Hamish*?'

'No, it's not Hamish's style. If he wanted rid of you he'd bash you over the head with a claymore.' Ewan grinned. 'I was just pointing out that it might not be someone pretending. Mind you, count your lucky stars that they haven't tried to burn you out – that's the tradition in these parts if you cross the natives.'

'Good God!'

8

Winter 1994

With another Christmas approaching, Colin was away at his mother's with the children so that she could give them their presents. Their absence suited her, for she was busy with her preparations. Also, she admitted to herself, it was pleasant just to have a weekend alone with Victoria: it was only two weeks until the baby was due.

Jillian was awake: Prince had a painful ear infection. Upset by his howling in the kitchen, she had brought him upstairs to her room and he lay on her bed, his head nestled in the crook of her arm – another bonus of Colin not being there. At last Prince was asleep, and Jillian lay in the dark listening to his calmer breathing. From a distance she heard a car. She sat up, alert: a car in these parts, at two in the morning, was rare. It stopped – by the spinney she judged, no doubt a courting couple. She smiled to herself – it was a cold night for that. But then Prince raised his head, his good ear pricked. He sat up and listened. Someone was walking outside the back court-yard. He growled. 'It's okay, boy. Shush.' She eased herself from the bed, crossed to the window and pulled back the curtains. As she peered out, she heard a whooshing noise then saw a blinding flash as flames burst into the air.

Not stopping for a dressing-gown, Jillian raced from the room and pounded on Victoria's door. 'Fire!' she cried, bursting in, an agitated, excited Prince barking at her heels. Once she was assured that her daughter was awake she ran to the phone and called 999. In the kitchen she wrenched the extinguisher from the wall and ran to the fire, which was in a back pantry and rapidly taking hold. It was quickly emptied and she fetched another, calling out to Victoria to collect more from the upper floors.

Although aware of the danger, aware of the heat and the flames, Jillian was conscious of how calm she was and how methodically she worked. She heard Victoria calling her. 'Here, darling, in here. I think we're winning,' she said, to keep Victoria calm.

Victoria, her face white despite the flames, stood in the doorway, leaning at a strange angle against the jamb. 'Mum, I'm sorry. The baby, it's started.'

'Why be sorry? Don't be frightened. It's probably a false alarm. Come with me. You'll be safer in the front.' She looked back at the fire, certain, in a few minutes, that it would burst into the main part of the house. She helped her daughter into the drawing room. There she picked up the telephone and this time asked for an ambulance.

'How did the fire start?' Victoria looked close to tears.

'An electrical fault, I expect. Will you be all right? I must get back to it.'

'Don't leave me alone, Mum.'

'Darling, I must. Keep Prince with you, keep him safe. Please, darling, be brave, just for a few minutes. The firemen will be here soon.'

Racing back to the seat of the fire she knew full well that she had lied. This was no electrical fire, and they were so isolated here that the firemen were all volunteers. If they arrived within half an hour she would be lucky. Jillian went outside, slipping and sliding on the snowy surface of the backyard. On the wall was a length of hose she'd put there for the garden. She had to pull and tug at it for, in these temperatures, it was frozen to the wall. One last pull and she landed flat on her back. She got up, winded, dusted herself down and dragged the heavy coil towards the kitchen, praying it would fit the tap and that it would be long enough to reach the fire.

The length of the hose was less of a problem: in the few minutes it had taken to get Victoria out of the kitchen, the blaze was encroaching further into the house. It had devoured the pantry and was now searching with its red hot tendrils through the door; snakes of fire were licking at skirting-boards. She was not calm now: she was in an anguish of terror at the flames bursting through and the inadequacy of her hose against them. There was so much wood in the house, old wood, dry wood, dry as tinder – all these words were tumbling through her head. And, with horror, she remembered the calor-gas cylinders in the still room next door – could she manhandle them out in time? She was not given the choice for a new danger came as the fire discovered a stack of plastic crates and dark, acrid smoke swirled about her. She began to choke. Somewhere she'd read that such smoke could kill in seconds. She left the water running, turned on her heels, fled from the back passage slamming doors shut as she ran. As she reached a frightened, crying

Victoria and a cowering Prince she herself cried out but with relief at the sound of a fire engine racing up the drive. When she opened the front door it was to find her mother in nightdress, winter coat and wellington boots in hot pursuit.

All through her pregnancy Victoria and Jillian had discussed what they would do when the baby arrived. Months ago Jillian had promised that she would remain by her daughter's side throughout the birth. This was not something that she wanted to do, in fact she dreaded it, and with the house on fire she had the perfect excuse to bundle Victoria alone into the ambulance, except that she couldn't. Assured by the firemen that there was nothing she could do, and reassured that her mother and Prince were safe, she clambered into the vehicle. There was no one else, and Victoria could not be expected to go through it by herself.

'I suppose it's silly of me. I've had two children of my own but I don't really want to be with her. I'm scared and I'm squeamish,' she confessed apologetically to one of the midwives outside the room, which she had been asked to leave while they examined her daughter.

'I can't think of anything more natural. It must be awful to see your own child in labour. I can assure you, a multitude of dads feel worse than you but they think they ought to see it through.'

'I suppose the brave ones are those who refuse.' She accepted the cup of tea, at least her third, she thought, and wondered how she could be making conversation at a time like this when she was so afraid – fear for Victoria and fear for the house played follow-my-leader through her mind.

'Oh, undoubtedly. But I shouldn't imagine they're ever allowed to forget that they didn't stay with their wives.' The midwife laughed.

'Have I time to make a phone call?'

'Masses. We'll be all night at this rate. A first baby. There's a call-box in the hall.'

Jillian had feared that the lines would have been burned, but the call went through and she listened to the ringing tone with a pounding heart. 'Thank God! I thought the whole place would have gone up in smoke,' she said with feeling, on hearing her mother's voice.

'And it's a miracle it didn't, if you ask me. You were lucky the firemen were on their way back from a chimney fire four miles away or you'd have lost the lot! You should see the back! The deep freezes have gone and it nearly got to your room – and that bloody dog's howling.' Mary was evidently relishing this litany.

'Poor Prince, he's got a bad ear. Could you give him his drops? They're beside my bed.'

'I've enough to do.'

'Mum, please, it's not his fault.'

'When do you think you'll be back?'

'I don't know.'

'You must have some idea.'

'It's her first child, Mum, who knows?'

'So it wasn't a false alarm?'

'No.'

'Only I'm up to my ears in it here with the mess and the mopping up,' Mary complained.

'Leave it, I don't expect you to do it. I'll clear up when I get back.'

'You should be more careful. You could have been burned in your beds.'

'I didn't exactly set light to it myself, Mum.' Despite the drama, despite the worry, her voice bubbled with amusement at her mother's predictability.

Back in the ward, she peered into Victoria's room. She was alone, looking tiny and scared in her hospital gown and not at all like the feisty young woman she normally was. 'You don't want to be here, do you, Mum?'

'Don't be silly! Whatever gave you that idea? Why, it's almost worth Lachlan doing a runner so I can be with you instead,' she lied through her teeth, plastering a cheerful smile on her face at the same time.

'You sure? Only I don't mind,' said Victoria, who looked as if she minded very much.

'Wild horses wouldn't drag me away.'

'Good, I hoped you'd say that. Any news of Altnahany?'

'I spoke to your grandmother, who's in her element, making tea and mopping up. She seemed to be implying that it was my fault, but then I suppose she would.'

'I think I heard a car, Mum. Did you?'

'At Altnahany at that time of night? Unlikely.'

'You don't think someone was trying to burn us down?'

'No, I think it was the wiring. We should have had the whole place done while we were about it.' The whole house *had* been rewired: it was one of the first things they'd had done. 'Don't worry about it, the insurance will pay. Fancy a game of Trivial Pursuit?'

'Don't let me win just because I'm in labour,' Victoria said, perky now that her mother was back.

'As if I would!'

The labour continued. The joking and cheerfulness subsided. At the beginning Jillian had left the room every time the doctors and midwives examined Victoria but now all modesty had been set aside, and as the pain increased Jillian stayed with her daughter. As she held her hand she kept a beady eye on the monitors, watching the graph for the slightest deviation. She mopped Victoria's brow, chatted to her, read to her, encouraged her, reminded her how to breathe – and felt totally inadequate, hating every moment of her daughter's agony. Only in the last few minutes was she swept into the excitement that everyone else in the room was feeling. Victoria held her mother's hand, so tight that her rings cut into her, and cursed Jillian, the nurses, the world but especially men. With one last enormous effort, the baby was born, and Jillian joined her granddaughter in crying.

In the morning, when she returned from the hospital, the house stank. Smoke and soot had permeated even to the top floor. Where the firemen had entered the house, trekking back and forth with their equipment, the carpets were ruined. Despite Mary's efforts at mopping up, there was water everywhere. Her lovely kitchen was smoke-blackened and would have to be totally redecorated. In the pantry, the freezers were melted black blobs, her stores ashes. There was nothing left of her little garden at the back of the house:

where her plants had been, there was only mud, churned up by the firemen's large boots as they had raced hither and thither. And, worst of all, Prince had run away. They were lucky to be alive, though, she kept telling herself to compensate. 'I heard a car. Parked by the spinney. Then I heard movement outside, which was what really alerted me. We were attacked, I'm sure. It was arson.' Anxiously she related her suspicions to the policeman who had called.

'That's a very serious accusation, Mrs Stirling.'

'Not nearly as serious as almost being burned to death in our beds, Inspector.'

'Quite. But, still, are you sure? I mean, you could have dreamed it. You could have imagined it. The mind plays funny games when you're sleepy.'

'I told you. I was wide awake. I was nursing my sick dog. Don't you think you should go and look for footprints, tyre marks in the snow?'

'I fear it would do no good, Mrs Stirling. There was a heavy fall of snow early this morning.'

'At least check. Please.'

But she knew he did not believe her, and wondered if he would even bother to walk over to the spinney. The insurance man, who called later, didn't bother to hide his deep suspicion of her story. As she answered his questions, she knew he thought she was lying. She did not like the way the questioning was going. How big a loss had the business made? Why such a large insurance? 'Are you accusing me of setting fire to the place? I told the police the circumstances. My daughter heard the car too. Ask her.'

Still the man looked unconvinced. 'Am I going to risk the life of my pregnant daughter? Think, man.' She knew she was not endearing herself to him, but on top of everything else his attitude was the last straw. 'In any case, this isn't my house. I work here, I'd be putting myself out of a job.'

'Where is the owner? Have you telephoned him?'

'I can't.' Even as she said it, she realised how unlikely that must sound to him.

'And why's that, Mrs Stirling?'

'Because I don't know where she is. She calls me.'

'So she could be anywhere, even here in Scotland?'

'No. No, she's in America. I'm sure she is.'

The man made a note. Jillian looked anxious and tried not to: it might be interpreted as guilt. This man's line of thought was ludicrous. 'She loves this house,' she added lamely, and feared she might be compounding the problem.

'And your husband, Mrs Stirling. Have you any idea of his whereabouts?'

'No, I haven't.' She felt physically sick and knew that she had to control herself, she must not lose her temper and deepen the man's scepticism further. She was on the point of saying that she did not wish or have to answer such questions, when Prince slunk into the room.

'Anyone home?'

'Ewan! Am I pleased to see you! And Prince.' She bent down to hug her dog, who looked deeply distrustful of the chaos that was now the kitchen and had once been his favourite place. 'You bad boy, where were you?'

'I found him wandering up the glen road, looking sorry for himself.' Ewan twisted round looking at the blackened room. 'Hello, Peter,' he said to the assessor. 'Hell, Jillian, what a mess! What caused it? I just heard. You should have rung me.'

'I couldn't, I was in Inverness. On top of everything else, Victoria had her baby this morning – Rose, isn't that a lovely name?'

'Congratulations, Granny.' Ewan grinned. 'Some night!'

'Some morning, too. Because of my errant husband, this gentlemen seems to think I set fire to the place myself. That I'm an arsonist.'

'What rubbish! Peter, you're on the wrong tack there. This wee lady lives for this house. She loves it as if it were a person. There's no way she'd do anything to harm it – she's worked too hard on it, you've my word on that.' The assessor looked more relaxed, but Jillian was left with the uncomfortable thought of what the outcome might have been if she hadn't had a friend like Ewan to vouch for her.

Although Ewan had invited her to go to stay at the Clansman until Altnahany was straight she reluctantly turned down his offer. The sooner she started work here, the faster everything would be back to normal, and with Victoria already champing at the bit to come home, she must get on. Not only was there the house to air and the kitchen to clean and paint, she also had to make a list for the insurance company of everything she had lost. Despite her penchant for list-making this was one she could have done without. It was not easy to remember what had been in the damaged rooms. She kept a notebook in her pocket for when she thought of something she had forgotten about.

Although she had expected Mary to surpass herself in moaning, her mother was a tower of strength. Even though she was desperate to go into Inverness to see her great-granddaughter she insisted on helping. 'The sooner this is done, the sooner little Rose can come home,' she said, donning an apron and rolling up her sleeves. She was indomitable, Jillian thought, as they set to work.

Colin had heard about the fire on the local television news and rushed in. 'Thank God you're all right. I wish I'd been here. You must have been terrified.'

'Not as much as I'd have thought. You often wonder, don't you, how you'd cope? The truth is, I was more scared being with Victoria.'

'Imagine. I've never slept with a granny before,' he teased her.

'It should be such a happy time, but now this.'

'We'll get it sorted out soon enough. It probably looks worse than it is.'

'I meant, the way the fire started. The police just won't take me seriously. They think I imagined the car. I'm hoping the insurance people will do tests for me, prove it was a petrol bomb or something.'

'Honestly, Jillian, you are being dramatic. A bomb! Here? And what would an investigation prove? Most people who burn down their own property use petrol, didn't you know? Best to drop all this talk – it can easily lead to worse suspicions and bad blood. Even the fearsome Pearlman woman wouldn't burn you in your beds.'

'Oh, no? I've been told it's local practice to do just that.'

'Rubbish! Whoever told you that was joking.'

'I don't think so, Colin.'

That Christmas was not at all as Jillian had planned. Within hours of her birth it was apparent that Rose had a problem with her digestive system. Victoria, though disappointed, patiently accepted her enforced incarceration in the hospital.

With all the building work and decoration needed it was perhaps as well the baby was not there. The volume of noise and the smell of soot, which still permeated the house, was not the best environment for her.

It was a worrying time, and it was as well that there were no guests for Jillian made a point of visiting her daughter every day. The drive to Inverness, in which she had once taken such pleasure, was more of a chore now that she had to do it so often. But, in February, the day she had longed for finally arrived. As she drove in to pick up Victoria and Rose, fire or no fire, bomb or no bomb, she sang all the way.

On their return Fenny was the first to call. She was somewhat distant and brisk, which puzzled Jillian, but she put it down to her being here in her professional capacity as health visitor.

'Anything wrong, Fenny?' she asked, to make sure.

'Nothing. Should there be?' Fenny replied, quite sharply.

Once Rose was installed in her bassinet, Victoria resting, and Mary tearfully making her way home after welcoming home her first great-granddaughter, Jillian had settled down with a cup of tea and a book when the telephone rang. 'Any chance of someone picking me up next month?' Esmée's voice asked.

Chapter Eleven

1

Spring 1995

Esmée arrived in Scotland thin, tired and with no hair.

'Sod it!' she exclaimed, as a gust of ice-cold wind tore viciously and violently across the car park. It lifted her hat, and as she grappled with bag and hair, it whipped off her wig and hurled it playfully among the cars like an airborne, long-haired animal.

'Esmée!' was the only word that came to Jillian. The 'What?' that followed was equally useless. But then, gathering her senses, she raced after the wig, retrieved it with difficulty from the top of a Range Rover and returned to her own car. 'Esmée?'

'Before you say another word, I don't want any fuss. Is that understood? Or I'll catch the next plane back to London.'

'Esmée!'

'Jill, darling, if you don't stop repeating my name like a mental defective I shall scream.' She eased herself into the car.

'What is it?' Jillian asked, getting in on the other side.

'Cancer, what else? See how well adjusted I am. I can even say the dreaded C word.'

'Oh, Esmée!'

'There you go again. Has running a hotel made you lose your vocabulary? Look, I'm fine, really. I'm sorry I've been away for so long but I didn't want you to know. If it hadn't been for that sodding wind you wouldn't have.'

'But look at you, how thin you are.'

'I'd have said I was on a diet. Now you know and it's spoiled everything. And you'll be a pain, I just know you will.' Esmée lit a cigarette.

'Should you? I mean . . .?'

483

'A bit late in the day for prevention, my sweet.' Esmée inhaled deeply, as if to underline her point.

'I feel so wretched, so selfish. I didn't think. I thought you were neglecting me. That you'd grown bored with Altnahany. But it was this . . .' Her words trailed off.

'Jill, my dear, I know you've a heart of gold, but if you get upset it makes it harder for me. So don't blub, there's a poppet. No long faces. Liz and Mungo were dreary – I had to piss off, they were pulling me down.'

'It's the shock.'

'I know. I honestly do.' She patted Jillian's hand comfortingly, as if it were she who was ill.

'So that's why I couldn't phone you? I'd have found out?'

'Exactly, Dr Watson. I couldn't risk me being out for the count and some busybody nurse picking up my phone. And, to be quite honest, Jill, my sweet, the treatments were such that, well, I didn't want to talk to anyone.'

'But you've been away so long. Have you been in hospitals all that time?'

'No, but I looked so bloody grim I couldn't inflict myself on you. You might think I'm looking ghastly now but, sweets, this is the best I've managed for yonks. Let's get going, I want to see all you've done. And hear all about that ghastly fire. You must have been going mental! And then there's my great-niece too. Imagine. I shall insist on being called Great Aunt Esmeralda. It has such a ring, don't you think?'

'But you hate your name.'

'Not in these circumstances, I don't. Are you ever going to get this car started or do you want me to drive? I'd better warn you, my sight's none too good these days.'

Jillian said little as they motored along. She couldn't: the words wouldn't come out. Esmée kept up a bright stream of chatter, only half of which she listened to. She stopped the car on the Struie lookout point as she always had for Esmée.

'Who's looking after you?'

'I've been to the best quacks in the world, Jill. You can be assured of that. It cost an arm and a leg but old Esmée here didn't want to pop her clogs without seeing anyone and everyone who might have a miracle cure.'

'You don't mean?' Jillian turned to her friend, her face etched with shock and sadness. 'You're not . . .' She couldn't bring herself to articulate the word when even thinking it made her stomach lurch.

'Dying? It's hard to say, isn't it? Yes, but then, darling, it comes to us all in time. It's just come a bit sooner to me than I'd wanted it to. But, then, I'm staring my golden-oldie bus pass in the face so I suppose I shouldn't complain.'

'Esmée, what rot. You're in your mid-fifties and you don't look it.'

'That costs a bundle too.'

'I was reading an article the other day . . .'

'If it's a cure for cancer I'll have tried it. Been there, got the T-shirt. You've no idea of the number of screwy crap treatments I've tried. I shall have "What have I got to lose?" inscribed on my tombstone.'

'Esmée!' Jillian began to cry.

'Don't!'

'I can't help it. You're so brave, joking about it.'

'I'm not brave, I'm scared shitless. Joking gives you fewer wrinkles.'

'So when . . .? How . . .?'

Over four years ago, it transpired, Esmée had found a lump but, being Esmée, had hoped that, if she ignored it it would go away. Of course it didn't. By the time she had sought help it was too late. Despite treatment in France, America and even Mexico, she confessed, the cancer had spread and, rather than face further treatments, she had decided to come home.

'Don't worry, I've no intention of dying here. It's not my style. So you won't have to be bothered with that.'

'You must stay.'

'I'm one of those people who can't stand fusses when I'm ill. I've found this adorable little hospice run by a nun who's an absolute poppet and she's promised me I can drink gin till it's coming out of my ears. I want to go there, Jillian, and you're to promise me that if I collapse, or anything, you'll parcel me up and send me. Promise?'

'I promise,' she replied doubtfully.

'And let's get all the bad news out of the way, shall we?'

Jillian's heart missed a beat.

'Dear Helen's dying, so at least I'll have decent company.'

'Don't talk like that, Esmée. Don't! Poor Helen, I so wanted her to come and stay.'

'I'm afraid she's not up to it. She told me not to tell you, but it wasn't fair for you not to know.'

'Where is she? In hospital?'

'No. She's with Mungo and Liz. That woman's a brick.'

'I always liked Liz. How long?'

'Days. I wasn't strictly honest just now. I didn't just scarper because of Liz fussing. I couldn't face it, not Helen. With Mum gaga she's the last link with Daddy. Good.' She shook herself, as if to shake away the sadness. 'I'm glad that's out of the way. How's Victoria, Miles, the baby, your mother? What a list!' Her voice had brightened.

'Victoria and Rose are fine. There was a small problem with her digestive system, but the doctor's solved that. Of course, Victoria couldn't tell you but she's Esmeralda Rose.'

'Sweet!' Esmée clapped her hands.

'I didn't realise I was going to love her this much. I thought nothing would surpass what I feel for my children, but I was wrong. Mum's the same.'

'And Miles, you didn't say anything about him.'

'I hardly ever see him, but he calls every week. He's doing well.'

'So what's wrong?'

'I didn't say anything was.'

'C'est moi here. You can tell me. I know that look – all prunes and prisms. Your face goes rigid when something's upsetting you.'

'What . . .' She had been about to say 'What nonsense', but changed her mind. 'You're right. I'm worried sick. He's unhappy. He hardly ever mentions his wife to me, so . . .' She shrugged her shoulders.

'So you presume it's not all hearts and roses? Pity. Nice boy. Is she playing around?'

'I've no idea. And Victoria says I'm silly, that since he hasn't said he's unhappy how can I possibly know?'

486

'But she's a mother now, perhaps she'll begin to understand. And there's nothing you can do about it, is there?'

'Nothing but wait until he wants to tell me. And that's hard.'

Returning to Scotland and Altnahany seemed to give Esmée a boost, despite the phone call they had dreaded, which told them that Helen had died in her sleep. Within days she looked rested, and Jillian was convinced she was putting on weight. She said she was eating better than she had in months. 'Your lovely cooking, no doubt.' But Jillian found she could not control the smoking and drinking. 'What the hell?' was Esmée's invariable response to her objections.

The baby was a godsend, for Esmée loved to spend hours of every day watching her, fussing over her, amusing her, comforting her. 'Isn't Victoria the most perfect little mother? No baby can be as well cared-for as this little scrap,' she said one day, when Victoria had brought her a bathed and beautifully dressed Rose.

'I thought she would be. She's always loved children and has a patience with them that she didn't have for most of the other things in her life. Colin was sure I'd be lumbered with Rose but, what with you and her, I virtually have to make an appointment to see my own granddaughter.'

'He would say that.' Jillian waited to see if Esmée was going to add anything further to this comment but she didn't. Not wanting to get into a discussion on the subject of Colin, she left it at that. 'You're lucky, you're assured of immortality, you'll go on in Rose's genes,' Esmée said instead. When Esmée spoke like that, reminding Jillian of her illness, she had to look the other way or make an excuse to get out of the room quickly so that Esmée would not see her tears.

'I'm very proud of you, Jillian,' Esmée said one night, when Colin and Victoria were long in bed. They had got into the habit of sitting up late chatting of all and everything, both aware that there was not much time left.

'This house has been a joy to restore. Even the fire had its advantage. I've got the laundry room exactly as I wanted it – we'd made a mistake there, it was far too small.'

'It's all lovely, just how I imagined it would be. But it's not what I meant. I was referring to the change in you. You've "found" yourself, as dear Patsy would say. You were such a sweet, adorable wimp when you were with my brother, and now you're a woman of strength and confidence.'

'Me?' Jillian laughed. 'There was a time when I thought I'd changed but I haven't, really. There's still too much of me caving in – you know, anything for a quiet life.'

'Ah, but therein lies a subtle difference. You used to give in to Jack because you were frightened of losing him, aren't I right? But now you do it because you can't be arsed with all the hassle of explanations and arguments. You do it because *you* want to.'

'Do I?' She sounded unconvinced.

'You're still afraid of being alone, but once you've resolved that, you will be truly your own woman. The day is so close when you'll be happy to love and not beg to be loved – not like me.'

'Esmée, don't say such things. You've had so many love you.'

'Did they? Only one, I realise now, dear old Toby, and I couldn't even see it until it was too late.'

'I'm sorry.'

'Don't be. I had a measure of fun finding out. I worked out the other day that I'd never been to bed with a Russian. That was remiss of me. I've enjoyed the EC.' She signalled to Jillian that she would like another drink, which Jillian poured against her better judgement.

'Who was best?'

'They all had their little points.' She spluttered. 'I think the Spanish were the biggest disappointment even though they were Alcock and bloody Brown.'

'I don't understand.' Jillian looked perplexed.

'All cock. I adore you, Jillian, you never could get jokes.' The spluttering became full-bodied laughter. Jillian watched, as Esmée rolled in her chair holding her sides, giggling as if she hadn't a care in the world.

'Should you laugh quite so violently, Esmée?'

'Sweetness, didn't you know that if you laugh for three minutes nonstop you get an orgasm?'

'That can't be true.'

'Yes, it is, I bloody well rely on it these days!' And Esmée was laughing again.

Jillian could not be sure but she thought that Colin might be drinking again; he was becoming moody and morose. It might be whisky, but on the other hand it might be Esmée. He did not like her being here, and made no bones about it to Jillian. Nothing personal, he was at pains to explain. It was just that he was worried for Jillian, that he thought caring for an invalid who, inevitably, would get worse would be too much for her to deal with.

'She's arranged to go to a hospice when she's really bad.' She bit her lip, still unable to speak of death.

'And when it comes to it, will she want to go? And, more to the point, will you let her go? I doubt it.'

'Honestly, Colin, I think you're worrying unnecessarily.'

'I wish she wasn't here, that's all.'

'It is her house, for heaven's sake.'

'I'm aware of that. You keep telling me.'

There were times after one of these conversations when she wondered if he were not jealous of Esmée and the attention she gave her. If he was, there was nothing she could do. It was his problem. Esmée needed her.

Fenny called regularly: not only did she have Rose to keep an eye on but Esmée too. The coolness was still there, which puzzled Jillian. She'd paid Hamish handsomely for the picture, which hung in Esmée's room since she had declared she adored it.

'What's wrong with Fenny? She seems a bit odd with us these days, Jill.'

'I hardly saw them in the summer – but that's normal around here, everyone's too busy during the season. I invited them to supper a couple of times in the autumn, and now I

489

remember she was a bit stiff turning me down. I didn't think much of it until Rose came home and I couldn't ignore it.'

'Have you asked her?'

'Yes. She says, "nothing," in that way you know damn well is a lie.'

'I can't bother myself with people like that. Have it out straight, don't sulk. She never said anything to you about me?'

'No, just asked after you whenever I saw her. Did she know?'

'Oh, yes. It was the doctor here who first sent me for tests.'

'Professional discretion obviously.'

2

The season approached and, with the new fire escape constructed, the bookings came in and Jillian was excited at the prospect of new people, new experiences. Esmée was full of anticipation too. Jillian had wondered if they should open, would it be too noisy for her? 'Don't talk daft. I've plenty of peace and quiet ahead of me,' Esmée joked, precipitating another of those occasions when Jillian had to leave the room.

'Mrs Stirling, might I have a word?'

'Of course, Margaret. What is it? You look worried.'

'If I tell you something, you won't ever tell anyone I told you?'

'No, I promise,' she said, without really thinking.

'It's about your board on the glen road being vandalised and about the fire.'

'I see.' Jillian crossed the kitchen and shut the door leading to the corridor. 'Yes? You know something?' She kept her voice as calm as possible.

'I've known about the board for ages.'

'And you didn't see fit to tell me?'

'I didn't think it was my place and, in any case, it was a silly

490

prank. I didn't want to get anyone into trouble. Most of the village knew and no one else thought to tell you.'

'I wonder why that was.' She spoke with irony.

'I'm sorry, Mrs Stirling, but this is a close community here. Why, most of us are related.'

'You're sure it's not because I'm English?'

'No, not at all. There's a lot of silly talk about that. I take it with a pinch of salt myself. English or from the Lowlands, it's all the same hereabouts. If you come from the next glen you're regarded as a foreigner, it's always been like that.'

'Who was it?'

'Hamish.'

Jillian had to sit down. 'But he's a friend.'

'Of course he is, and he still is. Trouble is, he's like so many here, he drinks. He was drunk when he did it and he's very ashamed of himself. It was a joke that went too far.'

'A joke!'

'Exactly. The minister had a word with him.'

'The "wee free" minister? Am I to take it I was the only person who didn't know?'

'As I said, it's a close community.'

'Closed, more like. And the fire. Are you telling me he was responsible for that too?'

'God in heaven, no. Not Hamish, he wouldn't hurt a fly. But, you see, when he's had a dram too many he's as likely to say he knows who did. I'm afraid they might be back to do it again. And I think you should know who did it, but you should also know it wasn't the persons who did your board.'

'Thank you, Margaret, but I wish you'd told me before.'

'I'm not the only person who knows. I'm the only one who wants to help you, though, aren't I?'

'What does that mean?'

'Nothing,' Margaret said, with steadfast stubbornness.

'It was a joke that got out of hand.' Hamish, for all his size, looked as sheepish as a guilty child.

'Some joke!

'Sit ye down. I was drunk.'

'So I was told.'

491

'Who told you, I'd like to know? I'll wring their scrawny neck.'

'Apparently you've quite a choice, since the whole village and glen knew. The board was petty, childish stupidity, which I'm prepared to overlook. But the fire, that's something else.'

'I had nothing to do with that. What do you take me for?' His red beard jutted out as he glared angrily at her.

'I've been told you know who did it. If I go to the police over this, you'll have to tell them all you know.' She looked up as a stony-faced Fenny entered the room. There was no greeting between them.

'They were outsiders,' he said hurriedly.

'You would have to say that, wouldn't you?'

'Honestly, they were. Firebrands, stupid folk. Full of talk on the devolution and white settlers.'

'Why, just like you, Hamish!'

'I met them in a pub. We got talking. I said too much. I said there were strangers here, in our glen, lording it over us.' He spoke hurriedly, and she knew he was lying.

'That was unfair of you. All we were doing was trying to save a lovely house and give work to people around here.'

'Aye, and took my sister's job from her just because Ewan's got the hots for you.' Fenny spoke for the first time as she removed her raincoat.

'Fenny? What do you mean? Ewan offered me a job. I'd no idea anyone else wanted it. I assumed there was no one else suitable.'

'Of course there bloody was! You don't need to be Einstein to work at the Clansman. No one suitable! There was an army of women out there who would have given anything to have that job, and some of them with bairns.' Fenny looked close to tears.

'The people here are the salt of the earth and they can't get work and the likes of you don't help. Ever since the clearances –'

'Hamish! It's time to stop wallowing in history and move on, for heaven's sake. You'll be going on about Culloden and

Bannockburn next!' Jillian's voice was raised as, once again, the history and tragedy of Scotland was laid at her feet.

'Oh, yes, and do what? Do you know what the unemployment is around here?' The arrival of Fenny seemed to have given him his confidence back.

'Of course I do. It's dreadful but with Altnahany we're trying to do something about it, aren't we?'

'A flea-bite on an elephant's arse, that is,' Hamish interjected.

'At least I'm trying. I'm not sitting about moaning and doing nothing. If I hear of someone starting up a venture I hope it will succeed, not look forward to it failing, which so many around here do – and don't deny it, I've heard them. And if someone I know had a fire I wouldn't automatically assume they'd done it themselves for the insurance money, as people have whispered about me.'

'If it and we are so fucking awful, then why stay?' Fenny leaned forward aggressively.

'I begin to wonder, Fenny, honestly I do.' She bent to pick up her bag from the floor. 'I'm truly sorry. I thought we were friends, but with all this historical bitterness between us, how can we be?' She turned towards the door.

'It was Colin who told you, wasn't it? It was that weasel welshed on me!'

On the glen road she met Ewan driving in the opposite direction. She pulled into the passing place, shut off the engine and rolled down the window as everyone did in these parts upon meeting a friend.

'You look in a wee lather.'

'I've just seen Hamish.'

'Ah!'

'Ewan! You didn't know as well, did you?'

'I'd heard rumours.'

'And you hadn't the decency to tell me?'

'It isn't that simple, Jillian. If I reacted to every scrap of gossip I hear in the bar . . . well, it would be ridiculous.'

'But it was me. My problem.'

'And it could have been malicious spite on someone's part.

493

Someone wanting to put them down. And in any case . . .' He reached for his ignition key.

'In any case what?'

'Oh, nothing.'

'I want to know.'

'And I can't tell you. I'm the last person who can.'

'What the hell does that mean, Ewan?' But Ewan looked steadfastly ahead. 'Oh, to hell with you all. Would you kindly move your car, Ewan, and let me pass?'

Once she was home Jillian kept her own counsel. She did not want to worry either Esmée or Victoria about this. But in the middle of the afternoon she poured herself a large whisky and drank it neat in one.

'How could you?' she said, the minute Colin walked in from the office.

'How could I what?' He poured himself a drink. 'You want one? My, my, had a shock, have you?'

'Hamish called you, then. I thought he might.'

'He told me of your visit and your little display of histrionics, yes. Not very nice of you, was it? You know how passionately he feels about his country.'

'Don't prevaricate, Colin. I can't believe you kept this information to yourself. Where's your loyalty? With Hamish and not me, obviously. You let me worry and wonder, blame other people. You're a bastard, Colin!'

'It was the drink got him.'

'Don't use that excuse to me. It's too easy. And was it the drink the second time the board was damaged?'

'No. I was sober for once.'

'And then there's . . .' She sat down on the kitchen chair with a thud. 'What did you just say?'

'You heard.' He busied himself pouring another drink.

Jillian sat in silence. She wanted to speak – enough words were crashing about in her mind, but she couldn't seem to put them in any order. She didn't even know if her vocal cords would work.

'I'm sorry. It was stupid of me. I was fed up. You were all over that creep Ewan. Wanting to fill the house with babies, the dying, plenty of time for others. But when did you ever think of me?'

That last sentence was the key to her marshalling her words. 'I want you out of this house and out of my life, Colin. And quickly. Now.'

'Oh, yes, and how long for? You're useless without a man, you've told me that often enough.'

'I shall be a thousand times better off without you. You have pulled me down and you have worn my patience to zero. God, I've been such a fool! I've done nothing but think and worry about you. And for what? I've protected you, defended you, made excuses for you, and why did I bother? You're an evil, pathetic little man and I want you gone. Run back to Morag and your lovely new conservatory.'

'I might just do that. At least she loves me. At least with her I won't have to drink to stave off the boredom. No wonder Jack did a runner!'

She let it pass. She had no intention of getting into a screaming match. Hysterics now would imply she cared, and the biggest shock of all today was to find that she didn't. She wasn't even surprised to find that he was one of the culprits. She'd hung on too long to something that had probably not been there in the first place.

3

Summer 1995

The only member of the household who made any comment about Colin's hasty departure was Mary. But then, Jillian decided, as she listened to Mary's diatribe, if her mother hadn't had something to say it would have meant that the end of the world was nigh. She thanked her mother for speaking so frankly, expecting Mary to say something about her sarcasm but surprisingly she didn't.

When she saw Ewan she thanked him for his obvious concern for her in not spreading the gossip that Hamish was not alone in damaging her sign. But next time he heard anything she'd appreciate being told.

'Let's hope there isn't a next time.' Ewan smiled.

'Undoubtedly there will be. I've still to solve the mystery of the fire. Sooner or later somebody will let something slip.'

'I hate even to suggest it, Jillian, but it couldn't have been Colin, could it?'

'No. Not Colin. He wouldn't have had the guts.'

Then she endeavoured to pack away these particular years of her life in that baggage compartment of her brain where she stored all the things she thought it best not to think about too much.

'You know what you need?' Esmée asked one evening as, with a mighty storm building outside, they sat by the fire in the small sitting room. It was more economical to heat than the drawing room.

'No, but no doubt you'll tell me.' Jillian looked up from the crossword puzzle she was doing.

'A *coup de foudre*.'

'What's that when it's at home?'

'French, of course, bless them. It's when you meet a fellow and the world tilts, love at first sight, like a lightning strike.'

'Jack.'

'Probably. But that was aeons ago. You need another.'

'At the moment I think that's the last thing I need – a man complicating my life.'

'Darling, you talk as if your life's been littered with the adorable souls. And how many lovers have you had?'

'Two – him and Colin.'

'God, you're positively virginal. And Colin was never a bolt from heaven, now was he?'

'No. I liked him, I knew him, and I needed someone, I suppose. Mum goes on about him using me but, if I'm honest, I used him too.'

'Don't make excuses, sweets.'

'I'm not. It's the truth. In any case, I've got you, Victoria, Rose and my mother – my little family. I don't need a man.'

'Then get a vibrator.'

'Oh, Esmée. You're such a shocker.' She chuckled.

'So much easier than a fellow. Use it, pop it in a drawer, and you don't need to cook it breakfast.'

'You fool.'

'You say you've a family, but you know I think you're the family. Without you none of us would be here, would we? It's you who creates the love and atmosphere that draws us like moths.'

'Esmée, that's such a lovely thing to say.'

'You can rely on me.' She grinned. 'Look at me. I owe you all these months. I'd have been dead by now but for you.'

'That's you fighting it. I just help you.'

'Oh, no, Jill. You keep me going.'

With a new season approaching she had to give up the job at the Clansman. With Rose well and Esmée better than she had been for months, Fenny no longer attended them. As Jillian returned from her shift at the Clansman she stopped at Hamish's cottage.

'I'm glad I caught you in, Fenny. I've spoken to Ewan. Your sister can have my job, if she's a mind to it.'

'Come away in, Jillian.'

'No thanks. That's all I came to say.' She turned to go back to her car.

'Jillian . . .' Fenny called. 'Look, I have to tell you, I lied. My sister never wanted that job. I lied because I was embarrassed over the signs. I wanted to put some of the blame on you, I suppose. I'm sorry.'

'Thank you, Fenny. But I'm afraid it's too late.' She unlatched the gate. 'You see, I don't want your apology. You're friends of Colin, and you've shown you can't be friends of mine too.'

As she got into her car she didn't look back. The degree of satisfaction that she felt from Fenny's astonished expression and her own intransigence took her by surprise: To sit on a high horse occasionally, when she was convinced she was right was a heady, strangely comforting position to be in.

From Lachlan Pearlman there was no word. Victoria had sent

him a card when Rose was born. 'He's her father, and no matter that he's been a shit, he's a right to know,' she had declared. But there was no note, no call, no fluffy rabbit. 'I might just as well have saved on the stamp!' Victoria said airily, but Jillian wondered if she said it to cover the hurt. It angered her to see her daughter alone with the child – those weeks in hospital when the mite had been ill had been so hard for her. And Victoria had been left with the fear that Rose's problems might return. She and Esmée were as supportive as they could possibly be, but how could it be the same as having Rose's father by her side to share the worries? Ever since she'd felt uncomfortable hating Theresa, it was an emotion she had fought; it was too damaging to one's own soul. But that had changed. She hated Lachlan for what he had failed to do, and Dotty quite as much.

Running the hotel and caring for Esmée was not the problem that everyone had foreseen. Esmée was fine. She admitted now that when she had arrived at Inverness it was with a death sentence of approximately three months. But Easter had come and gone, summer had arrived and Esmée felt better than she had in years. She needed no one to care for her.

Not so Mary. Strong, indomitable Mary sitting at the kitchen table, preparing vegetables for Jillian, complained of the heat, that she felt peculiar, that her feet were all tingly, and promptly keeled over into the colander of peas. That had been a chaotic day. Rose was poorly and needing Victoria's constant attention, Gretchen was off sick and Margaret had to be sent home with a migraine. But on having to accompany the ambulance to the hospital with her mother, Jillian had discovered how kind people could be. Although the hotel was full, the guests rallied round. One, a trained chef, took over the kitchen and cooked the dinner, others finished peeling the vegetables, laid the table, turned down the beds, cleared away and washed up. Esmée had insisted that she and no one else had the experience to dispense the drinks. When everything was settled and a degree of normality returned, the guests declared they had enjoyed themselves enormously, that it was a holiday with a difference, and to a man they refused to have their bills adjusted when it was time for them to go.

If pushed, Jillian would say that she loved her mother, but there was a distance between them. Their love for each other was somehow detached, not like the deep, passionate emotion she felt for her own children; she and Mary tolerated rather than liked each other. And Mary, she was sure, had never approved of her. But seeing her mother in the tall hospital bed, in the intensive care unit, all that was changing. She was unconscious, attached to myriad wires that led Jillian knew not where and of whose function she had no idea. She sat mutely, watching monitors flicker and flash. She saw the dots and pyramids of light, listened to the eerie bleep they made, electronic wizardry charting her mother's struggle for life. As she clutched Mary's hand and felt its roughness, saw the years etched into it, she knew she had been wrong. Jillian loved her deeply. As fear crawled freely over her, she prayed as she never had in her life, to that neglected God her father had worshipped, and begged him to spare this little woman whom, she was certain, she could never live without. And if Mary survived – Jillian shuddered at that awful word *if* – she would tell her how she loved her, and prayed again that she had not left it too late.

Summoned by the doctor she bent forward, kissed her mother and whispered she would be back. She half expected her to shy away, wipe the kiss from her skin as she said, 'I've no time for kissing, dirty habit!' but, of course, she didn't, for how could she know she'd been kissed?

'The doctor says that, with strokes, the next twenty-four hours are critical. They think she's in with a chance, but at this stage they can't ascertain the long-term damage.' She trotted out the words into the telephone just as they had been said to her.

'I'm coming.'

'Bless you, Patsy, I thought you would.'

Jillian met her sister off the train. If anything, she was even larger than the last time they had been together, so many years ago now. She realised, to her shame, that she knew little of what had happened to Patsy in the meantime. Even though a couple of years ago she had said she was coming, she never had, although the invitation was always there. Her clothes were the same, a whirling cape under which were what appeared to be several black skirts, perpetually spinning as she moved. Underneath these were what looked like baggy black pantaloons. She wore a snarl of beads about her neck, a large flat floppy black velvet cap was squashed on to her long tangled hair. The world might change, and the people in it, but Patsy's look was still the same constantly moving chaos it had always been.

'How's Mum?'

'Holding her own.'

'Christ, don't medics use some daft expressions? It makes it sound as if poor old Mum is hanging on to a leash for grim death.'

'She is,' said Jillian, without expanding further. 'Thanks for coming all this way.'

'We were lucky I wasn't out on the road. It's Glastonbury next week, and then you'd never have got hold of me.'

It was not until they were in the car, her knapsack stored in the boot, for Patsy would rather be seen dead than carry a case, and on their way to the hospital, that Jillian noticed her bright-red suede boots poking out from beneath the funereal black clothing.

'Lovely boots.'

'Cosmo made them. He said I reminded him of Dorothy in *The Wizard of Oz*, and she had red shoes.'

'Who's Cosmo? The latest?'

'My son.'

In the middle of Inverness Jillian stalled the car. Flustered and apologising to the other angry drivers, she restarted it. 'You never said.'

'I didn't want anyone to know. There would have been too much weeping and gnashing of teeth.'

'How old is he?'

'Twenty.'

'Does Mum know?'

'No. God forbid! He was adopted at birth. You know me, I never wanted children, best thing for him. You still not smoking?'

'Yes, but I don't mind if you do. Did he come and find you?'

'He did. I always knew he would when he was good and ready.'

'And you get on with him?'

'Wonderfully. We haven't got all that usual crap in the way – you know, the baggage that families gather. We met, we sussed each other and we liked, end of story. You're still a size six, aren't you? I bought you a grey pair, also Cosmo's. You used to only wear white and grey, now I see we've changed.'

Sitting at traffic lights, Jillian adjusted the collar of her pillar-box red dress. 'When Jack left, I altered my look. I suppose I was making a statement. Not straight away, but over the years. My wardrobe is as much of a mess as most people's now, colour-wise,' she added.

'I'm glad of that. Still tidy, though?'

'Sorry, but yes,'

'Don't apologise to me. You must be and do how *you* wish not how you think others want you to.'

'Still pontificating, I see.'

'Some things, my dear sister, never change.'

As they walked side by side into the hospital and climbed the stairs, Jillian was aware of what an odd couple they must make: she tall, slim, fair and neat, Patsy short, plump, dark and chaotic. In the same way that they didn't look like sisters, so they were different in character and attitudes. The nurture theorists should forget it, she thought.

As she watched Patsy fussing about her mother's bed, chatting to her, holding the hand she had sat patiently and held, she felt suddenly shut out again, as she often had in the past. As if Patsy's bustling manner was telling her, 'This is my mother, my responsibility, you're not needed any more.' She found she minded, in a way she had not minded way back in time.

'Mum, it's me, Patsy. What an old show-off you are!'

'Patsy!' Her mother had at last clawed her way back into consciousness. 'I knew you'd come,' she said before, with a contented smile, she slipped back into a deep sleep.

Jillian stood up from the hard chair which, for the last twenty-four hours, had been her perch. 'If you don't mind I'd like to go home, wash and change.' Her mother gaining consciousness at Patsy's voice, not hers, made her feel that Mary thought she was redundant too.

'You run along. We can manage now I'm here.'

From having been so seriously ill Mary's recovery was relatively fast. No one was surprised: that she had never had much truck with ill-health was another of the things she was fond of saying. She was left with a weakness on the right side, which would make looking after herself difficult, cooking dangerous, and she would be unable to get in and out of the bath. She would need physiotherapy for some time, her speech was slow and hesitant, but she was expected to do well.

'We can manage. I'll move her over here and we can let her cottage.'

'She won't like that.' Patsy was in the kitchen cooking herself a mess of tofu and vegetables. This daily ritual was a trial to Jillian for Patsy cooked with more passion than order. A strict vegan, she was suspicious of Jillian's kitchen, and had insisted that all the surfaces be scrubbed and cleaned with Dettox each time before she began, in case a trace of animal lurked there. This insulted Margaret, who was proud of the way she kept the kitchen spotless.

'There's no alternative, I can't run the hotel and keep popping back and forth to hers all day long. And I can't afford to employ someone full time to look after her. She'll have to move here.'

'I can stay for a month or two, get her back on her feet, or she can come with me. Which do you think?'

'I think that's up to Mum to decide, don't you?' Jillian did not like the idea of having Patsy here for a few months one little bit. 'Not now, though. I think we should give her a few days before we ask her.'

The initial euphoria of greeting her sister and hearing her news, of marvelling at her lifestyle and being curious, was wearing thin. Already there were signs that she was annoying Patsy by not understanding the importance of things like crystals and mantras, ley-lines and so on, which were of the utmost significance to her.

Jillian racked her brains, trying to remember how close they once had been, how happy with each other's company. But she couldn't. She could recall arguments, rows, accusations about possessions touched, borrowed, swiped, but no closeness, no happiness with each other. She knew she loved her, but was certain she didn't like her. But then she began to wonder about the love: she realised that not seeing Patsy for all those years hadn't bothered her, nor did the prospect of not seeing her in the future either. Some love! Poor Mary kept on about what a close family they were, but Jillian could not see it and doubted if it had ever been so.

'You've really found your niche here, haven't you, Jillian? A whole hotel means you can cook and do housework to your heart's delight,' Patsy said, as they sat round the table over a glass of wine.

'You make it sound as if that's all there is to Jillian,' Esmée said quietly.

'Well, that's so, isn't it? That and being a glorified geisha girl.'

'Are you drunk?'

'No, Esmée.'

'Then you are inexcusably rude.'

'Why? It's true. Jillian has devoted her life to caring for others, I'd have said that was highly commendable. After all, Esmée, you and I haven't exactly gone in for selflessness, have we?'

Jillian's head swivelled from one to the other as if at a tennis tournament.

'But that's not what you meant, is it, Patsy dear?' Esmée's smile was deceptively sweet. 'You were being a supercilious bitch. If you'd done anything with your life I might be able to find one iota of forgiveness. As it is, since you're just a layabout, I can't.'

'And you've succeeded with your life? Ha! What have you done?'

'Nothing. But then I'm not trying to be superior or patronising to anyone. Jillian works her cotton socks off in a difficult profession and comes up trumps. There's nothing housewifely about this operation.'

'She's slinging hash, like she's always done. Aided by her bloody lists, which prove how anally retentive she is.'

'Oh, yes? You think it's that easy? Jillian cooks like the professional she's become. You try getting the same menu spot on every time it's served. She can't have an off-day, the meat can't be tough one day and not the next. The punters look for consistency, and that's what she gives them. And,' Esmée got to her feet, 'while we're about it, I do hope you're not staying much longer. I find your attitude to my friend offensive. Now, if you'll excuse me, I'm off to bed.'

She left the room.

'I never did like that stuck-up cow. All trust funds and Lady Bountiful.'

'Don't even start belittling Esmée. She's worth a dozen of you.'

'What a sweet sister you are.'

'Yes, we're sisters, but only by accident. Esmée's more a real sister to me. I've never understood you, but the difference now is that I don't care that I don't.'

'You're jealous, aren't you? You always have been, just because Mum and Dad preferred me.'

'Yes, okay, I'm jealous. I'm jealous about Mum because I think it's unfair of her. I've done a lot for her and –'

'I thought your sort didn't expect rewards, that you do it for Love!'

'You're right. I don't look for thanks, but if you'd let me finish I'd have said that what struck me as unfair is that you do absolutely nothing. You merely swan in and she's all over you.'

'Of course. It's what being the favourite is all about. I've always been able to twirl them round my little finger.'

'And what about poor old Dad? Accusing him of molesting you.'

'He did.'

'Liar.'

'I was having hypnotic-regression treatment and it all came out then.' Patsy leaned forward angrily.

'Then it's false-memory syndrome that makes you think Dad touched you. And you bloody well know it.'

'Are you angry he didn't do it to you?' Patsy gloated.

'He wouldn't have touched any child, but least of all you. He made more fuss of you because he felt sorry for you – oh, you were clever enough, but I was beautiful while you were fat and ugly and he felt he had to try to make you feel better about yourself. And don't say I'm making it up because I'm not. He told me.'

Patsy lumbered to her feet, somewhat unsteadily after the amount of wine she'd drunk. 'You bitch!'

'I'd never have said that, but you persist in blackening our father's name and I won't have it. He loved us. As a dad. That's all.'

To her horror Patsy burst into tears. Big, ugly, rasping sobs shook her body. Jillian looked at her, put out her hand as if to touch her, but changed her mind. Her days of being a hypocrite were over.

Mary opted to go with Patsy. 'I can't say I enjoy the winters here, too cold by far. I think God either got bored or forgetful when he was making Scotland – all this beauty and he messes it up with midges and cleggies.'

'Are you sure, now, Mum? You know you're welcome here.'

'Jillian, you've enough on your plate with the business and Esmée, who surely will be getting worse soon. In any case, I've always fancied a commune. You never know, I might find myself a nice toy-boy who plays the guitar and wears leathers.'

Jillian was not sure how she felt about her mother leaving. On the one hand she had to admit to relief – it would have been hard looking after her as well as everything else. On the other hand, there was the disappointment that once again her mother had preferred Patsy. But, then, there was Mary's excitement at the new lifestyle she was embarking upon and it would be a hard-hearted person who put objections in her way. Saying goodbye to Patsy was easy.

Opening up the extra rooms to guests had been their saving. The occupancy rate, while still not as high as they wanted, was holding, and once people learned of them by word of mouth more bookings would come. The restaurant side was doing well. The locals liked the traditional food she served, the price at which she offered it and the kick they all got out of eating at Aunt Fiona's lodge which, in her day, had been closed to them.

.The season almost over, it was clear that she would pick up winter trade in the shape of functions. Already she had had inquiries from a bank and a firm of solicitors, not Colin's, asking about the tariff for office parties.

When Colin had left there had been silence from him for a month. But then the phone calls and letters began.

'Morag must have got fed up with him faster than I thought.'

'You won't take him back?' Victoria asked anxiously.

'No way. I'll never forgive him and, to be quite honest, I don't think I want to be involved with anyone else for ages.'

'What about Ewan?'

'Ewan and I are friends.'

'Pull the other one.' Victoria sniggered.

'Honestly. I value my friendship with him too much to contemplate an affair. That would spoil everything.'

'You don't hanker after Jack?' Esmée asked, from the sofa on which she was lying with her feet up.

Jillian thought for a moment. 'I think part of me will always love Jack. We had good times and I've the children to thank him for. But the trust was destroyed and when that goes . . .' She shrugged her shoulders dismissively.

Despite the isolation of Altnahany, Victoria had a steady stream of boyfriends who were brought in to be introduced and mostly never seen again. 'I've got to be careful who I choose next time. He's got to love Rose almost as much as me. And I've got to be certain he's right. I can't have a constant turnover of "uncles" in her life, can I? Why are you smiling? What have I said?'

'I was just thinking how Colin said that you would be an awful mother. How wrong could he be?'

'Oh, that creep, he was wrong about everything.'

4

Spring–Summer 1997

Another Christmas and New Year, another season came and went, Jillian's life had settled into a busy but satisfying routine. She was happy. The joy of watching her granddaughter grow, seeing her every day so that she had become a very special person in this little girl's life, was an added blessing. Jillian felt some days as if she had always been at Altnahany, and her past, especially the painful experiences, became a misty, shadowy otherworld, set in another time.

Esmée, who had come home to die, had astounded the medical profession for two and a half years. Tests and X-rays showed that her cancer had gone into remission and Jillian allowed herself to hope that it had disappeared for ever.

It was a different Esmée, though, a more settled, content woman, as if the trial she had been through had taught her what was best in life and what to appreciate most. She might talk of trips she intended to take, of lovers she would one day find, but she never went on them or searched. She read voraciously, catching up she called it, for she had always been too rushed before. She took long, healthy walks on the moor and in the forests. She ate sensibly, but still smoked and drank far too much. Jillian never interfered for Esmée was well, and that was all that mattered. Better not to change anything, she frequently told herself, when pouring another drink for her friend.

Spring was always late in these parts. Jillian would watch the television news and see cherry blossom blooming in southern streets and gardens, and would despair of it ever reaching Scotland. But she also knew that when it came it would be in a rush. Bare winter trees would suddenly turn green as if spring was making up for its tardiness. When it arrived the people changed she was certain. The long, cruel battle with the winter cold and blizzards behind them, they smiled more, were friendlier.

'Hamish!' She knew she sounded surprised as she opened the back door to find his bulk blocking out the light.

'I'm away and I wanted to talk.' He looked embarrassed as he shuffled his huge feet.

'You'd better come in. It's still cold, despite the sun.' Even though it was mid-morning she collected the whisky bottle and a glass from the dresser, and poured a large measure without asking.

'Slàinte.' He lifted the glass, downed it in one and she poured another.

'You're going away, you say. Where?'

'I've a job out Ullapool way, and Fenny's got a transfer.'

'That's good. So you came to say goodbye?'

'Aye.'

They sat in silence. 'You wanted to talk?'

'Aye.'

'Well?' Such taciturnity was completely out of character for Hamish.

'It's about the fire.' Again he paused. She wondered whether to prompt him, but decided to hold her tongue.

'I told you. I knew. That they were foreigners.'

'Yes?'

'I lied.'

'Yes.'

'I'm telling you this because I respect you and I think you should be told. Only Colin said I wasn't to, that it might make matters worse. That you'd go to the police. But I think he's wrong and you'd be right.'

'Yes.'

'Big Jo.'

'But I don't know anyone of that name.' She looked puzzled.

'He was instructed. He didnae want to, but his job depended on it – he said.'

'Who employs him?' It was a question that hardly needed asking. 'The Pearlmans, that's who you're going to say, aren't you?'

'Aye. That besom Dotty. An evil woman.'

'He – this Big Jo – didn't *have* to do anything.'

'But he did. He'd been cheating with their benefits and she knew. She threatened to shop him, and him with five bairns, and he'd done it before and he'd have gone to prison this time.'

'And Colin knew, you say?'

'Aye. He knew. He said he felt sorry for Big Jo.'

'Great.' She smiled briefly. 'Poor Big Jo mustn't be punished!'

'But nothing happened to you. And the insurance paid.'

'That's hardly the point, is it, Hamish? Oh, forget it,' she said, since she knew there was no point in pursuing this conversation with him.

She drove towards the Pearlmans, but parked first outside the croft where Hamish had told her Big Jo lived with his cluster of children. Although the view of the valley was gorgeous, it was a depressing place. The garden looked like a scrap-merchant's yard with rusting cars, bikes, old refrigerators among the rabbit hutches and strewn plastic toys. Jillian got out of her car.

'And to what do we owe this pleasure?' Dotty said sarcastically, upon opening the door to her. 'Money, I presume?'

'Don't panic, Dotty. We're managing fine. No, I've come to discuss the matter of a fire at Altnahany three years ago. You must have read about it in the papers? We even made it on to the TV.' She could hear her voice, calm and conversational in contrast to the anger seething inside her.

'I heard you were blaming us. I warn you, Jillian, if you persist I shall be forced to sue you for defamation.'

'Dotty, you've got it all wrong.' She used a patient tone this time. 'If anyone's going to be doing any suing it'll be me. You had that fire lit. You might hide behind an employee but I'm telling you I know it was you who hired him. Big Jo – he lives down the glen in squalor, mainly thanks to you.'

'What balderdash. Just because your daughter accuses my son of fathering her brat you do this to me.'

'Don't you dare refer to Rose as a brat! Ever. Understood? She's a lovely child – shame about the father. I know it was you, Dotty. Unfortunately for you, Big Jo has told me it was. And . . .' she delved into her handbag and produced a small tape-recorder Esmée had loaned her '. . . gave me permission to record him.'

Dotty made a grab for it, but she was heavy and cumbersome in her movements and Jillian moved away easily.

'If you'll calm down, Dotty, I've a proposition to put to you. You know, your colour is quite alarming. Sit down.' Dotty, as if hypnotised, did as she was told. Jillian remained standing. 'I can go to the police, of course I can, and you would be in serious trouble. Society here would drop you like a hot potato. But this is my proposal. You blackmailed that man into being an arsonist. I won't go to the police if you, one, double his wages and pay his National Insurance – as you should have done all along. I can see no point in his going to prison. Think of his poor children.'

'But –'

'No buts, Dotty. You're listening to me. Two, I want you to resign from the council. You're not fit to serve. Three, Lachlan pays all the money he owes Victoria. Rose was two last December. I'm afraid it'll be a tidy sum. And,' she held up her hand, 'he must continue monthly payments until Rose finishes her education.'

'You bitch!'

'Dotty, don't goad me. I want all three of these complied with. Fail in one of them and I'm off to the police.'

'This is blackmail.'

'Well, you'd be the one to know, wouldn't you?' She turned on her heel. 'Oh, and by the way, Dotty, no more fires, no accidents to come my way. I'm depositing this at my bank – just in case. Better to be on the safe side. 'Bye!'

Once back in her car she realised she was shaking. But 'Yes' she punched the air in imitation of Victoria. She'd handled that well, she congratulated herself.

A week later Victoria appeared in the door of the office. 'Mum, the oddest thing's happened: I've had a cheque from Lachlan for all the money he owes me. Isn't that extraordinary?'

'Must have had a guilty conscience after all.' Jillian smiled to herself.

With a start Jillian realised that this year she'd be fifty. 'How on earth could that be? It's a government plot, they're shortening the years. I can't be nearly fifty!'

'Sorry, poppet. It comes to us all. Start going backwards.'

'But the forties just scudded by. Where has all the time gone? What did I do with all those days?'

'Lived, loved and, hopefully, enjoyed. Well ... in the circumstances, some of them.' Esmée smiled. 'But don't flap. You're still lovely. You could pass any day for early forties.' She sat upright on the sofa, suddenly alert. 'We should have a party. We haven't had a party for so long. I miss parties ...'

'Do you think I want the world to know how old I am? No party,' she said, decisively.

In this house of women, and she counted Rose as one, there was a great harmony. She found that she and Victoria rarely argued there days, and she and Esmée never did. But sometimes she looked to the future and wondered what her life would be like when Victoria married, as no doubt she would, and Esmée ... but she couldn't even finish that thought.

One decision she made was to get divorced. She had put it off for too long. She wondered why. She rejected the idea that it was because she longed to be with Jack – she didn't. Maybe her mother had been right, that she used being married as an excuse not to marry anyone else. With Colin gone there was no need to hide any more – perhaps.

Since she and Jack had been apart for ten years it was a simple affair, and more so since she made no claim upon him. She had expected to find it depressing, but instead she felt nothing: it was just another load of forms to sign.

Ewan was her constant companion. Since the evening at the Clansman when Colin had fallen asleep he had never said another word about them being involved. She was grateful: she had told Victoria the truth. She really did value her friendship with him too much to put it at risk.

So, Ewan would join them for dinner at Altnahany one week and she, on her own, would dine at the Clansman with him the next. They would go to the theatre together and to the cinema. Once they'd gone to a catering fair in Birmingham. Victoria would not believe that they hadn't gone to bed with each other.

'There's more to life than sex.'

'Who says?' replied Victoria.

'Darling, you're not *that* old,' Esmée added.

Sometimes she wondered how she would feel if he appeared one day with a woman and announced that he was getting married. She was honest enough to admit that she wouldn't like it, but knew she'd wish him well.

5

Winter 1997

The day she had dreaded arrived. She answered a knock at the front door early one morning, before anyone else was about, to find Miles.

'Surprise!' he said brightly, pulled her to him and hugged her tight. 'I thought I'd just arrive, no warning.'

'What's up?'

'Why should there be anything "up"?' He laughed. 'You're getting like Gran! Any chance of a fry-up? I'm starving.'

'Of course. Get your bag later.' She led the way.

'No kitchen in the world smells like yours.' He was sniffing the air appreciatively. 'Is the hotel closed?'

'Yes. I've a couple of functions booked, not much else. It's for the best . . . Esmée has had a bad bout of bronchitis. She's stopped going to see her specialist. I nag her that she should. Then it's –' She stopped, realising he wasn't listening to her, but was staring distractedly into space. 'Are you all right?'

'Sorry. I'm tired, that's all. I drove through the night. You were saying?'

'It's Rose's third birthday next week. All the nursery-school children are coming and I've got a clown . . . You're not interested, Miles, not like you usually are. Something's happened. Please tell me.' She did not finish the sentence. Miles's face seemed to melt like wax and he sank, as if in slow motion, on to the nearest chair. He did not even cover his face, but allowed the tears to roll down his cheeks untouched. Immediately she was beside him, her arms around him. The years fell away and she was holding a young Miles whose bicycle had been stolen, the 'there, there' and the 'it'll be all right' were the same words she'd used then, she was sure.

'I found her . . . Shit, I can't even say it.' His face screwed up in disgust.

'Then don't even try.'

He shook his shoulders as if attempting to gain control. 'We went to a hunt ball. We always go . . . I missed Maxine . . . a friend said she'd gone . . . powder her nose . . . Tony's room . . . she said . . . we'd booked rooms, you see, what with the drink-driving . . . I went. Like a bloody fool I went . . . and I found them. Humping away . . . Tony's my best friend. Stupid how it makes it worse.' The disjointed account came to an end. Jillian sat silent, unsure what to say or even if he'd finished. 'So that's that,' he added. 'It's been coming a long time. But not like that, Mum. Not like that.' Now he covered his face with his hands as if to blot out some memory. 'All I see is Tony's bare, fat arse and my wife's splayed legs. I can't rid myself of it.'

'Oh, darling, I don't know what to say to help you. If only I could. If only there were magic words.'

'If I hadn't gone looking for her –'

'It would still have happened. You can't make it not happen, Miles. I'll make some tea.' That panacea for all their ills, she thought, as she put the kettle on.

Miles sat silent and then, as if the mundanity of her actions

513

calmed him, he began to talk, a long monologue of pain. She leaned against the cooker and let him get on without interruption. There was no satisfaction in knowing she'd been right. How much she wished she could have been wrong. 'None of our friends wanted us to get married. They said it wouldn't last. You were about the only person who didn't warn me.'

'And what if I had? Would you have listened?' She stood, tea-caddy in one hand, spoon in the other.

'Probably not.'

'Do you know if there have been others?' She loathed this conversation, loathed the woman who had made it necessary.

'I've heard rumours. Well, more than that, actually. A couple of mates tipped me off, said she was being unfaithful with a couple of blokes in our group of friends. I couldn't believe it. I bit their heads off and said I never wanted to speak to them again.' Once more he was off, telling her the sorry tale, the incompatibility, the awful, dawning realisation that it would not work, the incipient boredom. 'What I don't understand is, if I as much as looked at a woman she'd go ape-shit.' Wrong again, thought Jillian. She'd thought Maxine cold and unfeeling, apparently she was not. But then, she found herself thinking, women so often were bad judges of whether another woman was sexy, passionate or not. 'She was even jealous of you, called me a mummy's boy for phoning you each week.'

Jillian heard his words, the accusation, and nodded as if to affirm she wasn't surprised. The doubts, the dislike, the suspicions she had of Maxine always with her, but corralled in the back of her mind rattled free and mounted until she felt a surge of anger and loathing so strong it made her feel physically sick. She could quite happily have murdered both Maxine and Lachlan at this moment. Nothing changes. Victoria might be twenty-five and Miles thirty but she still felt the same protectiveness, the same need to keep them out of harm's way, to make them happy, to fill every waking day with joyful memories. They were still her children. She stood in her kitchen, and her own tears fell, at her inability to help, the impossibility of easing her son's pain. And she knew, without a doubt, that like other women she might play the charade of letting go, but it could never be. The cord remained, and their sorrow was hers.

Victoria had no inhibitions about telling her brother exactly what she thought of his wife. Jillian would not permit herself the same luxury. She had lived too long and knew that, despite how he felt now, whatever he said, how wildly he ranted, he might return to Maxine and any bitter words she had said could only create a damaging barrier between them. For, once said, maybe they would never be forgotten. And although she sympathised, although she entered enthusiastic-ally into his plans for the future – he wanted to join her at Altnahany – she said not one word against her daughter-in-law.

'Why do you always sit on the fence, Mum?'

'I'm not, Victoria. I'm seething inside. I loathe her, I wish she'd fall down a black hole. But I can't say it to him, don't you see?' Fortunately she was making bread and her energetic kneading of the dough released some of her anger.

'That should rise beautifully,' Esmée said, from the kitchen stool where she was perched, a drink in her hand. 'Your mother's right. She's the last person who can say a word.'

'Why? He says he hates her.'

'He probably does – for the time being. He's permitted to say it, Jill can't.'

'I say it.'

'Yes, and unwisely, Victoria. The world is full of people who have been dropped by friends to whom they said what they really thought of their partners.'

'If he goes back to her, will you have her to stay again?'

'With difficulty.' Jillian punched the dough.

'If he goes back I hope he makes her take an Aids test.'

'Oh, the folly of youth!' Esmée laughed.

'Altnahany, may I help you?' Jillian answered the phone.

'Is my husband there?'

'Maxine, hello.' She injected as much normality into her voice as she could.

'Is he?'

'He's out at the moment, walking the dog.'

'And I'm supposed to believe that?'

'Since it's the truth, yes.' Calm, she told herself.

'I'd have bet he'd come running to you. Typical!'

'Maxine, I don't know why you're being like this with me. Come on, it's not necessary.'

'Not necessary!' Maxine screeched, so loudly that Jillian had to pull the receiver away from her ear. 'From what I hear, all you've ever done is interfere in my marriage'

'Maxine, that's not fair. I haven't. I –'

'Oh, stuff it up your arse for all I care.' And the receiver went dead.

Esmée looked up from the book she was reading. 'The little wifey, I presume?'

'She's just been so rude to me. I can't believe what she's just said.' Jillian sat down in a daze.

'Little drinkie-poos needed here, methinks, sweets.' Esmée, with difficulty, stood up. 'I'm fine.' She waved Jillian away. 'I've been sitting too long and got stiff. What did she say?'

'Esmée, are you all right?'

'Don't flap!'

'She said I interfered.'

'What did you expect? If you were banged up in a closed order having taken a vow of silence, your son's wife would still say the same of you. You might just as well have done all the spuddling in the world, you'll be accused of it in any case. Now, if she said you fussed and worried too much, I'd agree. Drink that, it's Great Aunt Esmeralda's special dry martini.'

'Wow!' Jillian exclaimed, upon taking a sip.

'I reckon if I'd been so unfortunate as to be a mother-in-law I'd have died of cirrhosis of the liver in the first year of my son's *blissful* marriage!'

When Miles returned from his walk with Prince, Jillian told him of Maxine's call but refrained from telling him its content.

'You should have said something to cover your back,' said Esmée, once Miles had left the room to phone her back.

'Say what?'

'Defend yourself against the lying bitch.' Esmée moved on the sofa in the way of one trying to find a more comfortable position.

'Do you need some medicine?' Jillian asked her. Esmée was in pain, she could see, she knew the signs. 'Esmée, something's wrong?' She felt fear for her friend clutch at her.

'I didn't want to worry you.'

'Esmée! You must tell me.'

'It's nothing, really. Not like in the past. It's just an ache here.' She rubbed her stomach.

'How long have you had it?'

'Oh, just a day or two.'

'Esmée!'

'Well, a week.'

'Shall I call the doctor?' She was on her feet.

'I think another large martini might help.' Esmée smiled at her.

'The doctor told you not to drink.'

'Darling. Doctors have been telling me that for years. It helps, honestly.'

Jillian got up to mix it for her.

An hour later she wished she had told him something. Miles was prowling about the drawing room, picking up ornaments, inspecting them, then replacing them, though Jillian doubted he had really looked at any of them. She sat apparently reading when, in fact, she was steeling herself.

'Did you have to be rude to Maxine, Mother? It makes it difficult for me.'

She always hated it when Miles called her Mother rather than Mum: it always meant that he was about to be serious or angry. She closed her book slowly to give her time to think what to reply. 'Maxine says I was rude? Well, I wasn't. I didn't want to tell you what transpired, I was fully aware how difficult it could make things for you.'

'Exactly. So please don't speak to her like that again.'

'Have you not been listening, Miles? I said I was not horrible to her. In fact, quite the opposite.'

'Look, I don't know who said what to whom. It's just that I'd rather you didn't interfere.' He was playing agitatedly with the curtain tie-back, swinging the heavy rope back and forth, as if the large tassel was a silent bell.

Jillian stood up and picked up her book, checking carefully that the bookmark was in place. 'There seems little point in continuing this conversation since you don't intend to listen to what I've been saying. Of course it's right that you should take your wife's side in matters. I commend your loyalty. But I must repeat, I didn't lie to you, I've never lied to you.'

'Really? Who never told us what a bastard our father was? Who thought it best we didn't know that Dad was a by-blow of Granny Theresa's? If you can fib about things like that, what else can you lie about?'

'Stupidly, it transpires, I was protecting you and him, as I tried to tonight. Don't worry, Miles. I'll never bother again. Still, I presume from this conversation that you have decided to go back to Maxine?'

'I overreacted. It wasn't how I thought it was. Tony made her, he was forcing himself upon her. I arrived in the nick of time and saved her.'

'How gallant.' How could he be so gullible? She straightened an ornament. 'But before you go, Miles, there's just one thing I'd like to say. I sincerely hope that it works out for you. But I have to say that I don't believe her, I think she's lying and if saying that means I'm interfering in your affairs so be it. You may forgive her for what she has done, but don't expect me to. Don't ever imagine I can forget the pain she caused you.' She spoke calmly, deliberately, holding her book close to her, forcing herself to appear controlled.

'How is it that sometimes you can be so cold and reasonable about important things, Mum?'

'Miles, you can be so wrong about so many things!'

Jillian saw Esmée weakening before her eyes. The speed with which the disease took hold once more was terrifying. Esmée had refused to see the doctor, as if by doing so she felt she was admitting that it was back. But eventually even her stoicism faltered. Jillian felt a dreadful helplessness, which she combated by making tempting dishes to persuade her friend to eat more. She offered hot drinks, drives in the car, chocolates, ice cream, a crescendo of attention that she knew was useless, but what else could she do?

Esmée bore her ministrations patiently, and with surprising good humour when she'd been at such pains to tell her she hated anyone fussing over her. Even as her body betrayed her Esmée's spirit soared. She talked constantly of the future, plans for the house and Rose of which they both knew she would not be a part. She joked, she minimised her plight. The world still interested her. The hospice was never mentioned. Jillian hoped it never would be. She wanted to care for her until the end, not out of duty but because she loved her. Esmée's trauma put Maxine's lying and unpleasantness and Miles's attitude firmly into place for her. She was there if Miles needed her, that was all she could do. He would have to get on with it, she had other cares now.

And then there was Rose. She found with her granddaughter that so much of the hope and love she had had for her own children was, in some strange way, transferring to this little one. She tried not to let it happen, fearing the time when Rose would leave with her mother for another home and another life. But she found there was little she could do about it. The toddler ruled her heart far more strongly than any lover could.

'You'll never believe what's happened!' Victoria catapulted into the room, Rose bouncing on her hip. She was laughing, her hair awry, her cheeks red from the cold, exuding youth, health and happiness.

'You're in love,' Esmée volunteered, from the deep chair in which she spent most of the day now.

'How did you know?'

'Only a woman in love looks as you do, sweets. I can still remember, you know.'

'It was incredible. I mean we saw each other across the station buffet, it was like a scene from *Brief Encounter* and that

519

was it. I looked at him, my insides felt like water, my legs felt wobbly and I thought my heart was about to burst.'

'And the scientists say it's chemical. Poor sods can't ever have been in love.'

'Has it happened to you, Mum?'

'Once.'

'Who? Go on.'

'Need you ask, Victoria?' Esmée smiled kindly at her.

'Dad?'

'Yes, at a May Ball. I saw him getting a bottle of champagne and I knew I could love him. There's not a lot you can do about it when it happens – except hope it happens to him too.' Jillian continued with the tapestry cushion she was making.

'But it did. That's what's so brilliant. Murray looked at me and he said, "Wow," and we both knew.'

'So expressive!' Esmée drawled. 'What does he do?'

'He's a motor mechanic.'

'What a sensible choice. I always regret not having had a mechanic or a plumber as a lover. They'd have saved me a fortune.'

'Where's he from?' Jillian tried to make the question sound as low key as possible, praying she wouldn't say Australia or even Land's End.

'Fort William.' Jillian could have cried with relief. 'He has no money but I said that didn't matter, neither had I. He loves kids and Rose went a bundle on him. And I've invited him for the weekend, if that's all right?'

6

New Year 1998

Esmée slept in her tower room on the first floor and Jillian was at the back of the house in her old room. Beside her bed was the mobile phone, in case Esmée needed her. 'Like a baby alarm,' Esmée said.

Jillian was deeply asleep. It had been a busy month. She'd

met Murray and his parents, and the obvious love between him and Victoria had lifted a weight from her mind. It must have, for these days she slept better than she had for ages.

The birdlike chirping of the telephone penetrated her brain. 'Jill, darling, can you come? I'm in a bit of a pickle.'

Flinging on her dressing-gown, stepping over a disgruntled Prince, who was annoyed at being woken, Jillian flew down the stairs, through the hall and up the main staircase to Esmée's room.

'What is it?' Her heart, already pounding, jumped as if about to leap from her body at the sight of Esmée, on the floor, covered in blood. 'Hell, what happened?'

'I wanted to pee. Suddenly I felt so odd. Next thing I'm down here, covered in blood like something from the Rue Morgue.'

'Don't joke!' Jillian snapped, with agitation. 'Have you broken something?' In the half-light, she was feeling frantically for broken bones.

'Darling, it's coming from inside me.' Esmée's voice was weak. 'Jill, I'm so scared. And I've wet myself.'

'It doesn't matter. And there's nothing to be scared about.'

'Well, that's a load of crap if ever I heard one!' Esmée, despite the panic, despite the blood, despite her pain, laughed.

'Where's it coming from?'

'My mouth. I felt sick and then . . . It's stopped now. Christ, it hurts, though.' Esmée was covered in beads of sweat, yet the night was chilly.

'Can I get you up? Should I let you lie there? Esmée, I don't know what to do.' She felt more useless than she ever had before, even worse than when Victoria was having Rose.

'If you put your arm under me, maybe I can haul myself up.'

'But should we?'

'I'm not bloody lying here freezing to death. There has to be a more comfortable way to go!'

Esmée was now so thin that it was the easiest thing for Jillian to pick her up and gently place her on the bed. 'I'll call the doc.'

'Hang on, Jill. What's the point? You know, I know, that it's only a matter of time. Christ, I've had so much more than they expected.'

'But the pain. He can help you with the pain, and don't say you haven't got any because I can tell from your eyes. I've got to do something. I've got to help you in some way.'

Esmée patted the bed. 'Jill, my sweet, what he gives me is not working like it did. I didn't tell you, I didn't want you fussing. But, don't you see? It's over. The drugs aren't working. I'm dying.'

'Don't say that!'

'It's got to be said. You say it.'

'I can't. I won't.'

'Not saying it isn't going to make it go away. I'm scared enough without you being scared too.'

'Please let me call him.'

'No, I don't want him here. I've got something. You see that box over there? Can you get it for me?'

Jillian crossed the room and picked up a beautiful inlaid Regency box, which she had often admired, and carried it back to the bed. 'There's a key.' Esmée fumbled on her bedside table. 'Sod, I can't do it. My fingers won't work, they're shaking so.'

'What is it? What do you want?'

'Help me, Jill, in there . . .'

Jillian unlocked the box. Among the letters, the odd theatre programme, coloured ribbons from long-dead bouquets nestled a small vial. She picked it up, looked at it and then at Esmée. 'What's this?'

'I'm not going to tell you. What you don't know . . .'

'No.' Jillian put the vial back in the box and slammed it shut.

'Please, Jill, let me have it. A friendly doctor in Mexico made it up for me. I'll just go to sleep, no more pain. It's not detectable. No one will ever know.'

'I'd know. I'm calling the doctor.'

That night was long. The doctor had come. Later, in her kitchen, he marvelled at Esmée's courage. 'Her pain is considerable. She refuses point-blank to go to hospital. And I can't make her, though she would be more comfortable there, Jillian.'

'We can manage.'

'It's going to be hard.'

'I don't mind. I love her.'

'Quite.' He looked away, as if embarrassed by her words. As if love had no place with death. 'I've given her a large dose of analgesic and I'll call again in the morning after surgery. Until then, when that wears off, give her this and this. It will help.' He placed a collection of bottles on the table from his bag.

'What happened, Doctor?'

'I fear she had a stomach haemorrhage and, of course, there's always the chance of another. Her liver is failing fast – did you note the jaundiced colour?'

'No, I didn't. But now you mention it, the last few weeks – how stupid of me! Doctor, do you know how long before she . . . dies?' She said it, but brushed at her mouth as if to take the word away.

'I hate to say. I've had patients I thought wouldn't last the night and they've gone on for weeks. And others I thought had months didn't last a day. But not long, Jillian. I think, for her sake, we have to hope it's quick.'

If she had thought that that night was long, the next day was longer and the following night interminable. Victoria, eyes full of terror and compassion, helped her try to make the poor, wasted body more comfortable. There were moments of blessed relief when Esmée slept, more coma than fitful sleep. Once she called Toby's name and Jillian wished she had ignored her and phoned him as she had wanted to.

When Esmée screamed, and thrashed in the bed, clawing at her skin as if to wrest the pain away, Jillian knew what she had to do. She opened the box, took out the vial and picked up the orange juice to mix it. Then she changed her mind. She ran down the stairs to the drawing room and grabbed two bottles.

'Mum!' Victoria stood on the landing. 'Do you need me?'

'No, darling. She's fine. She wants a gin, would you

believe?' She bit back the tears and forced a laugh. 'Go to bed, I'll call you if I need you.'

Once more in the room, Esmée awake now, her dark eyes following every movement, Jillian mixed the liquid with the gin and a breath of vermouth. 'Here you are, my darling.' She sat on the side of the bed, gently lifted Esmée into a sitting position and cradled her in one arm. 'Here's your Mexican special, sweets.'

'Bless you.' Esmée grabbed the glass. Jillian helped her guide it to her lips. She took a sip. Some dribbled on to her nightdress. 'Wash or burn this,' Esmée advised, hoarse with pain. She sipped the rest, greedily, a slight smile on her face. It was done. She sank back on the pillow. 'Tell you what, Jill, you never could mix a dry martini!'

Jillian lay on the bed beside her as the time ticked by. She held her friend in her arms, stroked her hair, and sang to her softly, as slowly, relentlessly, death crept upon her. She wanted to cry, for the weight of her sorrow was heavy in her throat, but no tears came. This anguish was too great for them. 'I love you, Esmée,' she said, at one point.

'I love you too, Jillian,' Esmée said, her voice thick and barely audible. Jillian heard her, but did not register that she'd called her by her full name for the first, and the very last, time.

7

Esmée had planned her funeral meticulously. She had left instructions that no black clothes were to be worn; only martinis and champagne were to be served. Her will specified, it was rumoured, that anyone suggesting sherry was to be drawn and quartered. Caviare was available, as were marijuana and coke. She had never been a hypocrite, everyone agreed. She had stated that she wished to be buried in the churchyard close to Mede House beside her father. She wanted as many of her ex-lovers who were living, and could be found, invited to her funeral. Flowers were banned but donations could be made to a list of charities she had chosen. The music had initially been something of a problem with the vicar. Esmée had requested a jazz quartet, and she'd wanted her coffin carried into the church to 'Memories' and taken out to 'Moon River'. But Liz, who had been a stalwart fund-raiser for the church tower, won over the vicar by suggesting that her cousin, who was curate in an inner-city parish, and who lacked his musical sensibilities, should conduct the service. Honour satisfied, he'd agreed.

'Bless you for coming down from Scotland with her on the train, Jillian. Mungo couldn't have borne the idea of her rattling through the night on her own.' Liz loomed above her. 'It was when the girl from the airline referred to her as air-freight that, I knew we couldn't have her sent that way.'

'I think that might have amused Esmée no end. But, on second thoughts, she'd have been annoyed not to be in first class.' She looked about her in the crowded hall of Mede House. 'I see you found a goodly number of her lovers.'

'What a song and dance that was. Such a macabre sense of humour she had. I think she rather hoped some would arrive on Zimmer frames, but they all look amazingly hale, don't they? I'm sorry Victoria couldn't come – I'd love to have met Rose.'

'You know kids. She was fine the day before we left and then she had such a fever there was no way she could come.'

'And I suppose funerals are not for the young, are they? And what about the very old? I mean, is it tactful when they might be next? We agonised about whether to wheel Esmée's mother out for it, but sense prevailed.'

'How is Theresa?' Jillian asked, with no idea why apart from a morbid curiosity.

'Totally gone. No idea what day of the week it is or who she is. Mungo was flapping a bit, but I said, "What's the point? She won't even remember who Esmée was." Sad, really. Mind you,' Liz lowered her voice, but given its initial volume it was still audible to anyone who cared to listen, 'I wouldn't say this to Mungo, but I think she's much nicer now she's totally gaga. In fact, I'd go as far as to say that I quite like her now. Do you ever hear from Jack?' she asked suddenly.

'No, never. Do you?'

'Mungo won't allow his name to be mentioned. All rather over-dramatic, I think. I know he's a crook and treated you abominably, but I always had a bit of a soft spot for him, and it's not as if he mugged some poor pensioner, is it? I hope someone told him. He was very fond of Esmée.' She turned round as someone called her name. 'But if you'll excuse me – you will be staying?'

'Liz, I'd love to, but I've got to get back.'

As it progressed the wake became noisier and jollier as Esmée had, no doubt, planned. Jillian wandered around the room, looking at the pictures and ornaments, but not really seeing them. She did not like being here: the house held too many memories, too many echoes from the past. She fingered the ornate flower display and, with pleasure, discovered they were real. Liz had dispensed with the artificial ones.

'Excuse me, it is Jillian, isn't it? I'm –'

'Toby! How lovely to see you again.'

All that was different with Toby were a few grey hairs and a slight paunch. His face was still that of a mischievous boy – it looked at odds with his dark City suit. 'Esmée spoke of you often.'

'She did?'

'She loved you, but realised too late.'

'Oh, go on!'

'She told me so.'

Toby, at this, produced a large handkerchief and trumpeted loudly into it. 'I wanted to see her, you know, before it was too late. A friend told me she was unwell. I called her when she was in hospital in New York but she refused point-blank to see me. Actually, I was a bit hurt.'

'Don't you know why she refused?'

'Because she had no need to see me, I assumed.'

'There were two reasons. You had remarried and she didn't think that it was right to see you, feeling about you as she did. And there was her vanity. She didn't want you to see her as she had become. She wanted you to remember her as a beautiful young woman. I can understand that. And kinder for you because in your memories she's always lovely, isn't she? There's nothing romantic about age and ill-health is there?'

'Was it awful?'

'Awful.'

She stayed another hour. Esmée might have wanted her funeral to be like this but for Jillian it was hard. She didn't want to be jolly and happy with people she barely knew. She felt the enormous weight of the loss of her friend and she wanted peace and quiet to mourn her. She needed Altnahany and its calming influence. She spent another aimless hour before moving to the front door, intending to slip away.

'Jillian, you're not going?'

'I'm afraid so, Mungo. I've a train to catch.'

'If you could spare me just five minutes of your time? There's something I need to discuss with you.'

When she arrived at Inverness station in the early morning, weary and not looking forward to the drive home, Ewan was on the platform, waiting for her despite the early hour.

'You shouldn't have bothered. I've got my car.'

'No, you haven't. Victoria gave me the spare key and I arranged to have it driven back. It's safer. Cars get stolen, even here!' He grinned. 'How was it? Or is that a daft question?'

'It was different. And, I think, a resounding success. It was more like a party than a funeral. I left early. I couldn't take it. So many people. So much noise. I wanted to shout out, "Hang on, Esmée's dead. We can't be this happy." It wouldn't have endeared me to them.'

'I wasn't sure if I should come to meet you. If I would be in your way.'

'Ewan, it was the kindest thing you could do for me. And I can't think of anyone I would rather have meet me.'

On Struie Hill she asked him to stop the car. 'Esmée always liked to look at the view from here.' He pulled over and they both climbed out. It was still dark, the snow fresh on the ground, the air, as always, crystal clear. The world was crisp with frost, cold and expectant. She stood where she had stood so often with Esmée and felt that she was there beside her.

527

The pain in her throat eased as, at long last, the tears for her friend burst free. Ewan, at her side, took her in his arms. Jillian, who had so often consoled others, rocked them in her arms, crooned softly to them, stroked their hair and kissed away the pain, was in her turn comforted.

Victoria was waiting for her.

'How's Rose?' was Jillian's first question.

'She's fine. How are you?'

'I've known better weeks.'

'Tea, or something stronger?'

'Victoria! I'm not your aunt. It's the crack of dawn. Tea will do nicely. How's Murray? Is he here?'

'I wanted him to stay but he said no, you wouldn't want him around, not at a time like this.'

'He's wrong. I like him, I wouldn't have minded.' She sat and watched her daughter brew the tea.

'If this is the wrong time, tell me, but I've been worrying. What do we do now? What about Altnahany?'

'It's okay. Esmée left it to me in her will.'

'Bless her, I thought she might. What a relief. Only –' Victoria stopped.

'Tell me. Come on, don't look so scared.'

'It's Murray. He's asked me to go to Fort William to live with him. Actually, he asked me to marry him but I said I thought we should try it out first, what with Rose and everything. But I said you'd have to come too if we lost this. He said that was fine, but he's only got a small croft.'

'I think you were right about Murray. He's something special, isn't he? And before you ask, I'm pleased. I never wanted you to be here all the time. You're young, you've hardly tasted life yet. I shall miss you and Rose, but I've known since she was born that this day would come. And Fort William is no distance. Still, I've got news for you too. You'd better sit down.' She waited while Victoria pulled out a chair. 'Not only did Esmée leave me this house but a large annuity too to help out when business is bad and, as she put it, when I'm too crocked to manage. And I saw your uncle Mungo before I left. He has no children, and he and Esmée have arranged that their enormous trust fund will go to you and Miles upon his death. Until then, he's going to make you both an allowance and apologises for not thinking about it sooner. Esmée told him what a mean old bastard he'd become and that, he said, jogged his memory.' She laughed at the memory of Mungo's bluff, worried face as he confessed to such thoughtlessness. 'So, my darling, you're going to be a very rich lady. I hope Murray won't mind.'

In a squeal of excitement, Victoria was round the table and clutching at her mother, hugging her until the breath was almost squeezed out of her. 'Can I tell Lachlan and Dotty Pearlman?'

'Mungo said that Esmée left definite instructions that you must.'

'Oh, Mum.' Victoria let go of Jillian, stood back and looked wan, sad and all of ten. 'This is all fine, but I'd so much rather have her than the money.'

'So would I, my darling – so would I.'

8

Spring 1998–Autumn 1999

Another season passed. Another winter. One season melted into another, guests became faded memories – names in a book when once she'd thought she'd never forget them. But they hadn't yet become Ewan's 'skulls'. The summers were fine. She was busy. Word had spread and she was turning customers away.

There were times when she missed Esmée so much it was like a dull ache. There was the day when Victoria announced that she and Murray were getting married: Esmée would have enjoyed planning the wedding, which was such fun, so pretty, and to which Miles came, but no Maxine.

Later that summer Miles had telephoned to say his marriage was over, he'd had enough. Once more she didn't tell him what she thought, how relieved she was, just in case, but how she longed to pour her heart out to Esmée.

In summer, given the pace of their lives, she saw little of Ewan, but they phoned most days to check on business and each other. Winter was harder, with little to distract her, too little to do.

The first Christmas without Esmée was spent at Victoria's. She was pregnant now and they couldn't have been more welcoming, kinder, more attentive. But Jillian felt in the way, as if she was intruding on the little family. And Christmas, she found, was a time for remembering. In her practical way, she decided that mooning about the past and dead friends was not productive.

Spring, autumn and winter her week always included a dinner with Ewan, which they still took turns to provide and to which she looked forward just as much as when they'd first met.

'Jillian, I want to talk to you.'

'Don't we always?' She smiled at him across the table – his for this particular dinner in early autumn.

'Yes, but about something specific.' He topped up their glasses with wine, Châteauneuf, as always.

'Fire away.'

'I wondered if you'd marry me?'

The music on the CD player faded away, a huge blanket of silence descended, and Jillian sat still, as if playing Statues, her fork halfway to her mouth.

'Silly question. Forget I asked it.' Ewan returned to cutting the meat on his plate.

'No, no. Please, Ewan, I was just surprised.'

'So you're not turning me down out of hand?'

'Why now? We've known each other how long? Eight years? You've never said anything.'

'I did once.'

'Yes, but never again.'

'You mean if I had, if I'd badgered you, pursued you, we might have? Oh, bloody hell!' He banged his fist on the table.

'I don't know what I would have said. I didn't think you meant it. And we've been such good friends, I was happy with that.'

'But I love you, Jillian.'

'And I love you, Ewan. But I'm not sure if it's in the right way. Not in a marrying way. I'd hate to put this friendship at risk.'

'Jillian, love, I know what you're saying. I loved my wife. It was a special love. It's how, no doubt, you felt about Jack. Probably it will never be repeated, not at our age. But we can build a good life together, do things, be a couple. I've missed that more than anything. I think what I'm saying is that although I'd love to sleep with you I'd understand if you didn't want to. I'm retiring this year. I want, no, I *need* to be with someone when I haven't the Clansman to rule my life. I mean, what has either of us got to lose?'

That night she couldn't sleep. Was she a romantic fool, holding on to the dream of one day finding a romantic love? That had ended in disaster last time, after all. Was she ready to settle for the Darby and Joan existence Ewan was offering?

Still, that was hardly fair. She turned over, switched on the light and checked the time. Four! No, he'd said if that was what she wanted, he'd accept that, but he obviously wanted a full sexual relationship. It seemed to be her choice.

What if it didn't work? It had taken ages for the sexual frustration to subside when Jack left. But in those years alone she had finally sublimated it until she never gave it a second's thought. Then Colin had awoken the demon hormones, and when he'd gone it had taken time again to subside them. She didn't want to go through that again – ever. Esmée would have counselled her, Victoria couldn't, and she rarely heard from her own mother. Was it undignified to want a physical relationship again? To feel a man in her, on top of her, wanting her?

Ewan was a good, kind man. She did love him, if not as she would have wanted. But, then, perhaps Jack had ruined her for any other man.

What to do? When he said he needed someone to share his life, was he saying, in a roundabout way, if you don't want me then I have to find someone who does?

'Ewan's asked me to marry him, Victoria.' She had called her first thing.

'Mum! That's brill. Murray, did you hear that? Mum's getting married!'

'I didn't say I'd accepted. I said he'd asked.'

'But you've *got* to. And about time too! I don't know why he's put up with you for so long.'

'We'll see. Don't phone him. Don't say anything to anyone. Do you hear? I need to think to work this through.'

'Cross my heart . . .'

The autumn mist was descending outside the large pink house. Jillian loved this time of day, when the world disappeared and she was left alone on her own little island of Altnahany.

The noise of a car on the drive made her frown. She should have taken down the sign for winter. She knew that if it was someone wanting a bed she'd put herself out and give them one.

She straightened her skirt, pulled a comb through her hair and opened the door.

'Hello, Jillian.'

'Jack.'

He looked the same, yet different.

'Of course, your hair is white. It suits you, very distinguished.' Jillian's voice sounded odd to her. She opened the door to the drawing room and ushered him in. She felt her pulse race – from the shock, she told herself, which she knew had drained her face of blood and made her momentarily dizzy. 'Have you come far?'

'You could say that. Thanks.' He accepted the drink she gave him. She hadn't even asked him what he wanted but had poured it, remembering it had always been Glenfiddich. 'I'm glad Esmée left you this. It suits you. Makes up for . . . you know.'

'Fen Manor? The house I lost?'

'Well, yes. I suppose that's what I mean.'

'Nothing could ever make up for that house. This is different. Altnahany means different things to me.'

'Do you miss Esmée?'

'Desperately.'

'Did she give you my message years ago, back in the eighties? I often wondered when I didn't hear.'

'She did.'

'Ah.' He prowled the room, reminding her of Miles and another dramatic evening. 'Business good?'

'Couldn't be better.'

'Nice mirror.' He was still slim, she thought, not a hint of a paunch, still handsome – too handsome. He seemed to become aware of her watching him and smiled at her. Her heart leaped at his very special smile, warm, tantalising, full of promises. 'I was hacked off when you gave that money in the Swiss bank to the police.'

'I thought one criminal in the family was enough.'

'Ouch! Where's my sweet docile Jillian?'

'Not yours any more.'

'So there's someone else?'

'Could be.' She was wary of him, as if a wild animal was moving lithely about the room. 'Why have you come, Jack?'

'Looking up old friends.'

'Is that all I am?'

'Don't be silly. Of course not. I didn't want to alarm you by saying what I'm really thinking.'

'Which is?'

'What a bloody fool I've been.'

'Yes, you have, rather. And the police? Aren't you afraid of being picked up by them?'

He laughed. 'No. When you're as rich as I am it's no problem. I slip in and out of the country. When you're like me you write your own rules.'

'I see.' How arrogant that made him sound. 'Would you like some supper?'

'I thought you'd never ask.'

'It'll have to be in the kitchen. The dining room is too cold.'

In the kitchen it was his turn to sit and stare as she moved about preparing their meal.

'You're even more beautiful than you used to be, you know. There's a serenity in your face. And you've kept your figure. You're still stunning.'

'Thank you.' Had he always been so patronising? Were her looks and figure what had been most important about her to him?

'But you no longer blush – sad.'

'Thank goodness. I'm afraid the vegetables are frozen. It's difficult up here in winter. Did you know you're a grandfather?' She knew her conversation was all over the place, but she was finding it difficult to behave and speak normally.

'Yes, Mungo keeps me informed.'

'Really? I thought he wouldn't have your name mentioned in the house.'

'Ah, that's for Liz. No, I know everything that goes on in this family. Like Victoria and Miles's good fortune.'

She stopped slicing the potatoes and pointed her knife straight at him. 'Don't you even think it, Jack.'

'Think what?' He laughed his oh-so-attractive laugh.

'You keep your hands off anything of theirs.'

'Heavens, Jillian, what a protective vixen you can be.' There was the laugh again, happy, confident. Just having him in the room disturbed her. She busied herself at the cooker so that he could not see her face.

She sensed him behind her, rather than felt him. He breathed gently on her ear. 'Jillian,' he said softly, so softly and seductively. 'I'm sorry. I've been so cruel. But I love you. I've always loved you.' His hand was stroking the down on her neck. It slipped across her shoulder. 'Not one day has passed that I haven't regretted what I did,' he whispered. She felt her heart race, her loins melt. 'Can you forgive me?' Now she felt him slide his hand towards her breast. 'I want us to get back together, Jillian. You and me, as it used to be.'

Slowly she turned in his arms and stood facing him, seeing the look of triumph on his face, his oh-so-handsome face.

'You know, Jack, I've often imagined this scene.'

'Me too.' He kissed her forehead.

'I was never sure what the end would be.'

'There's only one possible conclusion.' He stroked her arm.

'Yes. How right you are. I see now. I don't hate you, Jack – hate would be too much of a compliment to you. I despise you, yes. But mostly I feel nothing. It's as if I never knew you. Do me the courtesy and go. But this time never come back.'

9

New Year 2000

New Year, even this important never-again-to-be-experienced one, was no different for Jillian. She had refused all the invitations she'd received and had half a bottle of champagne on ice, a plate of smoked salmon in the fridge. As always she would see the New Year in alone, with Prince beside her, millennium or no. She didn't even put on the television but sat in the silence and remembered.

Esmée would have partied tonight! Although she was gone, Jillian still felt her presence here. She had been there in the autumn when she'd shown Jack the door. She'd approved of that. She was at her side when she had told Ewan she could not marry him. She could almost hear her saying, 'Never settle for second best, sweets. You'd live to regret it.'

She opened the champagne. She'd hated hurting Ewan, but it was better in the long run: they'd only have hurt each other further down the line. Marriage was too important, too difficult, to be used merely to keep loneliness at bay. And that was what it would have been, as much for him as for her.

Loneliness, however, she'd learned to live with. She couldn't say she enjoyed it, or looked forward to it. It was there. She had learned, however, that she could be just as lonely when the hotel was full as now, in mid-winter, with just Prince beside her. In fact, the loneliness in a crowd, she thought, was the worst of all.

Prince could not settle. 'What is it, boy?' She patted him and, having attracted her attention, he padded to the door and looked back expectantly. 'Want to go out?' They moved through the large, empty hall – strange that she'd once been frightened here. She opened the heavy front door and stepped out into a wonder-world.

Shimmering down the sky, like oily water on a sheet of

glass, pink, blue and green lights rippled. The air was alive with static, which crackled in the frosty night. It smelt strange, as if the world were singed. She looked up with wonder at the glorious display of the northern lights. For a good half-hour she and Prince watched, silent companions, all she needed, she told him.

'Excuse me!'

Jillian jumped half out of her skin and Prince, taken unawares, stood alert, growling at the figure that had appeared . . .

'I'm sorry I made you jump. I walked across the grass. It's my car. I've broken down on the glen road and I saw your lights. I hope you don't mind, but might I use your telephone?'

'Of course. Come in.' Even as she pushed open the door she thought, This is madness. He could be a burglar, a rapist. But she smiled. Somehow she didn't think he was. Weirdly she felt quite safe, yet could not understand why. 'The phone's in here.' She pushed open the door, turned to face him and, in the light of the hall, she could see him clearly.

'Peter Macpherson.' He held out his hand.

'Jillian Stirling.'

She smiled at him. It was a smile of recognition of this total stranger. He responded and she knew from his smile, from the half-quizzical, half-surprised expression on his face that he felt it too.

She heard Esmée's voice echoing in her mind.

'What the hell! A coup de foudre if ever I saw one. Go for it, sweets!'